A Ho...

Helen Hollick is the a... ...t
Arthurian Britain, *The ...* ...l
Shadow of the King, as well ... *...old the King*. She lives in London.

Praise for Helen Hollick's novels

'Compelling, convincing and unforgettable' Sharon Penman

'A spellbinding novel . . . a fabulous read and one to be recommended unreservedly. If only all historical fiction could be this good' *Historical Novels Review*

'An epic retelling of the events leading to the Norman Conquest . . . most impressive' *The Lady*

'Hollick juggles a large cast of characters and a bloody, tangled plot with great skill . . . spirited retelling of the final days of King Arthur's court' *Publishers Weekly*

'Don't miss Helen Hollick's colourful recreation of the events leading up to the Norman Conquest in *Harold the King*' *Daily Mail*

'Helen Hollick has written a spell-binder of a historical novel, meaty and colourful' *Northern Echo*

'Uniquely compelling . . . bound to have a resounding and lasting impact on Arthurian fiction' *Books Magazine*

'Helen Hollick joins the ranks of Rosemary Sutcliff, Mary Stewart and Marion Bradley with this splendid novel' *Pendragon Magazine*

'Masterly and colourful recreation' *Bolton Evening News*

Also by Helen Hollick

THE PENDRAGON'S BANNER TRILOGY
The Kingmaking
Pendragon's Banner
Shadow of the King

Harold the King

A Hollow Crown

Helen Hollick

The story of Emma, Queen of Saxon England

arrow books

Published in the United Kingdom in 2005 by
Arrow Books

3 5 7 9 10 8 6 4 2

Copyright © Helen Hollick 2004

Helen Hollick has asserted her right under the
Copyright, Designs and Patents Act, 1988 to be identified
as the author of this work

This book is sold subject to the condition that it shall not,
by way of trade or otherwise, be lent, resold, hired out, or
otherwise circulated without the publisher's prior consent in
any form of binding or cover other than that in which it is
published and without a similar condition including this
condition being imposed on the subsequent purchaser

First published in the United Kingdom in 2004
by William Heinemann

Arrow Books
The Random House Group Limited
20 Vauxhall Bridge Road, London SW1V 2SA

Random House Australia (Pty) Limited
20 Alfred Street, Milsons Point, Sydney,
New South Wales 2061, Australia

Random House New Zealand Limited
18 Poland Road, Glenfield,
Auckland 10, New Zealand

Random House South Africa (Pty) Limited
Isle of Houghton, Corner of Boundary Road & Carse O'Gowrie,
Houghton 2198, South Africa

The Random House Group Limited Reg. No. 954009
Addresses for companies within
The Penguin Random House Group can be found at:
global.penguinrandomhouse.com

A CIP catalogue record for this book
is available from the British Library

Penguin Random House is committed to a sustainable future for
our business, our readers and our planet. This book is made from
Forest Stewardship Council® certified paper.

Printed and bound in Great Britain by Clays Ltd, Elcograf S.p.A.

ISBN 9780099272342

To Towse,
For her friendship and support.

And in memory of my Grandma Turner – Emma –
Who had the courage to do as this Emma did at Robin Hood's Bay,
Yorkshire.
I wish I had known her better; she was a remarkable woman.

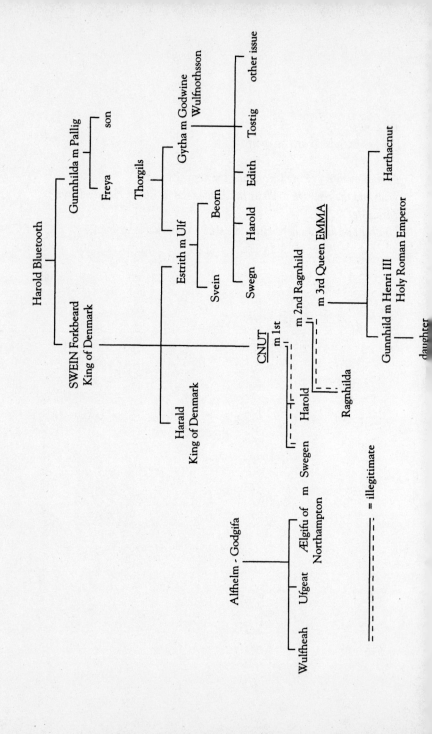

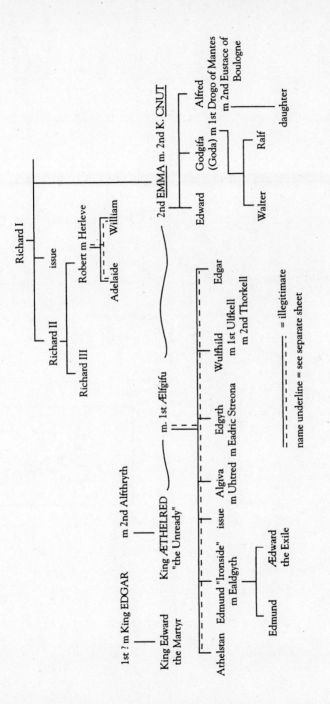

SCOTLAND

●Durham

NORTH
UMBRIA

DEIRA
●York

R. Humber
LINDSEY

●Chester MERCIA

Shrewsbury● ●Northampton

Peterborough● ●Thetford

WALES HWICCA ●Ely
Cambridge● EAST
ANGLIA

R. Severn ●Gloucester Epping Forest
Oxford● Stratford● ●Maldon
London● ●Ashingdon
Rochester● ●Canterbury
DEVON (WEST) WESSEX KENT Sandwich
Winchester● (EAST) SUSSEX
Bosham● ●Southampton
Isle of Wight

●Fécamp

Le Corentin● ●Rouen

Falaise● NORMANDY

Mont St Michel●

BRITANNY

GERMA
EMPIRE

●Bruges

LONDO

RIVER
LEA

St Pauls
Thorney
Island Southwark Greenwich
Lambeth

RIVER THAM

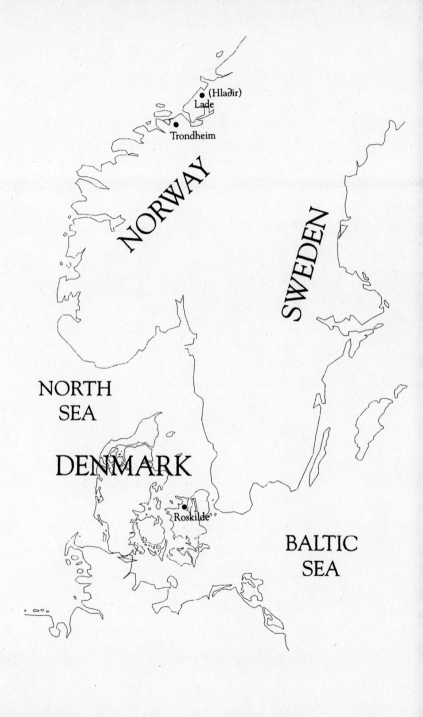

(Hlaðir)
Lade

Trondheim

NORWAY

SWEDEN

NORTH
SEA

DENMARK

Roskilde

BALTIC
SEA

Acknowledgements

For their patience and support – my agent, Mic Cheetham, and my editors, Susan Sandon and Kirsty Fowkes. Thank you. Also to Ilsa Yardley, who did an excellent job as copy editor, and to Georgina Hawtrey-Woore at Random House.

To Sharon Penman for always being there at the end of an e-mail, and for sharing that euphoric – and relieved – moment of actually finishing.

My thanks to my sister Margaret and her fiancé Tony, for coming with me on an enjoyable research weekend in Winchester and Bosham, and to John and Maggie Pollock for their kind and generous hospitality – especially to John for sharing his expertise and local knowledge of Bosham. I am indebted to him for several inspirational ideas.

Thank you to one of my dearest friends, Mal Phillips, for supervising the computer and my website, and to the staff of several museums who have been so helpful. Thank you also to the Royal Literary Fund for their support and encouragement. For their help with translation into French, Ferial McTavish and Linda Vann, and Anne Hansen for her help with the Danish.

Finally, to my family, Ron my husband, Kathy my daughter, and her partner Dave, for putting up with my moods, good and bad, during the ups and downs of writing, and to my special friend, Towse Harrison, to whom *A Hollow Crown* is dedicated. She always comes up with sensible advice, makes me laugh and has a comfortable shoulder to cry on when it's needed. What more describes the true meaning of the word 'friend'? Thank you.

For God's Sake let us sit upon the ground
And tell sad stories of the death of kings:
How some have been depos'd, some slain in war,
Some haunted by the ghosts they have depos'd.
Some poison'd by their wives, some sleeping kill'd.
All murdered – for within the hollow crown
That rounds the mortal temples of a king,
Keeps Death his court . . .
William Shakespeare, *Richard II*, Act 3 Scene 2

PART ONE

Æthelred

Anno Domini 1002–1013

That spring, Richard's daughter, the Lady Emma,
came to this land.

Anglo-Saxon Chronicle

1

Emma was uncertain whether it was a growing need to visit the privy, or the remaining queasiness of *mal de mer*, seasickness, that was making her feel so utterly dreadful. Or was it the man waiting at the top of the steps? The way he was looking at her, with the intensity of a hunting hawk, that was so unsettling? A man she had never seen until this moment, who was four and thirty years to her thirteen, spoke a language she barely understood and who, from the morrow, was to be her wedded husband.

Spring. Three days after the celebration of the Easter Mass, in the year of Christ 1002. Her brother had agreed this marriage of alliance between England and his Duchy of Normandy for reasons of his own gain. Richard ruled Normandy, and his brood of sisters, with an iron will that imaged their father's ruthless determination. Their father, Richard's namesake, Emma had adored. Her brother, who thought only of his self-advancement, and little else, she did not.

Her long fingers, with their bitten, uneven nails, rested with a slight tremble on Richard's left hand. Unlike her, he appeared calm and unperturbed as they ascended the flight of stone steps leading up to the great open-swung doors of the Cathedral of Canterbury. But why would Richard not be at ease? It was not he, after all, who was to wed with a stranger and be crowned as England's Queen.

With unbound, unveiled fair hair and her large shining eyes, Emma was passably pretty, but she was aware that Æthelred, surveying her from the top of the steps, was assessing that her legs were too long, her nose too large, her chin too pointed. Her breasts and hips not full and rounded. Her eldest sister had laughed when Emma had confided that she feared this Æthelred, King of England, would be disappointed with her.

'Please him in bed, *ma chérie*, and no husband will ever be disappointed with a young bride!'

Emma had not been convinced.

The drizzling rain had eased as the Norman entourage had ridden through Canterbury's gates, the swaths of mist, hanging across the Kent countryside like ill-fitted curtaining, not deterring the common folk from running out of their hovels to inspect her. England and the English might not hold much liking for the Normans and their sea-roving Viking cousins, but still they had laughed and applauded as she rode by; had strewn blossom and spring-green, new-budded branches in her path. They wanted peace, an end to the incessant *í-víking* raiding and pirating, to the killing and bloodshed. If a union between England and Normandy was the way to achieve it, then God's good blessings be upon the happy couple.

Whether this marriage would be of lasting benefit and achieve that ultimate aim, no one yet knew. The Northmen, with their lust for plunder and going *í-víking*, were not easy to dissuade and the substantial wealth of England had been, for many years, a potent lure. For a while, though, when the Duke, in consequence of this wedding, denied them winter access to his Norman harbours the raiders would search elsewhere for their ill-gotten gain or stay at home. Unless, of course, they elected to offer Richard a higher incentive than the one King Æthelred of England had paid.

If Emma minded being so blatantly used for political gain, it was of no consequence to anyone. Except to Emma herself.

Æthelred was stepping forward, reaching out to take her hand, a smile on his face, crow's-foot lines wrinkling at his eyes. She took in his sun-weathered, leathery face and fair, curling hair that tumbled to his shoulders, a moustache trailing down each side of his mouth to run into a trimmed beard with flecks of grey hair grizzling through it. She sank into a deep reverence, bending her head to hide the heat of crimson that was suddenly flushing into her cheeks. At her side, Richard snorted, disgruntled that she should be greeted before himself. He had not wanted to escort her to England, had vociferously balked at meeting face to face with this English King.

4

'I would not trust a man involved in the murder of his own brother to gain the wearing of a crown, any further than I could spew him.' How often had Richard proclaimed that opinion on the dreadful sea crossing? If they were his thoughts about this King, then why, in the name of sweet Jesu, had he arranged for Emma to wed him? Why was she here, feeling awkward and uncertain, fearing to look up at the man who would soon be bedding her and taking her innocence of maidenhood?

Non, Richard had not wanted to come to England, but he *had* wanted to ensure that the agreed terms were fully honoured. *Dieu!* To collect and count the dowry! He needed the financial gain and the respectability this absurd marriage would bring. Needed the prestige of having his youngest sister wed to one of the wealthiest kings in all Europe.

What if Æthelred was ugly? What if his breath and body stank worse than a six-month uncleaned pigpen? What if he does not like me? The questions had tumbled round and round in Emma's mind these three months since being told of the arrangement; had haunted her by night and day. She knew she had to be wed, Richard had been insistent on good marriages for all his sisters and it was a woman's duty to be a wife, to bear sons for her lord. Either that or drown in the monotonous daily misery of the nunnery. There would be no abbess's veil for Richard's sisters, though, he needed the alliances, the silver and the land. Normandy was a new young Duchy with no family honour or pride to fall back upon, only the hope of a future, which Richard was too impatient to wait for. This Emma understood on the very day that their father had died and Richard had set the Duke's golden circlet to the short-cropped hair on his head. Richard wanted all he could get and he wanted it not tomorrow or next year, but now. One by one her sisters had been paired to noble marriages, but they were all so much older than Emma. She had not expected to be bargained away so soon.

From somewhere she had to gather the courage and dignity to look up, to smile at Æthelred . . . she clung to the talisman of her mother's last parting words, as if they were a cask of holy relics: 'No matter how ill, how frightened or how angry you might be, child, censure *your feelings. Smile. Hold your chin high, show only pride, nothing else. Fear and tears are to be kept private. You are to be crowned and anointed as Queen of England. The wife and mother of kings. Remember that.'*

She took a breath, swallowed. Looked up at the man standing before her. Looked at Æthelred, who was to be her husband, and knew, instantly, that she disliked him.

2

Dismay gripped her with such force that she found she could not move. Her throat was dry, her heart jolted beneath her ribs; she felt as if the very air that she was breathing had been stolen away, that she was being suffocated, stifled. How could she go through with this thing? She could not! Suddenly she wanted to hitch up her gown, run back down the steps and flee from all these people staring at her, to be anywhere, anywhere but here with this old man who was bending forward to brush her cheek with his lips. He had a smile to his face that reached no further than the slight curve of his mouth, that certainly did not touch the empty coldness of his grey eyes. She wanted to go home . . . wanted her mother's arms, the security of places and people she knew.

Not that Gunnor had ever been the sort of mother to comfort her children. Emma could not remember the last time Mama had cuddled or kissed her. If she had ever done so, it must have been when she was a small child, before memories of such things lingered and took root. Not even when she had boarded that wretched ship had Gunnor shown any outward sign of affection. No farewell embrace, no wishing of good fortune, she had not even waited to watch the sail unfurl and the tide take her daughter away. Gunnor had merely ridden off without a backward glance once the plank was raised and the mooring ropes let go. Her son would be returning to her soon, but not Emma. She would quite probably never see her youngest daughter again.

Swallowing, Emma stretched her mouth into a tentative smile. To a girl of thirteen years, four and thirty seemed as ancient and worn as the hills. But at least he only smelt of male sweat and ale, not the stench of the common folk that had assaulted them as they rode through the narrow, sludge and detritus-strewn Canterbury streets. His beard had scratched at her delicate skin and his teeth, she noticed, were yellowing. Two were missing. His hand, holding hers, was large and clammy, the pads of skin at the base of his fingers calloused and feeling like unyielding, poorly oiled leather. The hands of a man used to wielding a sword or axe, or long hours in the saddle.

'*Wel cume in Engla-lond*,' he said, his voice low, gruff. 'I have arranged for you to stay at the nunnery this night, my dear. On the morrow, the good Abbess shall escort you here to the cathedral for our exchange of vows. From then, of course, you shall reside within the queen's quarters of my palaces, what is mine is yours.' Æthelred flapped his hand vaguely in the direction of the town's walls, to where a large timber-built Hall dominated the squat, reed-thatched commoners' cottages and workshops of Canterbury.

Emma took another steadying breath, retained her smile. She guessed the meaning of the first few words, but the rest? For all she knew, the King could have been insulting her beyond redemption. Some of the English tongue sounded similar to Danish, but the grammar and the lilt of speech was not what she had expected – she had believed them to be closely alike. Danish was her mother's tongue, but oh, this English was so different! She was on the verge of panic. *Sainte Marie, mère de Dieu* – Holy Mother of God, what was she to do? Was she to wed and bed with this man, give him children, be his Queen, and not fully understand the words that spilt from his mouth?

Richard, not noticing her silence, or her increased, terrified grip on his arm, proudly addressed Æthelred, speaking in Court French. He rarely used their mother's native speech, claiming it was uncivilised and uncultured. That was another of Richard's faults: his self-opinionated arrogance.

'*Mon Seigneur, je vous donne la garde de ma sœur.*' Irritably shaking aside his sister's gripping fingers, Richard offered an elaborate embrace of kinship. The false smile as wide as the spread of his arms.

Æthelred ignored him. Instead, frowning at not being able to decipher what this coxcomb upstart was bragging, he belligerently folded his arms and stared pointedly at his Archbishop of York, waiting for a translation.

That this English King spoke no French astonished Richard. It had not occurred to him that this man might not have an adequate knowledge of the language of Charlemagne. Perplexed, he tried again, with not such a wide smile, in his mother's tongue. 'I have brought, to your good care, my sister. As was agreed.'

Æthelred glowered. Danish. He had no liking for the Danes, a loathsome people with a pagan culture, an unreasonable temper and a damned language that he could not abide assaulting his ears. Murdering, bloody barbarians, the Danes. Disrespectful louts who thought no one else had an ounce of ability when it came to ships and the sea, and who took a perverse pleasure in raiding and looting, 'í-víking' was their term for it. To be more precise, taking that which was not theirs, be it land, property or women.

He had not been overpleased that this girl his Archbishop of York, Wulfstan Lupus, had persuaded him to marry, was half Danish, but alliances, like healing medicines, often came with a bitter taste. At least the taint was on the distaff side, not on the male, spear side, where it mattered. And the heavy dowry he had demanded compensated somewhat.

Sniffing loudly, Æthelred wiped a grime-nailed finger beneath his nose; glowered with a deeper-furrowed brow at his Archbishop.

Wulfstan, disregarding his King's tactlessness, dipped his head to the Duke and in fluent French welcomed him and his delightful sister to England. He fluttered his bone-thin hand, the huge, ruby archbishop's ring that appeared absurdly large against the stick-like finger glinting in the apologetic sunlight. 'Few at Court embrace French, nor, my Lord, while they raid our coasts and estuaries, while they burn our crops, murder our men and rape our women, do we listen kindly to the Danish speech.'

'You made no mention of this,' Richard searched for an appropriate word, 'inconvenience, when you came to bargain for my sister. Nor, I doubt, are you as fastidious when accepting taxation from Danish tradesmen.'

For good reason had Wulfstan been appointed as Archbishop of the diocese of York, as senior prelate of the wild, untamed land and people that spread northwards beyond the Humber river. His attributes included diplomacy and tactfulness, patience and a dignified humility that would not have been misplaced were he one of Christ's own chosen disciples. He was also a highly literate scholar and an orator, had an even better flare for government. A formidable man to deceive or gainsay. More than once had Æthelred remarked that it was as well that Wulfstan had chosen the Church as his living. Had he been of the warrior kind, no thegn or ealdorman, or even king, would have rested at night for fear of being overthrown.

With a barely perceptible shrug, the Archbishop answered the Duke of Normandy's accusations with simplicity. 'It did not seem of consequence, my Lord. It will not be yourself who will be staying here in England, but your sister.' With a placating smile the Archbishop proceeded to translate Richard's greeting, and his own response, to Æthelred.

'What of the girl?' Æthelred interrupted tersely. 'Does she not speak English either?' He glared suspiciously at Richard through narrowed eyes. Normans! Damned hell-spawn, bred of Danish pirates and pox-tainted whores. For all his protestations of piety and devotion to Christ, this pinch-mouthed Duke's ancestry was too closely connected to these present-day plundering whoresons for comfort. The grandsire had been nothing more than a raiding Viking himself, although, admittedly, one with a few brains between the gristle of his ears. Rollo had sweet-talked his way into the French King's favour and acquired a corner of France for himself and his followers. Northman's Land. Normandy, they had called it. Aye, well, as long as this present upstart had no ideas for extending his lands and grabbing a corner or two of England.

Cupping his hand under Emma's chin, Æthelred's rough-skinned fingers pinched into her cheeks as he tipped her head up and sideways to inspect her more closely. God's Breath, but she was young! And there was nothing of her – all skin and bone! He liked his women well padded, something to get his hands around, fingers into. Athelflade, his mistress, he had been moderately fond of, but then, she had been a quiet, dutiful woman who did his bidding without murmur. A pity she had given him all daughters and only the one son, and he a sickly, puking thing that had caused her death. His hand-fast wife, Ælfgifu, had understood his wants and needs, too, although with her sharp tongue and constant nagging he had not been sorry to set her aside when her cursed father had turned traitor. She had been chosen for him by his mother; to wed with Emma had been his decision. Already, he was wondering whether it had been a wise one, what would this infant know of a man's needs? He sighed, released Emma's face with a pat to her cheek, as if she were a favoured dog. He sniffed, nodded once. Right or wrong, there was no reneging on the agreement. 'She'll do.' Added half grudgingly, 'She will have to.' He laughed suddenly and, with more enthusiasm, kissed Emma again. Her face was fair and she would fill out as she grew, would learn as she matured, perhaps the teaching might be pleasurable? If not, well, she would not be the first wife to play mute to a man's whores.

'I am thinking,' he announced for all to hear, 'that I may be fortunate. A wife who does not know what I am saying could be a great blessing, eh?' He paused, watched the puzzled, tentative frowns. Laughed again, louder, a great belly roar of mirth. 'She'll not answer me back, nor make comment when I mumble about other women's bedchamber assets in my sleep!'

Understanding the jest, the array of English nobility joined his merriment enthusiastically. Men and women, in a dazzle of sumptuous garments; ealdormen, dignitaries and thegns with their wives, daughters and sisters. Richard slid a questioning frown at Wulfstan, signalling that he had not followed the conversation; tactfully, the Archbishop turned away, pretending that he had not seen the Duke's raised eyebrow.

Beyond realising that they did many things differently here in England – following laws and customs that were older and more entrenched than those directed by the Pope in Rome – Emma did not fully comprehend the previous marriage that Æthelred had made. The woman was his legal wife in English law, but had not been crowned Queen, nor received any right of status or recognition by the Christian Church. Therefore, technically, in Christian eyes, this Ælfgifu had been nothing but a concubine, yet the children she had birthed were not regarded as bastards. The eldest son was awarded the title 'ætheling', kingworthy, and could become, if thought able, king after his father. That concept alone was puzzling. In Normandy, as in France, the eldest legitimate son automatically inherited, the younger ones receiving next to nothing beyond a placement within the Church, becoming a squire to someone more fortunate, or finding what they could for themselves. In England, the most worthy, not necessarily the eldest, was elected as king by the Council.

The difference between that marriage and her own? Emma's was to be sanctified in the eyes of God, her vows exchanged and witnessed on hallowed ground, the Cathedral of Canterbury. The marriage band placed on her finger would be blessed by the Archbishop of Canterbury, the superiority of the blessing automatically dictating her higher status and the security of permanency. Unlike the woman, Ælfgifu, Emma could not be easily divorced, for immediately after her marriage she was to be anointed and crowned in solemn service as Queen of England. Another peculiarity of English law, there could only be the one crowned Queen; until she died or declared her lack of interest, no other could be anointed in her place, not even when that other was taken as wife to a new successive king. A commanding woman, such as Æthelred's mother had been, could effectively block the usurpation of her crown and position of authority. There had been no salient reason, before now, for Æthelred to decide on a Christian-blessed wife, for until she could be awarded the dignity of her title, any lasting alliance would be meaningless.

Emma's mother had been dismissive of the unconventional English law regarding marriage, and in Æthelred's case, his common-law wife, parade of mistresses and the children born to them. '_Dead whores are of no consequence,_' she had answered curtly when Emma had asked of them. '_You are to be Æthelred's Christian-blessed wife and his anointed Queen. One of your sons shall become king after him. It is made so in your marriage agreement, Richard has specifically seen to it._'

Sons. Emma was uncertain about that aspect also. Oh, she knew all about the mess of begetting and birthing, life within the walls of her brother's various crowded castles held little luxury of privacy. She had heard or witnessed all she need know about men, women and the subsequent children. She knew it hurt, both child getting and childbirth, for she had heard the moans for the getting and the screams for the producing. She knew also that death was often the end result, not that she feared death. At this moment, as her throat continued to run dry and her heart pound in her chest, she thought it might be most welcome.

The toll of bells from Canterbury's many chapels and monasteries had at last fallen silent and Æthelred's laughter trilled down to the people of the town. The tide of amusement scuttled through the streets, wafted along by a slight rise of wind, echoing and rippling along the narrow, stinking alleyways.

Richard, believing the laughter to be at his expense, was scowling, but Emma forced a stout-hearted smile to her cheeks as she placed her fingers within Æthelred's offered hand and kept it fixed there as her betrothed led her forward to introduce her to his Court.

First, the Archbishop of Canterbury who was to conduct the marriage and her crowning on the morrow. Emma wondered if he would have the strength to lift even a marriage ring, let alone a royal crown, for he was so old and frail. He had reached almost six and seventy years, Archbishop Wulfstan walking at her far side told her, she could barely believe such a great age. He was thin and small, wrinkled like a dried prune, could not manage to rise from his archbishop's chair. Nor could he hear well, for he had to cup his hand to his ear and exclaim, through toothless gums, 'Eh? What's that?' to her murmured greeting.

Æthelred moved on to the man standing beside the Archbishop. 'My son,' he announced stopping before a tall, handsome and quite ferocious-looking young man. 'Athelstan. One and twenty years of age. He has already proved himself capable with sword and axe, but he needs to curb his impatience. I have no intention of giving him opportunity to try for my place as king just yet.'

Athelstan flickered his iron-sharp, grey-eyed gaze disdainfully to

13

his father, then to her with a look that did not conceal his contempt for both of them. So, there was no love between father and son, then? Emma wondered why. Ambition on the son's part, perhaps? Indifferent, Athelstan bowed his head at her, a single curt nod. Polite, nothing else.

'And Edmund,' Æthelred continued as he introduced another, much younger lad, barely waiting for Archbishop Wulfstan to turn his words into French. 'Edmund is but eleven; I have strong hopes for him.' Æthelred playfully swiped at the boy's head, buffeting him round the ears. 'My other sons are sadly taken to God. My gaggle of unmarried daughters are over there.' He waved his hand in the direction of where the women of the Court were gathered. 'The last-born child I sired is a sickly brat, of no use to man or beast. I have sent him to the monastery at Ely.'

Emma had not dared to attempt making eye contact with Athelstan, but Edmund was nearer her own age, of her own height and not so daunting.

'*Gode fortune be wythe ye*,' she said in halting English, feeling confident enough to mimic the phrase that had been tossed at her by all those folk who had lined the road north from Dover. To her disappointment, and acute embarrassment, she had misjudged him. Apart from the aloof and disdainful glower he gave his father's new wife, Edmund, as with Athelstan, ignored her.

Richard did not look at them. His sneer more pronounced than their own, he walked on towards the line of waiting prelates and dignitaries, remarking only, 'Normandy does not acknowledge bastards born from a whore's spread legs.'

Mortified, Emma blushed crimson. She swung her eyes to Archbishop Wulfstan, pleading that he was not to repeat her brother's rudeness. She closed her eyes in a thankful prayer as, always the diplomat, he said nothing. She smiled her gratitude at him, received in return a conspirator's acknowledgement, the first genuine smile offered her this day. This alliance had been Wulfstan's idea; for the sake of England, and for his own reputation, the marriage had to succeed. If it failed, it would not be through the fault of the Archbishop of York!

As Æthelred escorted her along the line, Emma greeted each new face with courtesy and gestures of friendliness, repeating her few English words to each and every one of them, *Dieu*, how was she to remember them all? The ealdormen, Alfhelm of Deira, Goddwin of Lindsey, Leofwine, Leofsige, Ælfric, Athelmar. The important nobles, Uhtred of Bernicia, Ulfkell Snilling, Thurbrand the Hold, the Reeves of shire and port. Thegns – Morcar, Sigeferth, Eadric Streona and his brother . . . *Là!* Too many to remember – but she would have to. Tomorrow, after her marriage and crowning, these men would, one by one, kneel before her to pledge their service and loyalty. Another thing they did so very differently here in England.

Normans, if they wished to hold land, were obliged annually to swear their troth as vassals to their Duke's will – swear, or lose all. Whereas these English held their estates by right of legal tenure, their land could not be forfeit on a king's whim without grounds of legal justice. With free-given choice an Englishman honoured his king as overlord, the highest-ranked among them combining into a Council, the Witan, formed to advise and direct the King, even to elect the next king when death claimed the reigning monarch. Emma thought of Richard; had there been a choice, would he have become Duke? Would his nobles have considered him the most worthy to wear the ducal coronet? Hah! She very much doubted it.

Tomorrow also, robed in all her regal finery, Emma would greet and give her favour to those men who had agreed to become her own elite bodyguard of cnights. That any warrior would deem it worthwhile to serve, and protect without question, a skinny, awkward girl child was beyond Emma's comprehension. As was this English notion that these men were free to offer their pledge of loyalty and military service merely in return for keep and comfort. What was there to bind a vow? Honour, she had been told. In Normandy a man's honour could be out-bought. Did that not happen here in England? Ah, there was so much to learn!

On the outside, at least, these noblemen seemed approving of her, several showing smiles that were not based on a smirk of lust for a ripe bud, as many of Richard's lords had often done. For all that she was just a girl, these English, excepting the aloof Athelstan and his younger brother, were treating her with polite formality and respect. The women, perhaps, were not quite so comfortable with her, more than one eyeing her as a potential threat; but women, she knew well enough, were often kindred spirits to a kennel full of snarling bitches.

One thegn among the row of many, Wulfnoth his name, a bearded rogue of a sea dog – she could tell by the saline tang that clung to his body and clothes – raised both her hands to his lips and placed a lingering impertinent kiss there. 'Your servant, ma'am,' he crowed. 'This pious lack-laughter monk, Wulfstan here, told us you were a comely lass, but the old bugger never let on that you were on the verge of becoming a rare beauty! You are as a healing balm to sore eyes, my Lady. Well Come to England.'

To Emma's delight, Wulfnoth spoke in fluent French. 'There's naught so pleasant as a pretty face at Court to rattle these jealous old biddies,' he jested, nodding his head at the women. 'Their poor, shackled menfolk might not admit it, but I am wife-free, so I can safely acknowledge that I am afire with envy for our King. He is a fortunate man indeed, to be getting one as sweet as you for his own. You let me know if you decide you don't want him, lass, I'll be more'n happy to keep you warm in his stead!'

His exaggerated, playful wink was youthful and boisterous, belying the fact that his grizzled hair and beard made him appear older than he was. Emma laughed at his outrageous informality, surprised and pleased at the unexpected arousal of humour from within her. The women, however, did not share his gallant jesting. Did they truly fear that she might seduce their husbands away from their beds? Well, perhaps she had better not let them realise that their fears were built on shifting sand; as far as seducing a man went, she would not have the faintest idea of where, or how, to start!

And then, as Æthelred brought her back along the long line of people, someone spoke, plain and belligerent, in French. 'She might attempt to pleasure our father in his bed, she might even give him more sons, but here in England the most worthy is chosen as king. When the time comes, I defy any of her mewling half-breed brats to prove stronger than I!'

Emma faltered, forced the smile to stay on her lips and steeled herself not to look round. Athelstan! If he could speak French, then he had understood every discourtesy her brother had let slither from his tongue. Given that he obviously resented her coming, how he must now hate her! Suddenly she felt vulnerable and frightened. What was she doing here? More, how would she survive?

Given the vomit-spewing God-awfulness of that sea journey, though, Emma did not have a choice but to hold her chin high, ignore Æthelred's eldest born and remember her mother's advice that she was to shield her thoughts from marking her face. She *would* survive here in England. God help her, she would have to.

Nothing, not even the fear of a four-and-thirty-year-old husband or a surly braggart of a stepson would ever induce her to set foot on another of those damned, wallowing monsters that so calmly masqueraded as a ship!

3

Emma became Æthelred's wife as the heavens opened in a downpour of hail and thunder, their voices drowned by the crash and grumble of a turbulent, lightning-split sky. The folk who crowded into Canterbury to witness the occasion did not appear to notice, or mind, the sudden drenching and the torrent of water flash-flooding the streets.

Surely all England had come to see their King take Lady Emma of Normandy as wife? The narrow streets were crammed full of people, right up to and beyond the very gates of the town. Directly in front of the cathedral in the market place, empty of its stalls for this occasion, onlookers were packed as tight as salted pilchards in a barrel. There could never be any doubting the authenticity of this marriage, for too many eyes witnessed the public exchange of vows beneath the cathedral's arched porch-way. The outburst of cheering vied with the storm booming overhead, as Æthelred took up her hand and began to lead her inside. Mass, the formal blessing, and Emma's anointing as Queen would be conducted within. Always ready, on these crown-wearing days, to acknowledge his status, Æthelred turned to the crowd and raised his arm in salute, the enthusiastic response so great that Emma wondered whether these English would cheer anything if it appeared splendid enough. Dress a lop-eared, cow-hocked mule in fine silks and parade it before them, would they applaud that too?

Impulsively Emma also raised her arm, the response staggering, the cheering louder, wilder. All these people, men, women, children; well-off and poor; traders, shopkeepers, farmers, all of them acknowledging and greeting *her*. She risked a shy glance at Æthelred. Would he mind that her acclaim had been bolder than his own? She relaxed. He was smiling, laughing almost.

'It seems they approve of you. Not that it matters, the populace detested my mother. It made not the slightest difference to her; she cared nothing for them either. Nor for my father, if it came to that. Still, it helps to be liked.'

Emma understood one or two of his words, as for the rest, ah well, perhaps they were not important.

Inside the cathedral, Emma's shoes, expensive red leather slippers, scuffed gently on the red and black patchwork of tiles that led from the great western door to the altar steps. To either side, prestigious men dipped their heads as she passed by, her hand resting lightly on Æthelred's arm, the women sinking into curtsies of reverence. The interior was a haven of quiet and calm, a serene opposite to the storm turbulence outside. Candles burnt from every sconce in wall, rafter and free-standing candelabra; each an individual flickering halo of yellow flame, joining and merging to make a shimmering glow of enigmatic light. The heady aroma of incense mingled with the scent of tallow and the spirals of smoke, the whole conspiring to overpower the rain-damp, musty smell of men's cloaks and women's gowns.

Emma was enthralled. This homage paid to her without hesitation, the sheer beauty and atmosphere of the building with its painted walls of swirling patterns or religious scenes. How could she have believed Richard's prejudices? This whole thing was wonderful! Although, as she knelt before the altar to pledge her marriage vows, a tiny voice niggling in her mind whispered that the splendour of the occasion could be distorting her senses.

Richard's derogative assessment of England had prepared her to expect Canterbury Cathedral to be nothing more than a wooden chapel with mud floor and leaking roof. 'The English are poor builders,' he had declared to his companions before leaving Normandy. 'They have not the capacity of imagination or skill to create buildings of beauty for the glory of God. *Dieu*,' he had added with scorn, 'they even defend themselves behind timber – *incroyable*! I would have the English King come to Normandy, see our fortifications! *Sans doute*, how can a man proclaim his power unless he builds in stone?'

Æthelred's palace did, indeed comprise of a cluster of buildings constructed in wood and thatch, but not the cathedral. Christ Church, Canterbury was a building that could compare with any in Normandy. Emma's delight at seeing it yesterday had been twofold, England was not the uncouth, uncivilised land that Richard had vociferously declared it to be and, for the first time ever, she had realised that her brother could be wrong.

With the marriage ceremony completed, Æthelred seated himself comfortable on his king's throne, and Emma stood alone between the two Archbishops. Wulfstan tall and upright, and the old Archbishop of Canterbury with shoulders hunched, spine bent, his hand to his ear, his eyes squinting and peering to see through the fog of failing sight. The choir was singing, the beautiful blended voices of the monks raised high in musical prayer, the sound rippling and echoing up into the vaulted rafters of the arched roof, bouncing off the gay-painted stone walls. She understood these words, for the singing, as with the service, was in Latin, familiar and safe. '*Let thy hand be strengthened and be exalted. Let mercy and truth go before thy face.*' The soaring descant of the younger novices rising like a lark, high, to the very feet of God.

Prostrating herself, Emma lay flat along the tiles before the altar, their hard coldness seeping through her gown, the fine-woven linen beneath an over-garment that was elaborately embroidered with precious stones and pearls, that winked and glittered in the candlelight. Wulfstan intoned the prayers and blessing, and it was he who raised her, showed her to the congregation and asked, in stentorian voice, whether she was acceptable as their queen. The shouted answer shook the roof and quivered through the building, to be taken up and echoed outside by the people of Canterbury. 'Aye! Aye! Aye!' Even the flames flickered, as if a wind had rustled through the nave.

'Do you promise to keep good faith to God, and peace to your people?'

'*Oui*, I do so avow.' Her voice, quiet and timid, barely heard. More prayers, another blessing, further singing.

The Chrism, the holiest of oils, was poured on to the crown of her head and trickled down her forehead, where the gnarled and bent finger of the Archbishop of Canterbury traced the sign of the Cross. The anointing, the symbolism of her change from a mortal woman to that of a queen; the ring slipped on to her finger, the Queen's ring, signifying her union with the kingdom, as her marriage band had signified her union with her husband. The ring of eternity, a seal of Holy Faith. As Wulfstan placed it there, she repeated his words, that she would shun all heretical depravation and bring barbarian peoples to the power of God.

The crown was heavier than she expected, gold, encrusted with jewels, pressing on to her temples, into the back of her head.

'Receive the crown of glory and the public honour of delight so that you may shine out in your splendour and be crowned with eternal joy.' The crown, for health and prosperity, for mercy and honour.

'Lord, our font of all good things and giver of all, grant strength to Your servant to rule well in dignity and glory, shown by You to her.'

Overwhelmed, dazed – was this happening to her? – Emma felt her throat tighten, tears flood into her eyes at the enormity of Wulfstan's words. She bit her lip, bowed her head as the choir's splendour lifted into the *Laudes Regiæ*. She was Queen. Her spirit, her very soul, given to England and God for ever.

Æthelred was beside her, escorting her along the nave, and her vanity reached a new height of pride, the ceremony completed by her brother's obeisance. No other event throughout the passing of her life would impress upon her more the significance of a royal crown. Richard had cared nothing for his sisters, particularly herself, his youngest, save for what advantage they would bring him. To have him kneel before her, pay her public respect and homage – that, more than anything this day, made her appreciate this crown that she wore on her head. Even if the thing was a weight of uncomfortable heaviness that exacerbated the throb of a rising headache.

4

Several goblets of wine were doing very little to ease the drumming hooves that were now galloping behind Emma's temples, but at least she did not have to endure the noise within the King's Hall across the rain-puddled courtyard. Complying with expected tradition, the Queen and her women had withdrawn to this, the smaller, more sedate Queen's Hall. Abbesses and the higher-ranking holy sisters, wives, mothers and daughters, were enjoying conversation and entertainment more suited to their genteel sex. Not that a headache and several dozen chattering women, each one of them eager for a personal opinion to be expressed and heard, formed a suitable combination.

They had celebrated the Bride Ale feast together, she sitting at Æthelred's right hand, Richard to his left, on the King's high dais above the packed Hall. How the servants had managed to manoeuvre between the trestle tables and benches with their laden trays of sumptuous delights was a mystery. The dishes served had impressed even Richard: meats and fish of all kinds and varieties. Roasted, poached, baked. Fried. Cheeses, breads and butters; pastries, sauces, fruits and honeyed cakes; tarts and custards, never-tasted delicacies and sworn favourites; wines, cider and the seemingly never empty jars of amber, especially brewed, frothing Bride Ale. A king's feast fit for his new queen.

Bellowed laughter roared from the King's Hall, disturbing the wild birds, sparrows, blackbirds and finches, roosting among the high, cob-webbed and dusty, smoke-swirled rafters. The women nodded, muttering with a sense of wise pride that the men were deep into the mead, ale and cider barrels, and would be like bears with sore heads on the morrow. Gulping her English ale, Emma drained the goblet of heady, potent stuff. The morrow? Before tomorrow must come the night. Her wedding night. She was dreading it. How could she be intimate with a man she did not know, who stank of ale and spoke barely a word she understood?

Waving a servant forward to pour more Norman cider for herself, the woman seated beside her, Wilflad, Abbess of the Canterbury nunnery, indicated whether her Queen wished for any.

Emma shook her head, instantly regretting the movement, and placed her hand over her goblet. 'Non merci, madame. I am drinking Bride Ale.'

The Abbess beckoned another servant forward. 'My Lady's cup needs replenishing.'

About to say that she wanted no more, Emma changed her mind, allowed the servant to fill her goblet. Perhaps the drink would help steady her wavering nerve?

Sampling the golden liquid within her own cup, Wilflad licked her lips and nodded appreciatively. Said in French, 'This is a fine fermentation your brother has engifted us with. From where in Normandy are the apples harvested?'

'De la Côtentin,' Emma answered, appreciating the diversion of conversation. 'My apples, I suppose, my cider, now that I am wed. La Côtentin is my dowry land, I bring its revenue with me. Mama said for that alone I am a most valuable catch.'

Kindly, the Abbess squeezed Emma's arm, remarked, 'For yourself too, chérie. You will be a handsome woman come maturity. The King must be congratulating himself over there in that boisterous and rowdy Hall, the Côtentin and a lovely girl to bear him a brood of strong sons. How fortunate a man he is!' With careful deliberation, for the girl's sake, she shielded the sarcasm. If the Abbess had inadvertently let any of her feelings of dislike for the King slip, Emma did not notice.

Reading Emma's doubtful expression and guessing the thoughts that lay behind the sudden, obvious uprush of fear, Wilflad added gently, 'Come tomorrow morning you will be wondering what worried you. Æthelred has a short temper, one that is as brittle as dried kindling, but I have not known him to be unjust to a woman.' She spoke accurately, but not with the whole truth. As with so many wives and concubines, Æthelred's bed mates had not complained, but had endured in silence.

With practical kindness the woman advised, 'Serve your husband dutifully and he will treat you well.'

Emma appreciated the well-intentioned words, but they failed to reassure her. Æthelred was a virile and experienced man; she knew nothing of wedded intimacies. The day had been long, over-whelming and confusing, so many emotions surging, wave after wave, like a wind-driven high tide on an unsuspecting shore. She felt as though she had been half drowned, pulled from the surf and hung up to dry; had been left wrinkled, crumpled and drained. And soon she would have to face this next great surge of new experience. She gulped another mouthful of ale. Were the walls moving? Why were the faces blurring, the lilt of voices to-ing and fro-ing? She giggled, childish, into her goblet, suddenly aware that she was drunk.

5

In groups of twos or threes, women had been coming and going through the rear door to visit the especially dug latrine pit. Realising it would be prudent to follow their example, Emma motioned for her cloak to be brought, stood, was momentarily taken aback by everyone else coming immediately to their feet, the talk rapidly subsiding into silence. Not expecting her necessity to answer a requirement of nature to be so publicly acknowledged, she blushed, felt her face and neck burning with as much heat as the blazing hearth-fire. Unsure how to react – did she respond to the obligation of courtesy or did she ignore it? She opted for compromise. Giving a slight nod to no one in particular, she announced, 'Be seated. I attend a personal matter.'

She walked towards the door, her concentration focusing on putting one foot before the other without stumbling or zigzagging too noticeable a wavering path. Thank God for her appointed Captain of Cnights, a thegn, Pallig Thursson – bless the man, he strode beside her, his hand lightly guiding her elbow, his face stern and serious, daring any one of these tongue-wagging gossips to make, or think, a disparaging comment. Not until the bearskin had flapped back over the opening and the outer door had closed behind them did the rumble of talk inside resume.

'It does not take a seer to predict that they are taking this opportunity to talk about me,' she said, wearily leaning her head back against the welcome solidity of the doorpost. She closed her eyes, let the world spin by, breathed in the coolness of the evening air. 'Making fun of me.'

'In my experience, women spend more hours of the day deriding others of their sex than on anything else. Especially women who feel wrong-footed.'

Opening her eyes, Emma smiled at Pallig, marvelling at how a man could possibly be so superbly handsome. He wore his fair hair long, as did most of the English, and also like his fellow country-men, a moustache that trailed to either side of his expressive mouth, although, unlike Æthelred, his chin was beardless. An axe, that had a gleaming blade that could slice the wind, rested with nonchalant ease over his right, hard-muscled shoulder.

Pallig Thursson, Thegn of Exmouth in the Shire of Devon, had pledged his honour and service to her, his Queen, as she had sat enthroned beside the holy altar of Canterbury's cathedral. He, and fifty other free-born landholders in turn, had proclaimed their fealty and loyalty to her and her alone. The Queen's Cnights, her most especial and elite body of men, with Pallig as their captain. *Her* captain. Her and her alone would he obey and serve. In exchange for her gift of a heavily jewelled cloak pin, Pallig had taken his place at her side. From where he had declared, using the Danish tongue, that he would not, while there be breath in his body, be moved by so much as one step.

Not having the courage to ask, Emma wondered whether, in his enthusiasm, he had meant that literally and would escort her right to the latrine pit itself, or wait at a discreet distance while she relieved herself. Wondered, too, what he thought of playing nursemaid to a chit of a girl. What would a man prefer? The company of his own kind, a bellyful of fine ale and the teasing of the serving girls, or standing, brooding and bored, behind a bewildered child?

This was something else she would have to grow used to, this necessity to be escorted everywhere. The girlhood days of freedom suddenly seemed so far behind her. Dolls and games, and honey-sweetened cakes, were gone for ever.

'Ah well,' she said, to break the awkward silence, 'at least their gossip is providing entertainment.' She pushed herself from the door. 'I can be content that they are enjoying themselves, even if I am not.'

'Lady?' Pallig, falling into step beside her, queried her meaning. 'Are you not happy to be here in England?' He spread his broad hand, not understanding. 'As Queen, you now have everything.'

Emma forced a smile. '*Oui*, naturally I am happy to be here. It is an honour, *n'est ce pas?*'

'Indeed, Madam, that it is.' Gesturing with his hand, Pallig ushered her forward. Hiding her embarrassment she walked on, saying, with more authority than she felt as they neared the evil stench of the pit, 'I am capable of tending my own need. You may wait here.'

To her relief, the big-shouldered man made no argument. He merely nodded and, turning his back, planted himself, legs spread, arms folded, across the pathway to ensure her privacy.

Poor lass, he thought as he nursed his axe and watched the night clouds rolling in ahead of the wind that was swinging round to the north-east. There might be more snow yet, before the spring had fully flourished. The less well-off thought it must be wonderful to be born of the nobility, to be the daughter or sister of a duke. To be wedded to a king. Pallig hoiked a globule of spittle into the mud at his feet. Aye, well, that depended on the king, didn't it?

Fumbling with the wicker gate, Emma wrinkled her nose at the foul stench of human waste and, holding her breath, squatted quickly over the hole in the covering board. Rearranging her garments, she took several hasty steps away from the noisome place, gulping clean air into her choking lungs, swallowing down the nauseous churn of her stomach. Pallig was waiting patiently, his back towards her. Was she the fool to think that he liked her? That they might become friends? She smoothed her gown, admiring, yet again, the expensive decoration. She had been told that Pallig had chosen to serve her, but then, they had said similar in Normandy. '*It is a good choice, chérie, that you have made, to wed this English king.*'

The freedom of choice? Hah! She had good reason to be cynical of choice!

She shivered, gathered her cloak tighter. Now that the rain had cleared a mist was rising, creeping in over the palisade walls from the sodden forest beyond. Dusk. It would soon be night, and with night would come . . . Closing her eyes, Emma thrust the thought aside; instead, filled her nostrils with clean, spring-scented, rain-washed evening air. England smelt different to Normandy. Damper, more earthy.

She had not accounted for the deep breath mixing with the surfeit of ale and her head whirled and spun. '*Dieu!*' she gasped, feeling herself toppling forward, the nausea that had been churned to the surface by the stink of the latrine rising higher into her throat. She put out her hand, intending to steady herself against the granary wall, and was promptly sick.

Pallig was there, supporting her, his arm going around her waist, the great axe dropped, forgotten, to the muddy ground. His distorted face peered closely into her unfocused eyes. 'My Lady?' he asked, hurried, concerned. 'Are you all right?'

Sagging against his strength, Emma laid her pounding head on to his shoulder, feeling as if she would lose consciousness, but the swirl of red thankfully passed and her stomach sank down to where it belonged.

Fumbling to untie the linen kerchief tucked into the neckband of his hauberk, Pallig dabbed at her mouth, wiping away the unpleasant residue.

'I fear,' she said, attempting to lighten her embarrassment by a weak jest, 'that I have drunk over much of my Bride Ale.'

Pallig laughed, the sound deep and husky. Friendly. His arm firm and comforting. 'That is no bad thing for a wedding feasting, I am thinking!'

Her mouth twitched into a grateful smile, and he smiled back at her. 'Unfortunately,' he said with a grin, 'it may be a good thing for a feast, but too much drink can be bad for the head and stomach.' Removing his arm, he bent to retrieve his axe. 'Although there will be more than a few nursing sore heads on the morrow, I am thinking. The King included.' He stuffed the soiled kerchief through his leather baldric, rubbed his nose with his fingers, added, 'And if you forgive me my outspokenness, Lady, a shy maid such as yourself may be better off on the wrong side of sober this night.'

Pallig had his own young wife. He loved Gunnhilda and she him, yet their first bedding had been an anxious time for her. It was no easy thing for a maid to put her trust in a man so completely on that

28

first occasion. Was it so surprising? Too many men gave their wives no more regard than the hounds in the kennels and blatantly abused that given trust by caring nothing for the woman's part in the doing of a wedding night.

6

The men entering Emma's bedchamber were drunk with wine, cider, ale and laughter. It was a small room, perched above the eastern end of the Queen's Hall, reached by a narrow wooden stair, and seemed smaller with the great bulk of lewd-minded men crowding in. Furnished simply, it held two chests, one for bed linen, one for garments; two stools and a table, on which stood a pewter bowl of dried fruit, a jug of wine with two attendant goblets, Emma's jewel casket and her personal toilet equipment, combs and hairpins.

The wooden box bed with its goose-feather mattress, linen sheets and piled animal furs, was draped by heavy blue woollen curtains to provide privacy, and to keep out the cold and draughts. There would be plenty of those ushering in beneath the door and through the cracks in the timber walls and floor. Tomorrow, or some day soon, Emma intended to set about making the room more homely, hang on the walls some of the large embroideries that were becoming fashionable in France. Tapestries they were commonly called, though they were not woven but stitched by hand. She would find some suitable skins to place on the floor, too. Bear was best, as it was thick and hard-wearing. Perhaps a clay pot to put some spring flowers in? Add her modest collection of precious books and the rest of her personal possessions to the few that her women had already unpacked – with imagination and skill, she could make this a pleasant place for herself. A royal bower, where her command ruled, and solitude, should she require it, could be paramount. For tonight, though, command stood for naught and solitude was as far from her reach as were the stars in the sky. She would be obliged to share this bare place with her husband on most nights during the customary honey-mead moon-month of celebration. He was as raucously drunk as the dozen men who had escorted him here.

This was the way of things, Emma knew that, for her sisters had been put publicly to bed with their new husbands on their wedding nights. But, stupidly, she had thought that being a crowned queen, and wed to a king, she would be exempt from the embarrassing humiliation of it all. Sitting, hunched and naked in the bed, her arms clutched around her knees, with the bed furs pulled up to her chin, as much for warmth as modesty, she chided herself for being so naive. Being a queen would make it more necessary to be seen bedded with her husband. She had to provide him with legitimate sons, had to be seen to become the King's consummated wife.

Emma blinked aside tears. Her headache had worsened and her stomach was feeling queasy again; bit her lip as Lady Godgifa, appointed as her lady-in-waiting, stretched forward and, with a flick of her hand, exposed Emma's nakedness. 'Show yourself, girl. Let your husband see what he is getting.'

Lady Godgifa, wife to Alfhelm, one of the King's ealdormen. An arrogant woman who made no attempt to conceal her dislike of this Norman-born girl. Godgifa, able to speak both Danish and French, had agreed to do her duty to the best of her ability, but refused to step any further. She disapproved of this marriage and cared not who knew it, for her daughter ought to have married the King, not this foreign incomer.

Embarrassed, Emma wanted to cry out, to curl herself tight and hide from the glinting male eyes that were inspecting her breasts and body. It took courage for her to stare straight ahead, to straighten her legs and bring her arms away from covering herself. More courage to stop the cry of dismay from reaching her throat when her wretched brother, as drunk as the rest of them, said scornfully, 'Her teats are as flat as unleavened bread, but they should swell once her belly bloats with child.'

His words stung. In this vulnerable situation, could he not have offered her support? Damn him! Her one comfort, Æthelred and his lords would not have understood his slurred French.

'By God, there's nothing of her!' Æthelred declared, spreading his hands in dismay. 'I will be spending half the night trying to find her.'

Someone, answering with a great bellow of wit, indicated Æthelred's already rising manhood. 'Just point your pizzle in the right direction, it has the sense to find its way into harbour!'

If she had concentrated she might have worked out one or two of the English words, but she had no inclination to listen. All she wanted to do was burrow under the covers or run away. To scream, plead, be left alone. Join a nunnery. Die. Anything but be here, suffering this humiliating experience.

With more laughter and tawdry advice they put Æthelred into the bed beside her, tucking the furs around them as if they were babes needing swaddling. Æthelred's priest, the only man who had stayed mute in the background, sprinkled holy water over them both, and muttered a few liturgies about fruitfulness and the duties of marriage. Then her women were snuffing out the candles and chivvying the men from the chamber, the laughter and the increasing rude advice to aid the King's performance diminishing in volume as the door closed. Not that they went away. From the noise, it sounded as though all of them were huddled on the landing beyond the door, although, with the night-guard, there could be no room for more than three.

'My other wife, Ælfgifu, was barely older than you when I bedded her,' Æthelred said, stretching out his hand to tuck a strand of hair behind Emma's ear, 'but she knew of the world, knew already how to pleasure a man.' He snorted. 'Mama was unaware of her being a used whore. Once I took her into my bed she remained loyal to me, so it mattered not.' He did not add his private thought, that it was a simple thing to ensure: keep a woman busy with a child at her breast or in her belly and she would not have the chance to stray. He sighed, this girl was so young; what was he to do with her? More to the point, what could she do for him?

Would his mother, had she been alive, have approved of his choice of Emma? Æthelred studied her drawn, pale face, the tremble of her lip and the shiver of apprehension. Aye, Ælfthryth would have agreed to this Norman girl, for her worthiness of breeding would have been attractive to her personal vanity.

His hand dropped to cup Emma's breast; this had to be done, for

32

the child's sake he would get it over and finished as soon as possible.

Emma closed her eyes and, whether it was the ale or her fear, both perhaps, she found her conscious self drifting into a mist of unreality, a waking dream, as if the discomfort was happening to someone else. Vaguely, she was aware of his weight on top of her and that it hurt as he pushed himself in, but otherwise it was as if her whole being had become blank and numbed. He rolled from her, turned away and was instantly asleep.

She lay still, aware of an uncomfortable soreness between her thighs and the feel of a trickle of blood. Was that it? Was this what she could expect whenever he came to her bed? To be used and then discarded? She let her breath go, unaware that she had been holding it in.

'Tears are to be kept private,' her mother had said. What of pain and despair? Were they also to be hidden? Shut away out of sight, like soiled linen? How was she to endure this? Night after night? Time stretched ahead, a tunnel of black, stark loneliness.

Only one candle burnt, flickering as a draught toyed with the flame. Emma turned her head, watched the yellow glow flutter dark shadows along the walls. From down in the Hall the noise of celebration rumbled up through the floor. Some of the men had joined the women, resuming the dancing and pleasures of earlier in the evening. A crash; the shriek of a woman's drunken laughter; the deeper bellow of a man's voice. Had a trestle table been knocked over? From the clatter of pottery and metal it sounded as if it had.

The wick untrimmed, the candle began to smoke, then gutted out, the only light coming from the strip beneath the doorway.

Do not shed tears in public, Mama had instructed. Well, she was not in public, there was no one here to see her cry.

Beside her, Æthelred began to snore.

7

Pallig undressed quietly, not wishing to disturb the woman in the bed, or the child sleeping like an innocent angel in her cot. All the same, he could not resist a peep at the girl, her thumb stuffed into her mouth, fair hair framing her cherubic face. No doubt she had led her nurse a merry dance before settling to sleep. The little imp always did. He touched a kiss to his fingers, placed them tenderly on her forehead then, snuffing out the candle stub, climbed into bed beside his wife.

Gunnhilda stirred, disturbed by the ice coldness of his feet. 'Was it a good feasting?' she asked, her honey voice drowsy with sleep.

'Very good, but would have been all the better had you been there.'

She snuggled closer to him, her arms wrapping around the solidity of his muscled body. 'But you were too busy with your other woman to have noticed or cared about me.'

Her husband did not rise to her teasing. Gunnhilda was proud that her man had become Queen's Captain, although she had not been surprised. There were few men who could outshine Pallig, despite the ugly rumours that were still rumbling, concerning that awkward incident in Devon-Shire last summer.

'How are you feeling?' Pallig asked, smoothing his hand over her forehead to see if it were cool, brushing back the corn-gold hair that his daughter, asleep in her cradle, had inherited.

'I am well,' his wife answered, her own hand caressing his chest. 'Tired, that's all. I intend to start going about my normal life in a few days.'

Pulling back from her, Pallig immediately opposed the suggestion. 'You most certainly will not! I forbid it!'

Gunnhilda batted her hand at him. 'Oh, don't fuss! The bleeding and the pains have not been with me these last five days. I cannot lie abed for the rest of this pregnancy! October is too many months ahead for so much idleness.'

'But you nearly lost the child . . .' Pallig's protest was silenced by Gunnhilda touching her fingers to his lips.

She smiled, pulled him down into the warmth of the bed. 'My breath smells sweet and my urine is clear. I have rested and I am well. So is the child.'

Grinning into the darkness, Pallig kissed her forehead and settled himself comfortable. After a long silence he said, 'I feel for her, you know.'

Gunnhilda was almost asleep. 'Mm? Who do you feel for?'

'Our little Queen.'

Pallig had set eyes on Gunnhilda eight years past. A girl of fifteen and royal born, half-sister to the King of the Danes, Swein Forkbeard. Swein had brought her to England to find her a husband, although he had not quite foreseen the one she had then managed to find herself. That had been in 994. Pallig was one of Æthelred's thegns taking the raised tribute to pay the Danes to go away and leave England alone. That was all they came for, to fill their sacks with silver and gold, to take what wealth they could carry and then go home to Denmark. It made sense to pay the bastards outright and see them gone, cheaper too, in the long run. Better to concede taxes than suffer the consequences of bloody death, butchered cattle and violated women.

King Swein's plan, in 994, had been to ally with one of the northern lords, find himself a toehold for the next year's raiding and, if fortune smiled, the year after that also. Pallig grinned into the darkness, squeezed the soft, yielding skin of Gunnhilda's shoulder. Swein had reckoned his scheme without the unexpected interference of passionate young love.

It had been instant, their liking for each other. Pallig's eyes had met Gunnhilda's as she had served the cup of welcome to her brother's guests and when Pallig rode away from the King's camp the following morning she had ridden with him, perched behind his saddle, her arms tight-woven about his waist. Swein had bellowed his disapproval, had raged, ranted, pleaded and cajoled, but Gunnhilda had listened to none of it. Even the threat that he would think of her as dead were she to make the fool of herself with this Englishman held no sway.

After all this while of marriage, of bearing the three-year-old daughter who slept in the cot and losing two others before they saw more than four months of life, Gunnhilda thought she knew how to read Pallig's moods. If nothing else, she knew when to guess that something was mithering at him and that he would not sleep until he had talked whatever it was through to its end, chewed it up and spat the gristle from his mouth.

She asked, 'What is she like, then, this Emma of Normandy?'

'Fair-haired, fair-faced. Eyes that can seem black in a certain light, eyes that will one day, I am thinking, have the ability to look right through to a man's soul.'

'You liked her?'

Pallig answered slowly, uncertain. He felt pity for the lass, without question he would serve her honestly with loyalty and honour, but did he like her? 'Aye,' he at last said, 'I do like her. She's naught but a lonely, apprehensive child at the moment, more naive than ever my sisters were, but I like her. She has a quality about her that has been lacking in our English noblewomen for some years.' He rubbed his hand over the bristles of his chin. 'There's something about her, I know not what it is yet, just a *something* that has alerted my interest in her.' He ran his fingers through his hair, scratched at an itch on his scalp, rummaged through his thoughts for a thing more tangible to say.

'It's like looking at a tight-curled bud on a tree. You know it will blossom when the sun warms it through, but will it flower as pink or white? Will it develop into a succulent fruit, or wither away, get burnt by the frost or parched by a lack of rain?' He shifted his arm, grimacing as cramp niggled the muscles. 'Or the bud can be broken before it blooms, brushed aside by a clumsy man or beast, to die unnoticed by the wayside. It will be a great pity, and a loss for England I am thinking, if this particular little bud is not nurtured into fruition.'

'And you don't think Æthelred is the right man to do so?'

Pallig snorted contempt. 'Do you?'

Gunnhilda made no answer. Her husband knew well her contemptuous opinion of Æthelred. 'I would have liked to have been there to greet her,' she said, after a while. 'Do you think she would give me audience on the morrow?'

Alarmed, Pallig said too quickly, 'When you are stronger, perhaps. I do not want you tiring yourself.'

'So you do not want me to make a friendship with this shy bud who may turn into a plump fruit worth the plucking? Why is that I wonder?'

As hastily he answered, 'It is not that I do not want you to meet her, *elskede*, my beloved, just not yet, that's all. When you are stronger, when you are not so likely to tire yourself.'

'I see.' Gunnhilda half turned from her husband, folded her arms across her breasts.

'Oh, woman, see sense!' Pallig locked his hands around her wrists, tried to force her defensive arms apart, relented and kissed her with a husband's passionate feeling of love. He wanted her. Rolling aside, he lay quiet, breathing evenly and deeply, willing the need to subside. He welcomed the coming of this child, hoping for it to be a son, but missed the intimacies of lovemaking.

'I am worried that you might do too much too soon,' he said. 'You nearly lost our child, you must take care. This new queen of ours will be here for some long years, trust to God. There is no great urgency for you to meet her.'

'It would not be that you wish to keep me from her, because you fancy plucking her for yourself, then?'

'No, it would not!' The answer came hot and indignant. 'How could you suggest such a thing?'

Gunnhilda chuckled, teasing him, her voice like the merry trickle of a mountain stream. 'I suggest it, because you are hot for a woman and I have a suspicion that you are besotted with her!'

On the edge of denying that also, Pallig realised she was jesting.

'It is the other side round,' he admitted. 'The lass has taken a shine to me.' He laughed. 'Poor, misguided little whelp.'

Gunnhilda touched her lips to his, her taste cool and sensuous. If the truth were known, she wanted her husband as much as he wanted her, but dare not risk the safety of the child.

'Then she does indeed show sense. Only a blind beggar's maid would not see how wonderful a man you are.' She was laughing, but inside she understood Pallig's concern for the girl. Taken from her home, her family and all that she knew, to be set down instead in Æthelred's calloused and soiled hands? She might have a crown on her head, but she had still been abandoned in the midst of a stinking midden.

'Æthelred is an evil toad and one day God shall punish him for the wicked deeds he has committed. And for the way he doubted your honesty and loyalty.' The conviction in Gunnhilda's voice was as solid as the spread roots of an oak tree.

Gathering her to him, Pallig returned the kiss that she had given him. 'That is all in the past, beloved. Done and forgotten. We had a misunderstanding, Æthelred and I, but it was explained and our animosity buried. If he doubted me, would he have agreed this captaincy?'

'Did he have any choice? He needs the support of men who are murmuring dissent against him – needs it like a parched shrub needs drenching rain. Without it he will shrivel and die. You happen to be popular, he could not, therefore, deny them their wish.'

'Æthelred is trying to become an effective king, despite the hindrance of *i-víking* raids and the legacy of his interfering bitch of a mother. England is the better off now that she is dead. We are free of her meddling, and Æthelred has a chance to become his own man.'

'Provided he has the stomach to choose the advisers who are to replace his mother with wise care.'

Pallig grinned into the darkness. 'Your judgement of him is biased, my sweeting. You would never be admitting to his good points.'

'Has he any?'

He kissed the tip of her nose. 'I expect, were I to think on it for a year or two, I might manage to think of one.'

8

Her head hammered, as if a battalion of war drums were being pounded behind her temples, and if one more of these wrinkled baggages called her 'dear', she would . . . Ah, but what could Emma do? Lie on the floor? Kick her legs and bellow like a wayward toddler? Scowl and grimace, and earn for herself more contempt? For all their twittering, fussing and dutiful attention, it did not take intelligence to realise that it was most resentfully given. Lady Godgifa did not like Emma and as Godgifa was the matriarch among them, the women blindly followed her directive. Emma might as well be a churl's daughter for all the heed they were paying to her counter command over what Godgifa ordered. Not that she had yet 'commanded' anything. Tentatively, she had asked if she might have cider instead of ale to drink with her meagre breakfast of sheep's cheese and fresh-baked bread. Cautiously, she had murmured that she would rather wear the blue veil, not the pale rose; timidly, she had asked about the itinerary for this, her first day as Queen. But to give a direct command to someone as authoritative as Lady Godgifa? Sweet Jesu, Emma would rather face a hot-breathed dragon!

To her relief, Æthelred had already been gone from the chamber when she had awoken, muzzy-headed and aching in almost every muscle. Daylight flooded the room beyond the partially drawn bed curtains; with a groan, she had rolled over and buried herself beneath the furs, seeking sleep, but the women had surged in, chivvying her to be up and about, washing her, dressing her, as if she were a feeble child. She was a wife taken, no doubting that, for the stains on the linen and her thighs offered confirming proof. She had not missed the knowing nods and winks as two of them had stripped the bed sheet, removing it for anyone who wished to inspect the irrefutable evidence of her lost virginity.

Necessary formalities had trundled tediously through the morning, accompanied by an endless stream of obsequious faces, the leering and slavering of men bowing over her hand – God's Breath, did none of them wash?

At least the witnessing of granted charters might prove more interesting and the thought of flourishing her signature directly after Æthelred's filled her with an intense excitement. Silly, really, they were only legal documents that would be set aside in some musty old chest, probably never to see the light of day again, but written documents were in Latin, something familiar. She could read Latin for herself, would not need to rely on Archbishop Wulfstan to translate for her. This would also be a chance to show them that she was not a simpleton of a girl with no use beyond the bedchamber. Emma took great pride in her ability to read. Tutored on the Bible, she had avidly read all she could lay hands on, which was a considerable amount, given Richard's manic arrogance for proving his cultured status. His library was extensive: religious texts, the histories, Greek philosophy, the dramatic tragedies and comedies. He had not read one of them, always claiming he was too busy. Emma enjoyed the company that a book could bring, Richard's interest was limited to showing his collection to impressed guests and visitors. Hers had been the mental devouring of them.

Not that Richard had allowed her to read legal charters, save for those made obsolete and destined for the fire. He said she was too young and air-headed to understand legal matters. To her disappointment, she discovered later in the day that these Englishmen shared a similar view.

The Council Chamber was filled with the most important men of the kingdom, who turned, bowed an acknowledgement at her entrance, an act that sent a shiver of pleasure scurrying down her spine. The thrill was short-lived, for within moments they resumed huddled conversation and she was forgotten, left standing, uncertain what to do or where to go. Æthelred was engrossed with his eldest son, Athelstan, talking with his hands animated, shaking his head, scowling in disagreement. The other men were a sea of faces to which she could not pair names. Which one was Uhtred or Alfhelm? She flickered her eyes towards the door, was tempted to flee, half turned, found a man standing behind her, his weather-rugged face grinning, eyes sparking delight as he held out both hands to her and declared, 'By the gods, Madam, you are a sight for sore eyes this rain-ragged morning! If ever there was a cure for a mead-muddled head, it is the beauty of a lovely woman and you, my dear, must be among the loveliest!'

Emma blushed, dipped her head, flattered but flustered. She had met this man yesterday, but who was he? Oh! What was his name?

Did he read her face, realise her consternation? He bowed low, took her hand in his own and kissed it. 'Thegn Wulfnoth at your service, Lady. I am ship-master to the King.'

Another man, not a few yards away, spun round, his nose and mouth wrinkled, sneering. 'You flatter yourself, Wulfnoth, and exaggerate. This man, my Queen, is a sea merchant who boasts a fleet of ships, which earn more for him through his underhand methods of piracy than they do in providing taxed revenue for the King. I would advise you to salt his words to disguise any tainted flavour.' He spoke in Danish.

'Thank you, Sir, for your advice, I shall keep it in mind.' She could not remember his name, either.

The man nodded his head, returned to his discussion with two bishops. How many of them, she suddenly wondered, were perfectly capable of using a language she knew? But how many used it? And then a second thought. She glanced at Æthelred, who was now shouting angrily at his son. Was he, too, perfectly capable of speaking to her in familiar words?

Wulfnoth saw her apprehensive glance and, misinterpreting her thoughts, said in French, in a lowered voice, 'For temperament, the King takes after his mother, she was a harpy. I admit I was pleased to see the back of her.' He crossed himself, added hastily, 'May God assoil her soul.'

'I have not heard flattering things of the Lady Ælfthryth,' Emma confessed. 'My mother said she was a woman determined to keep hold of her power through the name of her son.'

The Thegn smiled appreciation. 'An astute woman, your mother. Ælfthryth was a bitch, although she had her share of supporters, men and women who wanted to shelter beneath the shade of her power.' Wulfnoth shook his head, had no one schooled this child on the more disreputable side of political necessity? 'A woman can only hold status through her father, husband or son. Without them she is nothing.' He gave a wry smile. 'Unless she becomes a queen who, even after widowhood, has nurtured enough power to retain her position. Ælfthryth retained her authority by ensuring that it was her own son who became king, not the elder stepson.'

Her hand going to her throat, Emma suppressed a squeak of fear. 'It is true, then? Æthelred's brother was murdered?'

Wulfnoth shrugged. 'There was no proof of who ordered it, but *oui*, Edward was cut down as he arrived in innocence at Ælfthryth's stronghold of Corfe.' Seeing the Queen's sudden alarm, Wulfnoth laughed. 'Take no notice of me, Madam. As our eminent Reeve, Eadric Streona said, I am prone to exaggeration!'

Emma laughed with him. *Mais oui*, Eadric – that was his name! An obsequious man, whom Emma had taken instant dislike to on that first day. Thegn Wulfnoth might be a rogue, but Emma judged, correctly, that he was no hypocrite. 'This England seems a dangerous place,' she said astutely. 'If a king cannot be safe from his own, what hope of protection is there from the *í-víking* pirates and cut-throats who persist in their bloody raiding? In Normandy our castles are built of stone, are defended by high walls and deep moats.' She indicated the wattle and timber of this, the King's Council Chamber, so flimsy in comparison with what she was accustomed to.

'In Normandy your noblemen spend their time bickering among each other over the accumulation of land and wealth. They wall themselves up behind great castles of stone to protect themselves against the greed of neighbours. In England, as a rule, we prefer to negotiate our way to peace, rather than shed the blood of our own.'

Emma could see an anomaly in that, but did not say so. In England, if a nobleman fell out with his king, exile, or a convenient accident, was often the result. At least in Normandy the fighting was open for all to see, dictated by the rules of war and battle. Æthelred's mother had apparently gained what she wanted through vicious murder. How essential was it to assure that your own son ascended to the throne, Emma wondered suddenly? Enough to risk the fires of Hell and eternal damnation?

'But what of protection against attack?' she asked, shying away from the uncomfortable thought. 'I am here, entered into this marriage to prevent the Danes from using our Norman harbours.' She fiddled with the ring placed on her finger, unfamiliar in its feel, resting next to the thinner marriage band. Her coronation ring, the symbol of her unity to God and the Kingdom.

'*Receive the symbols of honour so that you may shine out in your splendour, and be crowned with eternal joy.*' What in the name of God could she do for England if the Danes decided to run against Richard's treaty with Æthelred?

Seeing the doubt, Wulfnoth paternally patted her hand. 'The Vikings seek easy-come wealth; they care only to sail in on a flood tide and leave again on the ebb. You are quite safe, they do not have the balls to lay a lengthy siege to town or palace.'

Smiling politely Emma made no answer. Normans were men who lived and breathed – died – for the glory of the fight. They swaggered inside their stone-defended homes, awaiting the opportunity for a neighbour to lower his guard, and then took all for themselves. The *í-víking* raiders were no different. Was Æthelred aware that no stone battlements had ever stopped her father? And that the Danish and the Norman were no different when it came to the taking of easy-come spoil? God help England, and her, she thought, should the Danish King, Swein Forkbeard, ever decide to acquire more than a hoard of gold, or a chest full of silver.

A man, suddenly at her side, startled her. Emma had not realised that her attention had drifted and Archbishop Wulfstan of York was offering his arm. 'It is time to sign the charter of your *morgengifu*, my Lady, the morning gift that the King has granted you.' He pointed to the scroll of parchment the clerk was rolling open upon the table, the one Richard had been reading. Vaguely, Wulfstan indicated the close-written words. 'This witnessing will be your first public duty as Queen. To you is given the town of Winchester and in the Shire of Devon, Exeter. Winchester, of course, was held by the Dowager Queen, until her recent going to God.' Wulfstan crossed himself, as did they all, Emma included.

Winchester? Emma recollected reading about Winchester. Had that not been the Great King Alfred's royal town? The place from where he had ruled during the first encroachment into England by the Danes? But where Winchester was, and this obscure place of Exeter, she had no idea. On the far edge of the world, for all she knew.

'Did you say Devon-Shire, my Lord Archbishop?' she queried, realising a familiar name, her smile becoming relaxed, radiant. Devon she had heard of. She turned to Pallig, who stood, as ever, discreet a few paces to her left. 'Do you not hold an estate in the Shire of Devon? We shall be neighbours then, perhaps we can sit of a winter's evening and compare the yields of our crops and cattle!' She assumed that he did not laugh at her feeble jest because it was a poor one. Embarrassed, she turned attention back to the parchment. Was Devon, then, a place of deep forests or open marshes? Was there no corn or cattle there? She had, yet again, made herself look the fool.

Unaware of her discomfort, Æthelred scrawled his signature and made way for her to sign. Eagerly, she scanned the wording; voilà, it was as they said, the towns they had named and several more gifts listed. Tangible stuff: linens and brocades, silks, spices and jewels.

Wulfstan, at her elbow, coughed discreetly. Spoke to her, as always, in French. 'There is no necessity for you to read it for yourself, my Queen. The clerks have ascertained that the document is in order.'

'That they may have, but I wish to know what I am being given and what I am putting my name to.' Added with a light laugh, 'I know not what I might be signing away!'

Standing with his arms folded, awaiting his turn to sign, inwardly annoyed that his sister took precedence over him, Richard jabbed his finger at the parchment. 'You are signing for your lost maidenhood, girl, nothing more important than that. This is an exchange for your virginity, as was agreed between myself and England long before now. It is only the formalities of completion to be done. A woman has no necessity to read what she would not understand. Hurry and sign.'

Signing away her innocence? Emma took up the stylus, dipped its point in the ink. Were they worth it, these towns of Winchester and Exeter? These fineries and valuables? Were they worth the pain, embarrassment and discomfort that Æthelred had inflicted on her last night? She began writing, 'Emma . . .'

'*Non, madame*, not Emma, do not sign as Emma!' Wulfstan lurched forward, snatching the writing implement from her hand, causing her to gasp as the sticky ink spilled and smudged. He signalled for the clerk to blot the mess with sand and scrape the mistake away with a smoothed pebble. 'Do you not recall? You are now known as Ælfgifu. You were blessed with your new-taken English name yesterday, after your crowning.'

Emma blanched, a swirl of sickness surging in her stomach. She did not remember that! *Oui*, she remembered the Archbishop saying the name, but she had thought nothing of it, not among the confusion and bewilderment of that long service. So much of it had been unfamiliar and conducted in English, meaningless. Stupidly, she had thought Ælfgifu to have been assigned as an honorary title.

'Emma is too Norman a name for our English taste; you are to be called Ælfgifu, the name of Æthelred's grandmother.'

And his first wife. And the precocious daughter of Lady Godgifu.

'This also was agreed?' she asked of her brother, her eyes wide to hold back angry tears. Had no one, not once, considered seeking her thoughts and wishes?

'*Naturellement*. What difference does it make? A name is a name.'

She almost screamed, *They want; you want! What about me? Me! Me! Me! What about what I want?* They had taken everything from her. Her home, her family, her innocence. And now her name.

Well, they would not take away her pride! That, none of them could touch!

'I agree with you, Brother,' she said stiffly. 'A woman has no need to read what she would not understand, but I am no ordinary woman, I am a queen and this Queen can well understand what she is reading!' To herself she vowed, *And I am Emma. That is the name baptised upon me at birth; that is the name that shall accompany me to my grave. They may call me what they will, but in the privacy of my mind, and in my own home, I shall not, will not, give up what is mine.*

She motioned for a stool to be brought, sat and carefully read every word, steadfastly ignoring the surreptitious coughs and shuffling feet. Satisfied, she began to add her name, writing very precisely:

Ælfgifu Regina

9

The men were in the King's Hall, the noise of their shouting and bellowed laughter drowning the toll of the cathedral bell calling to Vespers. A single star was glistening low down on the horizon, bright and shining against the darkening blue. Soon it would be night and Emma would have to go through it all again. She walked stoically on, thrusting the fear of having to share her bed with a man she could never see herself liking, let alone loving. Pointing along a narrow alleyway between the two enormous granary barns, she asked Pallig, walking a respectful few feet behind her, 'What is down here?' She sniffed, 'Stabling?'

She had been determined to walk in the fresh air, to attempt to clear the stubborn headache that had persisted throughout the long, confusing day. She had upset them, she knew, those men who had muttered and tutted at her reading of that charter. Well, let them fuss and fume like puffs of smoke squinnying a way out through the peat of a burning charcoal mound. She was Queen, she could do what she wanted! Only, it was not all as simple as that.

'Aye, Lady, stabling and kennels. It is muddy underfoot along there, though.'

Pallig was indulging her, she could see it in his eyes, hear it in his patient voice, as if he were a father calming a fractious child. 'I want to walk,' she had said, 'to see something of what I am Queen of.' Politely, he had agreed to accompany her, only everything was wet from yesterday's rain and she had forgotten to change her soft house shoes for more robust boots; did not like to admit her error and return to her chamber.

'Is there another way around?' she asked. 'I would like to see the horses.'

Pallig nodded, indicated she was to continue ahead, stepping forward to show the way, his head whipping up and round as a noise burst from the narrow path and a brindle-coated dog, a leggy, gangling pup already the size of a small pony, raced down the side path and skidded round the corner, knocking Emma sideways, almost sending her sprawling into the mud. She screamed, from surprise more than fright, and fell heavily against a solid timber upright of the barn wall, wincing as pain twanged down her elbow and tingled uncomfortably into her fingers. Directly behind the dog came a boy, fair-haired, blue-eyed; about eight years of age and cursing as vehemently and colourfully as any grown man. 'God take your balls, you cur! Come here, Loki! Damn your hide, you whelp, come *here*!'

It had all happened so quickly. Pallig whirled as the dog appeared and collided with Emma, without thought raised his axe and swung it down to protect his Queen.

The boy saw the glint of the blade, his shout of fear echoing Emma's shrill cry, 'NO!' He darted forward, hand outstretched to push Pallig forcibly aside, throwing himself into the arc of that swinging death bringer to save his dog.

Emma shrieked, ''Tis but a dog, Pallig!'

Pallig cursed, minutely shifted his balance to let the falling axe traverse through an alternative curve that missed the dog's neck by the breadth of one of his own shaggy hairs. '*Det er fandens*, boy! By the Hammer, what the damn be you thinking of?' Angry, Pallig grabbed the lad's shoulder, shook and shook him, as if he were a rat caught in a yard dog's jaws.

Hitting out with his fists, the boy kicked and squirmed, demanding to be let go. The dog, unaware that it had been so near death, leapt, barking and cavorting around his young master, thinking this new thing a most splendid game. Irritated, his blood rush of instant reaction still pounding, Pallig kicked out with his boot, catching the pup on the muzzle. Yelping, the animal cowered away, batting at his bleeding gum with an absurdly large paw.

'Leave my dog alone, you bastard!' the boy yelled. 'He means no harm!'

'He attacked the Queen, you fly-blown slave-brat! I'll whip your hide raw for this – and that cur's!'

'I'm not slave-born! I'm a thegn's son! Let me go I say!' The boy slammed the heel of his boot into Pallig's shin, causing the man to curse and cuff harder.

The pain in Emma's elbow was receding, the shouting, however, was hurting her head. 'Pallig, please, leave it,' she implored, 'I am unharmed.'

The big man either did not hear or ignored her, for he went on with his vociferous reprimanding. Her nerves jangling, her head pounding, Emma had had enough. Angrily she stamped her foot, shouted, 'Let go of the child!' Louder, 'Let him go. I command it!'

More surprised by the unexpected authority in her voice than the order, Pallig released the lad who, glowering ferociously, ran to inspect the blood dripping from his pup's mouth.

Emma laid her hands against her bumping heart, stared at Pallig, her breath drawing in short bursts, quick and shaken. Had she really done that? Ordered someone in so forthright a manner? And he had obeyed her! It had never happened before, the lowest servants in her brother's castles had heeded her bidding only when it had suited them.

Bowing his head, Pallig said, by way of apology, 'My Queen, I feared you were threatened, that you would be harmed.'

With a steadying breath she recovered her composure. 'For that I thank you, but as you see,' she swept her hand to the boy, 'it is but a lad and his dog. Can they be so much danger to me?' She straightened her gown and the belt, with its dangle of iron keys, the symbol of her womanhood and mistress-ship of a household. 'Naught is hurt save my dignity.' She smiled. 'And I have little of that for it to be dented.'

She bent to examine the dog with the boy. 'The gum is split, if you bathe it with rosemary and comfrey it will soon heal.'

'The tooth is loose,' the boy said with concern, 'look.' With his fingers he wiggled one of the canines. 'He'll lose it for sure, just as well it is only a pup's tooth, not his full-grown one. I would not like him to be disadvantaged against the other dogs. My father's hounds can be a bad-tempered lot.'

'So can your father when roused,' Pallig growled, also squinting at the dog's bleeding gum.

The boy glanced up at him, grinned. 'Aye, you're right there! He'll whip the backside off me if he hears of this.' He turned to Emma, bowed his head, fell serious. 'Forgive me, Lady. This wayward dog of mine is not yet as obedient as I would like him to be. I trust you have come to no hurt? That you are not angry with me?'

'I am angry merely at the fact that you have an advantage. I have no knowledge of your name, nor of your rough-tempered father.'

Again the boy grinned as he looked square and unashamed into her eyes, his stance and bearing reflecting nothing but pride. 'You do know my father, he is Wulfnoth, Thegn of the Manor of Compton in the region of the South Saxons and Master of the Wessex contingent of the King's scyp fyrd. I am Godwine, his eldest son. We have the royal blood of Alfred in our veins.' He gave a slight shrug, admitted, 'Though I confess it is somewhat diluted.'

Wulfnoth? Emma clapped her hands, delighted. She liked Wulfnoth, one of the few who had made her feel welcome here in this godforsaken damp and dismal place called England. This boy did not have the beard, or the sea-weathered, tanned and crinkled skin of his father, but the likeness was there, now that she knew what to look for.

'When I am come to manhood, I intend to serve the King and become an ealdorman,' Godwine declared with forthright boasting.

Emma smiled. She did not doubt it! 'Or perhaps you could serve your Queen?' she suggested tentatively.

Chewing the corner of his lower lip, Godwine frowned. That had not occurred to him before. 'Aye,' he answered after a short pause to think on the matter. He grinned, suddenly liking the idea. 'Aye, perhaps I could.'

'You speak good Danish,' Emma said to keep the conversation alive, aware that she was deliberately avoiding a return to the Hall. 'It is most disconcerting to be unsure of what people are saying about you.'

'My grandfather was also a sea trader,' Godwine explained,

ignoring the snort of derision that Pallig made, 'before the joint ache got into his knees and forced him to stay abed. He spends most the day complaining that he would have no trouble setting the world to rights, if only his legs were able to carry him again. Father says he is a mithering old goat. He taught Papa the different tongues of a trader's world, as he is tutoring myself and my brother. My brother will probably go to the monastery before long; he has a lame leg, so he'll not be making a seaman. Or a thegn.' Almost in mid-sentence, Godwine changed to an attempt at French. '*Je parle très bien le français, n'est ce pas?*'

Delighted, Emma clapped her hands. '*Mais oui, très bien!*'

Godwine indicated her Captain, 'Thegn Pallig's father was from Oxford. *His* father was Danish, blood-kindred to King Erik of the Bloodaxe, so Pallig was able to claim a wife of the royal Danish line. She is a half-sister to Swein Forkbeard, King of the Danes.'

Clipping the back of his hand against the lad's ear, Pallig scolded, 'Hush, boy, we do not want our hearing scorched by your prattling.'

Emma had fallen silent, the smile that had been in her eyes faded. Pallig had a wife? Pallig, the man who was going to be her loyal friend? Always at her side, always there? He had a wife, another loyalty? 'You are wed?' she asked lamely, her large eyes imploring him to deny it.

But he did not. 'Aye, Lady, and a daughter of three years, with another child due, come the autumn.'

If Pallig had a wife she would have to share him, he would not devote himself solely to her, he . . . 'But you are my Captain!' she blurted, dismayed and disappointed.

'I am well capable of doing my duty to you, as your Captain of Cnights, and remain a loyal husband to my wife.'

Emma swallowed tears. There had been so much that was new and so bewilderingly frightening these last days. Everything of her life had been tossed high into the air and had landed again in a higgle-piggle muddle where she could find nothing, not even herself. Nothing was familiar, nothing was safe. 'I thought you were going to be my friend,' she mumbled lamely, her chin lowered, her hands linked, short nails biting into her own flesh. 'I do so need a friend.'

Pallig laid one finger beneath her chin, tipped her face upwards, said with gentle kindness, 'If I did not intend to become your friend, then never would I have agreed to taking the honour of being your Captain.'

'You will like Gunnhilda,' Godwine interrupted eagerly. 'She is one of the few women around here who is not stuffed as full as a pony's nosebag with her own importance. She's nice.' He grinned at Pallig. 'Isn't she?'

The man guffawed. 'I think so, but then, my opinion is heavily weighted.'

'What is all this? Straying from your wife, eh, Pallig? Does she know you are looking elsewhere for pleasure?'

At the sudden voice, Pallig turned, his brow furrowing. Emma took a step backwards, her face flushing crimson, aware the newcomer had seen the way her Captain had tilted her chin, had smiled at her. There had been nothing untoward in the gesture, but the King's eldest son was the sort of man who would see chalk where there was gold, if it suited him.

Pallig bent to retrieve his axe, wiped its blade edge with his thumb. Said nothing.

'My brother is searching for you, Godwine,' Athelstan said gruffly. 'Edmund will not be over-pleased to discover you have been consorting with the enemy.'

Godwine wiped his hand under his nose, sniffed. He was wary of Athelstan, who could be short-tempered and humourless, unlike his younger brother, who was a good friend and as adept as Godwine at getting into mischief.

Casually inspecting the edge of his axe blade, Pallig answered for the boy, in English, 'Spite is not a fitting companion for a future king, my Lord. Especially when it is directed at a lass who cannot defend herself in word or action.' He nodded at Emma. 'This marriage was your father's doing, not hers.'

'I have nothing against the girl,' Athelstan growled as he stalked away. 'As long as she proves to be barren.'

Emma looked from Pallig to Godwine, aware there had been an unpleasant exchange and that she had been the subject of it. Tilting her head, she regarded her Captain, her eyes staring steadfast into his. 'I think', she said, 'that the King's son does not like me.'

Pallig shrugged, making light of things. 'He will come round.'

Emma gave a small, shy, but knowing smile. 'No, Pallig, I think he will not.'

10

Athelstan was not in the best of moods. Too much ale from last night drummed in his head; late from his bed, the porridge in the kitchen breakfast cauldron had all but gone and he had been obliged to eat the burnt and congealed lump at the bottom. And he lost his temper with his father. Again.

He could never do right as far as Æthelred was concerned. If he stayed away from Council he was called a lazy imbecile, if he asked to attend, he was accused of stepping in his father's shadow. What did the damn man want from him? His blood? Add to that, it was raining again. The courtyard was awash with the slime of mud and judging by the grey monotony of the sky the foul weather was here for the entire day.

Striding into the stables, Athelstan paused at the sound of animated talk, his brother and that whelp, Thegn Wulfnoth's boy, Godwine. That lad could be as unruly and rebellious as his quarrelsome father and, to add to Athelstan's annoyance, they were talking of the Queen.

'Good God, boy!' Athelstan barked as he selected his saddle from the rack. 'You speak of her as if she were the Madonna, not a Norman interloper.'

Edmund scowled. 'I only said that the Queen was learning English quickly, what is wrong with that?' Why was his elder brother always so tetchy and belligerent? He never seemed to laugh or jest these days, nor have a good word to say of anybody, save for their dead grandmother.

Clicking to his stallion to make it move over, Athelstan busied himself harnessing the animal. 'The way you speak, anyone would think Ælfgifu was Godgifted,' Athelstan said scathingly.

'She prefers to be called Emma, you know that. You're only

jealous because she is in our grandmother's place.' Edmund's retort was as bloody-minded as his brother's. 'Well, Grandmama is dead and mouldering in her grave, and you should be forgetting about her now.'

'Forget Grandmama? If it had not been for her, I would have had nothing!'

'Aye, and it is because of her that I have nothing!' Edmund's response was abrupt and passionate. He was tired of having to compete with a memory, for unlike his brother he had every reason to be indifferent about their paternal grandmother, who had shown affection only for Athelstan.

Embarrassed at the argument, Godwine, brushing at the shedding winter coat of his pony, bent to clean the animal's belly. He was not yet nine and appreciated Edmund's friendship, realising that because of it he was more often at Court than most boys his age. Out of loyalty to his friend, or from his own precocious opinion, he had as little as possible to do with Athelstan. Godwine did not dislike the elder of the two brothers, but openly admitted he was afraid of the tall, hefty man. He never seemed to do or say the right thing whenever Athelstan was near, always managing to make a fool of himself, give the impression that he was a moon-tainted imbecile.

Athelstan led his horse from the stall and clipped his hand against Edmund's ear as he passed by. 'You do not want to have anything to do with this Queen, boy. If she has a son, where will that leave me? I intend to be king after Papa, me, not one of her bastards.'

Edmund's answer was hot with indignation. 'What if I am elected king instead of you? You never seem to think of that, do you?'

Athelstan roared amusement. 'You? King? Don't be absurd, boy! Grandmama trained me for the title, not you.'

Edmund returned, red-faced, to grooming his pony, bringing the tough-bristled brush over the coat with rough, angry sweeps of his arm. He and Godwine were intending to go up to the marshes with the dogs; it would be fun to catch something extra for the kitchen pots. 'No one has faith in me,' he muttered under his breath. 'I'll show you what I'm made of one day, then you'll be sorry.'

'I doubt the King shall be overpleased to hear that his sons are already trying the fit of his crown.'

Athelstan and the two boys swivelled their heads sharply at the sound of the intrusive voice in the doorway, each wearing a similar expression of loathing as they identified the speaker. Eadric Streona. Edmund and Godwine wore a scowled grimace, Athelstan assumed a glower of outright hatred. What his father liked about the man he could not understand, for himself, he had no more tolerance of Streona than a shepherd had for a prowling wolf.

'I am wondering', Eadric said as he sauntered into the barn, aware of the hostility but ignoring it, 'whether this animosity between you and your father, Athelstan, is because you are always alluding to when the crown becomes yours? It was a bad habit your grandmother nurtured in you. Any man, particularly one such as your father, does not care to be reminded so often of his mortality.'

Walking to his own stallion, Streona bent and picked up a hind hoof, checking whether his servant had taken him to the smith to have a lost shoe seen to. The inconvenience had been a nuisance yesterday, while out hunting with the King. Nodding satisfaction, he set the foot down again. No lasting damage done, now the shoe was replaced.

Indicating Athelstan's own mount, Streona said, 'You are not planning on riding out, are you? As I understood it, the King wishes to see you. I believe he has men looking for you.'

'Then they are not looking very hard, are they? Besides, I have no desire to see the King.'

'He wishes you to escort the Queen's brother to Dover.'

'She is his Queen, he can escort him. I am taking my brother and his friend hunting. Hurry and saddle up, you two, I cannot wait all day.'

Innocently, appalled at the idea, Godwine interrupted, 'No, Sir, we were going . . .' Edmund kicked his ankle and shushed him quiet. The brothers fought like rat and dog between themselves, but closed ranks with the solidity of a shield wall when it came to opposing the insidiousness of Eadric Streona.

Streona was dismissive; he shrugged one shoulder, sauntered

back towards the doorway. 'The King cannot go, he has matters to discuss here with his advisers. The situation with these damned Danish merchants is getting out of hand. Have you not heard? There are rumours of disruption spreading throughout the market towns. Traders are refusing to pay their due taxes on the goods they sell. Peasants making dictate to the King? Absurd. We will not tolerate it, and since your father has appointed me Reeve of Oxford-Shire, I intend to assure something is done about it.'

As far as Streona was concerned, this could become the opportunity he needed to act against these foreign incomers: an opportunity to acquire the acres of land that had been given away as tribute during these last two hundred years. Well, if truth be told, for him legally to redistribute the profits of Oxford's lucrative trading income into his own treasury.

Athelstan, assisting Edmund to harness his pony, answered with sarcasm, 'And the King wishes to portray me as his loyal son, no doubt? That makes a change. He usually treats me as something that he has trodden his boot into.' As an afterthought he added, 'Naturally, Eadric, you would have volunteered to escort the Duke, but I heard you recently encountered trouble in Oxford and are now reluctant to venture over far from the King's protection.'

Edmund, who only a moment before had been on the verge of ramming his fist into his brother's teeth, joined in by mischievously adding, 'I heard the market folk there pelted you with rotten fruit.'

Godwine sniggered.

His upper lip puckering in anger, Streona snarled at Wulfnoth's son with intense dislike, 'You think it amusing, do you, lad?' Pride was the one thing Streona nurtured above his first obsession of self-advancement; he would allow neither to be sullied or mocked. Especially not by a spot-faced boy who was the son of a God-cursed pirate trader.

This expected escort duty had, although Streona was unaware of it, been the cause of the argument between the King and his eldest son earlier in the morning. His intervention, now, added oil to a still smouldering fire.

'Do your own dirty work, Papa!' Athelstan had stormed. 'You are facing possible trouble from the Danish merchants settled in your towns? Well, I warned you to think carefully about raising a heregeld to pay Swein Forkbeard to go away; now you want to double the tax payments on the import of market goods as well? You cannot expect your people to pay twice over for your incompetence.'

'It was not called incompetence when my ancestor, Alfred, used the same tactic to protect his kingdom!' Æthelred had roared in retaliation.

'No, but then Alfred was buying time to regroup and gather strength. You are buying into an altogether different option.' Athelstan had turned on his heel and stormed from his father's Hall, having the sense to leave before adding the trail of thought that the difference between Alfred and Æthelred ran deep. Alfred had been a capable, competent king. Æthelred, with no one possessing an ounce of sense among his self-seeking advisers, was not.

Pride, too, was Athelstan's failing. Had his father asked him to escort the Duke of Normandy in a way that had flattered his son there would have been no disagreement, but as it was, Æthelred was a poor master in the art of tact. A severe disadvantage for a leader who, because of his mother's involvement with bloody murder, had begun his reign without a single mote of respect.

Athelstan knew damned well that he would capitulate to his father's wishes. Equally, he was damned if he would do so unless asked politely and, by God, he was certainly not going to take orders from a toad-spawned arse-wiper like Streona.

'Have those ponies saddled and get mounted,' he ordered tersely as he led his stallion past Eadric. 'I'll not hang about like salted herring strips drying in the wind for the likes of you ruffians.' He scowled at the two boys, said nothing until their mounts had clattered through the gateway and out on to the open marsh.

'Edmund, I would advise you to stay away from the Queen. She is not for us.'

Grimacing at Godwine, Edmund repeated, 'You hear that? My brother says you are to keep your distance from the Queen.'

Godwine's pony had been intent on snatching at grass and was a few yards behind. Hauling at the reins and kicking the animal forward to catch up, he muttered, 'Stuff your brother. I like her.'

Looking straight ahead, Edmund grinned. As it happened, he agreed with his friend's opinion, but knew better than to say so within Athelstan's hearing. He rarely agreed with his elder brother, barely a day passing without them exchanging some gruff word, but Edmund was a true Saxon and valued the belief in personal honour. Without good cause, he would never be publicly disloyal to Athelstan; aside, it was never a good idea to rile his brother when he was already hovering on the edge of a foul-mouthed bad mood.

The hunting was good, and Athelstan's temper was better suited when he returned, near dusk, with the boys and three brace of hare for the kitchens, but Godwine could not settle into sleep that night. Two men rolled in their cloaks near him were on their backs, open-mouthed, snoring; someone at the far end of the Hall was coughing and someone else was taking his pleasure with one of the serving girls, their coupling far from discreetly quiet and private. The elite and wealthy had their own chambers, or had found cramped rooms in the inns and taverns, but for the boys and the common men the Hall had to suffice, everyone squashed together, the trestle tables and benches stacked to the sides and hay pallets provided for the more fortunate, the floor rushes, with the fleas and lice, making do for the rest of them. Beside him, Loki was snoring almost as loud as the men, his paws twitching as he chased hares in his sleep. The boy lay, his arms behind his head, staring up into the dark abyss of the rafters that arched high overhead.

Edmund had warned him, a second time, to stay away from the Queen, advising that it was best not to antagonise Athelstan. 'After all,' he had reminded, 'my brother, in probability, will be the next king. It is him you will have to serve, not her.'

Godwine had disagreed, but kept his council. He was only a boy but even this early in life, he knew what he did, and did not, want to do. He adored Edmund and would walk into fire for him, but for Athelstan? No, Godwine could not see himself serving a man who filled him with feelings of apprehension.

He rolled over, put his arms around his dog and snuggled into the warmth of his coat. What could he do for Emma to show her he had taken her suggestion seriously? That he wanted to be a queen's man when he reached maturity? Loki licked his young master's face. It was good to have a dog. Godwine grinned into the darkness, ah, yes, that was what he would do – and bugger Athelstan when he found out! He would be off to Dover with the Duke of Normandy on the morrow, anyway, and by the end of the week the Court would have left Canterbury for the coastal town of Sandwich, Godwine himself returning home to Compton until his father next came to Court. Wulfnoth would soon be out with the ships patrolling the Kent and southern coast, blockading any new raiding from Danish seamen. Yes, it was a good plan.

The boy settled his head on the dog's belly. Fell instantly asleep.

11

Emma sat at the narrow window opening, looking down on the
scurry of the Canterbury streets. Everyone was so purposeful, with
somewhere to go, something to do, including the slaves. Shambling
along in their rags with dirty bare feet, bent heads and backs, they
carried a sense of purpose about them; knew their place and
position, even knew their value. Literally. She sighed, watched a
bedraggled man beating his stubborn donkey with a stick, smiled as
the disgruntled animal lashed out with a hind leg, and caught the
man in the privates. Good for you, little beast, she thought. Wished
she had the courage to kick out at those who were hurting her. Her
brother in particular. Damn him.

Richard had finally departed Canterbury this morning, leaving
with pomp and ceremony, demanding that his sister's guard, her
cnights, and in particular her Captain, be among his escort to
Dover. Was the King's eldest son and his men not enough? If
Richard were genuinely concerned for the matter of safety, she
could have tolerated the request, but Richard's motivations were
always self-centred. He could not bear the thought of a sister having
use of something that he did not.

Æthelred, not endeavouring to conceal from his wife his delight
at the Norman's departure, had gone hunting. The palace was
empty of men and hounds, quiet, and Emma was relieved that her
husband was gone for a few hours, for she felt awkward in his
company, unsure what to do, or say, with her limited ability to speak
in English, aware that after only a month of marriage he was already
growing tired of her. He lay with her at night, grunting at her body,
left their bed soon after sunrise and went about his day, leaving her
to see to her own amusement. In Normandy, her days had been full;
here, in England, she had nothing to do. Her ladies were efficient

and capable, Godgifa grumbling that it was quicker for her to do things herself than mess about translating and explaining to the Queen, never quite saying aloud that she thought of her as a girl with the brain of a mooncalf.

What would she be doing if she were back home? Walking by the river? Riding? Discussing history or literature with her tutor? Oh, this was no good! Normandy was no longer home, *this* was home, England. This depressing, dull palace with its wattle and timber walls, and its mizzle-faced women who whispered behind her back and averted their gaze whenever she turned to face them. She had tried to make friends. Had abandoned the effort as a lost cause.

They were talking, now, in undertones, Emma only understanding the occasional few words, although her use of English was improving daily.

'Disgraceful, the way the King treated my brother in the matter of those thieves of Oxford,' Ethelflad, Godgifa's constant companion, was complaining. 'Giving preference to that Trade Reeve, Thegn Edwine. My brother is ealdorman, he ought not to have had his decision overruled by Æthelred.'

Emma wandered across the room to where her books were piled on the floor, awaiting a safe place of keeping. There were a dozen or so; Richard had refused to allow her to bring more than those that were her own property. Perhaps there was some compensation in being a queen? She had her own entitlement to an income, could purchase what she wished; she would have shelving made and acquire more books. More than Richard would ever have!

'Edwine allowed their burial in the churchyard I believe?' Godgifa tutted as she twisted another handful of raw wool on to her distaff for spinning. 'Thieves have no right to Christian burial.'

'So say I, and my brother, but would the King listen? Nay, not him!'

Almost as if he were remembering an afterthought, Richard's last words to Emma had been, 'You will not suitably manage the dower properties your husband has gifted you with. For Winchester, I have no qualms, but for this backwater pigpen of Exeter I have designated my vassal, Hugh de Varaville, as overseer. He has volunteered to remain in England. The King has agreed to my concerns and has augmented Hugh as constable.' He had waved his hand disdainfully. 'Or reeve, as they say in their absurd language. He shall serve you well.'

'Serve *you* well,' Emma mumbled aloud, as she flicked idly through the heavy pages of parchment in one of the books. She disliked Hugh intensely. A man who would lick Richard's backside if asked and would as soon spit in her face rather than obey the command of a woman.

No farewell, no *bonne chance*, no endearment. Richard had mounted, spurred his horse into a canter and ridden out of Emma's life. She did not regret his going, but his leaving had exposed a great, gaping hole of emptiness; had left her facing the reality of a dismal eternity. She was on her own, a stranger among people she did not know, among women she disliked and who despised her. *Non*, she must not think like this, for she would go mad if she did not aim for a more positive and optimistic future.

'Who is this Exeter?' she asked in faltering English, mistaking who for where.

Exeter. To Emma, the name sounded intriguing and romantic. She pictured a busy and prosperous town that resembled her favourite childhood places in Normandy: Falaise, Aigle, Louviers. She carefully set down the book, her treasured copy of Virgil's *Aeneid*. Of course, there would be no stone castle in Exeter, like that at Falaise, but perhaps a comfortable manor house?

Godgifa was a woman of high status, her husband was Ealdorman Alfhelm of Deira, his guardianship extending from the hills and dales north of York, down to the Humber river and across to the wild mountains of the western coast. Ordinarily, she would have scorned the duty of playing nursemaid to a girl, but Godgifa loathed the barbaric North and dreaded the months she was forced to endure York, a crammed, stinking hovel of a town with its only boast of civilisation the cathedral and Alfhelm's palace. Though 'palace' was an exaggerated description of the complex of buildings that skulked in the shadows of York Minster. Godgifa was wealthy, a dutiful wife and an efficient mother. She was also severely annoyed that Æthelred had chosen this Norman as wife over the offer of her own daughter. Ælfgifu was younger than Emma, not yet ripe for bedding, but she was *English*, not foreign-born.

'Do we really want an outsider as our queen?' Godgifa said, as she often did, in a hushed, English, whisper. 'There is nothing of her, not in body or wit. My daughter would have made the better wife.'

Ethelflad always agreed.

Again, Emma asked her question. '*Où est* Exeter, *s'il vous plait?*'

'Exeter?' Godgifa answered with scorn, altering to French. 'Exeter is a Godforsaken wilderness of midden huts to the South-West. No one who mattered would wish to go there without due reason.'

Emma considered Godgifa's answer to be deliberately acrimonious. Tightly she answered, 'My Captain, Pallig, does not seem to find it so hideous a place.'

Lady Godgifa did not look up, nor falter with the drop spindle as she twisted the strands of wool between her fingers. 'He does not, but then Pallig's opinion is not worth considering, for he is a traitor, who gave his service to that heathen kinsman of his, Swein Forkbeard.'

12

'I want to see the Queen.' Godwine's demand was succinct and to the point.

The cnight's answer, guarding the foot of the stairs that led up to Emma's chamber, as plain. 'Get lost, urchin.'

The boy, ignoring the slur to his status, persisted. 'I have a gift for her. I want to see her.'

'The Lady has received gifts aplenty, ones of a higher value than the trinket you could offer. Now get you gone before I lose my patience with you.' The young man's rough-featured face scowled closely into Godwine's, showing bloodshot eyes, his breath stinking of an overindulgence of barley-brewed ale.

'This one is worth a fortune. To me and my Lady.'

With a head throbbing from last night's excess of feasting, the cnight's hand lashed out, aiming to clip the lad's ear, but Godwine dodged the clumsy movement with ease.

'I'll not go until I see her.' Godwine stated, planting his feet wide. 'Not if I have to stand by this stairway all day.'

'Then stand there you'll be doing. I'm not allowing you to pass.' The guard angled his spear across the first step, resting its tip on the wooden banister rail.

'I trust you shall allow me access to our Lady Queen, though, Leofstan Shortfist?'

Lady Gunnhilda's skin was pale, her cheeks hollow from recent illness, but her eyes, as ever, were bright and her smile dazzling. There was many a man who envied Pallig Thursson his beautiful wife.

Leofstan nodded acquiescently at her. 'I trust you are recovered now, Ma'am?'

Politely, Gunnhilda inclined her head, thanking him for his

concern. 'I had a scare over the babe I carry, and then caught a chill which has kept me longer abed than I would have wished. I am well now, however.' She pointed at the spear barring her way. Grinning sheepishly, Leofstan stamped to attention and withdrew it.

'Lady Gunnhilda?' Seizing his chance, Godwine plucked at her sleeve, hefting the bundle he carried between his arms. 'I have a gift for the Queen, only this mutton head,' he darted a withering look at Leofstan, 'will not let me pass.'

Gunnhilda frowned disapproval. 'I will have you remember that the men beneath my husband's command, master Godwine Wulfnothsson, are not mutton heads. They are men due respect and courtesy.'

Spitting on to the floor, Leofstan nodded vigorously. 'Quite right, Ma'am. Now clear off, you young devil, or I'll take my belt to your backside.'

'On the opposite side of the steerboard,' Gunnhilda continued, totally ignoring Leofstan's comments, 'it is not for a guard to decide who the Queen should, or should not, grant audience to.' She tossed a quick conspirator's grin at Godwine and indicated the bundle he was clutching. 'What is this gift?'

Delighted, Godwine showed her. 'I think she will like it, do you not agree?' he said earnestly.

Gunnhilda nodded, smiled. '*Ja*, I think she will.' Mindful of her condition, she mounted the stairway slowly, heard, through the open door at the top, every word spoken by Lady Godgifa regarding Exeter and her husband, Pallig. 'Some people, my Lady Godgifa,' Gunnhilda said tartly from the threshold, 'prefer the quiet and peace of the wilderness. It is more pleasing on the ear than the snarl of bitches in heat.'

Godgifa's cheeks tinged with pink but she made no answering comment as the Danish woman entered and made her obedience to the Queen.

'Madam, forgive my remiss at not greeting you 'ere now, but I have been confined to my bed. I am Gunnhilda, wife to Pallig Thursson.'

Emma checked an unexpected stab of jealousy. Pallig's wife!

Basing her on these other ladies, she had pictured her as a pinch-faced shrew of no consequence; ridiculous, really. Pallig, so handsome a man, would not have a wife who was less than perfect. The woman curtsying before her, dressed in the Danish style of fashion, with a loose-fitting embroidered tabard-like tunic over her linen shift, instead of one gathered at the waist in Saxon fashion, was confident and pretty. The two oval brooches at her shoulders were of engraved silver, each decorated with emeralds and rubies, both designs in a traditional Scandinavian pattern. Everything about her boasted her Danish origin, unlike Emma's mother, who had become Norman-French to the core on the day of her marriage. Even Gunnhilda's head-dress marked her for what she was, a non-English woman, for her hair, in its single thick braid, hung down her back beneath a linen kerchief covering her head and knotted at the nape of her neck. English women wore a loose veil, while the new fashion among Norman ladies, Emma included, was to wear the veil as a wimple covering both head and neck, fastened loosely at the throat. It was brave of Gunnhilda to retain her individuality against these intolerant English noblewomen.

Emma found herself liking her. The smile reached from Gunnhilda's heart directly into her eyes, her goodness pouring from her like sweet honey dripping from a harvested hive. She indicated that the woman could rise.

'These well-intentioned matrons', Gunnhilda said, 'will serve you well, but Pallig believes you ought to have someone nearer your age and character, to become a friend.' She put her hand on her bulge. 'I apologise that my child delayed my coming to you.'

'Is that not exceedingly presumptive of you both, Gunnhilda? How can your husband know what a queen ought to have?' Godgifa snapped a retort before Emma had a chance to respond. 'Older women have the benefit of experience and wisdom. The Queen does not need friends, she requires guidance and tutoring. I doubt you are able to offer sufficient of either. We,' she indicated Ethelflad, 'were here for my Lady Queen, despite personal difficulties.'

Gunnhilda answered, polite but succinct, 'But then, those who have husbands or brothers who are falling so often from favour with the King have a greater need than mine to prove their loyalty. Somewhat like a poorly made salver, such people often prove to be all shine and no substance.'

'Do the words loyalty and your husband fit together?' Godgifa snapped.

Emma was looking from Godgifa to this newcomer, Gunnhilda, enthralled. The younger woman, calm-voiced, in her mid twenties and beautiful, was outfacing the mid-aged, prune-wrinkled hag. A princess opposing a dragon! This was the stuff of tales and enchantments.

'The slur of my husband being a traitor is proven a false slander, as you well know, Godgifa. Your husband, however, has ignored the King's command on several occasions. Christmas last, he was not at Court, as I recall. Nor the Easter before that. A king can become justifiably suspicious when his ealdormen do not come to his Councils.'

Godgifa thrust herself to her feet, dropping her distaff into the rushes, rage infusing her face. 'My husband could not attend because he was ill!'

'My father says that any man who pleads sickness when faced with the prospect of a fight is not worthy of being called a man and ought to be instantly gelded.' The boy, Godwine, who had been standing outside the doorway, as entranced by the sparring as Emma, innocently added his own half pennyworth to the affray.

Unable to vent her rage on Gunnhilda, Godgifa lunged at him, striking her knuckles against his cheek, knocking him to the floor.

Enraged, Emma hurried forward. How dare this dour, miserable woman hold sway over what she wanted? Yes, she required advice and correct steering through unfamiliar tides, but to have a friend in a friendless place – oh, what she would give for that! She blessed Pallig for his sense and understanding, and for his pretty, young wife. 'Leave the boy alone!' she commanded. 'I will not have my guests ridiculed and abused.'

Breathing hard, her nostrils flaring, Godgifa responded curtly,

'These are not desirable people, Lady Ælfgifu. I advise you not to admit them to your chamber.'

Emma's indignation wafted into full flame. Perhaps it was Gunnhilda's obvious independence, or the encouraging shine in her eyes – or Godwine's tears as he scrabbled to inspect the bundle that had been knocked from his arms. Or perhaps it was nothing more than being addressed as Ælfgifu.

'In private I have asked to be called by my given name, Emma. I will not gainsay what is mine.' Added, with a deep breath of wavering courage, 'And I shall admit into my presence whom I please.'

A long pause of silence, with Emma aware that if she were to look away from Godgifa's glowering stare she would lose the day, skirmish, battle and war together. The opportunity to be her own woman, to rule as a queen should rule had been thrown before her, and she would be the prize fool to turn around and leave it lying, abandoned and untouched, on the floor. She kept her face passive, unreadable; breathe in, hold, release. Unclench the hands, relax the shoulders. Keep the eyes still, looking ahead. Blink slowly. Emma could hear, in her mind, her mother's instructions for remaining calm in any situation.

Outmanoeuvred, Lady Godgifa inclined her head. 'Very well, Madam, as you will. I shall check that the laundry has been dried and folded correctly.' She glanced at Ethelflad, who made no hesitation in leaving with her.

Emma turned to Godwine. 'And you, boy,' she announced, 'cannot expect me to come to your aid again when you rile an elder with your rudeness. If you persist in this insolence I shall have you whipped.'

His bundle retrieved, Godwine was wiping his grimed face with his hand, making the muck there all the worse. The tears were gone, replaced by an impudent grin.

'You were grand, my Lady! Just as a queen ought to be!' He thrust the wrapped bundle into Emma's arms. 'She's the last of the litter, so she's a bit on the small side, but I am certain she has the sweetest nature, like her mother. Papa said she would have to be drowned if no one took her before the end of the week when we leave Court. I thought you would like to have her?' A note of doubt crept into Godwine's voice. Had this been such a good idea after all?

Carefully, Emma unwrapped the old cloak, the thing within beginning to wriggle and whimper. A brindled pup, fat-bellied, recently weaned, poked her head out and began to lick enthusiastically at Emma's face. She smelt of dog and warmth and happiness.

'She is for me?' Emma queried, almost speechless. Of all the gifts and endowments that she had been presented with since coming to England, this was the best and most welcome. A pup of her own! Something that would not mind that she was struggling to learn this awkward language, that she felt so useless. Did, said, the wrong things. 'Does she yet have a name?'

Grinning his relief and pleasure, Godwine said, 'I have been calling her Saffron for the colouring around her chest, but you may name her what you please.'

Emma hugged the pup close, putting her cheek to the soft hair of her silky ears. 'Saffron is a good name. Besides,' she added, laughing, 'I am somewhat averse to having a given name altered.'

13

'Fight them, I say! If Forkbeard comes again with his heathens, we send them sculling back over the sea with their legs shit-stained!'

Drily, Alfhelm, Ealdorman of Deira, answered Athelstan's misplaced enthusiasm. 'And from where do we get the men who are going to do this fighting? How do we keep an army together when the harvest is soon to be brought in? And where do we send it?' He set both his palms flat on the trestle table that the King's son had thumped his fist into, said, 'We never know where the Danes will attack next. Confronting Swein Forkbeard is like attempting to chase a will o' the wisp across a marsh.'

The Hall was still half empty, not all the ships of the King's fleet were yet in harbour, although with the sun setting in less than an hour, the crews of those not assigned to night patrol of the Kent coast would soon be seeking the comfort of a solid bed and hot food.

From their seats close to the open window slit, Emma asked Gunnhilda anxiously, 'Will he come this year?' She pricked her thumb with the needle, winced as the blood began to well. If King Swein of Denmark raided England this summer season, then what would happen to the treaty made between her husband and brother? Would Richard keep his word and deny his shoreline to the Danes if they had to seek urgent shelter from either storm or Æthelred's fleet? She sucked at the blood, careful not to stain the linen. Richard? Keep his word? Not if he was paid enough to turn blind eyes!

She fashioned a few more stitches along the hem of what would become a new veil, had the confidence to say, 'I do not much like the King, but I do not want to be set aside, be forced to return to Normandy.' She shrugged, laughed, as if making a jest of her fears. 'I have my pride to consider.' Did not add that her stomach would not survive the sea crossing. It seemed absurd that with her Danish blood she should be so afraid of ships, an embarrassing absurdity that she was not willing to share with anyone, not even her friend Gunnhilda.

Gunnhilda bit off a thread and held her own sewing high to inspect. 'Your marriage will not fail because of the Danes.' She selected another skein of coloured silk, threaded it through her needle. 'The annual assault on England is not all my half-brother's doing, you know. There are many who are capable of gathering a crew, eager for an easy opportunity to better themselves. It has been the way of men for many hundred years. Sail a ship, make a fortune – acquire a duchy.' She added the last with a teasing smile. Emma's ancestor, Rollo, had been a Viking. His prize had been Normandy. 'Men from Dublin are inclined to harry the western coast, not Swein.'

Looking her straight in the eye, Emma challenged Gunnhilda's statement. 'It was not the Normans, nor the Irish, who raided Devon last year, so I hear.'

The men gathered before the King's dais were launching deeper, and louder, into their argument, Æthelred sitting among them, morose, nursing a head cold and a tankard of mead with equal attention.

'My half-brother is a proud man,' Gunnhilda acknowledged, ignoring the raised voices. 'He took it hard that I chose Pallig over him. We were fond of each other.' She rested her hands across the bulge of her pregnancy, smiled wistfully, remembering her child-hood. 'Swein would do anything to keep me from harm. It was because of me that he rebelled against our father, Harold Bluetooth.' She stabbed her needle into the linen. 'I hated Father, a spiteful man who wanted all for himself. I was six years old and I had committed some minor, childish thing that enraged him.' She shrugged. 'I cannot recall what it was now, but never will I forget that brute grabbing hold of my hair and hitting me with his fist. I remember the blood and the pain, my screams of terror. Swein intervened. He stood there with his warrior's axe, a great double-handed weapon. It must have been a sun-bright day, for I clearly recall a shaft of sunlight coming in, spear-straight, from the open door, to flare against the silver inlay of the haft. It sent little patterns of coloured light dancing over the floor.' She laughed suddenly, glanced up at Emma. 'I cried louder when my father stumped towards my brother and broke that sunray, chasing away what I thought to be a host of faery people!' She grew serious again. 'Swein hoisted me beneath his arm, called for his horse and his men, and rode away. He took me to safety and returned within the two-month with an army, defeated our father and claimed Denmark for his own. He was twenty years of age.'

Emma was not going to be diverted. 'And Devon, last year?'

At the far end of the Hall, where the servants were beginning to set the trestle tables for the evening meal, Gunnhilda watched her daughter toddling after the hens that scratched in the dust and debris. If she tried to clutch at their feathers, as she had yesterday, she would earn for herself another set of pecked fingers. Drawing her breath, the woman related the bare truth. 'Because our estate was left untroubled, my husband was accused of aiding Swein when he raided the Devon coast. Pallig did not join with my brother, but he was seen on his pony; he was not going to the Danes but to warn the villagers. There are those who dislike my husband for the royal-born Danish wife he has taken. They are always eager to discredit him. We were nigh on impoverished, buying our way back into the King's favour.'

Emma flickered her eyes towards Ealdorman Alfhelm, husband to Lady Godgifa, raised her eyebrows questioningly.

Gunnhilda nodded. 'Spite is a wicked vice. Those two are vindictive people.' She fashioned a few industrious stitches, smiled. 'I would like to believe that my brother came into Devon to see his niece, but I think I am being fanciful.' Then she added something startling. 'He is Freya's Godfather.'

Emma gasped, blurted, 'Given his tendency to steal from abbeys and churches, I would not have singled King Swein to be a Christian man!'

Gunnhilda laughed. 'Let us say he prefers to place one boot on either side of the fence regarding Christ and Odin, and that he gets

74

distracted from his faith by the lure of material gain over the spiritual.' She shrugged, stated, 'Many Danes follow both beliefs. Swein's children are all baptised, although it is only his daughter, Estrith, and myself his half-sister, who follow God with conviction. His eldest son, Harald, is more conscientious, but Cnut, my younger nephew, is inclined to the old gods. It is natural in a boy who sees nothing beyond the sharp edge of a blade, I suppose. Swein, whether Christian or pagan, will always follow the practicality of being a king; he must pay his men or they will melt away and follow someone else more worthy.'

'And it makes more sense for him to accept tribute payment than to risk an outright fight?' Emma asked astutely.

Gunnhilda nodded. Why risk bloodshed when there was a preferable option? 'Unfortunately people have a limit to the payment of taxes, and because of that there is unrest growing among the Danish settlers of the Mid Lands and the North who do not fear Swein.' She pointed her needle at the group of men, at Ealdorman Alfhelm, Eadric Streona and the King's son, Athelstan. 'Some men believe it is cheaper, in the long run, to pay an enemy to go away and will not fight, but young blood is always eager to initiate their swords into battle.'

Sitting quiet for a while, Emma concentrated on her sewing, her thoughts busy. Already she was unhappy with this marriage, could see nothing but bleakness spiralling away into the future, but there was nothing she could do about it. Finally, she confided what was troubling her. 'Gunnhilda?'

'Mm?'

'Is my husband a coward?'

How to answer? Gunnhilda chose the truth. 'No, he is not a coward, but he is a fool. He listens to the advice of those preoccupied with their own interests, because he does not have the ability to follow his own thinking.'

14

With the afternoon warm and sunny, Emma had urged Gunnhilda to walk with her along the river bank. She was bored. As a town she liked Sandwich, the people were pleasant, the market stalls interesting, but it was a male domain, centred around the fleet and fishing. All she had seen of England was Dover, Canterbury, Sandwich and the roads between. England, both Gunnhilda and Pallig assured her, was a wondrous variety of landscape: open, wind-whispering reed marsh and gorse and heather-clad moors, deep forests, soaring mountains and winding valleys. Idling her time away in her stuffy chamber within the King's Hall, Emma was beginning to wonder if she would ever see anything different from these four bland walls.

Kent she thought to be delightful, but what had she to compare it with? In its summer array the countryside looked beautiful but, probably, so did the rest of England. She wanted to do something, go somewhere; to explore, to see exactly what she was queen of.

That keeping a close eye on his fleet was a necessary duty for a king to undertake she accepted, but nothing, ever, would induce her to be interested in coracles, fishing boats, merchant vessels, or Æthelred's huge, sixty-oared warships.

The river seemed an appealing idea; a path wandered alongside its tranquil bank, an inviting place for the pup to run. Saffron was growing rapidly, all paws, long legs and boundless enthusiasm. The only enchantment to break the monotony of endless empty weeks.

Once cloaks were found and outdoor shoes donned, a small party of her serving women and their various children walked down through the water meadows of the estuary, swishing aside the long grass and shooing away over-inquisitive cows. Gunnhilda's daughter, Freya, clutched tightly at Emma's hand as one particularly shaggy beast loomed too near.

Reprimanding Saffron for barking at the animal, Emma was flattered that the child should trust her. She had limited experience with children, for as the youngest child born, it had been she who had received the mothering and cooing from a host of older siblings; servants' and courtiers' offspring had proven useful as casual playmates, but there had never been anyone suitable for a lasting friendship. Gunnhilda was the first real friend Emma had ever had.

She smiled down at the fair-haired child, squeezed her chubby hand.

'It is only a cow come to see you. I expect she is thinking, "*Who is this pretty girl crossing my meadow? I wonder if she wants a drink of my milk?*"' To Emma's pleasure, the girl giggled. Gunnhilda was so blessed to have such a child. And such a husband. Not for the first time these long, dreary days, Emma wondered what her life would have been like if Pallig had been her husband, not Æthelred.

Ever helpful, Leofstan Shortfist shooed the cattle away, prodding them with the butt of his spear and waving his arms about. The placid beasts regarded him balefully a moment, before shambling off to find a comfortable spot to chew the cud.

'Oh, look!' one of the women cried, as she stepped carefully over a fresh cow-pat buzzing with flies. 'The swans have come downriver – are they not the most elegant of birds?' The majestic creatures were floating with the current, cob, pen, and a trail of four dowdy grey-clad cygnets.

'Pallig says', Gunnhilda remarked, 'that like us, swans mate for life, if one of them dies the other dies of a broken heart, and before life fades from it for ever, it sings the most beautiful of songs.'

'I would not suffer a broken heart were Æthelred to die.' The words tripped from Emma's mouth before she could stop them. Fortunately, the other women had quickened on ahead and a sudden squabble from two of the children drowned the indiscretion. Gunnhilda said nothing, but placed her fingers on Emma's arm in mute sympathy. She shared passion and love with Pallig, and found it difficult to imagine a marriage without contentment. She was not so ignorant as to be unaware that many marriages were a tortured Hell, though, or that hers was a rare happiness.

A boy was fishing upstream, his crude pole and line dipping ponderously into the solemn water. Edmund scowled, gathered his things and moved further away.

'Do not go too near the edge!' Gunnhilda called to Freya, as the women spread their cloaks and settled themselves on the summer-dried grass. Some of the children began picking daisies to make neck and ankle chains; two of the younger boys, no more than five years old, found a stick which they tossed for Saffron to chase, although their aim was only a few yards. The dog did not mind; any game was eagerly enjoyed.

Tucking her hands behind her head, Emma lay back, her eyes gazing up at the white puffball clouds floating overhead. That one looked like a tree, that one a bird. What would it be like to sit on a cloud and gaze down at the world? She closed her eyes, drifted into a dozed sleep, the sound of laughter and chatter distant in her ears, the sun warm and comforting on her face. She had not slept well during the night, her mind unable to turn off the thoughts that whirled and muddled behind her eyes, and when she had slept, unpleasant dreams had troubled her. Falling into this lazy sleep, Emma wondered how it would feel to be loved as Gunnhilda was loved by Pallig. To have someone strong and firm beside you, watching over you. Someone who cared. Æthelred had no concern for her. Why should he? She was a child who had nothing to offer him, they did not converse, for she was still finding English, beyond a few tentative sentences, difficult to master, and apart from hawking, she had no liking for his interests, for she did not consider herself an accomplished horsewoman able to adapt to the faster pursuits of the chase. She knew nothing of government or politics, little of battle or fighting. There was no passion between them on those occasional nights when he came to her bed. What created love? Was it a thing that if not there from the start could never flourish? Or did it come with time and patience, creeping in like an unseen mouse hugging close to the shadows, waiting for an opportunity to grow bolder?

A shower of cold water sprayed over her, bringing her instantly awake. Saffron, her tongue lolling, tail wagging, stood shaking her wet, dripping coat, the stick dropped expectantly by her mistress's hand.

'Wretched dog!' Emma laughed, as sitting up, she threw the stick away, laughed louder as, landing far out into the river, the dog jumped in after it. 'I swear the daft animal would follow a stick were it tossed into Hell!'

She must have dozed longer and deeper than she had realised, for the sun had shifted and more clouds had ushered in. The swans, too, were gone – no, there they were, preening their feathers a short way along the bank. Edmund, Emma noticed, was fetching in his fishing line, winding the thread carefully around the birch pole, fastening the hook. She would like to have been friends with Edmund, but Athelstan had made that hope impossible.

Saffron, scrabbling up the bank, hauled herself from the river, shook herself again, showering the children this time. A contented afternoon, quiet and relaxed. Pleasant, but meaningless. Could she go through the rest of her life like this, drifting from one idle day to another with no ultimate aim or focus? Perhaps when children came it would be better for her, perhaps Æthelred would have some respect for her then? But how could she conceive children if she felt no pleasure in the trying? If there was no love between husband and wife, how could a child be started?

She stretched the ache in her shoulders, closed her eyes and breathed in the damp freshness of the riverside air, the scent of the grass, the summer drowsiness. She liked the smell of England, it was strong and dependable, the centuries of existence wrapped in its surrounding comfort, like an enshrouding mantle.

The dog started barking again. A girl screamed. Emma's eyes snapped open as two of her women, shrieking with fear, began frantically flapping their hands and skirts. The cob swan had waddled along the bank in search of food and the dog, not knowing better, had run at him barking, hoping to play. Swans and dogs were not a good combination. Enraged, the huge male bird spread his wings, lowered his long neck and lunged at the barking nuisance. Doing the sensible thing for once, Saffron hurriedly backed away, but the girl, Freya, was not so agile. She turned to run and tripped, falling headlong into a clump of nettles, her screams rising louder as the irritant poison of the leaves burnt into her skin.

The bird, annoyed by the noise, made straight for her.

Everything was so quick! Edmund, seeing what was happening, was running along the bank, waving his fishing pole and shouting. Leofstan was running too, but he had wandered over to a group of trees to relieve himself and was too far away. He took aim with his spear, but did not dare throw it for fear of hitting the girl. Gunnhilda was trying to lumber to her feet, the weight of the child she was carrying and her full skirt hampering her movement.

Thinking quickly, Emma bent to pick up the dog's discarded stick, and swishing it backwards and forwards, drove at the swan, making her own threatening, hissing noises through her teeth. Distracted, the bird swung away from Freya, but before he could open his wings to beat at Emma, the Queen darted forward, and without care of her own safety, threw herself on top of him, her arms straddling his body, pinning his wings down. 'Get the children away!' she screamed. 'And call my idiot dog! Get away!'

Someone was beside her, Edmund, a dagger in his hand, his intention to cut the creature's throat.

'No!' Emma yelled. 'He meant no harm' and before the boy could react, she had somehow twisted herself and shoved the startled bird, with a crash of spray, into the river.

Grinning, Edmund dragged her from the bank, the pair of them breathing hard, the laughter of reaction twitching at their mouths as the swan, indignant, his feathers ruffled, paddled out into the safety of the current.

'That was bravely done, Lady, though somewhat foolish. I have known a swan seriously injure a man.'

Calming her breath, Emma busied herself with brushing imaginary stains from her gown. She had known that too. One of her sisters had suffered many months of agony with a broken arm because of an angered swan.

'I would rather it was I who came to harm than the little one,' she said, nodding towards Freya, who was sobbing in her mother's arms. The women and the elder children were hastily gathering cool green dock leaves to put on the mass of white, stinging blisters that were erupting on her arms and legs.

'There is a better thing!' Edmund said as he hurriedly unlaced his braes. 'Hold her still . . .'

'What are you doing?' Gunnhilda shrieked, appalled, dragging her daughter aside as the boy promptly began to urinate over the girl.

'It is all right!' Emma reassured, suddenly remembering a long-forgotten incident from her own days of young childhood. 'Urine is not pleasant but it stops the stinging. My father did the same to me once, it took the pain away almost immediately.'

Gathering the girl into her cloak, Gunnhilda nodded her uncertain gratitude, and Edmund regarded Emma with a new look of respect. Two years younger than herself, he was, nonetheless, almost her height. A stocky boy, with the promise of a man's handsome face once his features fleshed out. 'I misjudged you,' he admitted generously. 'Godwine said you were a promising queen. I told him he didn't know shit from shingle.' Gallantly, he held out his hand in a gesture of surrender and offered friendship. 'He was right, I was wrong.'

Emma took the hand and the offer of peace with a pleased but embarrassed smile. She felt she had to say something significant. What?

'I had no more say for this marriage than did you or your brother. It was not my wish to be married to your father, nor that a son of mine might replace Athelstan's position.'

Not wanting to offend, Edmund rubbed his hand across his mouth and chin, was wary with his reply. Finally, with a grin, he responded, 'You might have courage, Lady, but you also have the empty brain of a barnyard hen! I can see, if I am going to make a half-decent queen out of you, that I will have to start teaching you some basic rules.'

At Emma's puzzled frown he laughed, a belly-rumble of

amusement. 'You must learn to look to yourself before bothering with the fate of others!'

Emma frowned, considered, said, 'Is that not somewhat selfish? Is it not my duty, as Queen, to care for the welfare of those who require the protection of their sovereign lady?'

Edmund shrugged. 'Aye, it is selfish to ignore the need of the poor or the sick, the young or old and those worse off. It is not selfish to grab hold of all you can – and keep tight hold of it – among the fools who inhabit my father's Court.'

'*You are going to be a queen*,' her mother had said. '*All will look to you for guidance and instruction.*'

It had not occurred to Emma, then, to ask her mother from where she was to obtain the knowledge, inner energy and emotional stability to do what was expected of her. If it were to come from God then He had, thus far, been most lax in His instruction.

'And what of Athelstan?' she asked.

'Athelstan', Edmund countered, 'likes to think that I do as he bids. For the most part I do not disillusion him.' He grinned. 'For the rest of it, he can go boil his head. Like I said, to survive you have to do what *you* want, not what others have in mind for you.'

15

Godgifa, her veil askew, her face flustered, was almost hysterical when the women returned to the Queen's chamber. Emma would have been flattered if she thought the fear was for her welfare, but it quickly became apparent that it was not. 'You could have been killed and I would have been blamed. I have always said you are a thoughtless child.'

Emma walked to her bed, sat down, calmly began to remove her outdoor shoes and replace them with soft, squirrel-fur slippers. The toe of one, she noticed, was slightly mauled. She smiled; Saffron's contribution. The pup was at that annoying stage when she would chew anything left lying around. She had ravaged one of Æthelred's boots the other night; Emma had been horrified, convinced the King would take his anger out on her, but to her surprise he had merely laughed and tossed the other boot to the dog, declaring the animal might as well have both of them. It seemed odd that her husband was so kindly disposed towards the waywardness of animals, and from the little she had observed, young children as well, yet was so indifferent with herself and his eldest son. She assumed that he was disappointed with her. Was he also disappointed with Athelstan? They showed each other no affection, only minimal respect from public necessity. Indifference. That could also describe this marriage.

On Emma's behalf, Gunnhilda answered Lady Godgifa's annoyed bluster. 'We are quite safe. My daughter is upset from the experience that is all, but we thank you for your concern.' As sarcasm went, it was blunt and to the point.

Indicating to one of the younger women that she would appreciate a goblet of wine, Emma accepted the drink and sipped slowly. Her hands were shaking; now that the incident and the heated blood rush had subsided, the after reaction was setting in. If that swan had caught her with a backlash from one of those powerful wings – Emma breathed out slowly, composed herself. She could have been badly hurt, but killed? *Non.* For the child, however, the consequences could have been horrendous.

'Edmund is spreading talk of it all over the place!' Godgifa snapped irritably, aware that Gunnhilda had neatly, but politely, reprimanded her discourtesy. 'What will the King think when he hears? He'll want to know why I was not with you; why I did not stop you.'

'It is nothing to be alarmed over,' Emma stated, flatly and without interest, wishing the subject could be dropped. 'I expect the King will realise that Edmund, in the way of boys, is exaggerating the incident into something it was not.'

The elder woman was not listening to plain common sense, for she was the sort of person who never listened to anything, save the sound of her own high opinions. In this instance, however, her discomfort was heightened by other fears that had been swelling out of all proportion these last few weeks. Her husband's position within the King's favour was becoming daily more precarious; there had been another heated disagreement between them yesterday evening, resulting in Alfhelm taking his disgruntled temper out on his wife. Would he blame her for any harm come to the Queen? The girl's well-being and education had been pressed into her care, although she had frequently stated that she did not want the responsibility. Alfhelm had waved aside her protests: typical man, never stopping to consider the possible consequences if things went wrong.

Mindful of Gunnhilda's sharp tongue, Godgifa expressed her relief for the girl, but added, 'It is well no one was hurt, but where was your guard, Madam? That fool, Leofstan Shortfist?' She removed her cloak and flung it at a servant to hang on a peg. 'He is slovenly and useless. I shall see to it that he receives a flogging.'

Emma swung around, angry. 'It was not Leofstan's fault, he was too far away to help.'

Godgifa seized on the excuse she needed to shift blame away from herself. 'Then he should not have been! What if you had been attacked, not by a swan but by a man? What if you had been assaulted or killed? Of course it was his fault!'

Emma's impatience, fuelled by the aftermath of shock, was rapidly expanding into fury. She felt the wrath building inside her, ready to spew out like a poorly sealed jar of over-fermented beer. If this damned insufferably selfish woman said one more thing, one more comment . . .

Godgifa continued, unaware of Emma's building hostility. 'The swan will have to be dealt with; we cannot have a rogue bird on the river. Have you thought to order its destruction? Oh, I'll see to it.' Godgifa flapped her hand for her cloak to be returned and swept imperiously towards the open door. About to leave, she set eyes on her friend, Ethelflad, hurrying across the courtyard. 'There, you see.' Godgifa turned to face Emma, her hand raised in a dramatic gesture. 'Here comes Lady Ethelflad in distress over your narrow escape from mortal injury.' To the woman hurrying towards her she said, 'The Queen is unharmed, although she does not seem to appreciate the danger she had placed herself in.'

Ethelflad faltered, puzzled. 'What are you prattling about?' She swept past Godgifa, her hair coming adrift beneath her veil, her cloak askew, went straight to Emma and sank to her knees. 'I beg you, Lady, help me. Help us.' A frustrated tear slithered down her cheek, tracing through the pattern of age-wrinkled skin. 'Æthelred is to banish my brother into exile. I plead with you to intercede, to petition your husband into rethinking this madness!'

From the doorway Godgifa snorted disdain. Ethelflad turned her head, pleading. 'Your husband must pursue Leofsige's innocence too, Godgifa!'

'And taint ourselves with your misfortune?' Godgifa answered, horrified, gathering her gown, as if avoiding contagion. 'Alfhelm warned Leofsige to be wary of overstepping the boundary, but your brother never was one to listen to sense. He is as foolish as you are.'

'He was doing his duty as an ealdorman!' Ethelflad exclaimed shrilly, grasping Emma's hands within her own, her face tragic, imploring.

From across the room Gunnhilda countered, 'By hanging a king's reeve in front of his wife and children? Without the legality of a trial?'

'The man refused to obey my brother's orders and evict a family who had not paid their rent. He was insubordinate.'

Emma withdrew her hands from Ethelflad's and wiped the intrusive feel of sweat from her palms on to her gown. How dare they? How dare these two conceited, assuming women attempt to use her so blatantly for their own gain?

'I have heard what happened,' she stated. 'I have learnt enough English to comprehend the whispered conversations and aggrieved protests that are rustling through my husband's Court. Is it not equally as insubordinate for your brother to presume the duties of an anointed king?'

She looked across at Gunnhilda and Freya, whose tears had at last subsided, helped along by the lump of sweet honeycomb that she was diligently sucking. Quite clearly Emma announced, 'Word appears to be spreading of our afternoon's excitement, Gunnhilda. Your husband will most assuredly hear of it and grasp the wrong end of the spear.' She went to her friend, embraced both the woman and the child, not minding the girl's sticky hands, delighting in the automatic response of Freya snuggling her face into her neck. To Gunnhilda she said, 'You look exhausted. Until my physician arrives, rest on my bed. I shall personally seek Pallig and send him to you.'

Walking to the doorway, Emma smiled at the apprehensive Leofstan, hovering on the threshold, his hands clenched, hopping from foot to foot. He was eight and ten years old, anxious to please, scared to offend and mortified to have failed. His worry turning to a radiant grin as Emma laid her hand on his arm, her words leaving him uncompromisingly devoted to her service.

'I am more than satisfied with your ability, Leofstan, and I am full aware that neither you, nor any of my men, would knowingly allow harm to come to me. You shall escort me to find Pallig.'

Appalled at being ignored, Ethelflad scrabbled to her feet. 'But my Lady, you cannot . . .'

Swivelling on her heel, Emma interrupted, angry, 'What can I not do? Your brother took it upon himself to hang a man. The King's man, his appointed Reeve. The *King's* Reeve, not your brother's. He hanged a man who had the right to a trial of judgement. Aside from that, why come to me for aid? You and Godgifa have often expressed the opinion that I am a child with no sense or intelligence, that Ælfgifu, Godgifa's daughter, would have made a better queen. I suggest, therefore, that you ask for her aid, not mine.'

Vengeance, so unexpectedly presented, came as sweet as Freya's honeycomb.

Gunnhilda found she had a sudden need to busy herself with wiping her daughter's face. *So,* she thought to herself, *our Queen does possess sharpened claws after all.*

16

Darkness had fallen an hour ago. The shutters had been closed at dusk, candles and lamps lit. Emma sat before her table, dressed only in her under-shift, with a soft lambswool mantle draped across her shoulders, her hair hanging unbraided. She had been combing it, but her hand had paused at the sound of the door-latch lifting, the tread of boots coming into the room, dread entering the pit of her stomach. Æthelred. What would he say about her afternoon's escapade? What would he do? Despite the bravado she had shown to Godgifa, she had been aware of the danger she had placed herself in, of the probable disapproval of her husband. She smiled at the only serving maid, a girl of no more than her own age.

'*Merci bien*, you may leave me now the King has come.' The girl, with a wary glance at Æthelred, bobbed a curtsy and withdrew.

The King helped himself to wine, sat on the edge of the bed to drink it. There was something different about him tonight, something less intense. He bent down to fondle Saffron's ears, then rub at her belly as the dog rolled on to her back, her absurdly large paws waving in the air.

'Dog's as daft as a mooncalf,' he said. 'She'll have no sense for hunting.'

'But I do not intend to hunt her,' Emma answered, surprised at her audacity. 'You have better dogs for that task.'

Draining the goblet, Æthelred nodded affably. 'You're right there, plenty far better than this absurd runt.' He glanced up at Emma, looked away. 'Would you like to see them working? Come hunting with me? I've not had chance to show you much sport yet, but now it is unlikely that bastard pain in the backside, Forkbeard, will be troubling us, I can devote some of my time to you.' He set the goblet down, started to unlace his tunic. 'I heard of your exploits today,' he said casually, without raising his eyes. 'There has been talk of nothing else. You are quite the heroine.'

His fingers stopped their fumbling, he looked at her from across the room, his eyes meeting hers, aware that he had treated her poorly these short months of marriage. He had not meant to, it had been the pressure of that damned Danish King nagging at him, the knowing that it would be impossible to gather an army together and see him off, once and for all. He felt inadequate and useless when those Viking longships were prowling the coast, and had a desperate need to prove his power and importance. He had never been permitted the initiative before, not while his mother had lived. Power? Importance? What did he know of either? She had held the reins of both in her talons, tossing him a sucked and chewed bone occasionally as compensation. Him? King? The only thing of kingship he had held were the symbols, the sceptre and the crown. Ælfthryth had taken everything else from him and used it for her own gain. From childhood she had controlled and commanded him, down to choosing which women should share his bed and bear his children. And when the first son came, had taken him too. What was left? Nothing! Oh, he knew they whispered and sneered behind his back, mocked him, insulted him because of it. As a counter, he blustered and shouted, ruled his kingdom by a pretence of wrath. Then he got drunk and took his impotence out on those who could not answer him back. Proved his manhood where he could, in bed.

He attempted a weak, apologetic smile at Emma. She was a child, it was not her fault that he had no idea how to govern a country or plan a successful counter-attack on Viking raiders; that he had to rely on the judgement of others. Others who were too busy lining their own money chests or working their way, rung by rung, up the ladder of power.

He stepped behind her, took the comb and lifted a strand of her hair. He stroked the comb through the softness, enjoying the silk feel on his fingers, the smell of scented herbs. He had made a mistake by wedding with this girl, a mouse who did not ignite a flame within him. Was that why he had agreed to the marriage? A timid creature who would not dare attempt to go against him? Who

89

would bow her head and think of him as God Almighty? Stark contrast to his damned mother?

'I expelled Ealdorman Leofsige from my kingdom today,' he said, selecting another strand of hair. 'He exceeded his authority and had the audacity to challenge my judgement. For the first time in my life I did something that I wanted to do and would not listen to anyone who would sway me from my decision.'

'It was a correct decision, my Lord,' Emma answered, boldly adding, 'I did not much like Ealdorman Leofsige, nor his sister.'

'He was my mother's man, one of the old kind who had served as Thegn to Papa. Some of them, I think, hope to continue as if she were alive, running things to their own whim and fancy.' He paused, set down the comb, ran his hand over the smoothness of Emma's head. 'And you had your own achievements this day. You bettered a vicious swan and Lady Ethelflad together?'

Emma dipped her head, chewed her lip, unsure whether he was about to reprimand her. She had been wed to him a few months, had learnt already that his moods were capable of savage and unexpected swings.

'Which was the more daunting? I would wager the lady. Dreadful woman,' Æthelred said, laughing, pleased at his jest. 'I always thought of her as a coracle being towed behind a merchant ship, bobbing and juddering in its wake.' He placed a light kiss on her head. 'You did well, my dear.'

Only then did Emma realise the difference in him, he was not drunk or foul-tempered and, even if it was somewhat mumbled, he was talking to her in Danish.

'Would you', he said, offering in his own embarrassed way a truce, 'like to see more of England? Shall I take you to London?'

Not daring to believe this change of fortune, enthusiasm sparkled in Emma's eyes, bringing a soft and attractive prettiness to her face. '*Oui*,' she began, then altered hastily to stumbling English. 'Yes, yes, my Lord, that I would like very much.'

Æthelred touched his finger to her cheek. She was so young, so much the child. 'And what else would you like? Ask and it shall be yours.'

What else? Oh, the stars and the moon, what else!

'To have Godgifa gone from Court?' she asked shyly, thinking, *to be rid of those who hate me, to have only those I am learning to love*.

'My first wife', he said with wry amusement, 'would have asked for her head.'

'But then, I am not your first wife. She was your uneducated concubine. I am your Queen.'

Æthelred raised his eyebrows, surprised. Others had said there was a spark somewhere in this Norman girl. He had not believed it himself and was unsure whether he was pleased at being proved wrong.

17

Emma's first view of London was as a haze of dark hearth-fire smoke breaking the bright blue of a perfect sky. Pallig, riding beside her, enthusiastically pointed it out. 'We shall go there on the morrow and get you a decent mare from the horse market at Smooth Field,' he said. 'That pony you are on is a good, sturdy old mount, but I expect you would like something finer?'

'Yes, I would.' Emma spoke with careful enthusiasm, aware her English was not always accurate, but her confidence in the language was growing rapidly, almost as quickly as the confidence she felt in herself. The change in her these past weeks had been remarkable and noticeable. The pallor that had clung obstinately to her face since April was blooming into a radiance of pink-tinged cheeks that had lost their hollow, gaunt look. Her eyes were alight with laughter, her mouth, more often, curved into a placid smile. Anyone who had previously complained that the Queen was a plain, not particularly pretty child, would need to think again, Pallig even daring to believe that, at last, his Queen was happy, despite Æthelred breaking his promise to escort her here. Or perhaps because of it.

'The King will be joining us at Thorney Island, at the end of the week when he has sorted the problem arisen in Dover?' Pallig asked congenially.

Emma's smile faltered at the polite question, but it swiftly returned. She would not have her pleasure tainted by something that was four whole days away. Pallig was right, she was happy, particularly when she was mistress of her own house and had no fear of offending the King. She turned in the saddle to wave at Gunnhilda, travelling in one of the pack wagons with the younger children of the household who could not ride or walk. Æthelred had sent word to suggest that the Queen's Court proceed to London ahead of him, that he would follow as soon as the legal issues over this tedious contest of trade agreements was settled to his satisfaction. Delighted, Emma had packed her possessions immediately; by the tenth hour they were already several miles from Canterbury along the London road.

Privately to his wife, Pallig had confided his assumption of Æthelred's reason for delay: a certain serving girl who had accompanied his retinue south to the coast. 'As long as our Queen does not come to hear of it,' he had remarked as he settled his wife comfortably into the wagon.

'I doubt she will mind if she does,' Gunnhilda answered, wrapping a shawl around her shoulders. The sun was bright, but there was a distinct chill in the air. 'Aside, I would wager she already guesses. She gives the appearance of a shy and naive innocent, but Lady Emma has a sharp mind. All she requires is to mature into the confidence to use it.'

'And you do not mind me being so often with her and not with you?' Pallig had asked as he lifted Freya on to her mother's lap.

'I am content with my daughter's company. I am delighted to be carrying your son within me, but you know I hate lumbering around, ungainly and ugly, with this great bulk. If you are with the Queen, then you are not under my feet and I can spend the day being as cross-tempered and irritable as I please.'

London, or at least the King's residence, Emma soon discovered, was to be a disappointment. Sited one and a half miles from the city, the West Monastery and its adjoining King's Palace was one of the most desolate and woeful places in southern England.

Leaving the city of London behind, the entourage turned left along a westward-running road, Pallig explaining that the River Thames ahead of them flowed in a great curve, running from its northward path to one that went almost directly east. 'It is quite a contrary old man, with its wide loops and ponderous meandering.' He indicated the flat vastness of the windswept marches. 'That's when it deigns to remain within its banks. Come heavy rain or winter snow melt, it is oft-times hard to know which is river and which is flood water.'

They crossed at low tide, when the river was at its shallowest. Emma was a courageous girl, not one given to imagining fears or horrors, but fording the Thames was not one of her better moments. The horses waded through hock-high water, their shod hooves scrunching on the firm shingle and hoggin that ran, straight as an arrow flight, across the wide expanse of river. None of the men appeared perturbed by the swirl of the current, or by what seemed to be endless minutes out in midstream, although several of her ladies were dragging their loose riding gowns up to an indecent height and giving screams of alarm every so often.

Looking behind her, Emma could see the ramble of the Lambeth buildings on the southern side: a tavern, a forge; a cluster of whores' bothies. On the outskirts of the small hamlet the palisade walls of several merchants' estates. Lambeth, like Southwark at the southern end of London Bridge, had the infamy of dual status, the wealthy side alongside with whores and beggars. Ahead lay their inhospitable destination: a rough, bramble-strewn island that was aptly named as Thorney Island. A squat of timber and thatch buildings was huddled behind river walls that were built in the vain hope of keeping the flood waters out. No more than five hundred by four hundred yards, the desolation housed a dour church dedicated to Saint Peter and an even duller monastery, serviced by nine monks and an abbot, all of whom looked as empty and drab as the leaden-skied landscape. The holy buildings had the advantage over Æthelred's apology of a residence, however, for they occupied the higher ground. The wattle and daub of the King's Hall and its accompaniment of outbuildings lay within a slight hollow which, even given the protection of the outer stone wall, was never dry in winter. The roof appeared in desperate need of rethatching, the walls replastering and the whole place tidying and cheering up. The ground, as Emma dismounted, was precarious with ruts that, as soon as the first heavy rain fell, would undoubtedly be awash with mud. This was a royal palace? *Dieu*, Emma thought as she handed the reins to a grime-faced servant who came scurrying from the Hall, *I thank providence that my brother did not come here!* How scornful Richard would have been! As they had ridden up out of the river, the horses shuddering up the bank, the castle of Falaise had come to Emma's mind, with its stout walls and safe haven of security. Falaise was also built beside a river, but did not smell of penetrating mould and the creeping decay of damp.

'The King's residence was relocated here several generations ago,' Pallig explained to Emma, as if that fact would suddenly improve the place. 'King Alfred moved the Saxon trade town of Ald Wych, further along the river, into the protection of the old Roman-built stone walls of Lun Dun when the Viking sea raiders first began their plundering. Plague prompted one of his descendants to remove the royal palace to the safety of upriver. Near enough to oversee London, far enough away to avoid disease.'

'And was there not anywhere else more suitable?' Emma asked cynically. 'No rat-infested hovel? No wind-torn peasant shack?'

Pallig grinned at her. 'Your husband declares, each time he comes here, that one day he will pull the lot down and rebuild.' He shrugged. *One day* was always a week, a month, a year away with Æthelred. He rarely did today what could be done tomorrow, and for Æthelred tomorrow never arrived. Emma made no answer, already she had learnt to understand that Æthelred's promises were as elusive as a rainbow's end.

Unlike her husband, Pallig always kept his word, and two hours after sunrise the next day he escorted Emma into London to buy her a horse. First, though, he took her to the market of West Cheap, and was pleased with the expression of delight that spread across her face.

'Better than anything you have seen in Normandy, is it not?' he declared as they dismounted their ponies and he swept his hand towards the ocean of trading stalls. Now, at last, Emma realised the importance of London. Of all the ports and harbours of Europe, Africa and beyond, the merchant ships, with their precious and varied cargoes, came to London. London had everything. Silks and exotic spices, jewels – garnets, sapphires, emeralds, topaz – too many to name. Jewellery of copper, bronze, silver and gold. Jars of olive oil; pots of olives and fruits and figs and dates. Pottery and baskets of all shapes, sizes and designs. Cloth. Leather. Iron pots and pans. Furs. And people. So many people! Tall, short, fat, thin. Rich. Poor. Fair-haired with pale-blue eyes or with skin as dark and shiny as a curried bay pony. Every tongue imaginable, Danish, French, German, Spanish, Greek . . . Was this, Emma wondered, the very centre of the world?

Where to start? What to buy?

Two hours of happy browsing passed quickly, Pallig passing her growing mound of purchases to the servants to carry. 'I expected you to buy a quality mare once we had finished here and moved on to the horse market,' he said with a suppressed grin. 'Perhaps we should consider a pack animal instead?'

Emma laughed and gaily paid a penny coin for a walrus ivory comb for Gunnhilda, to add to the amber necklace and bolt of sapphire-blue silk that she had already bought her, as compensation for not accompanying them. She had purchased gifts for all her ladies, and for Æthelred, although she was uncertain what he would like. She had chosen, in the end, a garnet-studded collar for his favourite hound.

From the market, they walked through the arch of the western gate out to the fields beyond the city, that were as busy and frenzied as the Cheap itself. The difference, instead of stalls and blankets spread with various wares, here there was nothing except horses, donkeys and mules. Every breed, every size, shape and colour. Dapples and bays, chestnuts and duns. Ponies, horses, mares and stallions, geldings. Native ponies from the moors, mountains and forests; foreign destriers, stocky carthorses, placid palfreys; dazzling Arabian and Spanish breeds. Some standing tied to the tethering lines, heads lowered, a hind foot resting. Others being trotted up for inspection, some, over in the further field, being ridden at a canter or gallop. One or two being urged to leap the fencing rails. Fat ponies, bony horses, some with gleaming coats, others with dull eyes and scabby sores.

'How do I find a suitable mare among all these?' Emma exclaimed, enthralled, holding her hands wide in wonder.

'With patience and a sharp eye,' Pallig answered, taking her arm by the elbow and steering her safely away from a stallion that was kicking out dangerously.

For more than an hour they inspected the horse lines, stopping occasionally for Pallig to look more closely at an animal; peering into its mouth to check the teeth for its age, picking up its feet or running his hand down a leg. Once, Emma exclaimed over a pretty roan, but Pallig pointed out the blemishes on her knees, explaining that it was possible she could be inclined to trip or fall. Nor would he let her look too closely at chestnuts. Too temperamental, he said with a firm shake of his head.

A grey was too small, a bay too thin. He spent some while looking at a black, even though she had three white legs. 'One white foot buy her, two white feet try her. Three white feet look with care, four white feet a good one's rare,' he quoted. He rode the black, trotting and cantering her in circles, but when he dismounted he shook his head, passed her reins back to the vendor and walked on.

Emma was disappointed. 'I liked her,' she said petulantly, looking back over her shoulder. 'She had nice eyes.'

'Aye, and an uneven pace. She'll be dead lame before many days pass.'

He rode two more, another roan and, despite his earlier warning, a chestnut of about thirteen and one half hands, although she looked smaller. Pallig set his hands horizontally along her side, building one up above the other from the foot to the withers, the highest point above the shoulder. He nodded, surprised. Thirteen and one half hands. The mare was attractive, with a flaxen gold mane and tail, a white star on her forehead and one white sock on a hind foot. She was underweight, and a white patch of hair on her back showed where a saddle or harness had once rubbed and left its mark. Her legs were not quite as Pallig would have liked either, a bony lump protruding beneath her knee. A splint, he said it was called, caused by too much concussion on too hard ground, but it was well formed, ought not give her any bother. He sniffed, shrugged and dismissed the eager seller, walking on to assess the next patient horse waiting in the row. An emaciated, broken-down nag, which he moved straight past.

'What was wrong with the chestnut?' Emma declared, exasperated, half running to keep up with his long stride. 'I liked her.'

'There's nothing wrong with her,' Pallig confirmed, 'but if we appear too keen, her price will double. We'll go back later.'

Emma wailed a protest. 'But she might be gone later!'

Philosophically Pallig answered, 'Then we will find something else equally as suitable.'

Not wishing to appear childish, Emma refrained from pouting, but could not stop herself from saying, 'But my feet are aching, Pallig. I feel as though I have walked more than one hundred miles!'

Laughing, Pallig answered, 'No more than four at the most, I assure you. She was a good mare, though, I will grant you that.' From his belt pouch he took several silver coins that he tossed to Leofstan, trudging doggedly in their wake.

'Go purchase the chestnut for the Queen, only ensure that rogue of a vendor thinks you are buying for yourself, pay no more than she is worth. We shall wait for you in the shade of that oak tree over there.'

Nodding and saluting simultaneously, Leofstan trotted off, anxious to please both Queen and Captain.

'He is young and slow with his thinking, but he is a good man, Leofstan Shortfist,' Pallig observed. 'He will serve you well through the years.'

'As you will.' Boldly, Emma slid her arm through his as they walked. Her heart was singing and for the first time since April she felt truly glad that she had come to England.

Away from the horse lines, the crowd had thinned, the noise diminishing, the smells of horse dung, urine and sweat, and the pungent odour of unwashed men and women, receding. Slipping away from Pallig, Emma skipped a few paces, then with her arms outstretched, whirled herself around, her head back, mouth open. She felt as light and free as the lark that was singing somewhere above them.

'Pallig,' she said, as she slowed to a breathless stop, 'I can scarcely believe that I am so content. Whatever happens to me, I shall never forget this day'

'Gunnhilda says that happy memories are to be collected and stored with care in a treasure box, to be brought out and examined when sadness visits uninvited.'

The horse came from nowhere. It must have broken free from its tether, for dangling from its halter rope was a length of broken rail thumping and banging against his forelegs, protruding nails cutting wickedly into the skin. Something must have alarmed him in the first place, but with this other creature biting and snarling at his legs, the stallion bolted faster, not realising that he carried the terror along with him. Men and boys were racing after the beast, shouting, waving sticks and ropes, making the animal more frightened. One boy, ahead of the others, leapt forward, making a grab at the horse's tail, missed and went sprawling into the dust.

With his eyes set to the side of his head, the stallion could see behind him and, maddened already by fear, he took the boy, grabbing at his tail, to be another predator; he swerved to the left, bucking and kicking to rid himself of the double torment.

Emma screamed as the animal plunged towards her. Uncertain which way to run she faltered, but Pallig was there, pushing her aside. The hot, blood-red breath of the horse, its rolling white eyes, the stink of drenching sweat as it rushed past. With a second cry, Emma fell, her gown catching between her legs; she lay winded, face down in the grass, her wimple askew. Voices. People. She opened her eyes, tried to move, felt a heavy weight lying across her, something wet and sticky dribbling on to her hand and cheek. Looked. Saw a mass of blood and gouged, splintered bone. She screamed, the sound going on and on, rising higher and higher in pitch.

The horse must have caught him, lashing out with its hind legs as it careered past. The men chasing the animal faltered, forgot the stallion, stood silent, with held breath. Leofstan was coming, walking with a grin, the chestnut, bought at a bargain, swinging easily, head down, at his side. He saw the gathered crowd, quickened his pace, realised suddenly, sickeningly, what was happening. He dropped the mare's lead rope and ran, arms pumping, the grin gone. It would be a long time before Leofstan felt like grinning again.

Pallig lay across his Queen. Were it not for him forcefully shoving her to safety, it would have been Emma lying dead, with her skull split open.

18

'I say we have paid enough in taxes already!'

'Aye, and what if Swein of Denmark comes again next year? Will we be asked to raise yet another geld to send him away? What do we, the market traders, get in return from the King, eh? Naught! That's what we get, naught!'

The mood in the Moot Hall at Oxford was ugly. Sending Streona away with his tail tucked between his legs, those months ago, had been a spur-of-the-moment impulse; Streona was not liked, and the King promoting the wretched man to Shire Reeve had not been a popular move.

'What have we to fear from Swein Forkbeard? He will not attack his own. We are of Danish blood, our fathers' fathers were once men of Denmark and Norway.'

'*Ja!* Were it not for our forefathers bringing their skills and crafts, Oxford would have remained nothing more than a cluster of piddle-stinking bothies.'

'You speak for yourself, Olaf Olafsson! Your house emanates more of a stench than do all the privy huts on Market Street!'

There was laughter at the jest. Olaf scowled.

'What have we to fear from Swein of Denmark? Mayhap we would be better off if he were to be our king!'

That last voice stilled the Hall into an uneasy silence. One thing to call a meeting to discuss a refusal to pay an increase in taxes, quite another to speak of treason. Yet it was not the content of the sentence that silenced the crowded place, but the implication. These traders, who lived through the buying and selling of necessities or trinkets, were all men of Danish descent, men whose forefathers had come in their longships from Scandinavia during the time of Alfred, originally to loot and plunder the wealth of the

Saxon kingdoms much as Swein Forkbeard was doing, but eventually to over-winter and then to settle, take root. The thing had sailed full circle and different men were now coming *i-víking*, under a new leader and with a new king ruling England. The reason was the same. For a man to do better for himself, in whatever way he could.

The fear for the English was that the northern and Mid Land Boroughs were not thought of as Anglo-Saxon, but Anglo-Dane. Was the South, in particular Wessex, now also vulnerable? Would Angle-Land become Dane-Land?

'Why should we pay, and pay again, to protect these rich English of the South? If they were men, they would arm themselves and fight for their security.'

'It is cheaper for the King to pay for peace with *our* hard-earned coin than it is for him to arm and feed his army, that is why!'

Edwine Thursson, Oxford's appointed Trade Reeve, his arms folded, his face grim, sat in the shadows at the rear of the Hall, listening. As a freeborn resident of Oxford he was entitled to attend any of these trade moots called to discuss important matters, although there were some among the folk here who resented his presence. He was a king's man and his brother, Pallig, God assoil his soul, had served the Queen. No one could deny that Edwine had, as vociferously as the rest of them, complained against this excessive tax demand, but if it was to rebellion that the wind was turning, would he decide to haul in his sail?

To add to the general grievance, there would soon be a new minting of coin, another legal way for the King to become richer and the poor poorer. Whenever the royal mints gathered in the old money and stamped a replacement, the new coins were of a lesser silver content, a lesser value. They used the excuse that these frequent mintings were to prevent fraud by counterfeiters, but who was there to stop the King's blatant fraud of clipping the coin?

As he listened to the debate, Edwine found himself growing more uneasy. It was his duty to serve this town where he and his brother had been born, where their sisters now raised families, and where their father and mother lay buried together in the churchyard. He enjoyed his work as Trade Reeve, took pleasure in seeing to it that every stallholder paid their allotted trading tithe and did not cheat the weights or sell bad meat or shoddy goods; that discipline and order of the King's law was kept on each and every market day. He sighed. For all that, he agreed with these men. If the harvest had been better, if last winter had not been so bleak ... If trade had not been disrupted by Danish plundering, ah, so many ifs! Swein would not risk tramping so far inland to bother this Shire, nor their immediate neighbours, but Oxford had been expected to pay the heregeld. Other areas, too, were grumbling: northern Mercia, Deira, Lindsey, Bernicia. The grumbles becoming louder, more insistent and more prolific, like a single spear falling in the spear rack, one knocking against the next until all the rack, one spear after another, was tumbling and crashing in a great muddled clamour to the ground.

And the hardest part for a king's man to swallow? Edwine had to agree with the undercurrent of feeling that was swirling with the disturbed dust and candle smoke in this echoing, draughty Hall. Would Swein be a better man than Æthelred as their King?

'So what do we do?' That was Thully the silversmith. He had suffered badly from the depletion of silver yields this year and would do so again when the King's Shire Reeve came to collect this extra demand of tax.

'We refuse to pay. That's what we do!'

'Aye! We refuse!'

'We pelt Streona with more than rotten plums this time, eh, lads?'

'We'll shove his geld where the sun can't shine!'

Edwine sighed, stood quietly and left. Perhaps it would be prudent for him not to hear any more of their anger.

Evening was settling like a woman's embrace around the town as he walked along the High Street and up the incline to where his family would be waiting to welcome him home. His wife was a comely lass who had presented him with two fine sons and a beautiful daughter. As with his brother's wife, she too was of Danish descent. Most of them around here were. He paused beside the

103

wicker gate that led into his property, the chickens had already been cooped for the night, the shutters of the house-place closed. Strands of rushlight filtered through the cracks and openings round the two small windows. From inside, he could hear his wife laughing with the children.

If push came to shove, would the traders act on their resolve? Would they refuse to pay the King's demands? Raise outright rebellion? That would be treason, could cause a whole barrel-full of trouble. He walked through the gate, ensured the latch clicked firmly into place as he shut it behind him. If the Shire Reeve had been anyone except Eadric Streona, then possibly the rise of bad feeling would have blown itself out like a blustering storm wind. But with Streona? Now there was a man who enjoyed poking a stick into a hornets' nest for the sheer pleasure of seeing what would happen.

The Queen being so close to Oxford was not helping matters to calm down either. What in God's name had Æthelred been thinking when he allowed her to come here? Who had advised him that she would be safe? At least Athelstan, in charge of the royal household, had seen the sense of housing her at the royal residence of Islip, not accommodating her here within the town.

He went indoors, was immediately knocked sideways by three children and several dogs.

'Papa! Papa is home!'

'Aye, I'm home – let me near the hearth-fire, then; it is getting a chill of frost out there you know. My hands are raw.'

His wife, Gilda, smiled up at him from her cooking. 'Supper is almost ready. Pour yourself some ale and wash your hands.' She looked attractive in the flicker of the candles and firelight. Her hair tied back in a tight, thick braid; the swell of the five-month child growing in her belly.

'Did the men come to a conclusion?' Gunnhilda, his widowed sister-in-law, was nursing her son to the far side of the hearth. It had not been an easy birthing and even though it was now four weeks since the child had been born, the colour had not returned to her cheeks, nor had the dark circles receded from beneath her eyes. Did

104

they expect her to recover so soon? Without Pallig, what was there for Gunnhilda? Perhaps those wives who had no love for or from their husbands were, after all, the fortunate ones. They had no reason to grieve when death ended a union.

Seating himself at the trestle table, Edwine considered his answer, said finally, 'I am thinking that it is not the best idea for you to be in Oxford.'

'From what I hear, nowhere north of London is a good place to be at this moment,' Gunnhilda answered, shifting the baby to her other breast. Were it not for Edwine's thoughtful sense and Gilda's quiet patience, she doubted she would have survived these last weeks. She was still not certain that she would, yet, survive. Without Pallig, there was a gaping, black and empty chasm within her, one that would never, ever, be refilled. The Queen, Emma, God bless her, had tried her best to be of comfort, but her own grief had been too deep, the shock of what had happened too vivid. It had hurt Emma when Gunnhilda had decided to leave Court to join Pallig's brother here in Oxford, but it had been a sensible decision. At the time.

Edwine puffed his cheeks and helped himself to an apple from the pewter bowl in the centre of the table. His wife kept a tidy, well-fed household, these little apples picked during the last days of late September were Edwine's favourite; the skin soft, the flesh sweet and juicy. 'As the traders see it, they are being asked to keep Wessex and Kent safe from attack by your half-brother. They are not vulnerable, yet they have to pay. They are asking, why is that?'

When neither Gunnhilda nor his wife, ladling vegetable and chicken stew into bowls, answered, Edwine continued, 'The South is where men of wealth live and trade. That is where the crops are grown, where the King has his residences. Who ever heard of a king travelling further north than Oxford? Northumbria might as well not exist as far as royalty is concerned; no king would dare set foot in that Godforsaken heathen wilderness. Christ on the Cross, they don't even speak recognisable English up there!' He swilled the ale around in his tankard, watching the froth make intricate patterns on its amber colouring. His sarcasm easing, added, 'Æthelred dare not offend Wessex or Kent by asking for the extra he needs, he must therefore raise his taxes elsewhere and he has been advised that a suitable elsewhere are the Boroughs of the Danelaw.'

Gilda called the children to the table, handed round the full bowls of stew. The baby fed, winded and settling to sleep, Gunnhilda placed him in his cradle, seated herself next to her daughter. Freya had said almost nothing since her father's death. The child was of an age to understand that he was gone away for ever, but not why. Gunnhilda slid her arm around her waist, gave a loving squeeze, was rewarded with a shy smile.

'And who advised the King!' Edwine asked rhetorically. 'Eadric Streona, that is who. Is it not well known that Streona has an abiding hatred for anyone who carries Danish blood in their veins?'

Again, neither of the women answered him, Edwine's children minding their own problems by squabbling over who had the largest chunk of bread to dip in the rich broth. Finally, Edwine set down his spoon and stated, 'I think it best that both you women take the children and go to Islip, to the Queen. It would be safer if things turn uglier than they already are.'

'And would that not be sending the wrong message to the people of Oxford?' Gunnhilda countered practically. 'You are already mistrusted. If we run away, what will be made of it? They may conclude that you are siding with Æthelred.'

'Nonsense.'

Gilda stood, began stacking the empty, dirty bowls ready to scour with wood ash. 'You are the one talking nonsense, husband. All this will blow away like hot steam escaping from a boiling pot. You'll see.'

Reaching for another of the apples, Edwine hoped she was right. Had a sickening feeling in the pit of his stomach that she would not be.

19

13 November 1002 – Oxford

Athelstan lay scratching at the flea bites to his legs and buttocks, his other arm draping across the naked flesh of his bed mate, the tavern keeper's daughter. He opened his eyes, looked direct at a louse struggling through the thick curls of her lank hair. Sunlight peered through the ill-fitting shutters, patterning the dust-matted floor, falling on his strewn clothing. He had not intended to stay the night in Oxford, but the girl had been available and the drink stronger than the desire to return to Islip.

He was the eldest son, the ætheling, kingworthy, and he was expected to play wet-nurse to the Queen. The girl had her cnights, there were others as capable as Pallig to protect her – why had the stupid man got himself killed? Athelstan turned over, buried his throbbing head in the lumpy, mildewed pillow, squeezed his eyes shut against the threat of tears. It was unmanly to weep, but he had admired Pallig, one of the few men not to belittle him, one of the few who had treated him with honour and respect. Amazing, really, for Athelstan did not think of himself as worthy of the accolade. Edmund had been right when he had once said that Æthelred loathed his eldest son because Ælfthryth had taken his firstborn away. Athelstan barely knew his father, he had always been a stranger, a bad-tempered man who never talked, but shouted, at Grandmama. And she had always shrilled back, condemning, belittling and mocking. Athelstan had come to manhood believing that the words worthless, ungrateful and pitiable were all synonymous with being king. He was learning, perhaps too late, that they could apply just as much to an eldest son.

'We've got to find him, Godwine! We've got to!' Edmund slithered off his lathered pony, ran to the tavern door and hammered on it with his bunched fist, Godwine leaning acrobatically from his own saddle to grab at the pony's trailing reins.

He had held such high hopes of excitement when they had left London two weeks past; where had it all gone wrong? The sullen looks from the Oxford townsfolk, the mistrust in the air that was as thick as the sludge of a slurry pit. Perhaps if the rain had eased, things might have improved, but as it was, there had been barely any hunting or hawking, and then the Queen had developed a fever that had sent her abed. At least she had kept boredom at bay in the Hall, but with her absent, everything had settled into a sullen gloom. A wasted journey and now this! Godwine regretted coming, wished he had heeded his father's expressed doubts and had not insisted that Edmund had specifically wanted his company. Well, he would remember next time, if there was to be a next time. If they did not find Athelstan soon, there would probably not.

Edmund thumped again on the door, his other hand clicking at the latch, rattling the bolted door. 'Open up! You must open up!' This was the third tavern they had tried; the Cock and the Bear had both yielded nothing save for a rough telling-off and a threatened beating. Oxford tavern keepers were not known as early risers.

'Hold hard! What be the fuss?' From inside, the bolts were drawn back, the door creaking inward, a beard-stubbled, half-clothed man in need of a thorough wash scowled through the narrow opening. 'What do you want? Getting me up at this hour? It had better be good, or I'll take my belt to you.'

'I'm looking for my brother. For Athelstan, the King's son.'

'Well, he ain't 'ere. Be off with you.'

Although eleven years old, Edmund felt the threat of tears. 'He's got to be!'

The door was closing.

'There'll be a bag of coin in it if you know where he is!' Godwine called. Added with quick insight, 'Sir.'

The door stayed open. 'Copper or silver?'

'Silver.'

Edmund turned to frown at his friend. Where would they get silver coin from, for God's sake?

Greed, as Godwine guessed it would, won the day.

'He's over yonder at the Feathered Duck. Can't see why he went there, my ale's far better'n their muck. Ain't fit for pig's swill their stuff. Just 'cos my two girls ain't got such big teats on 'em as the slut over there.'

Edmund was already haring across the street, pounding at the door, yelling Athelstan's name.

Sounds beyond the closed door, shuffling feet and curses. When it swung open, Edmund said nothing but darted straight through, ducking beneath the keeper's arm and running for the back of the dim-lit interior. He burst through a rear door into a small, foul-smelling chamber, startling the two who were coupling beneath the musty bed furs.

'There's no time for her!' Edmund panted, hauling back the covers and speaking in French to ensure the girl did not understand. 'We have to leave.'

Athelstan lifted his face from the whore's breasts, Edmund noting with an eleven-year-old's increasing curiosity that the taverner had been right about the size of the girl's assets.

'Go away,' his brother growled. 'I'm busy.'

'There's trouble. You have to get the Queen away – you, we, have to leave Oxford-Shire. Now.'

'The Queen, as I understand it, is ill. She is abed. As am I.'

Desperate, Edmund grasped his brother's shoulder, hauled him round. 'The Danish throughout England are preparing to raise rebellion against our father.' With another impatient shake, 'Streona is to put an end to the unrest here in Oxford. He came to Islip first, to tell the Queen to leave. He's hopping bloody mad that you were not there to take immediate care of it.'

His attention gained, Athelstan was at last listening. 'Streona can go to the Devil. I don't take orders from him.' He rolled from the bed, began dressing. 'Is Oxford armed, then?'

'Not yet. Papa has pre-empted trouble by ordering the arrest of all Danish troublemakers everywhere north of London.'

Athelstan was scathing. 'He has no hope of achieving that without starting a civil war. Who advised him of such folly?'

Edmund had an idea, but tactfully shrugged a non-committal answer.

'I can guess. Streona.' Pulling on his boots, Athelstan suddenly stopped, set the left boot down. 'Why must we take the Queen? Could we not leave her at Islip? She will come to no harm there and we can ride faster without her.'

Edmund crossed to the door. 'So,' he said with contempt, 'you are, after all, like Streona? A man who thinks only of himself, with no care for honour or the protection of the innocent. What if the Shire of Oxford does rebel and take up arms? The Queen will be the first one to die – after us – in case she is with child. I am only eleven and even I know that for a fact.'

Athelstan blew a snort of derision down his nose. 'They will not kill her, she is part Danish herself. They'll set her inside a nunnery until certain she is barren.'

Edmund said nothing, merely stood staring at his brother. If that was what he wanted to believe . . .

Athelstan picked up his braes, eased them over his buttocks, tied the lacings. Held his hands up in surrender. 'You are right. They will kill her. It was a passing thought, a bad one. I apologise.'

20

13 November 1002 – Islip, Oxfordshire

'Lady? Lady! Stir yourself!' Emma woke abruptly, confused and disorientated from a heavy and fevered sleep. There was a man in her chamber? Why? To murder her?

Her heart pounding with fear, only dignity salvaged her composure. If they thought she would plead and beg for mercy they were wrong. To her relief, she recognised Athelstan – and then a second thought burst into her mind: had he turned against the King?

'Lady. We must leave Islip at once.' Athelstan was leaning over her, his hand on her shoulder, gently shaking her.

Thank God! He held no dagger!

'Leave? But why? I am unwell, I do not wish to go anywhere.' This illness had seen her to bed for four days with an aching body, a blinding headache and alternate sweats and shivering. She had not eaten and had drunk only honey-sweetened watered wine. The symptoms were easing, but had left her weak and tired.

Despite being ill, she liked it here in the King's Palace at Islip, a handful of miles north of Oxford. A place clean, warm and well maintained. Especially she admired the beech woods, dressed in their splendid autumn finery, that crowded beyond the perimeter fencing. She had walked there several times with Saffron, enjoying the delight of kicking at the leaves piled in dishevelled heaps, and running, laughing, up and down the slopes and banks, the dog joyfully barking at her heels. She peered with bruised, tired eyes into her stepson's grave face. Her stay was to be a short happiness, then.

What had possessed Æthelred to command his eldest son to be her escort here she could not imagine. The young man had barely spoken a word to her, confining himself to nods and grunts; she assumed her husband had meant it as a gesture of peace between father and son. Whether it had been accepted she had no idea; if it had, the peace was likely to be short-lived. The two were always disagreeing and shouting at each other, every argument ending with one of them storming out in a rage that would last for days. Emma did not mind in the slightest when Athelstan retreated from Court to spend isolated weeks in one of his own manors, for his absences were a welcome relief from the tension that built between him and his father. The King's rages were not so easy to endure, particularly if there were other things already itching at him like aggravating bites.

Reaching for a mantle Emma asked, 'What is wrong?' It was an effort to talk, her throat and neck hurt, difficult to swallow, to make the words form in her dry mouth.

'Rebellion, Lady. We do not have the men to defend ourselves should Oxford decide to take up arms with the rest of the Danelaw. We are to join the King at Shaftesbury Abbey.'

This was not making sense to Emma's ears; perhaps she was still muzzy with sleep and illness? 'Am I in danger?'

Athelstan answered briefly and simply with one curt word: 'Yes.'

Her ladies, grasping the situation in a flutter of alarm, started to shoo Athelstan from the chamber, pulling clothing from the hanging poles, urging Emma to rise, get dressed.

'I do not think I can ride,' Emma protested wearily, swinging her legs from the bed, suppressing a wince of pain from her protesting body. 'I do not have the strength to stand.'

Running his hand through his fair hair, Athelstan stood, perplexed, within the open door. Below, in the Hall, there came sounds of hasty packing and preparing to leave. Outside, horses being led into the courtyard, chests and bundles being secured to harnessed pack ponies and mules. 'I did not want to take the wagons,' he said, 'they will slow us down.' Damn! This whole thing was becoming a nightmare.

Tentative, Emma pushed herself to her feet, tried a smile. 'I will do my best not to delay you,' she said. 'Give me time to dress.' Her face was pale, beads of sweat were scattered on her forehead. Athelstan, making a decision, shook his head.

'Get your ladies to wrap you warm and comfortable, then wait here. You shall ride up with me.'

'Pallig's widow and children are in Oxford,' Emma stated, already drawing on her woollen stockings, ignoring the presence of a man. 'Are they safely away?'

To his shame, Athelstan reddened. He had not thought of them, but then, why should he? It was only the troublemakers Eadric Streona would be going after, not the women and children. 'It is you I must get to safety, Lady,' he answered. 'Please, be as quick as you can.'

Wanting to argue, Emma opened her mouth to protest, but Athelstan had retreated from the chamber and she did not have the energy to summon him back.

Athelstan himself carried the Queen down the wooden stairs, his glower silencing any remark from his brother or young Godwine, who were mounted and ready to leave. She weighed no more than a merlin, so frail was her weakened body; she would not have been able to ride alone and a litter would be too slow. Lifting Emma on to his own stallion's withers, Athelstan vaulted into the saddle, his arm supportive around her waist. 'Forgive the intimacy,' he murmured. 'I can see no other way for you to travel.'

There was only the one good road south and it passed close to Oxford. From two miles away they saw the smoke palling into the sky, nearer, heard the cries and screams. Athelstan cursed, urged his horse into a canter. Damn Streona! He had ordered him to wait until the Queen was safely away, this was typical of the man, never waiting, never seeing sense above stark impatience and always blaming the outcome to be someone else's fault.

Emma's eyes were dull, her skin burning, she lifted her head from Athelstan's shoulder, looked towards the rise of Oxford's surrounding walls. 'What is it?' she asked, frowning, forcing her sluggish mind to concentrate. 'Why is the town burning, Athelstan? There is something wrong, we must stop.'

How he regretted, through the years to come, not heeding her instinctive concern, but what could he have done had he complied? Could he have stopped the killing and the slaughter? Would the lives of the innocent have been saved had he reined in and entered Oxford? Or would more have died on this Saint Brice's day, had he tried to curb Streona's vengeance? Who could say that the æthelings and the Queen, too, might not have fallen among those being savagely massacred? Once the smell of blood had been let loose in the air, the lust of killing always took hold. Regret only came after, when the blood has been washed away.

Tightening his grip around the Queen's waist, Athelstan dug his spurs into his grey's flanks and drove him forward into a reckless gallop, bellowing at his small emergency retinue to follow close behind, swords drawn. Exhausted, light-headed, Emma buried her head in his mantle, shutting out as well as she could the desperate cries of death and the sounds of its making, Athelstan's own vigorous blasphemy against God, and his contempt of the King and Eadric Streona, loud in her ears.

'Gunnhilda is in there,' she whimpered once, knowing that even had he heard, her stepson could do nothing about it.

Athelstan had liked Pallig. It had been Pallig who had taught him how to use a sword and axe, how to defend himself with a shield; Pallig who had first taken Athelstan as a young, greenstick lad, whoring. None of this Emma knew, nor, as the King's eldest son urged his horse down the road past Oxford's closed gates, did she realise that tears were streaming from his eyes.

Edwine Thursson had done his best, but his best had not been sufficient. He was arrested with the rest of the Danish traders as they fought to protect their women and children. Edwine himself had organised their safety by ushering the vulnerable, the wives, the mothers, the young, the elderly and infirm, into the sanctuary of Oxford's blessed church of Saint Frideswide. A typical Saxon church, plain but functional: rectangular, virtually windowless, the walls fashioned from split trunks, the roof reed-thatched.

Streona's mastiff dogs, bred for killing, attacked any who had not heeded Edwine's hasty orders to flee, their bloodstained fangs ripping at the throats of terrified women. Children, running screaming, their small hands slipping from the frantic clutch of their mothers' fingers, were scooped up by Streona's men, their heads slammed against stone walls or solid doorposts.

Eadric Streona had every prisoner hanged, without exception. The last view Edwine Thursson saw as the noose was set around his neck was the burning embers of a church. Charred timbers, piles of ash and rubble. Incongruously, the door lintel stood, soot-blackened but unharmed, the only part of the church that had been built of stone. As the rope tightened and his legs began to kick, the urine and faeces to scour from his body, he recognised what else lay among the red-hot debris of Saint Frideswide. Those weird, twisted items were not part of the church, were not benches or candelabra or decoration. He focused his eyes on one clear thing as his tongue slowly swelled and the blood was as slowly choked from reaching his brain. It was a woman's hand, gnarled, black. Burnt.

He prayed, as the life left him, that they would forgive him for his cowardice. For the fact that his death was so much easier than theirs.

21

Easter. A year, an entire year gone full circle. Emma sat at a side table in her chamber, unable to decide which rings to place upon her fingers. She pushed the casket away, not caring for the fine trinkets. She should have shed this melancholia that had plagued her through the dark, endless months of winter. What was there to replace it with, though? What excitement or enthusiasm was there to jolt her from this constant tiredness and the bereft feeling of utter despair?

The fever that had stricken her at Islip had remained virulent for several weeks, worsened, everyone at Court agreed, by that dreadful ride south, here to the King's Hall at Shaftesbury. Not until after the Nativity had she found the strength to rise from her bed, another month after that before she felt able to appear in public. Oh, they were all kind to her, the women fussing and mothering, the more affable men sending her trinkets and trifles to cheer her, but kindness was not what she wanted. She wanted someone to take away the memory of Oxford and that thirteenth day of November. Someone to remove from her mind the sound and stench of the dying.

She could have done more! She should have insisted that Athelstan halt, put a stop to the slaughter, not buried her head and passed on by. When the crown that stared at her from its elm-wood casket was set upon her head, her vow had been to defend her people. Yet she had ridden past the horrors and had done nothing at all to prevent evil. Nothing to help Gunnhilda. Queen? *Oui*, Queen of cowards, Queen of fools!

She did not know how Gunnhilda and the children had died, did not know, for certain, that they had been inside the church of Saint Frideswide, but the probability swung towards the assumption that they had. Emma had sent Leofstan to find out. He would, as Pallig had once said, make a fine captain one day. 'I want to know', she had said, her voice hoarse and frail, 'what happened to them.'

He had not been able to discover much. Those who were still alive were reluctant to talk about the horrors of that November day; the others, well, the others had only been able to tell their God. Neither Gunnhilda, her sister-in-law nor the children were in Edwine's house-place, for that had been looted by Eadric Streona's men and was empty of everything. Nor were they with Edwine when he had been herded into the market square and hanged along with all those others. All those others, more than sixty men.

Æthelred had ordered the immediate rebuilding of the burnt church, at his own expense, the contrition appeasing his conscience at the destruction of a holy building, but doing very little for the dead or his wife's grief.

Later, when word was gathered in, it transpired that only Eadric Streona had been so liberal with an interpretation of the King's orders. Oxford alone bore a tally of so many dead. At Winchester, London, Norwich, all those places where Danish merchantmen had settled to trade, there had been arrests and hangings, but few towns north of the Humber river had complied, shire reeves and ealdormen claiming they had not received the order. With the unrest stamped into oblivion, Æthelred did not pursue the matter, nor did he investigate that nowhere aside from Oxford had women and children died. What did it matter that a few innocents were caught in the net? They were, after all, only Danes.

The winter that had blown in from the north-east had been short and mild, spring had come wandering over the horizon early, bringing an abundance of blossom and hope. If the weather did not deteriorate into a bad summer, the harvest would be good, and England would forget the unrest and settle into the routine of existence. Provided Swein Forkbeard did not return. Word on the wind spoke of him having trouble of his own to contend with, difficulties with Sweden and Norway. It was never an easy thing for a king to carve for himself an empire, even harder to keep it intact.

'Madam? Will you not accompany me to dine? They are waiting to break the deprivation of the Easter fasting. The Abbess has promised us a fine supper.'

Emma gasped, looked round sharply, startled, had not heard her husband enter. 'I, I am not ready,' she faltered, her face reddening, her fingers again fumbling with her jewellery box.

'No rush,' Æthelred said. He selected an amber and silver ring, slid it on to Emma's right hand. 'I am looking forward to this feast; fasting for Lent and the holy days of Easter may be easy for monks and nuns, but my belly grumbles with great complaint at the necessity. Thank God our self-denial is to be ended.'

Emma smiled, although it was a half-hearted effort. Despite the deprivations of the holy season she did not feel much hunger. Fetching up her wimple, she called her handmaid to help fasten it. Holding the silver hairpins, she pointed at the small, square window that was unshuttered against the evening dusk. 'The sunset was beautiful,' she said, turning to Æthelred, 'the whole sky turned gold, as if filled by the glory of angels' wings. Did you see it?'

'Alas, I have more pressing things to think on than sunsets and golden skies.' What was he to do with this quiet, serious child? She had been thin when she had arrived from Normandy; there was even less of her after this prolonged illness. Wrong of him, he knew, but he had caught himself, on a few occasions over the long nights of winter, thinking it would be provident for God to take her.

'When I had been a consecrated King for ten years, a wondrous light appeared in the night sky,' he said suddenly remembering. 'A tailed star. Whether it was a new star or one that God had purpose-fully made brighter none could say, not even my holiest men.' Added sarcastically, 'Nor my mother who professed to know everything. It lit up the western sky for three whole months, from dark-fall to cock-crow.'

Emma's smile widened, spreading from her mouth to her eyes. 'I was born in the year of that dragon-tailed star!'

'Mayhap it was a sign for our future union?' A gallant thing to say, marred by the lack of conviction.

Not noticing, Emma shook her head. 'Oh no, Sir, such a mighty thing of God's sending could not have been for a woman such as myself.'

Æthelred was amused. Many another woman would have been flattered to have been so highly praised. If only she would flesh out, she would be a pretty young thing. He resolved to see that she ate well during the course of this evening's special feasting and give her more attention. Guilt occasionally rubbed Æthelred's uncertain conscience. The discomfort rarely lasted long.

'The Queen does still not look well, I see,' Alfhelm of Deira remarked to Ælfric of East Wessex, seated beside him. 'She ought to be breeding by now. My wife always said she was not strong; these foreign women are not made of the same stuff as us.'

'Mayhap that is why the Danes come over here to plunder our Saxon women, then?' Ælfric answered, adding, 'We will not be able to hold Swein if he returns this year, you know.'

Alfhelm made a snort of derision. 'You speak for yourself! The fyrdsmen of Deira are well rehearsed, I have ensured they were war-drilled every Sunday throughout winter.'

'But it will not be Deira he will be attacking, will it? He will come for the South, where the wealth is, where the King is. Rumour has it his blood is up because of that woman Gunnhilda's killing last November.'

Alfhelm had always thought Ealdorman Ælfric to be a weakling. He had accepted the honour of a title quick enough when offered it, wanting the wealth and comfort that the entitlement of office had brought him; a different matter when the more disagreeable side of duty lifted its ugly head. Coward, he had been called when he had failed to lead the fleet into battle. Was it his fault, he had countered, that he had suffered so appallingly from the sickness of the sea?

'And you are privy to Danish rumour, are you?' Alfhelm scoffed. 'Does the King know of your information?'

Ælfric beckoned one of the serving women to fill his tankard with ale, aware that Alfhelm's opinion of himself was always less than polite. Sourly he retorted, 'It is a poor leader who does not listen to the tattle that is spreading through his taverns and markets.'

Alfhelm had been one of the ealdormen to oppose the tactic of paying the Viking pirates to leave England in peace. But then, with the probability that Forkbeard would only be plundering the riches of the South, not the poorer North, he had good reason to resent the paying of a high tax for something that would be of no benefit to himself. Alfhelm reached into the bowl set before them and selected a fleshy wing of roasted chicken, preferring that to another portion of the baked swan, which he had found too oily for his taste. Already the two fish courses had been devoured, and the meats were being brought in, the fowl and birds first, then the larger joints of beef, lamb and boar. One thing for Æthelred's praise, he never stinted for excellence at table.

Grumbling, Ælfric continued, 'With Swein Forkbeard ruling virtually all of Norway as well as Denmark, he will be needing coin to pay his fighting men. It does not take intelligence to work out that he will come again to England to get it. I cannot afford to pay another geld. I have lost almost all I have as it is.'

'So you would prefer to fight him this time, then? I will ensure the King knows of it, shall I?' Alfhelm's retort was deliberately malicious. 'Do not fear, Ælfric, with good fortune, Swein will attack somewhere more convenient for you. East Anglia, perhaps? You will not need to stir from your Hampshire hearth. Thegn Ulfkell of Thetford is a capable man when it comes to warfare, though I think the King is remiss not to elevate him to the rank of Ealdorman. The fyrd of those boggy fenlands can be a temperamental and churlish lot. It's the constant damp, I judge, it addles their puny brains as much as it knots their joints. We have warned the King that there is the danger they may not rally to arm at the word of a thegn, but his adviser, Streona, thinks that to be nonsense and who are we, experienced ealdormen, to know better than Eadric Streona, the King's favourite?'

22

The nuns' singing was beautiful, the small timber chapel holding their voices like ripened grain cupped in joined hands. The hymn was one of thanksgiving, the words trilling up to the rafters and clinging under the thatch with the drift of candle smoke. Emma sat, relaxed, in her high-backed chair, her eyes closed, allowing the glorious music to surround and penetrate every fibre of her body, her lips moving, soundless, with the words. Wilton was a small but prestigious place, home to twenty nuns and several daughters of wealthy families, dwelling here for the benefit of their education, which the Abbess ensured they received with dedicated authority and dutiful obedience.

'It is to the glory of God', she maintained, 'that I send forth my girls as young women who can read, write and run a household as a household should be run.' And, of course, the better produced girls, the higher the gifts offered by their grateful fathers. Within the few years that the Abbess had been in command, the nunnery had doubled its wealth and students. Having the Queen herself as a temporary residential guest was the final accolade of respectability.

Surrounded by the grace of tall elm trees and the open swath of sheep-grazed downs stretching away behind, Wilton was situated in an ideal and serene location. The buildings were simple, nothing elaborate, with the guest chambers comfortably furnished. Æthelred had suggested Emma come here to restore her health, rather than traipse after a summer-travelling Court. 'And perhaps, when you are well again,' he had suggested with a parting kiss to her cheek, 'we can try for a child? A son will bring you joy and contentment, I am certain.'

Emma had not echoed his belief in the benefits of a child, but he had been right about Wilton. The colour had returned to her cheeks and a smile came more often to her lips; the dark rings lifting from beneath her eyes and from her troubled soul.

The winter had been like a waking nightmare for her, as if she had been flailing around in the bottom of a deep black pit, with four mud-slimed walls towering above her and only the stench of fear as company. She had tried and tried to claw her way out, to scramble into the light, but when she had struggled upwards, had slid down again, even deeper, even further into the abyss, until she had felt that the blessed sunlight would for ever be denied her. If only someone would toss her a rope, or reach down a hand, give her firm anchorage to haul upon. Help her! There had been nothing and no one at Court, only leering faces and callous sneers that had thrust her aside, refusing to help or offer hope.

The Abbess of Wilton had saved her. Hers had been the hand that stretched down and clasped tight at Emma's fingers. Hers had been the love that would not let go, the voice to coax and encourage. Hers had been the guiding calm to show Emma that, in the love of Christ, she would never be alone.

Strange, but Emma had always shied away from the thought of becoming a nun, possibly because it had never been a path open to her, but here at Wilton she felt she could happily take the Veil and spend her days in the comfort of God's embrace. Except, the decision would be for her own well-being, for her benefit, not for the right reason of worshipping God. Besides, it was impossible; if the path had never been open before, it was certainly shut now.

The hymn finished, the nuns knelt in prayer, then filed from the chapel. Emma sat a while, alone, staring at the one round glass-paned window. The crude thick glass was of expensive coloured panes, reds and blues and greens, and where the sun, darting in and out from behind scudding clouds, shone through, rainbow patches flickered on the stone-flagged floor. Like dancing faeries. Where had she heard that analogy before? Gunnhilda! Gunnhilda had told her of watching patterns on the floor, reflected there by the shine of the silver decoration on the haft of Swein Forkbeard's axe – or was it his sword? She could not fully remember. Emma felt the tears within her, the great well of grieving sorrow, clinging deep in the pit of her stomach, but nothing would come into her eyes. She missed Gunnhilda, her first and only friend, missed her so badly that it hurt, as if a knife were being twisted within her. So why could she not cry? Why could she not expel this weight of tears and weep? Let go of the pain that engulfed her, step out into the light? Release the pain of memory?

'Lady? Lady, be you all right?' One of the novices, a young girl who had no cares of the outside world to worry or trouble her, had entered, her leather boots soundless on the stone floor.

Emma opened her eyes, smiled reassurance. 'There is nothing wrong. The beauty of the singing caught at my heart, that is all. It was a lovely hymn.'

'There are men arrived from London. They ask to see you.'

The colour drained from Emma's face. This was it, then, Æthelred wanted her back. Of course he did. A king needed his queen, needed a son. She stood, took a steadying breath to quell the shaking in her legs and stomach. 'My husband?'

'No, Lady. I believe it to be his son, Lord Athelstan.'

The relief was intense, replaced immediately by guilt. She ought not to feel so pleased that her husband was not here.

Smoothing her gown, straight-backed, dignified, she left the chapel. The men had dismounted in the outer courtyard, had walked through the archway to the inner court on foot in respect for the holy place. Athelstan looked similar to his father, the same nose, hair colour, height and build. He had been kind to her at Oxford, but Emma had not been fooled. The kindness was committed through duty, nothing more. If ever she was to bear a son, Athelstan would turn further against her. He had made that plain on more than one occasion.

'My Lady.' He bowed, polite. There was no smile, no warmth in his greeting. 'I bring bad news.'

Emma's heart lurched, the guilt rekindled. Æthelred was dead. The shame ran through her, freezing her blood; she began to shake. How could she have felt so pleased that it was not he who had come? God forgive her! 'Is it my Lord the King?' she whispered, holding her breath.

'No, not the King.' Athelstan's answer was abrupt. Why should it be the King? Stupid child! 'I come because of Exeter, your dower land. Swein Forkbeard landed there several weeks ago.'

Not Æthelred. Emma closed her eyes, sighed her relief, then admitted the lie. Would she have been glad to have heard of his death, regain her freedom? Huh, how did you keep the lie from yourself? She would never be free, not while she was young and able to give birth to a child. Her brother would insist on her marrying someone else, there would never be the peace of the nunnery for her, not until she was old and haggard, with a shrivelled womb and of no more importance as a woman.

'Are many killed?' she asked, feeling she should say something of consequence.

'Very few.' Athelstan spoke terse, hard. His lips thin, his eyes narrowed.

Emma did not understand. Dreadful that the town had been ransacked, but if lives had not been lost . . .? 'The townsfolk managed to flee, then? To come back when the Danes passed through? I am glad.'

'No, Lady. They had no need to flee. The gates were opened, the Danes were allowed to pass through without one arrow being shot or one spear thrown at them.' He spoke with the utmost, deepest contempt, spoke as if it were her fault; as if she had given the order to make no resistance. 'Exeter', he continued, 'has therefore allowed the Danes access into Somerset and Wilt-Shire. Where they will go next we do not know. Here, or towards Oxford? East to London or Canterbury? South to Winchester? I wonder, will they be welcomed there, too, my Lady? Not since the time of Alfred have they successfully managed to reach so far inland.' His expression was cold, accusing and angry.

Gathering her pride, Emma answered with aroused indignation, 'I do not care for your tone, Sir. I thank you for informing me of the problem. I shall, naturally, ensure food and provisions are sent to ease any suffering or disruption. Beyond that, I know not how I can be of further assistance.' Was she being dull-witted? Had she missed some vital, important point? 'If you require the cnights of my bodyguard who accompanied me here to join your army, which I assume you are gathering to meet King Swein, then you must, of course, take them.'

Athelstan stared at her as if she were some noisome object. 'Your Reeve of Exeter, Hugh de Varaville, permitted Forkbeard the safe passage. We would very much like to know under whose orders he was acting.'

The words slammed into Emma as if she had been hit by a hammer blow. She put her hand up to her mouth to stop the incredulous gasp escaping. 'Are you implying that I am involved with this?'

God in His Heaven help her if that was what Æthelred also thought!

'He is your Reeve. You are half Danish, of distant kin to Forkbeard. We wonder with which wind your sympathy blows.'

Reacting in the only way she could, with an inner instinct for survival, Emma took a step towards Athelstan. With genuine fury at the insult her hand came out, fast, hard, slapping across his cheek. 'How dare you? I am no traitor!'

'The King thinks you are.'

'Then the King is wrong. Let him come here and accuse me of such himself! De Varaville is not my man, he is my brother's. If the King wishes to find someone to blame, then I suggest he has direct word with Duke Richard. For myself, I strongly recall protesting against Hugh being placed at Exeter. I did not choose him, any more than I chose your bloody father as my husband!'

Suddenly, she was furious at everybody and everything. None of this was her doing, none of it! Brought here to England against her will; losing Pallig and Gunnhilda; treated as nothing more than an inconvenient piece of baggage by her husband . . . and now this. It was too much! Too much!

Rage bubbled up inside her. How dare Richard do this to her? Oh, there was no doubt he had ordered de Varaville to allow the Danes safe passage, it was the sort of thing Richard would have agreed with Swein Forkbeard months ago. Richard would do anything for the right price. From selling his sister to the English to breaking an agreed treaty for a more prosperous offer.

Æthelred was as bad. Did he think so little of her? Did he truly think she was acting in league with Denmark? It seemed he did, but then, why should he not? He had made no effort to get to know her, he ignored her as often as not, occasionally for days on end. Beyond a casually tossed word, the odd glance or sexual attention for his own relief, what had he offered her? She suspected that her husband had been pleased to be rid of her for the entirety of the summer. Well, he was about to discover just who Emma of Normandy really was.

'You!' She pointed to one of Athelstan's men. 'Fetch up my mare and have her saddled.' To one of the nuns hovering in the background: 'Have my possessions packed and inform the Abbess that I am leaving.' At her hesitation, snapped, 'Now girl! Not this afternoon or the morrow, now!'

Athelstan rubbed at his stinging cheek, a twitch of mild amusement tipping the edge of his mouth. The slap had hurt, the lass had weight behind her fragile appearance. 'And where are you planning on going? To join your Danish cousin? The black mood that the King is in, you would be safer with Forkbeard than thinking of returning to Court, although it is there that I am ordered to take you.'

'Not that it is any of your business; I am going to Exeter, to hang Hugh de Varaville for acting as a traitor to his Queen.'

Alarmed, Athelstan blocked her path as she was about to stalk away towards the guest quarters. 'Whoa, hold hard, Madam! You are jesting, are you not? You cannot go to Exeter, the countryside round that area is crawling with Danes.'

'Sod the bloody Danes!'

Suddenly Athelstan laughed outright, his fists bunched on his hips, his head lolling back, a great shout of mirth bursting from his open mouth. 'God's Truth, Madam, I will wholeheartedly drink to that!'

A scathing retort hot on her breath, Emma realised that Athelstan had reassessed his anger, had listened to her and believed her innocence. Was laughing with her, not at her. 'If I were not so dreadful a sailor, after Exeter I would be tempted to go to Normandy to hang my brother also.' To her own surprise, she found that she meant her words, they were not merely hot air blowing from a cooling furnace. What did she owe Richard? Nothing! He had sold her to Æthelred and England; she was no longer Norman but English. Amen, so be it.

'De Varaville's death alone would do adequately, Lady, but it is a deed already completed. The people of Exeter strung him up immediately after the Danes had gone. He was not well liked, being a Norman.'

'How fortunate, then,' Emma answered succinctly, 'that by default I am now English and it is harder to be rid of a queen than it is to dispatch a reeve.'

23

September 1003 – Salisbury

Swein Forkbeard was a tall, muscular man with shoulders as broad as a bear's and a heart with the courage of a lion. He was firm, ruthless and his men worshipped him for the heroic warrior that he was.

His army was in good spirits, deservedly so. Had they not marched all this way into England without a single sword blade or axe head raised against them? There had been an English ealdorman called Ælfric leading the fyrd gathered at Shaftesbury, but he was a weakling who had spewed his guts into the ditch and then fled. The English army had scattered into the dawn behind him, leaving the road open for the Danes to pass by unhindered.

Swein pulled thoughtfully at his beard that was stiffened with white lime to hold it in its characteristic forked shape. The map spread before him, daubed on the underside of a clean-scraped calf hide, was crude, not explicit, but then the Danes had no need for the detail of careful-drawn maps. All they required was a talkative tongue and the knowing of where the English King was mustering his army, so it could be avoided. Information was easy to obtain. Peasants were willing to blab all they knew to save a farm from burning, or a wife and daughters from violation, and Swein saw to it that free-given talk was well rewarded. The farms that burnt held farmers with tight tongues.

The King of Denmark glanced across the boards of the trestle table at his trusted second in command, Thorkell, called the Tall, for his great height. Thorkell dwarfed even Swein, who stood the width of three fingers above the six feet. 'So we must decide. The younger men are all for fighting, such is the hot rush of their blood. We older, more cautious ramblers prefer to gather what we can with comfortable ease. Why go climbing up and down a rocky mountain track when a well-worn path winds its way along the bottom?'

Thorkell grinned at his King, 'It is always the way of the young, they have their weapons sharp and no blood staining the blades to prove their valour. They will go along with your thinking, though, if it is your wish. Provided our ships are brim-full of reward when we return home, none at the end of this day shall mind remaining all in one piece.'

Swein brought his calloused finger down his nose – he only had four on the right hand, having lost the middle finger in his first battle. He pinched the nostril together, considering. He was too proud a man to run a race if he was not certain to win it and he was not ready, or strong enough, to be the unchallenged victor of England. Yet. The men with him in his army were professional and experienced mercenaries hired for their spears, shields and double-handed axes, called the bearded axe, the *skaegøkse*, for its drooping lower edge to the blade and the yard-long haft. Some called it the Death Bringer. With more chests of silver and gold, with more hides and furs, he could, next year, hire more men. And more, and more, until he had an army so vast that England would yield the race without setting foot over the starting line. He wanted England and he was going to get it. But not this year, nor the next. Soon, though, very soon.

'We go to Wilton,' he announced, making up his mind to their course, 'then return to our ships. Æthelred thought it not unreasonable to attack and kill innocent women, let us follow his example at the nunnery.' The death of Gunnhilda had opened a wound that was festering. Swein had been fond of her, had wept at the manner of her dying and had vowed with his own blood, spilt from a dagger taken to his arm, that she would be, one day, avenged. Wilton nunnery seemed a suitable place to begin.

'And Wilton has treasure in plenty to satisfy our requirements.' Thorkell passed his remark with a grin, was answered by one as wide from Swein.

Laughing, the King returned to staring thoughtfully at his map. 'Can we send scouts ahead? Find whether that farmer told us aright? I have no wish to march into an ambush, mayhap this Ælfric has not run far, has more courage than is granted him?'

'That we can.' Thorkell pulled sheepishly at his right ear lobe, then grinned again. 'Truth to tell, Lord, they are already gone. I sent our best men ahead not an hour since.'

It could be a dangerous tactic anticipating Swein's intentions, for he was not a man to be gainsaid, nor did he tolerate others appearing more astute than he. Taking and holding a crown could be a precarious occupation, for there was always someone else who also wanted the wearing of it. Thorkell, however, was a good second in command and Swein Forkbeard valued his reliability, as long as he understood that the custodianship of the Danish crown was not negotiable.

Swein clapped his friend on the shoulder. 'Were it not for a lack of time, I would be tempted, after Wilton, to scald the shit from Æthelred's backside. He sits safe in Oxford, knowing full well that we are well away from his poxed town. Oxford tempts me, for my sister's sake, but I can wait to pay my respects to her. After my coronation, perhaps?'

'When you are King in Æthelred's place?'

'Ja!'

Thorkell laughed. 'Very soon, then, we shall be in Oxford!'

'Very soon. For now it will not be long before the leaves turn gold and frost will not be treading far behind. Our ships await our return. Come, let us strike camp and finish what we came for. If Wilton is as wealthy as I have heard, I can purchase twice, three times as many men for next summer's campaign.'

If the Danes had also discovered that the Queen, the Lady Emma, had been residing at Wilton for the better part of the year, they were disappointed to discover her gone. The Abbess and her nuns and students were not there either, having fled as soon as the Danish host set foot on the Wilton road. Some of the nunnery's riches the women managed to take with them, the important items, the holiest relics. Swein was content with what they left behind: the golden altar cross, the silver psalters, candlesticks, bowls and plate, the gold-bound books.

As September blew out with a strong westward wind, he stood at the prow of his dragon ship and felt the pleasure of the lift of the tide as she slid into the crest of the next wave. He turned as the English coastline grew smaller, his cloak billowing about his shoulders, his hair tangling with the wind. Until next year, England's King could sleep sound.

24

Winchester was a pleasant town, or perhaps Emma thought so because it was hers? This was her dower land, all revenue came direct to her, be it tenancy rents, market traders' tax, or import duty from the riverside wharf. Æthelred had promised that he would build her a house on the bedraggled plot that had been set aside for the Queen's use in the days when his mother had made this her own town. There was, as yet, no house.

Since her illness the King had avoided his wife, excuses at first: having always to be elsewhere; the attendance of legal courts throughout the Shires; the necessity to be with the fleet; the fyrd. Excuses Emma never queried, for she was too miserable to care. Now he also blamed her for Exeter, as did all his Court. No one said in as many words, but the looks were there, the sidelong glances, the hush descending whenever she walked into the Hall, the rapid change of conversation. She was Norman, had Danish blood, what else could be expected? Could none of them get into their thick English skulls that Hugh de Varaville had been Richard's man? That she was as disgusted as they at the treachery that had affected her property? She was grateful for Winchester, for she could be on her own here, with her men, her people, with the knowing that spite was not being whispered behind her back.

There had been rumour that Æthelred was considering annulling the marriage, on grounds of her being barren – one of the few acceptable reasons for divorcing a queen. Whether it was true or not she had never discovered, but he had not minded her coming to Winchester, staying here these long months without him. Had not insisted that she attend his Christmas Court at Shaftesbury. To send her in disgrace home to Normandy he would have to prove her involvement with Hugh and Swein Forkbeard, proof that he would never find for there was no foundation to the lie. And to break the treaty with Richard would mean losing the revenue from her Norman lands. Not that Richard had, thus far, been forthcoming with its payment.

Surprisingly, she had received support from an unexpected quarter, from Athelstan. Theirs was an uneasy settlement, one formed of a mutual desire to be plausibly absent from the King's company. It was a fragile reconciliation, one that Emma was full aware could be shattered as easily as thin ice. If ever she became pregnant and birthed a son, Athelstan's toleration of her would cease; given the present circumstances of her marriage, that was not too much of a worry.

'We'll head downriver, towards the coast, where that pool spreads beneath the ash trees,' Athelstan called over his shoulder as he nudged his stallion into a trot.

'Those banks just past there may be the best place to look for a holt,' Edmund offered, curbing his eager mount to remain alongside Emma's mare.

Emma only enjoyed hunting in small measures, but had accepted Athelstan's offer to accompany him on this day's outing. An otter had discovered the fish pools in the monastery grounds and was helping herself to the easy-come meals. Though not considered one of the more interesting sports, the thief had to be caught; sufficient reason to be out on horseback on a fine, bright day, with a nip of frost in the air and the smell of the sea wafting on the wind.

Edmund had taken it upon himself to be Emma's guide. 'Locating an otter takes skill,' he explained. 'The best hunting is in late September, when the rivers have a low water level, but at least this time of year the reed growth is limited.'

Reaching the suggested place, the dogs quested for a scent and the huntsman searched for sign of track or droppings in the mud at the river's edge, the party of followers waiting, dismounted. Sitting on a fallen log, Emma watched her chestnut mare graze, tearing hungrily at the grass as if she had not been fed for a week. The mare Pallig had chosen for her, a good choice, for she had proven herself to be a superb animal. Would the rawness of the hurt at losing her friends ever cease? Perhaps it would if she had another track to follow, one that had a destination. As it was, she rode round in circles, always coming back to the same landmark, seeing the same miserable scenery.

A horn sounded; they had found. Edmund boosted Emma into the saddle, swung himself up on to his own horse with a wide grin. 'There will not be much for us to do, except ride alongside the river, watching the dogs harry the otter into shallow water. It's interesting seeing them work together as a pack, but there'll be more happening once we reach the men waiting with the tridents. There's often something to laugh at, for you can wager that one of them falls over his own feet and gets a drenching.'

There was more excitement than Edmund had predicted, for this was a clever animal; three times it slipped past the men straddling the shallows, hounds having to search on downstream and find it again. Once, they thought they had lost it entirely when it dived into deeper water – Emma herself spotted it as it came up for air, some many yards further down.

'If it gets out on to the marshes, we'll lose the bugger,' Athelstan grumbled, frustrated that this damned animal was proving as slippery as an eel to catch. Hah, that was another reason to not fail; it was not only the fish pools that had been raided, the eel traps had been picked clean again last night.

One more shallow ahead, then the river twisted in a large meander and spread into the tendril fingers of the marsh and the deeper channel that widened into the estuary. If she escaped out into the reed banks she would be away.

'Get the nets,' someone shouted.

'There she is!' A flurry, a higgle-piggle of men darting into the knee-deep water, stabbing indiscriminately with spears and their barbed tridents. Someone yelled, his voice high and cursing.

'Have they got it?' Emma asked, craning her head forward and circling her excited chestnut. 'Is it caught?'

Edmund, knee deep in water with the men, waded to the bank, laughing, helping to half carry, half drag one of them.

'If it is,' Athelstan grinned, 'it is a damn bloody big otter.' His laughter spread at the expense of the unfortunate who had thrust downwards as the otter sped between his legs and driven his trident clean through his own foot. Emma shook her head, brushed away the tears of laughter as the spill of blood washed away with the current. A great jest among them all, save for the injured man himself.

Where it was difficult to decide what was river and what was marsh, a brown head bobbed up, its shiny black eyes and whiskered muzzle assessing the distance of the men and their dogs. Lazily, it rolled over, flicked its tail and was gone, lithe and beautiful. She would find another hunting run for now, return to the easy picking early next year, when the stink of men and baying of dogs had gone, and she needed a fine place to raise a litter of young.

25

The sagas and poems always told the battle songs as heroic adventures. The glory of the fight; the bravery of the deed. Burnished weapons and valiant hearts, victory and pride. Few spoke the truth. Of the blood and the stink; of boots ankle deep in gore and churned mud; the dreadful noise; the immense pain and fear. If the stories told of that, no man would ever fight again, even if it was to defend his home and family from those who had come, yet again, *í-víking*.

The heathland of Thetford was a rich, sandy soil, the rivers were plentiful and crops grew well. When East Anglia had been its own independent kingdom, before Alfred, Thetford had been its capital and now, in the fourth year of the new millennium, it still ranked high in importance, second only to the trading town of Norwich, one and thirty miles to the north-east. Over four thousand populated Thetford and its surrounding farmland settlements. The mills that ground the corn into flour along the Rivers Thet and Little Ouse were thriving businesses; trade was good and the expansion of ecclesiastical buildings was beginning to mirror the former status of the town's military might. It was only a matter of time before the Danish eyes of Swein Forkbeard were drawn towards its lure of wealth. If he had been expecting another easy passage from Norwich where he moored his ships, as he had at Exeter, however, he was to be disappointed, for he had reckoned without the King's most prestigious Thegn, Ulfkell *Snilling*, Ulfkell the Bold.

'Sir.' The soldier ducked into his Lord's tent, stood, saluted smartly, his right fist striking his chest to the left of his heart. 'The Danes are, as you feared, marching for Thetford. Do we intercept them?'

Ulfkell almost smiled with anticipatory delight. Forkbeard was marching into his trap. 'No, we do as planned. We hold hard where we are and defend the town. Have the women and children been evacuated?'

'Aye, Lord, they are scattering across the heath, are safe.'

'Then we wait for the morrow's sunrise and pray that enough of us live to see it set.'

The soldier saluted again, and turned to leave, but Ulfkell called him back. 'Have the harpers, or any who has a talent for the telling of tales, to wander the camp tonight. I would have the men hear of Maldon and the great battle we fought there.' The soldier nodded, smiled his understanding as he left the tent. That battle they had lost. Clever of Ulfkell to realise there was an amount of hurt pride to be regained, here at Thetford.

During the three days that Swein Forkbeard had been busy sacking Norwich of all it had, the Englishmen of Norfolk had decided what action to take. Three choices. Flee. Pay tribute. Fight. The first two, without a murmur from a single man, had been rejected. They had faith in Ulfkell, for was he not a man who had proved himself as a warrior at Maldon? Ulfkell was one of the few who had survived the slaughter with honour. Maldon, where the River Blackwater emptied into its Essex estuary, where the Danes had come raiding with three and ninety ships in the year of Our Lord 991. Byrhtnoth, then Ealdorman of East Anglia, had made a brave stand, despite his years of age, his silvered hair and stiffened bones. Wounded, he had fought on, though half his army, believing him dead, had fled in cowardness and panic. Byrhtnoth's own men, his cnights, would not leave him and when he fell, a spear-thrust finally taking his life, they chose to die rather than desert him. The Vikings had won the day, but not the honour. The heroic pride of the English cnights who had stood their ground to face certain death at the Battle Place of Maldon remained unconquerable.

Ulfkell had been there, a boy, no more than a handful of years turned to a man. He had fought in the shield wall, had killed Danes and seen his comrades, in turn, be killed. He had seen

Byrhtnoth fall and those miserable wretches run; had been there in that last gallant determination to fight on, but he had not seen the ending. A blow to the head had split his war cap in two, had sent his senses whirling into a red darkness from which he had not woken for two days and three nights. He had been left for dead, one of the few to survive the carnage. Ulfkell knew from personal experience that the stories the harpers told were exaggerated tales. He knew the truth, the horror of battle. But men had to fight and so the storytellers plied their craft well.

Thetford had to be protected. If the Danes could not be halted, at least they could be delayed and their numbers depleted. There would be no open-armed welcome for Swein Forkbeard here, as there had been at Exeter – only the sharpened tips of spears and the death-bringer edge of war axes awaited him at Thetford!

The English army consisted of Ulfkell's own hearth-troop of loyal men and the fighting men of the militia, the fyrd, the men of East Anglia – Norfolk, the North Folk, Suffolk, the South Folk and the East Saxons, Essex. He had no worry that, as at Maldon, these men would drop their weapons and run at the first excuse, for East Anglia had learnt its lesson and had carried its open shame ever since.

Across the military road that led from Norwich to Thetford, Ulfkell deployed his men in the standard, simple but effective formation of the war-hedge, the shield wall. Rank upon rank of men standing, straight, still, unmovable, the front line protected by the barrier of overlocking shields. It was not easy to break such a wall, for where one man fell another stepped forward to take his place, and another and another; and the wall never moved or wavered or fell, unless the attackers were lucky. Or skilled. Swein Forkbeard had great skill and determination in battle. But then, so did Ulfkell.

Forming a similar, triangular host, the front ranks protected by their shields, Forkbeard ordered his men into the attack. The Danish wedge bristled with spears and arrows, but the English had spears and arrows too, and the dull sky of a drizzling day turned darker with the shrieking clouds of shaft and haft, and the dreadful cries of the wounded and dying. They beat on forward, the Danes, ramming and forcing a way through, fighting hand to hand, eye to eye, battering at the solidity of the wall of men. The blood-gored blades of their axes bringing the scream of death. Pushing forward, inch by slow, laborious inch.

For three hours they fought. Neither side giving ground, neither side admitting defeat. The weight of one army pushing against the other. Where, at the start, the shouts had been raised to the low covering of cloud, where the English had called for Jesu Christ and the Holy God, and the Danes of Thor and Odin, they fought now in near silence. Only the grunts of effort, the gasp for breath and the clash of metal upon metal, the shattering of wooden shields and the startled cries of the wounded and slain breaking the slow settling of dusk.

The English tried their best to salvage the disgrace of Maldon, but the Danes had more to lose. The English, if they lost, could melt away into the gloom, could go home, mend their wounds and fight again another day. There was no going home for the men of Swein Forkbeard. This was their only chance to win or die. And so, with a final heave of effort, it was all over. Thetford fell to Swein Forkbeard, the town and the day was his. But not the glory. He could not be claiming that.

Ulfkell was a wise warrior. 'If we fail,' he had ordered, 'take your weapons and retreat into the woods.' Sensibly, he had additional plans for the Danes. He could have had more men defending Thetford, but instead, he had divided his army, left some deployed in the secreted hollows of the heath, hiding within the trees and the scrub. They were to wait and watch, to let the Danes pass by and then make their way to Norwich, to attack and kill those left behind, and to burn the Viking ships.

Except, Ulfkell was only a thegn, not the absolute lord of an ealdorman, and not everyone was happy to be obeying his orders. Norwich had been looted but was otherwise unharmed. Fire was always an untrustworthy element and with the wind blowing inshore, was it wise to risk a stray spark setting alight the reed-thatch of a house or workplace? What did a thegn of Thetford know of these things? Norwich elected to leave the war dragons to ride the sea and Swein, returning laden with treasure and victory, found nothing amiss with his fleet.

The chance to be rid of him gone, like chaff blown away on the wind.

26

The seventh month of the year, and with a string of inexcusable inadequacies stretching behind his noblemen, Æthelred was close to ordering the lot of them to be hanged. Above them all, Ælfric of eastern Wessex for his consistent and utter uselessness, with Richard of Normandy running a close second. The words he was applying to the manhood and existence of the Duke, were bordering on the blasphemous.

Twice, Æthelred had tried a diplomatic route of persuading Richard to honour the agreement of his sister's dowry. Twice, Normandy had blatantly ignored England's polite request.

'Damn the whoreson!' Æthelred stormed as he strode up and down the central aisle of his King's Hall, his feet kicking out at unsuspecting dogs, his hands sweeping goblets and wooden bowls from trestle tables. 'The revenue from the Côtentin is mine! How dare he refuse it me?'

Emma, seated with her ladies at the far end of the Hall, sat mute, her head bowed. Technically, the Côtentin revenue was hers, but she dare not say so aloud. The year, so far, had been unbearable. They told her, the priests and the nuns, that it was a sin to take a blade to your own wrists and let the blood drain away, or to set a noose purposefully at your neck and leap from a tree bough or rafter. Such a sin, they declared emphatically, sent the soul straight to Hell. Well, Hell could be no worse than this utter misery. She had tried to be a good wife, dutiful in bed, an efficient housekeeper – the accounts were accurate and never ran high over the expected allowance. That in itself, for a king's household, was an achievement. She played the part of queen and wife to the best of her ability, drawing on all the skills that her mother had planted and nurtured within her, but it was never enough. Never enough to please Æthelred.

'Duke Richard is aggrieved that you accused him of breaking the treaty between you, my Lord.' That was Alfhelm of Deira. It would have been better had he remained silent, for the King was in no mood for pertinent reminders of the North.

'An accusation that was justified. Is he not harbouring Danish longships yet again? Did he not pay that bastard Norman, Hugh de Varaville, to allow the Danish scum safe passage last summer? How many of the folk in Norwich, I wonder, had he bribed to disobey Ulfkell's orders?'

The last was a ridiculous statement, for no one could have foreseen the unfolding of events in East Anglia, but it was not prudent to contradict Æthelred when he was in a rage.

'I would that I had never listened to Wulfstan! What do archbishops know of marriage and political alliance, eh? Answer me that, someone?' No one dared remind him that the alliance with Normandy had been of his own making.

'Look what I get for the trouble. The Danes attacking ever more often, my treasury depleting before my very eyes, and her, a woman who has no spirit and no damned interest for me in bed!' Æthelred had reached the end of his Hall and instead of turning to stride back up its length, he stepped up to Emma, his bruising fingers grabbing hold of her by the cheeks, forcing her head up. 'Look at her! A skinny, sallow-faced cow who, it appears, is as barren as a mule!'

Shame flooded Emma's face. Do not allow your feelings to show, her mother had told her two years ago. Two years? Was that all? Surely a lifetime had passed her by?

'She does not give me pleasure or a son, and now she does not bring me the income I was promised! Normandy? To Hell with the place and to Hell with you, Madam!' He was angry and, as always, took that anger out on the vulnerable. His nobles fought and bickered among themselves, they disobeyed his orders and thought only of personal gain. That made him angry, angry because despite being King, he was impotent to do anything about it. Was angry because Richard of Normandy had reneged on the agreed treaty, had humiliated him, and again, he could do nothing about it. That made him angrier still.

142

He could not strike out at his nobles, nor could he lash the Norman Duke, but his wife was sitting there, silent, useless, her bone-thin figure a daily reminder of her childlessness. How many were whispering that perhaps it was not her fault that she did not conceive? How many were speculating that perhaps he was becoming as inadequate in bed as he was as a king? Angry, humiliated, Æthelred drew back his arm and brought his hand across Emma's face, knocking her from her stool. Several men gasped, her own bodyguard taking a hesitant step forward, but no one could intervene against a king's rage. No one, not for a woman, even if she was the Queen. Only one body defended her, only one loved Emma enough to leap up at her cry of pain and fear, and that was Saffron, her dog. As her beloved mistress fell, she sprang forward, teeth bared, snarling, unafraid to protect and defend. Æthelred was a big man, strong in muscle and build. Although he did not care to put himself in danger on a battlefield, he had been trained in weaponry and warfare, had the reactions of a man who could swing an axe or wield a sword.

He pivoted on his heel, his other boot jabbing out at the dog's exposed throat, knocking her aside. She yelped, fell, tumbled, was up, ready to spring again, but Æthelred was quicker. He ran the few paces to the Hall's white-plastered wattle wall, grabbed at one of the shining war axes hanging there and, turning, brought it down, clean through the dog's neck.

Emma watched the dog's severed head roll several yards, the blood gushing in grotesque fountains of spray over her gown and feet. Saffron. Dead. Slaughtered, murdered. The memory of Gunnhilda surged into her mind, and Pallig. The feel of his blood, hot and sticky on her skin, the stench of it in her nostrils . . . Her silent scream went on and on in her mind, rising higher, possessing her, but unable to reach her mouth to be let out and released into the world. Æthelred had his back to her, was gloating at the mess, pleased with the spectacular result and the silence it had brought. Emma had no weapon, had no idea how to fight, but reaction, fuelled by disappointment, bottled anger and desperate grief could be as powerful as any blade. Her fingers brushed against the stool she had been sitting on, touching the two carved arms that curved upwards like auroch's horns. Her hand tightened round one and, unaware of what she did, lifted the stool and brought it down, with the full force of all her strength, across Æthelred's shoulders. The King staggered forward on to his knees, his bodyguard as hesitant as Emma's had been. Shaken, bruised, but unharmed, he pushed himself upright, wincing, flexing his shoulders to explore any damage. He turned, with seething fury.

Realising what she had done, Emma paled, dropped the stool and backed away, her tongue moistening dried lips, her throat trying to swallow saliva that was not there. Instinct was shouting at her to be still, not to move, but she was a fifteen-year-old child and had not yet developed a trust for her own sense. She turned, ran and fled along the narrow corridor that led to her private chamber. In public, Æthelred may have struck her, then walked away, but in private a man may do as he wishes with his wife.

In two strides he was behind her, clutching at the swirl of her gown, his grip tearing the material along one of the seams, the skirt ripping, exposing her undergarments. Emma screamed, tried to kick out at him with her foot, but she only wore lightweight indoor slippers, what good were they? His hand, clamping on her wrist, hauled her after him. She struggled, her wimple coming away in his grasping hand amid a shower of hairpins, the thong tying one of her two braids snapping, cascading the plait loose.

'I have had my fill of women!' he roared as he dragged her into the chamber, his hand slapping twice across her mouth and cheek. 'Whores telling me what I can or cannot do, criticising my decisions, pouring cold water on my every plan and idea. You are no better than the rest of them!' His fist punched into her breast and belly. 'I will be obeyed, you bitch. I will be respected!' His nostrils were wide, his breathing heavy, the muscles at the side of his left eye ticking. He slammed the chamber door shut, bolted it. Quieter, ominously he added, 'And I will get you with child.'

Bruised and bleeding, her hair matted, her gown ripped, she lay half conscious, stiff and aching, on the floor, unaware of how many hours had passed, how many times and ways he had abused her. A square of night sky showed through the unshuttered window, no stars, for it was cloudy. No light cheered the room, only the strip of flickering torches hustling under the door from the lit corridor outside. No sound from the Hall. Beyond the window an owl screeched and then the bell from the monastery rang Matins. The second hour of the day.

A snore resounded from the bed, the curtaining undrawn, the man sprawled there semi-clothed, an empty tankard of ale clasped in his hand.

Her body shrilling protest, Emma crawled to the side table, feeling with her hands, found the jug of watered ale always set there. She felt for a drinking cup, knocked it, clattering, to the floor, drank instead from the jug, her swollen lip sore against the rim.

'So you are awake,' Æthelred said into the darkness, with no hint of compassion. 'Get you to bed.'

'If you were a man,' she slurred through the swelling of her mouth, as with shaking hands she set the jug down on the table, 'you would take what is owed from Richard, not from me.'

'I said, get you to bed.'

Æthelred felt no satisfaction or release from what he did to her. Intercourse was an act, a show of domination, of his power and manhood. Perhaps if she had fought or pleaded, if she had wept or screamed, it would have been different. Instead, she lay immobile and silent throughout the long night of rape.

She spoke only once more, an hour after dawn had slithered through the window and under the worn eaves. He was at the door, dressed, unbolting it, making to leave. To his back she said clearly, distinctly, 'But you are not a man, are you, Æthelred?'

27

December 1004 – Hedingham, Oxfordshire
Six entire months had passed in the relief of knowing that her
husband was many miles away and, with good fortune, would not be
returning. Six months, with the first four of them plagued by
sickness that had lasted throughout the day, not merely in the
morning. The child within Emma had been conceived through
violence and hatred, her body reacting with distaste and loathing.
If she had known how to be rid of it she would have done so, despite
being cursed by God for all eternity. Huh, was she not cursed by this
pregnancy anyway?

God was already punishing her, so it had not been difficult for
Emma to add to her sins by hoping – praying – for Æthelred's
ending. Ships floundered and war was a dangerous, bloody business.
But God had turned away, was not interested in the misery of a
young woman with nothing left her except despair.

Æthelred had not been harmed and his campaign to regain all
rights to the Côtentin had been a disaster. A total, outright and
complete failure.

'I told him to wait for a more favourable wind,' Athelstan was
grumbling, although no one was listening, for the same words had
been tossed around and around these past two hours.

With the threat of Danish aggression temporarily swept away
through Ulfkell's heroic challenge – the English had lost the fight,
but had also sent more than half of Swein's men to Valhalla –
Æthelred had seized the opportunity to make a challenge to the
Duke of Normandy. Two days after he had killed Emma's dog, that
had been. There were some who said he had decided on the idea to
escape the prospect of another hurled stool; others, who had a liking
for Emma, Edmund among them, used their eyes and thought it
more likely he was running away from the guilt of a dishonoured

conscience. Aye, it was for a husband to treat a wife how he willed, but no man who called himself a man of honour would want a wife to be seen as the Queen showed herself those two days. Even the hard bastards like Eadric Streona had gasped as she had entered the Hall that first morning, her face blackened by bruising, an eye so swollen she could not open it, her mouth so torn she could barely chew the bread of the break-fast meal. And that was the damage that could be seen. From the way she moved, there was more, worse, beneath her clothing. There was not a man that day, in that Hall, who had not felt admiration for Emma. They knew the significance of courage, recognised it when it stood so blatantly defiant in front of them.

If Æthelred had made sail for the Côtentin with the intention of claiming the land as a peace offering for his wife, he would need to think again for an alternative gift.

'Father's expeditions of the past went well,' Edmund said to his brother across the board game they were sharing, although neither was concentrating on the moves. 'Why did this one go so badly wrong? Papa rid both the Island of Man and the Strathclyde coast of Danish incomers.'

'They were successful', Athelstan answered with a growl, 'because they were planned with the forethought and knowledge of men of ability and worth. Men who are now in their graves. Papa was young then, with not so much ale paunched in his belly and stupidity clogged in his wool brain. He also had a mother who had the wit and talent to rule effectively.'

Edmund said nothing, stared at the smooth walrus ivory playing piece in his hand.

'Fifty ships,' Athelstan added. 'Our father sailed with fifty ships, expecting us to follow blindly in his wake and bare our teeth at Normandy. Only the wind changed and a storm blew up. We spent weeks scratching our arses in Bruges, those of us who managed to get that far. Until the seas run dry, a quarter of that fleet will never be seen again.'

Emma, sitting to the far side of the chamber, rested her hand on the bulge of her pregnancy. Every morning at Mass, since the day her monthly flux had failed to appear, she had prayed that she was carrying a girl. She did not want to give Æthelred a son, did not want to please him, did not want to do what they all expected of her. Did not want to break the frail friendship she had made with Athelstan. With a daughter born to a widowed queen, she could have taken the Veil and retired quietly from public sight, sound and mind. No one would have objected. Except Richard. He would never have allowed it, of course, would have insisted she marry some other loathsome creature. Immaterial thoughts, now that Æthelred was home and alive.

Setting the gaming piece in his hand aside, Edmund lifted his king, held it before his eyes, studying its fine carving. 'Is it for us to speak ill of a king's judgement? Even if that king is our father and is an incompetent fool?' He put the piece carefully down in the centre of the board and, selecting four of his jet soldiers, Athelstan set them in a square around it.

'Our papa, Edmund, intended to raid the Côtentin with the same efficiency, fear and havoc that the Viking kind bring to us. Only the wind was capricious, the tides uncooperative and the rain squalls treacherous. When we finally reached the Normandy coast, Richard's fleet was already there waiting for us. We turned tail and came home, without a single spear being thrown or sword drawn from its sheath. Papa is no seaman; he does not relish the misery of wet blankets, cramped quarters and a heaving stomach. He does, however, apparently welcome ridicule.'

Would his sons be talking like this, Emma wondered, if Æthelred were here to listen? Most certainly not, but then, the disparagement had been plain to read in every man's eyes. The words did not need to be spoken.

For the sake of the men, she had tried to warn Æthelred not to underestimate Richard, but he had mocked her. 'What do you know of it?' he had slammed at her, sneering at her before the entire Hall. 'My wife,' he had jeered, 'who cannot fulfil her duty to me by conceiving a child, thinks she knows of battle tactics.' Well, he could take both back now, couldn't he?

At the time, she had wanted to run, to hide her shame, as she had wanted to secrete away what he had done to her, but for the same reason that she had risen from her bed and entered the public Hall, she had held her head high and retained an impassive expression at his mockery. They would not witness her pain or her fear; she would not slide the truth under a barrel and allow it to disappear into the privacy of darkness. Would let them decide for themselves who knew more of Duke Richard of Normandy: the woman, their Queen, or their bastard of a King.

Sitting here, quietly listening to the discontented talk, these months later, Emma permitted herself the reward of a satisfied smile. The Côtentin, her dower land, was lost to England for good. Who, now, was the more humiliated? The smile was short-lived. Her ties to Normandy were severed, all she had left was a loveless marriage, an unwanted child and a hollow crown. There it was, resplendent on the outside, appearing solid and mighty, a thing of status and power, wealth and glory, but when you looked inside, all that was there was a gaping hole, filled with nothing more than the echo of disappointed dreams, with the only escape the promise of eventual death.

A tear rambled down her cheek, hastily wiped away. She still had her pride. Nothing, no one, not God nor the Devil himself would take that from her. Not while she had the breath in her body to lay claim to the authority that permitted her to wear this golden trinket on her head, for all its worthlessness.

The door was flung open and Æthelred strode through, removing his cloak and leather gloves, going straight to the fire to warm his backside. 'By God it is cold out there,' he declared, 'cold enough to freeze a man's essentials off.' He chuckled at his jest, did not notice that no one responded, or how silent the room had fallen.

Rubbing his hands he crossed to Emma, lifted her chin and roughly kissed her lips, his other hand resting on the bulge of the child. 'No matter about my balls now though, eh, Madam? Not now I have proven my ability and my manhood.'

She did not answer. No one did.

28

Nothing, ever, would induce Emma to want to give birth to another child. The pain was unbearable.

Beyond the Queen's chamber the snow lay thick, the roads impassable, the rivers frozen. Even the urine in the night pots had formed ice around the rim. Dawn had broken, the sky that threatened more snow, streaking with the first pale, frost-bitten fingers an hour or so ago. Daylight, however, was not warming into anything more than a sullen, dismal greyness.

Emma had awoken, yesterday, irritable and restless. Her back had ached, her swollen feet and hands had throbbed. She had not been able to lie, sit or stand comfortably these last few days, was tired and cold. She had eaten a light break-fast of cold chicken, but had brought it all up again. During the morning she had tried concentrating on her embroidery, had thrown the thing, spoilt beyond repair, into the hearth-fire.

Æthelred was not at Islip, he rarely stayed long at the manor, for as Emma had discovered soon into her marriage, he did not like the place that had been his mother's favoured residence. It suited Emma to be here, though, alone with her books, her ladies and her personal guard of cnights. She had delighted in making Islip hers, discarding most of what had been Ælfthryth's and furnishing both Hall and her private chamber with expensive care. All the comfort available, however, could not take away the agony that was now tearing her body apart. Her insides were being ripped open, she had sweated and gasped through the onset of labour yesterday afternoon, and had screamed through the long night. The pain had gone on and on, unstoppable and relentless for over eighteen hours. She was too tired to scream now, too tired to do anything.

On the far side of the chamber the two midwives were talking together, deciding between them what was best to do, their voices no more than a whisper.

'The babe is wrong within her, the arm is in the way, the head cannot push through.' The eldest, Unnor, a thin, elderly woman with white hair and prune-wrinkled skin, shook her head at her daughter, Ethelbyrne. Both of them experienced birthing women who, between them, had brought most of the children in and around Oxford into the world.

They had already tried most of their knowledge and arts to ease the labour; rubbing Emma's abdomen and women's parts with sweet-smelling oils, spooning spiced drinks into her mouth. In her hand, Emma clutched a small stone of jasper for its beneficial powers and, bound beneath her right foot, an unused new wax tablet with the words of a prayer scratched on it in Unnor's spidery hand:

> Mary a virgin bore Christ, the barren Elizabeth bore John.
> I charge thee, infant, if thou be male or female,
> by the Father, Son and Holy Spirit, that thou come forth.

So far, none of it was working.

Emma whimpered as another contraction heaved through her trembling body. She would have wept, but did not have the energy for that either. Her hair, long since come unbraided, was tangled; her linen undershift, soiled with blood, sweat and urine, was moulded to her drenched skin. Did all women go through this? Or was this torture visited on her because the child had been conceived through pain and violence? That fact Emma could not shift from her mind. Were babes formed from love born with love? As Gunnhilda's children had been? There had been no love when this child was started. Was this the Holy Mother's punishment for her not wanting the wretched thing? The conception had been painful, frightening and humiliating, the nine months between resented and now she had this agony to endure.

A few hours ago, during the slow-passing creep of darkness, she had asked, through her cracked lips and dry throat, if Æthelred had been summoned. Had received the answer that he was not expected to arrive until daylight. Would it help to have him there in the Hall below? To know he was listening to her pain? She doubted he would come, though he was only a few miles away, at Hedingham. The snow would prevent him, and his lack of concern. He already had sons and daughters. What did it matter to him that she was suffering to give him one more? If she lost her life because of this child, it would be no more than a nuisance to Æthelred. He wanted her gone anyway.

Emma shut her eyes and, throwing her head back and arching her body into the pain, moaned again.

'We must do something soon,' Ethelbyrne whispered insistent to her mother. 'We must try again to move the arm that is blocking the passage out, either by drawing it forward or pushing it back.'

'It did not succeed before; I am fearful to attempt it a third time.'

'As fearful as what may happen if we fail both mother and child? She is the Queen; we are expected to do all we can.'

Unnor clicked her tongue in reproof. 'It matters not whether she is a crowned queen or the poorest peasant, all of us suffer together when giving birth.' She rinsed a cloth in fresh-drawn cold water and wiped Emma's face, dribbling some of the moisture on to her lips and clutching at her hand as another contraction ripped through her body.

'We will try once more,' she said, her voice soothing and encouraging, masking her inner doubts that, as before, it would not be profitable. 'Ethelbyrne, you will do it, but first I will go below to the Hall and ask the priest to double his efforts for prayer. We need the aid of Jesu's good Lady Mother.'

To the woman's surprise there were new arrivals in the Hall, a party come not more than a few minutes before, their cloaks and hats snow-covered, their hands and faces blue-tinged with cold. They were clustered around the hearth-fire, servants scuttling to fetch broth and warmed wine, their backs to the narrow, dark stairway that led to the Queen's chamber above. Unnor assumed them to be the King's party and hurried forward, relieved that Æthelred himself could make a decision about what was best to do.

She had little faith in being able to move the trapped arm, which was, at the last inspection, beginning to bloat and swell. In her own mind there was only one thing left to do: to remove the arm with a sharp blade while in the womb. The child would undoubtedly bleed to death, but was probably dead already. Always, it was preferable to save the mother, though one in forty women did not survive childbirth.

To her disappointment it was not the King. The man who turned to face her approaching footsteps was older, thinner and taller. He wore the clothing and insignia of a high holy man and Unnor realised, with sudden elation, that this was someone even better than the King – Archbishop Wulfstan of York.

She fell to her knees at his feet, grasping the hem of his gown in her fingers and lifting it to her lips. 'My Lord, we desperately need your prayers. My Lady is suffering greatly; I have reason to fear for her safe deliverance.'

'It is for women to suffer for the anguish that Eve brought to mankind, but do not fear, I have brought something with me that may be of help.' Wulfstan beckoned a servant, no less cold and snow-covered, who, with numbed fingers, brought something forth from a small leather bag. 'This', Wulfstan announced proudly, 'is the very girdle that our Holy Mother wore when she bore Christ.' He took the length of braiding from the servant and handed it, with reverence, to the midwife. 'Allow my Lady Queen to wear it and I am certain all will become well, if it be God's wish.'

Delighted, smiling broadly, Unnor bobbed a reverence and, at a hobbling run, returned upstairs. 'Look,' she said, showing the intricately plaited woollen threads of faded blue and red and green to Emma. 'See what Wulfstan of York has brought you?' Deftly, she threaded and tied the thing round Emma's waist and nodded to Ethelbyrne that with the cessation of the next contraction she was to proceed.

Emma shrank from the touch of the woman's intrusive oiled hand, the scream shrieking from her, but almost immediately the pain subsided and as Ethelbyrne removed her bloodied fingers, eased almost entirely. Squatting back on her haunches, the younger

153

midwife grinned and, murmuring a prayer of thanks, stated, 'I have done it! I have moved it, the way is open for the head to present as it ought!'

'The pains will come again very soon,' Unnor advised Emma, as she gently massaged her swollen stomach. 'When they do, you must not push until we tell you and then you must bear down with all the strength left you.'

'I have none,' Emma gasped. 'I am finished.'

'What talk is that?' Unnor admonished. 'The Mother Mary herself is here with you. Did she give up on our Lord's entry into life? And she left alone within a stable?'

The contractions resumed, quicker, more insistent, but easier to bear, particularly when Unnor, moving behind Emma, grasped her around the waist and urged her to push – and the head was there, wet, dark hair, the shoulders covered in slime and filth, and the child was born, took its first breath and wailed pitifully. A boy. Emma had given birth to a son. Edward.

Quite the ugliest, most unpleasant thing she had ever seen.

29

August 1005 – Thorney Island

Staring dismally at the fading daylight beyond the unshuttered window, Emma watched as a heron stalked solemnly through the rushes along the mudbanked Thames. The water was low, despite it being high tide downriver towards London. Thorney, usually an island, was surrounded by dry land, the marshes stretching to either side, a brown, shrivelled expanse of straw-coloured earth. Even the trees, for lack of water, drooped with sad, crinkled, parchment-like leaves. Only along the river frontage was it green with reed and rush and summer water plants. The river itself, crystal clear, reflected the azure blue of the wide sky.

Few birds flew, for it was too hot. No breeze stirred; all southern England lay dehydrated, thirsty and desperate for rain that had not fallen in over ten weeks. The rivers, even this, the grandfather River Thames, were low and shallow, some had dried completely, leaving nothing of their existence except a course of hard-baked cracked mud. Where water still flowed it had become an ambling, sluggish trickle, where once it had gushed and tumbled.

All but the deepest wells had run dry, grassland meadows were browned into withered stubble beneath the scorch of the sun, and the young green crops had shrivelled and died. No grass to feed the cattle, goats and sheep that were growing thin and calling for water. No milk for calves or milk churn. No grain for flour, nothing to harvest. Nature had turned her benign bounty into the dust of death.

In the wake of drought the evil of plague had crept across Wessex and Kent, with its slow, menacing tread, spreading unstoppable through Sussex, Wilt-Shire and Hamp-Shire. Had leered a while at London, then drifted onwards, up through the County of Essex, to slither into Suffolk and Norfolk, taking all who fell in its virulent path.

Emma sat with her hands limp in her lap, her linen gown unlaced at her throat, her head, with her hair plaited into two braids, uncovered. Her palace bedchamber faced east and was, this late in the afternoon, in thankful shade. Death, if only he would come for her, would not be unwelcome. It was not death, nor its manner, that frightened her, but birth. She put her hand, the fingers bone-thin, on her abdomen, could feel nothing, no swelling, no movement, but the new child was there, growing inside her. Her lips barely moving, she counted the dates on those same fingers. February it would be born. Next February, in the year of the Lord 1006.

Perhaps if she could weep, she could be purged of this weight that lay like a milkmaid's yoke across her shoulders; but her eyes and her heart were as empty of moisture as the scorched earth.

He had claimed his rights as a husband soon after she had been purified by the solemnisation of her churching. If the eyes of God saw her fit to be a wife again, then so did the King. He had been drunk, foul-breathed and crude, had not listened to her pleading to be left alone, that she could not face bearing another child, not while the memory of the agony of Edward's birthing remained so vivid. What do men know of a woman's labour? What, beyond the act of begetting, do they care?

'If you had been there,' she had cried, 'you would know the agony I went through.'

'As we face the agony of the battlefield,' he had retorted, his hands clasped tight, too tight, on her wrists. 'We do not flinch when it is our duty to put on armour and take up sword and shield. Nor should you shy away from your duty to your husband.'

What choice had she? No more choice than the people of southern England who were dying, day by day, from slow starvation or the merciless ravages of plague.

The sky, eight miles away to the north-eastern horizon where the forest of Epping garlanded the hills of the Lea and Roding valleys, was grey and hazy. From heat or gathering clouds? Æthelred was there, in the woods, hunting for deer, although his huntsman had warned that the creatures had gone further north, following the shaded trails and the scent of water. He had been angry that she had not wanted to go with him. She would have to tell him, when he returned, that her monthly course had not appeared and that she was probably with child. He would expect another son.

In the courtyard below the window, Athelstan was about to mount his stallion. He had the boys with him, Edmund and Godwine. Despite Godwine's eleven years to Edmund's four and ten, the two lads were more like brothers than friends. Godwine, she had once hoped, would be her loyal friend too, but all that had been swept aside on the day Edward had been born. A son to the Queen was a threat to Athelstan, and Edmund's sense of honour gave his loyalty to his brother. Where Edmund led, the boy Godwine followed. For her part, Emma could not see the reasoning behind Athelstan's fearing of the child; all it did all day was puke, whimper or scream. If ever Emma steeled her resolve to take up the boy into her arms it shrilled louder, as if it was being agonisingly put to death. She knew it was a wicked thing to admit, but if plague or famine should take her son, she would not weep for his passing.

He was fretting now, on the far side of the room where his wet-nurse was attempting to soothe him. His fists were bunched, his puny legs waving, his mouth open in a thin, high wail. As a woman, Emma ought not to be concerned at the sight of a girl feeding a babe, but no matter how hard she tried, she could not stop the rising sense of revulsion. It was the girl's breasts that repulsed her. She was Emma's age, no more than sixteen, but already she had borne several children, all of whom, apparently, had not survived beyond the first year of life. The child she had brought into the world a day after Edward's birthing had been born dead. Emma considered it a cruel torture of nature to deprive a mother of her nine-month child, but to still bring in the flow of milk. On the dexter side of the coin, the girl had been available to nurse the young princeling.

Steadfastly, Emma watched out of the window opening, observing the sky darkening over the horizon. Was rain to come? If it did, it was too late for the harvest. She could not watch her son, not while the boy fed. Those huge milk-filled breasts were like grotesque cow's udders, the girl producing first one, then the other, with such pride from her unlaced gown and fitting the milk-

157

dripping teat into the babe's tiny mouth, swamping his face with bulging flesh. Emma shuddered, looked down at her own slender figure. They had bound her breasts tight with linen bands soon after the birth. When her milk had come in, the heat of the need to lactate had been almost as bad as the birthing, but the swollen mammary glands had soon subsided; her belly, too, had rapidly regained its shape, although it would never be as flat as before she had carried a child. Now pregnancy was to happen again.

Lightning flashed a zigzag path in the distant sky, soon after a low, rumbling growl of thunder. Rain. Too much of it and the little that remained of the summer crops would be washed away.

She would pray each day, ask for blessings, light candles; her quandary, whether to seek the protection of the Mother Mary during her labour, or beg the easier option of asking God to take her to His side. Day by day, death and despair reaped, side along side, their innocent victims. Could she not, please, be one of them?

30

December 1005 – Oxford

Emma hated it here. Why could they not reside at Woodstock or Islip? Why must they be here, in Eadric Streona's Oxford manor, where so many horrendous memories clung with bloodied talons to the city walls? The atmosphere in the town, less than a single mile from the manor's gate, was as thick as rancid butter. Oh, it might all be rebuilt now, the houses new, the church, Saint Frideswide, basking, erected in the glory of stone, but the resentment against the King and his devoted Reeve, Eadric Streona, was there, oozing beneath the surface like pus festering in an ill-healed wound.

There was nothing to show the blackening of smoke, the charred buildings; no bloodstains, no bodies. The horror had gone, had been tidied away; but the pretence was all on the outside, lime wash on a wattle wall to hide the rough mud and dung of the daub beneath. It made Emma feel sick to see that wretched man, pretentious and without conscience, so obsequious, so humble, twisting Æthelred round his finger as if he were a skein of wool. The pair of them oblivious to the sullen mumbling of Oxford's people. But then, the pair of them together had skin thicker than a scabby old boar.

'I will be pleased when the new year turns and Epiphany has passed. We can then, perhaps, leave here and reside somewhere more congenial,' she remarked to Archbishop Wulfstan, steadfastly ignoring the heated argument that Æthelred was conducting with two of his northern lords, Ealdorman Alfhelm of Deira and Uhtred, the eldest son of the ageing Ealdorman of Bernicia.

'Is there anywhere congenial?' Wulfstan asked in his dour, serious tone. 'It is written in scripture that with the millennium shall come the full sight of God and I fear that He does not like what He is seeing.'

Emma shifted to make herself more comfortable in the hard chair, pushing a feather-filled cushion firmer behind her back. More than seven months pregnant, she was feeling irritable and discontented. Was not in the mood for another of Wulfstan's doom-laden sermons. Too late, he was already launched into his personal diatribe against the sinners of the world.

'When God saw that wickedness had entered the Garden of Eden, He evicted Adam and Eve. When he saw that sin was running rife and people had forgotten His name, He sent the flood. As with Sodom and Gomorrah, if we do not bare our souls to His mercy and repent, He shall release the Horsemen and destroy all that is abhorrent, so that He may wash the world clean and begin again.'

The preaching of the end of the world, after one thousand years from the living of Christ among men, had run far and fast in the aftermath of famine and plague. So many had died, whole villages in places, with more dying by the day, for although the pestilence had burnt its course, there had been no harvest, and there was very little to eat, especially for the poor. The one good thing: the Danes had not come this year. It would have been a waste of effort, in southern England there was nothing to plunder.

Æthelred suddenly lost the last remnant of control on his temper and tipped up the trestle table before him, scattering men, dogs and chickens. 'I said no, Uhtred! No! Absolutely not! Do not pursue this, for you are trying my patience beyond endurance.' For good measure, Æthelred kicked at a dog and strode from the Hall, slamming the door to his private chamber behind him and bellowing for Eadric, as host, to fetch wine. Uhtred stood, running his hand through his thick black hair, puffing his cheeks.

Alfhelm folded his arms, glowering his own rage. 'I warned you not to go whining to the King, Uhtred, and now you have muddied the water for the both of us! Because of your persistence, neither of us will be receiving aid should we require it – and do not expect help from me. I have enough problems seeing to York's safety.'

There was no love lost between Uhtred and Alfhelm.

'It seems Uhtred has yet again been refused men to swell the fyrd of Bernicia,' Wulfstan said calmly. 'If it be God's will that Malcolm of the Scots should attack across the border, then there is naught we can do about it.'

'Except fight,' Emma promptly retorted, 'which it appears Uhtred is willing to do, while Alfhelm and my husband are not.'

Uhtred raised his head, saw Emma looking at him. He stepped over the debris and walked across the Hall to her, made his obedience to his Queen and the Archbishop. 'I cannot protect the North of England without adequate men,' he said bluntly. 'Malcolm is recent-made King of Scots; he has to prove his strength to the lords of the Isles, or wear his crown for but a short while. When he attacks Durham I cannot be certain that I can hold it.'

'The cathedral at Durham, where rests our blessed Saint Cuthbert, is stone built. If it be God's will, then it shall be kept safe,' Wulfstan asserted.

'With respect,' Uhtred said, masking his anger by inclining his head, 'the cathedral is stone, the town is not.'

'And is it not more prudent', Emma added, 'to see to England's security in the certainty of armed fyrdsmen, rather than the contrary whim of God?' It was bold of her to speak out before Wulfstan, but persistently, God had not shown much love or sympathy towards Emma and she was growing weary of hearing about His non-existent benevolence. How could God expect love and dutiful submission when the innocent died by the hundred? When she had to endure the humiliation of Æthelred's lust and the result of another child? Let the monks and nuns make it their business to pray for the salvation of souls; for herself, she was not impressed by God's performance.

To Uhtred she said, 'I acknowledge your concern, for I know that however thick the stone of solid-built walls, there are ways of tearing them down. Alas, I am only the Queen and I am not permitted an opinion, nor to help, if I had any to give.'

'God will show us the way,' Wulfstan insisted, annoyed at Emma's tetchiness but understanding of it, given her advanced condition. He did not know when the annihilation of the Apocalypse was to be brought upon the sinners of this world, the only thing certain, in the Archbishop's mind, was that to enter Heaven, all must be repented, or lost. The signs were there to be read by those who were aware: fire in the sky, flood upon the land, hunger in the bellies of men, women and children. Disease and death stalking through every town and settlement; raiding, rape and plunder coming from the sea. Or from the High Lands across the Scots border. It was the message of God and nothing could be done to stop it, except pray for forgiveness.

Uhtred took his leave and left Oxford, returning to Northumbria in disgust at the intolerable attitude of the King, but with an altered view of his Queen. She was not the timid mouse they had all taken her for. Lurking beneath that pale exterior was a Valkyrie, a warrior woman. One who had not yet found her voice, but would, soon, learn how to sing.

31

February 1006 – Winchester
Winchester was not as foul-smelling as London, even though the city shared the honour of being England's joint capital and was often full to bursting. Squatting in a fold of the Hampshire Downs, its chalky, navigable river, the Itchen, often as crowded as the streets, provided a convenient route into the market that attracted buyers and sellers from local villages and wider trade routes across the seas. A bustling town at the best of times, with pilgrims intent on visiting the holy shrine of Saint Swithin, a bishop revered as a worker of miracles and a man of humility, the arched gateways echoed almost constantly during daylight hours to the rumble of cartwheels, horseshoes, footsteps and the lowing of bewildered cattle.

Herded into pens of wicker hurdles set ready in Gar Street, the animals, if sold for meat, then passed on to Fleshmonger Street, which some were already beginning to call by its new nickname of 'Parchment Street' for the production of the vellum that was prized by the highest monastic scriptoriums. The butchers were tradesmen of efficient skill, who lived and worked on the same premises. Tanners' Street, in close proximity to the butchers, stank almost as much as the fullers' yards. Raw hides being processed into leather was not a quick or pleasant-smelling business, but Winchester's Shieldmakers' Street was an altogether more exciting experience, where craftsmen fashioned their trade by stretching the tanned leather over wickerwork or wooden boards. The streets had been designed into their grid pattern by the Great King, Alfred, when he had ordered the structural rebuilding and defence of his Wessex capital. Trade, business, commerce. Winchester could boast of its pottery, iron making, bell casting and leather working. The Royal Mint employed ten moneyers, while the Benedictines took responsibility for many of the numerous churches and chapels, and the New Minster, built to the north of Alfred's older building.

Emma avoided the wretchedness of the cattle market where possible, the hosier and shoemaker, leather worker and potter more easily drawing her fascination. Craftsmen with names like Godric Clean-hand, Ælfric Sheep-shanks and Cudbert Penny-feather. Particularly, this morning, the Queen intended to purchase pepper, for she understood that a trader's craft had moored yesterday, carrying the precious cargo obtained from Pavia in Italy, Europe's greatest centre of commercial exchange. The temptation to go and buy had been too great for her to resist, despite the inconvenient bulk of her pregnancy.

This February day the frosted air carried sounds sharp and clear: the calls of the traders to come see their fine wares, the haggling of bargain-wise women, the deeper voices of the men, the laughter of the children. A donkey brayed his reluctance to carry such a heavy load, two dogs fought a brief but vicious contest over a scrap of meat. Geese hissed, chickens crooned, caged birds whistled. It was good to be out here, to be among people who had no care beyond inspecting what lay on the next stall along. Æthelred had been in a black mood all morning, Alfhelm of Deria and Emma's brother, Duke Richard II of Normandy, once again being the joint cause. The one because he was at Court, the other because he was not. Mind, in this instance Emma could not disagree with her husband's grumbled opinion that Ealdorman Alfhelm and his family had outstayed their welcome and ought to return north to York.

Her peppers safely purchased, Emma picked over a bundle of woollen braiding, selecting a length an inch wide, with the colours of red, green and yellow intricately woven into an intriguingly delicate pattern. She studied it closely, sure there must be flaws in the weaving, a mismatch of colours, a knot in the thread, an inconsistency in the complex pattern? 'The woman who wove this', she said to the stallholder, 'must have exceptionally dexterous fingers and a sharp mind. I can find no fault with it.'

'My daughter does the weaving, Madam. You'll be hard pressed to find anything better.'

Emma paid her pennies. There was no possible chance that Lady Godgifa would allow her husband to leave Winchester without first attempting all she could to secure Æthelred's eldest son in marriage to their daughter, Ælfgifu. Emma had to admire Godgifa's persistence, although scorning her credulity. Athelstan was not in the slightest interested in the pinch-faced girl, nor in formal marriage. He was a man determined to become King after his father and, to ensure it, he would need to make a strong and strategic alliance when the time came. Who could foresee the important men of the future? To ally himself with Deira, now, could turn Bernicia or Lindsey against him. A man who wanted to be king did not take a legal-bound, Christian-blessed woman as wife until the crown was safe upon his head.

Athelstan was astute; he would not ally with Alfhelm, not while it was becoming obvious that the Ealdorman of Deira, through his own stupidity, was rapidly falling from Æthelred's favour. If only he and his unbearable wife would desist in their whining for recognition, then mayhap their prolonged presence at Court would be more equably tolerated, but as it was . . . Other lords, including Uhtred of Bernicia and the Archbishops of York and Canterbury, had returned to their estates soon after the twelfth night of the Christmas gathering, but not Alfhelm. Was there more that he wanted, beyond securing a marriage between his daughter and the King's son? If so, Æthelred could only wait and discover what the boorish man was fishing for, and as for her brother . . . Emma sighed, strolled on to the next stall. The child in her enlarged belly was heavy, due any day, her lower back was aching, her ankles and hands swollen. She ought to rest, but she needed to feel the fresh, crisp air on her cheeks, enjoy the pale February sun. Needed to be away from the cloying atmosphere of the palace.

Pope John, fifteenth to bear that name, was attempting to rekindle the broken treaty that had disintegrated between England and Normandy. In a letter to Æthelred he had declared his interest in re-establishing a workable agreement, the petty bickering, he had argued, must cease.

Had anyone seriously thought this marriage between Emma and

Æthelred would bring a lasting peace? Apparently, the Pope had, but then Rome was investing heavily in the profit of overseas trade and was interested in who, however subtly, controlled the ships that crossed the Channel Sea. Rome was none too pleased at the disruption of income, caused by the squabbling of two grown men. Neither was Emma, but she had resigned herself to the inevitable. Men might look like men, but all too often, some behaved more like children.

The frost had been hard and widespread overnight, the sun, as midday approached, bright but not sufficient to melt obstinate patches of ice that clung to shadowed puddles and ruts. Twice Emma had almost slipped and Leofstan had insisted that she take his arm for her safety. She had not objected, for he took his recent promotion to Captain with serious conviction. Towards the western end of the High Street, where the hill climbed steeper and the wind swirled all day, the stalls were wider spaced, the hiring tax for each pitch cheaper by half a penny. There was nothing more that Emma wanted, but she had been determined to walk the length of the street from East Gate to West and, as she passed, look in at her property, the cluster of humble dwellings ceded to her as a marriage portion by Æthelred. They needed pulling down and rebuilding, for several were nigh on uninhabitable, certainly not fit as a residence for herself. One day she would see to it. Huh, she was sounding like her husband!

A scuffle caught her attention, a woman shouted and a child, no more than eight years old, darted from behind a stall, a hunk of bread clutched in her hand. She ran in front of Emma, startled momentarily by Leofstan as he lunged forward to intercept her, but she was quick, used to running off, fast, with whatever she could steal. Ducking beneath grabbing hands, she was away and gone down a dark side street, curses rippling in her wake.

'Damned brat, this be the secon' time she's 'ad 'alf a loaf of bread from me.' The woman shook her fist in the direction the child had disappeared, declared, 'I 'ave 'er face now, though, I'll get 'er if she comes pesterin' again.'

'She looked hungry,' Emma said with compassion, having taken in the gaunt thinness of the girl. 'Is there nowhere those such as she may find food and shelter here in Winchester?'

'The nuns of Nunnaminster serve broth to those willing to work in exchange. There's never owt for nowt in this life, Lady.'

Handing the woman a copper penny, Emma refrained from agreeing. 'Take this for your trouble,' she said, then, as an afterthought, gave the woman another. 'And this for when the child comes again. Give her bread and bring her to the palace kitchens. Tell them the Queen commands that they are to find her work in exchange for her keep. There will be a silver coin awaiting for you for your trouble.'

'You'll have all the poor of Wessex turning up by the morrow,' Leofstan said with a chuckle as, offering his arm, he escorted Emma up the steep incline towards the gaping arch of the western gateway. He approved. It was a compassionate queen who helped the poor where and when she could. Æthelred's mother had offered no patience with them; a royal woman who had gone unloved by England.

Owt for nowt, Emma thought. How true. She had the security of never going cold or hungry, had furs, fine woollen gowns and soft leather boots. *Owt for nowt*. In return for her comforts had to give herself as wife to a man she loathed. Fair exchange? Emma was not certain, but then, she would never willingly give up this life for one of poverty, grime and discomfort.

At the gateway she turned north, drawn by the aroma of new-baked bread. Several Jews, trusted even less than the Danes, lived along here, making a handsome living from moneylending. The tavern, at the end of a small side street, was English, owned by a Saxon.

'It is amazing' Emma laughed as she signalled for Leofstan to see whether the place was suitable for her to enter, 'how tantalising smells can suddenly make you ravenously hungry.'

The Gate was a modest establishment, the trestle tables, wooden stew bowls and pewter tankards clean and in good repair. The tavern keeper enthusiastically welcoming such honoured customers of acceptable appearance. The bread, when it was served, was made from wheat grain, not cheap rye, and the meat fresh and well cooked, with a subtle seasoning of herbs. Emma enjoyed the meal, she had eaten only morsels these last few weeks, the size of the babe giving her indigestion if she overfilled her stomach. This stew, however, was appetising, the meat tender and, a rarity in England, rabbit.

'My brother is a wine merchant,' the taverner explained as he personally served the Queen. 'He fetches us back a few coney whenever he sails to Normandy or France. He got us through the worst of last year's difficulties; famine was bad for all of us down here in the South, but those across the sea thrived on our misfortune. There's many a Frenchman grown fat on our silver after trebling the price of meat and flour.'

'The King ordered grain from his own granaries to be distributed to the worst-affected areas,' Emma said, knowing as she spoke that his generosity had come too little too late. Tactfully, the taverner served his brother's best wine and said nothing.

Emma remained an hour, but with the afternoon sky beginning to cloud over, reluctantly pushed her ungainly weight up from the bench. As she came to her feet, a great gush of water burst from her womb and a pain simultaneously shot through her abdomen. She cried out, half fell, embarrassed and alarmed. Frightened.

Her maidservant, a quiet girl who served with enthusiasm but limited conversational talent, ran to her side, urging Leofstan to send quickly to the palace for a litter. 'The babe is coming,' she gabbled, flustered, her arms and hands whirling in anxiety as the busy tavern, attracted by the commotion, began to take an avid interest.

'The waters have broken, that is all,' Emma countered, sounding more in control than she felt. 'I am quite all right.' Another stab of intense pain and she stumbled to her knees, her head bowed, breath coming shallow and fast through her contorted face. 'God's mercy,' she gasped, her hands clutching at her belly.

'Holy Mother! You cannot let her have the bairn out here!' A woman, entering from the street, thrust her way through the crowd, removing her cloak as she walked. To Leofstan she ordered, 'You, bring her into the back,' and without waiting for an answer she opened a rear door and ushered Emma into the privacy of the living place beyond the public tavern.

'This is Leofgifu, my late wife's sister,' the taverner explained as he hovered, anxious. 'She was widowed in the Saint Brice's Day killings, came down from York to help me when my wife went to God.'

'A Dane?' Leofstan asked, eager to accept a distraction from the Queen's discomfort. All the same, his eyes were darting around the room, taking in the modest furnishing and the lime-washed walls that displayed a few pieces of weaponry and an embroidered tapestry depicting an í-víking longship, satisfying himself that this private house-place would be suitable, and safe, for his Queen.

'Get you gone!' the woman, Leofgifu, ordered, waving her hands at the men. 'If you want to be of help, fetch me hot water and send to the palace for my Lady's midwife.' For emphasis she ushered the Captain out. 'You had best hurry.' Without saying more, she slammed the door on the craning world.

Calm, capable, she guided Emma towards the hearth-place, sat her on a stool and robustly poked fresh life into the embers, sending sparks and a drift of smoke hurtling towards the escape hole in the low, red-tiled roof.

'Let's unfasten your veil, my dear, and these lacings on your gown. Give you a chance to . . . There, child, breathe with the pain, not against it.'

The contraction passing, Emma attempted a wan, brave smile. 'You seem to know what you are doing, Madam. I thank you for your assistance.' She grimaced as another wave swept through her.

'I've birthed six of my own and brought several more nieces and nephews into the world. You had these pains long? Backache, perhaps?' Her accent was different from the normal soft burr of Anglo-Saxon Wessex, some of her words with a distinct hint of the northern Danish dialect.

'I did not sleep for the discomfort,' Emma confided, 'but I have not been comfortable for several nights now.'

'Ah, birth works its own way. It is often only the first that takes the effort and trouble.' As another pain came, Leofgifu gently rubbed at Emma's lower back, then, with the contraction passing, helped remove her gown, boots and stockings. 'There's not going to be opportunity to get you away before this one makes an appearance.'

'I don't care where I have it!' Emma gasped through gritted teeth, trying to hold down a scream. 'I don't care about the damned thing at all. I did not ask for it, I do not want it!'

'Nay, none of us ever do, lass, not till the bairn's safely sucking at our breast. Were it men who had the bearing of them, there'd be precious few of us in the world!' Emma barely heard. She threw her head back and let the scream out as the pain of birth overwhelmed her.

She delivered her child on her hands and knees, down among the fresh straw that Leofgifu had quickly spread, the babe slipping into the world within an hour of the waters breaking. A girl, a daughter. Leofgifu, dressing Emma in one of her own clean undershifts, settled her into her curtained box bed that nestled in an alcove and handed her the child.

She was beautiful! Large, pale-blue eyes, pink wrinkled skin, soft downy hair. A face like an angel. She lay in Emma's cradling arms gazing, unfocused, at the face hovering above her, quiet and content. When Emma put her, tentatively, to her breast, she suckled with no fuss or whimpering. Why could Edward's birth not have been like this? Why could he not have been as utterly, divinely perfect as this child?

'Æthelred will be angry,' Emma said to Leofgifu who, after wrapping the afterbirth, was disposing of the soiled linen and straw. 'He expected a son. A daughter will not be to his liking.'

'He gets what God gives and is grateful for it,' Leofgifu answered tersely. 'Now you give that bairn to me and get yourself to sleep. If the palace comes meddlin' I'll send them away with a flea in their ear. You'll stay here until you're full rested, king or no king.' She was firm, in command, and her smile was like that of a serene Madonna, loving and warm.

'Leofgifu?' Emma said as she began to drowse. 'Would you consider coming with me? I am in much need of a companion.'

170

'I'll consider your asking, but there is my sister's husband to think on. It was good of him to take me in when my husband and sons were hanged, and I was left with nothing more than the gown I stood in.' Her answer was dismissive, but she had already made her mind. She would go with the Queen. Her brother-in-law had his eyes on a new wife and there would not be room for two women in a small tavern like this. The Queen's offer was a gift from God, even with its sting in the tail. She would be living beneath the roof of the man who had ordered the murder of her family.

32

Another Easter. Where did the weeks go? From the morrow the men of the Council of all England, the Witan, would start arriving at Canterbury. Another tedious round of bickering and petulant disagreement. It would all be the same thing. The Danes, taxes, Scotland; the King's failure to agree a truce with Duke Richard of Normandy. The next birthing day, Æthelred would reach eight and thirty years of age, not far from a tally of two score years, and he was tired and sick of it all. Had his murdered brother been the fortunate one? What pleasure was there in being King? His mother had revelled in the cut and thrust of political debate and intrigue, had thrived on the daily uncertainty. He loathed it. All of it.

Æthelred cursed and stalked away from the open Hall door, turning his back on the rain that poured down as if it were being emptied by the bucketful. He stumped across the new-lain rushes, his feet disturbing the scent of dried lavender and rosemary, his boot squelching into a pile of fresh dog mess, releasing another, not so pleasant, aroma. Used to the smells of his Hall, he paid no heed to either. At least here at Canterbury, unlike many of his palaces, there were separate king's and queen's apartments, he would not have to endure the screaming of that child Edward. Did the boy never cease crying? The girl, Goda, was a sweetheart, quite the most enchanting of all his children, but Æthelred, because of duties and judicial requirements, saw little of her. Emma doted on the girl – he had warned her several times to keep herself detached, that come a suitable age, Goda would be sent away into marriage.

'Daughters only have one use for a king,' he had said to Emma, rougher than he had intended, 'and that is for useful alliance.'

Emma had paid her husband small heed. She herself had not been wed until her thirteenth year and none of his elder daughters had husbands. Goda was barely two months old, there was no need to fret so soon about an enforced parting.

Athelstan sat before the hearth-fire, his wet boots stretched towards the blaze of the flames, his hands occupied with twisting three thin strips of leather into an endurable plaited thong. Æthelred scowled at him. Why was it that father and son so openly disliked each other? Antipathy? Distrust?

'Have you seen to those horses?'

His agile, capable fingers automatically weaving the strands in and out of each other, Athelstan looked up. 'Aye. They are comfortably settled.' He had never liked his father. He thought him a fool and a bully, but then Athelstan had loved his grandmother and would never forget or forgive the derision that Æthelred had constantly battered him with because of it.

'Fed? Dried? I do not want the Reaper coming to any harm.'

Like his father, Athelstan's hair, braes and boots were wet. Along the wall by the doorway their sodden cloaks had been hung on pegs to dry. The hunting this morning had been going well until the skies had opened and shed heavy rain that looked set for the rest of the day.

'He is muzzle deep into a warm bran-mash. As with my own fellow, he is dry, warm and content.'

The Reaper was one of Æthelred's best stallions, a sturdy fourteen hand, jet-black, of uncertain temper. Soon after acquiring him the animal had viciously lashed out and killed a stable boy by splitting his head open; only those who were competent around horses dare go near him, his reputation as grim as his name. There were servants capable of handling him, but Æthelred insisted that his sons care for the animals as much as possible, for any fool could set his backside in the saddle; it took a horseman to know how to care, properly, for the creatures.

Æthelred pushed aside his son's feet that were resting on the raised hearth bricks and walking past, seated himself on another stool; held his chilled hands to the warmth. 'I want you to keep close contact with Alfhelm,' the King ordered, 'throughout the duration of Council.'

173

Athelstan groaned.

'Am I asking too much of you, boy? Can I not depend on you for anything?'

'I have no liking for Ealdorman Alfhelm, nor his damned wife or daughter.'

'You'll have a liking for who I tell you to like! You had best start getting used to the girl. I have a mind to agree marriage between the two of you. I need to bind Alfhelm's loyalty tighter than it is.'

'Then you will need to find another way to do it,' Athelstan lashed his curt answer. 'I'll not wed the girl.'

'What? Are you squeamish because she has foul breath and crooked teeth?'

'There is nothing wrong with her breath or her teeth. It is her family that is foul and I have often stated my intention that I will not take a wife until I am crowned king.' Then he made a mistake: he added, half under his breath, 'That was Grandmama's advice and I will follow it.'

Furious, Æthelred stormed to his feet. 'You will do as I say, boy, not what that old hag told you!' He jabbed his finger at Athelstan, poking his shoulder. 'Nor will you be king. Edward is to follow me.'

'Edward? That fragile mushroom? He'll not make it past infancy!'

'I'll have you know that I was a sickly child – I survived, as will my legitimate son. And there'll be others to follow him, others who will take precedence over you.'

Casually, Athelstan rose to his feet, laid the partially plaited thongs across the stool. 'Then if Edward lives, and others are born and they are foolish enough to contest my claim, I will have to kill them. One by one.' It was not a threat, he meant it as a fact.

'I could as easily order you killed. Here and now,' Æthelred growled, low and menacing, his nostrils pinched, lip curled. Why did all the conversation with his eldest always disintegrate into argument?

Leaning forward so that his face was only an inch from his father's, Athelstan answered, 'Then why don't you?' He paused, pulled back, leered. 'I'll tell you why. Because I am all you have and you hate that fact, don't you? That brat the Norman bitch has given you will not live and there may not be others.' He took a step back, folded his arms, his expression mocking as his eyes surveyed the area of his father's manhood. 'There's talk, gossip, I find it most interesting to listen to. You lie with all these gutter-slut whores, yet you are rarely presented with their by-blows. Why is that, Papa? Are you getting old? Is your pizzle withering? Is it blunted, of no more use than a broken spear?' An effective taunt that rammed home straight to the mark.

His fists bunched, Æthelred leapt forward and drove his knuckles at Athelstan's jaw, but his son was agile, young and fit. With ease he tipped his head aside, felt no more than a brush of air across his skin. 'You are no match for me, old man. You never were and you never will be.' Giving a mocking salute, Athelstan turned away, took his cloak from its peg and sauntered towards the door.

Æthelred was shaking, enraged and angry, his face suffused purple, his hands white. Through clenched teeth, he spat, 'Get out! Get out of my sight, my Court, my kingdom!'

'With pleasure Papa, with great pleasure.'

'I'll show you, you ungrateful whoreson!' Æthelred screamed at his son's departing back. 'I'll bloody show you!' In three long strides, Æthelred caught up with Athelstan and shoving him aside, stepped out into the rain. Without slowing, head down, arms pumping, he splashed through the puddles and slammed open the door of the Queen's Hall on the opposite side of the courtyard.

Athelstan headed for the stables, shouting for his men to be roused as he walked. As always, Æthelred would take his anger out on someone of less strength. He felt a twinge of pity for Emma, but what could he do about it? She was a wife, wives expected to take the brunt of a husband's storm-raging moods.

Conscience was not an emotion a future king could afford to entertain.

Emma eased herself into the round wooden bathtub. Immersed in the comfort of hot water, she closed her eyes, willed her muscles to relax. Last night, she had stood up to Æthelred and had won. Releasing her breath in a long, slow sigh, she felt the tension ease from her body. She had won, God help her! She was seven and ten years of age, and had at last discovered the inner strength of assertive self-preservation and the delicious feeling of power that it gave.

Horses were in the courtyard, the sound of men's excited voices mingling with the singing of hounds. With the rain ceasing during the night and a clear blue sky overhead, there were several days of missed hunting for them to be catching up on. The palace would be depleted of men and noise until evening. A blissful day without the irritating presence of the King.

Opening her eyes, she reached for a tablet of goose fat, chamomile and lanolin soap and began to smooth it over her breasts, arms and belly. There were white stretch marks across her thighs and above the bush of pubic hair; would they increase in length, she wondered idly, with the carrying of a third child? With a sigh of resignation, said aloud, 'I do not want another child, did not want the first two.'

'Ah, but a wife cannot refuse her duties to her wedded husband. There is naught we can do but endure.'

Unaware that she had spoken her thoughts, Emma looked up at Leofgifu's submissive answer. 'And a husband', she retorted sharply, 'should remember his duty to his wife. Is it not sinful to ill use a woman?'

To that Leofgifu had to agree.

Emma smoothed the wash-cloth along her right leg. 'My husband gets drunk because he cannot bear the weight of his conscience. He shouts because he wants to be heard and no one cares to listen. He fears the night, and dancing shadows, because it is all too easy to hide a dagger blade where there is no light. He lives, day by day, hour by hour, in fear, afraid that one day someone is going to say to his face what troubles his mind. That without his mother he is nothing.' Filling a small jug with the bathwater, she poured it over her hair and vigorously applied the soap, the smile on her face enigmatic.

'He fears Athelstan because, in all but sex, the boy is the image of his grandmother.' She pointed at the last jug of clean, hot water, bent her head for Leofgifu to rinse her hair. Stripping the water from its long length, she stepped from the tub, allowed her friend to swaddle her in the warmed towel, begin to rub her dry.

'And now he also fears me, for I have done what he dreads most.' The satisfaction as she spoke her triumph aloud was invigorating. She felt free, reborn and renewed.

Leofgifu stopped rubbing, snatched her head up sharply, not understanding. 'Lady?'

Emma was dabbing a second towel at her face and shoulders. 'I am with child again, you must have noticed?'

The older woman nodded, aye, she had recognised the early signs.

'Yesterday, he again attempted to take me by force. He was drunk, angry – another row with his son, of course. He has always to prove himself to someone, and a wife comes in useful to beat and humiliate at will. Last night he came to my chamber with the same intention and I found the courage to tell him that if he ever dared touch me in violence again he would join his brother in his grave.'

Leofgifu gasped, her eyes wide with terror. 'Lady, you did not threaten to kill him? Madam, that is treason! He could have you hanged!'

Emma laughed. 'I am not a fool, of course I did not, I merely told him that if he abused me I would take my children and return to my brother, as is my right as a wronged wife. He cannot deny the charge, for his entire Hall has witnessed his mistreatment. I told him also that once in Normandy I would raise an army of Normans and French. Germany, too, would assist if I asked. The Pope, assuredly, would promote my cause, for I would see to it that I offered sufficient financial incentive.'

Puzzled, Leofgifu frowned. She was only a *lochorewif*, literally, the lockwife, the woman with the keys in charge of the household. The world of politics and men meant nothing. 'But what would you do with an army? How does this help you?'

With her hair all wet and glistening, Emma stood tall and straight, she smiled at Leofgifu indulgently. 'Damaged people', she said, 'are dangerous, for we have already drowned in the darkness and we know that if we kick strong enough we can survive, for we have proven it so.' She began to dress, her favourite blue wool with the yellow braiding. 'With an army I would put Edward on the throne and rule as Regent.' She fastened the shoulder brooch, delighting in how the sapphires gleamed in the caught light.

She closed her eyes, remembering. He had come bursting into her chamber, hurled her two women from the room and snatched at her, forcing his mouth on to hers. Where had Leofgifu been? Ah yes, with the children.

'You're a stupid, ignorant woman, with the brains of a sheep,' he had sneered, 'only fit for bedding.'

And quietly, without struggling, without attempting to push him away or cower from him, Emma had said, 'I heard of a woman, once, who disposed of a king so that she might rule, in her own right, through her son. Her name was Ælfthryth; she was your mother.'

He had stood there, silent, as she told him what she intended to do if ever he laid as much as one finger on her again, had realised that she was deadly, coldly, serious. What the mother of one future king could do, so could another, she told him. Rid the kingdom of a king, so that the mother could rule through her son.

33

'*Durham*', Uhtred's message read, sent urgent to Ealdorman Alfhelm in York, '*is in extreme danger. If you do not grant my father aid, Bernicia could fall.*'

'*Sod Bernicia,*' had been the terse reply.

Siege warfare was not a favoured method of fighting for an English warrior. Few towns and burghs were defended by stout-built stone walls; the majority, secured behind the limited protection of palisade fencing which, although constructed in seasoned oak, a wood difficult to burn, were not invulnerable. The border towns along the Welsh Marches, Hereford and Shrewsbury in particular, were used to attack, but the Welsh preferred the hit-and-run tactics of night raiding. Laying siege was too prolonged and cumbersome. To besiege a stubborn town, reluctant to bow to a demanded war-geld, was an effective procedure. As long as the besieging army was in no danger from counter-attack or the apathy of boredom.

By slaying his predecessor, Malcolm, the second king of that name, had escalated the ongoing blood-feud that ran between the noble families of the High Lands and the Isles of Scotland. Needing to prove his worth, he chose an inaugural foray across the border, often a profitable exercise for whichever side was doing the raiding. With Ealdorman Waltheof of Bernicia an old and feeble man, the Scot seized his opportunity and swept down towards Durham, setting camp beyond the walls to make ready to starve the inhabitants into submission.

A haphazard way of doing battle, a siege, for it required organisation, loyalty and vigilance. A poor leader could rarely sustain an effective long-term campaign: men were inclined, unless held under strict discipline, to wander off in search of more immediate gain, rather than sit arse-scratching, day after tedious day, watching ambivalent townsfolk skulk behind strong-held walls. Food, once everything within the near vicinity had been devoured, became scarce – a fact worsened after a famine year. The latrine pits soon began to stink and the edge of interest wear thin. To be successful, a siege needed planning, cunning and foresight. Malcolm had all those requirements and he was a determined man who had no intention of missing an opportunity for easy gain; but he had not bargained on the Ealdorman's son, Uhtred, taking over his dying father's authority.

Durham was not a faint-hearted town ready to surrender at the first thrown spear. This was Saint Cuthbert's resting place, his grand and beautiful cathedral dominating the huddle of inns, shops and bothies. A town increasing in wealth, that had an adequate supply of food and water, and the ability to withstand a siege for many months if need be, for the townsfolk believed that neither their saint nor their ealdorman would abandon them. All they had to do was sit and wait.

The drizzling rain had scuttled away with a change of the wind, and stars had pocked a bright, clear sky throughout the night. Tendrils of a new dawn purpled the eastern sky, and along Durham's rampart walls the sentries yawned, stretched and stamped dew-damp feet; spat at the enemy encampment below, ghostly in its swathe of slow-shifting ground mist. If the Scots were going to attempt another assault at the gateway with their battering ram, it would not be for an hour or two yet. No one was stirring down there among the ragged straggle of tents. Or were they?

One of the men peered closer. Was that movement at the outer edge of the camp? Something wading through the mist, like a boat being paddled slowly through water? He nudged his companion, pointed.

'What be that?'

His friend looked with squinting eyes against the glare of the rising sun. Laughed. 'Bloody fool, 'tis only strayed cattle. Frightened of your own shadow, are you?' He turned away, scornful, chuckling, but the first man, excited, grabbed at his tunic sleeve.

'It ain't just cows! Look!'

Through the dawn mist, the black, short-horned cattle of the borders were making their way down to the river, cattle driven by men huddled and bent low against their sides, men armed with shields and spears and swords. Uhtred's men. Malcolm, complacent, over-sure and caught unawares, escaped within inches of losing his life. For the majority of his men there was only death.

'What do we do with the dead?' The fifteen-year-old stood eagerly before his father. His boots, his leggings, his tunic, even his face blood-spattered, as if he had a plague of pox spots covering him. 'Do we leave them for the ravens? God's name, Papa, what a fight! Are all battles like this? No wonder the tales are so wonderful!'

Uhtred folded his arms and glowered at the boy. The killing had taken no longer than an hour, this had not been a battle, but a slaughter, as easy to herd cattle into a pen and slit their throats for the autumn butchering. There was much he wanted to say to the boy, that this was not glory, was not a game, a mock skirmish fought with wooden swords. This was real, this was death and maiming, misery and pain. But how could he say all that to an eager lad who had just encountered his first victory? Instead, Uhtred smiled and ruffled his son's hair, bright chestnut, like his own had been before the grizzle-grey had crept in.

'Our own dead, what few there are, will be buried with Christian honour, boy; as for the rest, it is wiser to dispose quickly of the dead, for a corpse soon begins to stink. We burn them.'

'And the Scots wounded?'

Uhtred lifted his eyes to the sky; the clouds were banking up again over to the west. More rain? It would be welcome, rain would clean away the spill of blood.

'We leave no Scotsman alive, son. The lesson here this day at Durham must be one to be remembered up above our northern boundary for many a year to come, remembered down to the grandsons of grandsons.'

The old Ealdorman might no longer be the formidable warrior he had once been, but his son was every bit as capable and Uhtred was determined to prove that it was not wise to set a wrong foot in

Bernicia while he had the holding of its protection, even if that was only by proxy in his father's name.

'How do we ensure they remember, Papa?' Eadulf was puzzled as he surveyed the carnage of the fighting, the grotesque dead, the suffering of the wounded. 'If we merely slit their throats and leave them with the rest of the dead, who will tell of that?'

Uhtred snorted. The glory was already beginning to lose its shine for the boy, then. He rubbed at his chin, at the straggle of beard growth, his eyes casting over the muddied, bloodied scene. Cattle to the pen . . . ? Aye, cattle to the slaughter.

'Hie! Eadulf!' He raised his axe, called to his brother, for whom the boy was named.

The man frowned, questioning, signalled he had heard, began making his way to Uhtred, stopping every now and then to speak a word of praise or comfort to one of their own wounded. 'Aye, brother? You wanted me?'

'It was a good fight, no?'

Eadulf grinned. 'It was a good fight, Uhtred. A pity Alfhelm of Deira was not with us to share our glory.'

Uhtred laughed at the sarcasm. 'A great pity!' It was good to laugh where there was so much death. 'I have a task for you, brother – for you and the boy here, I think.' He set his arm, proud, against the lad's shoulders. 'I wish all the Scots wounded herded together and beheaded. No exceptions. The bodies piled together and burnt, but not the heads. I want the heads.' He turned abruptly and strode away, heading for the gateway into Durham that, now, stood open for its people to pour through, jubilant and praising God. Uncle and nephew shrugged, a strange request, but orders must always be obeyed.

It took Uhtred longer to get into Durham than it had to raise the siege, for so many wanted to shake his hand, slap his shoulder; the children – there had been no chance to evacuate – dancing around his heels, the women offering him kisses, aye, and more. He reached the cathedral, endured with resignation the adulation and blessings of the monks; finally, finally, he called for a moment of quiet in which he might speak. It came, slow, reluctant, for the whole town

182

was like an excited child, too taut, too coiled for the discipline of silence and stillness.

He spoke, his voice booming across the square, of their endurance, of their courage and of the brave fight by his men. Then he asked for what he had come for. 'I require four women, four washerwomen, to help me cleanse the stain of disrespect from these walls of Durham. Four women who will help me ensure that slime shall never spit on us again.'

The four he selected did their work well and were each rewarded with the generous gift of one of Uhtred's own cows. Their task? To wash the hair of every decapitated head and braid it. An insult for the head of a warrior to be cleansed and tidied, to have the blood of war removed, and the soul left to wander for ever without the honour of the way of dying. An insult beyond all insults. And for each head, there was no hiding the shame, for Durham's walls were to show her reprisal to those who treated her with disrespect.

The pyre of bodies and remains belched black and acrid into the sky, its message carrying northwards on the wind, reaching the nostrils of those few who struggled and stumbled with Malcolm to reach the safety of home. To ensure he knew, Uhtred had the last man spared and set free to take Durham's message of warning.

They would come back, for the temptation to take what was on offer was always great, but it would not be for a long time. Not until the spears that had been set along Durham's walls, each spiked with a single head, had been taken down. And that would not happen until the skulls had rotted to bleached bone, after the crows had pecked the eyes and ravaged the flesh.

Durham would not be forgetting the Scots, nor, for some long while, would the Scots be forgetting Durham.

34

December 1006 – Shrewsbury

Alfhelm scowled as he watched the dogs flush a pair of ducks from the reeds. The easterly wind was cold, despite the clear sky and a bright sun; there would be another frost tonight, or snow. He shivered beneath the warmth of his otter-skin mantle, lined and edged with squirrel fur. He did not care for winter: short, dark days; hands and feet always numb; dismal weather. Dismal company. That was the trouble with winter, the falsehood gaiety of the Nativity festival, and the King's winter calling of Council. If there had been a way to circumvent attending Æthelred's Christmas Court, Alfhelm would have used it.

The King's Court was to assemble in Mercia this year, for Winchester and Canterbury were too close to Swein Forkbeard and his over-wintering scum. Alfhelm smiled to himself as he watched Eadric Streona release his goshawk after a pair of wild fowl. A splendid hawk, but too plump in Alfhelm's opinion.

The Danes had returned in early summer and as usual, had plundered and looted, then sailed away again with the autumn change of weather and wind. Only, unexpectedly, they had not sailed for their own lands, but had followed the Kent coast, rounded Dover and had made landfall along the many creeks and inlets of the Island of Wight. Watching Streona's hawk take the female bird with a scatter of feathers, Alfhelm's wry smile broadened. Swein Forkbeard's proximity would be giving Æthelred a headache that had the ferocity of a herd of stampeding horses. Serve the bastard right! If he had not whined and mithered and put deliberate obstacles in the way, Alfhelm's daughter would be wed to Athelstan and the alliance of Deira made firm. As it was, if the King had no wish to commit himself to his ealdormen, then mayhap those same men might reconsider their own commitment. Perhaps to a better man instead? To Swein Forkbeard.

Eadric Streona grinned as his hawksman lured the bird in.

'She's the finest north of the Thames river!' he declared with immense pride. 'I reckon there are few who could beat her to a kill.'

Affably, Alfhelm agreed but privately ridiculed the boasting. Why, he had several birds in his mews at York to put this overweight moulting crow to shame. There was an unwritten rule of hunting etiquette, however, never praise a bird in the mews over one in the hand. Alfhelm had learned that lesson when he had been a young man with barely a scratch of stubble to his chin. Unless certain beyond doubt of something, keep your mouth shut – as he prudently would with Forkbeard's tempting offer. No one knew of it, save Alfhelm and King Swein, not even Godgifa – Lord, tell her, and the world and his wife would hear of it within four and twenty hours!

The King of Denmark had his eye cast on England for his own, had a fancy for carving an empire. Already he held Denmark, Norway and Sweden, although adding England would not be easy. He would need a safe harbour and the security of not needing to watch his back. An alliance of royal marriage, Swein's second son, Cnut, with Alfhelm's daughter, was a sure way to receive all he required. Only one other knew of the proposed alliance, Swein Forkbeard's messenger, a man trusted for his discretion and loyalty. Through him, Alfhelm had sent acceptance of the offer, with condition of a suitable dower, his trust for secrecy being left with God and the blind belief that all poor men had only the wit to serve the one lord.

Streona's invitation for the Ealdorman to join him for a few days' hunting at his Shrewsbury manor had initially caused alarm. Did Æthelred know? How had he heard? Who had told? For several nights Alfhelm had not slept, sweat soaking the linen sheets, bruising blackening under his tired eyes. By day he could not concentrate, could not think straight . . . God help him, what if Æthelred knew? He delayed his answer to the invitation as long as might be possible, but if he were to decline, could that not also alert suspicion? Cause questions to be asked? Relations between Alfhelm and the King had fallen to an implacable hostility and Godgifa urged him to accept, insisting this was a gesture of reconciliation from the King through his Shire Reeve. He should go to Shrewsbury, she insisted, while she, with the rest of the family, would proceed to the Christmas Court and await him there.

'We have been quiet along the Welsh Borders these last few months,' Streona was saying as he nodded approvingly at his hawksman who, with the bird now hooded, returned the creature to his master's gloved fist. Stroking the soft feathers of her breast, Streona added, 'It can be dangerous here at Shrewsbury, for it is the only crossing of the Severn river for many miles.' He took hold of the hawk's jessies more firmly as she began to flap her wings, twining the leather laces through his fingers. 'The Welsh princes are too engrossed in their inter-family squabbles to be of any bother to us at present. With good fortune, they'll hack each other's heads off and save us the bother.' He turned to Alfhelm, said, with a bland, neutral expression, 'As will the Danes with Swein Forkbeard. I hear there are rumblings of unrest along his borders also? Æthelred is thinking that the man has bitten off a lump of ambition that is too large to swallow.'

Alfhelm could not give a clipped penny for the problems of the Welsh Borders, nor their interest in the squalid town of Shrewsbury. It boasted nothing more than a few peasants' huts, an apology for a market and an insignificant monastery of elderly and deaf monks. Let the damned Welsh have the place! He pricked his ears at Streona's comment on Swein Forkbeard, however. Was this a test? A sounding of how the river ran?

'I know nothing of Forkbeard's troubles,' Alfhelm stated with bald indifference. 'As long as he stays away from Deira I have no interest in him at all.' He shifted in his saddle, spread one hand and smiled. 'I am, however, concerned that my backside is blistered, my toes are frozen and my stomach is growling for food!'

Streona laughed, dug in his spurs and urged his horse into a canter. 'Then we shall return to my manor; I have a fine Italian wine I want you to sample.'

The track was narrow and winding, slippery in places, steep in others. Streona led the way, at ease in these woods, knowing the area well, for he had hunted here since childhood with his brothers and father. When the track widened, he slowed his horse to a walk, lengthened his reins to allow the animal to lower its head, gain its breath. Steam rose from its thick bay coat, its neck wet with sweat. Beckoning for Alfhelm to ride beside him, Streona deliberately dropped a few yards behind the two servants riding ahead.

'The King, Alfhelm, has asked me to intervene between you and him. He is aggrieved that there have been some unfortunate misunderstandings.'

'Not on my part!' Alfhelm answered with indignation. 'It is the King who wishes to throw honours at Bernicia instead of Deira.'

'With Waltheof dead, the King could not leave Bernicia without an ealdorman. Surely you can see that? And it seemed fitting for Æthelred to give Uhtred one of his elder daughters as wife.'

They rounded a bend and for a few strides the trees thinned, allowing a view of the river and the town. The low winter sun illuminated the calm water into a shimmer of sparkling light and reflected off the golden cross that topped Shrewsbury's abbey. The ash woods were silent, apart from the thud of the horses' hooves on the grass track and the slight ruffle of a breeze whispering through the bare winter branches.

As if he were remarking on the weather, or the condition of his horse, Eadric Streona added, 'Nor, my Lord Alfhelm, can Æthelred have you agreeing an alliance of marriage with Forkbeard's son.'

A blackbird, with a sudden shrilled alarm and a flutter of wings, hurtled from a thicket, causing Streona's stallion to shy, almost unseating his rider into the undergrowth. The dogs were running loose, their tongues lolling, short docked tails constantly waving. The two bitches were ahead, noses down following a scent; the dog stopped to cock his leg against a fallen, fungi-covered tree, pricked his ears at a sudden noise and plunged off to the left, disappearing into the tangle of a hazel thicket. He barked once, then yelped, was silent.

Alfhelm, his eyes closed, silently thanked God for the diversion.

'Curse that bloody dog,' Streona snapped. Halting, he drew the short-shafted hunting spear that rested in its holder alongside his saddle, dismounted. 'I have never once had him out without him causing some sort of inconvenience.' He called to the men ahead, who came trotting back. 'You two, see if you can get round the side and flush him out. I'll wager the damned animal has got himself stuck down a badger's hole again.' Striding forward, he slashed at the undergrowth, forging a path through, cursing as brambles caught at his cloak.

Alfhelm also dismounted, Streona waving his hand to direct him to the left. 'I can't see him,' Alfhelm said, thrusting his way through the tangle and peering into the wild undergrowth. 'No, wait, what's that?' Something was thrusting forward, moving fast and with much noise.

The boar, head down, squealing its sudden roused anger, shot out from beneath the entwined hazel, its small piggy eyes instantly seeing the men, its snout wrinkling at their unpleasant and intrusive odour. Eadric Streona and Alfhelm reacted together, both aware of the extreme danger a boar could bring to an unwary man on foot. Those tusks, stained with what could only be the dog's blood, as effective as any dagger blade. Eadric, his reaction quick and accurate, hurled the hunting spear he held, the point burrowing deep into its target.

Alfhelm had turned to run, intending to reach his horse and his own spear. He stumbled, fell forward, sprawling with a muffled groan to the ground.

The boar, already veering away from the smell of men, scuttled across the track and disappeared, and Streona, his eyes narrowed, stepped across the dead body of Ealdorman Alfhelm. 'It is not wise to make bargains with Vikings, my Lord Ealdorman,' he said as, with a twisting wrench, he pulled his spear out from between the dead man's shoulder blades. 'Nor to trust a messenger in my pay.'

A stroke of good fortune, the dog running off like that and disturbing a boar. Æthelred will be most pleased with the innocent account of a tragic accident. Most pleased. Enough, Streona hoped, to be rewarded, as Uhtred had been, with his own ealdormanry and the hand of a royal daughter.

35

December 1006 – Cookham, Berkshire

'Cold-blooded murder,' Ufgeat, Alfhelm's eldest son, hissed, his eyes wide and blazing with rage. 'It was nothing but planned murder!'

Wulfheah, younger by one year, clutched at his brother's arm, halting it from reaching for a dagger. His face was as blanched as Ufgeat's, his shock as deep, but his discretion more controlled.

To the women's side of the Hall, Lady Godgifa was slumped to the floor, her distressed sobbing penetrating as high as the smoke-wreathed roof beams. Her daughter, Ælfgifu, knelt at her side unsure what to do, her own tears coursing down her cheeks. All the Hall was in uproar, the women clustered beside Godgifa, the men on their feet, talking, shouting, waving their arms, all as unsure as the twelve-year-old girl. Only the King, Æthelred, and the man standing before him, Eadric Streona, appeared unruffled.

'That is a grave accusation,' Æthelred said, his back straight, his hands gripping the scrolled arms of his King's chair. 'Especially since my Shire Reeve has explained his account with succinct honesty.'

Streona spread his hands, palms uppermost, held low and placating. 'I was aiming at the boar, it came from nowhere. Your father stepped in the path of my spear . . . you must believe there was nothing I could do, Ufgeat. Nothing.'

'You lie!' Ufgeat shrugged aside his fifteen-year-old brother's grip, took a step towards Streona. 'I can read the lie on your face as plain as I can read the text in God's Bible. You lie!'

Raising his hands, the palms spread, Streona turned to the King. 'My Lord, I have explained the situation, have told openly of this tragic, most horrible accident. If there is anything I can do to help the widow Godgifa and her children, then pray tell me of it and I will undertake your wish. More than this I cannot do. It was an accident. An accident.'

The men had all come forward to gather before the raised dais, their feasting half completed, forgotten, the food abandoned to congeal and grow cold. Few of them, the lords and nobles of England, summoned to this King's Christmas Court, held any regard for Streona; among them all he was the most hated and contemptible of men, but to accuse him of murder before the King, and without sustainable evidence? Even if half of them did believe the accusation to be the truth, they could not condone the challenge.

Ufgeat was having none of it. 'I do not care for petty excuses and blatant lies, Streona. Papa was an experienced huntsman; he would never have walked in the path of a thrown spear, nor would he have stepped towards a charging boar. What do you think he was? A fool?'

Dropping his hands to his sides, Streona shook his head. This had to be handled carefully, for there could never be any proof or questioning. 'No, boy, your father was an efficient and loyal ealdorman. But nevertheless he . . .'

Ufgeat had heard enough. The dagger was somehow in his hand and he was leaping forward, plunging it down towards the elder man's chest. Streona screamed, twisted away, his mouth contorted with panic and horror. The King's cnights were plunging forward, grabbing hold of the boy, knocking the dagger from his hand and dragging his arms behind his back. To draw a blade in the presence of the King was a crime to carry the punishment of death.

Streona was unharmed, the blade had been turned and had not penetrated his tunic, but the sickness rose in his throat and piddle dripped from his bladder. He was an arrogant and ambitious man, and he possessed not a mouldering grain of courage.

'Grief is exercising your tongue and your sense, boy,' Æthelred roared, coming to his feet, his finger raised in warning. 'Both I and my Lord Shire Reeve of Shrop-Shire shall accept your spoken apology for this foolishness and think no more of it.' He paused, waiting for a response. Ufgeat, his arms pinioned behind his back, scowled, said nothing.

'I am waiting,' Æthelred snapped, patience wearing thin. 'Your father's death was an accident, admit to that and I shall be lenient of your indiscretion.'

His nose bleeding, his breath coming in gasps, Ufgeat struggled against the men holding him. He held his head high, stared directly at the King. 'My papa was convinced there was a reason for Streona inviting him to hunt at Shrewsbury. Now we know what that reason was. He was lured there to meet his death!'

The gasp of disbelief at Ufgeat's signing of his own order of death filled the Hall as if uttered by one single voice.

Æthelred ambled slowly to the edge of the dais, descended the four wooden steps and stooped to pick up Ufgeat's dropped blade. He lifted it, weighing its balance, before pointing its sharpened tip at the lad's throat, nicking the skin so that a dribble of blood trickled down the white flesh. Quietly, but with his eyes narrowed and his nostrils flared, he said, 'If I were you, boy, I would retract that accusation and plead for my forgiveness and mercy.'

The Hall was silent, breath held, no movement. The wind rustled through the reed thatch of the roof, the hearth-fire crackled and spat a dance of flaring yellow sparks as a log shifted. A dog scratched vigorously at his belly for fleas, his leg drubbing like a drum roll on the wooden floor.

Ufgeat's eyes wandered across the crowd, taking in the faces of Æthelred's ealdormen and his appointed reeves, men like Uhtred, and Ulfkell of East Anglia; Goddwin of Lindsey, Leofwine of the Shires of Hereford, Gloucester and Worcester. Men whose positions of authority were as insecure to the whims and fancies of a king as Alfhelm's had been. To a man, they sneered at Streona, condemning him for his arse-whipping and bootlicking. Well, now was the chance to be rid of him, to stand up for the rights and justice of English law!

His father had made some bargain that would bring great prestige and fortune to the family, that much Ufgeat and his brother and mother knew, but what the bargain had been Alfhelm had never said. No one save the bargainer and one messenger knew of it, he had claimed, and then this invitation to hunt had come.

192

Ufgeat looked into the King's eyes and realised that his father had been mistaken. Æthelred, somehow, had known. He glanced around at the stares of the waiting, immobile men and women, saw in every one of their embarrassed, cowardly eyes that no one was going to contest Streona's story. Not one of them was concerned for the truth. He turned back to the King, spat full into his face.

As if a storm wind had suddenly thrown open the Hall doors, men surged forward, shouting, protesting, their hands going to grasp his shoulders, to beat at his head, his back, their feet kicking at him. Down in the Hall a trestle table was knocked over, the food tumbling to the floor, the dogs, snarling and snapping at each other to devour the easy pickings, competing with a flurry of squawking chickens.

Fear tightening in her chest, as if someone had bound a cord around her heart and was pulling it tight, Godgifa blundered to her feet and staggered forward, half running, half falling, pushing her way through the clamour of angry men, ignoring their raised fists, their snarls of rage. She reached the dais, fell to her knees. 'My Lord King, I beg you, my son is distraught. He knows not what he says! Please, Sir, I am now widowed, do not take my son from me also!'

Wiping the spittle from his skin, Æthelred regarded her without a trace of compassion. He despised the wife as much as he had the husband. Without her scheming, without her nagging and whining Alfhelm might have been more obedient and manageable. Fool man, allowing himself to be so manipulated! Had the whisper been true? Had Alfhelm been plotting alliance with Forkbeard? Æthelred ignored the woman, whose tears were once again coursing down her cheeks, turned to the younger brother, to Wulfheah. 'And you? Do you accept that the death was accidental?'

Godgifa shambled forward on her knees, her hands reaching out to clutch at the hem of Æthelred's robe. 'Of course it was an accident, my Lord King. My husband always was an impetuous man and a blind fool!' Turning her head to Wulfheah, her eyes and mouth taut with fear, she added, 'Say something, boy! Tell him Eadric Streona was not to blame!'

193

Wulfheah was scared. His eyes darted from his mother to his brother. What to do, what to say?

'If you speak against justice for our father, Wulfheah, then your soul shall rot in Hell. As shall his, for his murder shall be unavenged.'

Wulfheah wanted to shrivel away and hide. He was a shy lad who had always relied on his elder brother's guidance and protection. Ufgeat was strong and clever, could do anything, knew everything. He swallowed. Ufgeat was never wrong.

'Streona lies,' he said, his voice small, cracking as it rose in frightened pitch.

Emma was not attending the Christmas Day feasting, that twenty-fifth day of December, for she was busy about a woman's duty in her own chamber. Labour had progressed slowly, the contractions swelling as the afternoon had drifted through the evening and into the star-pocked silence of a frosted night. The horse trough froze, as did the stream and buckets of water. With the dawn of Saint Stephen's Day, tree branches were coated in a white gown of hoar and spiders' webs glistened as if coated with a sprinkling of jewels.

The boy was born as a weak sun reluctantly lifted itself over the eastern horizon; the birthing not as quick as had been his sister's, but not as difficult as his elder brother's. Emma bore down on the birthing stool, sweat wetting her face and body, her undershift clinging, sodden, to her breasts and swollen belly, as she struggled through that last half-hour of pain.

Away from the Hall, across the white-rimed courtyard, other screams broke the sharp-tainted air of the crisp winter stillness. Piteous sounds that begged for mercy and a release from agony.

There were those who said that the sons of Alfhelm of Deira had escaped lightly not to be put to a hideous and protracted death, that Æthelred had forgiven an indiscretion caused by grief.

Godgifa, unable to do anything to save her sons, huddled outside the closed door of Emma's chamber, praying to God that the child should come soon, and that the Queen could intervene on her behalf and plead to the King to stop the nightmare that had so suddenly become her world. But it was all too late, all too hopeless. The child, a son, was born, and the King came to take him up in his arms and name him Alfred. Godgifa was not permitted admittance to the Queen.

It was done anyway, there was nothing Emma could do to help Alfhelm's sons. Lenient, they all said, and merciful of the King, merely to take their eyes, not their lives.

36

For their sins, God had deserted the English and released a scourge upon them. The Danes had not gone away, but had over-wintered in the sheltered harbours of the Island of Wight, adequately protected from weather and attack. Then, after the Yule feasting, Swein Forkbeard, King of the Danish, had called together his men and, in an unexpected move, broke winter camp to march inland across Hamp-Shire and into Berk-Shire as far as Reading, which they looted and burnt to the ground.

Armies do not march in winter. Winter was not the season for fighting. Mud bogged down cartwheels, ponies' hooves and men's boots alike; rain soaked through clothing, wind froze skin from the bone. Snow and ice hampered progress, life and the gathering of food in the same proportion. None of that bothered Swein Forkbeard. He was from a land of winter snow and ice, born and bred to cold conditions.

Reluctant to fight? Unprepared? Certain the Danes would take heed of the banks of approaching storm clouds and return south to their ships? For whatever reason or excuse, the English were not summoned to hinder their progress. Or perhaps it was a calling of bluff? One king attempting to outwit another? If so, Æthelred was a poor player in the game. No English army would have stayed in the field, the militias would have melted away like the scattering of a light snow in the reluctant warmth of a pale winter sun. The Danes, however, were not Englishmen. Æthelred had miscalculated. More than sixty miles from the sea and their ships, Swein's army met and slaughtered the thegns of three shires; men of Berk-Shire, Hamp-Shire and Wilt-Shire who, with no help from their King, had attempted to regain their shattered dignity. And failed.

Cuckhamsley Knob, where the three borders met, was a place

revered for its ancient holy origin. For more generations than any dared remember, from long before the rule of Alfred's ancestors, Council had met there on designated occasions to discuss matters of mutual need. Everyone attended; thegn and merchant, craftsman, tradesman and farmer – opportunist beggar and thief. A chance for holiday and festival, for the making of bargains and the seeking of wives or husbands; for buying and selling, and the exchange of gossip and speculation. Æthelred, responsible for inaugurating the system of the shires in order to improve and stabilise the annual collection of taxes, had implicitly honoured the Three Boroughs by promoting their joint meetings to the status of King's Council.

Swein was clever. To occupy Cuckhamsley Knob would promote outrage and indignation throughout southern England and would shame Æthelred as effectively as any ignominious clench-fisted gesture.

No one, from the King down, expected Swein Forkbeard to reach Cuckhamsley. No Englishman expected the Danes to march so easily and swiftly so far inland. No war horns boomed along the rain-flooded, mud-sucking valleys and trackways to resist him; instead, men cowered in their farmsteadings, protecting their families and livestock as well they might, and hoped the Danish would pass on by. Those who were not in the line of danger echoing their King's continuous assurance that it was not possible for a sea wolf to march as far as Cuckhamsley.

After three days of occupied encampment, Swein countered the apathy with his own boast: no Englishman had the balls to approach a Dane seated before a hearth-fire blazing on the brow of Cuckhamsley Knob. He had made his point, shown his skill, determination and opportunist bravado, and as quickly as they had arrived the Danes broke camp and, following the great curve of the Ridge Way, returned southwards.

God and their King may have deserted them, but the thegns and lords of the Three Shires had no stomach for choking down humiliation. They petitioned Æthelred for urgent aid and, on their own initiative, called out the militia. Cuckhamsley had been an embarrassment and a violation of pride. Forkbeard would not be permitted to gloat for long.

Had the King responded, seen reality and accepted the truth of events, then the Shires might have been successful, but as it was, Eadric Streona, in Oxford, assured the King that Swein was lacking in food and spirits, that his men were ill-tempered and belligerent. Eadric Streona was adept at telling the King what the King wanted to hear, regardless of truth or accuracy.

Avebury was a prosperous village, its handful of farmsteadings interspersed with craftsmans' halls and traders' shops. The same as any other Shire village of England. A main street, a mill, a well; a smithy, an inn. What made it different were the ancient stones erected in a time beyond time. The holiness of a long forgotten religion quivered through the centuries, refusing to be entirely thrust aside by the Christian belief of Jesu's followers. There were the barrows of the dead, the humped mounds of grass sheltering the remains of those of the past, the stone, man-built henges and avenues, with their significance and importance no longer comprehended, but nonetheless held in awe. Avebury, a village too close to the insult of Cuckhamsley, where with or without the King's blessing, vengeance had to be attempted.

Near to where the sweep of the Ridge Way crossed the River Kennet, the English militia of the Three Shires waited, fought and were slaughtered. Where even Thorkell, named the Tall, Swein's second in command, was appalled by the bloodbath of destruction.

He stood at the centre of what had once been a village, amid the stench of death, his sealskin cloak pulled tight at his neck against the sting of lashing rain, his eyes narrowed, heart heavy. The poor bastards had been cut down like harvested wheat. A man, his finely woven tunic smeared with mud and blood, lay face down, his skull split in two, the brain congealed with matted strands of hair that had, once, been fair. A woman, her skirt thrown over her head, her womanhood exposed, bloody and torn after she had been repeatedly used. Before or after death, Thorkell could not tell. He hoped after, but knew hope was futile. If he were to pull down her dress, cover her modesty, what would he find? Wide, frightened eyes? A mouth open in a death-frozen scream?

Children lay dead among the carcasses of dogs and horses, the girls used, regardless of age. Some of the boys, too. Nothing had been left alive or untouched. He stared down at his boots, mud-caked, blood-splashed, the grass beneath his feet churned, stained and gouged.

To his left a collected shout went up, half-cheer, half-warning, as the chapel roof caved in to the belch of flames devouring its burning walls. If there had been anyone inside they would have been long dead, but no one would have risked taking shelter within such a small timber and wattle building, surely? Save perhaps the priest. From experience Thorkell knew these men were loath to leave the sanctity of their post, preferring to die within sight of God. He was not a devout man to his own gods; Odin and Thor did not particularly draw him to their ways, nor had they, despite his many offerings and sacrifices, ever helped him. Freya had not answered his plea when his wife had laboured those long hours to bring their dead child into the world; the goddess had not cared to save either of them. Watching the fallen roof beams burn, Thorkell wondered whether this English Christ would have intervened and delivered her safe and well through childbirth. He was a caring God, so Thorkell had heard, just and wise. He puffed his cheeks, lifted his weary face to the fall of rain that had, this last half-hour, turned resolutely cold. They must have thrown oil on the walls to get that chapel to burn so well. Where had this Christ been for these people? Stepping across the scatter of mutilated bodies, Thorkell shook his head in dismissal. No god, pagan or Christian, gave a clipped coin for human kind. Dane or English.

'The fools were barely armed. A few rusted swords, hoes and pitchforks. Does this Æthelred not possess an army worth my while to fight?'

Thorkell brought his right fist up to his left shoulder in salute as his King, Swein, approached, a grin of white teeth showing clear through the blackened grime of his face. Even if poorly equipped, the fighting had been fierce.

'Has there been much of value found among the debris?' he asked. Men had to be paid. Especially men who had marched through the discomforts of winter.

'Enough to keep them satisfied.' Swein nodded his head over his shoulder, indicating the sacked village and the used women. He grinned, his eyes bright with pleasure. 'And we still have a geld to claim. After this day, Æthelred shall not be so reluctant to pay what I demand.'

That was something to ease a whispering conscience. If the English King had paid the demand last autumn this death would not have happened. The burden, then, lay with Æthelred, not the Danes. This death and destruction was his doing.

'Then, can we go home?' Thorkell asked tentatively. He had a new wife now, different entirely from Gotha. Where she had been fair, Judith was dark; where Gotha had been tall, plump and rounded, Judith was small, thin and shapely. The child would have been born by now. Had he a son or a daughter? Was it well? Was Judith?

The King slapped his friend and commander between the shoulder blades. He could read Thorkell as if he were a fresh footprint made clear in the snow. 'When Æthelred pays for his mistake, you can go home to bed that flat-chested woman you were a fool to wed last winter. Assuming she has not abandoned you for someone nearer her size!' It had been a matter of hilarity for everyone who knew Thorkell. His great height against her small stature.

Silent for a while, Swein surveyed the dead. Regret did not prick his conscience as it had Thorkell's. 'We lost a few of our men,' he said finally, twirling the end of his beard through his fingers, a thing he often did when pleased. 'With Thor's blessing I can now secure my hold on Norway and have plenty of gold left to plan our next campaign here in England.' He gave a short bark of laughter and again thumped his bear paw of a hand on to Thorkell's shoulder. 'Another year or so, my friend, and I shall have my empire, eh? What do you think? Swein Forkbeard, King of Denmark, Norway, Sweden *and* England. Shall we try for Ireland next? Scotland too, perhaps? Or look eastwards to Kiev?'

Thorkell returned the laughter, nodding, smiling, feigning enthusiasm. He kept his eyes from the crumpled bodies of two children lying close by. A young girl clinging in desperation to her elder brother.

A spear shaft had gone clean through both of them.

37

March 1007 – Winchester

The second day of March. A pewter sky hung low, brooding over a shrouding mist that sidled along the banks of the River Itchen and clung, wraithlike, between the clusters of alder and ash. Their shapes shifted and moved as the mist slithered through the trunks and oozed across the winter-bare ground; if spring was coming, it was a long way off. No bud showed on branch or bush, no fresh young shoots poked shyly up through the brown earth. It was as if everything alive was gone for ever and the mist had come to claim its own for the Other World. Sound was distorted, noises hollow and disorientating. Was that dog near the town's wall, or did his barking come from a distant farmsteading?

Emma clutched her bear-fur mantle tighter, her shiver not from the cold alone. They were coming. She knew it as certain as she knew that it was the mist creeping forward, not the gnarled old oak it encircled. The Vikings were headed straight for Winchester and she was alone, with only her cnights and the solid-hearted folk of the town to die with her. Where were Ealdorman Ælfric and the fyrd? He was Lord of eastern Wessex, was he not? Why had he not sounded the war horns and come to her aid? Why? Because Æthelred had summoned the fyrd into Kent and along the South Ridge and the Weald, to protect him should Swein Forkbeard swing that way after slaughtering his Queen and his youngest children.

From up here on the rampart walkway the view was usually spectacular: the roll of hills northwards, the rise of high ground to the east, the meander of the river winding its way down to the sea. The woods, the fields. Cattle grazing, men ploughing or sowing or reaping, depending on the need of the season. This still, malevolent March morning, Emma was discovering that there was more to being a queen than having a favourite town or admiring a view; was meeting, first-hand, the difficult side of responsibility. Within one or two hours, no more than that, Winchester might cease to exist. The gates and walls could be torn down, the children, nuns, the women, Queen included, left dead and raped in the streets, left to feed the crows. The mist, feeling its way ever closer, would breach the ruined gaps and come slinking inside, like a silent barn owl, ready to swallow up the wreckage.

Except, Emma had no fear of abuse by a man. She had already suffered it and, standing here, up on this walkway, waiting for the Danes, she suddenly discovered the power of her strength.

Below, the women were huddled in their houses, shielding their children, fearful for the men gathered beneath the walls, tense, anxious and waiting. Let Ælfric be a coward, let Æthelred skulk behind the walls at Thorney! Winchester was *her* town, these were *her* men, who would fight to their last breath to defend her and the babes in their cot within the royal palace. Let the Danes come! Let them destroy and kill; at least she would go to God knowing she had not failed her people in courage and determination. Unlike her wretched husband.

She turned, walked with care to the edge of the rampart and looked down at the anxious grey faces. 'Listen to me!' she called, raising her arms. 'I am Emma Ælfgifu, your Queen, and I am not frightened of this poxed, bearded rabble which threatens us! We may not have a comfortable number of fighting men to defend us, but we do have, among us, the best bowmen in all England, or so your Reeve, Godric Osgodsson, tells me. He is an honest and a good man. I have no reason to doubt him!'

Whether it was a true statement or not she did not care. The cheer they rewarded her with counted for more worth than accuracy.

The waiting. Silence, so loud when you listened for it.

Someone a few yards away dropped his spear, the sound clattering and echoing, loud and hostile, making them all jump as if stung. A nervous ripple of laughter, a few embarrassed coughs. They were all on edge, waiting. Waiting for their end.

'Will we see or hear them first?' Emma asked Godric, standing beside her. A reliable man, experienced and of practical sense.

'In this mist it is hard to tell, Madam. If they are marching in open formation we shall probably hear their approach first, or they may choose to come close with stealth, in which case we shall not know they are here until Swein Forkbeard launches his attack.' He glanced over his shoulder at the preparations being completed below. Buckets of water and sand made ready to douse fire arrows, hides being soaked with water for the same purpose. Fire was always the fear for timber walls and reed-thatched roofs; only the Minsters, Old and New, the nunnery church and the town's arched gateways were of stone. The gates themselves, two inches thick, studded with iron nails and bolts, were of seasoned oak.

'Do you think it true that they have fire-throwing engines, battering rams and siege towers with them?'

'You are remarkably acquainted with the weapons of war, Lady,' Godric said, replying with honesty, 'For answer, I cannot say. I doubt they would have dragged such stuff up to Reading and the Ridge Way, but there are plenty of trees a'tween there and here, and the Danes are no less skilled with woodcraft and the building of necessities than are we.'

It was better to talk, it took the edge off the waiting. Emma said, 'My father and brother often discussed tactics; I found it interesting to listen.' What would Richard make of laying siege to a town like Winchester, she wondered as she gazed into the crawl of eerie whiteness. Under Richard's command, Winchester would fall within hours. Was this Swein of Denmark as capable as her brother?

'It is possible', she continued without conviction, 'that the Danes have met with resistance further up the road.' It was a pathetic thing to say and Godric duly ignored it.

'There, Sir! Beyond the trees – look!' A young lad, no more than fourteen summers of age, pointed to a distant copse of birch. His helmet was too big for him, his chain-linked mail too loose – his father's armour, Emma wondered, or an uncle's? All the men, and boys, of the town had turned out to defend their own, dressed for war as well they could. Most had nothing except leather over-tunics or aprons. Many did not carry weapons beyond the everyday tools of pitchfork and chopping axe. Few outside those who served within the fyrd possessed the mighty death-bringer axes. Men to Emma's right lifted their heads and, on Godric Osgodsson's command, raised their bows, notched an arrow.

'Hold hard, lads,' Godric growled, raising his arm, palm outspread. 'We do not want to be killing them all too soon.'

One of the men grinned, lowered his bow. 'We wait till we see the whites of their eyes, eh, Sir?'

'Na, mate,' his companion chided, 'the coloured part of their eyes – more like the centre mark on our practice targets!'

'Aye, you're right there – an' the three of us can hit that every shot!'

A general flurry of laughter, a shifting of position as everyone straightened, straining their eyes to look where the boy had pointed.

The mist was moving, wavering, rippling outwards like the wash of a boat. No noise, no sound, just the mist rolling, being pushed aside. Then it came, a steady thrum of rhythm, the stamp of feet, the creak of leather, the jingle of metal. From out of the trees that covered the hill called Saint Giles, that rose up through the mist, men appeared, men carrying banners that lay limp, unwavering in the damp and heavy air. It did not matter, no one waiting on those Winchester ramparts needed to see the banners unfurled to know one of them was the black raven of Denmark and the golden hammer of Thor.

Many of them rode ponies, their winter coats thick, soaked with sweat, muddied and tired. Ponies stolen from farmsteadings, inns and fields. Several of them were lame, many winded and galled by saddle sores.

What had Emma expected of Swein's army? Great giants? Godlike warriors? Proud men brandishing their weapons, swaggering their arrogance. The Danes, emerging from the track that ran under the steep wooded slope of the hill, rode two abreast, those without a mount trudging in between, in twos and threes, some holding on to a pony's mane or tail. They were indeed tall men, they wore armour and carried shield, sword and axe, but they were of no more great stature than the men of Normandy. They looked no stronger than some of these waiting, expectant and ready, up here along the top of Winchester's walls.

As they marched nearer, following the river, taking the track called Chesil Street that ran along the far bank, she saw more detail, the smaller things. Some were wounded, some with arms in slings or with bloodied tunics or leaning on rough-made crutches. Many had grimed faces and damaged mail, cracked shields and broken spears. This was no rampaging army, no vast unstoppable force . . . these were tired men returning the quickest way possible to their ships. God in Heaven, and Æthelred was letting them pass unmolested? If the fyrd had been called together, had been waiting for them here on this Winchester road . . .

Drawing level with the walls, a man riding a tired chestnut pony drew rein, his hand going up to halt the column. Impetuous, his finger twitching, one of the men close to Emma loosened an arrow. It sailed outwards, lonely in its solitary flight, arched down and thrummed, harmless, into the cold, silver-grey of the river.

'You ought to withdraw, my Lady,' Godric whispered, his hand protective on Emma's elbow, urging her to step back.

'If our arrows cannot reach them, then they cannot reach me,' she answered, practical, calm.

The man on the chestnut was reaching up to his head, removing his war cap, his eyes studying the walls and the men arrayed along the top. He had no need to identify himself; from his stance, his very presence and quality of armour, Emma knew him to be Swein Forkbeard. Did he realise who she was? That he had the Queen standing before him?

'Fetch my banner up here, quickly,' Emma ordered suddenly. 'I would have him know that a queen of England is not afeared to outface him.'

A boy fetched it, running down the steps, jumping the last three. He hurtled through the archway into the inner courtyard of the King's palace, snatched up the banner and raced back to the wall, almost tripping as the material unravelled and caught between his legs.

'You have no need to fear us, this time, people of Winchester!'

Swein's voice boomed across the river, hitting against the town with all the might of a mangonel. 'We return to our ships with the geld your King has obligingly paid. You may go back to your hearth-fires, but I would advise you to keep a sharp edge on your blades, for I will not be gone long from Engla Lond.'

The boy reached Emma's side and she ordered the banner unfurled, a man grabbing for the linen, spreading wide the embroidered emblem of a crowned, rampant lioness.

'I do not fear you, Swein Forkbeard. The blood that runs through my veins is more noble than yours.'

'My Lady Queen,' Forkbeard answered with a laugh and a slight bow, 'I was not aware you were resident. Had I known, I might have decided to take you with me back to Denmark, but as it is I must pass on, for the tide awaits.'

'Step foot inside my city, Forkbeard, and you will be going nowhere except to Valhalla.'

'An honourable place, Madam, but as I have no wish to go there quite yet, I bid you fare well.' He laughed again, saluted with a careless gesture and returned his war cap to his head. Kicking his pony forward, he spoke to the person riding beside him who turned his face to stare up at Emma. She felt his eyes bore into her. Not a man, a boy, with fair hair spilling beneath his cap and no hint of hair to his upper lip or chin.

Emma sneered her astonishment. 'Do the *í-víking* fight with boys, now, then? Do they not have grown men to do their butchering?'

The boy rode proud, his fingers curled around the double-handed axe haft that was slung, almost lazily, across his shoulder. He returned her gaze, intent, as if he had heard her speak.

Godric Osgodsson shrugged; he could only guess. 'I have heard rumour that Forkbeard brought his younger son with him. That must be Cnut. He would be what age?' Godric turned to look at some of the faces clustered round, seeking help.

'Almost twelve, my Lord. Swein's eldest is fifteen, Cnut would be eleven or twelve.'

'And he lets the boy fight?' Emma asked, incredulous.

'No, Lady, I doubt it.' Godric shook his head. 'He would be with the baggage most part, I would warrant, but how else does a king train a prince for warfare? Not by leaving him at home to kick his heels and make mischief.' He did not add that there were plenty of eleven-year-old boys – aye and younger – swelling the men ranked along the top of these walls.

With the last of the Danish column disappearing southwards into the mist and the direction of their moored ships at Southampton, Emma forgot the boy. She lifted her skirts and whisked away down the steps, her face set in annoyed fury.

As humiliations went, Swein of Denmark had superseded all other degradations. He had deprived Æthelred of wealth and honour, and was walking away with a cocksure swagger. So, the King had paid the demand of six and thirty thousand pounds of silver? Had allowed the Danish army to march, virtually unchallenged, through more than sixty miles of English land and had permitted them to flaunt their arrogance before his Queen? How dare he! The Danish army had been nothing more than a hotchpotch of tired, ragged men who wanted to go home. Who in all Hell's name had advised Æthelred to pay the geld and remain hidden in London?

Oh, she knew the answer to that! Eadric Streona, new-made Ealdorman of all Mercia and recent married husband to a king's daughter. God in His heaven, if she knew how to fight, she would dress herself in armour and lead her own army against that damned, poxed Danish King and his son. Knew for a certainty that Æthelred would not.

38

'They say a man was cured of leprosy. Just by kneeling before his tomb!'

'And a woman, unable to bear children for the entirety of her ten-year marriage, became with child a month after prostrating herself there.'

Shaftesbury Abbey, Emma thought to herself, turning slightly more towards the lamplight, her back to the chattering women, *has much to answer for.*

She was not entirely convinced that the bones of a dead man, who had been no more mortal than any of them while alive, could be responsible for the curing of all ills. And yet . . . she fashioned three more stitches into the chair cover that she was embroidering . . . and yet there had been these miracles at Shaftesbury, almost from the very day that Æthelred had ordered his half-brother's remains to be transposed there seven years past. The tedium was that they went through this selfsame routine every year at the approach to the eighteenth day of March; Æthelred dreaded the anniversary of his brother's murder and Emma, too, was beginning to feel apprehensive.

Had Edward been a saint in life, a holy man or, at the very least, liked if not loved, then she could understand these beliefs that were growing up around the tomb; but he had been a boy, and a foolhardy one at that. What did God gain from permitting him this accession to martyrdom and allowing his soul to perform such perfect acts?

'A blind man was able to see, his sight was restored while he was there, kneeling in prayer.'

'I have heard that a woman who was desperate for a son to be born to her took her newborn daughter and left her on the tomb steps. In the morning she had changed into a boy!'

'Mayhap you ought to take yourself along to Shaftesbury, Judith,' Emma said, folding away her needlework, 'and pray for Edward the Martyr to grant you an ounce of common sense.'

The women laughed, Emma, after a moment's uncertain hesitation, joining in. It was not their fault that she was in this wretched, melancholy mood. Not their fault that she dreaded her husband's bouts of unyielding temper.

The door opened, the children's nurse creeping in as if she were about to enter a dragon's den. She was a conscientious girl, Wymarc, but short on discipline with the children, Emma thought, with young Edward in particular. On the face side of the coin, at least the boy did not whine and grizzle as much as he had used to.

'If you please, Madam.' Wymarc bobbed a reverence. 'The children are settled into bed, ready for you to bid them a good night.'

Emma managed to make her smile appear genuine. 'Thank you, girl, I shall be there presently.'

Leofgifu had found Wymarc in the Winchester slave market. A red-haired, grime-faced Breton child of five and ten years of age, with eyes as large as broth bowls and the sweet voice of a summer lark. Leofgifu was an excellent judge of character and after a few pertinent questions had purchased the girl. She had come from a large family of a dozen children, she being the next eldest, but when her father had died there had been no way to pay the rent for their farm and the landlord had thrown them out. Her mother had taken the younger children to relations in the south of Brittany, for the four eldest, slavery or starvation had been the only options. Wymarc's fortune had come when the slave master brought her to Winchester on the day Leofgifu was searching for someone to help care for the royal children.

'Little Goda is teething, I believe, Ma'am,' Wymarc added shyly, uncertain whether to speak. 'She is fretful and her cheeks are sorely red-spotted.'

'It is the great pity that children are not born with teeth,' Emma answered, rising from her seat. She was always reluctant to tend this pointless nightly ritual, but bidding children goodnight appeared to be an expected mother's duty. 'A full set of teeth would save us all many sleepless nights.' She flashed Wymarc a smile of encouragement, was rewarded with an amused chuckle.

'Aye, my Lady, but t'would be painful for the suckling nurse!'

The children's quarters were tucked to the side of the palace complex, in a separate lean-to building behind the royal apartments. Woodstock was a rambling, scattered arrangement of timber buildings with a central King's Hall. It was as if each successive generation of kings had added his own contribution of servants' quarters, stabling or kennels, without caring to remove any thing that already existed. Æthelred preferred Woodstock to all his estates; Emma loathed it, but then he cherished his hunting and she did not. Another nuisance, as with his Thorney Island palace, Woodstock could not boast of cobbling or paving to courtyard and pathway: the place was awash with mud. No bother to the men, who cared nothing for the state of boots and hose, but for women with their finely made ankle-length gowns and trailing sleeves, mud was a dreadful nuisance.

Gathering her over-gown of saffron wool and the under-tunic of pale-blue linen almost to her knees, Emma trod carefully across the yard. The wooden planking laid as walkways helped somewhat when rain persisted in earnest, but then the wood was often slippery and dangerous. Emma was never certain whether she preferred the task of ploughing through a quagmire or risking a broken neck.

Edward was snuggled beneath heavy bed furs of wolf and bearskin in a box bed shared with several other offspring of his father's highest cnights and noblemen. The younger two, Alfred and Goda, not yet of a status to leave their cots. From tomorrow when the ealdormen and thegns arrived, the children's chamber would be crowded with youngsters, an exciting time for them all, an opportunity to make friends and discover new games and mischiefs. Emma was glad their care went to nurses and slaves, that she would have little to do with them. Children's play held no interest for her, perhaps because her own childhood amusements had been restricted to the point of non-existence. She remembered a cloth doll and a wooden top. If there had been other toys she could not recall them.

Edward had no liking for change and unfamiliar faces. He lay, curled and hunched on the edge of the hay-filled mattress, afraid of the prospect of the next few weeks. His face was puckered and sullen, tears brimming from his eyes.

Emma stifled impatience as she brushed her lips against his cheek. 'You will have ample opportunity to enjoy yourself, Edward,' she said, sitting on the bed and stroking damp hair from his pale forehead. 'The calling of Council is always holiday for you boys, is it not?'

'They pull my hair and make fun of me.' Edward mumbled. 'I hate them.'

'But as my eldest, you are the ætheling, the next king. It is for you to command them not to.' Emma sighed. He was three years old. How did she instil courage and confidence into one so young? But if he was to be king after Æthelred he would have to learn, and learn quickly, how to stand up for himself and earn respect from his peers. She glanced at Wymarc who stood nearby.

'I will take care that there is no nonsense, my Lady.'

'Thank you, Wymarc, I know you have my children's interests always close to heart.'

Alfred, when she crossed to his cot, was already sleeping, his thumb firm in his mouth, his eyes closed, with the long fair lashes swept down to touch his cheeks. Emma felt an unexpected shudder ripple through her body as a memory of the daughter of Ealdorman Alfhelm swam into her vision. Ælfgifu, a child, forced to mature and accept the hideous side of life within a few short heartbeats. Would Emma ever forget that face of vengeance? Ælfgifu had burst in upon Emma, her fingernails going to claw at the face of her newborn son – thank God for the waiting women who fell upon the girl, hauling at her as they shrieked for the guard to come.

'Why do my brothers endure the agony of mutilation and blindness?' she had screamed as they dragged her away. 'Why should your sons not suffer as they do? They will, one day! I shall see to it that they will!'

It was an empty curse, thrown through grief and fear, but Emma had ordered the girl and her family removed from Court, not that any of them cared to stay. Had she been able, would Emma have done anything to stop her husband's ordered punishment of those boys? It was the way of things, their father had betrayed his King, the sons had defended his death and paid the price of kinship. Although it had been a high price, that blinding.

Emma slid the memory aside, touched the crown of Alfred's soft, golden hair. Why was she fond of this youngest son and not the eldest? Why did she so dislike Edward? They looked similar, the same coloured, slight-curled hair, the same blue eyes, slender fingers and upturned nose. Perhaps because Alfred was the more courageous and daring of the two, despite his younger age? He had toddled earlier than Edward, not minding the bumped knees and bruises when he fell. Alfred rarely cried or snivelled; he ate all put before him without fussing or pulling faces. Alfred, at two, already made it clear that he wanted to ride a pony and play among the rougher hounds. Edward picked at his food and shrank away from animals, fearing their size and noise.

As Wymarc had reported, Goda was red-faced and restless, her fist stuffed against her dribbling lips, her mouth sore and uncomfortable. 'Have you rubbed essence of cloves on her gums?' Emma queried. Wymarc confirmed that she had. 'Then there is no more we can do for her.'

It sounded hard and uncaring, but Emma was Queen; she did not have the opportunity, like Wymarc, to lift the fretful child and hug her and hold her close. She dare not, for if she were to begin to love the girl, her heart would all too soon be broken. Emma realised that now, now she had a daughter of her own, realised why her mother had been so cold and distant. Girl children were sent away as wives before they had a chance to grow into women; mothers dared not grow to love their daughters for the grief of having, so soon, to part.

Before the urge to lift her up, hold her, became overpowering, Emma turned away and left the stuffy chamber that smelt of breast milk and soiled linen. With her hand paused on the latch of her own chamber, a gruff voice from across the courtyard hailed her. She waited for Eadric Streona to come up to her, bow, although his obediences were never over-pronounced.

'Lady, I considered it best to summon you.'

'What is so wrong, Sir, that you must accost me in privacy like this?' Emma did so detest this grovelling weasel. She frowned, realised Streona, usually so self-assured, was floundering out of his depth, like a man who could not swim. He had the good grace to lower his head against the red flush of embarrassment that touched his cheeks. How it must be denting his pride to come to Emma for assistance!

'It is the King, Madam. He is in a bad way.'

The derisive laugh burst out of her mouth. 'His drunkenness is not my concern, Ealdorman. I suggest you seek his body servant or physician – or one of the slaves to clean the mess he has vomited over everything.'

'No, you misinterpret me. He is ill and I do not feel it wise to allow too many tongue tattlers to hear of it.'

Ill from too much drink, too much eaten? Let him suffer! Emma sighed. She was Æthelred's wife, duty had its expected rules. Reluctant, she nodded. 'I will come.'

Æthelred lay on his bed, hunched and crumpled, much as Edward had been, his arms over his head, knees drawn up. His skin, when Emma laid her hand on his forehead, felt hot, burning to the touch, yet he was shivering, his teeth chattering.

'How long has he been like this?' she asked, drawing another bed fur to cover him.

'These last two hours,' Streona admitted, aware he ought to have summoned aid before now. 'We returned early from hunting, the King was in a morose mood – the day was a disappointment, a poor scent.' He shrugged philosophically. 'He has been suffering a strange malaise these past days, Lady, but riding through the gates he heard this latest spread of gossip concerning his dead brother's healing powers.' The new Ealdorman of all Mercia was baffled; there was not this guilt of conscience over other men killed by what amounted to nothing less than murder – whatever the convenient excuse publicly given. Æthelred had barely turned a hair at Alfhelm's disposal, nor had his half-brother's death been of his doing. That was his mother's concern and she had either paid her penance or was burning in Hell for it.

'He dismounted without a word,' Streona continued, 'shut himself in here and gave orders not to be disturbed. His steward here,' he indicated a worried-looking Gilbertson, 'entered to help him ready himself for supper, found him crouched on the floor, gibbering nonsense. Sensibly, he ran straight to fetch me.'

Not me, Emma thought. *Does that not show how worthy I am to my husband?*

Bound to happen, of course. Every year, when the anniversary of murder came around, all the rumours, all the speculation, reappeared like muck floating to the surface of a pond. Had her own ladies not been full of Edward the Martyr's latest miraculous wonders?

'Fetch hot water and clean garments,' Emma instructed. 'I will send for herbs to calm him.' As reluctant as she was to agree with Streona, it would do Æthelred great harm for word of this to leak out and greater harm were he not to appear in Hall this night. A king who wished to keep his crown could never publicly display a weakness, and here was Æthelred whimpering, his thumb stuffed in his mouth.

Damn fool, she thought as she washed the sweat from his face and body, dressed him in clean garments. This was typical of Æthelred; run from the truth, hide in a jug of ale. Why could she not have a husband who faced his enemy with courage? One who feared nothing, not his failures or fears, from this world or the next?

Æthelred clung to her, as if he were a child, as Edward would. Tears streaked his face, his hands trembled. 'I saw them do it,' he slurred. 'I watched as he dismounted his horse and walked forward to greet me and my mother. They surrounded him and killed him.' He looked at his hands, began rubbing them, wiping at something there that only he could see. 'So much blood! It ran down the cobbles, puddling in the cracks. Bright red blood. So much of it.' He grabbed for Emma's arm, his fingernails digging through the linen of her sleeve, burning into the flesh beneath. He stared at her, eyes wide, frightened. 'Were you there? Did you see? Did you hear?' He let Emma go, his hands moving to cover his face, the sobs shaking his body. 'He took so long to die, it took so much to kill him!'

Lifting the cup of valerian mixed with wine, Emma encouraged

Æthelred to drink while murmuring soothing, childish words that she would normally use for little Goda. What a weakling, useless man this King of England was!

Later, wearing her Queen's crown and her best, finest gown, Emma walked into the King's Hall, her hand held high, clasped tight to her husband's. His face was ashen, his lips quivered, but the strength in her fingers flowed into his and her warning echoed in his ears.

'If you show them that you are afraid of a ghost, Æthelred, it shall be your end. There are only a few nobles gathered here as yet, but from the morrow all your Council will be in attendance. Do you think these few will avert their eyes and seal their lips? With the priests preaching that the end of all life is close and Swein Forkbeard God knows how much closer, how long will their loyalty remain intact if they see you dribbling like a milksop child because you cannot face the fact of your brother's death?'

She was angry, the anger spilling over into a boldness that had only partially raised its head before. She found it a welcome companion. When Swein Forkbeard had paraded his strength past the walls of Winchester, she had realised the prospect of losing all she had and realised, too, that she would do anything, anything at all, to ensure she kept it. That realisation had been growing stronger, inside her, ever since.

If Æthelred crumpled, she would fall with him. This was a loveless marriage, she had two sons, one of whom she detested, and a daughter she dare not show affection to. Her only assets were her crown and her pride. She was not prepared to relinquish either because Æthelred was too pathetic to lay a ghost to rest. As Queen, she could, now, understand why his mother had acted as she had. Why it had been imperative to have Edward killed, for the wearing, and the keeping, of a crown carried a heavy price and an even heavier burden.

They sat at the head of the Hall, the King's table resplendent with gold plate, silver and pewter, set on a white fine linen tablecloth. Emma dipped her hands in the offered wash bowl, dried them on a linen towel.

216

'Did you not say something of persuading your archbishops that your beloved brother ought to be canonised?' she said to Æthelred, knowing well that he had said no such thing. 'I recall you musing on whether the eighteenth day of March be declared, in future, as his feast day?' There were subtle ways of setting ideas into an anxious mind. 'It is fitting that you should mourn his passing, it shows your compassion, and as fitting that you should bring about his raising to eternal holy glory.'

Æthelred's head was pounding, his throat felt dry and his stomach was churning. For three consecutive nights, vivid and lurid dreams of daggers and gurgling death had haunted him. In all three, a youth's face, pleading for help as he lay dying. But if the truth were told, Æthelred had not objected to taking up the crown from that pool of blood, to putting it, straightway, on his head. Did not miss his brother, who had been a pompous brat in life. Have him canonised? How Edward would have gloated at the idea! A higher rank than king, a saint. But if Edward was to become a saint, would he forgive the losing of an earthly crown? Would he, perhaps, settle to rest in peace and leave his living brother alone?

It was a good idea. Æthelred was glad he had thought of it.

39

Enham, to the north of Andover in Hampshire, had been chosen especially for this White Sunday calling of the Witenagemot, the King's Council. Attending, in addition to the King, his Queen and his sons, were both Archbishops, four and ten bishops, six and ten abbots, six ealdormen and four and forty thegns who held various administrative offices. By Council standards an impressive group, only duplicated at Easter and occasionally Christmas. Spiritually and politically, England was in a state of upheaval. God, in despair, had turned His back on them all.

The assembly hoped, though doubted, that Æthelred would make some sensible decisions at this Council. The resentment that Eadric Streona had been awarded all he desired, while more worthy men were passed by, was gaining ground, although the shrugs and whispers were not loudly voiced. Æthelred had revived the old Ealdormanry of all Mercia solely for Streona's benefit, yet it was not Mercia that desperately required the solidity of a trusted and experienced commander. Without an overlord, East Anglia could be as vulnerable to disaster as a flat field was to an opened sluice gate.

While these worries were important, foremost in all minds was the fear of the wrath of God. This Council was for the special purpose of promoting a renewal of Christianity throughout the land. The Antichrist had been released into the world of men and doom was fast approaching. For England, that ending would be coming in the form of the *í-víking* warships and in the battleaxes of death. General belief was that unless God could be appeased and Æthelred could bring sanity into his rule, all would very soon be lost.

'We congratulate you, my Lord King,' said Eadric Streona, being the next to stand and speak, 'for agreeing to abolish that Danelaw custom practised in the northern lands of this, our realm. It was right to do away with a law by which a charge of murder could be brought against an innocent and not be challenged by trial of ordeal once any one person had sworn oath on behalf of the victim against the accused. It is to be hoped that further disreputable Danish iniquities shall also, soon, be abolished?'

Murmurs of agreement, resentfully offered as it was the unpopular Streona who had pre-empted the address. Uhtred, now made Ealdorman of Northumbria, Bernicia and Deira combined, stood abruptly, not to protest, as he too agreed that it had been a particularly vile law which had been in sore need of reform, but at Eadric Streona's pretentious attitude.

'I, too, add my appreciation of the King's wisdom, but I question what right my Lord the Ealdorman of Mercia has to presume that his Mid Land customs and traditions are necessarily proper over our northern ways? I remind Council that we are not all heathen savages north of the Humber.' Pointedly, he moved his eyes to locate Archbishop Wulfstan, who although tutored for a life within the Church from an early age at the desolate Fenland abbey of Ely, was a man dedicated to his diocese of York.

Wulfstan, perceiving a hostile retort from Streona, smiled amicably back at Uhtred and answered with humour, a suitable tactic to diffuse argument. 'I am sorry to say that there are some here, my Lord of Northumbria, who believe everyone outside his own town or village to be of a heathen nature!' He paused for the laughter to rumble and die down, then continued on to more pressing matters.

'My Lords,' he half bowed towards Emma, 'my Queen, we are here for the purpose of our collective welfare. This meeting place of Enham has been selected as a sanctuary for peace and a prospect of hope. Does its name not mean the "Place of Lambs"? Beyond this building,' dramatically, he swept his arm towards the closed doors, 'there are green fields where ewes are giving birth to their offspring. Are we not, during this Council, to adopt the lamb of the field and the Lamb of God as our symbol of hope and salvation?'

Æthelred, the only man present entitled to remain seated while speaking, made reply. 'I thank you for your compliments, Ealdorman Eadric, and to you all. As your King it is not always a simple thing to balance the wishes of one man against those of another. I humbly submit, however, that I do my best to attempt to please, but my priority has always been to do what is right above fawning to the individual.' He was rewarded by polite applause, knowing full well that his Council believed his sincerity while ridiculing his accuracy. He clapped his hands twice, cleared his throat. 'We must tend our business, there is much to discuss this Whit Sunday.'

Seizing his opportunity, Thegn Wulfnoth rose, scraping his stool across the tiled floor. 'My King, may I bring the Dane Tori before you? I believe it would be provident, at this stage, to finalise your financial arrangements with this man.'

Æthelred agreed by beckoning forward a stout-bellied Danishman, standing at the rear of the meeting hall. 'You have indicated through my thegn that you wish to purchase the estates of Beckley and Horton in Oxford-Shire? Tell me, why should I sell valuable land to an incomer Dane?'

Tori bowed, smiled. 'Because I am a merchantman who is reaching old age and I would prefer to enjoy retirement. My three sons now run my business and I wish to give up shipboard life and become a settled landowner.'

'Is there not land in Denmark for you?' Eadric Streona interrupted with a conspicuous sneer.

'Plenty, Sir, but a devout Christian is not always made welcome among the pagan farmsteads of my homeland.' The Dane spread his hands, showing the nodules and swellings of advanced joint ache. 'Many with my profound religious belief have found new homes in the far southern lands where the warmer days ease the pain of our old bones but I have no wish to travel so far. *Engla Lond* will be sufficient for me, and my gold, my Lord King, will be enough for you to equip and crew several ships.'

'We require more than gold!'

Tori ignored Streona's accusing tone and stubbornly continued talking to Æthelred. 'I offer, also, my knowledge of Thorkell the

Tall. Would the intended plans of Swein Forkbeard's second in command not be of use to you?'

Several men of the Council shuffled in their seats, notable among them Ulfkell of East Anglia. 'We already have word of him,' he said, slowly rising to his feet, aware that as a thegn he was not always accredited with the same respect he would be offered were he to be made Ealdorman, even with the reward of a king's daughter as wife. An awareness that galled like ill-fitting harness. 'It is said that Thorkell has disagreed with his King. That he and Forkbeard have fallen out of friendship?'

Tori laughed, his head back, his painful hands resting on his broad hips. 'If that is what you believe then you English are indeed poorly informed! Thorkell is a courageous and capable man. I have heard of none better than he on the battlefield, not even Swein himself, who values his commander as if he were a son.'

Bouncing to his feet, Eadric Streona again interrupted. 'Heard? Heard of none better? Have you not seen for yourself?'

The Dane was not a man easily riled to anger, but with considerable restraint, he answered the insult. 'I am a merchantman, my talent is for creating a profit from trade. I am not as adept with an axe as I am with a tally stick, and I have not spent my years amassing my wealth in order to toss it away on a battlefield. I leave the fighting to those who are good at it, and do my part by furnishing braver men than I with armour, weapons and ships.'

Several listeners grinned, appreciating a man who could get the better of Streona.

'However, King Swein is a man who has much employment to keep him occupied. He rules more than Denmark alone, is finding that multiple rule is no easy task.'

Æthelred leant forward, his chin cupped in his palm, his elbow propped on his knee, a mild grin lifting his lips. 'There is a saying that an ambitious man may bite off more meat than his teeth can chew. If Swein is finding it difficult to hold on to his conquests, I cannot say that I feel pity for his predicament.'

Tori smiled wryly. 'It is not for me to talk of his temporary dilemma, but when a king has a man like Thorkell to trust implicitly, then that king is a man to be envied. Knowing his back is securely protected, a man, whether he be thegn, *jarl*, or king, is able to look boldly in more than one direction at a time.'

Thegn Wulfnoth spoke up: 'My Lord King, you have ordered ships to be built of a number never before met under any king of England. We are gathered here to discuss ways of defeating the scourge of the Danes when next they come. It will not be this year, perhaps not the next, but when they do come, it shall be Thorkell who leads them, not Swein, and he will be more formidable than any other Dane who has tried to take England for his own.'

Superciliously, Eadric spat at his feet. 'I am not afraid, let him come! Let Thorkell meet with our ships and our armies; let him see what *real* fighting is!'

Several men cheered, but Tori interrupted, derisive. 'You do not fear Thorkell the Tall? Then you are all fools. Thorkell has a point of honour to prove, not to you but to Forkbeard. If he is to be entrusted with England's conquest, then he must show that he is capable of doing it. He will either succeed or die.'

Once again Streona shrugged an answer. 'Then he shall die.' He expected concurrence and agreement, received only silence, even from Æthelred.

'You may purchase the land you require, Tori.' With a grim smile, the King added, 'Although I suspect you would not desire Thorkell to come within an arrow distance of it. I doubt he is a man who takes kindly to deserters.'

Tori bowed, ignored the jibe, for it was justified. 'I dislike the man, Sir, as much as he dislikes me. I have no wish to be near him whether in Denmark or England.' He turned, left the Hall, pleased. All, save Eadric Streona, were content with the bargain.

As inclined to do when a lull in proceedings occurred, the men began to talk among themselves, discussing opinion, proffering advice, the babble of voices swelling louder. Archbishop Wulfstan stood, made no sound or movement, merely waited for silence to gradually resettle. Financing the King's needs was all well and good, but without God's provenance there was no advantage to long-term planning.

'Unless we repent our sins, we face a peril more mighty than Thorkell the Tall. I, in conjunction with my lord Archbishop Alfheah of Canterbury, wish to establish a new, Christian law code.'

Alfheah inclined his head, acknowledging Wulfstan's courtesy, appreciating the inclusion. In point of fact, the notion was entirely the Archbishop of York's; he was more experienced in the practicalities of politics, Alfheah being more spiritually adept. With deliberation, Wulfstan had involved himself with legal and secular law; he enjoyed the making and interpretation of rules, relishing his present challenge of introducing a moral reformation of practice for the laity, his ideas being widely respected and embraced. Though not loud or patronising, he was forceful and inspiring, his writing of an individual prose style, one that was potent and direct. Without pause or question, Wulfstan believed implicitly in a theocratic monarchy, with king, Church and people, whether thegn or peasant, fused into one, united and unchallenged Christian policy.

He was an imposing figure. At four and thirty years his hair had already turned white, his face become craggy and lined – features of acquired wisdom, not of age or weariness. If anyone could divert the wrath of God and bring salvation to His people, then the Archbishop of York, a statesman, a churchman and a profound advocate of God's Holy Word, was the man to do it.

'We are about to face the possibility of a hideous death and wanton destruction by the hand of God through the Viking sea pirate. It may be that not one of us will survive this curse that God is to send to punish us for the sins and transgressions that we, miserable men, have committed against Him.' For effect, Wulfstan pointed his slender finger at every man present, his eyes making individual contact with each one of them as his gaze moved slowly from man to man. 'We shall do public penance for our wrong-doings. We shall discard our apathy and commit ourselves to strict attendance to church, making our way there barefoot in

223

procession. From here forward, the psalms and prayers shall constantly be on our lips and in our minds. We shall honour God, and show Him that we regret and repent.'

The King's youngest sons had been seated in a corner to the side of the royal dais. Emma had not thought it prudent to bring them into Council, but Æthelred had been adamant. At her protest, Æthelred had retorted, 'I will have my younger sons seen as visibly as my elder. How else will they learn the ways of State?'

Not by sitting growing restless and bored in a Council chamber at two and three years of age, Emma had argued, but Æthelred would never listen to her practicality – God's Judgement, she was only included at Council because propriety demanded it. She certainly was not there for her intellect or opinion. Both of which few men, including her husband, had failed to realise she possessed in great amount.

Two-year-old Alfred, recently suckled and content with a belly full of milk, was drowsing in his nurse's arms, but Wymarc was finding it difficult to keep Edward distracted and busy. He had discovered his voice, independence and an ability to disrupt the affairs of adults by using an irritating, high-pitched tone, that could whine and mither with a monotony that grated on ear and nerve. He did not want to amuse himself quietly with his wooden animals. Most definitely did not want to sit still and listen to the drone of men talking about things he had no comprehension of. All he wanted to do was be outside in the sunshine with the lambs. Wymarc, attempting to entertain him by bouncing him on her knees, made a grab for his arm as he wriggled from her hold and ran, astonishingly fast, away from her reach. His boots thundering on the chequered red and green tiles, he dashed for the door, shrieking his laughter at the excitement of breaking loose, his shrill voice shouting, 'I want to see the lambs! I want to play with the lambs!'

Red-faced, Wymarc hurried after him, the King, annoyed, booming at Emma, 'For God's sake, woman, rid us of that wretched brat! Can you not control your children?'

Furious with both Edward and Æthelred, Emma stood, retorting heatedly, 'They are your children as much as mine. Do you not frequently take delight in reminding me that sons are the assets of their fathers, not of their mothers?' She walked with upright dignity from the Hall, steadfastly ignoring the gloating expression that had suffused Athelstan's smirking face.

40

If five and ten years was old enough to show the first sprouting of a beard and moustache, then it was certainly old enough to take an interest in the King's Council and in the prospect of fighting the Danes. The boy Godwine, on the brink of manhood, was intrigued by both, for the lure of adventure and for his friendship, that had strengthened over the years, with the ætheling, Edmund. Their pleasure in each other's company had not proven false for either of them, the elder boy happily sharing his own first forays into the mysteries of manhood with the younger.

Edmund and Godwine were everything that friends should be: fun, companionable, someone to brawl or laugh with when spirits were high; someone to shout at when anger steamed over, or to share grieving sorrows with. Someone to discuss the merits of women and horses, hounds and hawks. A true friend did not ask questions when answers could not be given, did not take offence at blustered bad tempers or lengthy and sullen silences. Loyalty was the measure of a friend, but whether their friendship was going to survive the next few stormy months remained to be seen. And whether Godwine's maturing courage was sufficient in quantity to carry him through the outcome.

Although his feelings for Edmund were stout and unbendable, Godwine had never felt the same ease with Athelstan; he admired and respected him, but trusted him, as his father, Wulfnoth, did? Ah, that was another matter. Even Edmund admitted occasionally, usually when too much ale had addled his brain, that he would not trust his brother a further distance than he could piss. The point was, however, when it came to the future safety of England, who could be trusted more to ensure its well-being? The King or his eldest son? Æthelred, becoming more entrenched with listening to the self-advancement advice of Eadric Streona, or the ætheling, Athelstan, who had his own reasons for seeking power?

Streona was a jealous man, who wanted all for himself and could not tolerate the concept of sharing. Athelstan had things to prove – to himself and his father – things that should have been examined, completed and set aside during childhood.

Eadric Streona's possessiveness emerged when it came to holding the confidence of the King in matters of state affairs. As Ealdorman of all Mercia, he saw himself as Æthelred's right-hand man, a second in command, and was striving hard to make the accolade officially recognised, taking every opportunity to promote his required usefulness. Athelstan considered that position, by right of birth, to be his; his hurt, frustration and disappointment being fuelled daily by his father's total lack of interest in him. There were occasions when Athelstan wondered if he actually existed; perhaps he was a spirit, doomed to walk behind the King for eternity and never once be seen in the living world of men? It certainly felt that way on occasion.

Two hundred ships rode at anchor in Sandwich harbour, manned by one thousand five hundred men. They had assembled, with hope and expectation, as April burst with a shower of blossom into May. Now, it was almost the end of June. Eight weeks and not one single ship had made sail. Excited hope had soon turned to boredom, expectation to disillusionment. Already, men were using the few short hours of darkness to slide away home. It would not be too long before men did so openly, in broad daylight, and in large groups, not in furtive ones and twos. Tension and temper were mounting. In the King's household it did not take the talents of a seer to predict that an eruption would come between Athelstan and Eadric Streona of Mercia.

'It will be sheer stupidity to take half the fleet up the Thames to London!' Athelstan stood before the Ealdorman, his anger surging upwards with his incredulity. 'We built this fleet with the express purpose of blockading the south coast.' Thorkell's muster was reported as being almost twice the size of the English – if it was true and the Dane made a successful landfall, then England, as an

227

English land, could be finished. Had they all forgotten, so quickly, the warnings of God's wrath? Of apocalypse and destruction?

'We cannot afford to allow Thorkell into harbour. We must use our ships to their best effect – out at sea.' Athelstan swung round, despairing. Was no one listening to good common sense? He pointed with a grand gesture towards the mass of ships, roped one to the other. They slept, their masts down, the square russet, saffron, or blue sails furled, oars at rest. To an eye that knew nothing of the sea, they appeared as no more than a host of abandoned boats bobbing on an incoming tide, but to one born with a saline tang in his blood they were the death shadows of the scyp fyrd. With the wind billowing and the spindrift leaping against the keel, with the strength of men driving the oars to lift her, each craft could come instantly and superbly alive; as lithe as a dolphin, as proud and graceful as a swan. As potentially lethal as an adder. These warships were lighter than traders' crafts, more manoeuvrable than the lumbering hulks of merchant ships, faster than fishing skips. With a master who knew the sea and all its changeable moods, and a crew who would caress their ship with a love and tenderness far greater than anything shared with a woman, a longship could become a weapon to equal any axe or sword.

But no craft could be made to sing without the skill of one who knew how to coax the tune into life. The men called to join the King's fleet were no less skilled than any seafaring *í-víking* Dane – the question, as yet unanswered, could the King use his scyp fyrd to its best effect? In Athelstan's opinion, if his father continued listening to this imbecile land crawler Eadric, the answer was a definite no.

His anger bursting, his bellow louder than the gulls swooping and screeching overhead for the new catch brought in by the coastal fishermen, Athelstan cried out his frustration. 'What do you know of the sea, Streona? You puke when ferrying across the mildest of rivers!'

Eadric responded with anger. How dare this boy insult his integrity? 'I grant that I do not have the skill of a sailor, but then, neither do you, Athelstan!'

'No, I have not personally commanded a ship, but unlike you, I am not too proud to listen to the judgement of those who have!'

The retorts were starting to fly like fire arrows released from a siege bow. Men loitering nearby turned, interested: local men mending fishing nets; merchants and traders buying and selling their wares along the quay; men of the scyp fyrd idling away their time in the brothels, taverns and ale houses. Sandwich was a busy harbour town that included the status of a king's palace, a centre for trade, justice, legislation, the collection of taxes – and the safe keeping of the king's fleet. The River Stour, the wool trade and an abundance of herring had heightened its importance through the years. Of its three hundred or so dwellings, the prime buildings were now occupied by wool merchants. As a diplomatic move to gain more Church approval, Æthelred was considering selling the Borough to Archbishop Alfheah of Christchurch, Canterbury, but at present the revenue of fifteen thousand pounds per annum for herring came in too useful. The monks would have to continue with their share of the wool that provided all their clothing.

'To listen to men like Wulfnoth, I assume?' Eadric insinuated, answering Athelstan's statement while inclining his hand towards the man in question, who lounged, unperturbed, against the doorway of a tavern, a half-empty tankard of ale clasped in his fist. 'You value the advice of rough-mannered pirates who have for their priority the lining of their own mantles?'

'As you do not?' Athelstan tossed back. 'Aye, good men like Thegn Wulfnoth, men who were born to men of the sea by women of the sea.'

Eadric Streona stood scornful, with his arms folded, his feet wide-planted, his derision as broad as the estuary of the Medway river. 'The King has better sense than to listen to men such as Wulfnoth. He portrays himself as an honest merchant, but is nothing more than a thief.' He spat the offence, his eyes holding directly to Wulfnoth, who said nothing. He had been on the receiving end of worse insults from better men. In good time, the opportunity to slit a cock's crowing throat always presented itself.

At his side, Godwine was not being so tolerant. His fingers tightened into a clenched ball as he glanced up at his father, astonished that he was taking no notice of the insult aimed so blatantly at him. Edmund, too, was angry, ready to draw his blade, would do so at the merest nod from either his brother or Wulfnoth. Who would care that Streona died this darkening evening? Who would notice? Certainly no one of the scyp fyrd, nor the merchants and tradesmen. As for the fishermen, well, they cared for nothing save the holes in their nets, the mood of the tide and the direction of the wind.

'There are moments', Athelstan declared to Eadric Streona, his stirred anger ploughing into a chill, controlled calm, 'when I wonder whether my father possesses any sense at all.' He swung away, bull neck jutting forward, jaw clenched, his steps long and impatient. Tossed over his shoulder, 'Those moments become more frequent when you are within my line of view.'

Wulfnoth, shrugging himself from the wall, handed his drained tankard to the nearby tavern girl and, making a low bow to the Ealdorman, strolled after the retreating Athelstan. 'I would get in the habit of watching the shadows,' he said softly to Streona as he passed by, the marten fur edging of his cloak brushing against the sable of the Ealdorman's. 'Æthelred will not always be King.'

'That he shall not,' Streona retorted, 'but Athelstan will not wear the crown after him.'

Wulfnoth raised his right hand into the vague area of his left shoulder, a mocking half-salute. 'We shall see,' he said evenly, 'we shall see.'

Edmund and Godwine, not so graciously taking their leave, followed in his wake. Was it deliberate that Edmund set his boot hard in the puddle, spraying salt-rimed water over Streona's expensive boots?

'This is it, then,' Godwine said as they jumped down the last three steps from the wharf and landed on the pebbled sand of the beach. Athelstan strode several yards ahead, his feet scrunching on shells and the stinking jetsam of rotting seaweed, fish bones and human refuse. 'Surely your brother will now rally the men to his own banner? He will rebel against this suggestion to move the fleet to London. I do not see that he has any other choice.'

'We,' Edmund hastily corrected, 'we will rebel. I will support Athelstan.'

'As will I, oh, as will I!'

Overhearing, Wulfnoth, midway between Athelstan and the younger lads, turned on his heel, the calmness that was a few moments before on his face clouding with rage. He marched back to them, clutched at his son's tunic, his other hand striking his cheek. 'Do not, ever, let me hear you talk so again!'

'But Papa, what have I said that is not the truth?' Godwine protested. 'Athelstan cannot hold off rebellion much longer and we will be with him, will we not?' He screwed his head round to plead for assistance from Edmund. 'It is what we have planned for months now.'

Ruefully Edmund returned his friend's gaze, then rested his hand on Wulfnoth's arm. 'Leave him, Sir, it is my error of judgement, not his. Godwine, if the need to defy my father arises, as my heart, sadly, is telling me that it one day will, we must keep our thoughts private.' He offered a placating smile at the Thegn. 'My brother cannot initiate a civil war. Not while we are threatened by Viking attack.'

Godwine bit his lip, deflated that the rise of excitement had been punctured, a little relieved, too. Treason was a dangerous path to follow, it was all right for Athelstan and Edmund, they were the King's sons, æthelings, men who were kingworthy, expected to be brave and honourable. Athelstan was three and twenty, Edmund eight and ten, men with boyhood long forgotten; for Godwine, manhood with all its independence, excitements and fears, was still waiting, hidden, beyond the corner. He scuffed the toe of his boot into the gritty sand. 'Then we accept Eadric Streona's part in all this and sit idle while England drowns?'

Wulfnoth guffawed, tousled his son's hair with his broad, calloused, hand. 'Nay, lad, I did not say that. I merely argue that we do not go broadcasting our intentions where our voices may carry to the wrong ears.'

41

Godwine's father, Wulfnoth, laced his fingers about his tankard of ale, looked solemnly into the liquid within. If Thorkell came, the English fleet would not be waiting for him, but would be dispersed: to London, the Medway estuary, Dover. There would be no blockade, no sailing out to meet him and destroy the dragon ships before they even as much as sighted England. All that effort, all that planning and organisation of muster? All for nothing. All for damned nothing! And now he was accused of treachery. Him? A traitor? God's Teeth but there was no one more loyal within the King's Court!

Æthelred was a fool. If only he would see that he could achieve more by putting his trust in his eldest son rather than Streona. Ah, but then if only Wulfnoth had not so openly backed the eldest son's protest at dispersing the fleet and had more readily towed the line that Eadric Streona advocated.

The King raised his head and met his Thegn's gaze, eye to eye. 'You have a strange meaning of the word faithful, Wulfnoth. I think it a dangerous thing for a king to have about him men who wrongly influence his eldest son's thinking.'

Wulfnoth pushed the tankard away, knowing that what he was to say next could be the ending of him, but saying it anyway because somebody had to. 'Sir, with all due respect, is it not more dangerous for a king to have about him men who do *not* influence his sons? Sons have a tendency to learn to think for themselves, a wise king trusts those loyal to him to guide that thinking. Only a fool follows a fool.'

'There are those', Eadric said from his side of the table, 'who question your knowledge of Thorkell. There are those who say you know him well.'

'Then those people are wrong,' Wulfnoth countered, forcing affability. It would not serve his cause to be losing his temper. 'I

232

have traded with him. It is what I do, I am a merchant trader. I trade with many men, Danes, Normans, French, Germans, even the Spanish. That does not mean I call them all friend.'

He was wasting his breath. The King had decided to listen to Eadric's advice and retreat from Sandwich into London. And Eadric had already realised that to be listened to again, on the morrow, he would have to be rid of men like Wulfnoth who knew what they were talking about.

'And I say you lie,' Eadric contradicted. 'We have proof that you are more than a trader where the Dane, Thorkell, is concerned.'

'Well, one of us is lying,' Wulfnoth growled. 'And it is not I.'

'Then I suggest we let God decide,' Eadric declared, low and menacing, knowing full well that whatever happened, Wulfnoth was finished as an English thegn.

'I will not do it! For you, Athelstan, for no one. I will not carry a red-heated bar of iron just to prove that I am no liar!'

'If you refuse, Wulfnoth, then you brand yourself guilty.' In exasperation Athelstan ran his hand through his tousled hair. This was a mess. He felt as if his feet were stuck firm in boggy ground. 'It is my fault. I ought not to have told Papa that he is an imbecilic puppet, but unless he ceases listening to Eadric Streona England will fall to the Danes. I know it as sure as the North Star shall be shining up there in the night sky within the hour.'

'Papa?' Godwine, standing beside his father rested his hand on Wulfnoth's arm. 'Papa, are we going to have to leave England?' Wulfnoth's son could see as clear as day the difficulty and the danger. Refuse a trial of ordeal and Wulfnoth was instantly branded traitor and faced exile or death. Go through with it and death was as much a risk.

Wulfnoth sighed, absently reached out his hand to ruffle his son's mop of fair hair. There were tears behind the boy's eyes; he was blinking them aside, bravely trying to stem them from falling. If only he knew that his father was desperately holding back his own! 'A man pledges his loyalty to his lord with his word of honour, son. If his word is not acceptable, then what is left for him?'

Slowly, Athelstan offered his hand. Reluctant, Wulfnoth took it, for this was goodbye. Resigned to his fate, the ætheling said, 'The day is coming nearer when I will have to attempt overthrowing my father, Wulfnoth. I cannot do so while the Danes threaten us, not unless I am certain that Englishmen will follow me wholeheartedly.'

'Aye,' Wulfnoth admitted, 'Æthelred can see that day too. He fears you, lad, and fears those who are your friends.'

'There is no truth in the rumour about you and Thorkell, is there, Wulfnoth?' Edmund said suddenly, leaning on the low sea wall a few yards to the left.

Godwine bunched his fists, rage swamping his face. 'You turd! Dare you ask that?'

Edmund ignored the outburst, looked across at the older man, an apology in his eyes for asking. He had to know, had to hear a denial for himself.

The tide had turned, was on the flood, creeping higher up the pebbles of the beach on the far side of the wall. The rows of ships, lashed one to the other, bobbed quietly, their wooden keels gently bumping as the water swelled below their bellies. There was always a special, different, smell when the tide turned. A saline excitement that hung, quivering, in the air.

'Nay, lad, there is no truth in it, I am no traitor.' Wulfnoth chuckled, a solitary snort of amusement. 'If Streona has so desperate a need to be rid of me, then I must be more of a nuisance than I realised!' It was a weak jest, but it brought a smile to their lips.

Chalk-white with fear, Godwine could see nothing to laugh at. He had witnessed men undergo the ordeal of trial, seen the writhing pain on their contorted faces as they had grasped a bar of red-hot iron by the right hand. Seen the agony as they had stepped – staggered – nine full paces without letting go or falling. He had smelt the burning, seared flesh; seen, as the bar was finally dropped, it peel away in smoking strips, exposing what lay beneath, the hand burnt to the bone. Had witnessed the pain of the next three days, the waiting for the dressings to be removed. If the wound was clean and healing, the man was professed innocent; if stinking of putrid rot, then death by hanging finished the thing. He had been sickened by it. What justice was there in mutilating a good, honest man? Oh aye, even if the wounds were healing and the man proven innocent, many died later of the blood fever, or never had the use of the hand again. The fingers were permanently gnarled and bent, clutched like a claw; the skin never grew back, the palm was withered and contorted, the flesh wrinkled and scarred. He did not want his father to go through that; but nor did he want to suffer the mortification of exile.

Setting his arm along his son's shoulder, Wulfnoth drew him inwards, guessing his thoughts. Thoughts that were shouting as loud in his own mind. 'I cannot serve a man who does no longer trust my honour-word, son.'

Athelstan smiled a wry expression. 'With you gone, the remaining scyp fyrd will go home. Men are already drifting in that direction. My father has been so ill-advised in this – what if we can persuade him to think again?'

Wulfnoth put his hand to Athelstan's arm. 'As you have just this moment said, this is not a suitable time to raise rebellion, lad.'

The wry smile became a grin. Athelstan was not his father; he had a quick mind, a grasp of politics, a flare for leadership and a passion for England. 'No, it is not, but a bit of local trouble along the south coast might well make the King think again. He has much land there, he would not wish to lose any assets to a pirate.'

For an honourable man such as Wulfnoth, exile held no more appeal than did a red-heated bar of iron. He grinned. 'You are right, my friend, he would not. And my land, too, is along that coast. I would not be content to leave the families of men loyal to me exposed and vulnerable to Danish raiding. I would be obliged to take my ships and crew to protect them, would I not?'

'Aye, and others of a similar mind may well go with you.' Athelstan grinned.

Wulfnoth guffawed, slapped his palm on to Athelstan's outstretched hand. 'The King is not going to appreciate the fact that I am about to do your rebelling for you, lad.'

'The King', Athelstan said with sincere feeling, 'can shove his head up his arse.'

42

The *Anglo-Saxon Chronicle*, produced by the Church clergy as a record of England's triumphs and disasters, was to state, when it was written retrospectively, that in the year Anno Domini 1009 King Æthelred '*carelessly wasted the nation's efforts*'.

It was a view his wife, Emma, unequivocally agreed with. 'All that cost and organisation. Everything wasted because of your misjudgement!'

'When I want the advice of a woman,' Æthelred snapped irritably, 'I shall ask for it. 'Though when I shall have the need of the intricacies of sewing, cooking or childbearing I cannot imagine.' As with most people, rich or poor, the edge of temper came into his voice because he knew the accusation to be justified. When in the wrong, losing your temper was a habit too many followed too frequently.

Emma's temper was also close to erupting. Her monthly flux was due and the uncomfortable cramp in her abdomen always caused her humours to be out of sorts. Added to that, the children were ill. All three of them with a fever and blister-like spots. Alfred and Goda were not so ill as to be a drain on their mother's strength and patience; indeed, Alfred was being a brave warrior by hiding the worst of his discomfort and trying hard to not scratch at the rash. Edward's grizzling was enough to try the patience of the Archangel Gabriel himself.

All night he had whimpered and cried, demanding to be sat with, sung to, amused and occupied. Much of it Emma left to his nurse, Wymarc, and the serving women, but as his mother she had to take her share of the responsibility – if for no other reason than to nip malicious gossip against her in the bud. Constantly, he had called for her when she had tried to slip away, believing him to be, at last, asleep, each time walking no more than a few yards before his screams all but woke the entire King's Palace at Thorney Island. By dawn, Emma herself was close to screaming.

'You appear to have no concern at what you have done. No regrets, no doubts. Can you not see that the people will not take much more of this?'

'The people', Æthelred sneered, 'can go to Hell.'

'Which is where they already are! You cannot go on raising tax after tax and not give them any return, Æthelred. You are raising twelve shillings per hide, more than half a man's expected income, and what have you shown for the use of it? Nothing, absolutely nothing!'

Æthelred pouted, aware he was not getting the better of the argument. 'It is not my fault, I have not been well advised.'

'God's Truth, but you whine like Edward! Nor is it your people's fault, yet they must pay. If they cannot pay, your reeves take in kind! How many good men have you made homeless this year alone, Æthelred? How many freeborn children, wives, mothers, and husbands, brothers and fathers have been forced to sell themselves into slavery because of your incompetence and Streona's greed? Reeves like him grow rich on the misfortune of the poor.' The anger was spilling over, flushing from the overfilled pot. These people were Emma's subjects too and she could no longer stand by and see their suffering ignored. It had come on gradually, this realisation that she was becoming fond of England and these Anglo-Saxon people, so gradually that she had not been aware of it until she had been on the verge of losing it all. Winchester, and standing so bold on the ramparts, had invigorated her, the cheering of the people reaching into her heart and giving her something worth living for – worth fighting for. And along with the realisation of her love for her adopted Country had come the awakening of ability and the possession of power, so that now she was not going to permit anyone to take this feeling of excitement, of being alive, away from her.

'You choose men to advise you on the content of their purse, not their capability. Is that how effective kingship works in England? God in Heaven, my brother will be laughing until his sides split open.'

Emma's outburst hit several sore nails square on the head. Æthelred was aware that he had made an almighty mess of this summer's campaigning, but he was damned if he was going to be reprimanded for it by a woman.

'Your brother?' He spat. 'I have every suspicion that your brother is directly involved with Thorkell's invasion! Who supplied the ships? The finances? It does not take imagination for a conclusion to fall upon Normandy!'

'But then you do not possess anything that remotely resembles an imagination, do you? If you did, you would never have listened to the stupidity of Eadric Streona and moved the fleet here to London. You would not have lost a capable and loyal man like Wulfnoth.' Emma thrust herself from her chair to pace the room. That wretched child was still screeching. 'You left Sandwich undefended. Despite all the money you raised to prevent it happening, Kent is left open and vulnerable. Nor does it take sense to understand that if you insult a man like Wulfnoth he will take his ships and abandon you.'

'Take his ships!' Æthelred roared. 'His ships? He has taken more than his bloody ships! I have lost a total of twenty craft to that traitorous bastard!'

'Yet you sit here, wringing your hands and cursing God because your strategy has gone wrong?' Emma retorted sarcastically and, dramatically flinging her arm into the air, announced, 'Strategy? What strategy? Were I king, I would be recalling Wulfnoth with all forgiveness, would ask my eldest, most competent son to take command of the fleet and, cladding myself in armour, take up my sword and personally go out there to slit Thorkell's throat if he should as much as dare to set one foot on English soil.'

'And if I were a queen,' Æthelred retorted, as he drained a fourth goblet of his best and strongest ale, 'I would not allow my damned son to afflict the entire palace with a thundering headache!'

43

'Eighty ships? You are telling me that you ordered eighty ships, under the command of Eadric Streona's brother, to go in pursuit of Wulfnoth?' Athelstan was incredulous. He said it again. 'You have lost us eighty ships because your sodding pride would not accept the plain, simple truth of common sense?'

Æthelred had ordered no such thing. Eadric had sent his brother off after Wulfnoth with the King's permission, but he had assumed the man would take five, eight ships at the most. Not eighty. On top of all the other blunders made, however, Æthelred was not about to admit to yet another mistake. Instead, he retaliated with blind temper. 'If you have no liking for the way I govern, then I suggest you leave my Court. In fact, until you can speak to me with a civil tongue in your head I suggest you leave my Kingdom. You have four and twenty hours to be gone.'

For a full minute Athelstan said nothing. He had ridden into Thorney not half an hour since from Kent, with the news that Thorkell had occupied Sandwich, and what was his father going to do about it? His nostrils were flaring, his breathing quickening, the rage, tumbling and twisting inside him, threatening to boil over and burst in a fountain from his mouth. His fists clenched, nails digging into his palms as he forced himself to remain calm, to speak polite and dignified, willing his hands not to clutch round that scraggy neck and squeeze the miserable life from it.

'I have no desire to stay within spitting distance of you, even were you to beg me, but do not expect me to leave England, Papa. Do not expect me to turn my back on those who will one day be my people. Unlike you, I honour my ancestors and my responsibilities. I will go from your Court, but I will be going out into the villages and the shires, the towns and the burghs. I will be gathering men to me, all those who can no longer stomach your indifference and incompetence. Expect to see me again, Father – at the head of an army!' Curt, he bowed his head and, with his cloak billowing behind him, swept from the Hall.

Edmund, tears weeping from his eyes, met him in the stables, his grabbing hand staying his brother from setting the saddle to his stallion's back. 'Athelstan! Please, do not do this! Go back to Papa, apologise, beg his forgiveness! Please!'

Compassionately, Athelstan took his hand within his own, squeezed it. 'I cannot do that, Edmund, things have gone beyond repentance and clemency.'

'Then wait a few minutes, allow me time to saddle my horse. I will ride with you.'

'No!' It came out harsher than Athelstan intended. He repeated himself gentler. 'Nay, lad, as much as I would like it, you cannot come with me, not to where I am going.'

'But . . .'

'No, Edmund. Father has declared me *nithing*, an outcast outside the law. We cannot both ride the same path. From here, you must follow your own fortune.'

Edmund threaded his fingers into his brother's, returned the squeeze. There was no point in arguing, he could see that. 'Then take care of yourself, Brother. And I vow, on the love that I have for you, that when you have need of me I shall be ready.'

Athelstan nodded. 'That is a vow I shall be glad to hold you to.'

The stable door was flung open, making the two lift their heads sharply. Emma. 'Is what I hear true?' she snapped, coming into the light of the lantern, not caring that her house shoes trod in the horse dung that had not been swept from the floor.

'That you no longer have to fear my presence?' Athelstan retorted. 'Aye, it is true. But I warn you, I shall be taking the crown as soon as I am able; I shall not be standing meekly aside to wait for your brat to come of age.'

Emma gave a sharp, impatient gesture with her hand. 'I was talking of more immediate issues. Is it true what I am hearing about Wulfnoth and Sandwich? That the one is dead and the other is lost?'

'They are both true. Eadric's brother pursued Wulfnoth with eighty of our war craft. All eighty were sunk in a storm off the south-west coast of the Island of Wight, along with Wulfnoth and many of his men. Thorkell occupies Sandwich and is ransacking most of the Kent coast.'

His tone had been harsh, scathing, as angry as he had been when telling his father all this. What senseless, pointless waste! To his surprise, Emma crumpled on to a pile of empty sacks, her head dropping into her hands.

When she looked up, there were tears in her eyes. 'Has Godwine been told?' she asked wearily.

Athelstan shook his head, said more kindly, 'I have not had opportunity to find him.'

Composing herself, wiping her fingers across her cheeks, Emma straightened her shoulders, stood. 'I shall find him and tell him. Thegn Wulfnoth was a good man; he was kind to me when I was in desperate need for kindness. I shall take it upon myself to look to Godwine now that you cannot.' She attempted a small smile. 'I believe you had agreed his wardship while Wulfnoth was absent from Court?'

'And why would you be doing that for me, eh, my Lady?' Athelstan said, the derision returning.

'I am not doing it for you,' Emma retorted, 'I am doing it for Godwine and for Wulfnoth, who was my friend as well as yours.' She turned on her heel, retraced her steps to the door, mindful of the dung this time. She paused in the doorway, silhouetted against the fading light of dusk. 'And I do it for the fact that I have no more respect for your father than do you. Given the right assurances for my future, Athelstan, I would be as pleased as you to be rid of him.'

44

Thorkell was immensely pleased with himself. Nor could he believe his good fortune. In the first week of September Sandwich, apart from the residents and a handful of rearguard wastrels, had been deserted and the Danish sea host had swept into harbour on a high night tide, their ships illuminated by the eerie light of a silver, three-quarter-full moon. After two days the land for five miles around had been secured, with minimal loss of life or blood on the raiders' side. Hemming, Thorkell's younger brother, who commanded half of the three-hundred-strong fleet, was forced to admit that the landing had been easier than he anticipated. He did believe that their luck would not hold, that there was bound to be an English army awaiting them a few miles further along the way, but then Hemming was noted for his pessimism.

'Canterbury will not fall so easily to us,' he said, his short, stubbed fingers automatically touching the Hammer of Thor pendant that hung on a thong at his neck. It was a special talisman, for it was made of an iron that possessed the magic power of Odin himself. If held aloft it would spin round and around, then settle, with its shaped, pointed tip, always towards the North Star. No matter how often or where he tried it: a clouded night, daylight, during storms, in perfect weather; without fail it located the north.

His folded arms set comfortably on the top rung of the closed gate, Thorkell remained quiet in his contemplation. Hemming had been foretelling danger since before they had set sail. There were some who said he was predicting doom from the day he fell out of his mother's womb, too early by a full month.

'That it may not,' Thorkell eventually answered his brother's bald statement evenly. 'But we did not come here believing we would face nothing more enterprising than an afternoon picnic.'

Resting his own arms on the gate, Hemming stared into the field. Most of the ponies were happily grazing, only a few remained unsettled, their heads up, ears back, ready to squeal and kick, unsure of each other and this unfamiliar territory. A few more days together as a herd and they would relax, once the squabbling for supremacy was established. Hemming grinned to himself. Were animals any different from men? Gather together a group of strangers, and always there was bickering and snarling until one among them proved his capability as a leader. For the ponies, it looked like the dun mare with the four white socks and the white face was to become the matriarch. She was a madam if ever there was one! Thorkell had claimed her for his own three days past, after they had taken her and several other ponies from that farm back down the valley. What they had not wanted they had killed or destroyed, the farmsteader and his sons included. A pity there had been no women, but any man of sense would have ensured the vulnerable were hidden away out of danger when Danes were within marching distance. Personally, if Hemming had farmed that steading, he would have sent that mare off with the women too. His grin quirked higher. In the case of his own nag-tongued, prune-faced wife, he would have sent only the mare and not bothered with the woman!

'Have you decided?' he asked, reaching down for a grass stalk to chew. 'Do we march direct to Canterbury?'

Deliberately, Thorkell avoided the question, for no other reason than he was uncertain what to do to retain this best advantage. He had been expecting more resistance, to have faced the English King and his army head on, soon after landing. All he had met, so far, were frightened villagers and farmsteaders intent on saving their property. Poor bastards. What chance had they against Thorkell's host, the largest ever seen in England?

Instead, he commented, 'We will need more ponies if we are to raid further afield than Kent. I'll not have the men march on foot, for we can too easily be separated from our ships.'

'We'll get the ponies.' Hemming casually flicked his left hand at the grazing animals. 'We've not done so bad this far with our acquisitions.' He turned his head, refusing to be ignored. 'Canterbury?'

'Canterbury will surrender before we reach the walls.'

'You are certain?' To Hemming's mind the holy city of Canterbury would hold fast, if not for the English King, then the English God. Sincerely, he hoped his brother had not misjudged things.

Dusk was enfolding the Kent countryside, the sky blending from a cornflower blue into a lazy purple, the meandering river, over to their right, a lavender ribbon of reflected mallow. Thorkell pointed to the far bank, directing Hemming's gaze to the ghostly white shape of a barn owl hunting on silent, gliding wings. It disappeared into a copse, the men listening for a while for its call. Nothing. Was her hunting successful? If not, was this a sign? Men, like ponies, were sometimes uneasy in strange terrain and the owl was the messenger bird of the gods.

The camp was on the far side of the burnt farmsteading, no need for tents, not on a night as warm as this. Fires, though, were necessary for cooking, and it was always more comfortable to sit around a hearth to eat and exchange stories and bravado. The sound of men talking, laughing, a few voices raised in good-natured argument. Metal stew pots clanging, wooden spoons rattling against wooden bowls. The steady scrape of a whetstone against an axe head. The ordinary and familiar sounds of an army at rest.

Thorkell barely heard, for he was listening, instead, to the unfamiliar sounds of England. The evening, when you cared to notice, was alive with noise. A few latecomer bees were humming among the meadowsweet, eager to gather that last bit of pollen before night fell; from the river the quiet plop of fish rising to suck insects from the surface. Birds whistling the boundaries of their territory; the ponies grazing, their tails swishing against the midges, the steady tear and chew at the grass. As dusk lengthened into night, the sounds grew louder, deeper, more insistent. There was the owl, calling its mate.

Pushing himself from the gate, Thorkell checked the latch was secure. He laughed. 'Hemming the doubter! Canterbury will not resist us – I wager you my new dun mare that it will not.'

Without hesitation, his younger brother spat on the palm of his right hand, thrust it out for Thorkell to take.

Thorkell kept his mare. And the three thousand pounds of silver that Canterbury prudently paid to see the *í-víkings* pass, in peace, on their way.

45

26 September 1009 – Dunmail Raise, Cumberland
Barefoot, the people who lived in the farmsteadings and fellside
crofts of the northern lonely land of eagles, lakes and mountains,
began the long climb up the crag that was known locally as the Lion
and the Lamb. It seemed a fitting place to conduct the Church-
ordained ceremony, perhaps the most fitting in all England. Even
slaves, for these next three special days of prayer and fasting, were
exempted from their work in order to attend compulsory Mass.
Although the loosely linked, self-contained communities who
scratched a meagre living from the high fells of the Cumbrian
mountains were uncertain how their participation could help in the
Archbishop of York's grand scheme of things.

Religious hysteria was mounting, the coming of Thorkell in the
South, his plundering, killing and burning the sign that opened the
sluice gates and released the flood of fear. This was it. The
apocalypse had come in the form of a Viking army. God was nigh
and was about to bring an end to all who had sinned. Evening had
come upon the world and there would be no tomorrow.

In the North, the motivation to seek God's forgiveness had been
slower to gather momentum, for the majority of farmsteaders were
of Norse origin. Even the names of their settlements reflected their
ancestry: Birkerthwaite, Dalegarth, Lowther, Rosgill, Rydal,
Threlkeld, Torver. The very hills themselves had lost their British
calling of *bryn*, replaced by the Norse *fjall*, fell. Only a handful of the
old kind remained, the Wealas, the British of Brigantia and
Strathclyde, a people who went further back into the past than the
Saxons, who had, in turn, settled the lower lands of Britain, and
created *Engla-Lond*. What possible threat was a raiding party
wreaking havoc more than three hundred miles away down in the
South to a remote hill farm a few miles from Scotland's wind-

hallowed border? Among the mountains and the lake-shimmering valleys, existence was from hand to mouth, every day was a struggle of Armageddon. If God ever remembered this lonely and harsh landscape, then He soon forgot it again. Only the thick-woolled, sturdy mountain sheep, and the copper mines, were an asset up here. That, and a talent to mind your own business and sit hunched for hours beneath the waterproof protection of an otter-skin cloak.

Fear, however, is not bound by reason or distance, and it can be so usefully and easily manipulated by those who have the sense and practicality to do so. Archbishop Wulfstan was a man blessed with both qualities and more besides. A clever man, who clung to his conviction that the Antichrist had arisen and was busy peddling his evil. When the end was to come, Wulfstan would not be caught bowed by sin and he saw it as his untiring duty to ensure that all others were equally ready to meet their God.

In the meantime there was the practical matter of funding his programme of repentance. Defence, whether against invading armies or unseen devils, drained coffers of gold and silver like water leaking from a holed bucket. A wide-held Church-engendered belief was that the wealthy saw to the poor, lame and sick, while God saw to the wealthy. Wulfstan was different from his peers in that he was not so naive as to rely solely on God's charity. Regular and appropriate finance came from organised taxation, and taxation came from labour. Honest or otherwise.

How much of the spreading fear was orchestrated? How much ran wild of its own generated accord? Who could say? Thorkell was leaving behind him a trail of blood and murder in Kent, his eyes and spears set towards Hamp-Shire. The King was barricaded in his Thorney Island palace, his various ealdormen as resolute for their own domains. Only the cynical, men such as Athelstan, and Wulfnoth before he had died, queried the tally of things.

The coin minted after the spring Council at Enham – a small, thin silver disc with the distinctive symbols of dove on one side and lamb on the other – had provided a great boost to a struggling economy. A well-timed and astute minting, that coin; particularly given that the silver content of the new was considerably lower than the old it replaced and the exchange rate had been biased towards the King's favour. Three new for four old. Ah, now that was a canny way to levy an extra tax, one that no one, from the richest merchant to the poorest peasant, could avoid. The Church's command of three days of especial Christian worship was carried along with a compulsory levy for charitable church purposes. Thorkell might be creating Hell in Kent, the Devil could be riding with black cloak flying and red mouth agape over the entirety of England, but neither Crown nor Church would be suffering financially.

Wulfstan was also astute with the choosing of his suggested period of mass prayer. With crops and livestock to tend, matters of religious welfare often came a poor second, particularly if the weather and the crops were good, but September was a sublime month if all went well. The harvest was in and the barns were full. If ever there was a period of leisure, then late September fitted well. In theory, it was also a month when raiders sailed for home and the fyrd could put away their weapons until the next spring. These Danes seemed to be ignoring the rules, however, which for Wulfstan was most annoying when it came to the fine planning of parading penitence before God.

It had been the local priest's idea to hold Mass on the summit of Helm Crag, as the fell was correctly called, an idea that received approval throughout his scattered communities and the personal blessing of York's Archbishop. A bold, detached hill, Helm Crag rose above the Grass Mere, its sentinel rocks, high on its summit, looking for all the world as if carved by God for, from whichever direction, the larger hump resembled a crouching lion with, between its paws, the unmistakable form of a lamb. God and Christ, manifest among the majesty of His mountains. More than this natural outcrop of rock, Helm Crag guarded the high, steep pass of Dunmail Raise, that toiled up and over the valley cleft beneath the great and mighty Helvellyn, the King of Mountains.

One man, old Gildas from Skelwith Valley, could remember another time of fear and fighting with King Dunmail and the tumultuous events of 945. In his five and seventieth year of life, his mind was as often unreliable as his limbs and bladder, but the battle of Dunmail Raise he could remember as clear as if it were yesterday. And even if his memory did fade, he had told the story so often that others were always able to tell it for him.

They carried him up Helm Crag on a wicker chair, for he was too frail to walk. Several of the stronger mountain men hoisted the carrying poles to their shoulders and lifted him aloft as if he were a processional totem or standard. Gildas sat, toothlessly grinning, his plaid cloak wrapped tight round his thin body, his wild grey hair billowing about his head, and his sing-song voice lifting as high and jagged as the hills.

Clouds were rolling down off Helvellyn, obscuring the brilliance of sunshine and darkening the Crag to a sombre blue-grey patchwork of shadow. Most of the inhabitants of the valleys had come, many from a prevailing fear of an uncertain future, a few from curiosity, most because it was reason for holiday. They gathered beside the shore of the lake, their chatter as excited as their expectation. Several had camped in the valley overnight, would sleep there throughout the days of designated prayer. Leather and canvas tents dotted the water meadows, the blue smoke of hearth-fires fading as the wood burnt down to ash. Some, those who knew of it, making use of the wide-mouthed cave over the far side of the Rydal Water. Children walked with their parents and grandparents. Men, women, young, old, their voices raised in song as the priest lifted his staff and began the long climb, the procession of people snaking in his wake.

No Viking raiding party would bother with these people, the mountains were too high, the passes too steep, the reward too low, but Wulfstan's word had been persuasive and insistent. If God no longer looked at the lakes and valleys, then perhaps it was because He was ashamed of their burden of sin. Thorkell might be many miles away, but the sheep still had lambs to birth each spring, the winter snows still brought death and hardship. For everyone, throughout all England, there were reasons to pray for salvation.

'A day such as this, it was,' Gildas creaked, pointing his bone-thin arm up at the wild, storm, sky. 'I were a lad, not far off my tenth summer. My da was Lord of all Skelwith and I carried his spears as we came up out of our valley to join with the host amassed in the Raise over yonder.'

The sun went from the remaining landscape and a veil of rain swept with hissing speed across the forested slope of Helvellyn, skimming quickly down the Raise and stinging across the surface of the lake, sending it shimmering and dancing as if it were a pot boiling. No one noticed the downpour save for a few of the women who carried young babes in their arms, but even they merely pulled their shawls the tighter and trudged on.

The path wound up the Crag in a zigzag pattern, some places steep, others easier to tread. A beck, bridged by flat stones of slate, ran down through the mossy grass, eager and chattering, swelling and rushing faster from the sudden torrent of rain. In the distance, over towards the saddle-shaped ridge of Blencathra, thunder grumbled. In answer, the priest at the head of the long winding column raised his voice higher in a more robust hymn. Those who had heard Gildas's story too often to listen to it joining him.

'King Edmond came here because our King, Dunmail, had allowed his kinsman, Olaf Gothfrithson of Dublin, to beach his ships over by the coast and to march his army along the High Street, laid down by the Red Crest Romans, then across the Pennine Hills to York. Edmond was aggrieved at that.' Gildas masticated his toothless gums a moment, before adding with unusual honesty, 'I suppose as King of England he had the right to be.'

He lifted his face and shook his fist at the rain clouds. 'You think Thorkell is a threat, eh, Æthelred? Ah, he's nought but a patch of mildewed reeds in comparison to the army King Dunmail led! I watched, from up there, beneath the Lion an' Lamb, me and the other lads my age, us on this side of the pass, and Helvellyn watching from the other. Aye, and when that fierce and mighty battle was over, when Dunmail lay dying, I knelt and wept my tears along with all the other lads. Our fathers were dead, not one of them left alive. The blood flowed down into Grasmere that day. Edmond swept on through the valley and away. He never paused, never came back. Huh, he never dared, for we might have been lads that dreadful day when our King was shamefully slain, but we grew from lads to men. And it would have been a different ending had Edmond dared show himself here again!'

'I heard another telling of that story,' one of the men a few rows back from Gildas whispered to his companion. 'I heard that Dunmail was not killed, but that he fled in terror, up over Helvellyn, dropping his crown and his treasure as he ran. That's why the mountain weeps its tears of cloud so often, for it mourns the shame of a king who fled from his men and left them to die.'

'Best not tell your version too loud in front of old Gildas, then.' The other man chuckled. 'Without his story to tell, I reckon he'd lose his hold on life.'

'Old Megan, his only surviving daughter, would not be too saddened to see him gone to God. She says he's a difficult old bugger to be takin' care of day after day.'

As sudden as it started, the rain ceased. Those at the head of the procession had reached the top of the Crag and there before them rose the black, towering solidity of the Lion, with the Lamb tucked safe between his paws. From close, the shape was not so convincing, but too many were familiar with its distant impression to notice or care. Below, a burst of sunlight illuminated the lake, and as the wind dropped away, reflected everything in its sudden calm surface; soft vertical bands of greens and browns shadowed by the dark grey of ghostly clouds.

And across the wide valley of Dunmail Raise, as if in tribute to the battle place of a king and the fallen dead, or the forgiving love of the Christian God, three rainbows arched, brilliant in their vivid, breathtaking beauty.

46

November 1009 – Bath

Reluctantly, Æthelred was forced to swallow his pride and recall Athelstan to Court. Worse, had to be civil to him. Either that, or lead the fyrd himself; of the two evils, enforced civility to his son offered the better option. Eadric Streona urged its doing and Æthelred had formed a natural habit of following Eadric's advice. Why should he not? Streona was a trusted friend, the only man who agreed with him, even if he did, often, later suggest alternatives to previous ideas and opinions.

Aside, ordering Athelstan's return could prove a suitable opportunity to teach the boy a lesson in humility. Graciously, the King gave command of an army to his eldest son, with the specific order to send Thorkell and his Danes either back to their ships or to their gods.

'Let him get on with it,' Eadric advised as he sat with the King, drinking the best imported wine. 'Let him see that it is one thing to brag and boast within the confines of a comfortable Hall, quite another out there, when winter is closing in.' Æthelred did not observe that his companion did more than his share of the bragging and boasting from within doors.

Although Thorkell's own dragon ship was an enormous beast, the majority of his fleet comprised of ships no more than seven and fifty feet in length by eight feet wide. Fully laden, with a crew of six and twenty oarsmen, the shallow-drafted keels required only eighteen inches of water in which to sail. Thorkell could go anywhere he chose. From out of a dawn mist his ships would appear, silent and unexpected, the men pouring from the decks to loot and plunder and be gone before the sun gained strength. Kent was bled dry before autumn had flushed the trees into vivid colour, Hamp-Shire and Sussex faring no better as the reds, golds and oranges withered to frost-tainted bareness. Wherever a tributary ran as a meandering vein from a main arterial river England slept uneasy.

Splitting his army into three, with himself, his brother Hemming and a trusted captain in command, the fellowship of Norse Men, the *faellag* swept across southern England unchecked. There was nothing Athelstan could do to be effective, for no one knew where next the sea wolves would strike. Again and again the war horns boomed the alert and the fyrd hastily assembled – but always, always, too late, the Danes had come and gone, as swift as a spring shower. Until they knew where and when Thorkell's men would appear, there was nothing the English could do as an opposing force. A fact Thorkell knew well. Outright battle was not what he wanted, or intended. That was for his King to do, for a united, disciplined army, not for a band of mercenaries out for the making of a quick and easy fortune. Deliberately, he kept his ships moving, never anchoring in the same place for more than the one night, never lingering along the reaches of the same river – his ships, the swift-oared, highly manoeuvrable craft of the *í-víking* so adept at playing this game of cat and mouse.

By mid November, Athelstan admitted defeat. There was no way that the English army could outwit the Danes, not unless they decided to make camp and stay put. And that, Athelstan began to realise, Thorkell would not do until he had destroyed the infrastructure of southern England and undermined the military strength and authority of the King. Hah! And that, too, he was doing very well!

Æthelred, safely skulking in London, solidly blamed the cock-crowing, oh so certain Athelstan for always being in the wrong place at the wrong time. In turn, Athelstan blamed the King for providing poor to non-existent information, useless spies and slovenly discipline. With king and ætheling fighting between themselves, what need had Thorkell to worry? Æthelred would not listen to excuses for a task he considered badly done, and Athelstan had been made to look the fool by both his father and Eadric. The fool he might be, but he would not give up as his father had, would not shelter behind barred doors and allow the Danes to get on with it, unharried and unopposed.

As spring began to stir with a reluctant, sleepy timidity, Thorkell reached Oxford and, in the name of Swein Forkbeard, burnt it to the ground. Athelstan chased after him, using his fastest horses and most experienced men, urging a forced marching, struggling along the muddied highways by both night and day, barely stopping to rest, water or feed the tired animals. As ever, they were too late. As they reached Oxford's smoke-blackened walls, footsore and exhausted, with lamed horses and dispirited men, they found the Danes to be long gone, heading direct to the coast, and as March blew, with ragged, searing winds, into a wet and miserable April, Thorkell ordered the sails set and disappeared over the horizon. Athelstan was frustrated and disappointed at his failure, but England breathed a sigh of relief. The Danes, they thought, were gone, had taken all they wanted and were gone.

It was a broken sigh and a short relief, for Thorkell had no intention of returning to Denmark, not yet. He spent a month in safe harbour along the Normandy coast, a chance to rest, to repair ships and men from damage received, and then returned, sailing direct for Ipswich in Suffolk, the town discovering that his shallow-drafted keels could sweep, like soundless, shrouded ghosts, upriver into their very heart, and as so often before, no Englishman had chance to lift an axe or spear in defence. Ipswich fell to the lust of the í-víking. One day, however, Thorkell would grow overconfident and find himself entangled with a man who knew what he was doing. One day the Dane would be tempted further into East Anglia and the domain of Æthelred's most capable warrior lord. His son-in-law Ulfkell.

47

4 May 1010 – Wretham Heath, Ringmere, near Thetford
Ulfkell Snilling, Ulfkell the Bold, had never professed to hankering
after great ambition; he was a humble man who devoted his loyalty
to God, King and Country. He had not hidden the smile of pleasure,
however, when Æthelred had offered a daughter as wife; nor, at the
last Christmas Council, his delight in finally receiving the prestigious award of the Ealdromanry of East Anglia. The wide space of
the open Fenlands of Anglia were vulnerable to attack; the pockets
of enormous wealth, at the abbey on the Isle Ely and towns such as
Norwich and Thetford, a profitable lure for any audacious Dane –
and to Ulfkell's certain knowledge there were those in plenty
lurking off the Anglian coast.

His was now the sole command, his voice alone, below the King,
gave orders that, on pain of death, had to be obeyed. For that reason
he praised God for the King's sense of wisdom. What Ulfkell lacked
in aspiration, he achieved in ability and determination. He was a
warrior lord who possessed the gifted instinct for battle; he put his
faith first in God and then in his double-handed battleaxe. Under
his command East Anglia would rise up and fight the next invasion.
Fight or die.

At Athelstan's command, and under his leadership, Essex was on
standby. If the war horns were to sound the fyrd was ready should
the Danes, after loitering in Ipswich, decide to swing south towards
London. If they turned north they would meet with Ulfkell. Only,
the new-made Ealdorman of East Anglia made certain they turned
northwards by offering Thorkell a challenge. For he called out the
entire levy of Norfolk, Suffolk and Cambridge-Shire, and bade
them wait a scatter of miles north of Thetford. Instinct, gut feeling
– God's protection – told him that Thorkell the Tall, for his own
honour, would not let the explicit bravado go unheeded.

Thetford, after the last devastation, had been rebuilt, houses, church and trade fully restored. With everything reed-thatched and built of timber and daub, it had taken a matter of weeks to complete. It was the men who were difficult to replace; men could not be reaped from the river, or felled from the forests.

An anxious week passed, a week that dragged slowly into a second. Ulfkell's men sat cross-legged around their campfires, mending war gear or resharpening an edge that was already lethal, their voices silent but minds restless; how many of them would see the summer come? Spring, the most beautiful season of the year, with the world awakening and everything fresh and new. A sad time to die. It did not seem right to go to God when the world was so vibrant with life.

A footfall behind him, Ulfkell turned with a smile, recognising the sound of his wife's light tread. He thought himself fortunate with Wulfhilde, for of Æthelred's four eldest daughters she was the most comely in fairness and temperament. The pious one had taken herself off to be Abbess at Wherwell, an action which Æthelred had not objected to, for she was too saintly a woman for any man to stomach. Algiva had been given to Uhtred of Northumbria as reward for victory against the Scots, although no one was in any doubt that the marriage was a sop to the reverberation of unrest after Alfhelm's death and his sons' blinding. Eadric Streona's wife, Edgyth, the youngest of the four, was shy-spoken and plain. Some whispered that what she lacked in speech she made up for in bed. Ulfkell snorted laughter – and how would they be knowing that?

'I thought you might have a thirst,' his wife said, offering a tankard of ale. 'It has been a hot day.'

Dutiful and compliant, that was Wulfhilde. Half his age, twice as patient. A thoughtful woman who put the needs of others before her own. Huh! More than once since their marriage Ulfkell had wondered whether Wulfhilde was truly Æthelred's daughter. He took the tankard, nodded appreciation and drank.

'Now the sun is setting the air will cool.' He reached out a hand and tucked a strand of her hair beneath her veil. She had yellow hair, the colour of sweet-smelling hay. 'I would prefer you to go to

Winchester where the Queen is,' Ulfkell said, concerned, knowing she would refuse. He had said it so many times before.

As before, she answered, 'I am as safe with you as I am with any other.'

'If Thorkell comes,' he said, his voice lowered and painfully sad, 'and I do not survive the battle, will you give me your vow that you will return to the protection of your father?'

Wulfhilde gazed towards the river and the darkening shadows of the forest beyond. How could she promise that? She had spent all her twenty years wishing and waiting to escape from Æthelred. How could she return to his vindictive spitefulness? 'Would you have me go where I would be unhappy? I had nothing but tears and a fear for the next day when I was at Court.'

Wulfhilde had wept the day she had been told that she was to wed Ulfkell of East Anglia. He was a grey-haired man in his fiftieth year, she, a young woman with her life before her. Even if that were to be a short life – as was the lot of many wives, for childbirth was a wicked killer – she had wanted more than to be the chattel of an ageing man full of bad breath, wind and the bone-ache. How wrong could a young woman be? She took the drained tankard from him, laid her other hand over his. 'I did not expect to love you,' she said, her eyes meeting with his. 'But . . .' She gave a small shrug, a half-smile. 'But I do.' She closed her fingers over his and stretched up to place a kiss on his cheek. Kindness, respect and tenderness had worked their magic well. 'I appreciate your concern for my safety, but I would ask you not to make me utter promises that I know I must break. I would rather die and follow you to the next world than live again beneath the same roof as my father.'

'You have brought contentment and love to an old, hoar-grimed man,' Ulfkell answered, returning the kiss. 'I would not see you unhappy. Do what you will, with my blessing, and if you decide to take for yourself another husband, see to it that he is worthy of you. That is all I ask.'

'There is no need for you to fear,' Wulfhilde said, moving away from him with a light laugh. 'Stay behind the battle line, keep your axe high, your shield low and have your men hack this Thorkell's head from his shoulders, so that we may never fear for our future again.'

It was a tall order, one that he was not sure he could complete. Still, he would have a damned good try at it.

48

Morale for the fyrd of East Anglia was high. Under their Lord, Ulfkell Snilling, they were ready and eager to fight. Overnight, the sight and sound of the Danish host, their campfires burning bright with the hot, quick blaze of gathered furze, three miles from Wretham Heath, had been suspiciously and intently watched. Thorkell was in no hurry to move. His men ate their fill, slept, awoke refreshed. Not all his warriors broke their fast, for even if they professed to bravery, stomachs often belied the truth. A fine day for fighting: overcast but with small chance of rain. Underfoot, the ground was dry and firm.

Ulfkell drew his men into two columns, one led by himself, the other by a trusted friend and able commander, brother to his wife's mother, a man of few words, who preferred farming to fighting.

Bending forward, Ulfkell stroked the brindle head of his dog, a great beast that stood almost as high as a pony. Hlaf had been a gangle-legged pup, quick to learn, eager to please. Loyal to serve. He was grizzled around the muzzle now, one ear torn from a fight over a bitch, one paw with two toes missing. The dog lifted his head, whined, caressed his master's hand with his lolling tongue.

'We'll have a day of it today, eh, my lad?' Ulfkell patted his flank, straightened, ran his finger along the blade of his axe.

Thorkell had advanced his men in line, ranked at a halt a mile to the far side of the open heath. To the left the dark reaches of the woods began, away to the right the grey ribbon of a dawdling river. Those first few moments of impending battle were always difficult. Who would move first? Shoot the first arrow, shout the first war cry, sound the first war horn? Both sides eager to fight, reluctant to begin. Often, it was some small thing that would initiate movement – a pony whinnying, a dog snarling, a bird flying up, startled, from the undergrowth. On this day at Wretham Heath it was the wind.

It came up out of the forest, a gushing whoosh of breath that rippled through Ulfkell's standards, whipping the fluttering banners into a whip-crack of life. His own banner, embroidered with a running hound, dipped as the bearer momentarily lost hold of the shaft, so strong was that gust. It was all the signal needed. The war horns assumed it to be the command they had been awaiting, and the great sound boomed and boomed with, in its wake, the Saxon fyrd, their fingers gripping tight to axe haft or sword hilt, moving forward, as if the columns were a single multi-legged creature. Their shout reaching to the very sky: 'Ulfkell! Ulfkell! Thorkell ut! Ut! Ut! Thorkell, out, out, out!' The words stamped to the rhythm of their marching feet.

Thorkell raised his hand and his warriors bellowed their own shout, began running. 'Thor's Hammer, Odin's Strength! Odin! Odin!' They met, somewhere in the middle, a mêlée of feet, arms, elbows and teeth as much as blade and weapon. The onrush from the Saxons halted the Danes, even made them give ground by several yards, but they were strong and determined, and had more to lose than did the army of Cambridge-Shire and East Anglian men. Thorkell had not wanted an outright fight, but could not refuse this one. What was the choice? Fight, or sail away to Denmark? There was no halfway decision, not when a famed warrior raised his fist and dared you to come fight him.

Fighting amid his surrounding guard of personal cnights, Ulfkell sent word to his right flank to bear more to the right, try to push the invaders over towards the river. It almost worked, would have succeeded if a spear had not been tossed with one of those lucky throws that bring about such devastation. It struck direct into his brother-in-law's throat, who was dead before a shout of surprise or pain could leave his mouth and, with his dying, the men under his command wavered, a small, almost unnoticed movement, but one that the Danes saw and seized upon. Three hours it had taken, three long hours for Thorkell to overpower an opponent that even he had to admit, after it was all over, was worthy of salute. Whether he would have been so magnanimous had Ulfkell not seen the sense in surrender, however, would never be certain, but as it was, honour had been satisfied and defeat accepted.

Leaving their weapons, but taking their dignity and their lives, Ulfkell submitted Thetford to Thorkell the Tall and withdrew. With head high, the Ealdorman led his men away; beside him, on his left side, his dog limped along, the other eye torn, a dagger wound on his shoulder. On his right Ulfkell's wife, her hand resting on his, her step equally proud.

Behind, the men carried the wounded and the shrouded body of her uncle. A pity that he would not fight again another day, but others would be doing it for him. In that Ulfkell was certain. This was only a battle, not the war.

49

For the second occasion these last years, Æthelred was forced to hold his winter Court in the crumbling town of Bath. It had once been a proud and beautiful Roman place, Aquæ Sulis, where hot springs and the blessing of the goddess had healed the sick of their ills. But the great baths were ruined, the waters fouled with scum and debris, there was nothing left of the might of Rome and, so it appeared, there was little left of England.

Thorkell had returned to Kent. The total of men, women and children slaughtered during the first months of winter had risen to eight hundred and four, not that the figure could be verified, as many peasant farmers could not count beyond the number of their fingers without the aid of a tally stick. It was a figure close enough to a truthful reckoning, though. The Dane was unstoppable. From his victory at Thetford he had bypassed Athelstan waiting in Essex, and had marched down into Wilt-Shire, ensuring Wessex ran with blood while the King huddled behind the walls of London, sheltering in King Alfred's old palace, built to the south-eastern corner beside the river embankment. A better place to defend than Thorney Island and easier to leave secretly, or in a hurry, should the unforeseen arise.

For Canterbury, there was no similar escape route, either by road or sea. Thorkell had chosen to over-winter his fleet at Sandwich – and why not? Æthelred was not making use of it. The Dane himself was encamped with half his men outside the walls of the cathedral city, laying siege.

Emma could imagine the horror the people were enduring, once all the food had been eaten and disease began to kill more inside those walls than Thorkell's arrows and spears were from the outside.

'If we do not send an army into Kent,' she shouted, uncharacteristically stamping her foot, 'then Archbishop Alfheah will be forced to submit. Can you so readily accept the loss of Canterbury?'

'Look about you, woman!' Æthelred yelled back. 'How many of my ealdormen and thegns have answered my summons to Court? Enough to count on two hands and still have fingers left over!'

'Well, mayhap if you were to string Eadric Streona up by his balls, as he deserves, then more would come!'

'I cannot aid Canterbury. It is the wrong time of the year to put an army into the field. How would we feed them? Tell me that. How do we march through this knee-high snow, through the thaws that will follow to swamp the roads with mud? The Medway is in flood, Athelstan cannot get into Kent from Essex and storms prevent us from launching ships. So tell me, how do I do it?'

Emma could make no answer, except, damn it, Thorkell had his men encamped outside the walls of Canterbury and winter weather had not sent him scuttling for shelter.

'All Alfheah can do is negotiate terms and buy his way out, and that the silly old fool is refusing to do, despite my ordering of it.'

'All right, I accept your reasoning,' Emma capitulated, reluctant, 'but you must assure me that you will send men as soon as may be possible.'

'Yes, yes,' Æthelred answered testily as he stamped from the room. His private chamber would be warmer than the Hall and less noisy. Would not have the prattled nagging of this woman hammering at his ears.

He had no need to promise. Someone in Canterbury grew tired of waiting for a slow death by starvation and took matters into his own hands. During the quiet hours of darkness, Canterbury's gates were opened and the Danes poured in.

At least Archbishop Alfheah was spared the distress of seeing his brethren hacked to death and his cathedral burning. He was captured and taken prisoner; secured with rope and chains, and thrust, semiconscious, into a donkey cart and taken away from the town. Sick of heart and stomach, he lay for four days in a stinking hovel, listening to the carousing of his captors and Thorkell's boasted achievement.

Eight and forty thousand pounds of silver was the demand for peace in Kent and, on top of that, the wanting of a separate ransom for the Archbishop.

The old man, stripped of vestments, freedom and dignity, closed his tired eyes and prayed for God's guidance and deliverance. Only God could offer that, for it would not be coming from the King.

50

What was the point of it all? The question tumbled through Thorkell's mind as he sat spooning porridge from a wooden bowl. It was coarse stuff, with a bland taste, agreeable to eat only because of the hunger that rumbled in his belly. Seeing the second half of the winter out, here at Greenwich, the ships pulled up along the river bank for cleaning and mending, had seemed a good idea after the Yule festivities had been enjoyed, when hope and enthusiasm had run high, but now? He scraped the last spoonful, swallowed and set the bowl down at his feet. Now that the snow was receding and a new spring blooming, the spark had gone out of the fire. The men wanted to go home. Damn it, he wanted to go home.

Thorkell glanced across at the young man sitting opposite him, a fair-faced youth, brash and full of self-confidence. Six and ten years old. By Thor's Hammer, Thorkell had been as confident at that age! He had arrived in England two weeks past. Was also anxious to return to Denmark, but for differing reasons. This boy had much to prove and was impatient to be doing it.

'King Swein is expecting to receive the English tribute of geld,' the boy said, finishing his own breakfast porridge. 'It is needed to pay his men for the summer's campaigning; are you certain it is today they are to bring it?'

Impatiently Thorkell answered – twice already since sunrise had he been asked the same question – 'Ja, I am certain. Æthelred has returned to London from Winchester; safe conduct downriver is arranged.'

As impatient, the boy glowered across the fortified compound, with its ramshackle accommodation and scatter of debris, to where Alfheah, Archbishop of Canterbury, sat, chained by the ankle to a solid-fixed post. For their own shelter the men had draped the sails as tents, the oars making effective ridge poles; for the Archbishop they had created a lean-to from wattle hurdles – there was a field somewhere with a hole in its fencing, but then, as the Danes had eaten all the domestic livestock in the immediate vicinity it was of no consequence. Alfheah had fared no worse than the rest of them, except for his loss of freedom, although it had been hard for an old man to endure the severity of a winter outdoors.

'And the extra we have demanded for his ransom?' the boy queried, tossing his head in the Archbishop's direction. 'Shall they pay that?'

Thorkell did not miss the use of the word 'we'. Full of his own importance, the lad already acted as if he were a commander. Thorkell shrugged. If he were the boy, would he behave any differently?

'You will not get more out of the English than has already been agreed,' Thorkell stated flatly, stretching his legs out before him. His bones ached. The young had the advantage of supple bodies and endless enthusiasm, did not mind sleeping on hard, cold ground, or the discomfort of an empty belly. What they lacked instead, most sorely, was wisdom.

'The Archbishop has ordered that no further money is to be paid on his account. His request will be obeyed. These high-ranking monks command great respect among their followers.' He had never complained, cursed or threatened; had offered polite thanks and a blessing to those who had served him food, or thought to bring him an extra blanket. Almost, Thorkell could believe he did not mind this relegation to humble endurance. Wished, now, that he had paid more heed to the Christian preachers who valiantly attempted to ply their trade back home in Denmark. Was it too late to sit with this old man and ask him the secret of his peace? Christianity was a lacklustre belief throughout the Netherlands, although there were several churches, some of them quite astonishingly beautiful buildings, but the nature of the White Christ did not appeal to a warrior used to the violence of war. Thor with his hammer and thunderbolts, Odin with his strength – these were the gods of a man who would often care for his battleaxe more than his wife.

Thorkell ran his hand over his chin. His beard and moustache needed trimming, they had grown straggly this last month; a bath, too, in hot, herb-scented water, would not go amiss; he had not enjoyed that pleasure for more than seven months. A quick sluice in cold water was not the same. He wrinkled his nose. Gods, but they must all stink! The men were nothing more than a rabble, unwashed, unkempt; rowdy and quick to squabble. More often drunk than sober. Mercenaries, the lot of them, interested only in the highest they could get for the least they could give. He would need to do something about his appearance before the royal envoy arrived. Shave, wash, find clean clothes.

He sighed. It would have been interesting to have talked in full with the old man. Ah well, the opportunity had been missed. 'The English will pay to see us gone,' Thorkell said, perhaps a little too patronisingly, to the boy. 'They will expect us to sail soon after the geld is delivered.'

The boy raised his eyebrows, scorn marking his words as he answered, 'They expect us to do their bidding? I think not, my friend!'

Suddenly irritated at being lectured by one who barely shaved, Thorkell got to his feet and fastened his cloak tighter. The wind, sweeping in off the river, had a bitter chill to it. 'I intend to meet the envoy with my pride intact. I go to bathe and change into something more fitting for King Swein's commander to be seen in.'

The young man made a derogatory gesture with his hand. 'Why do we need to impress? Æthelred has not managed to defeat us. This coming year will be no different from the last; we could change our minds and demand twice the amount they are to bring us.'

Thorkell jerked on his war cap. He did not need it, for they were secure here in camp, but a soldier's habit of a lifetime was difficult to break. 'We could, but we will not, because our men, sitting on their backsides around these campfires, are bored with England. They want to return to their families, show what they have achieved and gained. They will not fight again, not this year.' He stepped over the empty bowl at his feet, walked past the blaze of the wind-fanned fire and stood directly before the scowling youth.

'You have a lot to learn about what motivates a man to fight, son. It is the wolf defending cubs, or the stag brought to bay, who are the most dangerous. These men, here, fight for reward, not for loyalty. They want gain, not death. Englishmen, if someone ever finds the guts to rouse them, will be fighting for their homes and their families. There is your difference. Our men will not fight that sort of motivation, not for me, nor for you, Cnut, even if you are King Swein's son.'

51

Life for Emma had continued much as usual over the winter; the King had taken his Christmas Court to Woodstock to enjoy the seasonal hunting, then moved to Winchester to preside over the quarterly judgement courts of Wessex, and they were back now at Thorney Island for Easter and the paying of the heregeld. Except, Æthelred decided to send his wife into the Danish camp instead of going himself.

Londoners were not so happy with the lengthy delay of payment, the general opinion being that if a geld had to be paid, why could it not have been settled earlier? Trade had dwindled to virtual non-existence, for no ship had sailed further than the Viking encampment at Greenwich since their arrival. London was feeling the pinch of tightened belts and the constant watching over the shoulder for the ever-present expectation that wholesale slaughter was residing only a few miles downriver. Æthelred had not received a rapturous welcome when he arrived at Thorney. Had he ventured as far as London, he might have found the gates barred to him and more than a few rotting vegetables and stinking eggs thrown. *Unraed*, they were calling him, and not quietly in the privacy of a man's home but openly, out on the street. A play on his name, that taunt, *unraed*. Æthelred meant noble counsel. Huh! That was a jest! *Unraed* was the more suitable. Ill-counselled.

The King had used the high-running feeling against him as an excuse to spend a few days in the forests of Epping hunting deer – stag hunting, the does were breeding. Instead, his Queen was to escort the chests of silver from the palace to Greenwich, an obvious choice in Æthelred's opinion, as she needed no interpreter to bargain for the release of the Archbishop and they would not harm her, a woman and a half-Dane. If his sending her was thought odd or cowardly, no Londoner remarked upon it. But then, Emma held respect among her people. Æthelred did not.

They had argued, last night, when Æthelred had announced his change of plan; when did they not argue? Emma's contempt for her husband had reached the depths from where there could be no return. To honour a husband there had to be respect. For respect there had to be admiration and trust. Emma had none of either for Æthelred, only disgust for his ineptitude. Did this latest example surprise her? Was it so astonishing that he should prefer to chase deer rather than attempt to procure the release of his Archbishop? The argument had not been about Emma going to Greenwich, although her cnights, and those of the King, had vociferously objected, it had been the mode of transport that had fuelled a furious exchange of words. The collected tax of eight and forty thousand pounds of silver was aboard the King's ship, and Emma had flatly refused to travel downriver on it. Nothing would budge her, not her husband's scorn, entreatment, pleading or rage. Only under circumstances of the direst need would Emma, ever, voluntarily step aboard a ship again. Even if it were just to sail down the relatively calm waterway of the Thames. She had been adamant, the chests were to be loaded on to pack mules; she would ride to Greenwich.

Emma was aware that she looked resplendent as her retinue was admitted through the wide-flung wicker gates of the *í-víking* camp. She rode her favourite mount, the chestnut mare that Pallig had advised her to buy, a horse that had through the years proven her worth to be ten times the amount paid. She was no longer in her prime, but remained spirited, with a proud head carriage and a mettlesome pace, but for all her dancing and snorting, there was no vice in her, she did not buck, bite, or kick, did not pull at the bit or nap away from things she did not wish to go near. She would toss her froth of mane and cavort, her shod hooves striking sparks on cobbled streets or roadway stones, her arched tail held high as she jogged and pranced, her rider sitting erect but at ease, her hands light on the reins. If the effect was deliberately to impress, then it worked as intended.

Thorkell ducked out of his tent to greet the Queen and her guard of cnights, himself dressed in the full armour of a Danish warrior lord, but it was Cnut who stepped forward to help the lady from the saddle.

'We were expecting the King, not a woman,' he said, as he set her to the ground, his eyes looking partially over her shoulder as if expecting to find Æthelred riding behind.

'And I was expecting a man, not a boy,' Emma retorted, giving a dismissive nod of her head as she sidestepped him and walked towards Archbishop Alfheah.

'Do you not know who I am, Madam?' Cnut rebuked as he moved to stand in her path.

Emma stopped, disdainfully looked him up and down. She saw a youth with a hint of blond fluff on his upper lip, his limbs the wrong length for his lanky body, several puss-oozing spots marring his forehead and the side of his nose. His mantle was sable, his woollen tunic an expensive mustard-yellow dye. 'I do not know who you are, nor, if your name is not Thorkell the Tall, do I care to know.'

In turn, Cnut stared at the woman addressing him. She was as tall as he, as lean. She too wore sable, but her gown was a sumptuous forest-green, with an under-tunic of a lighter spring shade. Her wimple a pale, primrose-yellow, a delicate, fine-spun linen and above it, her gold and jewelled crown. Her eyes appeared dark in the shadows of the tents, a hint of gold hair frothing against her forehead, above high, arched eyebrows and features that could have been carved by a master sculptor. She was straight-backed, regal, every inch shouted her elegance.

When I am come king of England, Cnut thought, *this is how I would wish my consort to look.* He shunted aside the unbidden codicil that he would give anything to learn how to brandish this same authority and poise.

He tipped his head, lifting his chin, attempted to copy the detached composure that this woman was radiating. 'I am Cnut, son of Swein Forkbeard.'

'Then it is not you I am interested in,' she answered formidably. 'I speak only to the man at the helm, not his oarsman.'

The words stung. Cnut reddened, but he had the wisdom to hold a retort on his tongue. Thorkell, suppressing a smile, wished he had the ability, and nerve, to put this princeling upstart in his place as easily as this queen had just done.

Turning her attention again towards Alfheah, Emma was appalled at the Archbishop's shameful condition; he was bone-thin and ragged, his skin chafed with weeping sores. She knelt before him, not caring that the ground might muddy her gown, and taking his hands in her own, she kissed the gnarled fingers where his rings would have nestled, had his captors not stolen them. They had left him only his crucifix and that he had found the need to beg for.

'My Lord,' Emma said, concerned, 'they have not treated you well; this is not to be tolerated!' She rounded on Thorkell. 'How dare you, Sir? How dare you treat a gentle, innocent man who has committed you no harm, in deed or intention, with such shame? Where is your honour? Is it as non-existent as your manhood?'

'My honour is as intact as your impertinence, my Lady. Your Archbishop's prolonged captivity is none of my doing; had your King paid our demand before now, he would not have had to endure this delay. Have you brought the extra ransom we demand for his release?'

Indignantly, the Archbishop answered for Emma, 'She has not. I refuse to allow coin to be paid in my name.'

'I have brought the required geld,' Emma confirmed acerbically. 'But you shall receive nothing more, except the damnation of God, should you refuse to release the prelate of Canterbury.' The Archbishop's brave refusal of extra payment was not on the same level as Æthelred's. He had haughtily proclaimed that if Canterbury wanted their Archbishop back, they would have to pay for him themselves. A shaming statement, that had been one of his worst.

'Then I am damned by your God, but I had assumed I am already damned, so I do not have much more to lose, do I?' Thorkell's answer brought a roar of laughter from the gathered onlookers of his Danish army. They stood in groups, some leaning on their axes, others with their swords resting casually over their shoulders.

272

Several had not repressed the gawp of hungry lust that they dribbled at Emma. A few were edging towards the wooden caskets of silver being unloaded from the pack mules.

'We will not allow you to keep our Archbishop. He is to accompany me.'

'No, Lady, not until you pay his ransom. Not unless you care to take his place? I am sure my men would prefer staring at your face to his?'

Curt, Emma turned her back on Thorkell and mounted her mare. Leofstan, who had not moved more than one inch from her side, boosted her into the saddle, then swung on to his own horse, his hand ready at the hilt of his sword, relieved to be leaving this nest of vermin.

Gathering the reins, Emma nudged the chestnut into a walk. She regarded Thorkell disdainfully. 'As I am sure your men, in turn, would elect to live rather than be slain by my English fyrdsmen.'

Thorkell spread his hands, gave her the courtesy of a low bow. 'But the presence of the fyrd, Lady, is as noticeably absent as your husband.'

Emma halted her mare and gazed with loathing at the tall Danishman. 'The King did not come, Sir, because we considered it unworthy for him to concern himself with scum such as you.'

Thorkell raised his eyebrows. 'Yet you came? I am, then, not unworthy of a queen? I am flattered!'

'Then do not be. I came to see for myself how the Archbishop fares and my mare needed the exercise.' She kicked the chestnut into a canter, tossed over her shoulder, her words carrying, still in Danish, into the wind, 'Take your silver, pirate, and take yourself from this land over which I am Queen. Do not harm my Archbishop, for you will pay dearly for his pain, if not by the wrath of my husband then that of mine and God.'

Once through the gates, Emma urged the horse into a flat gallop, her cnights thundering after her, the Viking camp cheering and yelling their aroused excitement.

Impressed, Cnut ran a hand through his hair. 'I thought our warrior women were imposing, but that one . . .!'

273

'She is of Danish blood, what else do you expect?' Thorkell said, watching the riders diminish into the misted distance of the marshes. 'And think on this, if her brother had not married her to Æthelred you might have found her as wife. She is not more than a few years your senior.'

Cnut puffed his cheeks. 'Then glad I am that Æthelred has her – Thor's Hammer, I wonder if her claws are as sharp in bed?'

Hearing, someone called out, good-humoured, 'As I understand it, Æthelred has not the balls to find out!'

The geld had been paid, they could go home. Laughter filled the camp, except from the Archbishop, who retreated into his silent world of contemplative prayer.

Urging the mare faster, heedless of the ground beneath her flying hooves, Emma was thankful that the tears running from her eyes could be accounted for by the sting of the wind. Her wimple had blown askew, and her hair was streaming behind, her heart thundering, body shaking. Never, never had she been so terrified. Those men! The menace, the intimidation, the utter, sickening fear. In all the good names of God, if ever, ever Æthelred made her do such a thing again she would kill him. With her bare hands, if necessary.

52

Late Afternoon

Was that the wind rising? Thorkell raised his head, listening. Odd, there were few trees along these marsh-bound lees, yet it sounded as if a tempest was roaring down through wooded hills. He hoped it was not a storm, for these last few days had been bright with spring sunshine, the warmth coaxing out the budding leaves and spring flowers, bringing a similar warmth to cold bones and flesh. Winter was long and tedious; he had been pleased to see the end of it.

Alfheah murmured the final word to his prayer and, opening his eyes, laid his hands to rest on his lap. The knuckles were swollen, red with the pain of chilblains. These months of captivity had tested his faith almost to its limit; the squalor, the taunting, the isolation of being denied the companionship of his brethren. Gradually he had learnt to trust in his Lord God, realising that this was how Christ must have felt during those forty days alone in the wilderness. The acceptance of his situation had brought a calm, inner sanctity to him, one that lifted his fear of the unknown and brought the word of God louder to his ears. If this was to be the ending of the world, then he was in the hands of his Lord and, with that, he felt privileged and content.

As Thorkell walked past, Alfheah looked up, said in halting Danish, 'I see a self-importance about that boy, one that can only come from the son of a king. I see, also, that you do not like him.'

Thorkell laughed grimly. 'It is not for me to like or dislike him, old man. It is my place to serve.'

In his turn Alfheah laughed, his a lower, more subtle sound. 'I believe that no more than you do, Lord Thorkell. It takes a brave man to admit that his King has forsaken him for an untried boy.'

Derision snorted from Thorkell's nostrils. 'Swein has not forsaken me! What makes you think that? He is delighted with

275

what I have achieved here.' He walked on, intent on inspecting the security of the palisade fence. Unlikely that they were in danger here at Greenwich, for the openness of the marshes and the width of the river was adequate defence, but Thorkell was a commander who never took things for granted and men with beer in their bellies were too capable of shirking given orders.

Alfheah looked about with a puzzled frown, assessing the heaps of rubbish, the sloth, the naked foulness of the camp. 'And what achievement would that be then, Thorkell the Tall?' he asked. 'I see about me no great achievement.'

Cnut, returning with a swaggering stride from the latrine pit, heard his scathing words. He was new to English ways – new to leadership. New, but keen and anxious to learn. His father paid no more than a glancing interest in this green, fertile country, and that interest ran only as far as the amount and availability of silver and gold. He wanted to annex England as part of his growing empire, but only if it could be done with the least effort possible. Cnut thought of England in a different vein, that it would be a suitable kingdom for a boy who had a limited prospect of wearing a crown. That was the drawback if you were a North Man, born as the second son: the eldest inherited all, with precious else left for any younger siblings, unless they used their ingenuity.

'I will achieve what Thorkell will not be able to do,' he called confidently to Alfheah. 'I will make England my own.'

Compassionately Alfheah smiled. 'Not without the Grace of God, you will not, boy. Unless you set aside your heathen ways and embrace the true faith, God and England will never accept you. Without God, you cannot be anointed.'

'That's the trouble with you priests,' Cnut said, irritably striding away in the opposite direction to that of Thorkell. 'You mumble and mutter about your God as if there are no more important issues to concentrate on.'

Alfheah's smile remained unruffled. 'That, my son, is because there are no important issues over God.'

Annoyed that he had been so easily bettered twice in the one day, Cnut strolled down towards the river, to where the men were

276

gathering in noisy excitement. The incoming tide was causing a stir; he looked out at the water, his eyes lighting up with aroused pleasure. Odin's Joy! A bore tide! A high, fast-bowling bore tide! A spectacular surge wave, caused by the tide not swelling by degrees but rolling in, roaring and foaming as if it were an enraged, gape-mouthed sea dragon hurtling up the River Thames. Cnut, as with his fellow Danes, had no idea of the scientific logistics of the natural phenomenon, although as seafaring men they realised the cause to be the combination of the wide shape of an estuary and certain tidal conditions funnelling into a narrowing, shallower channel. The huge wave, as it sped and thundered its passage, heaved up the Thames at a rate of almost thirteen knots and a height of over twenty feet. As it plummeted by, men, whooping and yelling their delight, plunged into its wake, some taking their shields to lie flat upon, enjoying the sensation of tumbling, pounding waves. They were like children enjoying an unexpected holiday.

Cnut, stripping to his skin, jumped in, his exhilarated shouts as loud as any of them. Thorkell, watching from the palisade fence, was thinking on what Alfheah had said.

What achievement? *Ja*, he was right. What achievement?

53

The distant roar of sound from downriver alerted all of London, entreating screams of fear from the women, sending the men running for spears and axes. Had something gone amiss with the payment of tribute? Had the Queen been taken? Killed? Were they under attack? Was this it? Was this the coming of God?

The London militia hurried on to the wooden structure of London Bridge, alert, hearts hammering, weapons tight-held, waiting. If this was it, if this was Thorkell launching a raid . . . aye, well, if it was, they were ready.

Waiting, standing erect on the parapet wall running alongside the Queen's Wharf, Edmund reflected on another of the bitter arguments that last night had, yet again, torn his father and brother apart. Oh, there had been harsh words tossed between them before, words that had sent Athelstan storming from Court and Æthelred into a rage that often lasted for days, but always, eventually, Athelstan had ridden back, apologised, made his peace. Not this time. This last row had flared from bitter disagreement into outright hostility that no regret or apology would erase. Sending a woman to do a man's job, sending the Queen instead of the eldest son? That Athelstan could not, would not, tolerate.

Edmund winced at the ferocity of his brother's wrath. He felt wrenched in two over this, as if he were being dragged each way by straining horses, honour-bound to support his father, but oh, Athelstan was right! It was not Emma's place to deliver the geld – damn it, it ought not be a geld delivered but a full-armed fyrd!

Dismally, Edmund lifted his head, was struck straight in the face by a hammer-thrust rush of wind. Perhaps Thorkell had made further decision for them? If this was the Vikings making their attack . . . men were suddenly laughing, setting their weapons aside, thumping each other on the back, linking arms to dance in crazy circles. Edmund, too, grinned, released the tied straps of his war cap. What idiots! It was the bore! Only the bore tide! More than one of the London men, standing there or already turning to make his way home, felt a tinge of embarrassment on his cheeks. Mind, that showed how much of a dither London was in, how sense and everyday practicality had been swept aside by the presence of those heathens encamped at Greenwich. London had become as twitchy as a flea-riddled dog!

The women and children were coming out, running down to the wharves, their faces excited, frightened, in awe, as the great wave surged against the wooden pillars of the bridge, the water gushing through the man-made arches. London Bridge was solid-built, soundly constructed and kept in good repair, fire being its only enemy, but even so, those out on it clutched at the railings, or at each other, grim-faced, momentarily worried. It had shuddered, shrugged almost, as the tidal monster had passed, roaring and slavering, underneath.

Edmund laughed with the rest of them, a laugh of relief, then glancing at the shore where the after-waves were crashing and rippling, he cursed. Shouldering his way through the crush he began to shout, waving his spear, pointing, but no one heard above the din of excited, chattering voices. His stepbrothers had come into London with him from Thorney and had, when the alarm had been raised, been left, with strict orders to stay inside, at Edmund's favourite tavern. Godwine was supposed to be keeping an eye on them. Where was he? Angrily, fear heightening his temper, Edmund lashed out at someone, striking him round the face to urge him to move aside. Those stupid boys were down on the shoreline, jumping in and out of the waves, damn fools! Where in Hell was Godwine?

It had been Alfred's idea. The ideas were always Alfred's, even though he was only in his sixth year. Edward, a year older, did not have ideas as bold as Alfred's, but somehow he was always the one whipped twice as hard when they went wrong. As they usually did.

'Come on!' Alfred shouted as he jumped over another incoming wave, soaking himself further. He was already wet through from head to foot, so what did it matter? 'Try it! This is fun!'

Alfred had been the one wanting to come down into London. Edward would have been quite content to have remained at Thorney Island. The monks were practising the singing of a new psalm, he would have liked to have sat and listened, but no, Alfred wanted to come to London with Edmund. And what Alfred wanted, Alfred usually got. Edward did not like Alfred, he was only young, but already he realised that his brother was a troublemaker who had no realisation of the meaning of fear.

'When I grow up I am going to be England's greatest warrior!' Alfred often boasted. Edward had abandoned answering that it was the other Alfred, his brother's namesake, who already had claim to that title. As he had also abandoned answering what he wanted to be when he grew up. An archbishop.

'Don't be silly,' Alfred had taunted with that scathing harshness that only children could appropriate. 'You are going to be the king, you cannot be archbishop as well.'

Caution always rallied Edward not to reply that he did not want to be king, as no one seemed to like the present one, and being king meant strutting about shouting at people. Edward did not like shouting. In fact, there was not much that Edward did like, except the singing of the monks in church. Particularly, he did not like water, especially not this angry, boiling and churning River Thames. Bad enough to go out on it in a ship or coracle – but this! To step into this raging madness? Ah no!

'Come on!' Alfred repeated, 'if you don't join in I'll ask God to set Thorkell the Tall on you!'

What was worse? That evil, yellow-eyed monster Thorkell, or this rampaging river? Edward hesitated, took a tentative step forward, slipped and fell beneath the echo of the surge tide, a wave slurping over him, covering him and rolling him several yards upstream. He tried to scream, to shout for help. Water bubbled into his mouth, choking him. He could not see, could not hear . . . something had hold of him, was dragging him, trawling him like a fisherman's net. Edward had seen men drown, a vision he vividly remembered. He had been four years old and a ship had run aground in a storm. He could not remember the location, but he could still see the men crying for help, the ship breaking into pieces, the waves gulping and gnashing, eating the thing up as a dog rips and tears at a hare or wild fowl.

The sun hit Edward's face, something, someone was pounding his back. He felt sick, scrabbled forward on to hands and knees and vomited up the contents of his stomach. Beyond his watering eyes, Edmund's boots swam into view. The boy looked up at the tall, angry man, who stood with his hands on his hips.

Aye, Alfred's ideas always went wrong and were always blamed on Edward.

54

Cross-legged and deep in thought, Cnut sat before the fire, poking at the glow of burning wood with a stick. He watched its end catch light and the flames lick up the shaft, then tossed it into the heat. Watched it burn.

The men were feasting, eating and drinking their fill – there had been a special raid yesterday, taking three of the ships up the Lea river as far as the small Waltham monastery to acquire provisions. Dusk had barely settled, but already most of them were drunk. They were going home; mayhap not tomorrow, nor the next day, but soon. Very soon. When the Archbishop's ransom had been dealt with.

Prodding a log with the toe of his boot, Cnut shifted his backside more comfortable. 'What do you think of Thorkell?' he asked his father's friend, Erik Håkonsson, who had accompanied him from Denmark. 'Will he remain loyal?'

Erik was picking at a strand of meat caught between his teeth, alternately worrying at it with his tongue and fingernail. 'Thorkell is a good leader,' he answered, non-committal.

'That I grant. That my father grants, but will he remain a good leader?' The question had been nagging at Cnut these last few days, had grown stronger with the onrush of today's events, and he was not going to be sidestepped from an answer. 'My father', Cnut added, selecting another, stouter, stick to riddle the fire, 'is concerned that Thorkell is becoming,' he paused, considered, 'distracted.' He looked across the river at the empty marshes on the south bank that were turning dull and grey, now that the day's colour had gone. He was missing home, missing the deep, blue fjords that reflected every shadow of colour. It was too flat, too empty, here in this part of England. Too endlessly lonely.

'I would rather be sitting in a suitable Hall, on a comfortable stool, than here in this wilderness,' he confided.

'We sit here because here has a twofold advantage,' Erik pointed out. 'We cannot be attacked without foreknowledge of an army's approach, nor can London function efficiently as a trading town. Thorkell has tied a band tight round the vein that carries the lifeblood to Æthelred's heart.'

'There is more of a restlessness in Thorkell than in the men. For him, it is not the longing to return home, but something else. He is like a man who knows he has forgotten something important, but cannot remember what.'

Erik nodded in satisfaction as the meat came away. 'He has not been the same since hearing of his wife's death. It is a sorry thing for a man to lose one woman to childbirth, to lose a second . . . *ja* well, it must be hard.'

Cnut shrugged, dismissive. 'Women are easily found to warm a bed at night. It cannot be that which troubles him.'

The older man grunted laughter, as he slid another chunk of roasting lamb off the spit. He juggled it between his fingers, bit tentatively, the hot juice running down his chin. 'You have a lot to learn about women, then, boy,' he said, talking with his mouth open: the meat was scalding, hot on his tongue. 'There is the type of woman you love for your need and the type you need because of your love. The two are not the same and only the fortunate manage to find the second. Most of us have to make do with the first.'

Scornful, Cnut sneered a wry face. 'Love? Where does love come into it? A man takes a woman for passion. A wife is for the bearing of his children, for the cooking of his meals, running of his household and weaving his clothes.'

Erik sorrowfully shook his head. 'Ah, the innocence of youth! One day, lad, your eyes will light upon a woman and you will never forget that glint in her eye, that toss of her head, or sway of her hips. You will dream of her, whether you are asleep or awake. She will possess your mind and your body will be on fire for her. Nothing will ever erase the linger of her scent in your nostrils, the touch of her hand on your body, the feel of her flesh beneath your fingers.' Erik sucked the bone, tossed it aside and reached for another portion. The raiding had been good. 'When you find a woman to love, your life changes for ever.'

Busying himself with chewing a lump of gristle from his own chunk of lamb, Cnut had an excuse not to answer. Before today he would have told Erik he was talking the ale words of drunken speech. Before today he thought of women either as suitable for bedding, or did not think of them at all. *That glint in her eye, that toss of her head . . .*

'I will have no choice of wife,' he said after a moment. 'My father will want a useful alliance. My fortune will be that she does not have too many rotting teeth, foul breath and carries the pox.' There was a girl he had seen last Yule, a daughter of the Prince of Kiev. One year his junior, hair that was so fair it was almost silver, a slender, willow figure, a shy smile from bright blue eyes. He would eagerly have agreed marriage to her.

'Æthelred must have the brain of a mule to not value the woman he has as wife.' He said it quietly, offhand, as he concentrated on pulling a strip of meat from the bone.

'Emma of Normandy? She was a fine match, but as you say, this English King has wasted her advantages.'

'Thorkell said I might have had her as wife, had circumstances been different.'

Erik chuckled. 'At least she smells sweet, although I believe she can breathe fire on occasion!'

Ah, forget her! She was another's wife, a crowned queen. She could not be his. Cnut swilled his mouth with ale. 'She reminds me, in some ways, of a Kiev princess I met.'

'I am not a *scop*, a keeper of the oral records, so I do not know the certainty of it, but, *ja*, she would. Their mothers are distant kindred.'

That explained the similarity of the eyes, with the English Queen.

'She is pretty, this princess?' Erik asked it as a question, half hesitant, not wanting to pry.

284

'Some would think so,' Cnut answered casually, then grinned. 'I would think so.'

'Then I suggest you mention her to your father. Alliance with Kiev could be a judicious move. You may have to consider a Christian commitment before any approach can be made, though. They are as much God worshippers in Kiev as they are here in England.'

Cnut glared across at the Archbishop and Thorkell sitting beside him, deep in conversation. He would like to have believed that his father's commander was trying to persuade the old man to sanction a paid ransom. Had a gut feeling that he was not.

'That is one thing I have learnt in my short life,' he observed. 'There is always a snag where women are concerned.'

Erik, an older and wiser man, chuckled agreement.

The ale-skins were being brought round again; both Cnut and Erik raised their tankards for refills, laughing and jesting with the serving women. Oh, they had women with them, these roving armies, no mercenary would last more than a week without the whore camp for company and comfort. Some of them had followed from Denmark, others were Anglo-Danish or Anglo-Saxon. A whore plied her trade wherever there was a living to be made and a winter-camped army provided good pickings. Especially once the geld had been paid and distributed.

Confidentially, Cnut said, 'Father is concerned that Thorkell is no longer as devoted to his King's cause as once he was. Watching him, I too have my doubts.' To ease the sting, for he was not fully certain on which side of the ship Erik preferred to row, added, 'I think he is considering turning away from the old gods, is looking to this Christian Jesu.'

Erik shrugged. 'There are plenty who are devoted Christians who love your father, Cnut. Swein's sister, Gunnhilda, among them.' He gave a lopsided grin, 'Although she never ceased attempting to convert him fully from his divided faith. He pretended to believe in the White God for her sake, but once she was gone, well, her God had not lifted a finger to save her, even though she sought the sanctuary of a church, so why pursue it?'

285

Erik had found Thorkell to be a capable and formidable commander, and was uncertain why Cnut should be doubting him. Jealousy perhaps? It was possible: Swein had always held great respect and admiration for Thorkell; if a boy was trying to shine, he would have to eclipse the brighter star first. Thorkell was a man of honour, but honour could always be shifted if a deeper conviction overturned it. Had he converted to Christianity? If he had, was there any reason to suppose he would consider deserting Swein? Erik thought not. Not without good cause. Would a lack of king-given praise be reason? At the least, Thorkell had expected his King to offer him the regency of England once it fell into Danish control, but no, here was Cnut, come to preen over what he wanted. A king only retained his men if he could hold their unyielding loyalty clenched tight in his hand. If that loyalty should turn into sour vinegar, then it would trickle away like a handful of cupped water.

55

Was it the exhilaration of the bore tide, the receipt of the geld, or the longing for the open sea and the thought of home? Perhaps it was nothing more than the cumulative strength of a fine brew of ale. Whatever reason, the Danish *í-víkings* were more drunk than usual that April night. The air was clear, the sky full to bursting with stars; the many fires sending sparks crackling from dry timber, leaping up into the darkness.

Laughter from one of the groups, movement, as a man rose to stagger a short way into the darkness to relieve himself. Returning, had to pass the Archbishop's shelter. Out of habit, he tossed a defamatory curse at him. Alfheah, intent on prayer, ignored the taunt.

'Damn you, does nothing stir you from that odious piety?' He aimed a kick at Alfheah and, in his drunken stupor, missed and stubbed his toe on a water bucket, sending the thing tumbling. His comrades, lazing beside the fire, roared their laughter, and grumbling, the man sat, drank more ale and helped himself to a rib of beef, sizzling in the heat. Glancing at Alfheah he complained, 'Bloody man makes my flesh crawl.'

'They're all like that, these Christian monks,' observed the man opposite, as he wiped grease from his mouth, unconsciously spreading it into his thick, lice-riddled beard. 'It's because they have no balls.'

'Figuratively or literally?' someone else quipped.

'Both, I reckon,' answered the first man. 'They shrivel up with all that kneeling on the floor to pray.'

'Is that why they all sing so sweetly?' asked another.

'*Ja*, high-pitched, like little boys!'

Alfheah, had he chosen to listen, would have heard every word.

Did these imbeciles not understand the power of God when He entered your soul?

'Was this Christ a eunuch also?' someone asked.

'Well, he didn't have the guts to fight – all that turn the other cheek nonsense! How are men supposed to earn the reward of eternal honour by loving thy neighbour?'

'I love my neighbour' – the conversation had returned to the first man – 'she's got teats like a new-farrowed sow! Wasted on her dotard of a husband. I see she's well suckled, though!'

The bore tide of earlier in the day had roused a feeling of exuberance, sending a thrill coursing through the men as if the surge of water had stirred a great, restless need. Many were talking of going home, a few had even made ready their belongings. Such was the way of things with a fickle mercenary army. The ripple had swelled as the afternoon had grown older and became a persistent rustling by nightfall. No one spoke any intention aloud, but they were leaving, this was the last feast in England until they next returned.

Thorkell had sensed the restlessness as the men had leapt and cavorted in the rushing tide; no words, no gestures, it was like scenting rain coming in on the wind. They were tired, homesick; the geld had been delivered, there was no reason to fight for there was nothing more to take. He had talked a while with Alfheah, but found no answers to his questions and had returned to the solitude of his hearth. Picking over his own meat bone, he sat silent, watching the horseplay. Normally, he would have been laughing with them, enjoying the sharp exchanged wit, the jesting. Not this night. Why did he feel so remote? Because there was nothing of worth to go back to? Only an empty house and cold graves?

He tossed the bone into the fire, watched as the fat hissed and spat. Why could they not leave the English priest alone? It was not as if they were all Odin's men, several among them were Christian. Ah, but then that was Danish Christianity, faith packaged in a different cut of cloth. It had been a mistake taking the Archbishop as prisoner, Thorkell realised. The old man had been right, earlier, nothing had been achieved, except that his quiet dignity had stirred

Thorkell's interest. He had expected him to preach and attempt to convert his captors; to declare that woe would come upon them, the wrath of God, the evils of all that was bad and dark in the world, but he had not. He had sat there, day after day, calm, content in his meditation and prayer, impervious to the outer world. The men this night, were, as often they did, jeering at him, their ribaldry growing noisier, and Thorkell, sitting there watching, realised suddenly how much he admired the English monk. It took courage to believe, to truly, unwaveringly, believe.

On impulse, Thorkell made his decision. What had this man to do with them? There was enough grief to bear without punishing those who were guilty of nothing more than belief. He set his legs under himself, making to rise, was halfway up when it began.

'Want a bone to suck?' that first man jeered at Alfheah. Cackling, excited, he tossed a rib bone at him, an idle throw, not especially aimed, but it hit the Archbishop on the cheek, its sharp edge cutting the flesh, immediately drawing blood.

'Good throw – I'd wager you could not do it again!'

Another bone, another hit. Thorkell leapt forward, angry, his arms waving. 'Stop that!' he yelled. 'Where is your respect?'

No one listened, no one heard. Men were on their feet, flinging the remains of their meal, tossing anything that came to hand. Rib bones, chop bones, leg bones, lumps of gristle. Stones.

'Stop it I say!' Thorkell was shouting, stepping close to the Archbishop, attempting to bat aside the missiles, taking several injuries to his own face and hands.

Cnut was there, on the outskirts, cheering and applauding any good throw. 'Leave it, Thorkell,' he shouted, 'come away!'

Hemming, glaring at the boy for not attempting to stop the indiscipline, ran to his brother's side, shielding his face with an upraised arm, grabbed at him and forcefully dragged him beyond the circle of men and the flickering firelight. 'What in the name of sense are you doing, Thorkell? Leave them, they are drunk, beyond reasoning with!'

Blood dripping from a cut eyebrow and lacerations to his cheeks, Thorkell stared blankly at his younger brother. 'They do not obey me,' he said, baffled. 'If men do not obey me, then am I finished?'

Alfheah knelt in the centre of the menacing circle, his head lifted, hands clasped together and lips moving in prayer. 'Yea, though I walk through the valley of the shadow of death, I will fear no evil.'

A leg bone struck his shoulder, he half toppled, steadied himself. Continued praying.

'I cannot let this continue!' Thorkell bellowed, again trying to dodge in to protect the old man, but his brother grasped his arm, roughly swung him aside. 'Leave it! If you try to stop this, with the mood they're in they will turn on you too!'

'. . . For Thine is the kingdom, the power, and the glory.'

Shouting, jeering, laughing. Cnut, a grin on his face, relishing the frenzy of blood-rush enjoyment. Thorkell aghast, impotent.

A single, gasped cry. Abrupt silence.

Shrugging his brother off, Thorkell shouldered through the men, hauling and kicking, punching them aside, though they parted easily, now it was all over.

Alfheah lay sprawled, dead. His mouth open, his hands clasped. A knee joint, a great ox bone, larger than a clenched fist, beside him, the blood and hair and bone of an old man's shattered skull clinging stickily to it.

The circle of men fell silent, those holding bones, things they had been about to throw, surreptitiously dropped them, let them fall. The outer circle already melting away into the night, the rest shuffling, coughing, clearing throats. Ashamed.

Thorkell touched the oozing blood, eased aside a lock of matted hair. Lifted the dead man. He was so light, so frail, there was nothing of him, it was as if Thorkell held a sparrow in his arms. He looked up at the sullen men, tears streaming from his eyes.

'What heroes have I fought with these months? Men? Warriors? I see none of such before me, only cowards who have no shame, men so weak they must show their feeble strength in the killing of an old and defenceless man.'

Cnut ambled forward, the light of the fires illuminating the slim features of his youthful face, shining on his blue eyes and fair hair. 'You speak as if you have no respect for us, Thorkell. We are men of the í-víking, none shall call us coward to our faces.' A few murmurs of assent from the younger men; the older ones remained silent.

Carrying the dead man, Thorkell walked up to Swein's second-eldest son, stood before him. 'When it comes to murder such as this then I have no respect and I call you all coward.'

He shouldered through the circle, paused at the outer edge, his brother Hemming joining him, his face also grey-grim. 'You wish to become a king?' Thorkell said to Cnut. 'Well, there is more to being a lord than the killing of the old and weak. A king must know of his responsibilities and be a father to all who look to him for protection and justice. A king must know right from wrong, for if he does not, how can he govern the laws of his kingdom?'

'Nor can a king afford to dwell on his conscience, Thorkell, for if he did, he would never be more than a stomachless weakling.' With a sneer Cnut added, 'Like Æthelred.'

Dipping his head by way of a leave-taking, Thorkell turned, walked away towards the river and his ship, called, as he went into the darkness, 'You speak right, my Lord Prince, a king cannot dwell on his conscience, but a loved king will have an understanding of the word compassion. A hated king will not.'

Thorkell sailed with the turn of the flood tide; those who had not taken part in the blood-surge, and who had felt sickened by its doing, going with him. As the bows of the ships turned with the altering current and the pull of the river began to take command, they slipped the oars, raised sail and departed upriver towards London.

Deliberate, standing tall and straight beside the steerboard, Thorkell turned his back on the old gods, on Denmark, his King and the boy Cnut. He wanted no more of it, the killing of the innocent and the gratification of that poxed whore-master, greed. He did not know how he was to accomplish it, but he was determined to take the battered body of a devout, brave and honourable man to his people and somehow, somehow, make amends.

When the tide had turned again and had ebbed downriver,

Greenwich was deserted, only the trampled grass and detritus of occupation remained. Few of the men following the tide home felt no shame at what they had done. As Thorkell had said, there was nothing to boast of in the drunken killing of an old man.

Cnut, standing alone, feet wide-planted on the deck of his ship, felt the anger at the snub that Thorkell had made to him. He was a king's son. No one so deliberately insulted him. Not even when the insults were justified and were the truth.

56

Tempers were flaring high between two fathers and their sons on opposite shores of the cold, grey North Sea. Cnut and Edmund would have been surprised to discover that they were both arguing on the same side of the fence over the proposed marriage of the daughter of a dead English ealdorman. Swein of Denmark was irritated with the unhelpful attitude of his second son, Cnut, and Æthelred had been raging for most of the afternoon about his ingrate of an eldest-born.

'I cannot allow Thorkell to thrust his fist up my arse,' Swein exclaimed, exasperated. 'His deserting me to aid the English was an insult I cannot tolerate or allow. I thought you understood that, Cnut? He has deprived me of five and forty ships and crew, his experience and loyalty; has made me into a laughing stock.' Nor could Swein permit Thorkell to become Æthelred's military commander, for if the English found themselves a capable leader, they just might decide to make a fight of things. And win.

'That I understand,' Cnut answered, his hands spread, palms upwards, pleading. 'What I do not understand is why I have to wed this prawn-faced English girl!'

Swein swung away, his head bowed between his clasping hands. 'Woden's Beard, boy, but I thought you had intelligence? Have I nurtured a simpleton all these years?' Abruptly he took hold of his son's upper arms, shook him, his mind half registering that the lad, at one month short of seventeen, was already taller than himself. 'Alfhelm was murdered because I approached him with an offer of alliance. The Danelaw, even at that juncture, was weary of Æthelred's ineptitude.' He gave another, lighter, shake, said, trying to explain, 'It is an odd thing, son, but if a king rules for too long, his people grow bored with him. It is as if they have been rowing in the same direction, at the same speed, in the same conditions for year after year. All they have is dry biscuits for food and brackish water to drink. They want something different. A change of tack, to hoist sail, make landfall, anything. They need meat for dinner, ale in their tankards. Æthelred has been King of England for four and thirty years. Four and thirty *years*, boy! That is a damned long time to become as expertly useless as he has.'

Cnut thrust his father aside. 'I am not an idiot, Father, I am quite aware of the English situation. I realise that you are anxious to win these northern lords to your side by faith and trust, rather than by strength and killing – what I cannot comprehend is why does it have to be Alfhelm's daughter? He is dead. His sons are blinded, they do not hold any power or use for us. What good will Ælfgifu be to me?'

At least Swein was honest with his cynical reply. 'To you? Apart from pleasure in bed and a possible brood of sons, none at all.' He lifted his head slightly, said to a man hurrying from the wharf, '*Ja? What is it?*'

'We've found the leak, Lord. There is a patch the size of my fist that is rotten on the steerboard-side keel.'

Swein pursed his lips, further annoyed, as he stared down towards the fjord and the ship hauled on to the ice-hardened shore, her underside exposed to the scrutiny of the shipbuilders. The *Sea Serpent*, Swein's favourite dragon ship. She should not have required repair so soon after her building.

'I reckon the damage was done when she got scraped on those rocks last autumn. We were lucky not to have holed her.'

'Can you repair the patch or will the whole of the planking need to be replaced?' Damn! With only two weeks until Swein's plan to sail, weather permitting, this could cause an annoying delay. He could use a different ship, but since her launching he always sailed in the *Sea Serpent*, did not like to tempt Fate by using a sister ship.

'I think I can repair it, my Lord. If I start early tomorrow, it should not take more than a few days, the week at the most.'

Swein grinned, relieved. 'If you have her seaworthy by Thor's Day there will be an extra bag of silver in it for you.'

Saluting, the man hurried away, scowling up at the evening sky as he made rapid mental calculation. If he assembled his tools and searched for the right piece of wood straight away, he could make a start at first light.

Cnut, too, was squinting upwards. A crescent moon was glowing pale silver and the Evening Star sparkled, bright against the clear sky. Snow lay in deep rifts up on the higher ground and in the shadowed hollows. Some parts of the fjord, too, where the weak sunlight could not penetrate, were rimmed by ice. He loved the smell of Denmark. Crisp and intoxicating, the cold air rammed up your nostrils and hurtled into your brain, making you feel vibrant and alive. He would miss all this when they went to England. Miss it because he knew he might never come back, not after his father had his final victory over Æthelred, as he would, very soon.

A bell began to clang from the outer rafter of the wooden chapel further along the shoreline. Vespers, was it? Or was that a later service? He could not remember. A handful of Roskilde inhabitants came scurrying from the warmth of their houses, hooded cloaks drawn tight, five, six families? More women than men. Cnut sniggered, this Christ was a soft-bellied woman's God, fit only for virgins, eunuchs and peasants to worship. What was the attraction, then? Why had a warrior like Thorkell so suddenly deserted everything and everyone he valued, to have himself immersed in holy water and baptised into the family of this Christian God? All for the sake of an old monk who had done nothing but mumble and mutter prayers, and had been accidentally killed by an over-lively group of drunken men? Unease shifted uncomfortable in his conscience. A king could not afford to have a conscience, he had said that night. But what of leadership? Compassion? Duty? Without those, of what use was a king?

'To you, Son, this Ælfgifu will be nothing more than a concubine. When you are King of England in my stead,' Swein, unaware of his son's thought, held up one warning finger, 'and mark my word well, I do not intend that to be for many years yet, so do not be tempted to think much on it too soon – *when* you are eventually king, you will need a more fitting wife, a daughter of

295

another king or prince at the very least. For now, you must wed this northern girl because I need the lords of the English Danelaw to take the crown from Æthelred and put it on my head instead.'

To do that, he needed to show the North that he intended to replace Æthelred as king, ease the burden of exorbitant taxes, bring peace and respect for law and justice all at the one time. He almost had them, but the best, surest, way to capture a wild animal was to lure it in with tempting bait. Go slowly, slowly, make no sudden movements, speak calm, croon; offer comfort not fear or pain. Eventually it would come round.

'When we land in England, we must be certain that we will not face hostility. I have given assurances that if I am not hindered, not a farmsteading, not a man, woman or child, shall be harmed. Not one sheep or cow shall be butchered without fair payment; no hayrick shall be fired, no barn pulled down. We want to be welcomed with open arms. I want that crown secure on my head before my feet leave the deck of my ship. To do that it is imperative that I give the lords an assurance of my honour. I once made agreement of intermarriage with Alfhelm of Deira, I intend to show that my agreements hold good. By doing so I am making a statement both to Æthelred and his ealdormen, that I support, and have full sympathy with, the family of a wrongly and unjustifiably murdered Englishman. For that alone the North will flock to me.'

'You want a lot. What about what I want?' Cnut was turning sullen, his bottom lip pouting. 'I may not want to become King of England after you. You are assuming my elder brother will become King of Denmark, what if I want that crown for myself?'

Swein choked down amusement. 'You will have to take it from him first!'

'I could do that easily, with one hand tied behind my back!'

Swein did not doubt it, but he did not say so aloud. Cnut, for all that he was the younger of the two sons, showed the better promise as a warrior and a leader. Swein was proud of him. He did not say that aloud, either.

'I do not want Ælfigu, Alfhelm's daughter, as wife, a princess of Kiev will make a better queen.'

Swein tipped his head back and laughed, 'You aim high, boy! The Rus, Vladimir, Grand Prince of Kiev, is a powerful man.' He set his arm firmly along his son's shoulders and steered him towards the welcome of warmth that glowed from the inside of the royal Hall. 'If that is all that bothers you, lad, then it is easily settled. As Prince of Denmark you take the Kiev girl as wife, as the future king of England, you take Ælgifu as concubine. Once crowned in England, you set her aside and take your legal wife as your English queen.'

Petulant, Cnut countered, 'But I may prefer to have the one wife. I might turn fully to Orthodox Christianity, as you so often urge me.'

Swein guffawed. 'That you would have to if you want the Rus's daughter for wife! He is foot in boot with that pious Byzantine emperor, Basil.' Swein shrugged. 'Should you decide to embrace the Christ, it would give you adequate excuse to divorce Alfhelm's daughter when it suits. It is a damn silly thing to jeopardise my conquest of England just because you prefer one woman over another, though, boy.'

Glowering, Cnut allowed himself to be seated before the blaze of the fire, took the ale his father placatingly offered. 'And, of course,' he said sullenly, 'if I were to wed this Ælfgifu, it would bring you the benefit of no uncertain amount of gold as dowry from her grateful mother.'

Conceding the argument, Swein grinned. 'Well, ja, there is that to it also.'

57

'You must investigate the rumour of this marriage,' Emma insisted. 'If you allow it, it will constitute outright rebellion, a declaration of civil war.'

Æthelred, already halfway across the Hall, heading for the sanctuary of his private chamber, continued walking. It would not be sensible for him to abandon Council like this, but then, it would not be sensible for him to put his hands either side of his wife's throat in front of these snivelling few Southerners.

Apart from Eadric Streona, bless the man, he was always loyal, was always there whatever the trouble, not one single ealdorman had come to Court – not even Uhtred and Ulfkell, married to his own daughters! God rot them! God rot them all! There were no bishops, no thegns, no reeves or merchantmen. No one except the eminent men of Winchester, and they were here for the Queen, damn them, and Wulfstan. And he had only come out of duty to the Church, not to Æthelred, to lecture on God's punishment to them all.

'If Athelstan has something to say to me, boy,' Æthelred sniped at Edmund as he passed him, 'then let him come tell it to my face, not relay messages through that harpy I am wedded to.'

He carried on walking, but Edmund was striding after him, boldly grabbed his father's arm. 'My brother has sent word to you out of love for England and his duty as ætheling. He can not pretend he has not heard through his informers what is being planned, or ignore it as none of his business, as do you.'

Æthelred shook his son's hand off, brushed at his sleeve as if a dirt stain had been left there. 'His informants?' he hissed. 'Informants? Those sly dog turds who have gone against me? Those snivelling pig-shit wallowers, the brothers Sigeferth and Morcar?

They are not informants, they are traitors. If they truly cared that Swein Forkbeard intends to wed his son with that scum family of Alfhelm, then they would be here,' he pointed at his feet, 'here in Winchester in my King's Hall, planning our Council of War.' He thrust his face close to Edmund's, the sneer as ugly as a boar's snout. 'You want to be a warrior, Edmund? If you can do something about this absurd marriage alliance, then you – and her – deal with it.' He flung his hand towards Emma, who had remained, exasperated, on her Queen's chair on the dais. 'And for good measure, you can ask your new friend, Thorkell, to help.' Contemptuously, he spat in the direction of the Dane.

'My Lord King, I have no intention . . .' Thorkell began placatingly.

'No, Sir, nor have I.' Æthelred marched through the door, slamming it shut; rammed the bolts home.

Emma spread her hands. 'Such is the English way of a war council. The King loses his temper because he is in the wrong and he stamps off like a spoilt child.'

'That, Madam, given the public occasion of this calling of Council,' Eadric Streona chided with a frown of disapproval, 'is disrespectful to our Lord King.'

'He is my husband, Streona, I am entitled to be as disrespectful to him as I please.' Council? This was more like a mercers' meeting called on a pagan feasting night – only those few who preferred the martyrdom of a public display of Christian piety over an indulgence of ale and women attending.

Edmund sat, slapped his hands to his thighs in despair. 'Without the King's word in this we will not be able to summon out the fyrd. My brother tried it once, if you recall. He found a handful of men who had a taste for adventure. They supported him for all of three weeks.' He dropped his chin into his cupped palm. Was defeat so easy to accomplish, so hard to accept?

'If I may suggest?' The Dane, Thorkell, unfolded his height from where he had been leaning against the wall.

Emma stared at him with a frozen glare of ice. She detested him even more than she did her husband and Eadric Streona put together. From the day that Thorkell had stepped off his craft, his men showing hands empty of weapons, clutching only at green branches to show they came in peace, Emma could not bring herself to trust him. Why, was as difficult for her to understand as the question of why Edmund liked him. So he had brought Archbishop Alfheah's bloody and battered body to London for Christian burial, had done public penance and stood at the edge of the Thames river for baptism into the Christian faith. Did his attendance at Mass, his gifts to the Church, his diligent reading of the Bible, make him any less the murderer he was? Or was it that she disliked him because he was better than any of them? Because he was a man who was prepared to give up everything he had for personal honour?

'Yes, Sir,' Edmund asked the Dane, respectfully, ignoring Eadric Streona's scowl, 'what would you advise?'

Thorkell shrugged. 'To summon out the fyrd and march on Northampton. Cut out the pus before it sends the wound putrid. Cnut Sweinsson cannot be permitted to make alliance with this young woman, Ælfgifu. Once his father has a means to come into England without risk, then all will be lost. Allow a dog to snap once at its master's hand and next time it will bite and draw blood.'

'And what if Athelstan's information proves incorrect? What fools we will look?'

'Better fools than if you do not,' Thorkell answered simply.

'It is for the King to order out the armies. And the King believes his eldest son to be deliberately trouble seeking.' Eadric Streona had never been respected for his political or military sense. Indeed, there were many who doubted he possessed a featherweight of either.

'So,' Emma said, 'we sit here and play with our finger rings while Swein Forkbeard sails his ships into the Humber, marries his son to Alfhelm's plain daughter and calmly receives the submission of the North?'

Ælfgifu, the girl who had been intended, in her mother and father's eyes, for Æthelred and then, when that idea failed, for Athelstan. It seemed Lady Godgifa still wanted a crown for the snivelling bitch. Emma rose from her seat, began walking towards her own chamber. 'And my brother once thought there would be great advantage in marrying me into England? Remind me to ask him, one day, what he thought that advantage to be, for I am damned if I can decide what it is.'

58

This, then, was the horror of reality; now that it was actually here on her doorstep, Emma found it hard to comprehend. Had no one in all England dared to stand up to Swein Forkbeard? Had no one even so much as thrown a clod of earth to stop him? In the North, the Danish lords, she could understand it, for despite all their protestations, many of them remembered their Scandinavian heritage and had a justifiable grudge against Æthelred. But the South? Surrey, Sussex, Wessex? Her own Winchester? Why had they all given in so easily to Denmark? That hurt, Winchester's capitulation hurt like a gaping wound in her side, leaving an ache of despair. She could feel, now, why Æthelred had winced on hearing that Oxford-Shire had submitted; the pain had not been entirely for the loss of a shire, but for where the submissions had occurred. At Woodstock, Æthelred's favoured palace.

She glanced across at Eadric Streona who sat attentive to a board game with her husband – as if this was a suitable occasion to be playing *taefl*! Eadric had not lifted a finger to rouse the Shires of Mercia, claiming that he could not, that opinion ran too much against him, that if he called up an army it would be all too easy for the men to turn against him. Huh, he had done all the running! Once Swein had marched south from his base at Gainsborough, Streona had fled to the safety of the Court without waiting to lift his axe from its wall bracket. Of course no one rallied or fought! Who was there to lead them?

'You look troubled, my Lady. Can I be of service?'

Emma swung her head, gazed with loathing at Thorkell. Said nothing. Swein Forkbeard, having made rapid progress up the Winchester road, was a handful of miles from London. The rest of England, apart from the south-west, had capitulated to him. Only

London held for the King – and this Dane deserter had the gall to call himself Æthelred's friend?

'The King shall not allow harm to come to you,' Thorkell said, attempting to alleviate her concern, guessing it was that which bothered her. She had a pale, drawn face and fear startled her eyes. She looked tired, defeated. He felt sorry for her; it was hard to be a woman trapped in the peculiarities of a man's world.

Emma could not resist, too long, the given opportunity of a barbed answer. 'Which king do you mean, Traitor Man? Æthelred or Swein?'

Thorkell spread his hands, accepted her sardonicism. 'We have some of England's best fighting men here with us in London. My men are also experienced warriors and your husband's cnights, if used correctly, are no less formidable. Nor will Swein be contemplating a prolonged siege. London is not an easy city to bring down.'

She would not be drawn into further conversation. From an attacker's view, a siege was only undesirable if there was a possibility of counter-attack. With England declared for Swein, who was there to threaten him? Æthelred was finished and they all knew it. Those here at Court, Swein, and England.

Thorkell sighed, hooked a stool nearer and sat, ignoring the fact that the Queen had not given him permission. 'I fear you blame me for all this. If it were not for my deserting Swein's service, he would not have come to claim his honour rights.'

Emma snorted. 'You think this is because of you? You harbour grand deception, Sir! This is my husband's achievement alone. Were he not such an accomplished incompetent, we would not be in this situation.'

'Harsh words, Madam.'

'Accurate.' Ironic, she added, 'Aside, I thought God was responsible for changing your allegiance? Must we, therefore, blame God for this mess also?'

Thorkell chuckled. 'I would assume Archbishop Wulfstan would have stout recrimination against that theory. No, King Swein is a proud man, as are all kings. He would not have easily accepted the news of my desertion. My conscience obviously outweighs his. I will not serve with those who think it entertaining sport to pelt a holy man to death with animal bones. Nor will I serve those who condone it.'

'Although you are content to serve a man who is happy to accept the conquest of his entire realm without the slightest attempt to prevent it? And should you not have examined your squeamishness before taking our Archbishop prisoner?' Emma was terse, deliberately provoking. This was their first conversation, beyond the minimum of public politeness, since Thorkell's change of allegiance. There were some, Emma among them, who still queried the Dane's motives. Was he set here deliberately? Would he turn to bite as soon as the chain was unleashed?

'Had your brother known the outcome of your marriage, would he have pursued its blessing?' Thorkell asked in retaliation. If she had but known it, Thorkell did not fall asleep at night before asking himself similar questions. Why had he come? When push came to shove, to whom would he give his loyalty? Swein or Æthelred? He shrugged. While this English King offered him respect, he would stay. 'It is easy to be wise after the event, is it not?' He looked suddenly so remorseful that Emma found herself smiling.

'It is a novelty', she admitted, 'for me to hear a man willing to admit his mistakes. A pity there are not more like you.' Did she deliberately look towards her husband?

'Oh, I will not admit to anything, Lady. If I were to do that, my throat would run dry and my lips blister from excessive use.'

Emma had the graciousness to laugh. She did not approve of this tall, imposing man, for loyalty laid, ought to be paid, but on the other side of the door, she admired him for his courage. In that, she did truly regret that there were not more like him.

She fell silent, chewed at a hangnail. One of the advantages of being Queen was having nice hands. As a child she had bitten her nails; she felt an urge to gnaw at them now, at four and twenty years of age.

The question most prominent in her mind was one that, so far, had remained unanswered. If God had so easily deserted one of His own, if He had thrown no thunderbolt, brought no flood, plague nor

304

pestilence at the torment and death of His Archbishop, a holy and revered man, then how likely was it that He would judge, come the last day, any other with the pity of His favour?

If He did nothing to save Alfheah, was he likely to do anything to save the miserable wretches who were the rest of His servants?

'If London surrenders,' she said, troubled, very quiet, very afraid, knowing that the 'if' was, in reality, 'when', 'what shall become of me?' The question had been bundling through her mind these last few weeks, had leapt higher, more insistent at Winchester's capitulation and was ready to leap out from her in a shout of terror.

Thorkell was taken by surprise, a little puzzled. 'Has the King not informed you of our plans? He, you and the children as well, are to go into exile. I will be personally taking you. I do not have a death wish, it will not be sensible for me to remain in England.'

Dread congealed in Emma's stomach. Bile rose, she wanted to be sick. No, Æthelred had not told her. Her voice shook as she asked, 'And where are we to go?'

'Lady, London has not surrendered, you speak as if there is an inevitability in this.' Æthelred stood beside her, arms folded, face frowning disapproval. She had not heard him approach.

'And is there not?' she countered, raising her eyes to give a direct challenge at him. He glanced away. Æthelred was not a man who could stare into another's eyes, for fear of what could be reflected there from his own. 'Why should London be any different from the rest of England?'

Thorkell answered for the King; Emma was grateful for that, as she could try to believe him. With Æthelred, so very little was the truth.

'The North gave way to Swein without murmur because he has made promises. He is a clever man, the King of Denmark. He gave order that there was to be no looting or the spilling of blood of those who surrendered without resistance and he has kept his word. Not until he crossed Watling Street into Mercia did he allow his men free rein and, once homage was paid, there too they were curbed. What man of sense would choose conflict over the bending of a knee?'

'London has the balls to stand firm,' Æthelred interrupted

sharply. 'It shall hold for me, for the simple reason that my men are here to defend it.'

Thorkell held his council. Equipping a man with a sword or a spear was not sufficient to ensure he fought. Not if orders were inconsistent, not if families, wives and children, could suffer terrible consequences. Men had the courage to face death on the battlefield, but not to witness their loved ones being brutally slaughtered. And if defeat looms inevitable, men lose the motive to fight. They shrug their shoulders, lay down their weapons and simply go home.

Edmund burst into the King's Hall, breathing hard, his helmet straps swinging, his axe clenched in one hand. 'They are come!' he panted. 'They are on the far side of the river. Many, many of them.'

Alfred, Emma's son, clamped his fingers tighter to her gown; absent-minded, she lifted him into her arms, batted aside Edward who, at his brother's favouritism, was also demanding attention. Goda was safe in Leofgifu's arms, her eyes wide, fingers stuffed in her mouth.

'Is the bridge secure?' Thorkell asked, taking up his own axe from where it stood propped against the side of his stool. Edmund answered with a contemptuous look. Thorkell grimaced, raised his hand in submission, he had only been speaking his thoughts aloud, a commander's habit of running through a pre-battle routine. To smooth the lad's hackles he said quickly, 'It is an honour to stand beside a man as competent as yourself, Edmund. You would be surprised at how many fools there are in the command of armies.'

'No, Sir, I would not be at all surprised.' Graciously, Edmund accepted the oblique apology. 'The first ten yards of planking beyond the gate were removed some hours ago, only a narrow walkway remains to allow passage for those defending the bridge. If they fail to hold the far gate on the Southwark side, the militia men shall withdraw and London will be sealed.'

'Then Swein will need to march as far as Thorney for a first fording place?' Thorkell queried, again confirming his own thoughts.

'That, too, will be difficult,' Edmund answered, giving a sidelong glance at his father. It ought to be the King giving these instructions, ought to be the King overseeing the defence of London. Huh, what did he know of it? 'The posts marking the firm river-bed footing have been removed. Without a knowledgeable guide, many will take a wrong step and drown. The Thames looks benign when viewed from the surface, but the river has strong eddies and currents; it is not wise to stray from where it is known to be safe.'

The men waiting in the King's Hall nodded approval. *Give them leadership and they will follow*, Emma thought. *Give them nothing and they will drift away like dead leaves blown into a running river.*

Eadric Streona, Emma noticed, was the last to leave the Hall, making a pretence to retie his gaiter laces. Æthelred, clad in chain-mail armour, his axe, sword and standard bearers at his side, had gone ahead of his son and Thorkell, his cnights marching determinedly in his wake. He did not relish being in the thick of a fight, but if he wished to keep his crown, he had to be out there, up on the walls, encouraging the Londoners to stand firm. And strange, now that it came to it, Æthelred suddenly did not mind the thought of being killed. To die with glory would be to be remembered in honour. Look at Byrhtnoth of Maldon and Archbishop Alfheah.

Rallying her senses, Emma passed Alfred to his nurse, his thumb stuck firm between his teeth, brushed Edward aside and clapped her hands to gain attention. 'There will be wounded. It is our duty to ensure we do all we can for them.'

Her practical words animated the women. The children were ushered to a far corner, the hearth-fires and brazier replenished with wood and charcoal, water and broth set to boil. Emma herself, as the Key-carrier and head of the household, supervised laying out bottles and jars of unguents and herbs on a trestle table, pointed to where the rolled bandages should be placed; organised straw pallets to be set down the length of the Hall. Better to be busy, to keep the hands occupied, to stop the mind from the horror of exile. She need not have worried. It all came to nothing.

A few were carried into the Hall, men with arrow wounds, two boys – you could not call them men – with broken legs after falling from the steps that led to the wall parapet. Several with burns to hands and arms, fire arrows were always a curse. Nothing more. By dusk, Swein had decided London was not worth the effort and had marched away again, swinging his army about and heading back to complete his reduction of Wessex. London had withstood the aborted attack, had come through, unscathed but with a hollow, inglorious victory.

The Thames had saved them, the river with its deceptive dangers. Unable to cross the bridge, Swein had sent men to the ford upriver, with orders to come about on the northern side of the city. They had underestimated the care the river took of its own. With the ford unmarked and the marshes treacherous, even at low tide, less than half his men returned, unable to cross. The dead washed, bloated, beneath London Bridge, were taken by the tide downriver for the fishes to eat. Ever the pragmatist, Swein called off the attack. Senseless wasting men unnecessarily, Æthelred was going nowhere, except into the next world or exile. Either of which suited Swein, who had plenty of time to wait.

Before Christmas, Bath fell to him and the last of the western thegns sent their hostages and submitted. Swein returned across central England in triumph to Gainsborough and his waiting ships, while his seventeen-year-old son rode to Northampton and the estate of his English wife's mother. Ælfgifu had become his bride within the first week of Swein's landing; as a woman, she meant nothing to Cnut, she was neither plain nor pretty, passionate nor frigid, but she had conceived a child from their first union and that had pleased her young husband. By the time he reached Northampton the child would be born. All the more pleasing, should it be a boy.

Swein was not concerned about London. Once the worst of the winter weather became more favourable, it would be a simple task to sail down the coast and attack again from the river, as a seafarer would prefer to do.

As he had hoped, however, there was no sense in prolonging the death agony. Best to cut the poison out with a knife and have done with it. A few days after the Nativity London surrendered.

The King, Æthelred, following in the wake of his wife and her children, fled, in fear of his life, to Normandy.

PART TWO

Edmund

Anno Domini 1014–1016

*All the councillors chose Edmund as King
and he stoutly protected the
kingdom during his time.*

Anglo-Saxon Chronicle

1

Yet again Edmund squinted through the swirl of snow at his brother. Athelstan was slumped along his pony's neck, his white fingers frozen to the shaggy mane that glistened with frost. The pony was steady and sure-footed, but still a moan of pain left Athelstan's blue-tinged lips. They had three hours of light left, although it was only a short while past noon. Edmund wanted to kick on into a trot – a canter – but Athelstan was having difficulty coping with this slow walking pace. He would not survive anything faster, but then, if Edmund did not get him to warmth and shelter by nightfall, he would not survive anyway.

It had been nothing more stupid than a fall, an everyday tumble. The pony had slipped on ice, going down on his knees, and Athelstan had pitched over his shoulder, landing with a laugh to cover his embarrassment and, as it turned out, his injury. He was bruised, shaken, nothing more, he had declared, brushing snow off his mantle and inspecting the pony's knees for damage. Beyond wounded pride, neither of them hurt, he had assured, waving aside concern. Three days ago, that had been. Three furtive days of stealthy riding through hostile territory, startling at every sound, every movement beyond the quiet, lonely tracks that filed through forest land and open moors. Twice they had backed into the trees, gripping the ponies' muzzles with clamped fingers to keep them from whinnying; had squatted, breath held, as Danes passed by. Forkbeard's men, or those loyal to him, seemed everywhere. Was no one remaining loyal to the King? To Æthelred? A stupid question. Even Athelstan and Edmund had deserted him.

Then, last night, Athelstan's Captain of Cnights had woken Edmund, told him he was worried about his Lord. Rightfully, for Athelstan was sweating a fever, although the ground and air were hard with ice. Now, Edmund regretted the decision to stay in England and fight, if opportunity arose. Had he and Athelstan gone in Thorkell's ships to Normandy, then they would be safe, dry and Athelstan would not be dying.

Thegn Sigeferth's manor was only six or so miles ahead, but there was another valley and a few steep hills to negotiate yet. A river to cross, too. They had to push on!

Alfwine, Athelstan's chaplain, urged his weary pony into a reluctant trot and came up alongside Edmund. Like the rest of them, he needed a shave, a wash, a change of clothes. When you were on the run, nothing more than outlaws, there was not opportunity for the niceties of Court luxuries. Barely time to find food to eat. Aye, that was something else Athelstan desperately needed: hot, nourishing food inside his belly.

'Forgive me for saying, my Lord Edmund,' Alfwine faltered, 'but can you be sure of a welcome at Sigeferth's Hold? He gave hostages and pledged alliance to Swein with the rest of the northern lords, did he not?' Alfwine, along with a handful of cnights and servants, had remained loyal to the two brothers. The boy Godwine, too, was riding with them; Edmund was grateful for that, they had come a long way together from childhood.

For the ealdormen, particularly Uhtred of Northumbria, there had been some soul-searching before defecting to Swein Forkbeard, but what had Æthelred done to deserve the keeping of his loyalty? The King had nothing behind him save a list of rising taxes, no attempt at uniform defence, and reliance on a man who courted patronage through obsequious flattery and proffered wealth. Eadric Streona alone, in Edmund's opinion, would have turned the North against Æthelred. Riding in silence, Edmund shielded the thoughts, for they were not complimentary of the Ealdorman of Mercia. How often had Streona professed to be the most loyal of Æthelred's men? His friend, confidant – shield-bearer, shadow? How easily he had gone over to Swein of Denmark once London fell! God's Judgement, if ever a man deserved the fires of Hell, then it was Eadric Streona!

'There are some men', Edmund said at last, 'who will raise an angry question if Swein embraces Streona too close into his confidence. The Thegns Sigeferth and his brother Morcar numbered high among them. It was Sigeferth who sheltered Athelstan on many an occasion when my brother was sent from Court. Sigeferth who told of Swein's plans for Cnut to wed with Ælfgifu of Northampton. He and his brother have always been good friends with us.' He turned slightly in his saddle and attempted a brave smile. 'At least, I pray God they remain good friends.'

Beneath the warmth of his mantle, Alfwine made the sign of the cross, murmured a heartfelt, 'Amen.'

Neither of them need have worried. Sigeferth embraced Edmund with open arms and a wide, welcoming grin, his young wife, Ealdgyth, hastily organising the servants to carry Athelstan into her own bed, a separate chamber to the southern end of the Hall, the warmest and best room on the estate. Edmund had first met her when invited to the wedding feast, two years past, in happier days. She was quiet-spoken, capable and authoritative. If seeing a group of snow-matted outlaws riding through her gate alarmed her, then her face gave no sign of it. Indeed, the brief, chaste kiss of welcome that she placed on Edmund's cheek showed nothing but pleasure.

Edmund was chilled to the bone; he had removed his mantle several miles back and buckled it on over Athelstan's own to give him double warmth and protection. His hair was wet, his boots and clothes sodden from attempting to rescue a pack pony that had slithered on the ice and fallen into a river. The pony had drowned, the effort to save its pack a waste of energy.

Chivvying everyone into the Hall, Sigeferth sent servants to feed and rub down the horses, shouting, as he steered Edmund through the doorway, for stew to be heated, bread, cheese, ale to be brought.

Two strides within the inviting, homely warmth, Edmund halted, took hold of Sigeferth's arm, his expression earnest, anxious. 'My friend, I thank you for this hospitality. I assure you I do not intend to remain longer than necessary. If I may leave Athelstan in your care, I shall be on my way come tomorrow's dawn. I have no intention of putting you and your good lady in danger.'

Sigeferth laughed, slapped Edmund's shoulder and drew him nearer the hearth. 'You shall do no such thing, Edmund. You are always welcome beneath my roof, whoever designs to style himself King of England.'

Refusing to sit, Edmund persisted. 'If Swein discovers us here, Sigeferth, you will be hanged and your wife with you.' His body felt heavy, the ache in his limbs almost unbearable; he could sleep where he stood, were he permitted. He spread his hands, resigned. 'Yet, I confess I have no where else to go.'

'You have no need to go elsewhere, here is sufficient. Swein is entrenched at Gainsborough; he will not be leaving his camp while the snow falls. Did you hear, Ælfgifu has given Cnut a son? Swegen she has named him, but if its grandfather wishes to hold the North, then he must do more than prove his son knows how to make use of his manhood.'

Edmund looked up sharply. 'There is dissent?'

'There is. Swein could well find himself wearing the English crown for a very short duration if he continues to welcome men like Eadric Streona to his Court.'

'Streona is at Gainsborough?' Edmund was astounded, both at Eadric Streona's audacity and Swein Forkbeard's trusting stupidity.

Sigeferth's nod was grim. 'He is. With several chests full of silver, a gift for the newborn ætheling, so I hear tell.'

'Buying his way in. The slimy, belly-crawling, shit-faced bastard!'

Laughing, Sigeferth answered, 'I could not have put it better, though crawling is the only thing Streona is good at. For God's Sake, man, can we not sit? What with one thing and another, I have been on my feet most of the day, my boots are killing me!'

Edmund cracked his ice-stiff face into a smile, sat. It was good to have men who, despite all difficulties and dangers, remained stalwart friends. A pity his father had never discovered and utilised that fact.

Ealdgyth awoke Edmund from a sleep where he had been dreaming of snow smothering him. He had tried to get out by pushing with his arms, kicking with his feet, but the more he struggled, the deeper he fell. He was relieved to be shaken awake, to find that he was tangled only by a blanket.

314

'Edmund?' Ealdgyth's voice was low, whispering in his ear, reluctant to wake any of the others curled on their pallets in the Hall, those of rank nearest the hearth. 'Your brother is calling for you.'

Edmund sat up, plucked a few strands of dried bracken from his hair, said eagerly, hopeful, 'He is awake? He is better?'

The woman shook her head, laid her hand on Edmund's arm. 'I am sorry, there is nothing more I can do for him. He is dying.'

On his feet, the bedding tossed aside, Edmund lurched across the Hall, barely mindful of the sleeping bodies, several of whom he kicked or tripped over in his haste. Left behind him a trail of grumbled curses.

The bedchamber was lit by several candles and lamps, a brazier had been restoked with charcoal, and a faint smell of sweet-scented herbs permeated the air. Athelstan lay in the centre of the bed, pale, thin, every bone of his face visible. His eyes were burning brighter than the flames of the fire, his skin, when Edmund touched it, as hot.

'It seems there is some vital part within me that is damaged,' Athelstan said, his breath croaking in his throat. Blood, Edmund noted, was flecked in his spittle. 'I have made my confession to Alfwine.' Athelstan lifted his hand a few inches to indicate the chaplain, lingering in the shadows. 'But I would have you here while I dictate my will.'

'There is no need, Brother!' Edmund answered quickly, frightened. 'You are tired, a good night's rest and you will soon be well again . . .'

Athelstan cut him short. 'I am for God, Edmund. I beg you not to waste the short while I have left.'

Silent, Edmund sat, his hand clasped within Athelstan's, tears trailing.

'I have spoken my words for a letter that is to go to Papa, begging his forgiveness for my impatience. I would have you, as my executor, take this letter to him when – if – you are able. I can only trust that one day my last will may be legally ratified.'

Mouthing words that would not come, Edmund could only nod,

listen as his beloved brother listed the estates and items he wished to pass on. First came Æthelred himself; then, as second beneficiary, Edmund. Fresh tears trickling when he heard his brother was to leave him his own great sword that had once been carried by King Offa.

'I do not want your sword,' he choked, 'I want you, here, alive with me.'

'And I want you to be strong. I want you to take my sword and drive Swein from this land. With my death, you will be the next king. In my name, do your duty well.'

Among the legatees, Alfwine his chaplain was to receive a sword and a horse complete with trappings; Ælfmær, his seneschal, and Ælfmar and Æthelwine his most devoted cnights, Ælfnoth his sword polisher, his staghuntsman, his hawskman and his kennelman, were all to receive things of value. The estates not willed to his father or brother, those scattered throughout the Shires, were to go to the thegns who had shown their unswerving friendship, Sigeferth and Morcar. Nor was Godwine forgotten.

'When Thegn Wulfnoth was outlawed,' Athelstan gasped, his breath in his chest tighter, restricting, as if a hand was twisting into his lungs, 'Papa gave his confiscated land to me. I wish to hand the freehold back to Godwine. The estate and thegnship of Compton in Sussex is his.' He managed a weak half-smile, his fingers gripping tighter to his brother's hand. 'If it be in your power, see that it is all done, Edmund, for the sake of my soul.'

He slept then, having made his bequests and his peace with God. A sleep that slid into the deeper darkness where pain and suffering ceases, and the Light of God dazzles all else into insignificance.

2

3 February 1014 – Gainsborough

Cnut returned from Northampton in a glow of triumph. His son had been born lusty and healthy, a fine lad with a full head of hair and lungs with the bellow of a bull. He had decided to leave his wife and child at her family home, for her own comfort and his independence. She was with her mother and brothers, settled on her mother's own substantial estate, and wanted for nothing. If he was honest with himself, Ælfgifu had appeared relieved when he had suggested she stay. It was because of the child, of course, what woman, brought to recent birth, would want to be among the crowd of an army? Cnut did not like to think that just maybe, she was glad to be rid of him. That she had no more interest in him than he did for her. Arriving at Gainsborough, he was too astounded by his father's orders to fly into a rage. 'You are asking me to abandon Odin and Thor, and turn my face to Christianity?'

'No, I am not asking, I am telling. To be anointed as king over the English with the sacred and holy Chrism, I have totally renounced my heathenism and fully embraced the word of God. As will you.'

'I bloody well will not!'

'You bloody will, boy! I command it!'

Archbishop Wulfstan, seated at the far end of the Hall, glanced up from the Gospel he was reading and frowned. Faith was not a thing to be undertaken at the command of another, it had to come from within the heart, and this cock-proud boy, who had witnessed and laughed at the martyrdom of Archbishop Alfheah, was not ready for God's Grace to be marked on his forehead.

'We have done well for ourselves thus far with taking heed of both Odin and Christ in equal measure.' Cnut's remark was surly, he was almost pouting, like a child who was thwarted in getting his own way with pleading for a honeycomb or a sweet wafer. For good measure he added, 'Your father took up this Christian religion; it did little for your benefit.'

'It did nothing for me because Harold Bluetooth, like myself, only half turned to God. I now realise that you cannot combine the peace of Christ alongside the petty squabblings of our old gods. They are gone from us, they could not compete with the truth of Jesu Christ. They deserted us long ago, when Christ defeated them and sent them into the shadow lands. They no longer exist.'

Cnut laughed. 'And just how did He manage that? By waving loaves and fishes at them?'

Wulfstan despised these Danes with their hairy faces and crude manners; their vindictive bloodlust and barbaric paganism. The political situation, like it or not, had changed, however, and if he was to find the path of redemption, it would be better to swim with the current rather than struggle against it. Add to that, Wulfstan, with his unswerving faith in God, was always the pragmatist.

If the day of judgement was coming, then this, surely, was it. Chaos had come into the world – yet they were all still alive. The sun rose, the moon set; babes were being conceived and born. There was no pox, no plague, no flood or fire. The world went on. There was only Swein Forkbeard instead of Æthelred, and the Archbishop had to concede, even if only to his private thoughts, that there was more chance of survival with Swein as King than with Æthelred. If nothing else, it would put an end to the raiding and killing, and the raising of silver to pay the geld.

Wulfstan believed in the event of the apocalypse as God's punishment for all who had sinned, but he also believed that, by adequate and profound repentance, a final end could be averted, a new beginning made. Was not Sodom destroyed? The world flooded? The evils cleansed? Both Lot and Noah had been warned and spared. He, Wulfstan Lupus, Archbishop of York, too, had been warned and it was his duty to do God's work by cleansing all that was foul from this good land. If guiding Swein Forkbeard to the love of God was the task he had to do to find salvation, then so be it. The son was going to be more difficult, but Wulfstan never expected God's work to be easy.

'Jesu fought the old gods with truth, love and compassion,' he said sternly, setting his Bible aside. 'Who has seen Thor or Odin? Who has listened to Balder? What have they done for the good of mankind? Men, real men, walked with Jesus on this Earth and listened to what he had to say. Listened and told others, and their words were written down and passed to us.' He stood straight and unafraid as he raised his arms to pray. 'When the Saviour saw the crowds, He climbed up the mountain and His followers approached him. And He opened His mouth and taught them and said: blessed are the spiritually poor for theirs is the kingdom of the Heavens; blessed are the kind because they will possess the Earth; blessed are those who weep because they will be consoled; blessed are those who hunger and thirst for righteousness for they will be filled; blessed are the pure-hearted because they will see God; blessed are those who endure persecution because the kingdom of Heaven is theirs and blessed are you when they abuse you and persecute you and, lying, say every evil against you because of Me. Rejoice and be glad because reward is great in Heaven.'

Cnut sniggered. 'Fine words, but how do they apply to us? My father is King, he would not last half a day if he followed your doctrine of peace.'

'Mayhap not, but when called to God, he will last a lifetime in Heaven, rather than endure eternity in Hell.'

'I am content with Valhalla. It was good enough for my ancestors. It will be good enough for me.'

'Valhalla, Cnut, is ended,' Swein snapped. 'It has faded away, as the frost disappears with the coming of the sun. There is no Valhalla. Now, you will do as I say without further argument. My head is aching and my stomach grumbles for food. The nobles of all England have sent their hostages into my Hall, they have accepted me as their King, but that acceptance will last no more than a blink of an eye if I do not respect their land and customs. Come this Easter Council, I must be crowned as King, for that, I have committed myself to Christ and so, boy, shall you.' He made a dismissive gesture, turned to walk away. 'I go to inspect my hounds. When I return, Cnut, I expect you to have reconsidered. All my household has followed my example, as shall you. You, and your housecarls and servants, will publicly commit yourselves to God on the morrow. I order it.'

'So I am lowered to rank alongside servants, am I?' Cnut muttered, his anger unsated.

'No, you rank with me and with Christ. Is it not suitable for you?'

It was not. Cnut spun on his heel and stamped away, heading for where the preparations for the evening meal were being made.

'Do not turn your back on me, boy!' Swein bellowed, hurrying after him. 'You will not insult me and you will obey me!'

Ignoring him, Cnut walked on. 'You insult yourself,' he said, although not so loud that his father would hear. Swein's hand lingered over his dagger hilt, his fingers clenching and releasing. Finally, he let go his held breath and, turning on his heel, swept out of the door into the icy rain.

The air was cold, ice rimed the puddles and froze the breath. Four wooden steps led down from the Hall, a manor house that had been offered to Swein by its owner, Thegn Sigeferth. Aware Sigeferth had no liking whatsoever for him, Swein had graciously accepted the gesture for how it was intended, as a direct insult to Æthelred.

Turning his head, Swein shouted, 'You will regret opposing me, Cnut. Mark my word, you will regret it.' He had climbed and descended those steps so many times since occupying the Hall. His feet knew that the second step down had a worn hollow where so many had trod, that it needed replacing. He was looking back over his shoulder, glowering at his son. For all their differences, he was a good lad, had a good head on his shoulders. Saw sense. Usually.

Swein set his foot down on to the second step, did not see the ice. His boot skidded, he fell, his arms going out, a sharp cry of surprise whooshing from his mouth. The ground, when his head hit it, was rock hard. He lay still, unmoving, blood beginning to trickle from his open mouth and his ears, as a last breath sighed from his emptying lungs.

3

'*Où est Eduard?*' Emma was annoyed, more than she had been these
last two frustrating months. Exile did not agree with Emma. It was
humiliating. They were not impoverished, for there had been ample
time to load the Treasury aboard Thorkell's ships and to get away
from London with adequate personal items to ensure a life of
comfort. And Richard had been magnanimous with his generous
welcome, down to giving them their own residence here in Rouen,
a magnanimity that was spoilt by his triumphant gloating. The
shame of exile was bad enough on its own without her brother's
crowing. The one saving grace for Emma, her mother was no longer
alive to witness her mortification.

She repeated her question, 'Where is your brother?' Alfred was
engrossed in smoothing an ash branch for the haft of a boy-sized
spear that he was making with Leofstan, his sister, Goda, helping by
intently watching, fascinated by the thin, slivered coils of papery
wood that were descending to the floor like snow. Why could
Edward never do as he was told? Always slinking off somewhere,
sullen with his answers whenever she spoke to him; always
scowling. God's Breath, had she bred a mule head? Was he not,
indeed, Æthelred's son? But then, Alfred and Goda were also
Æthelred's, and they were not as dense as a tangled brier thicket.

His tongue poking through his lips in concentration, the seven-
year-old Alfred did not look up. 'Where he always is, Mama. In the
Cathedral.'

Emma exhaled an irritated breath. On occasion she wondered
why she was bothering with this effort to get them all back to
England. Æthelred spent most of his days, and nights, wringing his
hands and wailing loudly for the loss of his crown but doing
absolutely nothing to retrieve it. Edward, it appeared, preferred the

company of monks while Alfred was enjoying playing soldiers with the captain of her cnights. And Goda, ah, Goda was an angelic child who could find contentment wherever she was. The sort of child who would make anyone a suitable, dutiful wife. She sighed again, ah well, at least for Alfred that was a positive sign, playing would one day turn into reality. But not if she followed her husband's example of sitting on his backside when there was so much to be doing! Gathering ships, arms and armour – armies. Petitioning the Pope for a public condemnation of Swein Forkbeard; bargaining with men like Count Baldwin of Flanders, and the German Emperor, for aid. To return to England they needed planning, determination and support. None of which, so far, had been forthcoming because of Æthelred's abject moroseness.

This morning had brought wonderful news and a leap of hope that would end this waking nightmare of enforced exile. And now, when he was desperately needed, Edward was missing. Stupid, stupid boy!

Edward was fascinated by the abbey of St Ouen. As often as he could, he would listen to the chanted singing of the monks and was learning the services, down to the last detail, with only Matins and Compline outside his experience, for they were at the beginning and end of the day, and beyond his ability to attend. Lauds and Prime, at sunrise, he had managed on several occasions by rising at dawn and pretending to go down to the kitchens in search of something to break his fast. Although sometimes his ruse meant going without anything to eat. He did not mind that; he thought of it as a sacrifice for God.

The service had finished and, reluctantly, Edward waited for the monks to begin filing out of the church, knowing he would have to return home. There had been uproar earlier, with everyone flying into a panic because Godwine Wulfnothsson had arrived from England saying something about an envoy coming. Papa, after listening to what Godwine had to say, had fallen to his knees and wept, something Edward found to be acutely embarrassing. Papa often wept since they had come to Normandy, his shoulders would slump forward and begin to shake, then great sobs would burst from his mouth along with saliva and spittle. No one quite knew what to do when Æthelred cried. Mother always left the room, her mouth set in a firm, thin line, and if Edward found himself to be in her path, she would shout at him. He soon learnt to be out of her way whenever his father was sobbing.

His mother. Another advantage to being here in Normandy; he saw very little of her. She was too busy writing letters or inter-viewing messengers, or arguing with Papa. She rarely noticed her eldest son, which was highly acceptable to Edward.

He could not understand why Papa sobbed so often here, within the safe security of Rouen. So he was not King of England any more. What did that matter? He had never seemed to enjoy being king, had complained at the expectation put upon him, that sitting in a court of ruling was a waste of effort, that no one appreciated what he did, or listened to what he had to say. Edward thought that his father would have enjoyed being here in Normandy: the hunting was excellent, the living accommodation superior, the climate drier. To his mind he would prefer to stay in Normandy for ever.

A servant hurried in through the open church door and spoke in a muted whisper to one of the monks who stood inside. Edward shrank into the corner shadows where he had been squatting, as several faces peered in his direction. Through most of the day the monks were silent, the spoken word, beyond the requirement to praise God, forbidden, but Edward had learnt much of the sign language that was so efficiently used instead. The monk at the door stroked his tonsured scalp in a circular fashion and then rested his hand there, the sign for Queen, then he pointed at Edward and beckoned.

Reluctant, the boy shuffled to the door, his head bent, feet dragging.

'It is good that you worship with us so often, my son,' Brother Jerome said with an approving smile, 'but your mother has a more immediate need of you at this moment than does God. You are, after all, an anointed king's son.'

'God is my King!' Edward answered with specific conviction.

'Then that is also good, but God may one day want you to be a king here on Earth. You cannot turn aside from what He has ordained for you.'

Edward wanted to argue, to say that he would not be a king of England now they were exiled, but Jerome forestalled any answer by setting his hand on the boy's shoulder. 'The Englishman, Godwine Wulfnothsson, has brought word that King Swein of Denmark is dead. It is probable that you will be going home.' He said it with a broad smile, assuming the boy would be pleased.

Tears prickled Edward's eyes and he bit his lip. He would not cry because he knew what they all said about his father and did not want the same taunts said about him. They used words such as shameful and degrading, dishonourable, pathetic and pitiful. Edward had discovered early in his life what a sneer sounded like when it was used in speech. He only cried, now, when he was alone, because he did not want any of these mighty Normans to say of him, too, '*c'est un vaurien*', as worthless as chicken shit. Nor did he want to go back to England. He wanted to stay here, in the abbey cathedral of St Ouen, and dedicate his life to God.

'Does Mother know I am here?' he asked tremulously. If she did, would he be in trouble for it? Probably.

'It seems so,' Jerome answered, trying to be kind, assuming the boy was anxious not to have worried anyone. 'She knew where to send to fetch you.'

Sod, Edward thought and hastily crossed himself for swearing in God's House.

4

'Put these robes on,' Emma said, bustling Edward into a splendid tunic of richly dyed wool. 'You are at least to look the part of a prince of England, even if you cannot act it.'

'Why?' Edward asked argumentatively, refusing to co-operate as she manipulated his arms into the sleeves. 'Papa fled England, we are no longer wanted there.'

'We might be now,' Emma responded tersely. Really, this child was so annoying. 'If your father does not ruin our chances. Ealdorman Athelmar may be able to ensure we are home by Easter.'

Home, Emma thought, catching herself as she said it. Did she really think of England as home now? She looked about her. Stone, solid walls; oiled parchment covering the slit windows, the walls covered with coloured plaster and hung with animal skins alongside three of the best tapestries that she had brought with her from England. Comfortable, practical, but not home. Here, the Duke treated her as a younger sister, the populace in the street bowed their heads, but because she was the Duke's kinswoman, not because she was Queen of England. Here, she had no authority, no place and no pride. *Oui*, she wanted to go home. She wanted to return to being a queen, to having the status and the power. To being her own person with her own will and her own say, even if that did mean having to continue suffering the nuisance of having Æthelred as husband. England, with its green fields and soft rain, was now home. Not Normandy and its arrogant, insufferable Duke.

'Athelmar?' Edward queried, breaking her reverie. 'I thought he had retired to a monastery?' Edward had admired the old man for giving up everything of material worth for the simplicity of a monastic life. That option, he had decided, was what he would do when he became a man and they made him into a king. He would pass his crown to Alfred and retire into a monastery. How easy solutions were for a child.

Emma had no need to explain, but perhaps it would be useful and her earlier agitated temper was subsiding now that hope was blossoming into what could very well become reality. An end to this purgatory? Oh, blessed God, please let it be so!

Fastening a sable-lined mantle around Edward's shoulders, Emma licked her fingers and straightened a flop of his hair. 'He has left the abbey because the English Witan needs him. Our kingdom is in disarray and, being old and wise, he is the most suited to sort the chaos. He is a brave man, Athelmar, for alone among all of them, and by peaceful means, he tried to resist Swein of Denmark.'

'Is he here?'

For once, a silly question did not irritate. Fastidiously, Emma brushed fluff off Edward's shoulder, smiled. 'Athelmar is too old to come to Normandy; he has sent three men instead.' Bless Godwine for riding ahead to warn her of their coming!

Edward, hiding his disappointment, said, 'You're pretty when you smile.'

Emma was so often aware that she was unkind to the boy, that she scarcely bothered with him. The circumstances of his conception and birth were not his fault, but then, for her, neither was this antipathy of feelings. Perhaps this could be a chance to start afresh? Return to England, and be washed free of a soiled past, cleansed, an old skin shed. She would spend more time with her son, ensure he learnt his languages and read his books. Instil within him the importance of becoming king.

As he trotted at Emma's side, her long stride taking her quickly across the small courtyard towards the Hall, Edward dared to ask, 'Why am I wanted?'

'Because you are the King's eldest son, why else? Let me take a last look at you.' Emma squatted on her heels, minutely inspected him. '*Oui*, you'll do.'

'No I'm not,' Edward protested, scuffing his toes on each step as they climbed the stairway that led to an upper, private, chamber. 'Athelstan and Edmund are older than me.'

Emma halted before the door, smoothed her gown, patted her wimple to ensure wisps of hair were not straying. She was flustered, her heart thump-bumping in her chest. If Æthelred did not convince Athelmar's representatives that he was the better man to be England's king . . . if Richard, damn his eyes, did not agree to back their claim . . .

'Edmund is bastard-born, you are not. And Athelstan is dead.' Distracted, she was blunter than she had intended to be.

She entered the chamber, a room filled with men, Edward beside her, with all these eyes swivelling towards him, too scared to move. Emma dipped a curtsy at her husband, seated on the far side, and trundled her son forward as if he were an old barrel.

Æthelred had his head bent over a letter crumpled into his hand and was weeping loudly. Edward glanced up at his mother to see if she was angry, was surprised to see a rare soft expression of concern. Was more astonished when she went to Æthelred and slid her arm around his waist, placed her lips to his temple. No one was sniggering, no one was slyly nudging his neighbour, or rolling his eyes and making derisory gestures.

'My son, my poor son,' Æthelred sniffed, fumbling with his free hand for Emma's. 'How wrongly I treated him.'

Left to stand alone, Edward was tempted to run to his father and declare that Papa need not worry, he was quite all right, he had not minded, not really. As well he hesitated, for someone else said, 'He served England well, my Lord, right until his death. Athelstan was a man whose passing will be widely mourned.'

Edward felt his face burn. It was Athelstan his father was talking of, then, not himself.

'Be comforted that he did not suffer,' Emma offered, kneeling beside Æthelred, 'that he did not linger.'

'But to die alone? Abandoned by all who loved him!' Æthelred declared. 'It is too bad, too bad.'

Emma swallowed a tempting retort, retaining her carefully schooled pretence of compassion. If Æthelred had stood his ground, Athelstan would not have gone off alone to attempt to fight Swein Forkbeard; aside, Edmund had been with him, and Godwine. As for

327

Athelstan himself, her feelings were mixed. He had always declared that he would never allow Edward to come before him when it came to the wearing of the crown, but then, that declaration had been for the good of England, not for his own advancement. Being honest with herself, Emma would miss Athelstan far more than ever she would Æthelred, or Edward, but then, she could afford to be benevolent towards him now that he was dead and no longer a threat to her or her sons.

'It is my wish that my son's bequests shall be honoured and that my forgiveness of him be widespread notified,' Æthelred declared, shuddering down another sob. 'Tell me, Godwine, where is he buried?' The emotion quivered in Æthelred's voice, his lips trembled and no one censured grief for the losing of a son.

'He is at peace in a Derbyshire nunnery,' Godwine said. 'Edmund thought it wise to offer him a temporary resting place where none could contend its suitability.' A feminine grave among the nuns, an honourable burial for a royal prince, but one that gave no pretence for a right to the crown.

Æthelred frowned. 'I would have him transferred to the Minster at Winchester. It is more fitting.'

'Royal burial?' Duke Richard commented. 'With Cnut Sweinsson declared as King? There will be no chance of that!' Tactless, or a deliberate provocation?

Hastily interrupting any response her husband might make, and glowering at her brother to be silent, Emma beckoned Edward forward.

'My Lord husband, your living son, who has remained dutiful to you throughout, has come.' Surreptitiously she encouraged Edward to stand up straight.

As she had intended, Æthelred dramatically embraced him. 'Edward, my boy! Come, come here, sit beside me, lad!'

Enjoying the unexpected importance, Edward obeyed, having to wriggle slightly to seat himself on a stool which he realised, from his mother's frown, was rightfully hers. He squirmed, wondering indecisively whether he ought to move. Standing behind him, Emma hissed, 'Sit still, smile and, if spoken to, reply politely, in English. Do not speak French.'

Æthelred patted Edward's knee. The tears were gone, a smile beamed across his face. 'Is he not a fine boy?' he asked every one in general. 'Will he not make a fine king after me?'

From where he sat on his own splendid armed chair, Duke Richard listened to his interpreter. 'To become a king, he must have the prospect of a kingdom,' he stated in French. 'If what we hear is true, the Danish army has declared for Cnut.'

Ah, so the barbs *were* deliberate. Had Emma expected anything else from him? Richard had been lobbing arrows at them since the first day of their arrival, tired, weary and sea-soaked. The crossing had been more dreadful than she had feared; Thorkell's insistence that his ship was the best ever built and as seaworthy as a dolphin, had not impressed, nor held the seasickness at bay. That was the only drawback with her resolve to return to England. *When I get there*, she thought, *nothing, nothing whatsoever, shall induce me to leave again.*

'Then we must ensure that the Witan of England overrules the wanting of a mere rabble of Danish mercenaries,' Emma answered Richard, aware that Æthelred was too engrossed in stroking his son's hair and patting his cheek to be listening. Useless man! Did he not want his kingdom restored? Did England want him restored? Swein Forkbeard had been accepted as the better option. Could the same thinking count for his son, Cnut? And then there was Edmund, he was in England, he could be chosen in place of his dead brother. For all that she liked him as a man, Emma was not having that!

'In case of treachery, it will not be sensible for Æthelred to go to England,' she announced, placing her hands on Edward's shoulders. 'But I can see no practical reason why I cannot escort his eldest, legitimate, son there to plead his case.' And once in England, they would find it damned hard to depose her a second time. To take the crown, either Cnut or Edmund would have to kill her first.

5

Solid, unmoving land. Thank God! Emma's knees almost buckled beneath her, might well have done had Godwine not been there to hold her arm and support her.

'It gets you like that.' He grinned. 'After being aboard ship a while, the ground feels as if it's moving.'

'I do not care about the ground,' Emma answered, attempting a pale smile, 'it is my stomach heaving upwards that is finishing me.'

Thorkell's dragon craft had brought her passengers right into Winchester, judiciously flying the Queen's lioness emblem, with Emma, steeling herself to ignore her seasickness, standing at the bow with Edward. Her thanks to God, when setting foot ashore, heart-meant.

The city dignitaries and gathered nobles were there to meet her, on this first day of March, jubilant at her return, conveniently forgetting that not many months ago they had been doing exactly the same with Swein Forkbeard. It was so tempting to remind them, but she held her silence. If this journey was to restore her crown, she had to appear gracious and forgiving.

Suspicious looks were glanced at the corps of Thorkell's men, but Emma silenced the muted whispering by saying, 'My escort and their commander will require accommodation.'

The Reeve of Winchester coughed, embarrassed. 'I confess we are ill prepared for so many, er,' he hesitated, reluctant to say the word *Danes*, 'cnights.'

'Out of courtesy to my escort, we use their own term, housecarl. They are hardy men. I am sure they can manage with what is available; my manor in the High Street will suffice for their needs. For my own comfort, my son and I shall reside at Nunnaminster.'

That, Emma knew, would not cause a flurry. She and the Abbess were long-acquainted friends.

'The nunnery will indeed be suitable, Lady, for the royal residence is somewhat full,' Ealdorman Eadric Streona announced, staring with hostility at Thorkell. 'As you see, the most eminent men of England are here at Winchester to discuss matters.' He was polite but curt, annoyed because others had shouldered ahead of him to greet the Queen and she had steadfastly ignored him.

'I do not see Lindsey represented, nor Northumbria? And where is the King's son, Edmund? Has he not been included in these negotiations?' Emma asked.

A voice hailed from the lane that ran from the Minster to the river wharf, a man striding with a long gait, his cloak billowing, a gaggle of followers scurrying in his wake.

'Madam, my Lady Queen, Edward, I greet you both! You arrived before None was completed. I apologise for my delay.' Archbishop Wulfstan. Naturally he would be here. He swept Emma and her son a gracious bow, kissed her hand. 'I am here to speak for the Church, of course,' Wulfstan said, indicating that Emma was to proceed before him away from the crowded wharf, 'but additionally I represent Uhtred. It is impossible for him to leave the North. Too volatile a situation along the Scots border, you understand.'

Emma understood; quite clearly Uhtred was waiting to see on which side of the fence it would be more provident to graze.

'And Edmund?' she asked.

'Is on his way. He should be here by nightfall.'

She was anxious to meet with her stepson. According to the cast of his mind, he could put an end to her plans or help enforce them.

'I do not want to go to a boring meeting with Edmund.' Edward, half naked, stamped his foot and, wriggling out of Leofgifu's grasp, ran to the far side of the chamber to shuffle into a corner.

'You come here, child, and dress yourself. Prince Edmund will be here presently and he will not want to see your bare backside all reddened from where my hand has poached it.' Leofgifu had stayed loyal to Emma, going with the royal family to Normandy. She had never questioned her friendship with the Queen, but by God, this boy, on occasion, tried her patience!

'It's a meeting for old men.' Edward pouted. 'I shall not go. No one asked me if I wanted to come to this rotten place. No one bothered to consult what I might want.'

'That is because you are a horrid, rude child and have no say in these things,' Leofgifu answered tartly. No one had asked her either, come to that, but where the Queen went, Leofgifu went. She had not thought she would enjoy Normandy, but had, on the contrary, found it to be most enchanting. Well, if truth be told, the man she had met and felt drawn to had been the more attractive. A Norman horse trader who had promised to follow her to England. Leofgifu had no illusion that it would be a promise of the short-lived, easy-forgotten, kind.

The door opened and Edmund himself stepped through. He looked tired and gaunt; the past months of outlawry had taken a high toll, adding the look of years to a young man's face.

'What? Not ready, boy? Come, they are waiting for us in the Hall. Your mother and I have much to discuss with Council, we cannot be kept waiting because you wish to piddle about.'

Edmund's head was thumping and his body ached from the miles of riding he had accomplished since hearing of Swein's death. A week, two, asleep in bed would be most welcome. It was Edmund who had chivvied old Athelmar to send an envoy for the King, who had visited as many noblemen as he could, persuading them that it would be a wise move to call for Æthelred's return. Even if they could not see it, Edmund knew with certainty that if he were to take the crown for himself, he would be forced to fight to keep it. Cnut on the one side and his father on the other. Strange, he had never wanted the crown in his younger days, content to step aside for Athelstan, but now? Now he wanted it because, God help him, like his brother, he passionately cared about England. This way, by bringing Æthelred home, he only had Cnut to contend with. As they were boys, he had dismissed Emma's sons as rivals, although he conceded that the Queen had been clever in bringing Edward to plead Æthelred's pledge of good intention. He must not make the same mistake as Athelstan and underestimate her capability. Better, perhaps, to make a treaty of agreement with her? Out of them all, Emma could be the most daunting to face as an enemy and, if he had not misjudged her, the most steadfastly loyal.

'Be quick,' he said to the boy. 'I am wanted in the Hall and so are you. Æthelings do not keep their ealdormen waiting. Not unless they wish to be permanently exiled or openly ridiculed.'

Exile Edward wanted. Ridicule he did not. Shoving Leofgifu aside to finish dressing, he was not a child, whatever she said, he stamped out of the chamber. It was a short walk from the nunnery to the palace, but all the same, Edward found himself out of breath as they entered the crowded King's Hall. Edmund was a tall man and he had a long, fast stride; the boy had found that he had needed to trot most the way in order to keep up. His interest in the morning's events brightened when everyone stood at his entrance, they were standing for Edmund's honour, too, but were they not both sons of a king? And as Mama had often said, he was the legitimate born, so he had the precedence.

Much of what was heatedly discussed within the next half-hour meant nothing to Edward. He amused himself watching the motes of dust twist and dance in the sunrays that slanted in through the slit windows, and in studying the facial expressions of the most senior men. Old Athelmar, wrinkled and wizened, Archbishop Wulfstan, tall, dignified, and the Archbishop of Canterbury, who slept through most of it. Ulfkell of East Anglia, stern and imposing; the coward Ælfric, furtive, with darting eyes and a tongue constantly licking his lips; Eadric Streona, who insisted on being heard, bobbing up and down from his stool.

'My husband has sent a letter,' Emma finally announced, nudging Edward forward with her foot. 'My son, as your anointed King's representative, shall read it to you. Your King has considered all that you have had cause to complain against and he promises, henceforth, to be a true lord, to reform everything which causes you grievance and to forgive, without sanction, all that has been said and committed against him.' Occupied with trying not to drop the parchment that would not easily unroll, Edward did not see the express look of relief that flooded over Ealdorman Ælfric's sweat-pocked, fearful face at that.

Emma had rehearsed Edward over and over with the reading of this letter, determined that he should make a good and honest impression. Aware of the importance of his performance, Edward wanted to piss himself with fright, all those faces staring at him! He fumbled, cleared his throat, began, 'My Lords . . .' no one could hear him. Several men tutted and grumbled.

'Quiet for the boy!' Edmund demanded. 'Who among you has had to stand before such great company as a child and be expected to speak as a man? Let us show our respect to one who has not yet learnt our wisdom!'

Edward smiled shyly, perhaps he liked Edmund after all? Athelstan would never have been so nice to him. He swallowed a steadying breath, began to read. He could read well and, gaining in confidence, began to enjoy showing his prowess.

Archbishop Wulfstan, sitting at the foremost row of noblemen, listening intently, hid a smile behind a covering hand. Æthelred could not have written this letter; Emma must have had the doing of it, for it held her style, her character. Had also direct quotes from his own written works. Æthelred had never cared to read them in depth; Emma, with her intellectual cleverness, had used them to best advantage.

'People are made prosperous under a prudent king,' Edward read, 'but are made miserable under the misdirection of an unwise one.' That word, unwise, confirmed to the Archbishop that Æthelred had not written, nor read, the missive. Never would he have alluded to the detrimental mocking of his name.

'As your King, I, Æthelred, second king of that name, must be held responsible for injustice and hateful practices. I must govern justly and listen to my counsellors, even if their words do not please my ears. To command fair taxation and not extol profit for my own gain. It is my duty to protect my people against any attacking army, to meditate on wisdom and suppress evildoers.' Edward spoke clearer, slowing from the nervous pace he had started with, putting emphasis where it was required.

'Every merchant ship that passes the mouth of my rivers shall have peace, unless it is driven ashore by the wishes of God, who alone controls the waves of the sea and the wind of the air.' He read several adjustments to laws that Æthelred had been known to abuse, his words bringing approving nods from the men listening. 'If a man is accused of stealing cattle or killing another man, and the accusation is made by any man who pays taxes in the King's name who is not an Englishman, then the accused is not allowed to deny the charge unless proven innocent by trial.'

Wulfstan also nodded. Clever woman, the Queen, to have written that, for it had been a bone sticking in the Danelaw throat for many years. If an Englishman accused an Englishman, then justice had to be done through the process of law. If the same accusation was brought by a Dane against an Englishman, then it could be denied and acquitted. Laws that are all well and good for the English but prejudiced against the Dane settlers were, understandably, not welcome throughout the mid land and northern Boroughs of England.

There was impressed applause when Edward finished and bowed. Æthelred, it appeared, would be coming home, an apparently reformed and wiser king. Emma sat, her hands folded in her lap, pleased and proud of her son's heroic effort. Perhaps there was hope for him? Relief broadened her smile and the motherly kiss she placed on Edward's cheek was one of rare affection.

Edmund did not believe a word of the letter that he, too, had guessed had been written by Emma, not his father, but as Emma had politely indicated earlier in the day, her sons had the backing of the entire Duchy of Normandy which, in turn, had affiliation to the military might of France, Germany and Flanders.

'Would it be wise', she had said, with a charmed smile, 'to consider taking on such strength?'

Edmund had agreed that no, it would not. 'But neither would it be wise for a king to break the promises he has made.' It had been most satisfying to receive from Emma a similar nod of agreement.

6

'Cnut will not thank you for joining him in Gainsborough.' Alfhelm's widow, the Lady Godgifa, stood with her arms folded, barring the exit from her daughter's bedchamber.

Ælfgifu, thrusting her best gowns into a chest, attempting to squash them tighter so that she could close the lid, answered with venom, 'And what would you have me do instead? Sit here and wait for Æthelred to ride through the gate with a belated christening gift for my son Swegen? I wonder what it would be, Mama? A dagger blade, as with his own brother? Or perhaps he would prefer to have my babe's eyes put out, as he did with my brothers?'

Impatient, Godgifa pushed Ælfgifu aside and, throwing open the lid that refused to close, rearranged the muddled pile of clothing. 'Fold the things, girl, it will allow more room.' She lifted out a grey wool gown and tossed it aside. 'The sleeves are worn, you are a king's wife now, you cannot wear such rags.'

'I am not a king's wife, Mother, not until Cnut has dealt with Æthelred. His *i-víkings* have given him their support and claimed him king, but until he can be crowned it is a hollow claim.'

Godgifa snorted. 'To be so crowned he must be confirmed a Christian; will he prostrate himself before the Christ? Not that one!'

'Well, that is where you are wrong.' With more space in the chest, Ælgifu found she could add another mantle and several extra linen under-tunics. 'Archbishop Wulfstan welcomed Cnut to God the day after Swein's death. My husband realises that God has spoken to him and that He has need of him.'

In fact, Cnut had been appalled at the manner of his father's dying and the bitter argument that had caused it. What else could he do but turn to God and beg forgiveness? For had God not shown him, through his father's death, that God and Christ were the all powerful?

Godgifa shut the lid, began to buckle the straps. So that was how Cnut had managed to ensure his father was buried with dignity in York Minster? She had wondered. 'An army encampment is not the right place for you. It is not fitting for a woman, with a son at the breast, to go among so many men.'

'They are my husband's soldiers, they will honour me as their acclaimed king's wife, and where else can I be kept safe from Æthelred? Certainly not here!' Ælfgifu shuddered as she glanced around the room, checking to see if she had forgotten anything of importance. Who was there to guard her here at Northampton? A few lack-wits with quaking hands and piddled breeches? Two blinded brothers who sat huddled on stools before the fire all day, with nothing better to do than drink ale and curse Æthelred's name?

Ælfgifu had faith in Cnut. He was a strong young man and Æthelred was no match for him, but there were also niggling doubts scratching around in her mind. Why had Cnut not yet marched south from Gainsborough? Æthelred was on his way up through Huntingdon, could be in Northampton within the week. It did not take a quick mind to work out that he would soon send someone to ensure that Cnut's wife and son were efficiently disposed of, someone like that grime-rag Eadric Streona. Oh, how easily he had turned again! Scuttling back to Æthelred like the whipped cur that he was. Well, she was not going to sit here, wringing her hands and praying for deliverance, not when she was perfectly capable of riding a horse and taking herself and the babe to safety. Aside, there was also that other doubt.

Why had Cnut not taken her in formal marriage? For all these weeks, now, he had been dedicated to God; why had he not sent for her to have their union Christian blessed and acknowledged as an inseparable marriage? Without the blessing of the Church, he could, at a whim, set her aside, nor could she be crowned as queen. And that she wanted; oh, how she wanted it!

She might not especially like Cnut, but she very much liked what he was, and what he was going to be.

Ælfgifu had inherited several traits from her mother: a shrew's tongue, a calculating mind, and an insatiable wanting for more and better. Æthelred, by ordering the murder of her father and blinding of her brothers, had added something more potent and lasting: revenge. She was going to her husband's side to ensure he did not flee to Denmark without her, for if rumour was true and Cnut's men were not eager for a war campaign, then her husband could find himself in an untenable position, one that could only be solved by taking ship and running before the wind. And if Cnut chose to do that, she was fully intent on running with him. Or, if he refused to take her, to ensure for herself a secure sanctuary to await his return.

He would return, that she did not doubt, for he had nowhere else. His brother, Harald, would now be proclaimed King of Denmark and, while the brothers respected each other, there was no love between them. There would not be room in Denmark for both of them, not when they equally cherished the adornment of a crown. Æthelred might find himself, for reasons of practicality, unopposed this year but not the next or the next after that.

Nor did Ælfgifu have any intention of permitting Cnut to sail away without a memory of her firmly impressed on his mind and body. Particularly his body. This marriage had been made for convenience and political security; they had no love for each other, but when did love come into it? They shared a mutual heat of lust in bed and that was enough. When Cnut was with her, alone and naked beneath linen sheets, he had no thought of being parted from her. Ælfgifu saw to that, as she would see to it that if he sailed away he would be leaving a child planted within her. With God's blessing, a second son.

7

The noblemen of England had submitted to Swein of Denmark with such ease because he had promised no butchery and he had seemed infinitely preferable to Æthelred. They had been sick of their Saxon King. High taxation, year after year to pay the geld, and then the introduction of an additional tax to pay the scyp fyrd. What scyp fyrd? The one that he had assembled in Sandwich and then allowed to fall apart because he could not make sensible judgement or keep his lapdogs in line? His reign had been nothing but empty assurances and hollow promises. Not that any of them expected Swein to be any better, but he did offer a period of peace; women could be safe, crops grown and harvested, barns and hayricks left intact.

Cnut was a different matter. They liked the lad, one day he would be as good as his father, but not yet. That was why they went to Winchester to hear what Queen Emma had to say about her husband's regret for the past and his reform for the future, and why they had listened.

It all came down to the giving of land. The most powerful held the wealth and wealth was measured by the owning of land. Below the King, the Church was rapidly becoming a considerable land holder, for the reason that men who valued their soul saw the founding of religious houses and the giving of grants to those already existing as an assured path to God. And then there came the King's noblemen. Some had been under royal patronage for several generations, accruing estates and manors throughout England as payment for loyal service. Purchasing hidage from those who could not pay their taxes added to their holdings, as did receiving land taken from those who had fallen foul of the law. For those old elite families, the acres, the hides, steadily expanded.

Wealth brought more wealth, which bought more land. Land that could only be lost through forfeiture of non-payment of taxes or on the whim of the King. A king could give, a king could take away. That had been one of Æthelred's faults, the numerous unjust judgements that resulted in the confiscation of land. As for Cnut? What land did he hold that could be granted as reward to those who served him? To give land he first had to possess it and the only land he held was that belonging to the mother of his concubine wife, Ælfgifu.

Cnut stood in the bow of his father's ship, *Sea Serpent*, feeling the salt tang of the spray stinging his cheeks, the wind rummage through his hair and tug at his cloak. Like most of the men of his kind he loved the sea, its freedom, its moods. He stood, firm-footed, feet wide-planted, arms folded with his fingers pressed beneath his armpits. He was not appreciating the wind, or the spray, or the splendour of the ship. He was angry. By the wrath of all the gods, he was angry!

'Coast ahead, Sir!' his captain called, dipping his head towards the murk of a misted shore. 'Do you wish us all to put in, or just the ships with the hostages?' He waited, polite; no answer.

'Sir?'

Turning his head, Cnut's eyes flashed sparks of rage. 'Put in. All of us. I intend to leave something for the shit-scum of Lindsey to remember me by!'

Lindsey, the Boroughs of Leicester and Lincoln, Derby and Nottingham. Through Ælfgifu's kindred, Cnut had thought he had an understanding with Lindsey, had thought they had agreed to supply him with men and horses, when and if he needed them. Thought. How easily these lick-spits forgot their promises and their loyalties! What snivelling, cowardly whoresons they all were! Æthelred was leading an army into the south of Lindsey, had already plunged through Northampton and was destroying all that lay in his path – was retribution so unexpected? That was where Ælfgifu's family lands lay; of course Æthelred would confiscate those first! Cnut shifted his balance as the ship rolled. She would not like that, Ælfgifu. Another notch for her to mark on an arrow

341

shaft intended for Æthelred's heart. He glanced northwards, at the lour of grey cloud. She should be safe, by now, in the Wolds of York with her kinsman, the Hold, Thurbrand. Æthelred would not dare march beyond the Humber for Uhtred of Northumbria would be too much of a problem. Although he and the High Reeve, the Hold, of Holderness had never shared a similar view on anything, through a long-running feud that had caused outright hostility between them. Æthelred, marching too far north, could put their differences behind them. United, the North would be a dangerous enemy.

What hurt, what deeply punctured and stabbed into Cnut's spleen, was the added doubt from his own men, his own kind. They were his father's men, who had come as hired mercenaries to conquer England, men who had, at Swein's death, shouted for him to be their new king. So why were they now so unwilling to fight?

Because not a single stinking turd in all England had backed him! Because every ealdorman, thegn, lord, reeve and peasant farmer had applauded Æthelred's return, had said that Cnut was too young, too inexperienced and too naive to become king. Well, they would learn their mistake!

The ship was turning, the wind swinging to the steerboard as the sail flapped and the oarsmen sat alert, waiting for the order to run out the oars, the command to dip them into the water and pull. These men of the sea were brothers, they thought, lived, ate, slept and fought as one mind. When a ship was running, alive beneath their skilled hands, they were as one man. Cnut loved them, but they were wrong in not supporting him. He *was* ready, he *was* able to step out of his father's shadow and stand alone in the shine of the sun. He would have to prove it to them, then, wouldn't he? Show that he had the balls to do what a king must do.

'Set the hostages ashore,' Cnut ordered, as within the half of an hour the fleet of ships bobbed against the wharves of Sandwich harbour. The townsfolk had fled, or had scuttled into hiding, Cnut did not care which, as long as they left him alone to complete what he had come for.

They had all sent hostages to Swein when he had commanded it; every one of the empty-balled, pig-wallowing English ealdorman and high-ranking officials had complied. Every one of them had sent a son, grandson, brother or nephew to ensure their loyalty and augment their oath to the King of Denmark, Norway and England. And had considered the pledge void the minute Swein died; but Cnut did not see it like that. The army had unanimously declared for their dead king's son, and so should the noblemen have done. Had the ealdorman bowed to him, his army would have found the courage to fight . . . but on their own . . . on their own they just wanted to go home.

The grandson of the Ealdorman of Lindsey was brought before Cnut, eight years old, an innocent. Most of them were children. Children were more expendable than adults; children were not expected to be hurt if agreements were broken.

These children would.

Cnut looked at the boy dispassionately. The boy looked back, his head tilted upwards to see the tall man standing before him.

'Tell your father,' Cnut said, 'and tell him to tell Æthelred, that what I do is both a warning and a promise. Tell him that I will be back. Very soon.' Cnut studied the wary huddle of boys that his men were bringing ashore. The eldest was a son of the cowardly Ealdorman Ælfric of East Wessex, eighteen.

To his Captain of Housecarls, his personal bodyguard, men who would never, on pain of death, disobey his given command, he said, 'For each and every one of them, slit their noses and remove their ears and hands, then return to the ships. Leave them for their miserable fellow countrymen to find. I will have promises remembered and honoured.'

Lindsey, left to Æthelred's mercy, suffered. No farm was left unharried, livestock were slaughtered, women raped, even the young girls. Men and boys enslaved or killed where they stood. Estates were forfeited into the King's holding and punishment meted as if there was never again to be compassion or justice in the world of men.

After, even in the South where they had no care for the problems of the Mid Lands and the North, opinion ran in appalled whispers of muted shock. Cnut had been wrong to flee in his ship and abandon his allies to Æthelred, had been wrong to mutilate the innocent sons of the Shires, and they despised him for it. But Æthelred, too, was wrong. His vengeance was aimed at Cnut and the dead invader Swein, but taken out on the ordinary man, the trader, the farmer, the ploughman, and on their families. Had Archbishop Wulfstan not been warning them that the Devil was astride and that one day, soon, all evil would ride across the land? The people of England had not expected the annihilation to come in the guise of their own King Æthelred, however.

Then, on the twenty-eighth day of September, God delivered His final blow. The skies were torn apart as storms of crashing thunder and shattering bolts of lightning struck the world with doom. The wind, gusting with a force never before recalled, drove the high autumn tides inland across the open fens of East Anglia; sent them flooding up the waterways of Deira, along the Medway valley and the low lands of Kent and Gloucester, and as far up the Severn as Shrewsbury. Hundreds perished.

Blame for the suffering and misery of flood, and the following inevitable famine, the shame of mutilated children, misery and deprivation, was put entirely onto two men, hated with sudden equal intensity. On Æthelred and Cnut.

8

The stars speckled the black sky as if a sack of jewels had been torn open and spilt. The night was crisp with snow on the ground, the air sharp, sound carrying for miles across the sleeping winter landscape. From somewhere in the snow-bound forests a wolf howled, answered from a mile off by its mate.

Cnut pulled the bed furs up around his ears, the sweat on his naked skin cooling rapidly. He eased his wife, Ragnhild Sveinss-daughter, closer, enjoying the delicious sensation of her smooth warm body. Their lovemaking had been careful, for the child within her was almost five months grown, a distinct bulge in her belly. Five months? Their marriage seemed no more than five weeks! Drowsing into the comfort of the bed, her head heavy on his chest, Cnut allowed his mind to wander, thinking back, planning ahead.

In the balmy days of warm summer he had witnessed his brother, Harald, inaugurated as King, outwardly rejoicing for his acclaim, and as reward had received permission to raise an army to try again for England. An easy gesture for Harald to give, for with his younger brother away fighting wars elsewhere, Denmark and his crown were secure. If Cnut wanted a crown then he would need to find an empty one for himself. Cnut's problem, however, had manifested itself there at the coronation. Every *jarl* he approached, smiled, patted his shoulder, wished him good fortune and said the same thing: '*Ask me again when you are older. I'll not fight behind a green-stick lad.*'

Cnut could almost hear Æthelred laughing. And then Erik Håkonsson of Hlaðir had come forward. He, too, had rested his hand on Cnut's shoulder, but unlike the others his touch had not been patronising. 'Come with me to Hlaðir. You have nothing to gain by staying here, eclipsed by your brother's light.'

Cnut had been grateful to the older man, for his help and for his niece. Jarl Erik was one of the most respected warrior lords, and was placed among the highest-ranking noblemen of all Denmark and Norway combined. For more than thirty years he had been fighting and winning battles. It had been Erik who had ushered Cnut through childhood and early youth; Erik who had accompanied Cnut to England, had been there at that dreadful slaying of the old man, the Archbishop. Like Thorkell, that sickening episode had turned Erik to the full acceptance of Christianity, but unlike Thorkell, Erik had remained loyal to his king, to Swein and his youngest son. That sorrowful episode of the past haunted Cnut's dreams, the foolish pride of a boy holding sway over what was right. He had swaggered and preened because he had been jealous of his father's trust in Thorkell, a jealousy that had proved wasted and had made him behave like a spoilt child.

For the matter of a crowning, the jarls and anyone else of importance had come with their families to witness the occasion, the women especially pleased to have reason for the wearing of new gowns and the opportunity to display the wealth of jewellery their husbands lavished on them. With Ragnhild Sveinssdaughter, Erik's niece, Cnut had fallen in love immediately he had seen her. At first he had wondered whether Jarl Erik's offer of support had been intended as a jest for the obvious attraction between the two young people, had felt ashamed of his suspicion when, leaving Harald's Court for the sea journey to the western coast of Norway, Erik had admitted his reasons and they contained nothing but genuine friendship.

'I felt pained to see you brushed aside so out of hand, lad. Those fools cannot see the sea for the waves. You have more inside you, for courage, determination and strength, than ever your brother has. The Christ may show me that I am wrong, but I believe you to be the best of the two. It is not your fault, but the slowness of time, that makes you young and untried. With God's Grace, that will soon be remedied.'

Standing alongside Erik on the wind-blown deck, Cnut had felt the pride burst within him, had not dared to hope for more, but more had come.

Ragnhild stirred, mumbled in her sleep, the bulge of her belly jamming into his side. Cnut smiled into the darkness as he felt the babe kick.

She was his true-taken wife, the marriage blessed in God's sight in a Christian church – how Cnut now blessed his father's foresight in insisting on his commitment to God! Would Erik have been so eager to help had he not been embraced by Christ? Would Ragnhild have accepted his asking of marriage? Cnut shied away from the questions, fearing the answers. The small matter of Ælfgifu in England he shrugged aside more easily. She had known she was no more than a concubine wife, was only important as the mother of his son – sons – she had birthed another, Harold, named in honour of the new King of Denmark. Cnut frowned into the darkness. Ælfgifu was not going to take his rejection of her lightly; she was a shrew of a woman, determined and vindictive; everything about her was harsh and hard, as if she were made of wood with sharp edges and no soft, warm centre. Her temper was short and shrill, her eyes small and glaring. She demanded rather than asked, shouted rather than talked. Even her lovemaking was violent, her nails scratching his flesh, her wanting urgent, insistent. There was nothing tender about Ælfgifu. All she wanted was vengeance for her father's death and her brothers' blinding, and she did not care how she achieved it or who might suffer in her wake.

'I will help you, Cnut Sweinsson,' Erik had announced on that voyage. 'When the time is ready I will come with you to England and fight for you to wear Æthelred's crown!'

'And why would you be doing that, Erik Håkonsson?'

'I owed much to your father; alas, it was never in my power to repay him. At last I can settle my debt; aside, I have no liking for Æthelred Ill Counsel.'

In the spring, when the snow thawed and the ice on the fjords had melted, the men would come. Cnut did not mind that they would not be coming for his sake but for Erik's. What did it matter

347

who blew the war horn, as long as ears heard and men responded? And, for now, he had these few precious months with his beautiful love, Ragnhild.

9

The hope for kept promises died at the Easter Council, along with two men.

Where was Æthelred's reform of unjust laws? His willingness to put right the wrongs, the compassion and forgiveness for those who had only attempted to pursue the cause of peace? Even Archbishop Wulfstan's passionate and charged 'Sermon of the Wolf', a preached tirade against injustice, lawlessness and general wickedness, had made no effect in calming Æthelred's rage or the people's fear. England suffered and her noblemen began to realise they had allowed a wolf into the fold in the guise of a corrupt and inept man who happened to wear the privilege of a crown.

Emma had her own opinion. 'The absolute power of a king is given by God to be used wisely. Unfortunately, most who have been awarded this power are surrounded by those who profess themselves to be friends. They flutter like moths to a flame, drawn by greed to the light. Some fly too close and get their wings burnt; others, the majority, hover always just out of danger, so they gain all and risk nothing, but their presence eclipses the light and darkens it until it is of no practical use.' Exasperated from the tiring day, she was speaking her mind to Edmund in the privacy of her bedchamber at Woodstock.

She had always liked Edmund, who had the dedication, but not the stubborn single-mindedness, of his elder brother. Edmund was easygoing, quick to smile, willing to listen to alternative views; but now he was man-grown, he also had that essential formidability of one who would not tolerate being crossed. He was loyal to his friends and took his duty to the kingdom seriously, qualities Emma admired and respected. Similarly, Edmund respected Emma; he always had, only his love for Athelstan, by necessity, had taken precedence over his personal judgement. Emma, like Edmund, chose her friends from those she could trust beyond question. There were few of them; Wulfstan and her personal priest; Wymarc, who had dedicated herself to caring for the children and, above them, Leofgifu, her beloved companion, and Leofstan, Captain of her cnights – and Edmund. Edmund was more than a friend, for he was also an ally. He shared the same hope as Emma and travelled the same road, his hands easy on the reins, pacing at a steady walk, but constantly alert for ambush or unseen difficulties, which he was capable of combating with precision.

'It is a sorry fact', she continued, 'that wealthy and powerful men possess a driving need to acquire more of what they have already got. Corruption in a man is an insidious disease, akin to the cock pox.' She laughed cynically. 'It spreads unseen and unchecked. If chaste, without cheating or seeking extra illicit favours, he remains clean and uncontaminated, but once his pizzle has been dipped into the wrong pot, the fire takes hold and consumes him from the inside out.'

The hour was late, most of the royal household were rolled in blankets and asleep on straw mattresses. From the Hall emanated the steady sound of snoring. Æthelred was in his own chamber and, for all Emma knew or cared, was engrossed in the pursuit of her metaphor with a whore.

Candidly Edmund answered, 'The problem for my father is that he does not know how to rule. Grandmama had a hand on all its doing.' He was seated on a stool, hunched forward, his hands nursing a half-emptied goblet of Emma's finest wine. Even so, it tasted sour in his mouth. 'It is good policy', he continued, musing his grievances aloud, 'to appoint men who are solely responsible for a Shire or Borough. It is good because, with reliable men capable of their job, the defence of the Kingdom can remain intact if something should happen to the King. But', he added with a sigh, 'it is only good policy when the right men are appointed.' He rubbed his hand through his hair. He was tired, bone tired, in mind and spirit. 'Papa's ealdormen do not respect him, so they take what they can as often as they can, knowing they will never be challenged or punished for it. There are as many thieves and robbers among his reeves as there are outlawed and convicted felons.' He drank a mouthful of wine, wiped the residue from his moustache. 'If some-thing is not soon done to make Papa realise that his ill judgements are destroying England, the few good men at this Council will saddle their horses and leave. If the morrow goes as badly as today . . .' Wearily, Edmund shook his head, left his dismal sentence unfinished.

Council had consisted of raised voices and bitter argument. By mid afternoon Sigeferth and Morcar had been on their feet ready to walk out with Lord Uhtred; Archbishop Wulfstan had persuaded them to sit, be patient. Others had been on the verge of going with them, men who had previously been falling over their feet to placate the King and procure his forgiveness.

Old Athelmar had the right idea. With Æthelred returned to England he had quietly sought the sanctity of his monastery. At this precise moment Edmund felt greatly inclined to join him.

Leaving her chair, Emma fetched the wine jug, refilled his goblet. 'What, then, do you suggest we do about your father, Edmund? Slit his throat? Administer poison? I am sure, if I looked, I could find some hemlock along the hedgerows that will do the deed.' She spoke with a laugh in her voice, but there was an element of seriousness there also.

Edmund scowled, his chagrin made all the deeper because her suggestions had been swimming around in his own mind this last week.

'Or perhaps I could smother him with a pillow?' Emma quipped. 'None would question a wife wishing to be alone with her lord.' She paused, flicked her hand. 'Except for his whore.' Her sarcasm was acerbic. She had no proof of Æthelred's infidelities, only a suspicion, procured by the fact that he never wanted her in his bed. Or that could have something to do with the dagger she kept beneath her pillow. The one that, on the last occasion he had attempted to assault her, she had promised to use on his flaccid apology for a manhood.

Draining his wine, Edmund set the goblet down on the table

beside him and said conscientiously, 'Do not jest of murder, Madam. It is not seemly.'

'Nor is the King,' Emma retorted with a shrug to her shoulder.

They lapsed into silence, both aware that if Æthelred were to learn of this private meeting and the content of its conversation, for all its falsehood, the climate of this Easter calling of Council would rise higher in temperature than it already was.

'I am thinking that it was a mistake to have brought him back from Normandy.'

Privately, Emma agreed with Edmund, but then Æthelred had been the only way of getting back herself. Whatever she did from here on, she had to ensure that nothing would prevent Edward and Alfred from being accepted as æthelings and that, as Edmund had said, meant doing something about Æthelred.

She offered him more wine, he refused, his head was already heavy, his senses muzzy. 'It is a pity that there is no legal way in English law of removing an unwanted king.'

Edmund stared into the glowing embers of the brazier, at the red charcoal, the deeper yellow heat. 'Only God can take away what He has given. The King is anointed with holy Chrism, that makes him above mortal men and what mortal man has the right to remove one of God's chosen? It would be a sin as profound as the murdering of a priest.' He added, without glancing up, 'Or an archbishop.'

'That is a sin that does not appear to bother the Danish,' Emma answered flippantly. 'Perhaps we should take a spear out of their rack? Shall I ask Thorkell to do the deed for us?' She stared into the red liquid of her wine as she swilled it around in its cup. Not Thorkell, he had turned more pious than Wulfstan.

A long silence, each sitting with the company of their own thoughts. Then, speaking in almost a whisper, as if she did not want even the walls to hear, Emma said, slowly and deliberately, 'A mortal man could not murder a king, unless the slaying was done with honour on the battlefield, but what of a woman? A woman similarly anointed? A queen is above the law and is also chosen by God. She too has avowed to serve and protect her people.'

As slowly, his eyes fixing firmly on Emma, Edmund answered,

'And would a queen, then, be willing to risk burning for eternity in the fires of Hell for the sin of murder?'

Emma took a mouthful of wine, swallowed, almost gagged on it, for her throat was constricted. Was this how Æthelred's mother had felt the night before her stepson had arrived at Corfe? Had she felt the blood sticky on her hands? Was this what it meant to be a queen? To contemplate a decision that could blast you into eternal damnation? It would be easy to do – she could do it now, this moment. She could walk into his chamber, sink a blade into his back or across his throat. Or she could smother him, or put her fingers either side of his windpipe and squeeze . . . the darkness of evil gathered within her, grew, filling and consuming her, swelling through her body, dripping into her fingers and oozing into her feet.

'Do it!' a voice whispered. 'Do it and your crown will be safe!' The face of the Devil leered at her, a mask of emptiness, grinning eyes, bright and burning. Physically she drew back, found she was shaking.

'There must be another way,' she said lightly, her heart pounding fast, her voice, cracking. The demon that had been squeezing at her own throat, at her belly, fled as she rejected murder for the sin it was.

'Well,' Edmund said, rising from his stool, not noticing the cold hand that had attempted to enslave Emma's soul, 'mayhap God will have pity on us and solve our dilemma.' He half laughed. And mayhap the moon would rise and turn blue. 'I must take my leave; it is late and I am for my bed.' He ambled to the door; his thumb on the latch, stated, 'Athelstan never liked you because he did not trust you. It is in my heart that it is a sad thing he never discovered how wrong he was.'

Emma smiled, half shrugged. 'Who knows, it may yet be you who is in the wrong, not he.'

Shaking his head, Edmund answered, 'I do not think so. You have England's security as your priority because without England, you cannot exist.' He smiled. 'Good night to you, Lady. God protect you.'

Emma awoke from a deep sleep and a dream where she had been running naked through a forest of dark, brooding trees, a bloodied dagger in her hand, screams pursuing her. Or had it been her own

353

screaming? She lay in the dark, listening to her heart thump. Leofgifu, on her pallet, was lying on her back, open-mouthed, snoring. The reed thatch of the roof rustled as some rodent scuttled about up there. A floorboard creaked.

A shout. A man running. More shouting. Dogs began to bark, noise swelled from the Hall below, men waking, scrambling to their feet, hurrying into the courtyard. Were they under attack? Surely Cnut could not have returned? Emma stumbled in the darkness towards the faint glow of the brazier, cursed as her fingers fumbled for a taper. Leofgifu, groggy from sleep, was beside her, holding a beeswax candle. Light flickered, faded, then flared, bringing brightness to the room. Leofgifu, fearing they were to be slain in their beds, ran to bolt the door, but Emma, flinging her cloak across her shoulders and thrusting boots on to her bare feet, stopped her.

'I'll not skulk behind shuttered doors. If someone has come to murder us, then I would die honourably, not as a shivering whore.'

'Listen to you!' Leofgifu rebuked as she searched for her own boots. 'Anyone would think you were a spear-warrior like the menfolk. Like it or not, you are a woman and women ought not get in the way of men when they are about their business.'

Ignoring her, Emma was out of the door, running, her loose hair flying.

The courtyard was full of people, mostly men in a state of half-dress, some hopping on one foot pulling on a second boot, others drawing leather jerkins over their heads. Many barefoot, clad only in under-tunics. Chaos, confusion, no one seemed to know what was happening. More torches were being brought, lit, the smoke of the pitch turning the night air into a thick, stinking fug.

Someone blundered into Emma, trod on her foot, cursed. Recognising the voice if not the explicitly obscene word, Emma grabbed Godwine's arm, swung him round to face her. 'Godwine! What is happening?'

He was twenty and one now, a fine young man with fair hair and, as with most of his rank, a trailing moustache. One of the most handsome, intelligent and – a rarity – trustworthy of Æthelred's thegns.

'Lady!' he exclaimed, in turn swinging her round to hustle her away in the direction she had come from. 'This is no place for a woman.'

Disengaging herself from his grasp, Emma stood firm, refusing to move another step. 'Maybe not, but I am your Queen, I have a right to know what is happening.'

Godwine made one more futile attempt to steer her towards her chamber, gave up. 'Treachery. Someone has attempted to murder the King.'

Her head came up sharp, a temporary feeling of guilt flooded through her. Edmund? The damned stupid idiot had not taken their conversation seriously, had he?

None of her alarm showed on her face or quavered in her voice. Calm, she asked, 'Who and how?'

Godwine tried matching Emma's smooth control, found he could not. 'The Thegns Sigeferth and Morcar, Edmund's friends.' He hung his head to hide the tears of despair. 'They burst into the King's chamber with daggers drawn, slew his body servant and attempted to kill him.' He lifted his head, suddenly not caring that she saw him weeping. 'What possessed them? How did they think they would succeed? Get away with it?'

'They probably had no intention of getting away, Godwine,' Emma pointed out. She placed her hand on his arm, a comforting, understanding gesture. 'All they wanted was Æthelred dead.' *As do we all*, she thought bitterly.

'Shrewdly judged, my lady. Thank God they did not manage it.' Eadric Streona, striding out of the swelling crowd, swept Emma a patronising bow. Ordered his men to clear a path through the mêlée. 'The perpetrators' execution will be carried out immediately. This is, therefore, no place for a lady,' he said, ignoring the women gathering with husbands, fathers or masters. 'I would advise you to return to your chamber.'

'Any place of justice is the place of the Queen,' Emma retorted.

There was a commotion at the doorway to the far end of the Hall, people were pushing forward, jeering and shouting. Eadric inclined his head towards Emma, said simply, 'As you wish.'

They were brought out, their hands bound behind their backs, blood seeping from a wound to Sigeferth's left temple. Both were struggling, shouting. One of Streona's guards slammed the pommel of his sword into Morcar's mouth; teeth and blood gushed out.

'We are innocent!' Sigeferth was pleading to be heard, then he saw Emma. He tried to pull free from the hands restraining him, tried with all his strength to get to her. 'Lady! I beg you, we are innocent! We were summoned to see the King – Eadric Streona himself sent for us!'

Streona heard the accusation, laughed a response. 'That is a feeble lie! How dare you implicate me in your treachery?'

Men were bringing ropes, throwing them over the lower boughs of the oak tree that stood, majestic in its full maturity, outside the smith's forge. Two ponies were being led up. Excitement was expanding, rushing like wildfire spreading through dry grass.

Edmund came running, dishevelled, his underclothing partially unlaced, his feet bare. Valiantly he tried to stop Streona's men from setting his friends astride the ponies; swearing and cursing, he batted at them with the flat of his sword. Eadric Streona caught his flailing arm, dragged him aside. 'Justice must be done; come away!'

'Let go of me, you scum!'

'Give me the sword, boy. Or are you in this with them? Was this perhaps your idea?'

'Oh, I'll give you my sword, you bastard!'

Emma stepped in quickly, placing herself between Edmund and Streona, her hand going to the ætheling's arm, restraining him. Eadric's face had drained chalk white as the sword had pricked into the hollow of his throat, drawing a trickle of blood.

'Edmund, there is nothing you can do,' she commanded. At his continued struggle said again, sharper, 'Leave it I say!'

'We are innocent!' Sigeferth bellowed over and over as the noose was fitted to his neck. 'Look at our hands, we have no blood on them! We have killed no one! God help us, we are innocent!'

A woman, dressed only in her undershift, ploughed her way through the crowd, oblivious to the fact that she could be all but naked in some eyes. Ealdgyth, Sigeferth's wife.

356

'My God!' Emma cried, seeing her. 'Edmund!' She shook him, her nails digging into his flesh, shook him to get his attention. 'Edmund, do something about Ealdgyth! Get her away from here, she should not see this!'

Uncomprehending, Edmund stared at the Queen, then sense registered that Ealdgyth was attempting to claw at the pony Sigeferth was seated on, her hands trying to pull him down, save him.

Thrusting his sword into Emma's hands, Edmund ran to her, scooped her into his arms and carried her away, thrusting through the noise of the excited crowd, his long stride loping, almost running. His ears oblivious to Ealdgyth's frantic screaming, her fists and feet beating and kicking at him. Sigeferth's voice echoing, 'Take care of her, Edmund, for the sake of my innocent soul, take care of her!'

The men, the women of the King's palace, the nobles and their wives, servants, slaves stood, pushing together in a heaving mass of ghoulish hysteria, their combined wail of bloodlust reaching a crescendo as the ropes were tightened and burning torches were thrust into the ponies' rumps to frighten them forward into a bounding leap that left the two men dangling grotesquely.

It was not an easy death, for the ropes were knotted so as to not break the neck but to strangulate. For Sigeferth and Morcar, their eyes bulged, their tongues swelled, urine and faeces involuntarily evacuated, and their legs, bodies, jerked and twisted. A long, slow, horrible death.

Emma watched, her lips pressed silently together, her hand clutching her cloak tight at her throat. A slow, horrible, contrived death of two innocent men. Sigeferth had been telling the truth.

As he said, if they had slain Æthelred's body-servant, then where was the blood on their hands? The only blood that Emma had seen was from the injuries to Sigeferth's face and Morcar's mouth. Yet there had been blood on Eadric's hand, on his tunic, too.

And how was it, alone among all others save the two hanged men and the guard of the nightwatch, that Eadric Streona was full dressed?

10

'My Lady!' Godwine attempted to burst into Emma's chamber, jamming his foot into the half-open door before Leofgifu had a chance to slam it closed. 'I need to speak to the Queen, urgently!'

'The Queen is not dressed. Come back in a while.'

Stepping back a pace, Godwine thrust his boot into the door, slamming it open, sending Leofgifu sprawling. 'My apologies, I must see her now!' He paused to help the winded servant to her feet.

'Do come in, Godwine,' Emma drawled from where she sat at a table, a handmaid combing her hair. 'If you are seeking to break your fast, then I must advise that you will not be provided for in here.' She indicated a tray on a second table, the bowls and platters empty but for crumbs. 'As you see, I have already eaten.' She had on only her chemise, and a fine-woven lambswool shawl that did nothing to hide the shape of her slender body and the cleavage between her breasts. To his embarrassment, Godwine felt his manhood stirring.

'I am certain that you did not come barging into my chamber to gawp at my teats,' Emma said, masking her amusement, after the silent pause had lasted a little too long. 'Was there something more important on your mind, by chance?'

Blushing as red as a poppy, Godwine stared fixedly at a space on the pink-plastered wall. His mind had gone blank, all he could see was a tumble of fair hair . . . He cleared his throat, forced himself to concentrate; by God, this was urgent, how could he let himself become distracted? 'My Lord Edmund is with the King; they are amid a most heated argument. I fear things may get out of hand.'

Emma indicated that her maid was to braid her hair, asked Leofgifu to fetch her gown. 'Edmund is a man capable of looking after himself. I do not think he would welcome interference.'

'But Madam, it concerned the Lady Ealdgyth. Edmund promised Sigeferth that he would take care of her and the King has sent her away. On top of everything that has happened, I do not trust Lord Edmund to hold his sense!'

Emma had looked up sharply, half rising from her stool. 'What do you mean, sent her away?'

'At dawn. He has had her escorted to the nunnery at Malmesbury; she is to remain there until he orders otherwise.'

'Malmesbury? With that bitch, Abbess Mildrith?' She was fully to her feet now, beckoning Leofgifu to hurry and dress her. Within a handful of minutes she was out of the door and striding towards Æthelred's chamber, Godwine trotting at her heels.

As with Godwine, Emma did not wait to be announced, but walked straight into Æthelred's room, thrusting aside the half-hearted attempt by his guard to block her entry. Godwine judged it prudent to wait outside. He exchanged a grimace with the guard, who ducked his head towards the raised voices coming from within.

'I'm not poking my nose in there unless summoned,' he said. 'Not my business to interfere a'tween father and son.'

Godwine nodded agreement.

'Do you know what he has done?' Edmund roared as he saw Emma. 'He has imprisoned Ealdgyth, has sent her to Malmesbury. Malmesbury! God's Eyes, even priests and bishops quake at going there, so unyielding is Mildrith's view of life outside a virgin's cell. She'll destroy a fragile creature like Ealdgyth within the month!'

'Abbess Mildrith is an honourable and dedicated nun,' Æthelred countered. 'I have sent the woman there for her own protection.'

Removing several of Æthelred's tunics draped over a stool and disdainfully dropping them into a hovering servant's arms, Emma seated herself. She straightened her gown, smoothed away a wisp of straw that she must have picked up from walking through the Hall. The hem was stained, she noticed; she had worn this red dress too many occasions this month. 'Abbess Mildrith is a depraved, narrow-minded tribade. There is no nun in her convent below old age; they are all incontinent, grey hairs with stooped backs, gumless mouths and senile dementia. Mildrith's young noviciates relinquish their calling or plead to be removed elsewhere within the moon-month of arriving. More than one girl, from despair, has drowned herself in the river.'

'That is a lie! You insult an esteemed woman of God!'

'As she insults God, and it is no lie, it is a truth that has been carefully hidden. There is not a woman in England who would not spit on Mildrith.' Emma spoke with precise clarity, her voice lowered and even. Shrill words, quickly spoken, aroused a temper, doing more damage than a flame set to a tinder-dry hayrick. 'And why, may I ask, would Lady Ealdgyth require protection? From whom?' She finished fiddling with her girdle keys, looked up, staring direct at Æthelred, challenging him. Unable to meet her eyes, he glanced away, looked down. 'Surely this palace is safe for a grieving widow?' Emma added.

'It is not her safety he cares about, Madam,' Edmund interjected from where he stood, over by the narrow window, its shutters still bolted and secured. Æthelred's rooms were never aired while he was in residence, he complained at the draughts, the cold. The chamber stank of stale hearth-smoke and sweat, of puddled urine and passed wind. 'Ealdgyth was intent on slitting that bastard Eadric Streona's throat – I was all for helping her! It is for his safety that she has been sent away, to keep her mouth shut against the accusation that he murdered her husband.'

'She was distraught and spreading lies,' Æthelred bellowed, having heard enough of Edmund's diatribe. 'Eadric had no part in any injustice. He saved me from those two scum when they burst in here with daggers drawn, intent on my murder.' He stormed across the room, pointed at the fouled rushes. 'Here is the blood of the servant they killed to get to me! If you care to look outside, you will also see the blood of the man who stood guard. They stabbed him through the heart. How could I tolerate the lies that woman has been broadcasting about the man who saved my life?'

'How noble of Eadric Streona to be so conveniently on hand,' Emma said, examining her nails. One on her right hand was broken, that was riding yesterday. You could tell a lot about a person by studying their hands. Servants had rough, reddened skin; a

360

needlewoman calluses to her fingertips, a horseman or swordsman had the calluses along the padded flesh above the palm; all had short, torn and often dirty nails. A noblewoman boasted cared-for hands and long, shaped nails; women who spent much of their life cooking often showed their fingers as yellowed and smoke-tainted. Blood was another difficult stain to remove. Especially when congealed beneath the fingernails. Abruptly, she dropped the pretence of uninterest.

'Streona had this planned, that I know for fact. What I do not know is how much of it was your idea, Æthelred. I am sincerely hoping that you can assure me, in the name of the God who anointed you as King, that none of this was done in your name.'

Æthelred turned away, growled at his servant to fetch him ale. 'And make it the better-brewed stuff, the piss you brought me last evening was not fit for the pigs.' He busied himself with some rolls of parchment scattered across a table, said, with his back firmly to Emma and Edmund, 'My life was in danger and its cause has been remedied; those who attempted murder have been hanged and their estates laid forfeit to me.'

With a bellow of rage, Edmund pitched over a candle stand. 'You wanted the land, didn't you? Wanted to be rid of two troublemakers and make a profit into the bargain? How low can you stoop? You've been doing this ever since you became King, haven't you? You and Streona together, accusing the innocent of crimes they did not commit and taking all they had in forfeiture.' He flung his arm out, gesturing contempt. 'How long do you suppose ealdormen like Uhtred will remain loyal to you once they realise what you have done?'

Æthelred turned, a dagger in his quivering hand, its tip pointing vaguely in the area of Edmund's midriff. 'But they will not realise it, will they?'

The tension, as taut as a tent's guy rope, was shattered by Emma. Her hands flat on her knees, she tossed back her head and laughed. 'You poor, pathetic old fool,' she said, rising, walking towards him and removing the dagger as if she were taking away a toy from one of the children. 'Do you seriously think you could kill Edmund? And then me? For you would have to, you know, I have no more intention of keeping this from your lords than does your son.' She set her face very close to his, said into his ear, 'And do not think to have Streona do your filthy work for you. If he steps within sword length of me, I shall have my cnights cut him down and fed to the pigs with your pissed ale.'

She handed the dagger to Edmund who, staring at it a moment, threw it, with insipid distaste, into the floor rushes. 'You have imprisoned Ealdgyth because of the estates, haven't you, Father? By right of law they pass to her, unless she enters a nunnery.'

'Or unless she carries an unborn son,' Emma added. 'Abbess Mildrith can be relied upon to ensure that no unwanted pregnancy came to term.'

Edmund's face drained pale, panic flared through him. 'My God, I never thought of that! I promised Sigeferth I would take care of her, I promised!' His hands were raking his hair as he strode around the room, trying to think, trying to reason.

Emma, experienced, trained to show an outward serenity through an inner whirl of chaos, made up his mind for him. 'Then take the fastest horses from the stables and remove Ealdgyth from Malmesbury.' She went to the far side of the room, rummaged in her husband's jewel casket and, grunting satisfaction, handed one of Æthelred's recognisable rings to Edmund. 'Use this with wisdom. I suggest you take young Godwine with you, he will need no explanation, for I have a suspicion that he has had his ear nailed to the door throughout. Before you leave, I would see you in my own chamber.'

Edmund stood a moment, bewildered and confused.

'Hurry, man!' Emma said impatiently, shooing him towards the door.

He bowed to her; except for a curt, contemptuous glance, ignored his father. They heard him calling, a moment later, for his cnights, and the horses to be saddled.

'I will send men after him,' Æthelred announced. 'I shall order a galloper to race ahead of him. I shall . . .'

'You shall do nothing, Æthelred, for if you do I shall not

guarantee my silence. If your lords only guess at half-truths you have a chance of survival. If they learn of facts you will be dead before the summer. And I, for one, shall not regret your passing.'

What she had to say to Edmund in private impressed him, but did not come wholly as a surprise. Emma spoke forthright. 'We must do something about Æthelred. I suggest, after you have secured Ealdgyth's release, that you find a priest and witnesses, and take her as your legal Christian-blessed wife, then ride north. As her lawful husband her estates become yours. With Sigeferth's men joined with your own, you can also claim what was Morcar's. From there, I would suggest you rally the North to your own banner.'

'Civil war, you mean?' Edmund puffed his cheeks. How often had he talked his brother out of doing exactly what Emma was proposing? From where he now stood, too often. Perhaps he ought to have stood aside and let him get on with it?

As if she had been planning this for some while and not just thought of the idea, Emma took her crown from its casket. It was a band of purest gold, two inches in height and studded along its centre with sapphires and rubies.

'It is not in my power to give you Æthelred's crown,' she said, holding it out to him. 'That you must win for yourself, but it is in my ability to give you mine. I charge you to take it, for the good of England and the welfare of my people.'

Puzzled, Edmund had not understood. 'You are relinquishing your queenship?'

'Of course I am not! I am asking you to take care of this kingdom, as its king clearly cannot, to protect the laws and justice of England, in the name of the æthelings, Edward and Alfred, and myself, the Queen.'

'I could decide to sidestep you, take Father's crown and keep it,' he answered honestly.

'And there would be none who could stop you. Except my sons will not always be boys and, as I have often said to your father, you do not have the strength of Normandy to call upon to aid you. They, and I, do.' On every occasion that she mentioned this threat,

Emma said a silent prayer: *Please, God, do not let my brother fail me if ever I need ask help of him.* After the weeks of purgatory in Normandy she feared her threat was emptier than a dried well. Richard was too mean-minded to be helping anyone, but the bluff came with no one besides herself realising that the Duke of Normandy was as contemptibly useless as the King of England.

In the courtyard, ready to leave, Edmund mounted his horse and saluted her, not a mocking gesture but one of admiring sincerity. She stood in the doorway, her cloak gripped tight by her fingers so none might see the tremble in them. 'I will rule as king with your sons as æthelings to come after me. Is that sufficient for you?'

Emma nodded. It was not, but it would have to do.

11

Summers were warm in Norway; in Hlaðir, the fields were of fertile, rich, arable land that grew crops, or sweet, flower-strewn meadows. For that, the jarls of Hlaðir were wealthy men, their jurisdiction lusted after by those in search of wealth-making.

Cnut was fishing with Hakkon, Jarl Erik's son. They were good companions, these two men, of almost the same age, give a month or two, similar build, height, wit and temper. Hakkon was also much like his father, a warrior, who lived and breathed for the excitement of the fight. Since his fourteenth birthday he had gone *í-víking* with his father, both of them serving with King Swein. Their regret, that they had not been in England when he had died. Had Erik been there, Cnut would have been honoured as king, there would have been none of this waiting in Norway for men. Not that they had done too badly, for the harbour bobbed with ships; Erik's Hall and the numerous taverns bulged to bursting. But it was not enough, it was still not enough!

'You are not concentrating on this fishing, are you, Cnut?' Hakkon commented, seeing his companion's line dip below the surface, bob a few times, then go slack. 'We are supposed to be catching your supper, not sitting here feeding them theirs.'

Startled, Cnut jerked his line, which promptly broke, and laughed apologetically. 'No, I admit my mind is not here.'

'In England with that fool of a king? Ah, you will not have long to wait, lad! We almost have the ships and the crews, and even if we do not, I hear that Æthelred is despised more than ever. He might be dead now for all we know.'

'Ja, and he has a son capable of taking over from him.'

'What? The boy Edward? He is a ten-year-old!'

Cnut laughed again, realising Hakkon was teasing him. 'No, I meant the other son, Alfred,' he baited in turn.

'Well, I suggest you stop thinking of boys and set your mind to fishing, else you are likely to go hungry to bed tonight.'

Grinning, Cnut rethreaded a line, hook and bait to his pole. Confessed, 'It was not of the English boys that I was thinking but my own – unless he has arrived as a she.'

Hakkon stared, content, at the gentle swell on the water, looked out at the wonder that was this coastline of Norway, drowsy beneath the summer sun. Ragnhild had been about women's work this day. Cnut, pacing the Hall, banned from the women's chamber, had begun to grate on everyone's nerves, hence Hakkon's suggestion of fishing. Someone would come to the shore, attract their attention when it was suitable for them to return. Unless night came before the child which, with a first babe, was more than possible.

'I would not mind a daughter,' Cnut mused. 'I have two sons in England, although the one I have seen was a scrawny thing. He reminded me of a squirming newborn rat.'

'You tread on a young rat if you find one, hardly a suitable comparison, Cnut.'

His line sinking, Cnut began to haul it in, cursed, as with a snap this also broke, the fish darting away.

'With children, how do you know which are to grow into rats or cherubs? Which ones do you stamp on with your boots?'

'Children? Huh, looking at my cousins and the monsters that run around my father's Hall, I would say all of them are vermin! Hello? Is that someone calling our attention?' He peered across at the shore, saw a man standing, frantically waving. Hakkon pulled in his line and began to row. 'We are wanted.'

Cnut was out of the boat and plunging through the water before Hakkon had opportunity to beach it. The young man on the shore he did not recognise, but from the banner he carried he was one of Harald's men.

'There is news from Denmark?' Cnut panted as he waded ashore, oblivious of the cold water on his legs. 'Is there any word from Lord Erik's Hall? Has the babe come?'

The messenger looked puzzled. 'Babe, my Lord? I know nothing of a babe; I bring news direct from King Harald.'

'My brother is well? There is nothing amiss?' Cnut was on dry land, out of breath from excitement as much as the hurrying. 'Did they not ask you to bring me word of how my wife fares?'

'No, Lord, the news I bring is of far more importance.'

Folding his arms, Cnut frowned. The lad was not far past puberty, too young to have the birth of a child as a priority. Good-humoured he said, 'Tell me, then, what can be more important than the coming of my son?'

'Thorkell the Tall is harboured at Roskilde. He has come to Denmark with nine ships and crew to join with you against Æthelred. Your brother sends word that he grants permission for him to do so.'

Cnut was stunned. 'Is this a jest? Thorkell? The man who turned traitor against my father?'

'Ja, Thorkell. He has abandoned Æthelred as a man who breaks his promise and murders those of his own. He says the English King has no honour, that his blood is nothing more than piss and that his given word is shit.'

With the boat pulled above the tide line, the three men began to walk towards the complex of buildings that was Jarl Erik's homestead.

'So what has happened to make Thorkell so suddenly change his mind?' Hakkon wanted to know.

The messenger, finding that he had to jog to keep up alongside the two older men, explained, 'This is what I have been told to tell you, by the lips of Thorkell himself: "*Now that you, my Lord Cnut, have adopted the ways of a Christian, I am willing to serve you. If you do not want me, I will understand and go in peace with my ships to seek employment elsewhere. I will no longer support a man who has ordered my brother murdered and a corps of the finest Danish soldiers butchered, on an imagined charge of treason.*" '

Appalled, Cnut slammed to a halt. 'Hemming is dead?'

'Ja, my Lord, or so Thorkell tells.'

'By Thor's Hammer,' Hakkon exclaimed, 'if we care to wait long enough, Æthelred will kill off all his own for us!'

'Will you have him, Sir?' the messenger asked, anxious that his hard journey would not be wasted. 'Will you let Thorkell join you?'

Cnut clamped his hand on the lad's shoulder, confirmed that *ja*, he would. 'But first I have my child to greet and my wife to kiss. Then we will celebrate! We will lift the roof and sing all the songs of victory that we know.' He did not add that he had silently noted the insult his brother had tossed at him. *So he gives me permission to unite with Thorkell, does he? We'll see who'll be giving permission in a month or two!*

Unaware of Cnut's hidden anger, Hakkon laughed. 'And make up a few songs that we do not yet know, eh?'

Another was waiting at the doorway of the Jarl's Hall. The midwife. Cnut saw her face, the tears in her eyes and all joy of feasting scuttled from his heart like a stone skidding on a surface of ice.

The child had been born, a healthy daughter, the woman said, but the mother had begun to bleed. There was nothing to be done to save her.

As evening fell, the evening that in these northern lands never faded beyond the purple blueness of dusk, Cnut stood alone by the shore, alone but for the tiny bundle wrapped warm in lambswool in his tight-held arms. She was beautiful, this little girl. Fair hair, wide blue eyes that stared, bemused, up into his; a rosebud mouth that blew bubbles. She had made no cry, beyond that of a whimper for her milk. Ragnhilda, Cnut called her. An angel from God, the image of her mother, the pride of her father.

At the water's edge, where only God and the sky could look upon him, Cnut stood with the child cradled in his arms, rocking her to sleep, and wept for both of them the tears of grief.

12

Æthelred was ill, and Cnut's ships were prowling the south coast like a pack of hungry wolves waiting for the kill, but Edmund was not in a position to do anything about either. Not on his own.

Welcomed in the eastern Mid-Lands for his heroic rescuing of Ealdgyth, their marriage had soon become one of an ideal match, proven by the child she carried, due in late December. But the support of the Seven Boroughs was not enough to fight for a kingdom. Alfred, the Great King, had inaugurated the building of burghs during his time, to stem the incoming tide of Danes swamping English land. Designed as permanent, defendable places, each had expanded into larger areas, the Boroughs, taking their names from the original defended place: Derby, Nottingham, Leicester, Lincoln and such. One day Æthelred planned to promote them into his higher status of Shire, to have them more readily under the King's control and bring him more profitable taxation. Edmund wanted to make use of the Boroughs as Alfred had intended, as effective military places. While he could not go south to face Cnut, he could prepare to protect the men who had declared for him, for after Æthelred's wanton destruction, Edmund was determined to rebuild both houses and moral. Each fyrdsman was re-equipped with helmet, shield, byrnie and weapons. The war horns were polished, the horses were fed corn and new shod. When Cnut came, Edmund would be ready for him and he would come, for Æthelred had taken to his bed with a bowel flux. He was not, unfortunately, dying, but the physicians did not expect him to grow into an old man.

All Edmund needed was to consolidate the North. Uhtred of Northumbria was already wavering to his side, canny with choosing which water was best to dip his feet into, a man who could read the way the wind blew and observe the changes of the tide. He had submitted to Swein over Æthelred, because sense told him Forkbeard was the better man. He would fight alongside Edmund, when the time came, for the same reason. But Northumbria and the Boroughs would not be enough. Edmund needed Mercia and that meant Eadric Streona.

In appearance Leicester was no different from any other Saxon town, the usual huddle of houses, the rubbish strewn in the streets, the overall permeating stink. Edmund had suggested he meet with Eadric Streona under the auspices of the Abbot at the abbey, rather than the confine of a tavern, where a wrong word, or hidden dagger, could do unintentional damage. Edmund would rather slit Eadric's throat and have done with it, but a king's son who wanted to step into his father's boots the moment they became empty could not have the luxury of personal feelings. Not unless your name was Æthelred and you had already half destroyed your kingdom. With a view to the benefit of England, Edmund tried, he really tried, to be the diplomatic host who had shed the misunderstandings of the past.

'We must unite as friends,' he began, 'we are, after all, kinsmen, for your wife is my sister. The past has bled us dry, but after the physician has let blood we rest, take nourishment and then feel the life surge of reinvigorated energy. You and I, Eadric,' Edmund said, with as much enthusiastic conviction as he could stomach, 'can, together, be that nourishment. What do you say?'

The two men were alone in the Abbot's private chamber, a room that faced west, catching the last radiant burst of evening sunlight through the unshuttered window slits.

Eadric scratched at his nose. 'What is in it for me?'

Edmund retained the congenial smile. 'England's deliverance from Cnut's raiding. A return to the justice of law, an end to crime, robbery, murder and rape.'

Raising his hand, Eadric stopped Edmund there. 'No, lad, I said what is in it for *me*? I do not care an owl hoot for England. I am interested only in Mercia and my rights of profit.'

Angry, Edmund dropped the pretence of congeniality. 'Your ealdorman's payoffs, you mean? The dividend tax of one penny for every three paid? The right to purchase forfeiture land at a reduction of its value; to sell men, women and children into slavery because they cannot meet your excessive demands? Is that what you are talking about?'

This green-stick lad was starting to learn. 'I do not care which king I serve under,' Eadric stated bluntly. 'One is as similar as the other, as long as my service is made worth my while.'

'So you have become a mercenary, serving for pay and power, not loyalty and honour?'

Eadric rested his right elbow on the chair arm, half slouched, his fingers intertwined, legs spread out in front of him. 'You do not approve?'

'No, Sir, I do not approve. A mercenary is a man who fights because he has no king or country to call his own. Who has no soul and no honour. Who has nothing but a greed to gain more of what is not his.'

Eadric laughed, mocking. 'Nay, lad, who taught you that way of thinking? A mercenary is a man who bargains hard to get the best deal he can.'

'England's fate is of no concern to you?'

'Of course it is, but fate will happen whoever sits his backside on a throne or wears a tarnished crown on his head. You must make your own fate, your own future, regardless of what is happening around you.'

'That is a very cynical and selfish philosophy, is it not?'

'Possibly, but it is one that has served me well all these years.'

To cool his rising temper, Edmund went to a side table, selected cold meat and bread, gestured for his guest to join him. 'The Abbot has provided us with fine nourishment to fortify us through our discussion. It would be poor-mannered of us not to partake of his thoughtfulness.'

Lifting an open palm, Eadric shook his head. 'I thank you, but I have eaten. I partook of a meal before leaving my lodgings.'

Edmund sat, ate, listened as Eadric outlined some of his own plans for the improvement of administrative government within Mercia. If anyone, later, were to ask for a repeat of the one-sided

371

conversation, Edmund would not have been able to oblige. He listened, but did not hear.

Politely, he wiped his mouth and fingers with a napkin, replaced the pewter platter on the table. 'Cnut is devastating the southern coast. I do not intend to make the same mistake as my father and sit whistling to the wind in the hope that he may soon grow bored and sail away.'

Frowning, Eadric studied the man before him. He saw a younger version of Æthelred, the same nose, eyes, mouth. The chin was a little more pointed, he was taller, broader, perhaps; more confident, certainly. Then, abruptly, he changed his mind about Edmund. This lad was nothing like his father. He had his grandmother's character, her guile, her temper and her decisive independence. Edmund would not be for buying and, if he were king, then Eadric would not be receiving the extras that made his life comfortable.

'You are serious about fighting Cnut?' he asked.

Edmund nodded. 'I am serious about fighting Cnut.'

Throwing his hands in the air, Eadric guffawed a shout of gusted laughter. 'Whatever for? We allow him to burn a handful of peasant bothies, steal some cattle and carry off a few women; then we pay him to go away and we get on with our lives. Why stir a hornets' nest with a sharpened stick, when you can as easily leave well alone?'

Quietly, looking down at his hands, Edmund answered, 'Is that the advice you gave my father?'

'It was good advice.'

Edmund had run the length of his patience. He stood, marched to the door and flung it wide. 'It was bad advice. It did not work. Swein kept coming back, was intending to stay, only God took a hand in stopping him. Cnut, also, will stay. Unlike Swein, he does not already have a kingdom to call his own.'

Unperturbed at Edmund's hostility, Eadric fastened his cloak and strolled to the door. 'Wars cost money, money that can be better spent in buying peace.'

'You buy your peace. I intend to fight for mine.'

Opening the door, Eadric said with an expression that was no longer friendly or indulgent, 'There is one thing you are forgetting, boy. You are not yet king. If you put an army into the field, it could be misconstrued, by some, as treason.'

Edmund's answer was dignified. 'I am acting as ætheling, as my father's representative. I remind you, Sir, he lies abed, ill, unable to defend England for himself.'

Dipping his head in farewell, Eadric strode into the courtyard, calling for his horse. He mounted, curbing the stallion from an eagerness to be away, sneered, 'My congratulations, boy. You are almost as accomplished a liar as your father.'

13

Penned into the misery of Thorney Island during a dreary winter, Emma greeted her unexpected visitor with more warmth than he had expected. Godwine found himself blushing as she held him to her in an enthusiastic embrace and kissed both his cheeks in welcome. Gods, but how he wanted to kiss her back, and not in the chaste way that she had kissed him!

'What brings you to London? News? Not bad news? No, I see from your face that it is not, although equally, I think you do not bring good news either. Come, sit, let me pour you ale.' Emma was talking too fast, gabbling. Was she going mad in this winter Hellhole of a place? There was nothing to do, nowhere to go, no one to see or converse with.

'I have come with a message for the King, but I am told he is sleeping. I was sent, instead, to you.' Godwine grinned. 'I do not object to the diversion!'

'My husband sees no one before mid afternoon.' Emma laughed, a false sound. 'Not even me.' *Especially me*, she thought. 'He claims that I am too much the bully, for I order him to wash and get out of bed.' To stop moping, stop whining.

'He is no better, then?' Godwine asked rhetorically.

Emma shrugged. What constituted better? The stomach cramps and pains had ceased towards the end of October, but Æthelred had not quit his bed. His natural functions appeared normal, he ate well, drank even better. Wept and mithered and called for his priest throughout the day or night.

For almost fourteen years Emma had been his wife and during that long period he had rarely spoken a kind word to her, and yet, now, he expected her to love and comfort him, to hold his hand and forgive him his wrongs. Well, she would not! Let him suffer, let him reflect on all the cruelties that he had inflicted on her and others, let him contemplate the consequences. He could go to Hell. And the quicker the better.

Godwine altered tack. 'How are the children? Are they well?'

'Edward prays. Morning, noon and night, he prays for his father's soul. Alfred, the more practical, has already worked out the items he wants his father to leave him in his will; and as for Goda, my pretty angel, she is learning her lessons with enthusiasm at Wilton. They are turning her into a presentable young lady, so I understand. I do not envy them the task, I would have assumed it nigh on impossible to achieve.' She smiled, proud of her daughter. 'All I knew of her was constant squabbling, bruised knees and a determination to do everything better than her brothers. Including using a sword and spear. She was a chore, that child, I sincerely wish the nuns better fortune with her education than I had!' She meant none of it. Emma missed her daughter since her going away to be educated at the nunnery, but it had to be. Goda would become a woman and then a wife; Emma's prayers were dominated by if not a happy marriage for her, at least let it not be as miserable a one as her own. A pity Godwine was not higher born, he would make some woman a husband worth keeping.

'So,' she said, turning the subject away from the melancholy of an uncertain future. 'How does Edmund's war go?'

'You heard that Eadric Streona', Godwine spat the name, 'went to Cnut with forty ships?'

She nodded. She had heard.

'Wessex has fallen to the Danes and the Shires of Gloucester and Hereford; and, of course, Bedford and Buckingham, which are already Streona's, so Edmund's lands fall direct in the traitorous bastard's path.'

'I hear the English fyrds are calling Edmund "Ironside" for his strength of courage. It is a fitting title for a fine young man.'

'Streona is insisting that it is Ealdorman Uhtred's planning that has been the cause of our success.' Godwine spat into the fire, sending the flames into spluttered sizzling. 'He has no love for Edmund.'

'And was it Uhtred's strategy, then, to not meet Cnut's army head on, but to take the English into Chester-Shire and Shrop-Shire instead?' Emma was leaning forward, her elbows on her knees, wanting to gain every mote of information above the bare essentials she had learnt through the occasional messenger or trader.

Godwine grinned even wider than before. 'No, that was Edmund himself! We marched as bold as a tom-cat into Streona's lands, and instead of wasting our energy in burning farmsteadings or villages we headed straight for his estates. Burnt the lot to the ground, every one of them, taking his horses and armoury for our own use.'

Emma clapped her hands, delighted. 'And you are surprised that he has no love for Edmund?' She had heard that Eadric was furious at losing his personal property in that way. Good for Edmund! She indicated that her maid was to refill Godwine's ale, waited a while for him to drink, then said, 'But that was all good news, and it happened before the Nativity?' She set it as a question, suspecting there was bad news, now, to be told.

Stretching his legs and carefully setting his goblet to the table beside him, Godwine sighed. Pointless hiding the truth, she would have to know. 'We have done our best, my Queen, but it is a futile effort. We have hit them hard, but there is no more we can do. Without the re-enforcement of additional aid, Cnut will prove too strong for us.'

Emma did not state that if Streona had not turned traitor, then Cnut would have been stopped in his tracks. Eadric, however, was proclaiming that he did not see himself as a traitor. Cnut, he professed, had been declared king by his Danish army and Æthelred had fled abroad. That made Cnut the lawful king. How warped and twisted that man's mind could turn! Emma said, 'Uhtred is as wily as a fox; surely if he calls out the entire northern fyrd . . .?'

Godwine interrupted. Best say this quickly. 'Uhtred has had to return into Northumbria. There are several of his thegns who support Cnut, Thurbrand the Hold being one of them. A long-term enemy, as you know, and kindred to Ælfgifu of Northampton. Cnut's woman.'

Emma swallowed the sudden feeling of dread. She wanted to

cover her ears, not hear, not have to listen. Thurbrand, another man who could match Eadric Streona as a pair of boots cut from the same hide. 'As I last heard, Ælfgifu is still sheltering with him?'

'Aye, she is.' Godwine chuckled. 'She finds herself caught between a rocky shore and an incoming tide, for the lady is anxious for Cnut to walk into the North and join her and her two sons, but her husband is not as keen to oblige, for he has a large dose of explaining to do.'

Emma added her laughter to Godwine's humour, relieved to be able to turn away from the fear of implications that she did not want to think on. 'I do not see Ælfgifu as a woman who would easily forgive a man who fled direct from her bed straight into another.'

'And add to that . . .'

Raising her hands in mock horror, Emma quipped, 'There is more? Good God, the woman will not know which way to lace her gown if she swells herself with so much grievance!'

'. . . There is the insult of alliance with Streona; after all, he was responsible for her father's murder. For that alone I reckon she will take a dagger to Cnut's balls.'

The laughter died. The fire crackled, the wind moaned through ill-fitting window shutters. Godwine spread his hands on his thighs, uneasily rubbed them up and down. 'The Boroughs of Lindsey have only accepted Edmund halfway up the blade. The fyrd were happy with raiding into Streona's lands, they've been itching to do so these God knows how many years, but Cnut is now on their doorstep and without Uhtred . . .' He let his words trail off, then, impassioned, 'Lady! There have been too many rumours that Æthelred has outlawed his son, that Edmund is fighting on his own and not for the King. For all that they like and admire him, the men will not rally to Edmund if they think wrong of him. If Cnut marches up the Great North Road, I fear they will stand aside and let him pass.'

Despair knotted in Emma's stomach, her laughter and pleasure drained away. It was all happening over again. The North would submit to Cnut and then he would turn on London. From there would come nothing except the bleakness of enforced exile. She closed her eyes. Not Normandy! She could not stand the indignity of having to beg for her brother's aid again so soon. Sickness rose into her mouth: the nausea of the memory of the sea.

'We have able men,' Godwine said apologetically. 'Each man would fight as if he were two, three men, if they had the knowing that Æthelred himself asked it of them.' Godwine fiddled with the hem of his tunic, picking at a hanging thread, working it looser. 'Æthelred cut the heart out of his people when he devastated Lindsey. They are afraid to anger him a second time and someone has seen to it that they think he will be angered if they rally to Edmund.'

Emma's head shot up as if she were a hound hearing the music of the hunting horn. 'Cnut?'

Godwine shook his head. 'Possibly his idea, but no, we believe it to be Streona spreading the lies.' Said, his eyes meeting hers, pleading, 'We need the King.'

How Godwine wished he had not spoken, how he so desperately wanted to comfort her, hold her, tell her it would be all right, in the end it *would* be all right.

'He will not get from his bed, Godwine.' Emma hung her head, her hands clasped, her fingernails digging into her palms. 'The King is frail. He is truly ill, dying.' Guilt was a terrible burden to carry. She should have had some patience with him, have been more compassionate. It must be hard to know you are old and can no longer do the simple things of daily need for yourself. To accept that winter has come and that permanent darkness will soon be following. Emma argued with herself that he deserved to be shunned by her, why should she care that he was fragile and incontinent? That God was calling him? She wanted to be rid of him, did she not? But if that was her attitude, one of total, callous indifference, then was she no better than he?

Godwine stood before her, put his fingers under her chin and tipped her head up. If he was going to kiss her it would have to be now, while he was standing so close, drowning in the scent, the touch, the nearness of her. The moment passed. She was his Queen, he a mere thegn.

'Dying or not, Lady, he has to lead a militia north. He has to show his support for his son or everything will be lost to Cnut. Everything, Lady.' He repeated it, so that she clearly understood: 'Everything.'

14

As the last week of February drew to a close, the King's entourage, escorted by his and his Queen's cnights and the militia of London, were heading north. It had been slow going. The road, Ermine Street, that ran for miles as straight as a harpstring, was treacherous with mud and half-melted snow. The unforgiving wind, howling across the East Anglian fens direct from the sea, was bitter in its vehemence; the pewter-skied days were short, the frosted nights long. They had covered less than fifty miles in six days and Huntingdon was still more than four miles ahead.

Every few yards Æthelred's litter became bogged down and had to be hauled free. Tempers were as short as the days, and impatience was running as high as the fenland skies.

Emma had never travelled with an army before and this was only a militia, three hundred and fifty men including the permanent cnights. The logistics of moving these few was a headache, how in God's Name were full armies moved about in winter conditions? She began to admire the fortitude of Edmund and Cnut. Her body ached from riding, the insides of her thighs were chafed raw and she was certain that she would never be able to sit down properly again. Some nights they had not been able to find a hunting lodge or manor house; twice they had slept in a farmsteading bothy; once out in the open, sheltering from the bitter cold beside winter-bare hedging, although Emma and her husband had tents of horse-hide leather stretched over hazel poles. They at least provided shelter from the wind, if nothing else.

The column halted again; the litter was stuck. A distinct grumble murmured along the line of shivering, tired men, like a sullen wave rippling in across a wide, flat beach of shingle.

Godwine rode up to Emma, halted, saluted. 'The King is calling for you, Lady.'

'Can his body servant not deal with it?' she asked, sharper than she ought.

'I think not in this case, Madam.' Godwine lowered his voice, leant across his horse's neck to whisper, 'He wants to turn round, return to London.'

'He has been wanting to do that after half an hour from leaving!' She sighed. 'I will come.'

Throwing her leg over the high, square saddle pommel, she slid to the ground, grimaced as her boot sank ankle deep in mud. She wore male apparel beneath her gown, breeches, gaitered leggings. It was warmer and more comfortable for riding, although more difficult to relieve herself. The skirt of her gown was fuller than it would be normally, and slit at front and back, so that it fell either side of the saddle when mounted, but appeared loose and appropriately modest when not. Modesty, however, on this interminable journey, had long been thrown out with the piss in the pot. Emma hitched the gown to above her knees as she made her way towards the King's litter, not caring who might glimpse the trousered legs beneath.

He was weak and thin, his face more like the mask of a skull than a live man's warmth of flesh. With sunken eyes and hollow cheeks, Æthelred's body had shrivelled into itself like a fallen plum left too long in the autumn sun. It was plain to see that he could not go on much further, but he would have to.

Emma sent a servant for water, spooned a little into her husband's mouth, although most of it dribbled out again. His breathing was shallow, his skin yellow-tinged and his breath stank sour. As much as she wanted to taunt him that this was his own fault, that God was punishing him for all the wrongs and evils that he had committed through his life, she could not, for that would be cruel. Emma had realised soon into her marriage that to survive she had to keep herself hard and remote, detached, but that was the outward persona, the woman everyone else saw. For herself, her inward eye that watched into the privacy of her soul, she knew she had an expanse of compassion and love. No one had brought it to the fore, that was all. No one except Pallig, all those years ago, and Godwine maybe; and her daughter, Goda. No, not Goda, she had let go of her, played the indifferent, mimicked the impervious. How else did one survive, and endure, a shattered heart?

'It is not far to Huntingdon,' she said to Æthelred, wiping his mouth. 'We will rest there.'

He became agitated, his fingers plucking at the furs covering him. He kicked his legs, trying to sit, climb out of the litter. 'No! Not Huntingdon!' he screeched in a high, tinny voice. 'I cannot go to Huntingdon!'

'It will be comfortable there. Riders have gone ahead, have made preparations for us. If you wish we can, perhaps, stay a day. Give you a chance to rebuild your strength. Edmund awaits us at the Burgh of Stamford, you will not have to travel further north than there. Once it is seen that you readily embrace him as your son, you can rest.'

'North? I am not going north! There are men waiting to kill me in the North!' Æthelred's disquiet became more pronounced, for all his apparent feebleness there was strength in his arms as he pushed Emma aside. He was half out of the litter, his stockinged feet sinking into the mire.

As befitted a king, a guard was set around the low-slung, wallowing conveyance, two men to each corner, two behind, two walking with the sturdy ponies pulling it. A conscientious man always kept his weapons sharp and ready, and it was something to do to pass the time during these irritating stops to reach into your pouch and pull out the small whetstone that every soldier carried there to keep an edge to his dagger or sword blade.

Scrabbling in the mud, with Emma calling for assistance, and trying to induce him to not be such a fool, Æthelred heard the rasp of the coarse stone on the steel, he saw the gleam of the blade and screamed.

'They were right! They were right! I am to be murdered, I am to be killed!' Where to go to be safe? Where to hide? Where to get away from these men come to do away with him? Æthelred flung himself into the litter, pulled the furs up, covering himself as he lay curled beneath, alternately whimpering and screaming.

'Take me to London!' he demanded, his voice shrill and insanely intense. 'Take me back, I order it, take me back!'

There was nothing Emma could do, short of gagging and binding him, but even that would have served no purpose. Æthelred's wailing had carried up along the line of men and the Londoners, already weary and discontented, none of them caring for this miserable march into a fight that was not theirs, heard and, in an unspoken unanimous decision, swung around. When men have decided they have had enough and their King is ordering them to turn about and go home there is no asking of questions. Strange how the reverse of the route was to be accomplished so much more efficiently than the outward one.

Whether he had imagined it, or overheard some mischievous or careless talk, Æthelred was convinced that treachery awaited him at Huntingdon. He gibbered and whimpered all along the road and Emma, furious, betrayed and ashamed at his spineless weakness, rode behind his litter in stiff-backed silence, all her guilt at her lack of tender kindness quite gone. He had forsaken England for his own imagined terrors and yielded to the pull of his weakness. He was no king; he was worthless.

His friends, those few who had stayed loyal to him throughout, his Captain of Cnights, his body servant, his seneschal, his priest, they opined that he could not have travelled further, that he was mortally ill, was dying. Edmund was abandoned and with him the opportunity to outmanoeuvre Cnut. Except for London, Æthelred had lost his kingdom.

Whether he was mortally ill or not, was irrelevant as far as Emma was concerned. Æthelred, to her mind, was already dead.

15

Bad news always spread with the rapidity of a swelling flood. With the fyrd unwilling to fight, Cnut moved swiftly up the Great North Road, sweeping all before him, as a housewife takes a new-made broom to the spring cleaning.

Uhtred was the best ealdorman Æthelred had, one of the North's greatest magnates, whose kindred spread back through generations; powerful men, who had not served but had ruled over an extensive kingdom. For both those reasons Cnut had to hold Northumbria; without Uhtred's submission, England was nothing. In turn, without the support of his King, Uhtred could not hold Cnut at bay. With the Danish army marching closer to York, and for the sake of his people he surrendered. A bitter potion to swallow, for Cnut would be demanding hostages – and what had happened to those he had taken once before? There was not a noble family in all England, save for the King's own immediate, which had not suffered the result of those wicked mutilations that Cnut had ordered done at Sandwich harbour.

The manor estate of Wighill, a few miles off the Roman Road that led from Tadcaster to York, was chosen as a neutral place for Uhtred's public submission. Thurbrand the Hold, the northern term for reeve, brought Ælfgifu there to reunite with her Lord, to wait beside him for the Ealdorman and his escort of no more than forty men. An agreement that was not to Uhtred's liking, but the defeated were not in a position to dictate demand. And how hard could it be to bend a knee to Cnut? To kiss his hand and swear oath? No harder than when he had done so to Swein Forkbeard. Except, then, it had been of Uhtred's choosing.

The March day was sun-bright, a vivid blue sky tingled with the keenness of the frosted night that had gone before, and the promise of an early-come spring was bursting from the hedgerows, meadows and trees. Uhtred rode at the head of his men, sitting easily, hiding the sour mixture of displeasure that galloped in his stomach. He did not want to do this thing, but neither did he want death and destruction for his people. It was not right that they should suffer because a man could not relinquish his pride.

The manor stood on a rise of ground, safe from where the River Wharfe could touch it on those many occasions when it burst its banks. The fields were fertile, the cattle, sheep and ponies plump. Birds were already busy about their nesting, although it was too early for the summer visitors of swallow, swift and martin. Uhtred was not paying attention to the progress of nature, however, his eyes were fixed on the nearing Hall, the tents of Cnut's men, the noise and bustle that lay ahead. He rode through the open gateway into the courtyard, had to wait for one of his own men to dismount and come to hold his horse. That ought to have been a courtesy offered by the host, a traditional welcome that was obviously not extended to a man coming to submit away his king-given power.

He was dressed in splendour, his body armour gleaming, his weapons of the finest quality. From his shoulders hung a cloak lined with marten; at his throat a torque of gold. No one would guess, in the pride of his step, the shame that hung like a stone in his stomach. They had to leave the weapons on the threshold, as etiquette demanded, but safe conduct had been pledged and a man's word was his honour. Uhtred clung to that as a litany. If he murmured it often enough he might come to believe it.

Inside, the Hall was ill-lit and smoke-fugged. Embroidered hangings hid the bare plaster of the walls, curtaining screened the side alcoves. A wind squinnied in through the open door and scurried down the roof hole, puffing the spiral of hearth-smoke into curls and eddies beneath the arching crests of the weight-bearing roof beams. The place rustled as the draught twitched at anything that it could lift and tweak, as it ran, like a light-footed mouse, through the spread floor rushes. Birds' feet rattled on the wooden shingles of the roof, mixing with the clatter of the women's cooking pots, and the general hubbub of a busy manor. Uhtred, with his men ranged nervously behind him, paused inside the doorway, their eyes blinded by the contrasting darkness of the interior to the bright sunlight outside. The talk and laughter faded to a hush as Uhtred stood there, letting his sight adjust, all heads turning in his direction. Cnut sat at the far end of the Hall; at his side the woman, Ælfgifu, cold and austere.

They have made well their difference, then, Uhtred thought. *She has seen that it is better for a woman with two sons born to hold her tongue if a man should choose to take another to his bed.* He stepped forward, three, four, five paces into the centre of the Hall, brought his clenched right fist up, sharp, smart, to his left shoulder in salute. Cnut made no movement, no attempt to rise and greet him or bid him welcome. Uhtred swallowed his dignity. The Dane intended to make this hard, then. He lowered his head and bent his knee to the ground, his men, to soften their lord's humiliation, following his lead.

They came from behind the curtaining, from down the ladder steps that led to an upper chamber. From a smaller side door. Thurbrand's men, daggers drawn, swords gleaming, blood-bringing. It was soon over, three, four minutes? Unarmed, unprepared, trusting to the honour of a safe-given conduct, lying in pools of seeping blood, one and forty men lay dead. Cnut sat, unmoving and silent. He could not be allowing Uhtred opportunity to submit and then break his oath again, as he had with his father – but had it needed to be done like this?

Ælfgifu was laughing, clapping her hands at the success of the ruse. Thurbrand wiped his soiled blade on Uhtred's fine, bloodied and torn cloak, saluted Cnut, but it was Ælfgifu who acknowledged him, Ælfgifu who ran down the steps from the dais and hugged him. Cnut said nothing, sat in silence. He would have accepted the submission, but not Ælfgifu. She had wanted Uhtred dead and he had not found the inclination to argue. He groaned. He was sick to the stomach of death.

A man's pride was his honour and what honour was there in cutting down unarmed men? Cnut looked at Ælfgifu, her wide, smirking mouth, the way she was prodding at the dead, her head back, drunk with laughter and the smell of spilt blood. And suddenly Cnut realised how much he despised her.

16

It seemed no one had the option of choice that spring, it was as if the world was treading a preordained path that lurched and twisted through dark woods, up stony hillsides and then plunged, without pause for breath, into a bottomless ravine.

Emma had recalled Edmund to London, with those of the Witan who remained loyal, Ulfkell of East Anglia, the thegns and bishops of Kent, a few from eastern Wessex. Edmund was yet to arrive. Her urgent summons had been because Æthelred was close to death, but the hushed talk in the King's Hall centred not around the King, but on Uhtred. Treachery stank and to foreswear an agreement of safe passage reeked the worst of all. There was not an Englishman in all England who would proclaim Cnut's honour, for he had none.

Archbishop Wulfstan, a subdued and bewildered man, had managed to make his way by sea from York. He had been so certain that with King Swein's death the culmination of God's wrath had reached its crisis and passed, yet here it all was, swelling larger than ever before; blood and battle, killing and dishonourable slaying. He was on the verge of wanting God to end it all, to send his fireballs, his plagues and floods, to make a finish to it. What more could a mortal do to appease Him? Wulfstan had published his 'Sermon of the Wolf', a tirade against evil, a work that was being read aloud in nigh on every church, chapel and cathedral from east to west, north to south – and aye, beyond! Even the great places of France were preaching his words, but to what avail? Here in England? None! A great renewal of Christian building, to the glory of God, as occurring in Italy and France. What was it someone had written? Raoul Glaber in his 'Historia'? 'It is as if the world has shaken itself and cast off the old garments, to dress itself in a new white robe of churches.' Is that where England had gone wrong? Instead of repenting sins and righting wrongs, ought they to have been urging the building of churches?

Wulfstan sat silent in a corner of the Hall, nursing his puzzled thoughts, only half listening to the outrage of Uhtred's shameful killing, finding himself wondering whether it was the death of Æthelred that God was wanting and waiting for. By the rattle of breath in his throat, and the yellow colour to his skin, that wanting was not far off.

A hand touched his shoulder, making him start. He leapt to his feet. Emma.

'I bid you to come, Archbishop, my husband is lucid and he would have you hear his confession.'

Wulfstan nodded, gathered his Bible and his thoughts. She was drawn and pale, the Queen, had not slept for many nights now, having refused to move from the King's side. For the sake of her son she could not.

'Edmund will not harm either of your sons, Lady,' Wulfstan said as he walked with her. 'He is not Cnut.'

Emma sighed, she was tired to the bone. 'At my marriage it was agreed and contracted that any male child of the union must take precedence over any already born; you know this, you were the one to draw the contract. But what good are agreements written on parchment when my eldest son is no more than eleven years old and there is another born before him more than twice that age?'

They were at the chamber door. Emma halted, let the Archbishop enter alone. All she wanted, all these years, was to be rid of Æthelred, yet now, when all he had to do was to die, she was frightened at the dreadful nearness of being a widow.

The door opened, rustling the heavy covering of deer hide, the draught toying with the candle flames, sending them leaping and skittering; Emma looked up, round, as Edmund entered. He put his finger to his lips to silence her from saying anything and moved to the bed, stood, staring down at the limp, gaunt frame of the man who had been his father. His boots were muddied, his chin beard-stubbled and he stank of his own and his horse's sweat. He still wore his cloak, in his hand his gloves.

'To think I have been afraid of him all these years,' he said at last in a respectful whisper. 'He never loved me, never spoke words of kindness or encouragement. Yet I so wanted to love and respect him. I wanted the people to cheer him and bless his name, for England to fall on its knees and weep when this moment came.' He reached forward, took the claw that was his father's bone-thin hand. 'We rarely have what we want, do we?'

'You had no need to be afraid of him, Edmund,' Emma said, folding her hands in her lap. 'He was proud of you, of you and Athelstan.'

'Was he? A pity he never made mention of it to us.' Edmund sat on the edge of the bed, holding those thin fingers between his own, the weariness as pronounced in his face as it was on Emma's, for he had ridden without stopping from Huntingdon.

'I was afraid of him because I did not want to be like him, was scared that he would demand that I emulate him, to do as he did. Even as a boy I could see that he had no authority of kingship, that he had no talent for knowing the right thing to do and when to do it. Grandmama had the saying and doing in all that. I did not want to come to manhood being a puppet who danced to whatever tune was being played as he had.'

'With Eadric Streona playing the pipes in place of your grandmother?'

'Aye.' Edmund gently laid the withered hand down on the bed furs. 'Can he hear us?'

Emma shook her head. 'We think not. His soul has already departed. It is the shell of his body that has yet to pass over to God.'

'You know the stupid thing?' Edmund said, gazing directly at her. 'I have done all I can to be my own man, yet here I am, sitting in this wretched place, dancing to the tune that Cnut is piping.' He laughed. 'I suppose that is what it is to be royal-born. You forfeit all right to a say in what to do with your life.'

'No peasant farmer, slave, or woman would allow you that single privilege,' she answered derisively.

She was right, of course, this nonsense was the melancholy within him speaking.

The physician entered, peered at Æthelred, inspecting his eyes, smelling his breath and feeling for the faint, erratic life-beat that fluttered in his ragged, loose-skinned neck. He shook his head, left the chamber, saying he would return shortly.

'They are to elect me King,' Edmund said suddenly, louder than he had intended, into the silence. 'I am sorry that it cannot be your son, but how can he fight against Cnut?'

Emma shrugged, unable to answer. How could he?'

He walked around the room, laid his gloves down, took off his cloak. Said, in a rush, 'I admire you; as Queen you have more than proved your worth to England. As King I will return the crown you once lent me, and will honour your position as Dowager. You may retain Winchester and Exeter as your own.'

Her hand was on her throat, the words stuck there. Managed to stammer, 'And my sons? What of them?'

'They will have no fear of me. I cannot guarantee either of them a crown, but they will have their life and freedom. When the time comes, it will be for the Witan to decide which among your sons, or mine, is to follow me. I can say no fairer than that.'

Ah, yes, Edmund's son, Ædward, the child that the widow of Sigeferth had borne. There was another child on the way too, so Emma had heard. Strange how she had not bred for Sigeferth, but was ripe for Edmund? But then, Sigeferth would not have been the first man to possess a blunted spear.

'You are certain that Ædward is your child? Not from the seed of Sigeferth? It is a question I shall ensure any Witan must ask, even from beyond my grave.'

Edmund frowned a candid half-smile; it was not a question she should be asking, for it insulted his honour and integrity and that of his wife, but in her position he would have asked the same. 'She bled her monthly course during the moon-month that we shared the honey cup, conceived my child soon after. He was born more than ten months after Sigeferth's death.'

Graciously, Emma nodded acceptance.

Aimlessly strolling, Edmund was uncertain what else to say. He touched things, picking them up, looking at them, setting them down again without seeing what it was he held. A Bible, a glass bottle containing some unguent or other. A jewelled cloak pin.

Emma glanced at the hour candle that had burnt down through the marks indented in the wax. 'It is tomorrow,' she said wearily. 'Midnight has passed, it is the twenty-third day of April.'

'At the Cathedral of Saint Paul, they will crown me as King as soon as they entomb my father before the altar, as is the way when danger threatens. The one king stepping into the footprints of the other.'

'And then what will you do, Edmund?' It was not a challenge, at least it was not intended so. Now that she had his assurance that she was to keep her crown she would be content to support him. At least until Edward was grown older.

'Do? I shall take what men will rally to me and go out to meet Cnut. With every breath that remains in my body I will attempt to kill him for the destruction that he has cursed upon my Country, and for the way he slaughtered my friend and kinsman, Uhtred.'

'Then as the anointed Queen,' Emma answered, ensuring that, for all his fine words he understood that she would not be giving up her God-blessed right, 'I shall issue my own order that any man who serves me is to take up his weapons and follow you in my name.' She spread her hands in a helpless gesture. The fear had gone, the impatience returned. 'For the good of England, all we need do now is to wait for your father to hurry and go to God.'

Edmund nodded, grateful. She could so easily try for Edward to become king. As his grandmother had ensured for her son. Thank God that Emma had the more sense and wisdom!

The third hour of the morning. The candle had burnt almost to its end. Emma peered at it through red-rimmed, tired eyes; she had been dozing, her head resting on her arms cushioned on the bed. She sat up, stretching the ache of pain from her stiffened shoulders. The priest was asleep in his chair, his head tipped back, mouth open, snoring. There was no one else, Edmund had gone, probably to wait within the Hall.

She could hear nothing, no sound. With a muted gasp she leant forward, her fingers going to the life-beat beneath Æthelred's jaw, put her ear to his mouth, felt the faint warmth of his breath and his bloody-minded determination to cling to life. Why did he not let go, leave all the mess that he had made of everything for others with more guts than he to sort out and put right?

Her fingers were on his neck, a scrawny, wasted little neck that was no wider or stronger than a chicken's throat. She remembered his hands around her own neck that time, long ago now, the fear and the choking pain as he had squeezed his fingers on to her windpipe. Recalled the hatred that had been in his eyes. It would take so little to press there, below the lump of his Adam's apple. So very little to finish it . . .

The hour candle guttered out with a spluttered fizz as the flame fell into the puddle of molten wax; the priest awoke with a jerked start, momentarily confused. For more than ten years he had served as Æthelred's chaplain, was one of the King's devoted friends, one of the few who never queried or blamed his many inadequacies. Emma was stroking the lank white hair from Æthelred's face.

'You had best summon in the ealdormen,' she said. 'And the King, Edmund. Æthelred is with God.' Or with the Devil. She did not much care which.

17

A long-drawn, tiring and bloody summer loomed ahead. If this was what it took to be a proper king, then was it any wonder Æthelred had shirked in his duty? Edmund had been torn in deciding how best to start a defensive attack against Cnut, with his decision, finally, reaching an obvious conclusion. He had to win back those lords who had deserted his father for Cnut. That meant a campaign in Wessex, for he had no intention of going begging to Eadric Streona. He had not been certain of Emma's suggestion that he take the two boys, Edward and Alfred, with him, not wanting to be tied by children; but as she had said, they were eleven and ten years of age respectively; they were the æthelings, ought to learn about fighting and kingship. There were extra advantages also. Any ealdorman or thegn who disputed Edmund's right to the crown, through his mother not being a queen, could not use the same excuse against Edward. Edmund was well aware of another motive – that of Emma ensuring Edward was seen, in case anything happened to his elder half-brother. The only risk in the strategy, once Edmund had ridden south-west, Cnut was left free to harry where he wanted.

He chose London.

During the second week of May Cnut's ships took possession of Greenwich and, soon after, moved upriver to anchor at Bermondsey, where he was barred from further progress by London Bridge.

'Lady?' Leofstan Shortfist, who had remained loyal to Emma throughout the years, respectfully coughed to draw her attention. She had given orders that she was not to be disturbed from her prayers, but this was urgent. She finished, crossed herself and turned her head, her eyes and expression querying the intrusion.

'They are digging a channel around the southern end of the bridge, Ma'am. The brothels and bothies of Southwark they burnt yesterday evening, as you know. We assume that Cnut is determined to control the Thames. He cannot pass under the bridge, so he intends to take his ships round it.'

Emma swore a soldier's word that Leofstan was surprised she knew, then remembered with a half-smile that it had been a favoured word of Pallig. With a suppressed wince Emma pushed herself upright, her knees ached often these days, although she was only seven and twenty years old. A hazard of kneeling too long and too often on the cold stone of a chapel floor.

'Take me there,' she commanded. 'I would see for myself.' Not that she doubted Leofstan's words, he was a good soldier, quick-witted and intelligent, but she needed to think, to plan. If Cnut decided to set a prolonged siege on London and if London then fell ... She steadied her nerve; whatever happened, she would not leave England. But her sons were a different matter; if Cnut got hold of them they would be killed. Another reason for their being out of Danish reach with Edmund.

Edmund's own son, and his again pregnant wife, were also made safe, not that Emma concerned herself about them. They had gone north under the personal protection of Wulfstan, who had promised to find them suitable lodging.

'How long will it take him to complete this work?' she asked, looking out as Cnut's men laboured to dig a curving channel from river bank to river bank, in a wide arc around the end of London Bridge, a discreet distance beyond arrow range. The Aldermen of London, standing with her, forlorn and filled with misgivings, could only shrug and woefully shake their heads. No one knew. A feat of engineering such as what Cnut was attempting had never been tried before.

'What will he do once it is finished?' Emma mused aloud.

'Drag his ships through, Lady. He will then have access to all the upper reaches of the Thames.' The Alderman's answer came in a patronising tone, as if Emma was only a woman, not a queen.

'I have managed to work that out for myself.' When would these fools learn that she had as much intellect as they? Probably more, in some cases! 'The question was rhetorical,' she snapped, irritated. The answer was obvious, he would ensure London submitted.

Edmund was not here to see to London's safety, but Emma was, therefore the responsibility had become hers, and she was determined to make a good job of it. 'We must be ready', she said with authority, 'to send word to Edmund. If Cnut decides to lay siege, we will need help.' To Leofstan, at her side, ordered, 'Select two suitable men, have them leave now and make camp up beyond the fields of the Corn Hill. Arrange some signal that can be sent from the walls, a smoking beacon, perhaps? When it is lit, they must make haste to ford the Thames at Thorney – no, too near, Brent Ford would be more suitable – and ride with all speed to fetch the King.' She surprised herself; here she was, giving orders to men about men's business and they were obeying her without murmur. She liked the feel of it. If London fell, it was possible that she could die along with these good people. They had cheered her when she had ridden through the gates and ordered them barred, saying, before them all, that they would not be opened again to any but their King, to Edmund Ironside. They still cheered her whenever she rode along the streets, still blessed her with God's mercy. The poor, simple fools. If Cnut attacked, what did she know of holding him off? On the dexter side of the argument, winning the admiration of the Londoners was no easy achievement, done by showing that she, their Queen, was willing to die alongside them.

The ships took hard effort to move, but the Danes were tough, resilient men, and once on the far side of the bridge there was more work. Cnut ordered a line of earthworks constructed outside London's walls and then, hunkered behind their protection, he settled down to what could be a tedious blockade. London was the pivot of all England; when London fell the rest, by default, would follow. Unfortunate for Cnut, Emma discovered that she knew more about sitting out a siege than she had realised, her knowledge gained by listening to her brother's insistence on recounting his numerous triumphs.

Looking over the rampart walkway of the city, one morning as

396

the sun rose in the east, its pink fingers turning the Thames to a glow of red-tipped gold, she smiled at the irony of finally being grateful to Richard for his interminable bragging. He had come through worse situations, or so he had claimed, therefore, so would she. Emma felt frightened, apprehensive, yes, but also elated and excited, her feelings all tumbled and mixed together, like a stew of varied ingredients tossed into the same pot. She was aware of the blood coursing through her veins, the beat of her heart, the breath in her lungs. Was aware, too, of that clenched knot that hung in the pit of her stomach. This was what it was to be alive, to be at the edge, facing eye-to-eye at survival, knowing, knowing, you would win through.

London, under the command of its valiant Queen, squatted on its heels and prepared for a long wait.

18

Cnut had not expected an organised and effective counter-attack to his overall strategy. Had he been a fool not to think of the possibility that Æthelred's son might be the opposite in character to his father? Everything had all seemed so easy when he had talked and planned with Erik around the hearth in Norway. Ah, plans always sounded so simple when discussed as hopes and dreams. You never looked for the pitfalls, the things that could go wrong, or even when you did think of the counter-side, there was always something else unexpected lurking in the shadows, waiting to leap out and surprise you. Like that damned woman in London. A woman! *Ja,* she was also a queen, but women were supposed to content themselves with weaving and spinning and suckling brats at their breast, not defending cities from siege! If it had not been for her rallying London to stand firm, the bloody place would have fallen by now; as it was, he had been forced to leave half his army sitting below the walls arse-scratching the interminable days away, while he hurried south-east to deal with Edmund.

Slamming his boot into a molehill, Cnut sent a spray of earth scattering over the summer-heated dry grass. Edmund, the one they were calling Ironside, was not the King – he was. Cnut, son of Swein Forkbeard, Cnut Sweinsson, was King! He kicked again at another mound of earth, taking his temper and frustration out on the habitat of a creature no larger than the palm of his hand.

Damn him – *damn* him! Cnut stamped the disturbed earth flat. Wessex had reverted to Edmund, along with East Anglia, Essex and Kent. What did Cnut have? Eadric bloody Streona of Mercia and a sullen, resentful thegn called Thurbrand! He walked on down the hill, heading to where he could hear men bathing in the river that wound between a copse of trees. It was all right for them, they could take an afternoon to enjoy themselves in the summer sunshine, could wash away the grime and the sweat and the cares. How could he shrug off this weight of frustration that lay heavy on his soul?

It had been a mistake, ridding himself of Uhtred. He realised that now, now that it was too late. The motive had been to show that he was not a man to be gainsaid or betrayed by broken promises. Instead, he had established that he was a man of dishonour, who courted lies and deceit, and who extolled murder over negotiation and compromise. Uhtred's death may have been essential, but not the way of doing it.

Ducking through the trees, Cnut walked from the dappled light into the full sun, found himself grinning at the men, stripped naked, playing like children in the curved meander of the river. He had a sudden flashed memory of walking with his father along the shore of a fjord, back home in Denmark. He had been a child, seven, eight years old? What was it Swein had said?

'Everyone makes mistakes, boy, but not everyone cares to learn the lesson.'

Using Thurbrand, the Hold of Holderness, to dispatch Uhtred had been Ælfgifu's suggestion. Another mistake, listening to and trusting that woman. 'Everyone makes mistakes. Not everyone cares to learn the lesson.'

Damn it, that water looked inviting. Cnut sat, began pulling off his boots. A lesson to remember. No one, ever, did something for nothing.

Thurbrand had been anticipating reward for his services. Cnut had intended a rich payment of gold and the hand of friendship. Whether Ælfgifu had made promises without consulting him Cnut did not know, probably she had. A full week after Uhtred's disposal, all Hell had broken loose with Thurbrand; he had expected to be made Jarl of Northumbria, or Ealdorman, as they called the title here in England. That favoured distinction Cnut had awarded to Erik of Hlaðir. *Earl* Erik – these English always did turn the Scandinavian tongue so quickly into their own pattern! Jarl in its English pronunciation became earl. He must learn and use that term.

So here he was, skulking, useless, somewhere in Wilt-Shire, waiting for his scouts to inform him of Edmund's whereabouts, and Thurbrand, in a mood as black as winter clouds, refused to leave Holderness to support Erik who was struggling to establish his claim on Northumbria. What a God-Almighty mess!

Naked, Cnut dived into the water, plunging down into the cool greenness, his strong arms propelling him forward. He came up again several yards from the bank, gasping for breath and tossing water from his hair and eyes. He lay back, allowing the gentle current to rock him along, giving only the feeblest of paddles with his hands and feet. Above, the sky spread into infinity in an unbroken stretch of sapphire blue.

Nearly all England was clamouring for Edmund. No one, beyond Mercia and Northumbria, was shouting for Cnut.

'My Lord! My Lord Cnut!'

Startled from his reverie, Cnut lost his buoyancy, coughing and spluttering, went under, then ploughed to the surface and, regaining his bearings, struck out for the bank with strong, swift strokes. Pulling himself from the water, he indicated for his clothes to be brought. 'What is it, Thorkell? I can see from your face it is urgent.' Perhaps it was the invigorating cold water, or the sudden heart-beat excitement of something happening at last? Whatever, Cnut's dark mood lifted as swiftly as a hawk snatched upwards with her prey.

'Edmund has come. Two, maybe three miles to the north of here.'

'The north? Gods curse it! The *north* of us? How in Thor's Name has he managed that? He was to the south, Thorkell. We fought a skirmish with him not two weeks past at Penselwood, that is to the south, in Dorset-Shire. How in the name of God has that whore-poxed Englishman managed to get to the north of us?'

Cnut cursed again, lengthily, colourfully and explicitly. Why in all the names of all the gods that had been or were yet to come, was Edmund not an incompetent fool like his damned bloody father had been?

Thorkell could only shrug. 'I told you he was one to be reckoned with, although I had no insight to him being this wily.' Personally, in Thorkell's opinion, the brain behind the English campaign was

Godwine Wulfnothsson. Now *there* had been a schemer! His father, Wulfnoth, would have been able to outwit the most cunning wolf. Had he passed his skills on to his son? Thorkell would be most surprised to find he had not.

Cnut dressed, not bothering to dry his skin. He nodded angrily towards the river. 'Get them out of there, get them armed and set them ready.' His eyes screwed against the sun, he estimated the hours of daylight left.

'At least we are keeping Edmund occupied and away from London,' Thorkell said, after he had passed on the order. 'While he is pursuing us, our men left behind to barricade London are not being disturbed.'

Cnut's answer was saturated with frustration. 'I came into Wessex to remind the nobles that I will not tolerate their defection to Edmund. What have I achieved? I have been harassed and tormented, chivvied and chased. I feel like a man on the run, watching my back at every move.' He pulled on his boots, wrinkling his nose at the uncomfortable feel of wet feet sliding into sweat-soaked leather. 'Well, no more. Edmund will not make the fool of me. Make formation. We go out to fight him here and now, and whatever way this ill meeting goes, we use the coming darkness to disperse.'

Thorkell frowned, drawing his bushed eyebrows close together.

'Do not look at me like that, Tall One. I know what I am doing,' Cnut barked. 'I intend to forget about Wessex and concentrate on London. As I should have done in the first place.'

Thorkell, Cnut's second in command, made no comment, but his grunt of satisfaction spoke his approving thoughts for him.

19

Late June 1016 – Brent Ford

The longest day had come and gone, it was all downhill, now, to winter. With the sun blazing in a clear sky these last weeks, the short nights held only a few dark hours and, even then, the horizon remained a dusky, purplish blue. Ideal for an army on the march, especially an army avoiding all the familiar roads and taking, instead, side-lane track-ways and scarce-known paths.

The skirmish by the river at Sherston had not solved any great outcome, but it had wounded a good few of Cnut's men and tired many more. Edmund had the advantage of being able to call on several different fyrds, Cnut only had his Danes and Eadric Streona's personal cnights. The fyrds of Mercia would not fight outside their own boundaries, not for Streona, nor Cnut. The pity, from Edmund's view, was that they would not fight for him, either.

Deliberately, Edmund had ordered the clash of arms at Sherston to be limited and at half scale. The only way he could beat Cnut was to grind him down, smaller and smaller as a woman takes patience to grind the corn into flour on the quernstone. He could not be having all his men out into the field at once and, cleverly, he had used only the Wilt-Shire fyrd, those willing to fight for their own in their home territory. They had enjoyed the contest, winning no honours but gaining no disgrace. His cnights, those of the King's permanent army, he had held at bay, ready should things go bad and they be needed in a hurry. Come dusk, Cnut had melted away into the woodland and Edmund had let him go, let the Danes run, he had time on his side, the leisure to pick his way via the quiet routes to London. The Wilt-Shire fyrd he dispersed, his cnights he scattered into small groups and ordered them to travel as secretly as possible.

'We meet in the last week of June in the woods up behind the

Clayhill Farm at Tottenham, north of the Thames. Make your circle wide and keep well to the north of London. Cnut will be returning by the familiar roads, he will not be knowing the lesser tracks, as we do.'

'What if London cannot hold out once he reaches there?' someone had asked.

'London will hold,' Edmund had answered, sure in his certainty. 'I have sent word to the Queen that we are coming. She will see to it that London sits tight. Like a broody hen on her nest.'

It was a good plan and it worked well, better than Edmund had expected.

The last few days of the siege had been a Hell on Earth for the Londoners. Cnut, as soon as he arrived, attempted an assault that should have worn down the most stoic of defenders, but London, rallying to Emma's insistence that Edmund was coming, did not give in, despite all that Cnut had to throw at its walls and gateways: battering rams and towers, fire carts and burning ships. The walls held, the gateways shuddered, but did not break. The bridge remained firm. Nor had the lengthy blockade been successful – if the idea had been to starve London into submission, it had not worked. With Cnut fighting in Wessex, discipline had been lax, particularly at night after the ale-skins had been passed from hand to hand and the Danes had slept sound, drunk. All too easy for Edmund's messengers to reach the Queen with news.

Cnut's cursing had no effect on the men, for their own expletives were on the same level of profanity as his. It was utterly unbelievable that this Edmund Ironside had done it again, had managed a surprise attack, even with numerous scouts sent to patrol the northern marshes. No amount of filthy language would save the situation however, for the area of a siege was not suited to open fighting. Cnut's only option was to disband, take to the ships and flee. Except that, too, was not so easy. The Londoners were manning the bridge, in turn blockading the Danes. Any ship that tried to escape between the wooden uprights and duck under the boarding of the walkway would never reach the other side. Londoners knew how to stop a ship going under their bridge, the most effective deterrent being fired pitch tipped through the metal sluice holes. Every sailor's fear, fire.

Cursing, unable to run towards the sea, Cnut ordered the ships upriver, clinging to the southern bank, ensuring that his best and most experienced men remained behind to hold the ford at Thorney. He could not be allowing Edmund to cross behind them, not until he could reposition on his own terms at a place of his own choosing. He chose well. The next most suitable fording place, Brent Ford.

Hand-to-hand fighting. No niceties or opportunity for leisurely decision making. Cnut himself was in the affray, using his axe, his feet, fists, anything and everything. Close-quarter combat and chaos. Weapons clashing, men grunting, shouting and screaming. The stink of sweat, blood and urine. The numbers evenly matched – again Cnut cursed Edmund for his ability; his men were fresh and eager with much to gain, little to lose. The Danes were tired and were fighting for survival.

Several thoughts skimmed through Cnut's mind as he met, head on, with one opponent after another. Tactics, plans, all inter-mingled alongside idle thoughts as he hacked and slashed and fought to live. Who would care for his daughter, Ragnhilda, if he was killed here? A damned stupid thought, one that he drove instantly aside. Another thought. His death would irritate Ælfgifu, she would have no hope of installing either of her sons above Edmund or the offspring of Emma of Normandy. She was there, in London, Emma; he had seen her himself as she stood on the wall rampart looking down at his army. Cnut had even fancied that he had seen a smile of triumph on her face, that had been this morning . . . this morning! God take the bitch! She had known! London had known Edmund was in position, ready to break the siege!

He struck out with his axe, using it two-handed in the figure of eight swing that brought it down and up in one flowing movement. It struck home, cleaving through a man's shoulder, taking the arm off in that single slice. The man screamed, blood pumped in a fountain from the severed stump. Cnut, barely giving the dying man a second glance, merely stepping over him and aiming for the next man. The haft split, he dropped it, used his sword instead. He had ordered one tactic only: to avoid a long drawn-out fight. That was not for here, not for this place. He would need more men to defeat Edmund in a decisive battle, men that he would have to draw from Northumbria and Mercia. The tactic here was to kill or mortally wound as many English as possible, and to thrust through, direct and as rapidly as possible, to this bastard of a man who was calling himself King.

A good tactic, but one difficult to perform, for the other side was trying the selfsame thing.

Edward and Alfred were ordered to stay with the ponies. It was not an order Edward had any inclination to break, for he hated these last months, each morning had felt sick, each night had piddled his bedding. Thank God it was only bracken or hay or straw; had it been the linen he was used to he would never have stopped Alfred from seeing and laughing. Alfred, along with the other boys, was revelling in all this nightmare horror. He stood there now, perched on the bough of a tree, intently watching the fighting, giving a vivid and lurid commentary on what was happening. Edward squatted beneath the sweep of the low branches, his arms over his head, hands against his ears, his face pushed tight into his knees. He hated the squalor, hated the hardship, and hated his mother for sending him into this fear and danger. What if he were to be killed? Had she thought of that? *He* had. He thought of it constantly, which is why he wet himself and spewed up his food as soon as he had swallowed it. He stuffed his fingers in his ears, trying to drown out the sounds, tried to curl tighter into a ball like a hedgepig rolling up to defend itself. He was supposedly here to learn how to fight, how to lead. Aye, he had learnt all right! He had learnt that battle was a foul, evil, stinking thing; that battle was to be avoided at all cost. At *all* cost!

Something made him look up, some disturbance of the ground, a movement, a shadow in the grass. A man! A man coming towards him – a man with chain-mail armour and an axe. No helmet. Fair hair, a bushed beard. A huge man, an ogre, titan, giant. God save his soul – a Viking!

405

Edward screamed. The branches caught at his clothing, whipped his face, grabbed his hair as he tried to scramble away, crawling backwards into nettles that bit and stung at his legs and arms. He could hear his brother and the other boys shouting, hear them scrabbling about in the tree. The man kept coming forward, a grinned leer on his face, his axe raised. Edward felt something under his hand, something hard and heavy. A stone. His fingers clamped around it and he was throwing, his full weight and desperation giving the missile momentum. By luck, not aim, it struck home; the man lurched, dropped the axe, his hands going to his face, blood seeping from between his fingers and with a rattled groan he toppled and crashed to the grass, quite dead.

Alfred was swarming down from the tree and running to Edward, who was sitting, ash-faced, his stomach heaving. The boys crowded close, some kicking at the dead man with their boots or spitting on him; others stood, thumping Edward between his shoulders, impressed.

'You've killed him, Edward,' Alfred said proudly, scarce believing the evidence of his eyes. 'Well done, Brother, well done!'

Edward could not take it all in. His hands were shaking and stinging; he was going to be sick again any minute. He had killed someone, killed a man. Oh, God's Wonder, what if it was Cnut himself? What would Edmund or his mother say to that? He would be a hero, they would write poems and sagas about him, the monks would write his name in the chronicles that they so industriously kept. '*In this year, Edward, ætheling, son of Æthelred, did slay the invader Cnut, with one stone, as did David slay Goliath.*' How England would cheer and praise him. And best of all, if this was Cnut, how his mother would love him. The hugs, the kisses, the devotion. All he had ever wanted – for the throwing of one large stone!

It was not until later, when the men came wearily back to camp, many of them wounded, as many left dead down by the river, that Edward realised the truth. It had not been Cnut, Cnut had gone, had sailed on upriver. Depleted of so many, Edmund had not been able to follow, the end would have to come another day.

The man Edward had killed had been a rough-necked nobody, a

whore-born deserter who had fled from his Danish army with the idea of taking what he could carry and getting as far away as possible. Tired men praised Edward, some ruffled his hair, Edmund squeezed his shoulder, said he would make a fine warrior some day. Beyond that, nothing. They were all too damned weary to notice, and his mother, Emma, was never told of it.

20

After a great effort and some brilliant successes, Edmund failed to pursue the fleeing Danes because he did not have the men to make that final demanding push. Too many years of apathy, too cynical a view of leadership, had soured the English from ealdorman to churl. No one was willing to drop everything, take up their weapons and come out and fight beyond the service of their compulsory duty.

He could have followed Cnut up the Thames, trapped him in the shallower waters and dealt with him there. Could have, but his men were dead on their feet. He had to let them go, bid them return to their farms and their villages of Essex and Hertford-Shire, to rest, recover, gather in the harvest and join him again at the next meeting with these poxed Danes.

Cnut had blessed God for the reprieve, as he had moored his ships as far up the Thames as they could sail. He had fortified a camp and settled to lick his wounds, but before mid July, found the audacity to squat outside London again, renewing his incompleted siege. Within the week, had realised, dismally, that it was a mistake to attempt to pick up where he had left off for the strategy was untenable.

With one last, valiant effort, he had thrown all he had into an attack on the city by land and river combined. He failed. Realising the inevitable, as the first dainty edge of morning crept timidly into the eastern sky, his ships had quietly sailed away under London Bridge, the Londoners, this time, allowing them to go. Instead, he turned to East Anglia to obtain all the supplies he needed, food, beer, horses, weapons, then sailed for the Medway river and Kent, where he waited, hoping to draw the English king to him. The prospect of victory, so golden at the start of the year, was rapidly diminishing. Edmund was winning but all was not lost. There were opportunities for another battle, and another, and another beyond that. As far as Cnut was concerned, the fighting would go on until either he or Edmund lay dead. To the ordinary people, the farmers, the peasants, those who only wanted to bring in and enjoy their harvest, there was little care over which one would win during those dry, balmy days when summer drifted into the first early stirrings of autumn. It only mattered, or so it seemed, to the two leaders themselves, to Cnut and Edmund. And to Emma and Eadric Streona, who had their own reasons for the wanting of victory.

After skirmished fighting at Otford, where Edmund had managed, somehow – God alone knew how – to overtake Cnut's Danes and defeat them yet again, the end appeared closer. With a might of effort Edmund had driven Cnut's ships into Sheppey and he looked, for all the world, as if he was going to achieve the ultimate victory.

Others certainly thought so.

Godwine skidded into Edmund's tent, his heel scooping up a divot of the worn grass. 'We have a visitor, Edmund. Come quick. Now!'

Edmund muttered an oath. He had been asleep, dreaming of some pleasant, appreciable thing, he forgot entirely what it was now he was so abruptly awake. Groaning, he opened his eyes, did not otherwise move from his cot. He was bone weary. Had he been asleep? It did not feel as if he had. All these months of marching, riding, fighting – thinking. That was as tiring as the physical stuff, the mental energy that was required, the necessity always to be alert, ready, expecting the unexpected. The one consolation for his aching, throbbing temples, Cnut was probably feeling as numbed as he did.

'Who is it? If it is Emma, send her back to Canterbury, I'll not be seeing her. The two boys have returned to her care and that is final. I'll not read another of her letters of protest, nor listen to one more of her sent messengers. Nor to her.' He turned over, pulled the blanket up to his ears and tried to reach the sleep he had been disturbed from.

Godwine was across the tent in three strides, pulling the blanket away. 'Ach, man, it is not the Queen! It is Eadric. Eadric Streona is outside the camp looking sheepish and waving a green branch about his head, hoping we'll not shoot an arrow straight through his throat before he has chance to grovel before you.'

Edmund was up, on his feet, lacing his tunic. 'Eadric? Here? God Almighty, are you serious?'

Godwine fetched Edmund's boots, nodded.

'I'll hang the bastard.' Edmund threatened, buckling on his sword belt. 'I'll flay him alive, roast him on a spit. Behead him.'

'What, all at once?' Godwine laughed. 'And before you hear what he has to say?'

'I do not wish to listen to one word that evil-minded, foul-mouthed dog turd cares to mutter. He can explain himself to God, not to me.' Edmund ducked out of the tent, was striding towards the shuttered gateway.

Godwine caught him up as he took the steps to the rampart walkway two at a time. 'Not even if he has come to offer you Mercia?'

That stopped Edmund. 'I would have Mercia, but not Streona.'

Godwine spread his hands, half apologetic, half sympathetic. 'It is a sorry fact, my Lord King, you may not be able to have the one without the other.'

Edmund walked, slower, to the palisade, looked out and over at the solitary man sitting astride his horse beyond arrow range before the gate. Eadric had not come alone, but prudently, he had left his men ranged in a semi-circle some distance behind. They all carried the green-leafed branch of peace, appeared weaponless. Withdrawing behind a pillar, Edmund ordered a servant, who had come trotting up behind him, to fetch his crown. 'And my best mantle. Hurry.'

It was not often he had the chance to parade dressed for a crown-wearing as befitted his status as King. Since the opportunity had arisen, he would take every full advantage of it.

Suitably attired, he stepped out to where Eadric could see him, stood, arms folded, Godwine to his right with his axe provocatively poised over his shoulder.

'So, Eadric, the dog returns to his vomit. What have you to say to me that I ought listen to? I can think of nothing.'

'I come in peace to talk peace. To admit that I have been wrong and am ashamed of what I have done.'

'Bloody liar,' Godwine whispered.

'Rats, skulking from a sinking ship?' Edmund answered.

'The question is, my Lord, do we let them scurry into the sewer ditches, or burn the nest?'

Edmund scowled. 'It sticks in my throat to talk to this bastard, Godwine, but as you say, I do so desperately need Mercia.'

'Then order him to call out the fyrd in the name of Edmund Ironside, King of England. Mayhap, somewhere along the line, after Cnut is dead and England has started to settle into a new prosperity, Eadric can meet with an accident. While out hunting, perhaps?' Godwine's reference was pointed, referring to Alfhelm's murder.

Edmund nodded, his face as passive as his friend's. A sensible idea, but if it was sensible, why did he not like it?

There was one wholly unexpected advantage to welcoming Eadric back as a King's ealdorman, however. The Queen sent no more letters or messengers to Edmund about Edward and Alfred, beyond one curt missive: '*I will not, under any circumstances, trust the life of my sons while that man is in your company. Be warned. Blood stains his hands.*'

Edmund never expected to be grateful to Eadric Streona for something.

411

21

17 October 1016 – *Ashingdon, Essex*

As Emma had warned, there was reason not to trust Eadric Streona, but Edmund needed him now that the Danes had once again found the audacity to enter the Thames estuary. This ring of to-and-fro advance and retreat had to be ended. Cnut had to be stopped with a final confrontation, but so much depended on a concerted, united effort, and with men like Streona at your back Edmund could not feel easy with that dependence. All the same, he could not allow Cnut to entrench himself somewhere, well supplied, for the winter. He would have preferred to have more proof of Eadric's new-found sense of regret, but then, what higher proof could the man give than to fight in battle for his acknowledged King? With misgivings, that same King sent out the war call and, to his relief, southern England responded to the mournful booming of the war horns. Eadric, with typical effrontery, informing anyone who cared to listen that the fyrds had rallied because of his expression of faith in Edmund. On hearing the boasting for himself, Edmund gritted his teeth and tactfully made no comment. Godwine, not so level-tempered and coming very close to connecting his fist with Eadric's mouth, consoled himself that he could do whatever he wanted to the cursed man later. After Ashingdon.

It was as good a place as any to fight a last battle. Ashingdon was nothing more than a hamlet of two farmsteadings, three peasant bothies and a chapel. Beyond the settlement a long, low hill projected into the flat country between the Rivers Crouch and Thames. Although Edmund had not taken Cnut by surprise – the Dane had become too wary for that – he had managed to come up on him quicker than expected. In open battle experience the English were lacking, but their numbers were impressive and they had among them a leader who knew all there was to know about tactics: Ulfkell of East Anglia. Men anxious to repair loss of face had also responded to Edmund's call, among them the man branded as coward, Ælfric of Hamp-Shire, although his presence was, as ever, questionable. There were more than a few men sitting around the campfires, that star-bright night, laying wagers on how soon Ælfric's stomach sickness would recur and take him running to squat, groaning, beneath the hedgerows. Edmund had wisely countered any doubt by ensuring that the man fought in the King's wing and that his men were under the King's command, not their Ealdorman's. If Ælfric wanted to spend the day puking somewhere, then let him. Edmund needed the men of his fyrd, not him.

The enemy camp was in full view, no more than one and a half miles away towards the next, larger, settlement of Canewden, their distant fires looking like a meadow scattered with clumps of white daisies. If it were not for their own noise, Danish voices could have been heard across the quiet waiting of the tense, breath-held darkness.

Sharing his meagre supper of mutton stew with his ealdormen, Godwine, the Bishop of Dorchester-on-Thames and the Abbot of Ramsey Abbey, Edmund forced himself to be pleasant in manner and conversation with the two men whom he doubted, Eadric and Ælfric. A task, that in Streona's instance, stuck like a bone in his throat.

'He'll not run in the darkness, do you think?' Ælfric asked, anxious, referring to Cnut, gathering his mantle tighter. The night was clear but chill, offering a foretaste of the winter that would soon be trundling its cold breath over the countryside. He was starting to shiver, did not want anyone to assume his shaking was through fear.

'No, Ælfric, I am sorry to disappoint you, he will not be running,' Edmund answered, giving the Ealdorman a friendly, sympathetic pat on his shoulder.

'No, no, do not get me wrong,' the man answered quickly. Too quickly. 'I am eager for a fight, I just thought . . .'

'You just thought it would save your stomach a lot of bile if Cnut were to pack up camp and sail quietly away.' Eadric Streona's comment was acerbic. 'We well know your past history, Ælfric.'

413

Edmund could not hold in the retort that sprang to his mouth, did not even try. 'But then you are not exactly clean and shining behind the ears yourself, are you, Eadric?'

'I have never run from a battlefield in my life!' Eadric protested, vehemently. The fact that he had only fought in minor skirmishes was tactfully not mentioned. It was not what Edmund had meant anyway and Eadric well knew it. The King, however, prudently did not pursue the matter. Here, now, was not the place to quarrel.

'Cnut is in a position where he will have to fight,' Ulfkell explained, ignoring the squalled flurry of tension as he stretched his long legs to the crackling fire. 'He is laden with spoil, if he were to attempt an escape by land, he would be obliged to leave behind all he has looted and abandon his ships. Alternatively, it would be foolhardy to attempt an embarkation with us so close; he could never put up an adequate defence. Therefore, on the morrow we fight.' For his part, Ulfkell was looking forward to the affray. On behalf of Thetford, he had his own score of honour to settle with these Danes.

'And on the morrow we win!' Godwine raised his ale tankard high, slopping some of it over the rim in his enthusiasm, the others cheerfully following suit. The Bishop of Dorchester endorsing the optimism with a loud 'Amen' and forming the sign of the cross in the air, a gesture echoed by them all. He, like the Abbot and several other men of God, were not permitted to shed blood, but that did not stop them from entering a fight that was of a magnitude such as this. The clergy would stride into battle with their cassocks girded high and solid, wooden clubs tight-clasped in their hands. The damage such a weapon could do to a man's skull was formidable.

Later, when the men had settled into their cloaks, or dozed where they sat, Edmund found that he could not sleep. He had not sought his bed until after midnight had passed and dawn, now, would not be far away. His thoughts kept returning to his wife and son, to the child she would be birthing soon. When was it due? Mid November? His first son was a bonny lad, with bright, interested eyes and a grip as firm as a mastiff's jaws. Ædward. He prayed to God that the three of them would be kept safe, had asked Godwine to ensure it, as he

414

had asked Emma, too, but he doubted she would keep her word, not with her own Edward and Alfred to consider. He supposed he could not blame her. The strange thing was that he had taken Ealdgyth as wife to spite his father – oh, he had been attracted to her, what hot-blooded man would not have been? But love? That had grown between them in these short months of marriage. It was love, not lust, he was certain. If it were only the wanting of a woman in his bed he could have had any one of the whores following behind the army, but he wanted only Ealdgyth. Wanted her here with him, now, this night, to feel her, smell her. Love her. If she were here, perhaps he could sleep, could tear his mind away from the fear that was within him about the coming day.

Skirmishes, unplanned attacks, were one thing, this was different, this would be a last, final thing, and it would be foul and bloody. How did men like Ulfkell, and those sitting, sleeping, around the dying fire, relish the prospect of battle? Did the thought of what they would see, do, feel, not sicken them? He rolled on to his back, put his hands behind his head and stared up into the darkness that was the low leather roof of his tent. What was it Ulfkell had said once, long ago, when Edmund was a child and he had asked him about combat?

'It is a thing you do, boy, without thought or question, because it is a thing that has to be done. You go into battle knowing you have put an edge to cut the wind on your axe and sword, knowing that you have done your best to learn how to use them, and knowing that your comrades beside you, all those men to left and right of you, are as shit scared as you are.' Edmund smiled, puffed his cheeks and ran his hands through his hair. There was something else Ulfkell had said, not when he had asked as a boy but at Æthelred's funeral, in that waiting hour between his father's burial and his own coronation. 'Success, whether it be as a sovereign on a throne or a peasant farmer fighting in battle, is based on trust. You have to trust those next to you to do their best, in whatever it is you are expecting them to do. And to trust these other men, you must trust your own judgement.' That was the rub. How to trust his own judgement? Edmund sighed, shut his eyes. There was one thing for certain: one of them, either Cnut or himself, tomorrow –

no, today, it was already today – would not be leaving Ashingdon alive, or at least, would not be living long after it. That scared him too, the thought of a long, drawn-out death. Better to be killed outright in battle, where so much was happening that you did not, perhaps, notice the manner of an ending.

He must have dozed, slept, for Godwine was shaking him awake. 'Dawn, my Lord. The Danish camp is already astir.'

Edmund grunted, swung his legs from his cot and called for his mail hauberk. No profit in thinking on the endless possibilities now. Now was for the doing and only the doing.

22

18 October 1016 – Ashingdon

Eadric Streona was appalled at what was happening in front of him and at his own stupidity. This was something he had not anticipated, had never imagined, not even when listening to the stories the harpers so graphically told. How in God's Name were they going to defeat so many? How in all the fires of Hell was any one of them going to emerge alive from what was about to happen?

A slight rise on the Danish side of the field meant that Cnut had managed to move forward without losing any of the advantage of the high ground. Edmund, taking the advice of Ulfkell, had deployed into three divisions, Wessex under his own command at the centre, Ulfkell's East Anglians to the left flank and Eadric on the right.

The sight of so many, rank, upon rank, of Danes standing facing him had churned Eadric's stomach. The noise was dreadful; the shouting, the jeering, the clashing of spear or axe on shield – and no advance had yet been made, there was not yet any close fighting. What would it be like then, when the two armies met together? Eadric Streona swallowed, felt the sweat drip from beneath his armpits. His palms felt sticky, the axe haft in his hand slippery, the felt padding beneath his mail was sodden and heavy from the sweat soaked up from his back. He regretted, now, mocking Ealdorman Ælfric's fear. He looked to his left. Ælfric was standing thirty or so yards from Edmund, not in the forefront of things but near enough to know that he would be fighting, not merely observing. And he had done this before? Had faced this monstrous prospect? No wonder the man had feigned illness and refused to fight! It was not normally in Eadric's nature to feel admiration for someone, but on this occasion he had to concede that he was impressed by Ælfric, who stood, rigid to attention, ready and waiting. A pity, Eadric thought to himself, that the damned man did not break his resolve, drop his weapon and run. It would have given Eadric an excuse to chase after him.

The sun was well risen, noon would be less than two hours away, were they just going to stand here all day, shouting profanities at each other? God's Truth, Eadric hoped so! He damned, bloody hoped so!

Edmund half turned to his right and nodded his head in salute to the Ealdorman, Ælfric. That was courage, he thought with pride, to stand in line, to wait for the order to go, knowing that your guts had been left in camp and that there was nothing left to shit from your backside. Ælfric was terrified, his face was the white of chalk and Edmund fancied he could see him shaking, even from this distance; he stood there, ready, determined not to let his young King down. There would be reward for Ælfric when this was all over, Edmund decided, appropriate recognition. He looked up as a flock of geese skimmed overhead, their wings whistling in flight. A good omen? Bad? Enough of this! Someone had to make a move, had to get things started and it did not look as if Cnut was eager to take the initiative.

Lifting his axe above his head, Edmund swung it three times in a circle, the war horns boomed into the saline-crisp air and chaos was let loose.

'We must keep together,' Ulfkell had said last night, when they had squatted beside the rough plan he had drawn in the hearth ashes. 'It will do us no good to have one flank outpace the other.'

Enthusiasm? Eagerness? Or merely the easier curve of the terrain? Whatever cause, Ulfkell's flank advanced quicker than the right, opening a gap that rapidly widened with every yard. Eadric, watching, holding his men at a steady walk, knew it would all go wrong. 'We are to advance in a steady line,' Edmund had said.

'Walk!' Eadric yelled, turning his head to left and right, holding his axe out to one side, shield to the other, as a barrier. 'We will not spend our breath in the first few minutes, we will walk!'

Those ahead of him had not listened, they had gone, the fools, were up with Edmund and the centre, closing in on Cnut's men,

418

who were rushing forward. This was madness! Could Edmund not see it for himself? They were vastly outnumbered, Cnut had the advantage of the high ground – in the names of the Saints, they would be massacred! Horrified, Eadric halted abruptly, the ranks of men behind bumping to a stop. He had never seriously fought, had never been one to listen to the advice or wisdom of those who knew more than he did. Nor was Eadric the type of man who would admit to his own failing.

The gap between the right flank and the rest of the field had widened so much that as the two armies clashed in a great uprush roar of sound, the entire third of Eadric's command remained behind, uncommitted. He had said that it was a fool plan, that they would be better to wait, choose a more suitable location. Eadric Streona had *said*, but had anyone listened? And here he was, being proved right! The Danes were too superior in strength, look at them! Look how their left was coming forward, turning inwards to envelop the rear of Edmund's centre!

There was nothing he could do to help, the tactics had been flawed from the start. Was that his fault? He had to make a quick, practical solution; this battle had been badly commanded, badly led. Best to get his men out, serve their interests as well he may.

Convinced, Eadric fled the field, taking the men of Hereford-Shire and Shrop-Shire, the entire right flank, with him. The remainder of them died, those who had not turned tail to run. With the right flank gone, the rest stood as much chance as a field of corn surviving the reaper's scythe.

Ælfric never felt the axe that took his head from his neck. Ulfkell fought on with a spear rammed through his thigh, agonisingly hanging there until he could find a moment to twist it out. Fifteen minutes later, a sword curving into his arm amputated it above the elbow and he bled to death on his feet, still fighting. The Bishop was killed and the Abbot of Ramsey. His death was significant, for Ramsey was responsible for the recording of the Chronicles. He was a man much loved by the monks under his supervision and they would see to it, later, that his death was honoured and the manner of its treacherous doing preserved, in their careful, scripted writing.

So many of them dead or left to die. Ah, the glories of battle? Glory belonged only to the harpers' songs, not to the reality that was the battlefield.

Godwine, wounded, but able to stay on his feet, got Edmund away with the help of a small group of cnights. A small group. Such a small, bloodied, bewildered group. They half carried, half dragged their King, for he was unable to walk without aid. It had seemed such an innocent wound, one that he barely noticed at first, but the sword had bitten deep into his groin, thrusting up into his guts and stomach. He fought for as long as he could, but the bleeding disabled him and he fell, useless, to the mashed and mud-bloodied grass. And then it was all over.

He was in great pain, the redness of agony swinging in and out of the swaying blackness of nothing. Edmund was unaware that they managed to get him to the horse lines, to put him across a pony and ride, so slowly, so damned slowly, away. Was unaware of those left behind as fodder for the ravens and that Cnut had won for himself a crown.

23

October 1016 – Alney Island, Gloucester

Emma took the bold and nerve-racking decision to join Edmund, with her sons, at his manor on Alney Island in Deerhurst. If she was to fight for Edward's right as ætheling, then this was the day she had to do it. She told herself that the unease fluttering inside her was from the importance of the occasion, that so much of the future rested on this one afternoon's work. That there was no reason for her stomach to be churning, or her heart to be thumping so fast, but if this day did not go as Edmund planned . . . no, she would not think of that. All the same, the flicker of unease lurched more persistent when Cnut's ship came into sight downriver.

She stood up on the wooden rampart walkway to see him come in; that should have been the King's prerogative, but Edmund had asked her to do it on this occasion on his behalf. Why was it she was so pleased to oblige? Why did she feel like some silly, giggling maiden? Because Edmund trusted her? Because after all these years, she was beginning to realise what it meant to be a woman in command of her own destiny? She convinced herself, as the ship came closer, that her eagerness to be done with these next few hours was to satisfy her fears about Godwine. He was with Cnut as a surety of safe conduct – aye, and all knew Cnut's reputation there! No, her heart was skittering, her throat and lips were dry because she was nervous. Nervous of making a fool of herself, nervous of doing, saying, the wrong thing. Nervous? She was almost scared witless! So much, so very much depended on this day's work!

The negotiations for this meeting of truce had swung to and fro like a dangled plumb line these last weeks. As the victor of Ashingdon, Cnut had demanded that Edmund attend him, Edmund, as the crowned and anointed King of England, had politely refused, on the justifiable grounds that Cnut was not a man to be trusted,

421

even with his given word. Instead, Edmund made his own alternative demand. Southern England was in disarray, but he was holding on to it through the sheer bravado of will-power and the respect that he had earned as a formidable leader and opponent. Those with him at Deerhurst were well aware that the holding was by the skin of his teeth, but Cnut was not. The ability to bluff your opponent convincingly could often be the more discerning side of valour.

Cnut stood in the bows, behind the high, carved dragon prow, his legs braced against the movement of the ship as she nosed in against the jetty. He was a fine-looking man, Emma conceded as she watched him disembark and make his way up the slope towards the open gateway with his escort of ten unarmed men. The remainder of his guard stayed aboard, their eyes watching every movement the English made, ears pricked, alert for a shout or the clash of weapons. With them Godwine, who placed himself where Cnut had stood, beneath the dragon prow, plainly seen.

Unsure of this called meeting, Cnut was aware, from his own doing, that treachery was too easy a thing to organise. What he had done to Uhtred of Northumbria could be replicated here at Deerhurst, with the spear-point turned against him. His safe passage up the Severn, therefore, had been elaborately arranged and the exchange of hostages undertaken with almost as much ceremony as the meeting proper, although Cnut's record of the treatment of hostages was not admired among the English either, a fact that the Dane used, in this instance, in his favour. He had made it quite clear that if he did not return to his base by the setting of the sun, neither would the Englishmen and boys in his temporary keeping be watching the next dawn appear.

Of her own choosing Emma had decided to attend this meeting, a decision that Edmund had generously, and gratefully, welcomed. It was her place as Queen, and as the mother of the eldest æthelings, to ensure her voice was heard in any undertaking that affected the governing of England. And whether she could add her own bluff by convincing Cnut that Normandy would take great umbrage at a usurpation of her crown remained to be seen. She was determined to have a good try at it.

Gathering her gown to her knees, Emma descended the wooden steps. At the bottom, she rearranged her skirt, ensured her wimple and crown were straight, and walked, proud, across the bailey towards the centre of the open courtyard, to where Edmund was already seated beneath an erected canopy. She settled herself beside him, chiding Edward, perched on his own stool, for his fidgeting.

'Sit still, boy,' she rasped as Cnut paused in the gateway and then entered. 'Else I'll toss you to those murderous Vikings waiting outside.'

Edward bit his lip and stared hard at his boots, rapidly blinking his eyes against threatening tears, afraid of the big man coming towards him.

'I greet you, my Lord Prince,' Emma said, rising to acknowledge Cnut and speaking in Danish. As head woman, she offered him the traditional welcome cup of wine, discreetly sipping from it first to show that it was not tainted.

Aware that poison could take many forms and be spread on the edge of drinking vessels as well as added to the liquid, Cnut deliberately turned the goblet to drink from the edge that had touched her lips. He took the obligatory sip, but one that barely wet his mouth, and poured the remainder to puddle at his feet.

'Is it customary to be greeted by the widow of a dead and mouldering king?' he asked condescendingly, meeting her eye to eye. He turned to Edmund. 'I was expecting your wedded wife to accompany you, my Lord.'

Indicating the cushioned stool that had been set ready for Cnut, Edmund answered, courteously using Cnut's own tongue. 'My wife is about women's work, she is close to her time for bearing my second son. But, surely, you know that she is not our anointed Queen? My Lady Emma Ælfgifu is Dowager, and bears the honour of that title.'

Polite, Cnut bowed his head, sat, smiled. Ah, that was why his Ælfgifu, up in Northampton, was so persistent in wanting Emma gone.

She was not as tall as he remembered, thinner of face; for the rest, he recalled her well, every nuance, every flexion of her voice, movement of hand and head. Remembered the flash of her eyes, the control of her voice. Had he ever forgotten that day in Greenwich? How she must have looked upon him with loathing, a spot-faced, ignorant youth. If she still thought of him with contempt, she hid it well. Huh, of course she despised him, foolish of him to consider otherwise.

'May I present my sons,' Emma said, chivvying them both to their feet. 'My Lord King Edmund's brothers, the æthelings, Edward and Alfred.'

'Half-brothers,' Cnut drawled, 'they are of no consequence to me.'

'But they are of a consequence to England, Sir, and to my brother, Duke Richard of Normandy.'

Outmanoeuvred, Cnut acknowledged them with the barest of nods.

'My brother thought he had killed you once,' Alfred announced, unabashed and unafraid. 'It turned out to be a Viking deserter, though. Do you get many deserting their service to you?'

If the Queen's own face had not mirrored his annoyance, Cnut would have sworn that statement had been a deliberately planted contrivance. As it was she ordered her sons to sit, and be silent and still. For his part, Cnut could not imagine the elder boy, a scrawny twig of lad, capable of killing anything larger than a blow fly. For the younger, though, ja, there was spirit behind his gawky childishness.

'Let us to business,' Edmund said, waving for a servant to bring forward wine and sweetmeats. 'I would ask you to be gone from my Kingdom before any more blood is shed and wasted.'

Cnut tossed his head back and laughed outright. 'Well, that is bold and to the point! I have to confess that I admire your nerve. You certainly have balls, Edmund, if nothing else!'

Emma, alarmed, glanced at her stepson with a sideways look, uncertain how he might react to such bluntness, relaxed at his apparent calm composure.

Folding his arms, Cnut's poise and attitude of self-assurance gave an impression of arrogant haughtiness although, in fact, he was as nervous as an unbroken colt. 'Your army is grossly depleted, your leaders are dead. What have you got left to send against me, Edmund? I could take England now, like that.' He snapped his thumb and finger together in a loud, expressive gesture of contempt. Bluff. He too had lost men at Ashingdon.

'I have lost good friends, yes,' Edmund answered quietly, the memory painful, 'but you made a grave and irreversible error in sending Eadric Streona to me as your harnessed traitor. What he did by running from the battlefield without a drop of blood staining a single weapon has sickened all England, even his own Mercia. Because of that one act of cowardice and betrayal, there is now no one who would not rally to me, if I asked it of them.'

Listening intently to every word, his eyes not missing a single movement or subtle gesture, Cnut stroked his short blond beard. *If I asked it.* Was there some doubt, then, that Edmund intended to carry on with this fight? Surely he was not prepared to capitulate so easily? Disappointment plunged through Cnut. He liked this man sitting before him, for all he was an Englishman and his enemy. No, it was more than liking, this was respect; but there could be no admiring a man who laid down his spear on the first night of darkness. What was it he had heard about Edmund? That he had refused to leave the field at Ashingdon, although he was sorely wounded? That he had insisted on continuing the fight, swearing to see it through to its ending? Close to death they had carried him away, his sword clasped in his hand, refusing to set it aside for a full seven-day around. Or so Cnut had heard tell.

He could see no sign of wounding, there was no pallid complexion, sweating, or death rattle in his throat. A healing gash to his forehead and yellowing bruising to his cheek, that was all. No more than Cnut himself sported as a reminder of recent combat.

'Eadric Streona is nothing to do with me, Edmund,' he said. 'He is his own man, with his own mind, and I am thinking that he has proven, beyond speculation, that any king who trusts him must be a king prepared eternally to watch the shadows that creep behind him.'

Edmund was unhappy with this Dane using his name as if he were a friend, but he could not afford to be churlish; he let it pass. 'I

425

would advise you to remember that we were to come to some amicable agreement between us here this day.'

Cnut leant forward, propping his elbow on his thigh, his eyes bright, eager. 'And you have some suggestion for an agreement?'

'I think you know well that I have. The messengers going between us through these last days of flurried activity have, I would wager, spoken more than I permitted in your ear.' Edmund's smile was honeyed sweetness. 'And in my ear, too, of course.'

So Edmund had his spies listening and watching, as Cnut had his. Interesting. Why make the information public? What was this game that Edmund was so astutely playing? Cnut was aware that this man was making strategic moves, lifting and placing his ivory-carved men across the board, aiming to surround and capture his opponent. Why was it that Cnut felt that, already, he was hemmed in on three sides, with only the fourth remaining, for a short while, open? Bluntly he said, 'I am intrigued that you have the gall to offer me terms of agreement. As I stated initially, England is open to me, like a whore lying with her legs invitingly widespread.'

'Your only problem with that, Cnut,' Emma interrupted sweetly, 'is that you cannot be certain whether the whore carries the pox, or whether she has a sharpened dagger concealed beneath her bed.'

Cnut looked at her, said nothing. She was sharp, this woman, barbed, like a boar-spear. Was she valuable, though? For hunting, a man could get a suitable spear from anywhere, but he preferred his favourite, the one that fitted comfortable in his hand, the one that balanced right, cast well. He had thought it before, thought it again. Æthelred had been a fool not to appreciate his Queen. He turned his attention back to Edmund and realised, suddenly, that *ja*, Edmund was not the fool like his father, for he had Emma here with him and he was making full use of her wisdom.

'You have appointed a man as Earl of Northumbria,' Edmund continued, unaware of Cnut's speculative thoughts, his English tongue tripping over the Danish word for ealdorman. 'Placing one of your own in a governmental position is not the same thing as governing. There are many in the North who will stay loyal to me, for through my wife and children they are kindred. In addition,

426

there are many who resent the manner of Uhtred's killing and such men are already realising that I am not my father.'

'Are you saying they will defy Earl Erik and rally to you?' Cnut asked.

For answer Edmund lightly shrugged.

'And I remind you', Emma added, 'that my brother has an interest in the English throne.'

Cnut guffawed. 'He has made no attempt to keep hold of it thus far, Lady!'

She retained the smile, serene, her hand going to maternally caress Edward's hair. She looked at Cnut, straight and direct in the eye. 'Did he not?' she said. 'Your father died and you, in your own turn, fled home like a child with a scraped knee seeking his mother's solace. The weight of Normandy's strength was therefore not tested.' Bluff. She was getting good at this.

Biding his time, Cnut sipped his ale. He had refused the offered food and was not certain of the drink, but Edmund and the Lady had been served theirs from the same pitcher and they had been sampling it freely. If death was awaiting him, he felt confident that it would not be coming by the stealth of bitter poison. Was she telling the truth in this? Had Duke Richard been planning a counter-attack on England on behalf of his sister? It was possible. Richard was a proud and pompous man, he would not tolerate humiliation, but he was also lazy and indifferent.

Loath as Cnut was to admit it, Edmund was not talking nonsense. His Danish army had been battered at Ashingdon; many longships would be half empty when the men decided to return home. If it had not been for Eadric Streona's fortuitous cowardice, this meeting of truce would not be taking place, Ashingdon would have been lost and he himself probably killed. Not that that fact made Cnut any more agreeable towards that wretched man, Eadric Streona. A traitor was to be treated with contempt, no matter what field he grazed in.

'So,' he said finally, 'what is this thing you wish to propose?'

Relieved that this had been easier than expected, Edmund answered straight and blunt, 'I wish to retain the South as my own.

You may have all the land north of the Trent river. Including Mercia, you are welcome to that. It will be fitting punishment for them.'

Cnut blew disdainful air through his nose. 'The North alone is worthless to me.'

'Other Danes have thought it worth the having.'

'Other Danes have not wished to be King. I do.' As it was, it was a good offer, but not good enough for Cnut to readily agree. It was more than he had been expecting, though. 'Tell me this, why should I allow you to keep Wessex and the South for your own? I won the victory at Ashingdon, not you.'

Gravely, Edmund nodded agreement. 'Aye, you won at Ashingdon, but you did not win England. You cannot win England, not while I am alive.'

Cnut spread his hands, stood. 'Then I shall wait for you to die. If your death comes soon, then the waiting will not be too hard to endure. If it does not, well, I shall harry your coast, take your women, grain and cattle, and demand tribute, as did my father. I can wait.'

Edmund remained seated, said plainly, 'Unlike my father, I will not pay tribute, and Englishmen shall defend their women, crops and livestock against your coming. Are you so certain that in such adverse circumstances you will find men willing to sail with you? I think not. My offer is a good offer, it is one of peace and mutual satisfaction. We both get what we want. We both win.'

'I will think on it,' Cnut said. 'I shall send word by the morrow noon.'

Edmund conceded. That was fair. Cnut would never accept the terms as they stood, but if Edmund's spies spoke right, he would be willing to bargain.

From respect, Cnut bowed his head, turned, left, was partially annoyed that Edmund had not risen to return the politeness. He remarked upon it to the hostage, Godwine Wulfnothsson, as his ship pulled away from the shore, her oars dipping, hungry, into the smooth waves.

'Does your King not honour his guests by getting off his backside

428

as they are taking leave? Where I come from, that is a mark of disrespect.'

'So, where you come from,' Godwine answered, looking direct ahead and riding out the roll of the craft with spread legs and a spear-straight back, 'do you dishonour your warriors by expecting a wounded man to stand on his feet?'

Cnut's head shot up, alert. 'He is wounded? I saw no sign.'

Godwine kept his face impassive, *nor were you meant to*, he thought. 'He took a sword blade into his groin, it heals slow.'

'But it heals?'

'It heals.'

Silence. Cnut's mind was buzzing with a torrent of whirling thoughts. Why had he not known this? How much was being concealed? How much the truth?

'It is not mortal?'

'It is not mortal.'

The wind caught at Cnut's cloak, sent it flapping about his head like the black wings of the raven on his banner. He was certain that Godwine was lying.

'I do not know whether to believe you,' Cnut said, speaking with honesty.

'That is for you to decide, but I am permitted to tell you this, that you would gain much, and lose little, if you were to accept King Edmund's terms.'

Cnut sent reply to Edmund by the following noon. He agreed to take the North for his own, but he wanted more than Edmund had offered. As the victor of Ashingdon, Cnut demanded all that lay above the Thames. Edmund was to have Wessex and Kent. It was how England had been divided in Alfred's time and Edmund was content with the agreement, with the provision that London was to be free to see to an own decision and that his heirs, the æthelings, had their lawful right to take up his crown when he no longer had use of it. Cnut accepted, for within that short space he had made his own private enquiries. Godwine, for the honour and dignity of his lord and friend, had indeed lied. The sword blade had gone deep and the wound was festering. The physicians had cut away

Edmund's manhood in an attempt to stem the putrid spread of gangrene, but to no avail. Honour and respect were two things valuable to a warrior, for by these they were judged, in this life and the next. It made sense to agree Edmund's terms, for as Godwine had said, what had Cnut to lose by doing so? Plain also, why the Queen had been there, to ensure her eldest son acquired the crown for himself.

It had been a difficult thing for Edmund to sit there in front of Cnut and act as if he were fit and well, knowing that he was rotting inside. More difficult still to have swallowed that remark the Dane had innocently made: '*I have to confess that I admire your nerve. You certainly have balls!*'

That was something, Edmund, physically, no longer had.

In York, safe within the protection of the nunnery, Ealdgyth, wife to Edmund Ironside, now made King of Wessex, delivered their second child, a son in the first week of the October month.

Edmund did not hear word of it until the twenty-ninth day, and it pleased him to know that he was leaving behind two healthy boys. He asked Godwine to ensure that they were kept safe, thanked God for all He had blessed him with and, in the early hours of the thirtieth, died.

24

The smells of the Thames, where it flowed past the city of London, were mixed together in a blend of the natural and the noxious. A wet earth scent of the mudbanks that had not been covered by the high tide, and the lingering decay of the rubbish and sewage that freely filtered into the flow from where it was tossed over the city's walls, or emptied direct into the water. It was preferable to be down here by the river on a full or ebb tide, never at low tide, for that was when the smell became worse, especially in a summer heat.

This was winter and the frost crackled on puddles beneath their feet as the small group of cloaked people had stolen out of the gateway, opened by the minimum of gaps, and made their way by the light of a single heavily shaded sheep's horn lantern to the last jetty, downriver. The aroma of the ship met their nostrils: the caulking, the ropes, the sails. The sailors themselves, unwashed, their skin and hair salt-smeared from their days at sea. This was a trader's boat, smaller, more squat than the huge warships and not so manoeuvrable, for she did not have the ranks of oars that could propel a boat forward, fast, in any weather, any wind. Traders' craft were sedate, matronly things, that relied heavily on the wind and the turn of the tide. They were also, on a moonless night such as this, able to glide silently past Cnut's drink-sodden men and his fleet of ships moored at Greenwich.

Godwine steadied Edward as he stepped aboard, the boy's nose and mouth puckering in a grimace of disapproval. 'It stinks of sheep shit,' he said. 'We cannot go in this, it is not a ship suitable as transport for the son of a king.' Edward was petulant because he did not see why he and his brother had to leave London in darkness and secrecy. He wanted to go to Normandy, he had been happy there after that first flight into exile when he had been eight years old, and this exile would be even better, for Mother was not coming, at least, not straight away. The problem was the manner of going. The Danes would be only too happy to see the royal princes gone, so why all this secretive nonsense?

'A head severed from the neck stinks even more,' Emma snapped in answer, her voice a low whisper, 'as we shall all discover if you insist on making so much noise.'

'I'm sorry, Mother, but I do not see why we have to leave like this,' Edward persisted. 'We sailed to Normandy in a dragon craft last time.'

'I'll whistle Thorkell up for you, then, shall I? Seeing as it was he who took you,' Godwine answered, as irritated as Emma. 'I am sure his new master, Cnut, will be only too pleased to see you.'

'Come on, Edward,' Alfred chided, pushing past him, 'this is fun, an adventure, I have never sailed on a trading ship!'

Petulant. 'I don't want an adventure. I was asleep in my warm bed and I would rather have stayed there. Cnut will be pleased to see us go; why can we not leave with our heads high, in daylight?'

Alfred grinned. 'Are you serious? He would never let us walk innocently out of here. Exiled æthelings, Edward, have a tendency to return with an army following close behind. At first opportunity Cnut would make certain we were of no more nuisance by stringing us up by our pizzles and cutting off our ears and noses. If we were lucky, he might not bother with the niceties, he might simply decide to slit our throats.'

Edward bit his lip to refrain from making a retort. All he had to do was make a pledge with Cnut, explain to him that he wanted to become a monk and that he was welcome to England. All of it. Alfred was becoming such a know-it-all lately. Pouting, he sat where Godwine pointed, Alfred thumping down next to him, grinning and making the boat rock.

The ship was Godwine's, it had been one of his father's trading vessels, a good, solid craft with a dependable, solid crew. She had carried various things during her long sea career: wool, wine, ale, timber. Never the two sons of a dead king, having to flee for a second time into exile.

'You will be following soon, Mother, won't you?' Alfred said anxiously, peering through the darkness at Emma who stood at the edge of the jetty, her cloak clutched tight at her breast.

'As soon as I can,' she said, shuddering at the looming prospect of having to step on board a ship in the dead hours of the night. 'If I abandoned London now, there would never be any coming back for us. The people would shun me, and you, as if we carried the plague. If I stay until the last possible moment, then we might have a chance of rallying a Norman army to put you on the English throne by force, Edward.'

The boy muttered something into the blanket that he was hauling up to his shoulders against the damp cold. 'I don't want to be put on a throne.' His mother, fortunately, did not hear, but Alfred did.

'Then I'll have it!' he hissed, snuggling into his own blanket. He was only eleven, but he knew his own mind and what he wanted when he became a man. England, and a crown. It was so annoying that everyone talked about Edward being the next king, he was nothing but a girl's squit. Edward hated being unwashed and dirty, he hated sleeping on the earth in a tent, wearing old, worn clothes. He timidly held a sword, had no idea how to use a shield and fainted at the sight of blood. Him? King? If there had not been the need for quiet, Alfred would have laughed aloud.

'Kings on thrones get killed,' Edward added when Alfred said nothing.

His brother looked at him with a contemptuous sneer. 'Not good kings. And anyway, the eldest-born ætheling is more likely to be killed.' Alfred's leer widened. 'Usually by a better younger brother.'

Shuddering, Edward drew away from Alfred, tucking the blanket tighter as if it would protect him. 'You're beastly to me,' he whined, 'just plain beastly. I hope you do become king and I hope someone poisons you or lops your head off.'

Alfred ignored him. 'You will take care, won't you, Mother?' he said, his inner anxiousness overriding the bravado teasing of his brother. 'We will need you in Normandy to help raise the army.'

Emma hesitated before answering. If only she could ride to Normandy, or fly on the shoulders of some enormous bird. The sea did frighten her so!

Her silence suddenly alarmed Alfred, he half stood, dropping the blanket. 'You are coming, aren't you, Mother? You're not sending us away from you?'

Ah, the last was easier to answer. 'No, dear, I am merely sending you away from danger, not from me. You were right to realise that Cnut would not allow you to live if he captured you. You will be safe in Normandy with your uncle.'

'But he will not help us return to England,' Alfred persisted, 'not if there is nothing of direct benefit to him, and not if you are not there to make him.'

Emma was impressed. Her younger son had sense and intelligence, then. He had certainly not inherited either from his father.

'See you take them direct to Rouen, my friend,' Godwine instructed his merchant master, 'deliver them, personally, with this letter from the Queen, into the Duke's care.'

'Aye, Lord, I will.' To Emma, 'Do not worry, Lady, they will arrive safe. I pledge my life on it.'

Godwine handed him a leather pouch. 'My Lady Queen knows that I trust you above all whom I employ, but this is by way of something extra from her to you.'

The ship's master weighed the pouch in his hand. It was heavy and it chinked. Gold coin. He smiled at Emma. 'I trust this has our good King Edmund's head upon it by way of its minting, Lady?'

'Who else?' Not Æthelred. Most of the coin minted during his long but feeble reign had either gone into Danish hands, or had been melted down by Edmund for his use as coin of the realm. Very few cared to remember Æthelred, not even by his image stamped into valuable gold.

'Tide's turning, Sir,' one of the sailors remarked. 'The wind with it, we'll be able to drift along without a water vole knowing, let alone a snoring Viking rat.'

434

As the ebbing current took the ship and the four oars dipped to guide her out into mid river, Emma threaded her way, careful in the darkness, away from the river and up the sloping pathway. They would steal, like thieves in the night, back into London through the gateway held ajar for them by one trusted guard of the watch and none would be the wiser of this night's events. No one would know that the Queen's sons had been taken away, safe, to her brother in Normandy, not unless she or Godwine cared to tell, and not until Richard came with a fleet and an army. Although that was a vain hope. As Alfred had realised, Richard would do nothing if it was an inconvenience to himself; without her there in Normandy to nag and pester at him, things would be left to moulder.

She turned, once, as she trudged up the slope, to look for the ship, but she could see nothing in the darkness, only the black shape of the river snaking through the blacker grasslands of the river meadows that spread wide beneath a black, clouded sky. She listened. Could hear nothing except Godwine's breathing and the moan of an ice-chilled wind. They were gone. The elder son who irritated her because of his likeness to his father and the younger one who, if he had not been sired by Æthelred, she might have come to love more. Goda, her beloved daughter, was already gone from Wilton to Normandy. Godwine had seen to that as he had hurried to London and his Queen, on the very day of Edmund's death. Richard would find her a good husband. One better than he had found for her mother, Emma hoped.

'God speed you, my children,' Emma said to where the black ribbon of the river wound its way through the night. 'God speed all of you.'

Was this how her mother had felt, that day when she left Normandy to come to England and marry Æthelred? She had not thought of her mother in a long while, she had been dead these many years. Why think of her now? Emma could picture her stern face, her straight back, erect stance. Could not remember her voice. She strained to hear it, but nothing came.

And after all these interim years, Emma discovered why her

mother had turned away and not watched as her ship had left Normandy, bound for England. Discovered how a mother's feelings of loss for her children, when she well knew that she might never see them again, cut with such unbearable pain, deep into the heart.

PART THREE

Cnut

Anno Domini 1017–1035

The King commanded brought to him the widow of the other King, Æthelred, that he might have her as Queen.

Ango-Saxon Chronicle

1

The snow had made it hard for everyone; the cold gnawed at fingers, toes and face, bit into the empty bellies. They were down to eating the dogs, now, in London and, in the poorer hovels, even the rats. The royal household was faring no better, for the sacks of grain were almost emptied, a thin and watery porridge, bolstered by the last of the stored root vegetables, was a diet Emma was beginning to detest. The start of a thaw had not made any difference, they were still hungry, the only consolation, those on the outside of London's walls, Cnut's men, were worse off. Londoners had the shelter of their houses, the Vikings had only their tents.

Through most of the day the sun had been shining, although too weak to melt more than the tips of a few hanging icicles, that would refreeze overnight. Emma, as she did every day, was up on the rampart wall, observing the comings and goings of the besieging army. How did you gauge misery? By men shuffling on frost-bitten feet, or huddled beneath damp, mouldering blankets? By the cries of dying children who could not suck milk from an empty breast?

What more could they do? Wait out this Hell until the last one among them died? 'We cannot go on, Bishop,' Emma said to her good friend Alfward, Bishop of London, who stood, haggard and shivering, beside her. 'London is on its knees. I have to put an end to this.'

On her other side, Godwine, his arms leaning on the parapet, said, 'It is a pity we have to surrender after putting up such a strong resistance. I reckon Cnut has lost as many men as we have.'

'That he has,' the Bishop answered, 'but unlike us, beyond his camp whores he has not lost women and children, the elderly and the infirm.'

'We must face reality, Godwine,' Emma said with a sad, resigned smile. 'We have lost England. Cnut has won. London may as well seek a truce.' With Edmund gone, this ending had been inevitable, but better to fail trying than not trying at all.

Godwine sighed, long and slow, pushed his chin even tighter into his crossed arms. 'Then I shall find a secret way out for you tonight, Lady. We can, perhaps, make our way across the ice to the south bank, from there reach the coast and find a ship to take you to Normandy.'

Emma did not answer. A ship to Normandy? Oh, Good God, she could not face that, not a ship, not Normandy! If she must flee she would go to her kinsman, Count Baldwin of Flanders. Bruges was a more attractive prospect than Normandy. To go aboard a ship again . . . She could not, could not do it. But what was the alternative? The rest of her life locked within the confines of a nunnery? Wilton would not be too bad, or perhaps Shaftesbury, but what if Cnut decided to be vindictive and locked her away in somewhere like Malmesbury? There was no Edmund to arrive suddenly and whisk her away to safety. She missed Edmund, he had been a good friend. Had been a brave and honourable man, and she had not been ashamed to weep for him. For Æthelred she had shed not a single tear.

She snapped her shoulders back. She could not afford to be standing here dwelling on the past, there were things to be discussing, doing. There would be time to mourn Edmund later. Through the night, the long hours of not being able to sleep because of hunger and the despair of facing another tomorrow, she had been nurturing a daring – frightening – idea. Night, she had found, was good for thinking, to use the quiet and the solitude to look inside your head. At night, there were more thoughts to be shared around between those still awake and God was more attentive.

The idea had wormed its way in, initially, some while ago and she had instantly dismissed it, but today? Today it had begun to take tangible form, the doubts giving ground to more positive thinking. It would take an enormity of courage and strength, this thing that she was planning, but it could mean an ending with dignity for London and, perhaps, England, and she cared about that, about

England. As for herself, it could go well or horribly wrong, but how much worse could things be than the years she had spent as wife to Æthelred? And, Dear God, she would rather face anything than crossing that Channel Sea again! She gazed across the frozen Thames. A few days ago Cnut's *i-víkings* had been skating and sliding on it, having a day of holiday to rub salt into London's gaping wound. Godwine's plan of escape would not work, there could be no walking out of here across the river, for now it was thawing, the ice subtly shifting as the current moved and battered the surface sheet from below. What would be the point of going to Normandy anyway? Repeatedly she had begged help from Richard and repeatedly he had ignored her. All the bluff, all the pretence that she had made to others of Richard's promised aid? Ah, she was so weary of it. So bone weary.

A noise split suddenly through the winter-still air with an explosive sound that shot from river bank to river bank and boomed across the flat, frozen marshes. Godwine's head lifted up, his hand clutching automatically at his dagger; the Bishop, alarmed, crossed himself; Emma gasped, her fingers going to her throat. In a world where the loudest noise was a clap of overhead thunder, sounds were sharp on the ear, this great shuddering roar was both fearful and exciting.

'My God,' Emma said, shaken. 'What was that?'

A great crack was appearing before their startled eyes, running straight as a thrown spear across the frozen water, splitting the ice in two, the widening tear shouting its appearance with the force of Thor striking a hammer blow.

Others had come running up on to the wall, fearing some awful new attack. Men and women pouring into the slush-trampled street, screaming, weeping, expecting this to be their end. Expecting to find the sky torn open and all manner of fearful creatures descending to bring their doom. Beyond the walls, by contrast, the besiegers were sprinting for the river bank, chattering and laughing their excitement at the ice so spectacularly parting. The phenomenon, for people used to a world of winter ice, quite accepted.

'So, there will be no escaping across the river,' Emma said, shrugging her shoulders as they watched Cnut's men hauling chunks of broken ice on to the bank. 'I will have to do what I have decided. I think, I pray, that it will be for the best.'

Cnut was astonished, and somewhat mystified, to receive word that an emissary was asking permission to come out of the south gate to talk terms with him. Disappointed too, in a way, for he thought Londoners were made of sterner stuff – and he had a wager with Thorkell as to the day of surrender. His estimate was not for a further eight and forty hours.

He had been inspecting the hulls of the ships, the craft drawn up on to the high ground and upturned for over-wintering and repairs. Ships were always pulled up out of the water when the season turned cold, for compressing ice could do much unseen damage to the keel. It never ceased to amaze Cnut how many barnacles could cling to a ship's underside during the course of a year. The job of scraping them off was a messy, tiresome business, fortunately, not one he had to do, although he had taken his share of the work as a child.

With the thaw coming, the snow in the encampment had turned to a muddy slush that had splashed up his boots and smeared the hem of his tunic and cloak. His beard needed trimming too, he felt as ragged as a blind beggar; he half turned, intending to go to his tent to tidy himself, shrugged, set the notion aside. If someone wanted to speak with him, they could speak as easily with him dirty as clean.

'I'll come,' he said, feeling churlish for his lack of enthusiasm. If London was seeking to discuss terms, then it was all over, he had won, he had his crown. Was that the rub, though? Any man could set a crown on his head and call himself king, but a real king, a true king, was one loved and cheered by his people, who was mourned with genuine grief after he had gone. How was that achieved? Edmund had managed it; in a few short months most of England had turned to him with respect, admiration and affection. How was he, Cnut, to do the same thing? It was a puzzle that had bothered him through these last weeks when he had nothing to do except sit and wait and watch outside the defensive walls of London.

The west gate opened and two people emerged. A man and, to Cnut's sudden interest, a woman. The man he recognised instantly, Godwine Wulfnothsson, who had been hostage at the treaty of Alney Island. The woman . . .? Cnut swore at the stupidity of not tidying himself, damn and all Hell, it was the Queen!

He rubbed the palms of his hands on his backside before they reached him, masked his embarrassment as he bowed, with a slow nod of his head, as she stopped and stood before him. Emma remained spear-shaft straight, not condescending to acknowledge his rank; he supposed she deserved the authority. On the other side of the shield, it was damned bloody annoying to be deliberately snubbed by a woman. Even if she did wear jewels and a crown.

'Lady, you do honour me. I was not expecting one of such beauty to beg my solicitude.'

Emma took a deep, steadying breath; this was it, then, the gamble that could save England but ruin what was left of her life. She would have given anything at this moment for a gulp at a strong brew of barley beer. She was shaking, hoped Cnut was unaware of it. She exhaled slowly, tipped her head a little higher. She was a queen, Queen of England, and by God, this pip of a boy was not going to take that away from her! 'I have come, Sir, to beg nothing. And senseless flattery does not become your rank or position.'

Cnut raised his eyebrows. So, her tongue was as spiked as ever.

He smiled insolently. 'Have you come to beguile me instead, then, Madam? To seduce me perhaps?' A crowd of his men, interested in the exchange, had gathered around; they laughed, a full, belly-mirth sound.

'I'd wager you're up for that, Sir!' someone shouted lewdly.

Emma ignored them, although Godwine coloured at the insult to his Queen, his hand going to where his dagger would be, had he been permitted to carry it. 'What I intend to say to you is between my lips and your ears only,' Emma remarked. 'It is not for the low-life entertainment of your slug-slimed, illiterate barbarians.'

Cnut shrugged, raised his hands in defeat, grinned as he said to his men, 'It seems the lady does not appreciate your sense of humour, my lads. I will have to instruct her on our charm and wit by myself.' The laughter increased.

Polite, and with another small bow, Cnut gestured for her to precede him to his tent. With the dour-faced Godwine remaining outside, she ducked beneath the opening, waited for the Dane to chivvy out his ear-wagging servant, then fetch her a stool. He poured her a pewter tankard of watered ale.

'Would you care for something to eat?' Cnut asked, noticing that she was thin, but did not look starved or hungry.

'I thank you, but I have eaten.' A broth that had more water than vegetables, but that she was not going to divulge. 'I will say what I have come to say without the preliminary niceties of formality. Conquest by force and tyranny is never satisfactory, even the red-crested legions of Rome could not rest easy when there were those who resented their presence.'

Cnut said nothing, sipped his ale. He had heard of the Roman Legions and their Empire from his childhood tutors, but had never taken heed of their tedious and long-buried history. Fighting and the tactics of warfare had been his interest, but the tutors had always dwelt on the political murders of a succession of emperors and their relentless persecution of the Christians. Some of their histories had pricked his ears, the writings of Caesar and Tacitus, but nothing else.

Her nerve strengthening, Emma smiled to herself. Ah, he was not as well read or educated as she. Good, that was useful to know. 'I take it you can read?' she queried, being deliberately insolent.

If anyone else had so insulted him, Cnut might well have had them hanged, but somehow he could not take offence at Emma's blunt rudeness. Why was that? He had no cause to crawl on his belly before her like a whimpering lapdog.

'We can exchange debate on some great work of authority if you wish,' he answered flippantly, desperately praying that she would not take him at his word. 'I did not bring my books with me to besiege your capital city, but I know a few of them well enough.' He rubbed his chin, fingering the curls of his blond beard as if thinking.

He could read, but he rarely did so for pleasure – Thor's Hammer where did he ever find spare moments to sit still and read? He plucked a title from memory, something that he and his brother had studied as children. 'Bede's *Ecclesiastical History* I found fascinating.'

'Gregory's *Consolations of Philosophy* was always my favourite,' Emma countered.

Cnut had never heard of it. 'It was interesting, but I have read more that were, what shall I say, unbiased?'

Emma smiled, he was an accomplished liar, if nothing else. 'It was Boethius who wrote the *Philosophy*, not Gregory.'

'Ah well,' Cnut answered, unembarrassed, 'I never was one for remembering names, especially those of boring old farts who had nothing more interesting to do with their life than grind ink stains permanently into their fingers.'

Emma laughed.

Resting his hands on his thighs, Cnut regarded the woman sitting opposite him. He would not describe her as beautiful, not even pretty. There were lines beside her eyes, her mouth was too thin, her nose too straight. How old was she? Not far from her thirtieth year? She had been three and ten when she had come to England to marry Æthelred, when was that? Ah, he could not calculate it in his head. Did it matter?

Ragnhild had been beautiful, and Ælfgifu was irresistible, her lust for sport in bed overriding her plain features. Did she, in her family home of Northampton, sleep with other men? Cnut doubted she would be so stupid, but then, she was capable of ensuring he never knew of it.

What of Emma? Emma would never cheat on a husband, because she was a queen and because she did not need to be beautiful or alluring. There was something more to her, more important than the surface layer that everyone saw. She was regal, stately, every inch of her shouted royal pride. Ælfgifu was uncouth, with no subtlety or gift for political astuteness. Beside Emma, she was an embarrassment. *Ja*, Cnut could admire a woman like Emma.

'So, are we to debate history?' he questioned.

In turn, Emma had been studying Cnut. He had matured since

they had first met, his face had filled out, his shoulders broadened. He carried more confidence as an adult, more self-assurance. He was one and twenty years of age, she six years his senior – what in all the names of the Christian God, and of all those He had defeated and sent into obscurity, was she doing here? He had shown himself to be cruel and ruthless, to act on the impulse of the blood-heat, not the cool calculation of sense. More than once he had proven himself dishonourable, that his word was not binding, that he could not be trusted. But then, had Æthelred been any different? How many promises had he made and broken? Cnut had shown himself to be without conscience against those who crossed him but was that a bad thing for a king? All morning, Godwine had blustered, '*What in God's name are you thinking of? Have you lost your sense?*' She had made no answer to his protestations: where, for a queen, did sense end and survival begin?

She smiled in answer to Cnut's question. 'I have not come to discuss history, but your place in it.' She inhaled, forced her mind to concentrate, to ignore the wild pounding that was skittering about inside her chest and churning up her stomach. 'You will not last as King of England because you are no Englishman. Sooner or later some ealdorman or ambitious thegn will take it upon himself to be rid of you and the English shall be so busy rejoicing that they will fail to notice that they have crowned yet another fool who does not know how to govern with wisdom and authority, or lead with courage and honour.'

'So you are telling me that I may as well take my ship and sail away now, for I have no future here?'

'If I were to suggest such naivety, would you comply with it?'

Cnut shook his head.

'You know nothing of England,' Emma continued, feeling the trembling rekindle in her body, but steadfastly ignoring it. 'You do not know our ways, traditions or customs. Our expectations. Despite reading Bede, you have no knowledge of our ways. Especially of our laws.'

'I confess you confuse me, Lady. You speak as if you are English. My education must have been sorely lacking somewhere, for I was

446

led to believe that you are Norman-born?'

'I forfeited my identity as a Norman when I pledged my vows to take care of the English peoples as their Queen. I would not compromise that vow by serving one while being obliged to the other. If you are ever to be accepted, and loved, as a king of the English, then you will have to become more English than the people you rule. As I have.'

The hairs at the nape of Cnut's neck tingled. How had she known that this had been precisely what he had been thinking these past days?

'The English', she continued, unaware of his inner superstitious discomfort, 'have been demoralised by thirty years of war and by a king who did not deserve the authority placed upon him. Unlike Æthelred, Alfred was called Great because he took his responsibilities to God, and to England, seriously.' Her ale finished, Emma set the tankard down on the floor beside her feet. She looked up, held Cnut's eyes with an intensity that he found unnerving. She added sincerely, 'As do I.'

Standing, Cnut strolled to the table, refilled his own tankard, offered her more. She refused. 'Are you trying to tell me, in some subtle way, that I will not make a good king?'

'Do you think you will?' she countered.

Cnut faced her, eye to eye, his expression as intense as hers had been a moment ago. 'Ja, I do! I do not want to be some mere blood-axe warrior who rules because he is the strongest man to wield a sword. I do not want to have my name scratched from the English Chronicles in a few months to come, because I am already dead and forgotten.'

Laughing scornfully, Emma remarked, 'You think you are important enough to be written into our church-kept records? I think not, Sir, unless perhaps it is as a passing mention for an entry in my son's name.' She paused, composing in her mind, '*And Edward did come with a great fleet of ships, and with him came his brother Alfred and his mother's brother, Richard, and together they did drive the usurper from the land. And England was restored to God, and the Dane did perish and become forgotten.*' She smiled to herself, she liked the sound of that; she would repeat it to the Bishop, encourage him to have it written in the London Annal, if ever, eventually – by some God-sent miracle – it happened that way.

Angry, frustrated, because he knew she was right, Cnut hurled his tankard across the tent, sending it clattering against the ridge pole. A stir at the door, two anxious faces peering in, Godwine's and the Danish guard.

'All is well,' Cnut snapped irritably, waving them away. 'I stumbled, all is well.'

He squatted beside the brazier, his head down, fingers locking and interlocking, the bones of his knuckles cracking.

Emma sat straight, dignified. 'I do not wish to see England torn into any more shreds. I do not wish to lie awake at night wondering whether, on the morrow, I shall lose my crown.' Her heart was beginning to thump again, did not add, *and I do not want to set foot on board a ship*. 'You want to become a beloved king and I want to retain my position as Queen. It seems, to my mind, that we are in need one of the other.'

Snapping his head up, Cnut stared at her. 'I do not follow you, Madam?'

'Do you not? England will never accept you unless the English are persuaded that you were sent for their salvation by God. To do that, you must ensure there will be peace and prosperity throughout this land. I have the power to destroy that peace by sending Normandy against you. My brother is vassal to the French King; where my brother requires aid, it is the duty of France to grant it. Where France requires aid, it is the duty of the Holy Roman Emperor to grant it.' She smiled silkily. 'And where he requires aid, it is the duty of the Pope to grant it.' The same old repeated lie. She had said it so often, now, she was almost beginning to believe it. At least enough to sound convincing.

Cnut was astounded. How had she done it? How had she managed so easily to reduce all his confidence into nothing but dust? Gods, but if this woman were at the head of an army . . .!

'Or', she added slowly, persuasive, 'I could ensure that Normandy never has cause to set foot on English soil, that France and the Holy

448

Roman Emperor never wage war on you and that the Pope, far from excommunicating you from God's Truth, shall welcome you as a beloved brother.' She swallowed, her throat dry. If her spies had been wrong in this and if her intuition played her false . . .

Cnut spread his hands, incredulous. 'And how, my Lady, do you think you could manage all that?'

She answered simply with four words that totally and utterly stunned him.

'By becoming your wife.'

2

March 1017 – Thorney Island

Erik of Hlaðir had been a good friend to Cnut, more like a cherished uncle. He had been well pleased with the reward of Northumbria as an Earldom. Well pleased.

The King's palace at Thorney was full to bursting and London, downriver, was no better, with every tavern, boarding house and spare bed taken. Even most of the common land, that which was not flooded for the spring high tides, was dotted with tents and makeshift bothies. Everyone in the world, or so it seemed, had made their way to London for Cnut's coronation, everyone from earl to pick-purse thief.

Erik, who had only arrived himself yesterday, paused before entering Cnut's chamber and rubbed his hands together nervously. Cnut should be awake now, a servant had emerged five minutes ago with the night pot. He gathered his courage, knocked quickly on the door and marched in.

Cnut was sitting sprawled in bed, finishing the remains of a break-fast meal. 'Erik!' he called enthusiastically, waving at the man to come in. 'Well come, my friend! How are all my nobles this fine morning? Still grumbling that their lodgings have more fleas than a mangy street dog?'

Brushing spilt crumbs from his beard, Cnut pointed to a side table. 'Fetch a tankard, there is plenty ale here to be finished. I do not know what they complain about, I mean, look at this place.' He gestured at the room. 'Call this a king's chamber? The walls are damp, the smoke hole is blocked; you cannot see the embroidery on those wall hangings for the grime and dust that covers them. I have no wonder that Lady Emma finds Thorney undesirable.'

'She is more comfortable in her lodgings in the city, I

understand?' Erik asked, declining the ale and seating himself on the bench beside the table.

'More appropriate. Until that wretched brother of hers deigns to reply to my messengers seeking his permission to wed her, we must observe formalities, or so Archbishop Wulfstan regularly reminds me.' Cnut grinned. Erik knew well Cnut's liking of women and he was already learning about the formidable Archbishop.

'There is no news from Normandy, then?' he asked.

Cnut thumped an extra pillow in place behind his back. He had already decided this was to be a lazy day. Tomorrow he would be crowned King and after that there would be no opportunity for lying abed, with or without a female companion. 'Nothing.' He leaned forward eagerly. 'I could not believe my luck, Erik, when Lady Emma came right out with her proposition – and there I had been, the previous few weeks, trying to think of a way to wed her without her ripping my balls off in demented indignation!' They laughed together, friends and kindred. Sobering, Cnut added, 'Whether I can convince Duke Richard that my proposal is a good one is a another matter.'

Erik shrugged, from personal experience he knew the Duke to be an obstinate autocrat. He detested him. 'All that man wants is dignified recognition. As a vassal to the French King he is unlikely to get it in Normandy, but as an uncle to a king of England? He would thus have the prestige he seeks.' Erik paused, he already had unwelcome news to impart, this was a second burden. 'He may decide that it would be worth his while to put Edward on the throne and rule as Regent.'

Certain of himself, Cnut shook his head. 'I too know Richard; do not forget, my father had many a dealing with him. He has one weakness that can be exploited, he likes to keep his treasure chests full. My approach of negotiation has already included a financial offer he will find difficult to turn down.' Cnut grinned. 'And of course I have suggested that my emissary reminds Richard that a long and protracted war because of a nephew who is a mere boy could prove expensive.'

Erik grinned. 'And if the Lady Emma were to deliver you with a son he will have a firmer link with England through his own Danish blood.'

'A son of mine or those two cockles of Æthelred's? Is there comparison?'

'For the lady's sake you may need to agree not to pursue them.'

'If Richard agrees not to contest their birthright, then I will have no need to bother them. Why swat a fly that is not buzzing about your head?' Cnut lay back, brought his arms up behind his head. 'It all seems so simple, Erik. Too simple. What gaping hole have I missed that I am about to fall unwittingly into?'

Erik fell silent, suddenly interested in a broken fingernail.

Cnut noticed the silence. 'What is wrong? I could read the wrath of doom on your face the moment you came through the door. Tomorrow is my coronation day, I was looking forward to it, but that frown tells me my expectations may not be rewarded. Has Saint Paul's burnt down during the night? Has the good Archbishop of Canterbury received some dreadful blow to the head and cannot remember the order of service?' Cnut laughed. 'I promise you, my friend, whatever is the black news that you come so early in the day to tell me, I shall receive it in good humour.'

'I doubt it, my Lord.'

Cnut spread his hands. 'Try me.'

Erik took a breath and spoke very fast, as if saying it quicker would make it sound the better. 'Your wife has come from Northampton. Your first wife, Ælfgifu, with your two sons. Their ship moored at the wharf half an hour ago.'

Silence. A long pause of uneasy silence.

'She was not invited.'

'No, my lord.'

Cnut shot from the bed, heedless of his nakedness. 'What bloody fool allowed her out of Northampton? Who gave permission for her to take ship?'

'I believe she came with Thegn Thurbrand's fleet.'

Cnut snatched a bed fur and draped it modestly about himself. 'Thurbrand? I might have guessed.' Ælfgifu had been growing closer to that man these last few years. How close? If anyone had been sharing her bed, Cnut would not be surprised to find it was Thurbrand. The man had too much ambition for his own good and was not particular about how he achieved it. Come to that, neither was she.

'I suppose it is naive of me to ask what she wants?'

Erik did not insult Cnut by replying.

'Where is she?'

'King's Hall.'

'Shit.' Repeated, with feeling: 'Shit, shite, shit!' Cnut began to pace the chamber, pausing every few strides as if he were about to say something but changing his mind, strode on. Jerked to a halt in front of Erik. 'What do I do?'

Relieved that he had unburdened himself, Erik spread his hands and shook his head. In truth, he had no idea. 'My Lord, no mortal man knows how to handle a woman in the heat of a jealous rage.'

Cnut poured himself ale, drank half the tankard straight down, wiped the residue from his lips. 'One answer from two choices, Erik. She must be silenced and distanced; for that, I either kill her or,' he ran his hands through his hair, the fur he was clutching to his body slipping to the floor. 'Or woo her.'

Erik indicated if he might help himself to the ale. Cnut nodded agreement. 'I do not advocate killing her, my Lord. I govern the North for you, but it is a difficult governing. If you do away with Ælfgifu, even through an arranged accident, her kindred could rise against you; they are a close-woven lot and as untrustworthy as a wounded boar.'

Ambling to the bed, Cnut sat. His father had instigated this marriage precisely for the allegiance of the woman's kindred. He did not want war in northern England, for his only hope of being accepted as king, as Emma had so succinctly said, was to promise, and deliver, a lasting peace.

Cnut scratched at his manhood. 'You know, Erik, I am beginning to see the point of a monk's celibacy. It leads for a quieter life in several directions.'

3

She came through the door with a rustle of a fine silk gown, covered by a sable-lined mantle. Her jewels, and there were many of them, sparkling where the early morning beams of sunlight filtering through the small windows caught them. She had both boys with her, Swegen and Harold.

'I informed Earl Erik that he is an imbecile,' she said, sweeping into the room. 'It is nonsense that you would not be eager to greet your sons, even if you are still abed. Go to Papa,' she ordered, pushing the two reluctant children forward.

Cnut leant from the bed and lifted both of them to sit either side of him; they were silent, wide-eyed lads, frightened by this man they had rarely seen.

'They are good, fine boys,' Cnut lied, hiding his disappointment at their sullen shyness. 'Why have you come, Ælfgifu? You must have received my letter.'

Ælfgifu removed her cloak, dropping it to the bed as she approached, her hand smoothing over the fur. 'Of course I received it. Do you sleep here alone, or do you share with some cow-teated doxy?'

'If you received it, why are you here?'

The two boys, nervous of this big man, wriggled towards their mother, their hands clutching at her gown. She smacked the fingers aside. 'Do not touch, children, your fingers will mark the fabric.'

The younger boy, Harold, began to grizzle, his tears setting the elder one whimpering.

'See what you have done by neglecting them?' Ælfgifu complained unfairly. 'Have you no feeling for your own sons?' She strode to the door, flung it open and irritably waved in the nursemaid waiting outside. 'Take the boys away, feed them or something.'

454

Alone with Cnut she slammed the door shut and swung herself around to face him, her fists bunched in fury. 'Swegen turned three years old a month past. Could you not bother to send your eldest child a birthing day gift?'

She was as slender as the day he wedded her. The gown she wore was expertly sewn, cut to show the curve of her hips, the roundness of her breasts. A Saxon, Ælfgifu wore only a loose veil, not the covering restriction of a wimple that hid her hair from sight, its rose colour complementing the pale hair that tumbled unbound over her shoulders and down her back. Cnut knew it would smell of sweet-scented herbs were he to press his face into it.

He answered her with sarcasm. 'In case it has escaped your notice, I have been somewhat busy.'

Dramatically pointing at the bed, Ælfgifu shouted, 'Busy fornicating with that strumpet who calls herself Queen, I suppose?'

It took a great deal of effort for Cnut to keep his temper in control, but he knew by experience that to enter into a shouting match with Ælfgifu was to instantly lose. She could outbellow a wharfside fishwife.

'I apologise for neglecting the boy's birthing day,' he conceded. 'I shall see to it that he receives a grant of land, Harold too, for his day when it comes.'

'I will not be set aside, Cnut. No amount of polite letters telling me that my marriage is void and ended will alter that. I will not quietly fade into the background while you take her to your bed and leave me without my rightful crown.'

Cnut, preoccupied with brushing crumbs from the bed, did not answer immediately. 'And just how do you work out that the queen's crown should become yours, Ælfgifu?' he finally said. 'There is no legal church-blessed marriage between us, nor will there ever be. What we did have, I have annulled. Tomorrow, I am to be crowned as King and some time soon I will be exchanging marriage vows with Emma of Normandy. She comes with the package of kingship. She is already the anointed Queen, the crown remains hers.'

'And I come with the sharing of your bed, the birthing of your sons and the loyalty of my kindred. You will not set any of us aside, for if you do you will face rebellion.'

Emma had warned him of this – not Ælfgifu, he had shied away from discussing her – of the matter of the Mid Lands and the North.

Lady Emma had proved, as she had said she would, invaluable. With many of the older and established nobility dead, killed at Ashingdon, she was one of the few people who held an extensive knowledge of England and the earldoms – ealdormanries, she had initially called them, but had quickly slipped into the use of the Danish term, although Cnut had insisted they talk in English, for as she had said, to be a successful king he had to become more English than the English. A few Danish words made more practical sense, though, where the law and government were concerned. Ealdormen were earls, and the royal bodyguard were no longer cnights but housecarls.

'You will find hostility in the North,' Emma had advised, 'too many of them are linked by blood and too many of the others are linked by feud. They either fight *for* each other or *against* each other. No wonder anywhere north of the Trent is regarded as a land of savage barbarians.'

'And what do I do about them? He asked, genuinely interested in her sound advice.

'Tame them with bribes and flattery, or if they do not care to be yoked to your plough, then quietly and quickly do away with them.'

'That is easier said than done.'

'Not if you enlist the full co-operation of Archbishop Wulfstan, by wholeheartedly adopting his beliefs and principles for the government of England and the worship of God.'

By God, Emma was a clever woman!

Cnut smiled at Ælfgifu, but there was nothing of liking in the expression. This one was a bitter, scheming bitch. Oh, Emma was scheming and she could probably be as much the bitch if need arose, but there any resemblance between the two women ended. Ælfgifu thought in black and white patterns of revenge for wrongs committed against her; Emma thought in a careful and considered blend of colour to obtain, by skill, what she wanted. He wished, now, that he had sought Emma's advice on what to do about Ælfgifu as well, although he could guess her answer: do away with her. Ælfgifu would never be harnessed but, and he knew he would regret this, he could not bring himself to have her killed. Her family connections were too useful, her body too alluring. Could she be bought or bribed? It was worth trying.

Cnut pushed aside the bed coverings, revealing his naked body. He patted the linen sheet. 'Come here,' he said.

'You cannot do without me,' Ælfgifu whispered, as within a few moments, she slid in, naked, next to him. 'Both you and I know it.'

She was wrong, but this was not the place to contest the issue. If she wished to believe a lie, Cnut was not prepared to disillusion her.

After, when they lay breathing hard, the sweat streaking their bodies, she said, 'There are two things I want from you, Cnut. Promise them me and I will leave you in peace.'

He had been drowsing, with his eyes closed. He answered cautiously. 'I make no promises until I know what I must avow to.'

'Make your promise that you will not set me aside; that whenever you ride north, you will come to my bed, even if it only be once in a year.'

Cnut considered. It was a reasonable request. 'I will not promise, but I shall try.'

Good enough. For now. She smoothed the hair on his chest, her palm sensuous, sliding to his stomach, lower.

'And the second?' he asked, feeling his arousal at her touch.

'Eadric Streona's head.'

Cnut rolled her over, entered her quickly, making her gasp as he took his pleasure of this second coupling. As he spilt his seed into her he said, 'That I can promise you, Madam. It will be done.'

4

If Edward knew that Alfred had been weeping he would never allow his brother to forget it. Therefore Alfred ensured that he was quite alone before allowing the release of his grief.

His uncle had been discussing his mother for months, but adult talk was so confusing, and most of it heard in snatches, for whenever they realised he was listening they would stop, or change the subject. That had not happened today. Uncle Richard's son, the eldest one, almost an adult himself also called Richard, had come out with it, straight and plain.

'So what are you two brats going to do now that your mother is to wed Cnut?'

Edward had said nothing, but then he never did defend Mama. It had been left to Alfred to shout, 'It is not true! Why are you always so horrid to us? Edward will be King of England one day, then you'll be sorry!'

'*Êtes-vous un imbécile? Edouard ne sera jamais roi*, he will not be king, not now that Cnut is crowned and is to take your mother as his queen. There will be no place for you in England, especially once she is breeding for him, and I shall not want homeless brats at my Court when I inherit from Papa.'

'You lie! Mama is coming to join us here in Normandy. She is to persuade Uncle Richard to equip a fleet, and we will attack England and return in triumph! She said so!'

Richard had started to walk away, laughing in that high-pitched donkey whine of his. 'What a woman says and what a woman does, boy, are two different things entirely, *n'est ce pas*? There will be no fleet, no army. Your mother will never come to Normandy and neither you, nor your brother, will ever be king. My papa, your uncle, has agreed the marriage by negotiation. Cnut gets to become

458

recognised and honoured as a legitimate king by marrying an anointed queen, and Normandy gets a new, lucrative trade agreement *et voilà?*'

'What do we get?' Edward had asked, at last opening his mouth. Alfred secretly wishing that he had thought to ask the question.

'*Vous? Ne vaut rien.* You are worthless, you have been abandoned into the obscurity of exile.'

To stop the tears, Alfred had bitten hard into his lip. Edward, damn his eyes, after Richard had walked away, had smiled, actually smiled, and capered a few ecstatic, jigged steps.

'God be praised,' he had exclaimed, elated. 'I can go into my monastery!'

Alfred had hit him, his fist ramming into Edward's face. Blood had burst everywhere and Edward had started to scream. Alfred had run before Wymarc came to investigate the noise.

Richard was wrong! They *would* return to England, Alfred would, even if Edward did not want to. That crown was his and he was going to have it!

Only, a boy who was in his twelfth year had no way of getting it without adult help, so all he could do was find a dark place beneath the trees down by the river and weep for the desolation of having nothing. Not even a mother who could tell him herself that she no longer wanted him.

5

From the start of his reign, Cnut set out to win the respect and the hearts of the English people, aware that his past mistakes were going to make the task harder. He made it known that he intended to honour God and the Christian religion; to bring peace, renew the old laws and make some new. He vowed to rule with compassion but, equally, would demand respect and intended to rule with absolute authority. To spread his word and the glory of his coronation, a new coin, bearing his image, was minted. There were only a few unpleasantries to be got out the way. He had men to pay and the cost of a finished war to finance. There were protests at his demand for 72,000 pounds of silver, but dissenters who thought he might be as weak and fallible as Æthelred soon discovered how wrong they were.

'We cannot afford what you ask!' Leofric, the eldest son of one of Æthelred's lesser ealdormen, had objected. 'There is nothing left in England except mould and mud at the bottom of the well.'

'Then you will collect the mould and the mud,' Cnut had answered, dispassionate.

Those who had helped him were rewarded. To Erik, his friend, he had given Northumbria, Thorkell, to Emma's disgust, received East Anglia, Cnut kept Wessex for himself – and Eadric Streona, for his betraying Edmund at Ashingdon, received the rest.

Emma found herself wondering about Eadric Streona on the morning of her wedding day. Why had Cnut allowed that man to retain his status? It was a riddle she had asked him more than once these past weeks, but Cnut had always answered the same, that there was no justified reason to be rid of him. No justified reason, indeed! Emma could name several without thinking. Then there was the other matter that Cnut had not satisfactorily explained. Ælfgifu of Northampton.

Emma had been displeased at her appearance at his coronation; if it had not been for the woman's departure immediately after, this day's wedding might never have been about to happen, although Emma was aware that a physical departure was not the same as a mental one. Did Cnut still want Ælfgifu? She had no idea; tactfully she had opted to not ask of the woman. There were other ways to discover what was needed to be known, after all. She knew that Ælfgifu had been in Cnut's bed the day before his crowning and had ensured that it had not happened the night after. A pity the potion that had sent Ælfgifu puking from the feasting, and then repeatedly running for the cesspits, had not been more than an inconveniencing discomfort, but more would have been too obvious, and murder, as Æthelred had discovered, was not a good thing to bring to a coronation. Ælfgifu of Northampton had to be legally, totally and completely set aside, her sons declared illegitimate and unable to lay claim to the title ætheling. For her own children? Aye, well, they were safe in Normandy. In her brother's household, they would be wanting for nothing. She was under no disillusion that Cnut would have the boys killed if ever he found opportunity, but at least Goda was safe. Would still have the promise of a high-status marriage. And for herself? She was saddened, but relieved, to let the past go. How many women had a chance to start again from the same exalted position? To have had a crown and on widowhood keep it? For Edward and Alfred, how many sons of dead, deposed kings were permitted to remain alive?

Emma smiled to herself as she placed her crown over the saffron linen wimple. She wore a gown of mustard-yellow, with her mantle a darker shade, to match the wrist-tight cuffs. Was Ælfgifu aware of the spies who kept a discreet watch on her movements? Oh, Emma had learnt a lot about ruling a kingdom these last years! Spies were the most valuable asset a queen could have. Through them, she had known, even before Edmund had died, that Cnut had tentatively approached her brother with a proposed option of marriage and that Richard had curtly refused. That information she would be keeping

461

a close-guarded secret, for she would not be having Cnut know that the first part of her gamble, that he would accept her suggestion, had been played with a weighted dice. She also knew that Cnut's brother, Harald of Denmark, had no tolerance of his younger sibling and that jealousies between the two rumbled across the horizon like summer thunder storms. And she would know if ever Cnut renewed interest in his whore.

Her escort was waiting in the outer courtyard of the nunnery, for she had chosen to stay with the Sisters for privacy and suitability. The secular buildings of Nunnaminster were on Colebrook Street, for the Benedictine Order preferred its peace and seclusion from the world, but enjoyed the financial gain from guests who paid well for comfortable lodgings. The solitude had also suited Emma, for she welcomed the opportunity to sit and think, to pray. This was her wedding day and a guard of honour, her own and Cnut's housecarls, were awaiting her, yet instead of going out to them she made her way to the nuns' chapel, indicating to her handmaids that except for the ever-faithful Leofgifu she wished to go alone. She could hear the restless crowd lining the streets of Winchester beyond the high walls, anxious to see her, to witness the union of these two unique people, but they would have to wait.

Situated on the south side of the cloister range the chapel, at this hour of the early afternoon, was empty and quiet. She liked the building, for it was pleasant and welcoming, its greensand ashlar blocks cut straight and smooth, while its flint and red-detailed patterns leant an air of joviality and gaiety, as opposed to the solemn structure of the New Minster church, which shortly she would be entering as wife to Cnut. The inside of the chapel smelt of fresh-strewn herbs and spring flowers, of beeswax candles and exotic spices. It was light and airy, with its white-plastered walls, decorated with thin red lines to represent the outer stonework. She sat at a bench halfway along the nave, her friend Leofgifu sitting beside her.

'It is good to be here in Winchester,' Emma said, after a few minutes of quiet contemplation.

'Aye, Lady, it is that.'

'Have you visited your brother-in-law in his tavern? Is he well?'

462

Again Leofgifu answered that, aye, all was well. Topics of conversation already discussed. Emma was nervous, uncertain of herself and this thing she must do, was searching for neutral, uncomplicated talk.

'I am thinking that I shall ask Cnut for permission to rebuild the hovel on the Godbigot land that Æthelred gave me. I would like my own house, something fitting for a queen's personal residence.'

'Will you build in stone, do you think? As they build in Normandy?'

'Definitely. It will be two-storeyed, with the public Hall below and my chambers above. Æthelred would never give me permission; he said it would be too costly and a waste of my money.'

'Cnut will think different?' Leofgifu was sceptical, but then she always was with men. None of them could be trusted; they covered you in kisses and promises then vanished, leaving nothing but a torn heart, and oft times a swelling belly, behind. They had not come here to discuss building plans, but Leofgifu was a patient woman, she could wait.

Emma answered with a coy shrug. 'Cnut wishes to give anything I ask. He is anxious to prove that he is a man of vision and wisdom.' She snorted, as sceptical as Leofgifu had been. 'He is desperate to prove to me – to England – that he is not the dishonourable murderer we have hitherto taken him for, that he is interested in the cultured things of the civilised, of the Christian world. Expect churches and abbeys to spring up like autumn mushrooms, Leofgifu!'

They laughed together, companions, trusting friends.

Several sparrows were busy about their nest-making under the eaves of the tiled roof, their high voices chirruping and echoing among the rafters of the vaulted emptiness. Emma watched them, enthralled at their acrobatics, for a while.

'How uncomplicated life is for God's feathered creatures.' She sighed as a pair fluttered from beam to beam. 'They meet, mate, build a nest, lay their eggs and hatch their youngsters. For a few busy weeks they devote all their waking hours to feeding and nurturing their fledglings and then, one morning, the nest is empty, the babies are grown and gone, with no more need of their parents.'

'Would you be wishing for it to be that simple for us, then?' Leofgifu queried. 'Would you not be wanting the lasting love and pleasure that childer bring?'

Emma answered aggressively, 'What love and pleasure has Edward brought me? I detest the boy. There, I have admitted it openly. He repels me because whenever I see him I think of Æthelred. Whenever I touch him I am reminded of the way I was forced when conceiving him.' The birds had gone, squeezing out through whatever hole they had found their way in by. For a moment the church was totally silent.

Emma turned to look at Leofgifu, clasped her hands in her own. 'You have been my good friend and constant companion, you above all others know me for what I am. You have been more of a mother to me than ever my own was, tell me, am I doing right in marrying Cnut? I hardly know him, what little I have seen I have thought of as an arrogant stripling of a boy, who wants to hold more in his hand than he has room for.' She dropped Leofgifu's hands, stood, began to pace up and down the nave. 'Am I fooling myself, Leofgifu? Am I doing this because it is the only way I know of repaying Æthelred's soul for the hurt and pain he caused me?'

'Maybe you are,' Leofgifu answered, remaining seated, 'but are there not other reasons that run close alongside?'

Emma paused before the altar steps, gazed at the wooden crucifix that stood central between two tall candles. Should she answer with honesty? But if she spoke anything less than the truth what was the point of this delay, this seeking of solace? 'I wanted to be in control of my life,' she said slowly, examining her thoughts before she spoke. 'I have enjoyed these last months of freedom, being my own keeper. I did not want to return to Normandy to be sold to the highest bidder by my brother, even if that bidder should turn out to be Cnut. I have found the wit and intelligence to make my own judgements and decisions, but how do I know that I have made the right choices? I was frightened of going back to Normandy, frightened of what my brother might plan, frightened of the sea voyage – oh, especially that! God grant me the mercy that I need never take ship across the sea ever again!' She knelt, crossed herself, murmured an amen. 'But now I am frightened at what I am about to do.' She turned to look at Leofgifu pleadingly. 'I have abandoned my children and my widowhood – what if Cnut is as bad as Æthelred? Worse? Tonight I have to bed with him. Leofgifu, I cannot go through with this, I cannot!'

The older woman was up, encircling Emma with her arms, allowing her to bury her head in her bosom and weep. To weep for loss and sorrow, for the empty, wasted days and the wasted longing for what might have been.

'There, child, you stress yourself for no reason. You have hatched your eggs, fed your fledglings and seen them fly from the nest. The boys are in no danger in Normandy and little Goda would soon have been leaving you for her own marriage anyway. As for Cnut, well, he is young and handsome, and I have seen the way he watches you when you have sat near him in Council or at feastings. He listens, respecting your words, your advice and suggestions. A man who is willing to listen to what a woman has to say is not likely to be a man who will treat her harshly in the privacy of his bed.' Leofgifu lifted Emma's face, dried the tears with the hem of her gown. 'If you wish to hear the thought that is in my heart,' Leofgifu smiled, 'then I would give all I own to be in your place this night!'

Emma smiled back at her, jested weakly, 'Then, if he does not please me, I will let you have him.'

Lumbering to her feet – Leofgifu had severely increased her girth during her years with the Queen – she helped Emma to rise. 'If you do not mind my impertinence, I will hold you to that pledge, Lady!'

Emma laughed, felt better now, having voiced her fears and allowed them their liberty.

The church door opened with a slow creak of its hinges. One of Emma's maids, a slight young red-haired girl with eyes as large as milk pails and a timidity that would have made a mouse appear brave, peeped into the church. She bobbed a curtsy. 'If you please, Ma'am, the King has sent word that he is awaiting you on the steps of the Minster and that he grows impatient.'

Emma exchanged a conspiratorial look with Leofgifu, then

465

smoothed her gown, gathered her breath. 'I am coming, child, I was but making my peace with God.'

Unfair of them to send the girl, had it been anyone else seeking to hurry her, Emma would have snapped their head off with one bite.

Thorkell, Earl of East Anglia, was awaiting her in the courtyard. He bowed, his face grave, serious, announced so that all might hear, 'The King has commanded brought to him the widow of the other king, Æthelred, so that he might have her as Queen.'

Emma had never liked Thorkell, even when circumstances dictated he had the safe keeping of her life. She understood his reasons for deserting Æthelred and again turning traitor; could she blame him, for abandoning the man who had murdered his brother? She understood, but could not, would not, condone. Tempted to retort that Cnut could await her pleasure, Emma caught sight of the merriment in Leofgifu's eyes.

'He is eager for you, Madam, let you be going to him and make a start, this day, on a new, pleasanter life than the one you had before.'

He greeted her with a smile as broad as the ocean, taking her hands in his, placed a kiss on her cheek. If this courtesy was a sham, an act put on for the benefit of his nobles and people, then it was performed well.

With the public part of the exchange of vows completed upon the steps of the New Minster, Cnut proudly led his wife inside to make their pledge in the sight of God. There was a second ceremony to perform also; for the glory of God and to acclaim the sanctity and happiness of their marriage, the happy couple were to present the Minster with a fine and beautiful crucifix made of gold and silver, an exquisite, and expensive, marvel. Cnut was determined to start on this particular journey on the right foot. And after darkness had fallen, and with the feasting of celebration under way, he lifted her and carried her to his king's chamber, not permitting the usual ceremony of bedding to proceed.

'My wife is a woman who has borne children, she has no virgin

466

purity to prove, nor have I any manly prowess to parade before your prying eyes, so be gone! We would have our privacy, if you please.' He set her down inside his chamber and, laughing companionably at those who had come clamouring behind, shut the door on them and, firmly bolting it, called out, 'There is Bride Ale aplenty to be compensating your disappointment!'

He stood looking at her. She had come to him as Queen, dressed in the finest silk, with braiding of gold and silver thread. At her throat a ruby the size of her thumbnail hanging from a golden chain woven in intertwined links. She dripped jewels and wealth and superiority, and he could not believe his good fortune. She was seven years his senior, a crowned Queen, and she was everything that Cnut had ever wanted. He was King; *he* was *King*, and with this woman as wife no one, not one person in the entirety of England, could deny him his place on the throne or the crown on his head. He wanted to leap, punch the air with his fist and shout out, 'Yes!'

'Well,' Emma said after a few moments of awkward silence. 'Are we to stand here the rest of the night staring at each other, or are we to find some other form of amusement? I could send for a chequered board and some gaming pieces if you wish, or would you prefer to play dice?' She smiled impishly, her face lighting into girlish amusement as her mouth quirked upwards at one corner. 'Or I could suggest a book worth reading?'

He laughed, a snort of mirth, appreciating the jest, said, with honesty, 'I would prefer to take you into that waiting bed.' He paused, chewed his lip, suddenly found his boots interesting. 'But I confess I am as nervous as an innocent youth. I am suddenly aware that you are so much more' he paused, searched for the word he wanted, 'important than I am.'

Emma was suddenly, deliciously happy. 'Hardly that, Sir, and I am, despite what you said to those barbarians who insisted on hammering on our door, feeling as nervous and naive as any virgin on her wedding night.'

Her answer pleased him, for he stepped forward and gently pulling her towards him, kissed her. His lovemaking was slow and tender, with careful concern for her comfort and enjoyment; his

467

delight complete as she responded, with wonder at first, then desire, as she discovered, after all the disillusioned years of marriage to Æthelred, the intense pleasure that intimate loving could bring to a woman who had passion locked inside her, desperately waiting for it to be released.

6

Emma lay dozing, content in the warmth of the bed. The heavy woollen curtaining pulled close for privacy and to deter the worst draught, was not yet drawn aside and she could hear Cnut's body servant snorting from his pallet beside the door. Through a slight chink where the curtains did not quite meet, the room beyond this private world was a dim, colourless grey. Dawn was breaking and soon this luxury of idleness would be broken, too. She stretched lazily, like a she cat purring in the heat of the kitchen cooking fire; beside her, Cnut stirred and slid his arm over the thickness of her pregnant waist. She was five months gone, another four until knowing whether she carried a son or daughter, the first pregnancy that she was enjoying. Cnut treated her as special, a woman to be cosseted and fussed, a novel experience and one she was making the most of.

For his part, Cnut could not understand her astonishment at his concern. A woman with child was in a delicate situation, she needed to be nurtured and cared for, lest the unborn babe, his child, his son or daughter, be harmed. Emma had delayed telling him of her condition, not through any wish of secrecy or anxiety, but because of past experience. Cnut's delight, when she finally summoned courage to admit she had missed a monthly flux for two months, had astounded her. He had swept her into an embracing hug, twirled her around in his arms as if she were a little girl, sat her down, brought her wine, sweetmeats, asked what she needed; all the while bearing a grin that seemed sure to split his face in two. Æthelred had grunted and muttered about his personal inconvenience. Not once during her pregnancies had he asked over her health, how she and the babe fared. Goda had been four months old before he took interest in her. By contrast, Cnut asked almost every hour if she felt well.

She had thought Cnut to be asleep and was surprised when he said, with a yawn, his head tucked into her shoulder, 'The child is awake, even if the rest of my Court is abed snoring. He kicks like a mule.'

'You should feel him from my side, there are some nights I get little sleep from his antics.'

'Then it is a girl, not a boy,' he prophesied. 'Women can never remain still for more than a minute.'

Emma laughed at his absurdity. She hoped it was a boy, for a son would gild their union with an edge of gold, would put an end to some of the nastier comments that had been spouting as gossip from evil tongues.

Cnut yawned again, snuggled closer, enjoying the lazy warmth as much as Emma had on first waking. This marriage was going to be a success, despite his initial misgivings and the ugly rumour-mongering coming from Normandy. It was true that he had explored the possibility of political alliance by marriage before the mortally wounded Edmund had died. True also that there were those in Normandy who called her Jezebel and hussy, those who deplored her audacity at not shutting herself away from the world in mourning for her first husband and for not seeking exile with her children. Emma was an intelligent, politically astute woman who had suffered mentally and physically under the slovenly attitude of Æthelred; why should she mourn him? No one else in England did. That these foul rumours against Emma's integrity came from the direction of Cnut's enemies was plain.

He had no problem with dismissing the gossip, but it hurt Emma, so he attempted to suppress most of it, aware he could not do so successfully with every tattled piece of spit. What amazed him was the fact that he cared and that he wanted to protect Emma from the intentional spite. That even, if perhaps he had not loved her at first, he had respected and admired her, and that was as good a basis for a happy marriage as any. He lifted his head, placed a kiss on her lips. It was growing light outside, he ought be up, getting dressed. So should she for that matter. This was Christmas Day, there was Mass to attend and then the delight of the Yule festivities. He was

470

looking forward to the day, for he was the King and the King was entitled to enjoy himself to the full.

Thrusting aside the curtaining, Cnut tossed a pillow at his sleeping servant, startling the poor man awake.

'Hie there, Torchil, stir your lazy bones out of that blanket and get yourself busy. The King is awake and I want a piss and my breakfast.'

Emma rolled into the hollow where Cnut had been lying and closed her eyes. There was plenty of time until she need attend Mass. Until then, she would stay away from the prying eyes and slanderous tongue of the world, and sleep. Could she be any more content? When she thought back to those first, so unhappy, months of marriage with Æthelred and compared them with these . . . compared? Could you compare an onion with an apple? A boar with a stag or a dead twig with the beauty of a flower?

7

Godwine had never cared for Æthelred's Ealdorman, Leofwine, nor for his cocksure brood of pig-headed sons. Whether the dislike had originally come from his own contempt, or had been inherited from his father's opinion Godwine did not know or care. All he was concerned with was that the eldest son, Leofric, a man near Godwine's own age, was a loud-mouthed braggart who, if he did not soon shut up, would find a fistful of knuckles rammed into his mouth. What Godwine found totally incredible was that Leofric should find anything to brag about. His father had been a minor ealdorman of the Hwicce, the Welsh March lands from Gloucester-Shire to Worcester-Shire, but now, under Cnut's reorganisation, was nothing more than a demoted under-earl in the command of Eadric Streona. True, Leofric had been promoted to Shire Reeve of Worcester and had taken in marriage a most becoming Coventry girl of ten and five years old, but what was there in that to boast of? Ah, but then Leofric was the sort of man who, even if he had a boil on his backside, would crow about it. The new wife was only interesting in appearance. She was too pious in all else for Godwine's liking.

'I reckon she kept her legs crossed even in the marriage bed,' he remarked to Erik of Northumbria, who laughed.

'Nay, lad, Godgiva was safe enough. Leofric is too mean-minded to give anything away, even his seed!'

'And what is it you find so amusing?' Eadric Streona said, walking past the two men and overhearing the last three words. The King's Hall was crowded, stuffy and hot, filled to capacity with Cnut's nobles, their wives, sons and daughters. Everyone had come to the Christmas Court, for to miss it would imply the wrong impression and no one wanted to antagonise Cnut, not after the summer and autumn that had just passed, and not with such a high burden of taxation remaining outstanding.

Cnut's purge of those who seemed likely to oppose him had been thorough and complete. Anyone who had said a word against him, refused to pay his demand of taxes or obey his law, had been efficiently dealt with. No dissenters now existed in England; at least, none who would dare speak aloud their discontent. The lucky ones had escaped with having their ears or hands removed, the not so fortunate had been hanged. Harsh judgement, but Cnut could not afford to be seen as a weak king.

The query on everyone's lips was how Eadric Streona had managed to outflank punishment. If anyone should pay for rebellion and disloyalty it should be the Earl of Mercia.

'We were admiring the merits of Leofric's wife,' Erik said, resenting the interruption. 'I understand she is opposed to the burden of taxation that her husband is having to acquire from the people of Coventry. She has become a champion of the poor man's cause.'

'She could champion my cause any day!' Godwine laughed, drawing the lady's shapely figure in the air with his hands. 'I'd willingly pay my taxes if I could inspect her merits for myself!'

'Or weigh them,' Erik answered, his humour returning as he gestured hands cupping large, ample, breasts.

'If I were Leofric,' Eadric tossed at them as he began to walk away, 'I would have you whipped naked through the streets for your crude insults.'

'Now there's a thought,' Godwine guffawed, slapping his hand on Erik's shoulder, 'those merits paraded naked through the streets!'

'With a quick feel for every penny of tax paid.'

'You're disgusting. The both of you.' Eadric answered, his nose wrinkling in disgust.

The amusement gone, Godwine jeered, 'That we might be, but we are loyal to the King. I am not a man who changes side mid-battle.' The exchange had shifted balance from light-hearted humour to something more destructive and sinister.

'I did not see you aiding Cnut at Ashingdon, Godwine. I am

473

astonished that you have the gall to show your face here at Court, I'd have you hanged, if judgement was left to my decision.'

'The King recognises a good, loyal, man when he sees one,' Erik countered on Godwine's behalf, taking a menacing step towards Eadric, who puffed out his chest, ready to meet head-on.

'Then Cnut is an ass.'

A hush had fallen, attention drawn to the rising voices and the passionate exchange. Strange how in a Hall such as this, with its high-raftered roof, its wide-spaced walls and the mill of people within, how words could echo and carry to the ears of a king.

'Is that your considered opinion, Eadric Streona?' Cnut asked through the sudden fall of breath-held silence, 'or a mere, general, observation?'

Eadric blanched, he bowed, sweeping a reverence almost to the floor. 'My Lord, you heard an inadvertent comment out of context, it is not what you think.'

Cnut had been deep in conversation with Emma. 'So, my Lord Earl? Please explain. How should I think of it?'

He walked slowly down the Hall towards Streona, his nobles and their women opening before him like the churn of the Red Sea parting for Moses.

Eadric backed away a pace as Cnut came close, his hands held wide, placatingly. 'I am loyal to you, my Lord. How can you doubt it? Leofric here will vouch for me. I have explained my conduct at Ashingdon. I was coerced into joining with Edmund, but I had no intention of doing his dirty work. As soon as I could, I quit the field, leaving the way open for your victory. If it were not for me, who knows how that day might have gone?'

'Ja,' Cnut answered, 'who knows? Maybe a king who had been lawfully anointed and crowned in the sight of God would not have been betrayed by scum such as you. What honour was there in that winning for me, eh, Eadric? Can I ever reflect on that battle and not feel the red heat of shame?'

'You were pleased enough with the outcome at the time!' Ah, that proud temper of Eadric Streona's. He never was capable of controlling it.

He held his breath, released it, thought Cnut had ignored the careless remark, for the King was silent, and had started to turn away, to walk back towards the dais and the Queen.

'Where are my taxes?' he suddenly barked, wheeling around to point a finger accusingly at the Earl. 'Why have you not paid them? It is Christmas, and I asked for full settlement by Christmas.'

Eadric spread both hands wide, spluttering incredulity. 'But no one else has paid, my Lord! Everyone has asked for an extension until Easter, and extension you have granted.'

'I do not recall you asking, though, Eadric,' Cnut snapped. 'I want payment, now.'

'But I have not got it! I would have to pay out of my own coffers, I would lose all I have!'

Men were shuffling uneasily, women clinging to their husbands' or fathers' arms, fingers over mouths to keep the fear tucked in. Few cared for Streona, but did he deserve such public humiliation? No one was prepared to speak for him, however.

'Then lose all you have,' Cnut said with a simple, careless shrug. He turned away, nodded slightly to Erik of Northumbria.

And then the women did scream and the men draw back, afraid and alarmed. No one carried weapons within the King's Hall, but there were still the bright, gleaming war axes arrayed on the walls to show the King's strength and power. It only took a moment for Erik to have one of them down and in his hands, a further moment to have the blade scything, with a dull, sucking thud, through the neck below Eadric Streona's open-mouthed, horrified expression.

A long minute of stunned and total silence. Leofric stood, swallowing bile, his mouth working, no sound coming from it, his face white. He had not liked Eadric, but liked less the smell of blood and murder. He looked from the fountain spouting from the grotesque neck stump to Godwine, to Erik. They were not grinning, but their expressions were those of fulfilled satisfaction. Had this whole thing been a deliberately organised drama? Had Eadric, unwittingly, been lured into assuring the manner of his own death? Leofric wiped his hand over his face, found that it was shaking. This had been murder, planned, calculated murder.

Cnut stepped forward, grimaced at the mess on the floor. He clicked his fingers at two servants. 'Spread sawdust and clean rushes over all this, and have the body thrown into the stagnant water of the marshes. Traitors like him do not warrant Christian burial.' To Erik, with a single brief touch to his shoulder, said, 'I would be obliged if you could take the trouble to find a suitable container and send the head to my former wife. It is a thing I promised her some while ago.'

Erik did not query the choice of gift, nor, surprisingly, from her chair on the dais did Emma. But then Emma was the sort of woman who appreciated the significance of such a gesture. Leofric, with his advocation for moral standards, was the sort of man who did not.

8

Cnut was furious, his rage made worse by the fact that the renewed raids on England's coast, and a direct challenge to the legitimacy of his crown, were commanded by his own brother, Harald. The problem was that Cnut's hired mercenaries wanted payment and did not care to wait any longer for it; dogs turning to bite the hand that fed them. They had scuttled to Harald with their grievance and, gleefully seizing his chance to better his brother, he had agreed to help.

'Does he think he has some God given right to deliberately annoy me?' Cnut bellowed as he strode about the chamber, semi-clothed, picking things up and throwing them angrily away. From the bed Emma watched, half amused, half sympathetic with his annoyance.

'You must admit it was astute of him to take advantage of this rare lull in what is normally foul winter weather.'

'Astute? Astute!' Cnut lifted his hands in the air. 'Harald has never been that. Greedy, lazy, good for nothing, *ja*, but astute? Never!' One of the reasons for Swein to have brought Cnut with him to England was that he and his brother had always squabbled as boys. He had hoped that the expanse of sea between the two would put an end to the bickering, that each would be content with his own and call truce with their warring. Wasted hopes for, if anything, the antagonism had increased twofold.

'Pay the men their geld and he will have nothing to goad you with,' Emma said simply. 'It is coming, is it not? Will be paid by Easter in full?'

The reason behind his strutting anger was that Cnut had been taken by surprise by the fleet of Danish ships entering the Medway estuary two days past. The havoc they had created was, according to the messenger arrived at first light, devastating in its intensity of violence. Two settlements and one of Cnut's own manors had been destroyed, the people slain, the buildings gutted and cattle slaughtered. The cycle of raiding and killing, started again. Would it never end? Would peace never be allowed to settle and prosper?

'I'll damn show him who is the better king!' Cnut said suddenly. He whirled to the door, hauled it open and bellowed for his captain of housecarls to be fetched. Swirling back into the room – leaving the door wide open for the world and a fluster of draughts to peer in, he tore on his clothes, shouting his orders to the servants who had come running.

'My fleet is moored at Greenwich for the winter. See to it that the ships are immediately made ready and launched. By noon. I want to be sea-bound by noon, do you hear?'

'Is that possible, my dear?' Emma asked, shuddering at the thought of ships, her calm tempering his flurried agitation.

He was pulling off a boot that he had put on the wrong foot in his haste to be dressed. 'Possible? Of course it is. The keels are all repaired, all that is needed is for them to be launched and for the sails and rigging to be hauled out.' He stamped his foot into the correct boot. 'I'll have the bastard! He'll not be expecting me so soon. He always did underestimate my ability.'

'If I didn't know better,' Emma said, leaning back on the pillows and resting her arms behind her head, 'I would say that all this bluster was nothing but show. I think,' she leant forward, wagged a finger at her husband, 'I think you are enjoying this!'

Cnut grinned, crossed the room and placed a lingering kiss on her lips. 'I am. When the Archbishop placed that crown on my head, I pledged that I would not be another Æthelred, vowing that once all owed debts were paid, there would be no more tribute, no more *i-víking* looting for spoils and gain. I promised that England would be safe in my hands and by God, Emma, I intend to show that I can be trusted as a man who keeps my word.'

Emma ran her finger across his cheek and over his lips. With all seriousness, said, 'Keep just one promise and you will prove that you are not Æthelred. He could not do even that.'

In some respects fighting at sea was easier to command than the shambling array of undrilled men in a land battle. There, among the mud and the blood, it was often every man for himself; at sea, the macabre dance of each warship was easier to choreograph, for a crew sailed and fought as one, a united brotherhood of blood comrades. The *í-víking* thought of the sea as his natural element, he was born to the sea, saw no fear of dying at sea, although there were fewer options of manoeuvre with a ship, for the rules were confined by the mood of the tide and the humour of the weather. As on land, where the selection of terrain was important, calm, sheltered stretches of water were preferred for a fight at sea, the advantage often going to the commander who could block a narrow entrance or exit and have his flanks protected by rocks. Or who could blockade a wide river mouth.

In the Medway estuary, Cnut took the initiative by doing just that. He could have had the option of sailing upriver and picking a fight somewhere along the muddy banks, or in one of the many boggy marshes – a fool's choice, for one who knew the river, although one that Harald, who did not know its temperaments, had hoped to entice him into. Cnut, listening to local knowledge, was content to sit and wait at anchor, riding the flood and ebb currents of the estuary, waiting for Harald to grow bored and make his move. By sun-up on the third day, Harald had decided on his limited options; he had no intention of running the blockade, of escaping under full sail and oar by attempting to dodge and weave the waiting line of ships, but neither could he risk being holed up along a river where supplies would rapidly decrease; and abandoning his ships to march away overland was out of the question. Instead, he attempted to draw Cnut forward, by lashing his ships together, keel to keel, to make a joined bridge of boats, over which his men could move with ease and fight where necessary. Harald, after all, had more than fifty ships, Cnut a mere twenty.

Another advantage of sail over a land army: the initial inspection and probing of strengths and weaknesses was easier to establish.

Godwine's ship was alongside his King's dragon craft, a high-sided monster that boasted thirty benches carrying one hundred and twenty men. She had been Swein's ship, his joy and pleasure.

'See the state of their rigging?' Cnut said to Godwine, pointing to Harald's fleet. 'It is old, some of the sails are salt-worn and wind-battered, too. These men have not pampered their craft through the winter, they've been too busy mithering about how hard-done-by they are. A ship is like a woman, my friend, she prefers to have her hair clean and shining, her gown new-woven. She likes to wear expensive jewellery and to feel the gentle, caressing hand of her lover on the curve of her back. Leave a ship to wear last year's rags, and to sit alone in the cold and damp, then she will sulk and not serve you well.'

Much of this Godwine knew, for his father had told him the same thing, indeed, Godwine's mother had often complained that Wulfnoth treated his ships better than he did his wife. The moment of nostalgia at the unbidden memory of his parents passed. They were gone to God, resting at peace; this was the here, the *now*. *His* life.

'At sea it is not easy to keep the secrets of your strength from an enemy. On land you can pitch fewer or more tents, scatter your campfires to confuse a watching spy of your numbers. You cannot do so at sea, for it is easy to count the oars and the men rowing them.' Cnut indicated the end ship of the lashed row, her steerboard side hull easily viewed.

'See how she has not been cleaned of barnacles? Nor had her dragon crest repainted? I would wager there is rotten wood below her sea-line.'

'Her height is impressive, though, my Lord. She will be hard to board if we manage to get in close.'

Cnut nodded, *ja*, Godwine was right there, but it was a problem that could be overcome – *Sea Serpent* was no stunted shrimp, either. Enough of the talk! Cracking her fingers together, he grinned at Godwine. 'Get your best men forward, and let us fight!'

They were ready, each of Cnut's ships cleared for action, anything movable on the deck stowed beneath the rowing benches or, if not entirely necessary, ditched overboard. Weapons were to hand, first the spears for throwing, then swords, daggers and axes for close combat, each man's shield slung across his shoulders. It hampered movement only slightly, kept a great amount of wind and salt spray from their backs, and the death-bringer of a thrown spear. The bravado of hanging them out along the side was for decoration alone, and confined to the swaggering entry into harbour.

Cnut brought his ships up slowly, the equivalent to a walk, no point in wasting effort before it was needed. Gradually, he fanned the fleet out to form the attack, initially, a horseshoe shape in front of the enemy line, held until they could swing aside, to left and right and approach from the rear. The elite fighters, and those of proven worth with accurate spear throwing, were mustered in the bows for maximum effect, the strategy to surround and come in close, grappling and then boarding. It was then close-quarter fighting, every man for himself. The difference from a land battle? Burial of the dead was easier at sea.

Cnut was leading the centre, to fight head on; Godwine had been given command of the left flank and the Captain of Cnut's housecarls, Halfdan, the right, or steerboard side. He was a good man, Halfdan, having served alongside Cnut's father, and transferred his loyalty with fervour and enthusiasm to the son. Godwine was a little green behind the ears in experience, but he was one of England's most proficient sailors, and knew as much about the sea and the handling of ships as did Cnut. Perhaps more, if truth were told. Ideally, the great men such as Erik and Thorkell would have been preferable to take command, but they were not in London when Harald cleaved into the Medway and made his presence known, and besides, it was not always the men who carried the highest titles who made the best fighters.

'Do me well, today,' Cnut had called to the both of them, his hand raised in salute, his head high, eyes and heart alight with anticipation, 'and you shall be handsomely rewarded.'

'To fight as your companion and friend is reward enough!' Godwine had shouted in eager response. A man clever with his words who would, as Emma had once judged, go far.

There was much Godwine wanted, and he was astute enough to

realise that this was his opportunity to go out and get it. Already, through his service to the Queen, he had shown he was a man to be trusted; now he could add to that by showing he was also a man to be reckoned with. Recklessly, some would say, he drove his crew into the ship's full capacity of oar power as Cnut signalled for the pace to increase, the thresh of spindrift, the grunts of effort, as muscles strained and pulled; the creak of wood as the oars plunged and rose in perfect unison. It helped Godwine's cause that he liked this new King – as a king, a man and a friend.

'Lift her! Lift her!' the oarmaster cried, as the ship sprang into life and the spray flew, salt-tinged, to their lips and hair, blown by the wind and the speed of their passing.

'Pause, steerboard side!' Godwine called, signalling with his hand, to bring the craft round in a tight curve. 'Lift!' he bellowed a few seconds later, and the oars swooped and the craft leapt forward, as if she were a horse, released at last into a gallop.

She rammed, bow on, into the poor-maintained craft that Cnut had pointed out, and the enemy hull shattered, splintering like summer-dried kindling beneath a man's stamping boot. Their spears were thrown, the men, braced for the collision, using the momentum of force to leap on to the tilting deck, their axes swinging, swords plunging, mouths open, yelling the war cry, 'Cnut! Cnut!' Leaving a skeleton crew behind to steady the oars, the men hurtled on to the disabled craft and plunged on to the next, not stopping, not wavering except to kill or maim. From the centre, from the far flank, the same was happening, the cries of the wounded and the dying muffling the agitation of the gulls swooping and diving overhead.

The fighting was fierce, vicious, and soon done. The disadvantage of war at sea, for ships that were lashed together: if the tactic failed, escape was impossible.

Godwine had reached the sixth ship, if he had paused to look behind, would have seen decks slippery with blood and the steam of men's spilt guts and severed limbs. The carnage of battle resembling the butcher's table after the autumn slaughter. He stumbled, landing awkwardly as he jumped from one ship to the next, his ankle giving way beneath his weight. He cursed, aware that a man

482

on his knees was vulnerable, heard the sound of a sword as its blade whistled through the air, tried to throw himself to the side – and the man fell, the sword still gripped in his clasped hands, his head, from eye sockets upwards, gone, brains and gore and blood spraying over Godwine's already bloodied and rented chain hauberk.

'Thank you, Eadric Sheepshanks,' Godwine breathed, thrusting himself to his feet, briefly taking the hand offered to help him up. 'I will not forget that you saved my life.'

Eadric grinned. He was a man of no especial status, although freeborn, the eldest brother of eight, who held the tenancy of a small farm in a wooded vale of Wessex, a mile or so from the coast, Godwine being his manor lord. By chance, he had been serving his fyrd tithe of arms, had been one of those selected to serve as crew to Godwine's own craft, *Seagull*. He nodded his gratitude at Godwine's recognition, reasoned that if his fortune held, he would receive a pouch of silver or bag of gold by way of reward.

Fortune was smiling, that day, on Eadric and Godwine and Cnut. Thirty of the *í-víking* ships were destroyed, and Harald was forced to bow to his younger brother in surrender and acknowledge his underestimation of Cnut's judgement and capability. A bitter blow for the elder man, elation for the younger.

With pride swelling his chest almost to bursting, Cnut and his fleet escorted his humbled brother to the safety of harbour at Sandwich. As reward, the King offered Godwine a tribute beyond expectation. 'At my next Council,' Cnut declared, 'when we meet at Oxford for the holy celebration of Easter, I shall bestow upon you an earldom. To you, Godwine, will go Wessex.'

In turn, for Eadric, called Sheepshanks for the width of his thighs, Godwine granted more than a pouch of coin: he bestowed the status of thegn and, to go with it, the gold to purchase a better farm in a better, more fertile valley, one where Eadric's mother had been born, at a place called Nazeing, near the River Lea in the County of Essex. A good place to farm, to take a wife, raise a family.

Halfdan received nothing, for he had no use of reward, save for the dignity of the Christian words of blessing spoken over him as he went to his grave within the salt embrace of the ebbing tide.

9

Aware that he was unwanted, disliked and very much in the way, Harald was in no hurry to go home to Denmark. There was more than one way to kill a rat and if he had been unable to defeat his younger brother at sea, well, maybe he could find another way to dislodge him.

'I am not so certain about the wisdom of this proposed charter,' he said to Emma, stretching out his long legs and folding his arms behind his head. He sat in Cnut's favourite chair, the one with the high back and embroidered, padded cushioning. Cnut would be annoyed if he knew, for he allowed no one to sit there, but he had been cloistered with the Archbishops Wulfstan and Ælfstan this past hour, discussing the wording of the charter Harald referred to.

Emma made no answer, pretending to be engrossed with a particularly difficult stitch on the embroidery she was working. She understood why Cnut had insisted that his brother stay at Court – as an honoured guest – but for the love of her sanity, she wished he could find an alternative way of keeping the wretched man under close observation!

The silence stretched into the discomfort of embarrassment. Emma finished the stitch, sat back to admire her handiwork; with deliberation she turned her head to stare with dislike at her brother-in-law. 'And may I ask, why you are not certain?'

Harald shrugged, lumbered to his feet and wandered around the room, making a show of closely inspecting the weaponry displayed on the walls. Emma did not approve of the axes, swords and spears arranged across the white lime-washed plaster; this was their personal room, where she and Cnut enjoyed privacy and the rare luxury of relaxation. She would have preferred embroideries, or painted patterns on a more pleasing background colour. A yellow, perhaps? She had insisted on her choice for the bedchamber, however, so felt obliged to defer to Cnut for this room.

'I query the wisdom of granting so much land into the hands of the Church, that's all,' Harald said, testing an edge to a sword blade and finding it sharp. He sucked the blood welling from his thumb. 'The Church is getting enough, in my view, without Cnut giving more.' He half laughed. 'I feel, if my brother truly intends to give half his kingdom away, he could give it to me. After all, I could make more use of it than a fusty old bishop.'

'It is my charter,' Emma said scathingly, her hand on the swell of her pregnancy. 'It is at my request that Cnut gives this parcel of land to Christ Church, as a gift to God for my safe delivery when my time comes.'

Another short silence.

'Ah,' Harald replied, placing a false grin across his mouth. 'Then I defer to your feminine wisdom.' He proffered her a bow, then, with quick steps, crossed the room, took her hand and kissed it. 'You are a handsome woman, Emma. I can see why my brother was so intent on securing you.'

Emma attempted to withdraw her fingers, but Harald held them firm.

'Ragnhild, his Norwegian wife, was a beauty. Has he told you about her? He was besotted with her.'

'How fortunate, then, that she is dead,' Emma answered, trying again to release her hand.

'My wife is a hag. She has hairs sprouting from her nose. Making love to her is like caressing a grim-breathed troll.' Harald moved closer, pressing himself against the bulge of Emma's abdomen. 'Cnut seems to have no problem. I would expect he receives much pleasure from you in bed.'

Emma slapped his face. 'I would advise you not to attempt to insult me again, Harald, I am not as restrained as my husband when it comes to dealing with my enemies.'

'What enemies would they be?' a voice asked from the doorway.

Harald spun around, his face blanching, to see Cnut entering. Composed, behaving as if nothing untoward had occurred, Emma smiled delightedly at her husband. 'You have finished? How wonderful! May I read it?'

Cnut kissed her cheek, motioned for her to sit. 'How often must I tell you not to stand on your feet so much? You must rest, *elskede*, I insist upon it.' He set a scroll of ragged parchment in her hand. 'This is one of the drafts, the scribe is copying out the final agreed version as we speak. What enemies?'

Eagerly, Emma sat and began to read, saying absently, 'I am perfectly all right. And there are no enemies, I have none.' Her eyes scanned the first few lines, her lips moving silently, then she began to read aloud, '*I, Cnut, King of the English at the request of my Queen, Ælfgifu,*' Emma detested the continuing use of that official name, but there was nothing she could do about it '*grant to the venerable Archbishop Ælfstan a certain grove of woodland commonly called Hazelgrove in the famous forest of Andredesweald, that he may have it for his lifetime with all the things rightly pertaining to it, free from all earthly service, and after his death may leave it to whatever heir he pleases in perpetual inheritance.*' Her smile broadening, Emma looked up at Cnut's benign expression. 'Thank you, my Lord, I am delighted to be giving this gift.'

'Valuable land, is it?' Harald asked.

'Of course it is. Of what use would poor scrub be as a gift?' Cnut snapped.

'I only thought that perhaps you ought not be giving away assets that may be needed,' Harald answered, making himself comfortable in one of the other chairs. 'If there is no tithe collected by Easter, then you must find alternative payment for my men.' His eyes held Cnut's, unblinking, plain in their meaning. 'We will not wait longer than Easter.'

'Your men? We?' Stifling the inclination to call in the guard and have this irritating bastard executed here and now, Cnut poured himself ale, sat in his chair after thumping the cushions. 'I was under the impression that my fleet decimated *your* men, Harald. That I thrashed those who rebelled. Most of them have only God, and the fishes of the sea, to receive anything from. There will not be payment for those who survived, to live is sufficient. Cnut's voice rose as he neared the end of the sentence and, with it, his temper. He flung the ale aside and lurching to his feet, bore down on Harald, his fingers curling into the folds of his brother's tunic.

With his face very close Cnut said, slowly and explicitly so that Harald should understand every word, 'London has sent its ten thousand pound tribute, it came yester eve. In full. I intend to keep forty ships for my own, those who wish to stay are welcome to join my English scyp fyrd. The rest of you will be paid at sunrise on the morrow and may leave in what ships remain on the noon tide.' The material tightened at Harald's neck as Cnut's fingers gripped harder, choking him. 'You shall be with them and if you ever so much as glance in England's direction again, or dare to insult my wife as I overheard, then you will regret the day our mother spewed you from her womb!' Cnut flung Harald from him, causing him to over-balance, fall to one knee.

With the false congeniality swept aside, Harald brushed off imaginary dirt from his sleeves and backed towards the door, his face puckered in livid hatred. 'You shall regret this, Brother. I do not tolerate insults.'

Cnut stood his ground, defiant, fists on hips. 'Neither do I, Brother, and it is you who shall do the regretting. You have a choice: you board one of those ships and be gone from my sight, or I shall find some form of appropriate accommodation for you here in England. Something that closely resembles six feet of soil.'

For reply, Harald made an obscene gesture with his arm and slammed from the room.

'I think you have offended him,' Emma said with an approving smile.

10

Cnut's political genius was so successful at the Easter gathering of Court, that the chroniclers, in later years, found little more to write of him beyond the recording of his virtues and generosity. The achievement at Oxford was partly due to Archbishop Wulfstan who saw, with relieved delight, an end to the horrors and deprivations of the Devil's work. Their suffering was over, God's wrath was appeased, and all would be right and golden with the Christian world, and, ironically, because of Cnut's coming. Could it have been the black presence of murder that had tainted Æthelred's reign? To gain a crown by the spilling of a brother's blood, had that been the cause of God's anger?

Wulfstan spoke forthright to the Council, standing beside the King on the dais, his arms raised high.

'We have a King who has repented his sins and his wrong doings, who has pledged to rule as a just and Godly King. A King who believes in the wisdom of that earlier, wise King, Edgar, who made for us the laws of our land. I am ashamed that I feared and despaired of the testing by our Lord God during these long years of deprivation through which we have suffered; I would not have believed that a Dane could lay claim to our land and bring us into salvation, but here is the proof of my doubting!' He swept his right hand towards Cnut. 'It humbles me to admit before you all that I questioned the will of God, but he has delivered us and has rewarded our faith with a King who will guide us into the eternal light of righteousness.'

There was more to this meeting of Council than the religious rhetoric of Archbishop Wulfstan for, with the demanded tribute finally paid, the assembly at Oxford was to become the watershed of Cnut's acceptance as King by the people of England. He was to offer more than his pledge to rule as a king should rule, vowing that the English would henceforth live in peace, as one united nation of Anglo-Danes. Every man, from earl to thegn, pledged his honour to Cnut and eagerly took a binding oath, sworn in the name God, to obey Edgar's revived laws.

'Sir? My Lord King?' Leofgifu edged on to the dais, trying not to disrupt what she privately thought of as long-winded speech making. 'Sir, it is my Lady Queen.'

Cnut swivelled in his chair, his brows shooting downwards into a frown.

'The babe? It has come?'

Leofgifu hesitated, she had not wanted to be the messenger, but someone had to tell him. 'It has come,' she said, 'the babe is born.'

Cnut jumped up, waving Earl Thorkell, who was making an opulent and praising oration, to silence. 'Well, woman? How is it? What is it? How does my lady wife?'

Taking a breath, Leofgifu blurted everything in one sentence. 'The babe is well, as is my Lady Queen, although she be tired. You have a daughter, a baby girl.' She almost flinched, expecting a bellow of disappointed rage, but it did not happen. Instead, Cnut laughed, punched the air with his fist.

'I have a daughter!' he shouted, 'another daughter, praise be to God!' After twirling Leofgifu around, not an easy task, given her ample girth, he jumped from the dais and, grasping mens' hands as he passed, hurried to the doorway.

'Forgive me, my Lords, this meeting is concluded. I have a daughter to greet and you have several barrels of my finest barley ale to break open in celebration!' He was gone, whisking away to Emma's chamber.

'You would have thought he would have preferred a son,' someone said, as men scraped back their stools, began to fasten cloaks, or collect up scrolls of parchment.

'He wanted a girl child,' someone else said. 'Mark my words, if the Queen gives him a son there'll be all Hell let loose from the direction of Northampton.'

*

'What do we call her?' Cnut asked, his voice hushed as the babe lay asleep in his arms, her tiny fingers curled tight around one of his own.

'It is for you to choose, but I would call her Gunnhild, after the good friend I once had, your father's half-sister.'

'Then Gunnhild it is.' Cnut looked down at the child's sleeping face, a week old, already grown so much, yet still so vulnerably small. She was perfect, absolutely perfect.

Moving slowly, he sat on the edge of Emma's bed, his wife shifting her legs to make room for him. Carefully he tucked the shawl under Gunnhild's chin, rocked her as she stirred.

Watching him, the love that was pouring from him to his daughter as if it were a waterfall in full spate, Emma asked, 'You have another daughter, Ragnhilda. Why do you never speak of her?'

Cnut wiped dribble from the babe's lips with his finger. 'She was a beautiful child, too.' He glanced, with a smile, at Emma. 'Like her mother, as this little one is like you.'

'Ragnhild? I have heard that you loved her.'

Chewing his lip, Cnut looked back into the past, those stolen months of happiness in Norway. Then, when he had lost Ragnhild, he had thought that happiness would never find him again. Was that why he had pushed himself to come to England? Why he had taken risks against Edmund – and he had taken them, he had the battle scars on his arms and legs to prove it. Edmund had not been the only one to keep secret the damage done by sword and spear. Except Cnut's wounds had been minor compared with that mortal injury, although some of them persistently ached when the wind moaned at night from far-distant lands away to the north-east.

'I thought I would die when I lost her; some part of me, I think, did die.'

'Strange,' Emma said, touching her hand lightly, lovingly, on his arm. 'A part of me died when I was wed to Æthelred. I only came alive when he died and I married you.' She was not envious or jealous of Ragnhild. How could she be? The woman, unlike Ælfgifu of Northampton, was gone, was no threat. The living caused the mischief, not the dead.

490

'You know, of course, that Norway was lost to Denmark soon after Erik Håkonsson left to come to England with me?'

She nodded, aye, she knew that.

'We left Erik's son and his brother, Ragnhild's father, in charge of Norway. Capable men, the both of them, but a man called Olaf Haroldsson, an old enemy of my father's, proved more capable. With Hlaðir fallen, they fled, taking my daughter, Ragnhilda, with them, intent on joining me here in England.' Cnut paused, rocked the child. 'But the winds of the North Sea can be treacherous, and the ships were blown and tossed about as if they were wooden toys bobbing in a spring-flood mountain stream. A few who had fled reached safety on the shores of the Isles of Orkney. Only a few, Erik's son and brother were not among them.'

Cnut laid his lips lightly against Gunnhild's forehead. The child, Ragnhilda, had survived. Somehow, in the name of God, the child had been saved.

'She remains in Orkney, up in the High Islands, where I have friends and kindred to take care of her. I had hoped, one day, to send for her, but . . .'

'But?'

He shrugged.

Emma answered for him. 'But now you are wed to me and we have a daughter born, and you did not think I would approve of having another child, of a different woman, within my household?'

He shrugged again. *Ja*, he had thought that.

'The two brats dropped from that whore in the north, no, I would not allow within spitting distance, but the child, Ragnhilda, is different.' A daughter could not be a threat to a son. 'Send for her. Bring her to Court.'

It took a while for Cnut to swallow the lump that had hurried into his throat, to blink back stupid tears, to raise his eyes and look at his wife. What did this intelligent, proud, clever woman see in him?

'One day soon, not too far into the future, I will have to sail to Denmark to sort matters there. When I return to England I shall personally collect her, if you are certain you do not object.'

491

'Why should I object? She will be company for this little one.'

Cnut laughed suddenly, wrinkled his nose. 'She may only be a small bundle, this second daughter of mine, but when she decides to fill her swaddling linen, the smell she produces can outshine a barn-full of swine!'

11

After fifteen years of waiting, Emma had finally seen her estates of Exeter in Devon and was relieved to find that the old memories were no longer raw. Cnut's primary intention had been to consolidate the south-western counties, but there was opportunity, too, for him to enjoy the delights of family life with his wife and baby daughter, particularly during the Nativity, which they spent together at Buckfast Abbey. The deer were plentiful on the moorland regions of Exmoor and Dartmoor, and although Emma did not share her husband's enthusiasm for the chase, she found the scenery as enchanting as Pallig had once described it to be. She had told Cnut about Pallig, forgetting that he had known of the man, for Gunnhilda had been Cnut's aunt.

'I grieved for them for so long,' she had confided to him one night, as they lay close together after making love. 'They were the only people to be kind to me when first I came to England as a shy and frightened girl. My only friends.'

Cnut had laughed. 'You? Shy and frightened? Pull the other oar, lass!'

She had laughed with him, but inside the memory had rekindled those fearful, lonely, months of emptiness. It was a sorry thing not to have a friend and, now that she had found one, one to cherish, she was not going to let Cnut go. Prayed that God would grant them long years of happiness together.

Devon had not entirely been hunting and holiday, for there were duties to attend, judgements of law to make, charters to grant, but the winter months had passed pleasantly, with only a few minor falls of snow hindering them for no more than a handful of days. An enjoyable experience, but Emma was delighted to be back in

493

Winchester, for her house was almost completed, her Queen's hall. At last, her own private residence.

They had arrived, weary and saddle-sore, the previous evening, Gunnhild red-cheeked and irritable. Emma had thrown herself into bed, with barely the energy to remove her travel-grimed clothing, had fallen instantly asleep. When Cnut joined her she had woken, briefly, to feel his shivering body against hers, but had slept on. Come morning he was gone, with only a dent in the pillow and his own scatter of muddied clothing to show for his being there.

By midday, Cnut felt as if he were drowning in the demand of duties of government and called a halt to the tedium. 'I am a man born of a wind-rippled fjord and the open toss of the sea,' he said, rubbing at his aching temples. 'I need fresh air to fill my lungs, or I swear I shall suffocate.' By way of added excuse, he sought Emma out and offered to accompany her to inspect her new Hall.

'They are so stubbornly pedantic, these sombre-faced clerics,' he confided to her as they walked, arm linked through arm, along the wide stretch of the High Street that ran from east to west, with their escort of four stalwart housecarls, two making way ahead and two trudging discreetly behind. 'Have they no sense of humour? I swear these clerics of mine would argue with Saint Peter at the very gates of Heaven over some triviality of written legislation!'

Emma laughed and squeezed his arm affectionately. 'They fall over their feet in an attempt to impress you, to show how competent and efficient they are.'

'Ah, so that is what they are doing. I wondered.'

The eastern end of the High Street was broad and flat, for here it was low ground and often flooded from an overspill of the three brooks that provided a living for several families. Constant running water was essential for so many trades; in this instance the brooks made income for a fuller and several leather workers. On hot days Winchester stank, from the debris and waste-strewn stagnant water, and the obnoxious stench of the fuller's yard. On a windy March day, after a gentle fall of rain, the aroma was bearable. It was a busy, cluttered thoroughfare, even on days such as this, when there were no market stalls set out along the cobbled street. The Saint

Swithin's Priory, the Old Minster, was a much patronised place and Winchester itself, with its royal importance, a central focus for trade and legal jurisdiction.

The two housecarls ahead cleared a pathway through the crowd, their shields and spears allowing no one to linger or push by, the few grumbles at their casual roughness lost among the general hubbub made by so many busy people. Footsteps, talk, laughter; the occasional angry exchange. A donkey's stubborn braying, a dog's anxious barking. Traders, craftsmen, housewives, servants; slaves, children, monks, they were all here in Winchester, and most were used to the presence of royalty walking up their main street. A crippled beggar chanced his luck for a tossed penny, but received only a scowl and the threatening end of a spear from one of the housecarls; a child, playing football with three other boys, almost collided into Cnut, but the King, chuckling, kicked the pig's bladder aside, sending it rolling and bumping back down the hill, the boys whooping their delight in pursuit. Cnut was the King, Emma his Queen and Winchester, unequivocally loved the both of them.

With the High Street beginning to climb, Emma slowed their brisk pace to an amble. She was a fit woman who enjoyed walking, but she so rarely found the chance to have her husband to herself that she took the opportunity to stretch the stolen hour into something longer.

Ahead, the archway and squat tower of the west gate dominated the final rise of the hill and the High Street split into two, one way sweeping out underneath the gateway, the other arm swinging to the right into the gold-lenders' street: the Jewish quarter, where several Jews were settled in a small, enclaved community. Emma had no care for them and shared the common feeling that one or two would, before long, encourage the coming of many, but Winchester, as with any trading town, was a centre for the business of buying and selling, and where you had merchants you had money. And that attracted the Jewish moneyers. They were taxed high and brought considerable revenue, so they were tolerated. Ever it was so, money talked loud, often at a shout.

Emma's Hall was before the right-hand turn, the high wall, higher than a man on horseback, giving it both protection and privacy. The gateway stood open and, dramatically, Cnut paused at its threshold and bowed. 'My Lady, should I carry you across as if you were a new-come bride?' He did not wait for reply, but bent and swooped her into his arms, strode purposefully under the arch and set her down again, with her giggling like a virgin maid, in the courtyard beyond.

Builders' scaffolding was in place along two of the main Hall walls and despite the workmen the place seemed oddly hollow. Standing, looking around, her arms folded critically, Emma took a while to realise why. There were no servants, no dogs nosed for food, no chickens scratched and squawked at a midden heap or crooned to themselves on hidden nests. No horses looking, prick-eared, from the stables. No smoke or smell of baking bread or roasting meat drifted from the kitchens. It was an empty building, soulless and lifeless, just a house, not a home.

Seeing their arrival, the Master Mason climbed down the cross-tied beams of scaffolding, his feet sure and confident as he swung along the narrow slippery rungs of the ladders and, wiping his roughened hands on his leather apron, forced a smile on to his harassed face and bowed. 'You are welcome, Master, Mistress. Had I known you were coming I would have had the place tidied.' His voice trailed off as he looked, mournfully, at the mess that builders invariably left behind: a coil of frayed rope, a broken pulley wheel, piles of rubble, stone dust, wood shavings.

Emma waved his concern aside. 'I would have been more displeased to find my Hall abandoned and neglected.' She smiled reassuringly. 'Here I can see for myself that work is in progress. Is there much more to do?'

Pleased to be able to impart good news, the Mason grinned. 'Anther four or five days, Madam, that is all.'

Like Emma, the Master Mason was Norman; he had worked on several of her brother's castles and, in part, on the cathedral at Rouen. This, Emma's house, to the best of his knowledge was the first stone building, outside of a religious complex, to be built in

England. Given free rein and a full purse, Emma had been set on rivalling the Norman Duke for grandeur and comfort. The style of her house was large in design, but modest in size, a two-storeyed building, with stone walls and vaulting on the ground floor of the public Hall, the more traditional timber, daub and wattle for the upper private chambers.

With pride open on his bearded face, the Mason pointed to the red-tiled roof. 'The tiles are all laid, Madam, most of the construction finished. The chimneys I am especially pleased with.'

With curiosity, Cnut strolled over to one of the two high-reaching stone stacks that protruded from the outer long wall, patted its solidity. They were firm structures of mortared block stone, stretching up, square and solid, towards the sky. A new conception, one totally alien to Cnut, who doubted their usefulness. He shrugged, held his counsel until he had chance to inspect them more thoroughly.

Emma was already entering through the doorway, the inside smelt of sawdust and chiselled stone, of tarred rope and slopped water; of toil and sweat. The walls were bare, the floor dusty with a weird, patterned dance of interwoven footsteps. Swept, tidied, with embroidered tapestries on the walls, benches and tables, fresh rushes flickering lamps and tallow candles, it would soon be transformed into a living place, where a heart did beat and a voice did speak. At the far end a staircase, the wood new, pale and unscuffed. Gathering her gown, she climbed, pushed open the doorway at the top and entered what would become her solar, her private sitting room. Her breath came in a gasp, held in her throat, and tears of excited joy prickled behind her eyes. The room, although devoid of any homeliness, was flooded with light from the three small-paned glass windows. Crude glass, thick and not very opaque, but windows were not for looking through, only for keeping out the elements and letting in the light. Glass was so much better than the thin sheets of stiff, oiled parchment. Wooden shutters, folded back to each side, would shut out the night and the worst storms.

Cnut strolled across to the chimney – the second would be in the chamber beyond. He stepped inside the huge, cold and empty hearth and peered upwards into the square of sky above. Personally, he could not see the point. If the hearth-place was not central to the room, how could you sit around it to talk, or laugh, or argue?

'How much rain and wind will sweep downwards?' he asked the Mason. 'Given some of our English downpours, I should think any fire would be washed away before it throws out any heat.'

Emma saved the Mason from embarrassment by answering for him. 'I am assuming that work on them is not quite finished, my lover, hence the scaffolding and our Master Mason being grieved at the distraction from his task.' She moved across the room to peer up the shaft herself, shuddered at the height that felt as if it were about to fall down upon her. 'Are tiles not placed at specific angles across the sky hole to channel away the rain but allow the escape of smoke?'

The Mason smiled, could not have put it better himself. Even so, Cnut was eventually proved right, there was often no sufficient draught to draw the smoke upwards and on days when the wind blew particularly malevolently, more of it tended to blow into the room than drift up. But then, what Hall was never smoke-filled?

From the solar, a second room, Emma's bedchamber with, to one corner, a private chapel, and to the far end an oak door leading to a small, windowless room. Cnut peered in, nodded satisfaction. This was for the holding of the King's Treasury, the chests of valuables that he owned; a sensible way of doing things, for the King must be ready to face his enemies at any time and not have need to pause for the securing of his wealth. The fact that the Queen was responsible for its keeping was the source of her power, of course. Cnut wondered what would happen if one day, after he had been away, fighting in Denmark, for instance, Emma should refuse to give it back. The anomaly had never arisen before; there had been a queen, Alfred's daughter, who had held the treasury of Mercia and ruled in her own name, but then, that had been during the war years when the Danes and the English had first been at each other's throats. Her own brother had soon put a stop to a woman's bid for ultimate power. Since then, the only capable women had been Æthelred's dominating mother, and Emma. What would Emma do if she had sole control of the King's Treasury? Cnut had an uncomfortable feeling that she would become as formidable as a fire-breathing, gold-guarding dragon creature.

Finished with his squinting into the darkness, he asked, 'I assume the floor is solid? Chests weigh heavy.'

Emma entered the windowless room, jumped up and down, her outdoor boots thudding on the timber floor. 'The floor is oak, double planked, on sturdy beams.'

'And, of course, your great weight is ten times that of my gold.'

They laughed together, Cnut sliding his arm around Emma's slender waist, for she was still slender, despite having given birth to four children. He bent his head, put his lips to hers, enjoying the taste of her mouth against his. 'It will be good', he said softly, 'when you have a bed in this chamber and your Master Mason has the sense to turn his sour gaze in the opposite direction.'

Giggling, Emma put her hand to his chest, pushing him slightly away. 'Then I suggest we leave him to his work. The quicker he is finished, the quicker I can see about furnishings and making this into a room we can enjoy.'

It seemed an ideal opportunity.

'I am pleased your house is almost ready for you. Its finishing will give you amusement while I am gone.' Cnut realised, as he said it, that perhaps the opportunity was not as ideal as he had imagined.

Hurt, annoyed that her happiness had been so easily and abruptly shattered, Emma turned away from him, went to one of the windows, stared out. From this side of the chamber the view was down into the crowded High Street. She watched a woman drop her basket, bundles of wool, skeins of thread and packets of needles and thimbles cascading to the floor. No one stopped to help her retrieve anything, everyone stepping over the muddle, leaving the distraught woman to sort everything for herself. As Cnut wanted to leave her.

'I see,' she said tartly. 'Where will you be going? For how long?' If he said to the North she would scream, hit him. Oh, she knew all about Ælfgifu! All about the letters and messages she constantly bombarded him with. Knew about the occasional letter Cnut sent as reply.

Cnut came to stand behind her, set his hands to either shoulder. 'I go to Denmark, where else?'

Not to the Northampton Bitch, then. Could she believe him?

'I have no intention of allowing my brother to yoke more men to his command and to try again for what I will not let him have. It is in my mind to anchor him to harbour before he plucks courage to set sail again.'

Emma could see the sense of it, but seeing sense never made the doing any easier. 'When do you leave?' she asked curtly, not wanting to know the answer.

'After Easter. Mid April. I intend to announce that I am sailing north to deal with the unrest on my borders with Scotland. Erik has asked for my help. My brother shall not expect me to turn east, after, towards Denmark.' He slid his hands lower, holding her to him, folding them beneath her breasts, resting his chin on her head. 'Will you take care of England for me while I am gone?' he asked, trundling her around and, ignoring the presence of the Mason, kissing her with a passion of trust and need.

Deliberately, he did not tell her that he would also be visiting Northampton on his way. There were one or two things he had to settle there. Nor did he tell his Queen that while he trusted her, he did not feel it right to leave a woman in charge of his crown or his kingdom without male guidance. Thorkell, Earl of East Anglia, was to be his official regent, if the man could manage to overstep the Queen's precocious command. Cnut had found only one sure way of doing so and that way was not an option open to a man who was not her lawful husband.

12

The Christmas court was held at Winchester, and the hope had been that Cnut himself would have returned from Denmark and been here for it, but the Nativity had come and gone, and only three days were wanting for yet another old year to turn around into the new.

Thorkell held the Court at Cnut's palace while, heavy with child, Emma preferred to reside in her own house at the west end of the High Street. The year had been long for her, on occasion lonely, but for the most part interesting and eventful. This was the year, above all previous, that Emma felt her worth as Queen. Cnut may have charged that contemptible man Thorkell with the title Regent, to be the first to witness charters and make final judgement, but Emma held the reins, decided which road to follow. And she did it while swelling with child and through the birthing of a son.

He was born in late December, during a wind-blustering night of a tempest that rattled at the doors and moaned through the eaves. Born with ease and happiness, even though Emma was in her one and thirtieth year, and no longer a young girl with a supple and pliant body that bent to the whims of labour.

Harthacnut, a legitimate son for England's King, a red-faced, angry little man, demanding absolute attention. How hard it was, looking down at him as he suckled her breast, for Emma to forget the two potential rivals, the sons residing in Northampton with their bitch of a mother. Easy, by comparison, to forget the other two, the ones exiled in Normandy.

The Northampton Bitch, as Emma insisted on calling Ælfgifu, had steadily become a problem during Cnut's absence, growing almost in unison with the pregnancy. Cnut had taken a risk to leave

England so early in his sovereignty, but it had been a risk weighed against the prospect of a second invasion from his brother. That possibility Cnut was determined to erase before he could turn to other, English, matters.

'She wants a crown for her own son, doesn't she, my *skat*,' Emma whispered, using the Danish endearment, as she moved the babe to her other breast. 'But it is not his, it is yours.' The child gazed up at her with unfocused blue eyes, his mouth drawing greedily at the essential first days of his mother's milk.

'He'll be one with his own mind, that lad,' Leofgifu said in passing as she cleared away the debris of the babe's soiled linen. 'There'll be no messing with him when he's grown to manhood.'

'Then I trust the Whore of Northampton learns of it and ensures her two brats remember their place.'

'Aye, she's one with a grudge, that woman.' Leofgifu took the sated child, winded him. Laying him in his cot, added, 'Do you think there be any truth in this rumour of Thurbrand? Is it likely she was behind his murder?'

Emma laughed. 'What? Murdered so soon after he had denounced her as a cast-off whore? No, of course she had nothing to do with it!'

It was known that the two had quarrelled, but uncertain whether Ælfgifu had been involved in the killing, which had been done by Uhtred of Northumbria's son in revenge for his father's murder. Ælfgifu would never work side alongside with that young man, but Emma had no intention of damping tattled gossip with opposing fact.

With the wind knocking, impatient, at the shuttered windows, moaning down the chimney and creaking at the rafters, all sound beyond this, Emma's small private world, was muffled. The hammering at the outer door to the solar startled both women and the child, who jerked, arms thrown above his head, but slept on. Stumping across the bedchamber and through the far room, like a dragon ship under full sail, Leofgifu hauled the door open, prepared to unleash her displeasure at the interruption, her scorn rising to a scream before one word had left her lips.

Armed men were rushing in, knocking Leofgifu aside as she tried to bar entry. She fell heavily, her head hitting the edge of a table; she lay still, blood dribbling. Their leader crossed to the bedchamber, kicking the two barking and snarling dogs aside.

'I am grateful that you have come to give honour to your Lord King's new son, Lord Athelweard,' Emma said, deceptively calm, to the man standing, legs apart, sword drawn, in the open doorway, 'but perhaps this is not the most appropriate of moments? As you see, he is but a few hours old and I am not from childbed.'

The man made no move to leave, or rebuke his handful of men who were ransacking the solar for things of value. Athelweard, who had married the only daughter of a minor ealdorman of western Wessex, had fancied for himself the inheritance of his father-in-law's title, but had been disappointed by Cnut's lack of sharing the same aspiration. Athelweard. So Emma's spies had been right, he was one of the dissenters who hoped that Cnut would not be coming home.

'I have taken control of Winchester,' he announced gruffly. 'The crown is mine, as is the treasury. I wish to take it. Now.'

Had it not been for the dour seriousness of his expression and the gleam of the blade in his hand, Emma would have burst into laughter. 'You want the crown?' she echoed, incredulous. 'Has my Lord Thorkell not uttered some word of objection to that? After all, I believe he is anxious to try its fit as soon as he finds the courage.' There was no proof for that statement, only suspicion, but strong suspicion, fuelled by well-whispered rumour.

'Thorkell cannot leave the palace,' Athelweard answered, his speech slurred. He was drunk, then. All the easier to deal with. 'My men hold him captive there.'

'Your men? You have an army?'

'I have half of Wessex with me,' Athelweard boasted. 'Cnut ought not have denied me my rights.'

'Only half of Wessex? Not the whole? Did the more important half, Godwine's, not like the idea of following your stupidity, then?'

503

Athelweard growled, waved his sword in her direction, his balance slightly top heavy.

Emma gathered a mantle to her shoulders, for the draught was intense with the outer door open. Where were her men? Those who ought be in the Hall below? Was her daughter, in the children's quarters, safe? 'The King did not slight you, he is waiting to offer you something greater when opportunity rises.' She might as well attempt bluff, while deciding what to do.

'Bull's shit.'

'If you think so.'

'I think so.' Athelweard's eyes flickered to the bolted door at the far end of the room. 'I want the King's Treasury.'

Emma waved her hand towards it. 'Then take it, there is nothing I can do to stop you.' *Where are my guards?* she was frantically thinking. *My servants? My housecarls? Oh God, what if Leofgifu is hurt . . . what if they harm my son?*

Apart from the persistence of the wind, its determination to gain entry as forcibly as this rabble, and the banging of a door somewhere, the Hall below was ominously quiet. Were they all dead? Why had she heard nothing? Huh, of course! Ale barrels had been taken around the town this evening for Winchester to celebrate the birth of her son. How many of her household were lying drunk in the streets? Athelweard had been at this Winter Council since the first week of December, clever of him to use the distraction of this given opportunity; he must have spent many hours convincing men to join him when chance presented itself, except Emma would never have credited the man to have been so cunning. If she had, she would have had him closer watched.

Shouting, suddenly, from the courtyard, the sound of fighting.

Athelweard ran for the door, his men ahead of him. Emma slid from the bed, stiff and sore – for all the ease of its coming, a babe leaves its mark on a woman's body during its birthing. The room was reeling, but she reached her son, lifted him from the cradle, waking him from sleep into shuddering wails of protest.

Slamming the outer door, Athelweard shouted for it to be barred, looked frantically for another route to leave by. The windows were small, not wide enough for a man to crawl through. Footsteps on the stairs, hammering on the door, a man desperately shouting Emma's name.

Leofstan! Oh, thank God, Emma thought, holding Harthacnut closer, jiggling him to attempt to quieten his distress.

Stunned, dizzy and disorientated, Leofgifu sat up, her face already bruising blue-black, blood matted into her hair. On her knees, she crawled across the floor, valiantly tried to stand, to shield her mistress and the boy.

The door was quivering, the wood splitting as an axe broke through, a face, angry, anxious, on the other side. Again the axe thundered down, the door shattered and Leofstan crashed into the room, rolling as he hit the floor and coming instantly to his feet. One of the men, hurrying forward to meet him, met instead with that axe. Leofgifu screamed as, shouldering her aside, Athelweard grabbed at Emma and the child, hauling her as a shield in front of him, his sword blade at her throat.

'Come one step closer, soldier, and I'll kill them both!'

Leofstan halted, stood half bent, the axe haft across his hands. 'Hurt the Queen or her son,' he breathed, eyes narrowed, talking low, 'and you'll regret the day the whore who spawned you ever spread her legs for the runt who sired you.'

Three more of Leofstan's men were coming through the door, their eyes locking with the scum who were standing, uncertain, looking from their master to the Queen, to Leofstan. One let his sword drop to the floor, the others followed his example.

'Sensible, your men,' Leofstan said, his voice growling menace. 'Let her go.'

Athelweard's arm tightened, the blade biting into her throat. She was barefooted, her chemise thin, the mantle only of light wool. Was her shivering from the cold, or fear? Athelweard let go of her waist, twined her loose hair into his fist, pulling her head back, pressing the sword deeper. 'I swear it,' he threatened, 'I'll cut her throat!' . . . And suddenly he was falling, taking Emma and the child down with him, the crash of the chamber pot crunching into skin and bone as Leofgifu smashed it hard across the nape of his neck,

505

urine and broken pottery scattering everywhere. An inglorious end to a foolish attempt at futile ambition.

Emma's inclination was to have Athelweard strung up by his privates there and then, but to kill him could prove damaging, for he had kindred and kindred were too often eager for the taking up of the blood-feud, and there was too much unrest in the West Country to risk fanning a few stray sparks into a full, burning blaze. Aside, death was too good, too quick for him, and a queen, a woman, was not permitted, through the respect of decency, to issue the order of a man to be killed. Ælfgifu of Northampton might stoop to the depth of indecency but she, Emma, would not.

For one month she left Athelweard to moulder, chained in the stink of a pigpen, while she decided what to do with him. When she had been purified from childbirth in the sight of God and was able to resume her duties as Queen, she had him publicly blinded and gelded, and declaring him *nithing*, outlaw, sent him into the dishonourable state of exile. A pity she could not deal as easily with Ælfgifu and Thorkell. Both were harbouring ideas beyond their reach, both, Emma would have been happy to see the back of. Both were as constantly irritating as winter chilblains, rubbed raw by a too-tight boot. And for both, she could do nothing, except sit and watch, and wait.

13

The rumour that Cnut had been personally responsible for murdering his brother was a whisper that rattled with the persistent March winds and wormed through every knot hole and under every ill-fitting door. Unlike some of the other, wilder rumours, this was one that Emma could quite believe and would have no trouble in accepting, for Harald was a lascivious rat and rats were better off dead, but until Cnut came home there would be no knowing of the details, or the truth. It was wrong to speculate, but with no counter advice, what could be done? Then, on the first day of the Easter calling of Council, a man and his wife came to Court with news that was to be received with opposite feelings by the Queen and England's appointed Regent.

Godwine, Earl of Wessex, brought home to England his bride, Gytha, sister-in-law to Cnut's sister, Estrith.

'By God's Grace, Godwine!' Emma declared as he sheepishly escorted his new wife into the Queen's chamber, 'I allow you to go off with my husband and you return, these months later, not only married but with a child on the way!'

The Danish woman, Gytha, blushed, but was content with the good-natured teasing. Smiling, she accepted the seat Emma indicated and joined in the entertainment of her husband's tale-telling.

'The King's fleet had not been in harbour at Roskilde for, I swear, more than an hour, before I saw this vision of loveliness before my eyes. Naturally, I asked her name and was delighted to discover her to be the sister of Ulf, husband to Estrith! I swept her a bow, kissed her hand and asked that I might make her my wife.'

'It was not like that at all,' Gytha protested, batting at him with her hand, 'my husband exaggerates somewhat, Madam.'

'Oh, I know Godwine well, Lady Gytha, you have no need to tell me of his storytelling capabilities!' Emma laughed. Instantly she had a liking for this bright-eyed, smiling woman who, although mild-mannered, had an air of one who would not tolerate nonsense within her household. Stern but fair, that was Gytha.

'Does it matter how we met?' Godwine interceded, laughing, 'I found the woman who has, through all my life, walked my dreams, and took her as wife.'

'Then such a blessed find must have reward,' Emma declared. 'What honour can I give you as a wedding gift?'

Gytha blushed, her hand coiling into Godwine's. 'The King has given us the manor of Bosham for our own,' Godwine said proudly. 'It will be a fitting place for my wife to bear our first child.'

Delighted, Emma clapped her hands. Bosham, across the inlet creek from Cnut's own highly favoured hunting manor on the south coast, a few miles from the town of Chichester. 'Then I insist on finding something of value for you to put in it. The place is sparsely furnished as I recall.' She thought a moment, glancing around the chamber, eyeing tapestries and wall hangings, furs on the floor, the carved chairs, oak table.

'I shall have a bed ordered made for you. Something grand, with a headboard carved from the finest elm, the faerie wood, to protect your sleep and guide in pleasant dreams.'

Godwine had always been a favourite and Emma was content that he had found the joy of happiness. Was pleased, and relieved also, that he brought her more than the prospect of a new and treasured friend, for he brought news of Cnut.

'Your husband has sent a letter to Thorkell. It is to be read at Council, and then copied and repeated by each priest of each church or chapel, abbey or minster, to be heard by all people throughout the land.'

Emma folded her hands in her lap, the laughter gone, replaced by annoyed jealousy. 'I see. The King wrote to Thorkell. Does he so easily trust the man?'

For his own mind, Godwine had thought it wrong of Cnut to give so much power to Thorkell, for if a man could change allegiance once, then twice again, could he not, as easily, change it on a third occasion?

Quickly he added, 'I have a copy for you, with the addition of a private letter, of course.' He clicked his fingers for a servant to fetch his saddlebag, rummaged inside, brought out two scrolls of parchment, one larger than the other. Graciously Emma took them and set the private one on a table. How she wanted to break the seal and read it! To remember the feel of Cnut's hands on her body, rekindle his scent, his voice, his touch. But she had guests and politeness dictated that she must wait for privacy.

Although only a wife of several months, Gytha was already learning her husband's frailties. Tact was not there among his strengths. 'I confess', she said, putting her hand to the swell of her abdomen, 'that the journey has tired me. May I beg your indulgence, my Lady, to retire to our chamber at the inn?'

Bless her, oh bless the woman! Emma thought.

The private letter was brief but sincere. After reporting that he was well, and that he had much to tell her, he wrote:

As you once suggested, I have decided to fetch my daughter, Ragnhilda, from the Isle of Orkney. I can no longer risk her falling into the hands of the Scots' King. I like it not that there is as much of a struggle between the lairds of the Clans as there was between myself and my brother. My dear, as you will learn from the letter I ask my trusted friend and aide, Thorkell, to recite, I had no option but to be done with Harald, for the good of Denmark, and for the peace of England. My fear is that there may also come a bloody ending in Scotland before long. I will not have my daughter ensnared within it.

He had killed Harald, then. She would not be shedding tears for him, an obnoxious man who deserved to die. So Cnut was to go to Orkney first, would then sail to York to ensure the North was aware of his homecoming? Did he intend to visit the Bitch in Northampton, as he had on the outward journey? Oh, Emma knew of the diversion! Knew that he had stayed a day and a night at her manor.

How to stop him? Thoughtfully Emma rolled the parchment and put it within her jewel casket, among her other personal treasures. How to stop him making a repeat visit to his whore?

'So Cnut is homeward bound?' Thorkell said to Leofric of Mercia, a man with whom he had found he shared much in common. A dislike of Godwine Wulfnothsson being high among the tally.

'And the Queen is to go to York to meet him?'

'We all know why she is going northwards, Leofric, and it is not to meet the King, but to stop him meeting someone else.'

'Aye, my kinswoman, Ælfgifu.' Leofric grimaced. He had no fondness for Ælfgifu, a woman who held too high an opinion of herself, who came close, too often, to bringing shame into the family. 'She wants her son as king after Cnut.'

'What we want and what we get', Thorkell remarked tartly, 'are often two different things.' There was much that he wanted, would possibly never get.

Leofric snorted disdain, aye, he would drink to that remark! He wanted to be made Earl of Mercia in the place of authority that Eadric Streona had occupied, but Emma, the Queen, had consistently blocked its giving and Cnut had sailed to Denmark before anything further could be done.

'What of you, Thorkell?' he asked. 'You are already Earl and Regent, what more could you wish granted?' It was said in all innocence, as casual conversation. Leofric did not expect the answer he got.

'England, my friend. I want England.'

14

York had been a pleasant place to stay, but now that the heat was increasing, Emma desired somewhere cooler, for York was cramped and crowded, and as with all cities had, once the days began to grow warmer, soon become aromatically unbearable. Cnut was supposed to have arrived several weeks ago, but something was delaying him – how glad Emma was that she was here, for otherwise she would have been convinced the delay was an excuse for a planned diversion. He knew she was waiting for him, for Cnut insisted on keeping a close eye on the set of a sail, his letters came weekly, giving orders, making suggestions, reminding her of things she had remembered perfectly well for herself. They had been welcome at first, but now Emma was at the point of tossing the next one direct into the fire. Damn the man, if he did not trust her judgement, then why did he not stir himself and come home? And if he wrote, once more, that he had much to tell her that was for her ears alone she would scream aloud!

Her choice of riding north to the abbey at Whitby had been a good one; the coast was cooler, the ride enjoyable and the destination, hopefully, inspiring. Only there was someone at Whitby, within the nunnery, who was not pleased to see her. The coming of the Queen, in fact, briefly turned the abbey inside out.

Ealdgyth, widow of Edmund Ironside, sat on a rock watching the ceaseless movement of the sea, the evening sun warm on her face, the sea wind whispering in her ears and toying with her hair. She had removed her veil and shoes to walk along the sand, and unbound the tight braid of her chestnut hair, for she enjoyed the feel of the freedom. If she had the courage she would have stripped naked to plunge into the breakers, but someone was bound to see and such immodesty would upset the nuns. She had no wish to do that, for apart from the austerity of the Abbess, who ruled with iron discipline, they had been kind to her and kindness in an unkind, hostile world was a thing to be richly cherished.

The tide had turned, was retreating, leaving a widening ribbon of wet, soft sand. She ought to return up the cliff path, for it would be Compline soon and the children would be wanting to say goodnight. She sat, her elbows resting on her knees, chin on her laced hands. Usually the unaltering daily rhythm of the abbey was as soothing and comforting as the regular pulse of the tide, but not this evening. This afternoon, everything had been flung up in the air, to fall again, higgle-piggle, muddled and fraught with danger.

The sky began to turn from its azure blue into streaks of reds and golds as the sun dipped lower, and was suddenly filled by a rushing of wings as birds gathered to follow the falling tide line. Widgeon whistling ahead of the wind, geese in their family groups, alighting on the sand and unsettling the flocks of dunlin. Turnstones were already rooting busily among the tide-stranded lines of decaying seaweed. The air was filled with noise and the heady scent of wet sand, seaweed and the salt tang of the sea. Still she sat there, staring, her thoughts blank, her heart heavy. The only movement a single tear that trailed, like a glistening diamond, down her cheek. A curlew flew out over the water, its forlorn cry so eternally lonely. A second tear rolled after the first.

She was a fool to have thought that this sanctuary would have remained undiscovered for ever. Someone was bound to have found her eventually, was it provident that the finder was the Queen? Surely she would understand? She was a mother. A man, a king, would not turn blind eyes to the sons of the king who had come before him. But would Emma?

The sun sank into the sea, modifying the sky to vibrant shades of glorious colour. If she did not go soon, the nunnery gates would be closed and the porter would grumble at her. Shells crunching underfoot alerted her, someone else was walking on the beach, another woman. Ealdgyth knew she ought to stand, bob a reverence, but the effort was too much, the feeling that she did not care what the Queen thought of her poor manners flooded her misery.

Emma's shadow fell between Ealdgyth and the shouted remnant of the spectacular sunset. Respecting the other woman's silence and solitude, she seated herself on another nearby rock. Said nothing.

'Those are oystercatchers out there,' Ealdgyth said, her voice distant, blank. 'Do you see them, hacking and stabbing at the mussels? The creatures in their blue-black shells try to burrow deeper into the sand, to hide, but the birds find them, jab at them with their spear-like beaks and they are caught, exposed and devoured.' She turned her head to look steadily at Emma, her eyes, tearless now, unblinking. 'I understand how it feels to be a mussel desperately trying to hide in my shell, knowing that at any moment I shall be torn open and ended.'

Emma sat, much as Ealdgyth had done, elbows on knees, chin on hand. The surprise at discovering her here at Whitby had stunned her – the Abbess had informed her almost immediately upon her arrival, covering herself, no doubt, in case Cnut should be angry. Which he would. He had been wanting to know the whereabouts of Ealdgyth and her sons since the day of Edmund's death. It was a mark of lasting respect for Edmund, and for his widow, that the silence had been held so long.

'They are devoured in great quantity, as you say,' Emma said into the twilight, 'yet, on the morrow there will be as many more mussels in the sand. And on the day after that, and the day after that. As with most things, it is the strong, or the cunning, who survive.'

'*The Lady Ealdgyth is here with her two sons and a few servants,*' the Abbess had declared with defensive haste and, shifting the blame, should there be any, had added, '*She came at the request of our Archbishop, Wulfstan.*'

Through the years Emma had learnt to judge people by her first impression. So far, her initial assessment had rarely proved wrong. Save perhaps for Cnut himself, but then, if she was to be honest with herself, her first thoughts of him had been accurate: ambitious, vain, his presumptuous brashness a public shield against his inner self-doubt. For the Abbess, dislike. If there was any compassion or pity within this woman it had been sucked from her years ago.

513

'*Cnut has no care for the widow of a dead king,*' Emma had lied. All the same, she had seen her two children settled into their guest quarters and walked down the steep cliff pathway of cut steps to the beach.

'I was told I would find you here,' Emma explained, deliberately keeping her voice friendly and companionable. 'I understand you often walk along the beach of an evening.' She laughed lightly. 'The Abbess told me all this as if you were a heathen worshipping the Devil, or selling your body as a whore!'

Ealdgyth forced a timid smile. 'The Abbess is a good woman at heart, but she worries about what others may think of her. She wants to be remembered as a good and holy woman, who did her duty to God. She has forgotten that sometimes, holiness begins with the living, not the evermore of the afterlife.'

Brushing the dried sand from her feet, Ealdgyth started pulling on her boots, then reached for her hair and nimbly began its rebraiding. Said, on an indrawn breath, 'I would like to trust that now he has found them, the King will not harm my children, but I have seen for myself what he has done to the sons of other mothers. Sons with far less importance than my two lambs.' The heartache wrenched at her faltering voice and with difficulty she swallowed the tears. All these years of hoping that she would be forgotten, that no one would come looking for her, knowing, knowing, that one day someone would.

'I did not wholly love Edmund, how could I? I barely knew him, but he was a good man and he treated me with kindness. Love would have grown between us for it was there, in bud, ready to break into bloom. He came for me when I needed someone to pull me from the drowning mud. For that alone I began to love him.' She said it as if she had to justify herself, explain something, something she herself did not fully understand.

In her way, Emma knew what she meant. Had the mud, once, a lifetime ago, not almost choked her too? She remembered the darkness, the sensation of being unable to breathe, to feel nothing but cold emptiness clammy on your skin; to ache for the solidity of friendship and that butterfly touch of love.

514

'I loved Sigeferth; he was my light, my life. I could not believe that he chose me as his wife.' Ealdgyth paused, her eyes drifting over the swaying movement of the sea. 'He did not deserve that hideous death.' She again looked at Emma and the Queen recognised the wild despair of hopelessness in her eyes. 'I see him every night in my dreams. I see that death over and over in my mind. The light going from his eyes, the life straining from his swollen tongue. And then I see the same death for my sons, only it is a different king laughing as they hang there. It is your other husband, Cnut.'

A single orb of brightness, low down on the horizon, glinted against the darkening blue of the sky. The Evening Star, Venus.

'My husband is not with me,' Emma answered, her hand moving to cover the other woman's. It was cold to Emma's touch, shaking slightly. 'He is in the Orkney Islands still, although he will be coming any day soon. It is by chance that I came to pay my respect to the shrine of Saint Hilda. I did not know you were here.'

'But you know now.' Her despair was absolute.

Yes, she knew now. Those two living sons were a threat to Cnut. Their father had been the lawful anointed King, a king who had died honourably from wounds received in battle defending his kingdom and his people. They had every right to the title ætheling, to claim their legitimacy as kingworthy. And once they were grown, they would be a threat to Cnut and to his son, her son, Harthacnut, who lay even now, sleeping in a bed alongside these other two boys.

'I am tired of hiding,' Ealdgyth said, the weariness evident. 'I can run no more. Not even for my sons.'

'Then would you give them up?' Emma said sharply. As she had given up hers? Ah, but then her giving had been different; by sending them into Normandy, she had saved Edward and Alfred from a certain death. Cnut could not have permitted them to live had they remained in England. And it had been no hardship for Emma to see them go, they were Æthelred's sons and she had been only too pleased to shed everything that reminded her of his foul stink, his loathsome touch. If she had to part with Harthacnut . . . that she could not, would not, do.

'Your sons are a danger to my son,' Emma said candidly, 'but they are also a danger to other sons of Cnut. Sons who are older than the child I bore seven months past, sons who have the tainted blood of a whore in their veins.'

Emma stood, brushed sand from her gown, her decision made. Mayhap it was the wrong one, but how could the killing of the innocent be right? 'It grows late and the sea air and the ride here have tired me. I would seek my bed. And we have yet to climb all those steps to the top of this cliff.' She held out her hand to Ealdgyth. 'I would be friends with you, for there is no reason for us to be enemies, provided I have your word that you will not send your sons against mine.' This was foolishness and Emma knew it. Even if Ealdgyth gave her word, what was to guarantee that those sons would not go against it when they were grown? But every woman was entitled to be a fool once in her life.

Ealdgyth's smile as she hesitantly took Emma's hand in her own was infinitely sad. 'I have no wish to see my sons dead, my Lady Queen. I have seen enough of death for it to sicken me to the pit of my stomach. All I want is peace and somewhere safe to sleep at night, without the fear of dreams.'

The moon was rising, its great, smiling circle coming up out of the sea, turning the world silver beneath its benign breath. Emma felt that all she had to do was step on to the reflected path that shimmered across the shifting waves and she would be able to touch it with her outstretched fingers. Soon, there would be ships on that sea, dragon ships with their colourful sails proud-filled, the spindrift curling at their prows. Cnut's ships.

'The moon is bright,' Emma said, 'bright enough to light any road that a woman might wish to take, where eyes cannot follow her, or death stalk in her wake. Follow the moon,' she advised, 'for she is one of us, a mother, with the cycle of the month around and who cares for, and loves, her children.'

Emma remained at Whitby Abbey for three days and not once during her stay did she mention her first evening, her walk along the shore or her meeting with a woman seated there on a rock, a tired woman, who had watched the oystercatchers rummaging for hidden prey. Emma stayed silent, even when, much later, the rumours came that a ship had sailed from York, with a sad-eyed woman and her two small sons, heading across the North Sea to a distant land beyond the reach of Denmark, no matter how long an arm the King might have; to where they spoke in a different tongue and followed different ways.

If ever Emma heard that this woman had found a new life for her sons in a place called Prague, and that one day the boy called Ædward would find a wife and raise his own son and two daughters near the straggling town of Budapest, she never said anything.

15

Cnut's ships sailed into York along the Ouse, their coming causing
a stir of excitement that brought the townsfolk running to the river,
with Archbishop Wulfstan approaching at a more dignified pace,
but nonetheless eager to greet his King. Hope that God had
benevolently set aside his wrath for another millennium had taken
root in the Archbishop. With Cnut's ship, *Sea Serpent*, turning out
of the current, her sail lowered and oars stroking the water to bring
her around, he felt he could at last believe in the prospect of lasting
peace.

The wharves were always busy, without the influx of gawping
sightseers and Cnut's fleet of twenty warships making the river itself
as crowded, for York, the capital of the North, was a trading centre
on a par with London. Ships were being loaded or unloaded with
cargo: fish, oil, salt; cloth, wool, pottery, everything and anything
that could be bought, sold or traded was stacked high or stored in
barrels and bales.

To the far side of the river were the sailmakers' bothies, the
huge looms, the spars and frames to shape and stretch the wool
into the great square sails. Wool from the fell and dale sheep,
with their double-layered coat used as the most efficient cloth for
sails, the outer waterproof layer proving light in weight but strong
in resilience and wear, while the softer inner layer served for
warm garments for seafaring men. To the right of the sailmakers
the rope makers, with the bales of raw hemp towering in stacked
piles; then the shipbuilders, the repair workers; the bank of the
river, as far as the eye could see, busy with the people of a water
world.

On the townward side of the living waterway the warehouses, the
traders' stalls, the bustle and clamour of a crowded dockside. Cnut

stood on the deck of his ship looking at it all, his men grinning, as eager as he to throw the mooring ropes ashore and make fast.

'Wulfstan!' Cnut called, seeing the Archbishop standing surrounded by an array of monks and priests, 'it is good to see you, my friend!'

'As it is good to see you, my Lord!' Wulfstan tossed back, lifting his voice to be heard above the cacophony of noise.

At the last minute the oarsmen lifted the oars out of the water, holding them upright; as if a leafless forest had suddenly sprung from the decks, and Sea Serpent bumped gently against the wharfside, men on land reaching eagerly to secure her. Cnut leapt from the deck, strode to the Archbishop and greeted him with an embrace of enthusiasm. A greeting as warmly returned.

'What, no wife to hale me also?' Cnut boomed good-natured, looking about him, searching through the faces and the out-stretched hands reaching forward to touch him, slap his shoulders, clasp his arm. 'Where is she? Waiting to greet me at the palace, I assume, disgruntled because I took longer than I intended?'

Wulfstan spread his hands, placating. 'Alas, not expecting you, she is not here. The Queen rode to Whitby to worship at the shrine of Saint Hilda. We hope for her return within the day or two.'

Hiding his disappointment, Cnut made the best of it, keeping the grin, making a jest of things. 'Perhaps it is as well. I can hardly be berated for my late homecoming if she is later than me, eh?'

A woman, a maidservant, was being helped from the ship, in her arms a bewildered girl child. Cnut caught sight of her, hurried forward to take the girl, her face immediately lighting into pleasure, her arms and legs winding tight around his body.

'My lord Archbishop,' Cnut announced, 'may I present my daughter, the Princess Ragnhilda? She has been in Orkney this past while, but is to live with me now, as befits the daughter of a king.' Quieter, the frustration showing through, added, 'I was hoping my wife would be here to meet her.'

He shrugged, joggled the girl in his arms, playfully bouncing her up and down until she giggled, and became more at ease among all these strange faces and voices. 'We'll not let that bother us, though, will we, my honeycomb *skat*? Gone to Whitby you say, Wulfstan? Hie then, bring up the horses, my daughter and I shall ride to join her!'

16

The sky was as blue as a kingfisher's feather, the day as hot as a smith's forge and as airless as a wax-sealed barrel. Divesting herself of her wimple and cloak had made little difference, Emma had felt as if she were melting. If only there were a wind, a breeze! Deciding to take the coastal road south, the Queen's entourage had made slow progress, for it was too hot to push the ponies into anything more than an amble; aside, what was the rush? There was no need to hurry to York, and Emma was enjoying her holiday from routine and the responsibilities and restraints of Court. The sea route beckoned more than the high, desolate sweep of lonely moorland, and the intrigue of visiting Leofgifu's place of childhood irresistible. The woman had spoken of nothing else since coming north. York had been interesting, Whitby spiritually uplifting, but the cove near to where Leofgifu had been born and raised was alluring. The full delights of paddling in rock pools were beyond the enjoyment of the children, for Harthacnut was barely turned the seven-month and Gunnhild only in her second year, but Emma had developed a liking for this wild, rough coast and wanted more of its exciting freedom, while she had chance to enjoy it for herself alone. The dull, flat beaches of Normandy, with their windswept, shape-shifting dunes, were expanses of sand that went on for ever. She had never much liked those beaches. Dramatic cliffs hovering above a restless, sparkling sea, islands of warm sand all entangled within outcrops of jumbled seaweed and barnacle-encrusted rock, was a lure too tempting for Emma to ignore. She was not, however, prepared for the heart-stopping fear of the narrow track along the grass-covered clifftop abruptly toppling into the nowhere infinity of the sky.

'Oh my God!' she exclaimed with a high, girlish laugh as the three men ahead of her suddenly disappeared over the edge. 'This is like leaping off the world!' Leofgifu, riding a similar sturdy hill pony, chuckled. This was her home, these moors and cliffs; married, she had lived amid the stench and confine of York, but as a child she had intimately known this coast, its high cliffs and ragged rocks, the sweep and curve of the bays, the constant voice of the sea.

'You keep your weight backward in the saddle, my Lady, and let the pony pick his way down; you'll be safe, don't fret, these ponies are as surefooted as goats.' For Leofgifu, this was the memory of childhood and younger years, when every day had been filled with sunshine and the heat of summer. That the winters had been harsh, the seas unforgiving and her merchant father often gone for months at a time entirely forgotten.

'Our steading', Leofgifu explained, 'was two miles over yonder.' She tossed her hand westward. 'But my brothers and me, well, we came down here to Green Man Bay nigh on every day, when it were not thick with snow or raining fit to drown us.'

It was all gone now, her childhood, the steading burnt out by raiders, her family, save for a favourite nephew and a scatter of cousins, all dead. The nephew, a lanky youth on the verge of manhood, to his exuberant delight, was riding with them.

The track was steep, almost sheer in places, winding downwards through a straggle of woodland and undergrowth that abounded to either side of a tumbling stream that leapt and gurgled from rock to rock in a torrent of white, chattering foam.

Once, in the lives of the little dark people who populated the hills and dales before the coming of the Roman Red Crests, all the coast was woodland, thick, heavy forests that began at the cliff edge and swept inwards up and across the moors, harbouring wolf and bear, and the spirit people. The Green Man, the Hooded Man of the Woods – he had the honour of several titles – once lived here it was said, in this steep-sided ravine that ran down through the sheer cliff to the sea. His hut had been built in the cleft of the valley above the shoreline, and he had lived on the fish of the ocean and the roots and berries of the earth. One night, he had fallen during a storm and had lain among the rocks, his back broken, unable to move, crawl or heave himself away from the incoming crash of the tide. They had found him, drowned. You could hear him, the local fishermen said, on those nights when the wind moaned and the sea roared, hear him calling for the gods of that time to help him, but they had not listened.

'All he had to do was call on Christ,' Leofgifu recounted as the ponies picked their way, one steady foot after the other, down the worn path. 'If he had turned his face from those heathen, mean-spirited evildoers and called for God, then he would have been saved. The Green Man cared for the woodland creatures and the birds of the air, and for the human people who came here to this cove for the skill of his healing.' Leofgifu sighed, shook her head. 'God would have saved him, had he only called.'

Turning to check the children were safe, held tight within the firm clutches of two housecarls, Emma smiled. She had heard the tale of the Green Man already; another reason to come here, to see for herself where the legend had begun.

With the incline shallowing, the trees parted and the blue sea, beyond a wide expanse of sand, opened up before them. Kicking her pony to a trot, Emma urged it out into the open and turned, gawp-mouthed to crane upwards at the height of the soaring cliffs, the V of the ravine, cutting direct through them, as if sliced with a sharpened sword. She kicked her feet from the stirrups and jumped to the sand, laughing as her boots sank into the sun-warmed softness.

'Come,' she called to Leofgifu as she reached up to take the babe, Harthacnut, 'I would like nothing more than to sit here and let the sun bake me.'

Lulled by the song of the outward-going sea and the whisper of the wind, they all slept, stretched out on the sand or the flat rocks, the children included; even the ponies, hind hooves resting, heads down, ears lolling, eyes closed. The men on guard dozed. What harm would come to them here on an isolated beach at the foot of the cliffs?

Harthacnut woke first, demanding the attention of his wet-nurse, who took him away to the shade of a sentinel rock beneath the cliff to satisfy his appetite. Emma, awake now, stretched lazily, stood, brushed the sand from her gown. The tide was far out, exposing the wide sweep of the curved bay, sun-gold sand and blue, blue sea. She bent, dabbled her hand in the cool bubble of the freshwater steam, moistened her lips and bathed her hot face and neck. How long would it be before Cnut returned? She had begun to think this journey north to meet him had been a fool's errand, that perhaps he had no intention of coming to York, but of going straight to the Humber and that bitch. She splashed her hand into the rush of the water, sending up a fountain of spray. Damn him! Damn all men.

The wet-nurse was winding Harthacnut, the child sprawled over her shoulder, her hand patting his back, a task Emma did not object to doing herself. Strange how she enjoyed tending these two babes, but had so loathed the touch of the two boys, Edward and Alfred.

'Let me take him,' Emma offered, lifting her son into her arms and wandering along the sand as she soothed his whimpering. He was not a fretful child, but he took a while to settle after feeding; colic, the wet-nurse said, but Emma thought it interest and intelligence, for he would look keenly at the world through his wide babe's eyes, instantly attracted by movement, colour and sound.

'Look at the gulls!' Emma said, turning him to watch the swoop of the birds as they dived on what appeared to be the beached carcass of a dolphin. Wandering along, in the way that mothers do, Emma pointed out other things: the waders at the sea edge, the dazzle of the sun on the shining blueness, the white-patterned foam of the rolling breakers. Here and there, tables of flat rocks that peeped through the shingly sand, as if some giant child had stamped on them in a fit of temper.

She paused by a shallow pool, poked in it with her fingers, disturbing a crab that scuttled sideways, its claws snapping irritably at the intrusion. Whether Harthacnut watched or understood she did not care or mind, for she felt at ease, comfortable, were it not for that niggling doubt of Cnut's intentions, happy.

With the child draped, content, over her shoulder, she wandered on, deep in thoughts of everything and nothing, drifting along the beach as if she were tide-nudged flotsam. A lullaby that she remembered her mother singing came to mind and she hummed its tune, hesitantly at first, the memory of the words rekindling as she gained confidence in her singing voice. Emma walked, relishing the quiet, the unique pleasure of being alone with her son.

The bay curved, imperceptibly as she wandered, only obvious from the bend of the cliffs running ahead and behind, flanked by the two arms of jutting headland, three miles apart as the gull flew, an added mile along the sweeping arc of the beach. Beneath the cliffs, a massive tumble of rocks lurched into the sand. She had walked far enough. Gathering her gown in one hand, she seated herself on a boulder that had a worn hollow the size and shape of her behind. The others of her party, she was surprised to see as she looked back along the meander of the beach, were far off, more than a mile away; they must still be sleeping for she could not see them moving about. Hah! Lazy lumps! She would retrace her steps in a moment, but Harthacnut was sleeping soundly and the walk had tired her, harder work than she had realised, trudging through that sand. Resting her free shoulder on the rocks, she tipped her head, closed her eyes. Dozed. Dreamt of Cnut beckoning her into a haze of white, brilliant light; dreamt of distant voices calling from across a vast and empty ocean, voices that changed to the high, persistent scream of the gulls and the rasping cough of the corncrakes.

Spindrift, carried by the wind, touched her face, jerking her awake. She was startled, momentarily lost and disorientated, the dream of the gulls and kittiwakes interloping into reality. Automatically, her fingers clasped at the baby, gripping into the linen folds that swaddled him as he stirred and grumbled, her eyes widening into circles of horror, an indrawn breath gasping into her throat. The sea was returning, the tide sweeping in! She stood, her foot slipping on a frond of seaweed, the curve of the beach obvious now, now that the sea had filled more than half of it! She started walking, forcing her mind from another bay she knew, one somewhat larger, admitted, but Mont Saint-Michel was a place both beautiful and deadly, the island where the new abbey stood, the buildings clinging like goats to the rock face, more notorious for the speed of the incoming tide than its religious fervour. As a child, Emma had always been afraid of going there, fancying she could hear the cries of the dead as they drowned in the sea that came in across the flat sands faster than a man could run. This was not Normandy, she chided herself as she walked, willing her feet to push quicker through the cloying sand that seemed determined to slow her down. She could see the others, tiny specks in the distance running towards her, two of the men attempting to urge ponies into the spreading water of a channel that separated her from them, the animals refusing to move forward, perhaps for fear of the sea, or the shifting sand beneath their hooves. Leofgifu was waving her arms, shouting, but not a word reached Emma's ears. She stopped walking, her path was barred, the sea had run in over the sand, galloping up the flat expanse and flooding into the hollows. There remained the wide half-moon crescent of gold beneath the dominating cliffs, but without a boat there was now no way off this beach. Emma stared out at the sea, its bobbing blueness, the sun sparkle, the dance of foam, willing a sail to appear over the horizon. The one moment in her life when she would board a ship without hesitation, and there was nothing here to carry her away.

Panic began to swell. In her mind, she heard, again, the moans of the drowned at Mont Saint-Michel. She clutched Harthacnut in her arms; the child, sensing her growing unease, starting to whimper. How far did the sea come in? Would there be enough beach for her to sit, wait it out? Think! Keep calm! Use your brain, woman!

A line of debris nuzzled close against the cliff base. Driftwood, rotting seaweed, fish bones, the remains of dead marine life; broken barrel staves, half a cracked wine jar; a tangle of frayed rope. Incongruously, a torn and battered boot. The cliffs were the tide line, then. Could she swim? The current would be strong for the tide was not coming in straight but from several angles and, aside, she was no fine swimmer. She remembered asking her papa why the men caught in the tide at Saint-Michel did not swim.

'They do, *ma petite*, but their boots weigh them down, their clothing becomes saturated and clings, and they tire. They try to swim, but the tide is stronger than the muscles of a man's arms. The tide always wins.'

526

And what of Harthacnut? How could she swim with him in her arms? She looked again at the cliffs, soaring upwards seemingly to touch against the blue sky. There were patterns, horizontal lines in the rock, as if someone had built them in layers, one set down on top of another. Further along, to her left, the lines split, offset, one side pushed lower than the other. How could she know that this massive cliff-face had once lain beneath a primeval ocean, at a distance of time immeasurable in human understanding? That these rocks had formed, over a period of millions and millions of years, from the crushing weight of mud, grains of silt and the bones and shells of weird and wonderful creatures?

She was not a fish, she could not swim, nor a bird able to fly. As she looked and watched, she could see the unstoppable encroachment of the sea coming closer. She did not know how long she had left, but sense told her that she could not remain standing here, doing nothing. Quicker to die trying to swim, to drown in a matter of moments, rather than wait, let death come slowly creeping? She looked again up the sheer face, at the crannies and pockets where tufts of sea grass clawed a life and scattered puddles of colour bloomed in mats of salt-tolerant flowers; at the birds, the gulls, kittiwakes and guillemots. Leofgifu had told her of the birds, how her brothers used to climb down for the eggs; the kittiwakes clinging precariously to solitary perches, the guillemots standing in long, serried ranks along straight ledges. The razorbills who preferred nooks and crevices. Out on the jagged crops of rocks, most of them now surrounded by sea, the cormorants and gannets were busy fishing, diving into the swirl of the current, emerging, feathers wet and glistening, with a shining silver fish between their spear-beaks.

Leofgifu's brothers had climbed down these cliffs to collect eggs. Always, their mother boxed their ears for risking the danger; always, she had been pleased at the clutch of carefully held eggs. Climbed down? If they came down, they must have gone up again? Concentrating, Emma studied the rock face, jiggling Harthacnut in her arms against his increasing fretfulness. There was a foothold, there a handhold. From that crevice to that niche . . . could she?

527

Dare she? The tide had slithered another ten yards. Carefully she laid Harthacnut down, propping him between two rocks and cushioned on a bed of sand, she would try a yard or two, see if it were possible, found as she set her foot in a hollow that the apparent solid rock crumbled into flakes of shale. She tried again, choosing something that looked firmer to take her weight, felt with her fingers, and pushing and pulling climbed to a height of eight feet, then her boot slipped and, with a gasp, she found herself dangling, holding on by her fingertips. She kicked with her feet, trying to locate a hollow, then fell, bundling into the sand. She was no more hurt than if she had taken a tumble from a horse, but she had been fortunate to land on soft sand not hard rock. A fall of a few feet was no difficulty, but how high did these cliffs soar? A hundred, two hundred feet? More? To fall would be to die. To stay would be to die.

Her boots and stockings must go, the leather sole had no grip and she would do better to feel with her toes. Harthacnut? How was she to carry him, yet keep her hands free? A sling? Yes, it would give her more freedom of movement to remove her outer tunic, the over-dress hung in more elaborate folds than the under-dress. Quickly, her fingers trembling, she unthreaded the side lacings and slipped out of the garment. The under-dress was of linen also, but plainer and draped straighter, she would have to gather it up to allow for climbing. She bunched the gown through the braiding of her girdle, so that the skirt hung to her knees, not her ankles, then pondered how best to make a carrying sling for the baby. If only she had her veil, had not left it with Leofgifu! Ah, but then it was made of a fine weave, thin enough to be almost gauze, perhaps it would not have been suitable. Her over-gown had been one of exceptional quality, a shame to rip it, but rip it she must. Tearing along the side seam, she split the garment in two, then worked on loosening the one front panel, using her teeth to cut through the stitching at the neck. She had no cloak pins or brooches, they were on the pack ponies, but there was sufficient material to wind criss-cross round her chest and neck, to make a safe and secure knot. For extra security she tucked the ends through the girdle band, tied it tighter, a thick braid of strong, coloured silks.

Harthacnut was crying. She lifted him, jiggled him in her arms, distracting his attention, then eased him into the crossed sling so that he lay against her breasts, aware that his weight was more than she had allowed for. He seemed of no consequence sleeping across her shoulder, but was heavy slung across her chest, the drag on her neck already causing the muscles to ache. She checked the knots, looked again at the horizon. No proud fleet of dragon ships, no flotilla of fishing craft. Along the beach the men had not persuaded the ponies to swim, they could not reach her. Through the trees of the descending ravine she caught a glimpse of movement going upwards at speed, the bright red of a tunic. Elfric Wihtgarsson, Leofgifu's nephew. They had teased the young man mercilessly about the brightness of that tunic. Was he racing up to the clifftop to summon help? Who from? There were no farms or fishermen's huts along this wind-tousled stretch of coast and Whitby was miles away.

'Ssh, baby,' she soothed, stroking Harthacnut's curl of red-gold hair. Taking a breath, she reached up and clasped her fingers into a crevice, and lifted her foot into another. Began nervously humming the lullaby again. But perhaps because she had come from Whitby, or because of the story of the Green Man, who would have been helped had he only called on God, a holy song filled her mind. Cædmon had once been a monk and a poet at the abbey, unable to sing until inspired by a dream sent by God. Between breaths and cautious movement, she sang Cædmon's hymn, 'Nü scylum hergen hefænrïcdæs Uard':

> Now must we praise the Guardian of Heaven,
> The power and conception of the Lord,
> And all His works, as He, eternal Lord,
> Father of glory, started every wonder.

She swallowed hard, bit down the scream as her hand missed a hold and rocks crumbled.

> First He created Heaven as a roof.
> The holy Maker, for the sons of man . . .

Grasping at a grass tussock she paused, steadied her breathing, dared a glance downwards, regretted it. She had climbed fifteen feet, too far to fall. Harthacnut had ceased his crying, was silent. She smiled at him. 'Well, my sweeting, this is a fine way to journey, is it not?' Her legs were shaking, her arms aching. She climbed on, feeling carefully with her fingers, touching with her toes, ignored the sweat as it trickled down her back and between her breasts, the abrasive sores on her hands and feet that were already become scraped raw.

> Then the eternal Keeper of mankind
> Furnished the earth below, the land for men . . .

'Almightly God and everlasting Lord . . . Why in damned Hell did you have to create the bloody sea and these sodding cliffs?' The words sobbed from her as she shoved loose rock from a crevice, startling a nesting bird a few yards to her right. Many of them were in flight, one alerted by another, flocks of kittiwakes screaming their annoyance, gulls swooping at her. There had been no wind on the beach, but up here it was cold, a salt breeze blowing in off the sea. She risked another look down. The first waves were lapping at the base of the cliff, the tide almost full in. As far to go upwards now, as it was to go down.

In a bird-dropping-filled crack, her fingers moved a stone, cold and hard. She made to toss it aside, noticed its coiled shape. She had seen these at Whitby, lying on the beach or embedded in the rocks, some small, as tiny as a thumbnail, others as large as a cartwheel. Sea snakes, they called them, Saint Hilda's Serpents, for her command had petrified the evil creatures, turned them all to stone. There were other shapes in the rock, solidified bones, the imprints of shells and fronds that looked like bracken. Shapes that to a mind already filled with fear added more dread.

'Will we be turned to stone, eh, my dumpling?' Emma said to the child through ragged, uneven breath. 'If we cling here long enough, will someone, one day, find our bones squashed into this rock face?'

A clump of samphire fell from above, hitting her shoulder, as well it was nothing more than earth and plant. She looked up, distant faces, small against the sky, were peering down at her, Elfric in his red tunic; his aunt, Leofgifu, her veil askew, tears streaming; Leofstan, her Captain, white-faced, at a loss what to do. If they were calling to her she could not hear for the singing of the wind and the shrilling of the birds. Incongruously – she ought to be concentrating on where next to grip her hand, set her foot – she noticed a family of black ravens swirling among the clamour of the white gulls.

'Odin's birds,' Emma explained to Harthacnut as she hauled herself up through another four agonising yards. Every muscle in her body was shrilling as loud as those gulls. 'His two messengers were ravens, "Hugin" and "Munin", Thought and Memory.' Another yard, slightly to the left to avoid a solid outcrop that yielded no handhold. 'The birds of the battlefield.' Wished she had not considered that aspect of the great black birds. Were they hovering, waiting for her to fall, waiting to pick her bones? Their croak could be heard from a distance of more than half a mile, their flight graceful and spectacular, a mating pair tumbling and playing together in flight, rolling to their backs and dropping downwards . . . another thought that Emma wished had not entered her mind.

Blood was oozing from the cuts and grazes on her fingers and palms, the fingers themselves swollen, too stiff to move, often locking, refusing to bend. Her feet, too, although she could only feel, not see, were as badly mauled. She was tiring. Should she stop, rest? She set her forehead against the rock, closed her eyes; her legs felt like lead, shook like the jelly-ooze of bone-marrow, her arms a dead weight. Just let go . . . Harthacnut, whimpering again: it felt as if she had slung a millstone weight around her neck. Best to keep going, find the strength, the energy. So much easier to push off into the clear air and fly with the birds . . . keep going! Easing slowly, right hand, left. Left foot, right. They were trying to lower a rope made from joined reins, stirrup leathers, harness; Elfric and Leofstan lying on their stomachs, leaning over, leaning down. It would not be long enough! Nothing would be long enough! Her foot crunched into something, an abandoned nest, cracking open the eggs, the pungent sulphur smell wafting into her nose, gagging in her throat. On. Climb! Climb!

Then the sling ripped, Emma heard it, the tear as the weakened material gave way. Felt the weight suddenly ease from her neck as Harthacnut began to slide down her chest and stomach, what was left of her tunic fluttering away from her legs, sailing lazily, turning and twisting in the breeze. She did not have the breath to scream, but her heart lurched, the sickness rising from her stomach and her head spinning dizzily. Every fibre of her body was trembling as she pressed inwards to stop the baby from falling, hold him tight between the cliff face and her abdomen. What to do? Oh Good God's mercy what to do? Think! Steady the rattling breath; breathe in; slow the frightened heart-rush of heat.

Carefully, she let go her clinging hold with her right hand, gripping tighter to a jutting rock with her left. She shifted her weight from left foot to right, lowered her hand, feeling for the child – she dared not look down, for the swirl of dizziness would come again and she would fall. Felt his curl of fine hair, his cheek, his neck, dug her fingers – those cramped, sore, swollen fingers – into the swaddling linen. Slowly, slowly dragged him up her body, ignoring his rising wails of protest, hoping the cries were nothing more than fretful indignation and soiled swaddling – the smell indicated it was no more than that. She had him at her breast, his head at her left shoulder, tears would come if only she had the spare energy to shed them. She nestled her cheek against his hair, her breath sobbing, shaking, dared not let go that clamped hold of him, though the pain in her hand was shrieking as if the muscles and sinews were afire.

She closed heer eyes, breathed in through her nose, out through her mouth. What to do now? She needed here hand free to climb . . . pushed him higher, so that he lay across her shoulder and bit with her teeth into the folds of the linen, praying that the wet-nurse had swaddled him tight, that the encircling binding would hold. Loudly, he protested; silently, Emma climbed.

Breathing was hard now, for she had only her nose, not her mouth. Her jaws were aching, the muscles locked in spasm, sweat dribbled into her eyes, her hands were clammy, wet, sticky. But she would not stop or give in. Would not listen to the voice that shouted and screamed at her to let go. Give up.

Inch by inch she climbed, hauling herself up the cliff face. Inch by slow, pain-racked, agonising, stubborn-minded inch.

And hands were on her shoulders, twining into her hair, grabbing her arms, the baby; hauling her over the edge, rolling her on to the flower-speckled sweet grass, the wind hitting her sweating face, her sodden clothing. Her body trembling uncontrollably, the blood pounding through the taught, clamped fingers, the aching shoulders. They were crying together, laughing, jubilant – afraid. Unbelieving that she had done it, had climbed cliffs with a babe carried in her teeth.

Below, all those many, many feet below, the birds gradually settled to their perches and the full, high tide waited, sullen in its suspended motion. At the base of the cliffs the waves played with their earned trophies, the debris of the natural flotsam of the beach, and a length of colourful, ripped and ragged linen; a pair of quality leather boots.

17

18 October 1020 – Ashingdon

Cnut finished his prayer, crossed himself, then turned and smiled radiantly at Emma. The consecration had been a moving service, one he could boast of for many years to come, as he could of this church, the first of his to be completed in England. And what more fitting place than to set it here, at Ashingdon? The Holy Minster of Saint Andrew had a specific and intentional remit: to offer prayers for the souls of those slain in this place of battle, whether they be English or Dane.

He had personally suggested its siting, overlooking the Crouch estuary, and had commanded its square tower to be of several storeys and of multi purpose. Naturally its prime intention was for the greater glory of God, but more practically, it also served as a watch-tower. From its height the expanse of the estuary could be observed and should any unwelcome craft sail into view – how better to summon out the militia than the urgent tolling of the church bell?

Emma smiled up at her husband as he helped her from her knees, the dedication prayers had been long and her joints were always stiff since that nightmare climb. She still shuddered when she thought of it, breaking out in a sweat, feeling her stomach lurch, her muscles lock in remembered fear. When she dwelt on what could have happened . . . she stood, her hand clasped firmly in Cnut's. No good would come of the might-have-beens, nightmares were for children who did not face the reality of the day. What could have been had not happened, she was here, alive and well, except for the occasional creak to the knees and knuckles.

She turned her dazzling smile to Archbishop Wulfstan. 'A moving service, my Lord. You have such a gift for the use of words, too often you bring tears into my heart for the beauty you speak.'

'Thank you, Ma'am, but if gift I have, then it is a gift from God.'

'Indeed so, Archbishop, indeed so,' she answered with a polite incline of her head. Was there never any penetrating that austere outer shell of this serious-minded man? She had rarely seen Wulfstan smile, never heard him laugh. Had God not created mirth to run as opposite to sadness and gloom? Although, perhaps on this occasion he had cause to be of solemn humour, for it ought not be Wulfstan officiating, but the Canterbury Archbishop: old Ælfstan had died on the twelfth day of June and his replacement not yet appointed. A disadvantage of the hierarchical position, by the nature of their required knowledge, wisdom and experience, Archbishops tended to be old men and old men were, all too often, soon called to God. Wulfstan was one of the rarities, a man who had entered his professional calling at a moderate age. At least the priest appointed to Saint Andrew's was a young man – almost a child in comparison with old Ælfstan, Stigand was fresh-faced, enthusiastic and dedicated. Emma liked him, if for no other reason than his mouth quirked naturally, and often, into a curving smile.

'So, Wulfstan,' Cnut said jovially, proud, 'what do you think of my church? Will it suffice?'

Looking about him as if this were his first view of the place, Wulfstan nodded his dour approval. It was a good church, stone-built of flint and Roman brick. If those Roman Red Crests of the distant past had served no other purpose, the rubble of their ruined buildings were always of use.

'I understand you have received a letter from his Holiness, Pope Benedict? He exhorts you to suppress injustices and use your strength in the service of peace, I believe?' he answered.

'You are remarkably familiar with my personal correspondence,' Cnut retorted with raised eyebrows.

And to Emma's surprise – and delight – she saw Wulfstan smile in response, a shy and meagre expression, no more than an uplifting of the corners of his mouth but, unmistakably, a smile.

'The Pope is, how shall I say, a resourceful man? He believes in ensuring that, should there be an unfortunate accident, his collected eggs are not all in the one dropped basket. He wrote to me also, praising your efforts and congratulating you on your foresight.'

Cnut grinned broadly, pleased. 'In other words, Archbishop, my programme of combining the building of churches with the implementation of strategic defence towers meets wholeheartedly with Rome's approval. I have pleased him with my foundings at Bosham and Hadstock and elsewhere?'

'There are some who doubt the necessity of a watchtower at Hadstock,' Godwine, at Cnut's shoulder interceded, 'though I admit it can oversee the Granta river.'

'Believe me, Godwine, the Granta is a strategic waterway; I certainly made use of it. Although it is not a river to be sailed when there is a possibility of a long and dry summer, eh, Thorkell?'

Cnut had not been the only seaman to learn the value of the inland waterways that navigated the outlying fenlands of East Anglia and Cambridge-Shire.

'Ja, there are dead among the ash trees of Hadstock. I recall we twice fought inconclusive skirmishes there. It is good to lay souls to rest by the building of churches and buying the Pope's approval will always bring its benefits. Whether God can be so easily appeased is another question entirely.' The sardonic words caused everyone to turn, to stare at the Earl of East Anglia, as if he had suddenly erupted into pus-oozing boils or sprouted devil horns and tail.

'By which, you mean . . .?' Cnut queried, his head tilting, brows dipping.

Shaking his head, spreading his hands, Thorkell answered with an air of innocence, 'Merely that sin must be paid for, one way or another.'

Stigand, a quick-witted, intelligent young man, who had ambition much more far-reaching than the priesthood of some back-of-beyond church, was the first to think of something tactful to say to break the ensuing uncomfortable silence. 'Penance for sin must always be paid, my Lord Earl. The greater the sin, the greater the atonement.'

'If I read my Earl's attempt at subtlety correct,' Cnut intoned, scowling at Thorkell, 'he asks how many churches must be founded by an individual to ensure God's forgiveness?'

'That would depend on the depth of the sin, would it not, my

Lord?' Thorkell bounced back at him, unperturbed by the penetrating glare of the King's blue eyes, satisfied that Cnut had correctly interpreted his ambiguous meaning.

Animosity had been rough-edged between the two men for several months now, almost as many months as the tongue-wagging, critical gossip against the King and his Queen had been systematically whispered through the trading towns and market centres of the south-east.

'I remind you, Thorkell,' Cnut snapped, suddenly losing patience, 'that contrary to recent popular speculation, it was not me who tossed meat bones at Archbishop Alfheah. Nor, as the spread gossip seems to imply, was I in command of the men who did. You were. Poor command as it turned out, perhaps the one who began the recent spate of tongue-tattling ought think of that?'

'But you were there,' Thorkell insisted very quietly. 'You watched and did nothing to stop it.'

That, Cnut could not deny.

The new-built church of Saint Andrew was full of men, Cnut's Council, his noblemen, the earls, thegns, commanders of his housecarls; men of the Church hierarchy, bishops and abbots. His Queen, his family. Men and women who felt themselves redden with uncertain embarrassment at Thorkell's outspokenness. One woman, however, stood at the chancel steps with her head high, her stare as rigid as Cnut's. The woman Cnut guessed to be behind the initiation of the tale-telling.

The King had been reluctant to invite her to the ceremony, but it would have been churlish, and unwise, to ignore her. Her sisters, Algiva and Edgyth, had been more accommodating women, for when their husbands were dead they had taken themselves off into the obscurity of the nunnery, happy to remain there quietly. Granted, their circumstances were different, their husbands had been traitors who had paid the price of going against their King. Ulfkell, on the other hand, had been an acclaimed heroic warrior. Why should his widow, King Edmund Ironside's beloved sister, hide herself beneath the dark habit of a recluse? Wulfhilde had never any intention of doing so. Nor had she the inclination to allow the stirred dust of the past to settle and lie undisturbed. Cnut, as far as she was concerned, was a murderous usurping tyrant who had stolen her brother's throne. A throne she wanted for the son she had borne to Ealdorman Ulfkell eight months after his death. Her only son, delivered with pain and difficulty, for she had not been a young woman and had lost all her other children either before or at their birth. Her son, Æthelred's grandson, Edmund's nephew, now aged three, thrived.

Cnut's eyes were drawn to her and his lips thinned. Wulfhilde. This was not the place, nor the occasion, to rant and throw a tantrum against her as if he were no older than the son she carried in her arms.

'It is a frailty of man to make mistakes, Thorkell. I am not God. I admit I have done things that were wrong, things that, perhaps, condemn me in His sight, but I can do no more than I am already doing to set right those wrongs. The rest is not for you to judge, but for me and God to settle when I eventually stand in His presence.' Deliberately he levelled his voice, put the sound of an agreeable smile into it, treating the difficult exchange as if it were no more than lively debate.

'Come!' Cnut declared, clapping his hands. 'There is ale and wine and feasting awaiting us at the manor. We have accomplished the ecclesiastical side of the ceremony, let us finish the day's praise in the human way by making merry and getting drunk!'

A raised cheer, the return of congenial laughter and chatter as the guests filed from the church, Thorkell acknowledging the King's prudent diplomacy with a discreet bow. All the same, it was Thorkell who escorted the Lady Wulfhilde along the lane to the King's manor, also new-built. Thorkell who sat attentive beside her throughout the feasting.

With men and women watching, ears straining, tongues gaping to spew more gossip, Cnut steered clear of the incident throughout the evening. He could wait his opportunity to react, for he was a patient man.

Come morning, with the ebb of the tide, the leave-taking was under way, the host of guests dispersing for their own lands and homes, some by sea, others on horseback. Wulfhilde had gone with her retinue to her manor in the heart of Essex. Thorkell, too, to sail north along the coast to Norwich. Wulfstan had left with the bishops and thegns. Godwine was to travel south with the King, his wife, Gytha, riding alongside the Queen.

'The boy is settled?' Emma asked Gytha as their horses walked lazily in step behind the loud, masculine banter of their menfolk. She swivelled her head to glance at the swaying litter some distance behind, amid the winding line of housecarls, militia men and baggage carts.

'Swegn is an independent child, even at these tender months,' said Gytha. 'I swear to God if a second child is as full of temper as this one I'll not be birthing a third!'

'A little warrior, I have heard Godwine call him.'

'*Ja*, for the way he kicks and screams when he cannot get his own way – God help me when the lad grows older, at least in his cot I know where he is. Once he learns to walk . . .!'

Emma laughed. She had recently discovered the same problem with Harthacnut, now that he was learning to shuffle his own way about. In comparison, Gunnhild was a cherub, but then girls were often the more amenable. Little Goda certainly had been.

'What of Ragnhilda? Is she not the sweetest child?' Gytha asked. She found it so easy to talk to Emma, who had no patronising airs of arrogance and had become an easy friend, although almost twice Gytha's sixteen years of age.

'I confess our circumstances of meeting were not ideal.' Emma shivered, pulled her cloak tighter, although the day was pleasant and warm. Shrugging aside the lurch of memory, said, 'She is the happiest, sun-bright child. I swear I could part with Harthacnut on occasion, but I would never be pleased to see the back of Ragnhilda!'

They had met on the cliff path, only an hour after that dreadful climb. Leofgifu's nephew had ridden ahead to summon help, instead, had met with the King's retinue.

There had been uproar. Cnut shouting and cursing everyone for their slackness and stupidity, Emma included, his hand striking out at anyone who came too close to dodge his wrath. His words, churned by a surge of fear, mingling into incoherence: 'Could have been killed, or drowned! Why were you men not alert? Lazy imbeciles! Fools! Incompetents! What if you had fallen, woman? Damn stupid . . .!'

Emma, dishevelled and ragged, wanting only to bathe and sleep, had knelt on the grass at the top of those cliffs and wept. Great sobs shattering through her aching, scratched and battered body, her hair loose, matted and tangled, her bloodied, swollen fingers covering her face. And a hand had come out and touched her, a tentative touch, light, as delicate as a butterfly's wing. Emma had lifted her head and seen a girl standing there before her, a small child with golden hair and a puzzled face.

'Are you to be my mama?' the child had asked. 'I do hope so, you are more pretty than the big lady over there,' and she had pointed to plump Leofgifu, cradling the wailing Harthacnut.

Unable to speak and only vaguely realising who the girl was, Emma had only managed to nod. Satisfied, Ragnhilda had sat herself down beside Emma and announced. 'I am glad of that. Glad also that you do not mind weeping, 'cos I was worried about that. My nurse says I'm too big to cry and slaps me whenever I do, which is quite often, because so many things make me sad, but you're sad too, and you are bigger than me and no one is slapping you.' Her chatter had been nonsense and delightfully comforting.

Cnut in mid-stream of blasphemic oaths had overheard, in mid sentence had broken off and laughed, had gone to Emma and cradled her to him, stroking her hair, holding her close and safe, realising the futility of losing his temper.

'You new mama', he had confided to his daughter, 'is a brave and remarkable woman.'

Matter of factly, Ragnhilda had answered, 'Of course she is, Papa. You would not choose her to be my mama if she was not.'

Ah, the sweet innocence of children!

Emma's attention was brought abruptly to the present. Leofric, at last made Earl of Mercia, was making some point of argument with Godwine. The two men detested each other, their petty squabblings building into something grander now that they were so often vying for the King's favour. Emma agreed with Godwine's opinion, although Cnut determinedly disagreed that Leofric was not a man to be trusted, as with those in the past, he would be looking for his self-interest above all else. Although, Emma had to concede, sometimes, when a snake hissed its presence in the grass it was better to leave it alone and burn it out later from a safer distance.

The chance opening so conveniently before her, Emma altered the subject to one her husband had asked her discreetly to broach. 'Gytha, I would have you talk to your husband at some personal moment on a private matter of the King's business.'

Instinctively Gytha curled her hands tighter around her mount's reins, slowing its pace. Gytha could be trusted and Godwine over and again had proved his loyalty.

'Where there has been a first marriage, a husband's daughters can be as much a difficulty as his sons, especially when they are sisters of kings,' Emma said.

She was talking, Gytha realised, of the Lady Wulfhilde.

'The King is concerned that Thorkell may be wanting more than he already has,' Emma stated bluntly.

Gytha nodded, this she knew from Godwine, who had confided to her that it might not be politically wise to grant over-much power to Thorkell. Making him Regent of England while Cnut was away had been a hazardous risk.

'Your husband is not yet aware, for the information has been private to the King,' Emma said, steadying her own mount to a slower walk so as to not be overheard, 'Thorkell wishes to remarry.'

Gytha kicked her gelding forward from his attempt to lower his head and nibble grass, asked, surprised, 'He has a lady in mind?' A question that, by adding two and two to her own observations, she could reckon an answer to be four.

Emma nodded. 'He wishes to take the widow of Ulfkell, the daughter of Æthelred, sister to Edmund.'

'And from there pursue the claim of her infant son for the wearing of a crown?'

Again, Emma nodded. As Cnut had said last night in the

intimacy of their bed, Gytha was an astute woman and her husband even more so. 'If I am to face rebellion from my own lords,' he had said, as they lay within each other's arms, 'then I would be wise, early on, to begin standing the one against the other.'

And Godwine, always discreet, always reliable, and with an ambition as broad as Thorkell's would, now that he knew of it, not be permitting this man who was not an English Saxon to outclass him in rank and desire.

18

Council was nearing the end of a long and tedious day, one full of bickering and sallow temper. It was always so when the tax levies were being set.

'But with no threat from Denmark,' Leofric grumbled, 'why must the cost of the fyrd levy rise yet again? Are we, now, under new threat? If so, by whom?'

'Norway is not secure,' Cnut said, justifying his reasons.

Thorkell, rising to his feet, Leofric sitting to allow his turn to speak, lifted his arm, palm spread. 'But Norway will not send ships to England. Olaf would not risk leaving himself so exposed.'

'You too oppose this, Thorkell?' Cnut asked less than mildly. He was finding it difficult to keep his temper in check. Would these imbeciles never understand that England had been left wide open to attack because Æthelred had not always ensured the fyrd was ready, well-armed, well-trained, to be called into action whenever required? Peace was the occasion to ensure your defences were maintained at full strength. Why shut the stable door after the horse had galloped out?

'I ask only an annual rise of one penny on every hide or ploughland household. Dependants are also to give one penny extra and lords are to pay for any who cannot afford it. Is that so unreasonable an expectation? In return I offer safety and peace.'

Leofric again: 'But we have that with what is already raised. Why do you need more?' Cnut was beginning to regret promoting the man into the position of earl. Godwine had warned him . . . ah well, the thing was done and in other respects outside of his tight purse, Leofric was an honest and dedicated man.

'Can we be certain', Thorkell interrupted, 'that this raised tax is for the benefit of England? What have you to assure us that this

543

extra geld will not be used for your intention of subduing Norway? Does not Denmark, after all, bring you sufficient finances for the doing of that? We, some of us,' he indicated the men of the Witan, 'do not believe that you can successfully be a king to both Denmark and England.'

'Yet you had no such qualms when you fought with my father,' Cnut answered quietly, annoyance slithering into his voice. 'It was accepted that he could be King of both lands. But you were expecting to be made supreme overlord of England, were you not, Thorkell? You would have had nothing but praise for the venture.'

'The men of Denmark think poorly of you, so you have no hope of seeking power there, eh, Thorkell?' Godwine added. 'You have only England and that you see slipping through your fingers like water.'

The mood had turned, Thorkell felt it. The disagreement of the afternoon's debate had veered against him, like a temperamental wind. Had he been at sea, he would be ordering the sail reefed, anything loose roped down, waterproof sealskin jerkins pulled on. The squall hit him side on.

'You have been doubting the King's intention since his return from Denmark. How many occasions, now, have you disagreed with his decisions, queried his proposals? Who was it who refused to support the revival of King Alfred's fyrd? The forming of one single army beneath the control of the King? An army of men able to fight when and where they are wanted, not merely in their own district and for the expected tithe period of service? Who was it who opposed increasing the scyp fyrd?' Godwine listed several more accusations, marking them off on his fingers. 'And who is it, Thorkell, who wears a sour face and a blackened heart because he cannot wear a king's crown?'

Thorkell had sat through the tirade biting his tongue, could not remain silent at that last. He leapt to his feet, his arm raised, fist clenched. Anger spitting from his eyes. 'I served with loyalty and honour while my Lord King was away abroad. As I will always serve if asked. I have nothing more than a wish to do as my King bids, to the best of my ability whenever and whatever he asks of me.'

Godwine remained seated, his legs spread before him, thumbs hooked through the bronze-embossed belt at his waist. 'How noble of you,' he said sardonically. 'A pity it is all lies.'

'How dare you . . .'

'And how dare you?' Godwine countered, coming alert to his feet, his arm also waving, his fist also clenched. 'Just when, Thorkell called the Tall, were you proposing to inform this Council of your recent marriage?'

Consternation, muttering, the men exchanging glances, whispered questions. All eyes on Earl Godwine of Wessex and Thorkell of East Anglia.

'You marriage', Godwine continued, his eyes boring into Thorkell, 'to the widow of Ulfkell Snilling, Ulfkell the Bold, daughter of the old King, Æthelred. A daughter of the royal line, a daughter who, as wife, could give you the right to be elected king. A marriage this present King forbade.'

Uproar.

Godwine sat, his arms folded, watching the slow smile come across Cnut's face. It had been nicely and so completely done. None had known of the marriage; at least, Thorkell had assumed none had known. Even the priest who had married them had been despatched a day or so later, quietly poisoned. None could have known. Could they? She had said it would not work, Wulfhilde had warned him that Cnut was not the man her father had been, was not the man Thorkell judged him to be. Swein Forkbeard had been a man of stature and strength; Cnut, it seemed was developing into a man twice that of his father's capability.

Thorkell laughed, cynical, half bowed to his King. 'Is there any point in denying it?' he asked.

Cnut sat, stone-faced, disappointed, angry. Why could men not accept what they had been given and be thankful for it? Godwine, for instance, cherished his role as earl for the power it brought him. It was enough, more than enough. Why did men like Thorkell, men who already had power and status, have to prove they were better than others when they were already the best? Why could they not just do their job with good will and an eager heart, prove themselves

545

by Christian acts, not those of hate and evil? Resigned, he said, 'No, my friend, there is no point.'

Thorkell shrugged, spread his hands in submission. 'Then, with regret, I must take my leave of this Council.'

'*Ja,*' Cnut said. 'Take your leave of my Council and my Kingdom. You have three days to be gone.'

'And may I take my wife and her child into exile with me?'

'That is your choice, but if you do not, the both of them shall enter the service of God. You have my word they shall not be harmed.'

'And if I choose against that?'

'Then I shall follow you and send you, her and the child to serve God in a different, more eternal, manner.'

19

Godwine found his brother-in-law, Ulf, to be a God-damned pain in the arse, with Eilaf, Gytha's younger brother, running a close second. His one consolation, Gytha matched her husband's opinion of them both. No matter what you thought of someone, however, if they were a guest in your house they had to be treated civilly. Even if their company was unwanted and uninvited.

'Ulf has always considered himself to be a bigger and better braggart than anyone else,' Gytha had confessed to Godwine last night, in the quiet pleasantness of their bed. 'And where Ulf goes, Eilaf follows. The pair of them are like empty iron pots, their tinny voices making nothing more than a hollow clang.'

With Thorkell outlawed and expelled, Godwine had accepted that Cnut had been honour bound to offer Ulf a position of authority because of Estrith; the King could hardly refuse his own sister's husband a title when one became available. Countess sat well for her, but it had been a sad day for England when it had to join alongside Ulf, Earl of East Anglia.

Thorkell had stormed in a rage from Court in a flurry of pulsating language and foul threats, had taken his ships, his men, his wife and adopted child to Sweden. Where he was stirring muddy-watered puddles into bore-tide waves. Through Wulfhilde's son, he wanted England and had decided to take it by using the restless manpower of the Netherlands. He had the ships and the finances, but whether he could retain the loyalty remained to be seen. Mercenaries were wary of following a leader who changed the set of his sail with each shift of the wind, and two could play at the buying of men's loyalty. Putting Ulf as earl in his place had been an intentional insult, for Godwine was not the only man to dislike Ulf's arrogance. If it were possible,

Thorkell despised Ulf even more than the rest of them put together.

The summer had passed slowly, with the King's fleet patrolling the waters off the Island of Wight, Godwine taking his turn of command alongside other earls; huh, Ulf had made a mess of that simple task too, by allowing six of Thorkell's mercenary ships to slip past one moonless night. He had been sleeping, curled beneath a blanket in the stern, his back propped against the steerboard. Consequently his crew, leaving the ship to drift, had slipped from the rowing benches and snored the night away as well. Bloody fool.

Eilaf had spent the better part of this blustering afternoon bemoaning Cnut's overlooking an appointment of title for himself.

'I am Ulf's brother, in Jesu's name, and I am the only one without rank, even Gytha can call herself Countess. What honour is there for me?'

'My brother shall find something for you,' Estrith had snapped, after hearing the complaint once too often. Few had heard her added mutter of, 'Preferably something tight that will fit your neck and strangle you!' But then, Estrith was entitled to a bad-tempered humour, her child was overdue by two weeks and she felt herself to be broader than the entire width of Godwine's manor house.

Escaping the incessant mithering, Godwine had come from the Hall to walk by the shore, despite the rough wind blowing off the sea. Decided, first, to inspect progress at the church. Only the tower to be completed now, once the scaffolding was removed Holy Trinity would be ready for dedication to God. He stood for a while at its south-east end, inspecting the length of the nave before him, watching, in admiration, the builders running up and down ladders, scampering about as if they were squirrels. Catch him up there, even if it were only two floors high! He had climbed up the internal ladder-way three days ago to peep out through one of the window slits at the incoming tide, the ground below sending his head spinning into dizziness – and he had argued for a third storey to be built? He smiled to himself. Perhaps Cnut was as wary of heights as he, hence the stubborn refusal to make the porticus any higher than it was.

Beyond the shelter of the tower Godwine stepped over the plank bridge spanning the stream, and was nigh on knocked sideways by the blast of wind that whipped at his clothes and stung his cheeks. He grabbed at his cloak and, ducking his head, strode along the promontory, following above the tide line of exposed mud, his passing disturbing the busy waders poking about for their low-tide feast. Bearing left along the curve of the headland he puffed his cheeks, grateful to turn away from the strength of the wind, saw Gytha with the Queen and the children coming towards him, returning from their own walk. Emma was often at Bosham, though her husband's manor was on the opposite side of the creek at Cnut Bourne; it was lonely for her with Cnut gone to Denmark in pursuit of stopping Thorkell's nuisance. Made sense to be more frequently this side, with her joint Regent of England, the Earl of Wessex. Gytha had seen him, raised her arm to wave, the wind tearing her veil almost from her head. He saw her catch at it, laugh, although the sound was carried away with the screech of the gulls. Emma held Godwine's second son, Harold, not yet three months, draped sound asleep over her shoulder, the other children prancing beneath their mother's feet, excited by the boisterous game the sea-wind was playing with them. Gunnhild, four, with her brother, Harthacnut nearing his third birthday; his own son, Swegn at two, toddling bravely along with a determination of stamina, and Cnut's Ragnhilda, six going on sixty, a child born with the wisdom of a grandmother. Godwine halted, waited for them to approach, Emma was teaching Ragnhilda a poem, one he recognised as 'The Wanderer'.

'. . . "The Ice-cold sea on many waterways
Travel the exile's path; fate is relentless."
So spoke a wanderer who called to mind
Hardships and cruel wars and deaths of lords.'

The little girl, serious at her side, solemnly repeated the words as her stepmother spoke them.

Wrãþra wælsleahta, winemæga hryre.

'Very good!' Emma praised, as the girl turned her face up to her for approval of her use of English. The Queen, remembering her own difficulty, appreciated the child's desire to learn, to leave behind her Danish tongue. Godwine smiled as he hunkered down to catch the unsteady Swegn as he lurched into his papa's outstretched arms.

'Hey, a lad with legs as sturdy as oak trunks!' Godwine praised, as he lifted his son and swung him round and round, making the boy crow with laughter. He had never seen Emma as content as she had been these last months, even the going away of the King, this time, had not unduly saddened her. Motherhood with Cnut as husband suited her. Playing with Swegn made the other children clamour for a turn, Gunnhild happily insistent; Harthacnut, feet spread, fists clenched, angrily demanding; Ragnhilda shyly polite.

'Do I get one too?' Gytha asked, her eyes sparkling like the sun shining on the sea. She was eight and ten years old, and Godwine loved her. Setting Harthacnut down from his second swing Godwine, feigning a frown, eyed his wife critically. She had not lost the extra weight she had inherited while carrying Harold, but then, Godwine liked his women to be on the plump side.

'It will strain my back, but aye, I suppose what is good for the childer . . .' and grabbing her by the waist, he energetically twirled her round, sending the children, and Gytha, into fresh shrieks of raucous laugher.

The babe over Emma's shoulder stirred and she soothed him, humming a lullaby, stroking his silk-soft fair hair, her own smile echoing the pleasure of the others.

'I'd not recommend going by way of the point,' Godwine advised, setting his wife down with a fond pat of his hand to her backside and indicated the way he had come. He pointed to the children. 'The wind will blow this lot away as if they were spindrift.'

'We were about to turn into the Hall when we saw you,' Gytha explained. 'Did you leave by the north door, then? We did not see you come out through the south.'

550

Godwine, lifting Swegn to his shoulders, nodded assent. 'I could not stomach your younger brother recounting his wretched Welsh expedition once more. *Guds skyld*, you would think Eilaf had conquered the whole of the damned place and slaughtered every last Welshman into the bargain! All right, so he ravaged Dyfed, but can he not see that we are not impressed by his sacking of Saint David's? It might be Welsh – God must have his own reasons for accepting their barbaric ways – but to burn a church down? Ah no, that is not a civilised Christian thing to do.'

'He wants Gloucester-Shire as an earldom,' Emma explained, 'is hoping his prowess will satisfy the King of his ability.' Sucking in her cheeks to stop the laugh bursting through, added, 'You are supposed to be impressed.'

'Oh, I am,' Godwine stated, pretending to be equally as serious and hoisting Swegn higher. 'But then, I have never encountered such a prolific bore before. No, Harthacnut, I am carrying Swegn, he is smaller than you, he cannot walk so far.' This last was to the boy, tugging insistently at his tunic, demanding also to be carried. Pouting at the flat refusal, Harthacnut stood still, fists bunched, the petulant look setting harder.

'Come on, Harthacnut,' Ragnhilda coaxed, holding her hand out to him, 'we'll be left behind, else.'

'Shan't. Want a carry.'

'Uncle Godwine has Swegn and Mama has baby Harold. You cannot be carried.'

'Shall. Mama will have to throw Harold away.'

'Don't be silly!'

'Not silly – you're silly. You're only a stupid girl.' He stuck his tongue out at her.

Ragnhilda bit her lip, unsure what to do. The adults were almost at the Hall, were busy talking, had not noticed the two of them trailing behind. She did not care for Harthacnut; he was churlish and spiteful, and not only to Ragnhilda. Yesterday she had caught him throwing stones at the chickens and she was sure it had been Harthacnut who had made the baby, Harold, cry this morning. Harthacnut had innocently claimed that he had only been trying to soothe the child, the adults not noticing that he had not been crying before Harthacnut had poked into his crib. Nor had they noticed the angry red pinch mark on the babe's cheek.

The insults she could tolerate, for mostly they were untrue, although sometimes they struck near the heart. Like last week when he had called her a bastard brat. 'You're not proper born like I am,' he had sneered. 'Your real mama is dead and she wasn't the Queen; my mama is.'

He had heard the disparagement of Ragnhild from Ulf's indiscreet words, the man said often that Cnut was bloody lucky to have got away with bedding a whore like Ragnhild without having his balls cut off by Ælfgifu. Ragnhilda could never imagine Emma doing anything so horrid to Papa, so why would this woman, Ælfgifu? She knew nothing of her, except that Ælfgifu was the woman whose sons ought to be drowned in a vat of oil. Emma had said so on the eve of Papa's going to Denmark. Ragnhilda was supposed to have been asleep, but had crept from the children's quarters to say a last goodnight to Cnut, knowing she would not be seeing him again until next spring. She had gone around by the outside wall, not wishing to go through a Hall full of sleeping men, had paused outside the open window to her father's chamber and heard them arguing, shouting at each other, Emma saying to Papa that if he dared visit that bitch he had best not think on coming home again. He had shouted back that he would damn well do as he pleased, Swegen and Harold were his sons and he would see them as often as he liked. Ragnhilda had turned away and tiptoed back to her bed, pretending nothing was amiss. Come morning, though, they all asked why her eyes were so red and her face puffy.

'Come on, Harthacnut, I'm getting cold. Please?'

'Want a carry.'

He was heavy, for although younger than her, he was stocky and well-fleshed. Even so, Ragnhilda managed to hoist him into her arms and stagger to the Hall with him. Without being tempted more than twice to toss him head first into the mud.

20

Sweat glistened between Ælfgifu's ample and shapely breasts. Cnut, tempted to remove the enticing trickle with his tongue, judiciously refrained; he had not the energy to make love a third time this night. She lay naked, her hair spilled in a cascade across the pillows, her arms stretched, careless, above her head. She was not beautiful, not as Ragnhild had been, but there was a sensuous allure about Ælfgifu that drew Cnut to her, wanting her for himself, not allowing him to let her go. He fooled himself that he only visited her because of the boys, huh! What care had he for those two squabbling, bad-mannered brats? They were eight to her eight and twenty, both of them snarled up with the bitterness of feeling hard-done-by, their looks surly, their demands caustic. And had it been deliberate, as a reminder to her own hatred, that the first men he had met on entering this Hall at Northampton had been Ælfgifu's pitiful brothers? Shadows of men, blind of eye and soul alike, nothing could have served better purpose to ram a spear home than to ensure the King noticed those empty and puckered eye sockets. What more could he do to exorcise her revenge? Æthelred was dead and Eadric Streona's weather-beaten mouldered skull stood sentinel on its spike over her entrance gateway. As sightless and lifeless as Wulfheah and Ufgeat.

He stretched, easing a twinge of cramp from his calf, ignored her fingers as she moved her arm to trace the curl of his chest hair with her cat-claw nails.

'Can you not let the past rest?' he said. 'It is over, done. Those responsible dead and punished.'

'She is alive, her sons also.'

Cnut knew full well whom she meant, but was not going to fall into the trap of playing her mind-twisted games. 'The boys are exiled, would be dead if I were able to get at them. Edward and Alfred are nothing to you, as your brothers' blinding and father's murder is nothing to do with the Queen.' He used the term deliberately, not using the more personal Emma, to emphasise her status.

Ælfgifu, unimpressed, merely snorted.

'I visit with you, make love to you. I am generous with funding the education of our sons. What more do you want from me, Ælfgifu?' He raised a warning finger to silence the intake of breath that signalled a tirade. 'And do not say a crown. You cannot, nor shall not, have one.'

Pouting, she rolled from him, leant from the bed to retrieve a sable mantle to throw about her shoulders. 'Is that all you credit me with? The wanting of a poxed crown to weigh heavy on my head? I do not want her stupid bauble – I want you to pass your kingdom on to my eldest son. Our son, not hers.'

'Harthacnut is also my son.'

'Huh!'

'Yes, huh.'

'Are you sure he is your son?'

'Am I sure yours are?' Cnut was wryly amused when she did not answer. He slid his hand across the satin feel of her shoulder beneath the mantle; irritably, she shrugged him aside. Very well, if she wanted no more of his attention he would dress, the day was already busy about its passing. He fumbled on the floor for his clothes, left in a muddle from their hasty discarding last night. Three days he had been in Northampton, perhaps his welcome was becoming stale?

'I'm sailing later today,' he announced, suddenly making his mind to it as he fastened the bronze buckle of his elaborate belt.

Ælfgifu responded with a non-committal twitch of her shoulder, a toss of her hair. 'What do I care? Three days of your company is the most I can expect from you. I will never get anything else. Your pleasuring is pointless for you can never satisfy me in ways that are outside the bed. Not even there, truth to tell.' Her words stung, said with intentional spite.

554

'As I said, I do what I can for you; you want for nothing save my presence. What you receive is more than many concubines dare hope for.'

'Dare hope for? What I dare hope for?' She jumped up, was on her feet, her hand holding the mantle close to her breasts to dignify her nakedness. 'I hope for nothing from you, I know I shall never get it! I am your first-taken wife, the mother of your firstborn son. It is my right to be kept in the manner I am accustomed to. It is my right to expect you to be here to protect me and my kindred, to see to the punishment of those who commit evils against us!'

Ah, so that was it. Cnut stood, arms folded, regarding her. Her face was plain, her eyes unremarkable, nothing exceptional. And yet . . . and yet something kept drawing him back to her bed every few months. The longest he had been away from her, discounting his journeying to Denmark, had been six months. He spaced the visits deliberately and rarely announced them in advance, for he trusted her as far as a legless grasshopper could leap. Emma, he thought, knew nothing of his coming here, or if she did, held her own council. A pity the pleasure Ælfgifu's body provided did not match her company. In bed, she took him to Heaven, outside it, while with her he was skirting on Hell's threshold.

'So what is it I have not done?' he droned. Something minor to him, major to her, he knew her well enough for that by now.

'You should know.'

'Well, I do not.'

'Are you so stupid, then? Do you take so little interest in your northern provinces? Your northern lords?'

'I take great interest in both, Madam, but through Earl Erik, who has charge of them.'

'Earl Erik? A pox on Earl bloody Erik! What does he care for my kinsman Thurbrand?'

'The Hold of Holderness? Thurbrand? What in *Guds Naun*, in God's Name, has Thurbrand to do with this?' Cnut spread his arms wide, at a loss. 'He is dead.'

Erupting as if she had been a simmering volcano, Ælfgifu was across the room, the expensive mantle dropped and forgotten, kicking at him, raking his cheek with her nails, hissing and spitting, cursing. Only his longer arms held her off, for the full spate of her fury was a match to equal his strength.

'Yes, he is dead! Murdered! Stabbed through the heart, a dagger in his guts, butchered by a madman who has had no reprimand, no punishment for the deed! A man who swaggers his freedom as if he is royal-born and God-shriven! Thurbrand's murder was done by Uhtred of Bernicia's son and you have had nothing to say or do on the matter!'

'I have had the pressing matter of Thorkell's treachery to deal with, *elskede* . . .'

Wrenching free, Ælfgifu ducked beneath his arm and slapped his face, drawing blood with her rings. 'Don't you "my beloved" me! My kinsman was murdered nigh on three years past!'

'General gossip gives the organising of it to you.'

'I have consistently contested that slur. Why would I work in yoke with the spawned slime of Uhtred? Against my own kinsman?'

Dabbing at the seeping blood, Cnut inspected his finger for the amount. A few spots, nothing more. 'The rumour was that you and Thurbrand fell out.' Cnut put his face closer to hers. 'Displease you in bed, did he? Not as good as me at satisfying you, eh?'

She slapped him again.

Cnut was losing patience, he did not have to come here and put up with her childish tantrums. 'Thurbrand', he snapped, 'got himself into a brawl with Ealdred. He could easily have sidestepped it, but no, he had to taunt the lad about the manner of his father's dying. What did he expect? A pat on the head as if he were a good dog?' He drew breath, lifted his cloak from the wall peg and swung it to his shoulder. 'Ealdred did the killing, but Thurbrand did the provoking, and in that I agree with rumour. Thurbrand was not clever enough to think of its doing on his own. Someone prodded him from behind. I wonder who that someone could have been?' He pushed the nine-inch long pin, with a head of gem-encrusted silver the size of his clenched fist, into the folds of the cloak to secure it at his shoulder. 'I did not like the way Thurbrand dealt with Uhtred's killing. That, too, was of your doing. Now the son has slain his father's murderer and no doubt the blood-feud will dribble on through another generation. I hold nothing against the lad. Perhaps he'll come for you next.'

'You bastard.'

'That I might be, but you will have either to accept it, or find yourself another man to keep you and your brats fed with fresh meat and clothed in silks and furs.' He turned on his heel and marched from the chamber, deliberately leaving the door wide so anyone in the Hall beyond might see Ælfgifu's state of undress, knowing most of them would be wide-eyed ogling.

She snatched up the sable and covered herself, ran after him. 'Cnut! Do not go yet, my Lord! It is several hours till you must sail. Please, stay with me?'

Cnut felt like hurling an insult, telling her to go choke on her own hatching plots. Instead, without pausing, he raised a hand, called, 'After I've dealt with Thorkell to my satisfaction I'll be back. Perhaps.'

The two boys, he noted, were fighting on the far side of the Hall, punching each other in a way that was not a friendly bout of brother against brother but with all the ferocity of meaning harm. Bugger them. Let them maim each other, then he'd not have the added burden of what to do with them when they grew into more than boys.

21

7 June 1023 – Thorney Island

Harthacnut, three and a half years old, could not quite figure this thing called death. Its concept was baffling and it drew even more peculiar reactions from the grown-ups. No one had bothered with those rats that Uncle Godwine had destroyed last month down at Bosham, yet here everyone was, wailing and weeping over the death of that fusty old Archbishop Wulfstan, and going on about moving the bones of another Archbishop, Alfheah, who had died years ago. What was the problem? Papa wanted the bones taken to the cathedral in Canterbury, the people of London wanted them kept where they were; no one had made this great fuss when Papa had ordered the removal of those monster's bones, found when they had started digging the foundations of his church at Ashingdon. Harthacnut liked that story and asked his father to recount it often.

'I had decided on where I wanted my church to be, up on the hill. All the men came, with mattocks, picks and shovels to start clearing the land marking the pattern of the church, to build the start of the walls, and as one man drove his spade in there was a crunch and a skull appeared. A gape-mouthed skull with huge eye sockets, long snout and sharp pointed teeth, a creature that, had it been alive, would have ripped the throat out of a man. Well, they kept on digging and found more: the backbone, the ribs, legs, feet, claws – a whole skeleton of a great beast longer than this Hall!'

'What did they do with the bones, Papa?'

'Oh, they were the remains of a devil creature, the men called in the priest – Stigand, it was – and he organised the thing to be burnt and the ground blessed.'

Harthacnut delighted in picturing the monster biting the heads off people, ripping their guts out. Perhaps the moving of Alfheah was a problem because he had been a holy man and did not need burning and blessing? Oh, it was all most odd!

And then there was the added fuss of Earl Erik dying. Harthacnut disliked him as much as he had Wulfstan. Both had been wont to lecture him: 'A *son of a king would not do that, Harthacnut,*' or, '*Try to behave as an ætheling should, Harthacnut.*' A musty, frowsy pair; the boy was glad to be rid of them. The only interesting part was the manner of Erik dying; that Harthacnut had listened to with relish.

He had been returning from attending the burial of Wulfstan and his horse had stumbled. Erik had somersaulted off and snapped his leg, which had turned bad, gang . . . something or other, Harthacnut could not remember the exact word. The surgeon had to saw the leg off, the blood had fountained everywhere and Erik had bled to death. Harthacnut had tried it for himself a few days after hearing his parents talk of it by stealing a small saw from the carpenter and sawing off a dead stable cat's leg. It had been difficult, but eventually he had severed the leg. The lack of blood had been very disappointing.

'Will there be any blood coming out of the Archbishop?' he asked his mother, who was concentrating on reading a parchment by the poor glow of a rushlight.

'What do you mean, blood? Of course there will be no blood, you silly lamb.' Completely misunderstanding, she laid the parchment aside and with an indulgent chuckle knelt beside her son, her arms going maternally around him. 'The tomb is to be opened and the remains transferred into a coffin. When we rebury the Archbishop at Canterbury, I promise there will be nothing nasty for you to see, my little *skat.*'

Harthacnut squirmed out of her embrace, scowling, Emma taking the expression to indicate his boyish pride in not wanting to be coddled by his mother. In fact, he was cross that she would insist on using that soppy Danish endearment, and would not be able to see any gore for himself.

'What's wrong with the boy now?' Cnut said gruffly, entering the room and throwing his cloak aside; missing the coffer, it slid to the floor. It had been a bugger of a day. He unbuckled his sword, added it to the crumpled cloak, sat on a stool and held his foot aloft for his servant to pull the boot off. 'What's the puckered face for, boy? If the wind should change you could be caught like that for ever.'

'He is anxious about the ceremonies here at London and Canterbury,' Emma answered coolly. The relationship between her and Cnut had been strained this last six weeks since his return from Denmark. Oh, how happiness fluctuated, was so easily spoilt! He had recounted very little of the expedition, save that Thorkell had no chance of raising a full fleet to come against England, although, to ensure it, Cnut had been forced to leave the majority of his own scyp fyrd in Danish waters with orders to keep regular patrol and a watchful eye. A matter of weeks, maybe a couple of months, and Thorkell would capitulate, bow to the pressure. All it needed was the patience to wait and the financial resources to pay the English fleet to remain vigilant. A gall that rubbed, for Thorkell had predicted Cnut would need to rely on Englishmen to sort Danish problems.

Not surprisingly, London had refused to pay the higher taxes demanded, the merchants' indignation fuelled by a London-wide increase in anti-Dane feeling that had begun to swell against the King and his men who, Londoners claimed, spent more months in Denmark than in England. Denmark and its troubles, whether raised by Thorkell the Tall or What's-his-name the Short, was no business of London. Denmark was for the King to sort out, from his Danish funds and nothing else. All puff and wind, of course, with the basic point of Cnut's strategy, to protect London, being deliberately obscured. Petty-minded people causing petty-minded squabbles. Ah, but it had ever been so in London, for the merchant guilds were a law unto themselves, no mind which king set his backside on the throne.

For the defiance Cnut had been angry, his annoyance heightened by the less than enthusiastic welcome home that he had received from his wife. Emma had been made aware of his tryst with Ælfgifu and although she saw no reason to let him know she had an efficient network of spies, neither was she going to allow him to pull a hood over her eyes. Had the Northampton Bitch been a bawdy-house whore she would not have cared a bent copper penny, providing she did not carry the pox, but Ælfgifu was an ongoing, annoying problem, with or without a sexually transmitted disease.

Both situations, London and his wife, were beginning to wear thin for Cnut.

'Well there is now another matter for him to worry on. That old crone has been preaching her evil curses again.'

Emma lifted her head sharply, concerned.

With the second boot removed, Cnut examined a hole worn in the toe of his woollen sock. 'Apparently, unless I leave the Archbishop where he is, my skin shall erupt into pustules and my vitals shrivel, black and rancid.' He laughed nervously.

'She is a hag, Cnut, pay no heed to her. She professes to desire a man of God to remain undisturbed, yet calls on the Devil to secure it? I think not!'

'That is what I concluded. I had her arrested, she is to be executed on the morrow at sunrise.' Feeling happier, Cnut beckoned his servant to fetch him wine.

Emma ushered Harthacnut off to play with his wooden soldiers, said vehemently, 'She is Satan's witch. The Church should be dealing with her, not you.'

'I have made it quite clear that any Londoner who protests at her punishment shall be deemed as being in league with her and face charges of heresy themselves. I will not be overruled in this matter, no more than I will over the decision to reinter Alfheah's relics.

'So the transfer goes ahead on the morrow?'

'It does. After the witch has been burnt.'

Playing with his toy soldiers, Harthacnut's attention to the adult talk had been waning, but his ears pricked at the incredulous gasp that left his mother's mouth.

'Burnt? Alive? Are you jesting? There has never been such a manner of public execution before.'

Cnut raised his goblet in a mocking half-salute as a concession to her observation. 'We have never had to condemn a Devil's whore of a witch before. I suggested the Bishop of London choose the way of it, seeing as this woman is one of his own parishioners. He may

561

protest loud about an archbishop's bones, but he can see the danger of someone casting the Devil's incantations on the steps of his own cathedral, which is where she was standing when she cursed me.'

Picking up the scrolled parchment and reseating herself, Emma shook her head, worried. 'Will there be trouble?'

'Possibly. Probably, but not with the witch, London will revel in her burning.' Cnut drank deeply of his wine, watched his wife with half-lidded eyes from above the rim of his goblet. She was a striking woman, not pretty, but handsome in her own way. She was elegant in her dress and manner of walking, was always immaculate, always polite, never coarse or foul-mouthed in public. Rarely in private come to that, even when they argued, she kept her language more or less within decorum. Cnut finished his wine, held out the goblet for a refill. If it were not for Swegen and Harold he would have abandoned Ælfgifu years ago. Beside Emma, she was dross against gold.

'I queried the wisdom of her execution being set for the morrow, but that was an argument I could not win, for it was pointed out to me that I would be wise to have her done with before the tomb is opened, in case Satan has been heeding her blasphemies. The fire will be built as soon as the tide ebbs; she'll be burnt on the river shore, beside London Bridge, and then, when the river rises, the water will take her and cleanse the area. A double death, you see, burning and drowning, both being methods apparently prescribed by God for those such as she.'

They lapsed into silence. Glancing at her letter again, Emma read a few of the words, found she could not concentrate.

'A letter?' Cnut asked after a while, indicating the parchment. 'From anyone interesting?' He played a smile on his mouth, not wanting to appear intrusive or possessive. Treading on hot coals, lest he break this apparent truce and she should snap his head off again.

'It is from my brother Richard,' she said, the quiver in her fingers belying the rigidity of her voice. She faltered, continued, her eyes lifting to stare at Cnut, the pain of need so suddenly, dreadfully obvious. 'He has arranged for my daughter, for Goda, to wed with Drogo, Count of Amiens and the Vexin.'

Cnut raised an eyebrow, impressed and unconcerned. Drogo could be of no possible threat to England. Now, if it were one of Æthelred's boys marrying into an area where an army could be raised . . . ah, but the Duke would not be so stupid as to follow down that route. 'An honourable and ideal match,' he said truthfully.

The choke faltered Emma's cry as she flung the parchment away. 'It is a decision I should have been a party to! She is my daughter!' Emma buried her face in her hands, her shoulders heaving, her entire body trembling. Instantly, Cnut was beside her, with Leofgifu hovering, concerned, nearby.

'I know nothing of Drogo,' Cnut confessed, 'but through my father I knew of his. A good man, so I have heard.' He embraced her, brought her close, his strong hand firm on her back, allowing her to weep privately into his tunic.

'Look at it this way,' he said, practically, after a moment. 'Had you been the arranger, would you have approved the match?'

Bleakly Emma nodded.

'Well, then, there you are.' Cnut kissed the top of her head, her braided hair bare in this, their private chamber. She smelt of summer flowers.

Emma kicked him, not hard, but with a force to let him know he was an insufferable pragmatist.

He yelped, laughed, tipped her face to his and kissed her on the lips. 'I love you,' he said, meaning it. 'Whatever I do, wherever I go – whoever curses me – I want you always to remember that.'

Emma drew away from him, wiping her long sleeve against her moist eyes. 'And, no doubt, you said exact the same to her?'

Momentarily, Cnut frowned, pursed his lips. Her? Did she know of Ælfgifu? Well, it was to be expected. How could he answer? Patronising? Placating? He decided to settle on the truth. 'I do not love Ælfgifu. As you have often observed, she is a scheming, plotting, traitorous bitch. I go to her for one reason and one reason only . . .'

'To bed her!'

'No! To ensure her leash remains tight secured!' Cnut had kept his hands on Emma's shoulders, brought her close to him again, held her. 'If I were to allow Ælfgifu her freedom, she would have an army at my gateway faster than a hare breaks cover from the hounds. She would take a suitable husband and fight me until the death for my crown for her sons.' He shrugged, grinned, 'Leaving aside the fact that no one could better me in the first place, that is.' He put his mouth against Emma's, kissed her, hard, with passionate wanting. 'This way, for the sake of those sons, my first wife has to behave herself.'

'She will never get the crown for those brats!'

Cnut held his council. Strange, he had held virtually the same, but reversed conversation with Ælfgifu about Emma.

A tug at his tunic hem. Cnut glanced down, found Harthacnut standing there, attempting to gain his attention. 'Papa,' he demanded, lifting up the carved toy in his hand to show him, 'Papa, you promised to play soldiers with me.'

'Not now, Harthacnut,' Emma answered briskly, moving away from Cnut and scooping the boy into her arms. 'It is late, skat, you ought to be abed.'

'But Papa promised!'

'He did no such thing.'

'I hate you!' Furious at the attention his father had paid to his mother but not to himself, Harthacnut smacked the wooden soldier into Emma's face, catching her brow above her eye and drawing an impressive gush of blood.

Leofgifu grabbed the nearest thing to hand, the embroidery she had been working, and Cnut, snatching it from her, slapped it against the cut, held it there with firm pressure.

'Take the boy away,' he gruffly ordered. 'As my wife says, he ought be abed.' He ought to have his backside whipped raw. Kept his thought to himself, Emma would never have the allowing of it.

One of Emma's maids came forward, but Harthacnut angrily kicked her shin.

'Now, none of that, young man!' Leofgifu commanded, grasping hold of his shoulders. 'You have done damage already, do not make matters worse.'

Harthacnut tipped back his head and wailed. Leofgifu, oblivious

564

to his shrieking, tucked him under her arm and bore him away.

Critically dabbing at the coagulating cut, Cnut observed, 'He is getting too wilful, that boy, he'll soon be needing a firmer hand.'

'He is bewildered,' Emma answered, going to the polished mirror to examine her reflection and tenderly investigate the wound for herself. 'The immediate now is the only importance to a young child.' Why was she so lenient with Harthacnut? She was aware that she ought to be more strict with him, but he was a child, a little boy, and she had been offered nothing except the rigour of discipline through all her own childhood. Surely there was room for understanding of how he felt? For giving love, not censure? He would behave the better as he grew, as he realised the importance of self-discipline, honour and respect. 'How can a child his age know right from wrong? He will learn. In time, he will learn.'

Cnut was not so certain, but let it pass. 'As the immediate now is of importance to me also,' he said huskily as he stepped behind her, inspected the eyebrow and satisfied himself that the sudden bleeding had looked worse than it actually was. His hands cupped her breasts, his thumb running over the feel of her nipples beneath her gown. 'Get you gone,' he growled to the servants, 'I have private business with my wife.'

Emma thought of objecting. She was not convinced about Ælfgifu, but then, why cut off your nose to spite your face?

Harthacnut went to bed in a rage, his face red, his body rigid. Only having that soldier clutched in his hand diverted him, silencing the fury. Interesting, the side of the man's helmet was stained. Harthacnut touched it, examined the stickiness that transferred to his finger. Blood fascinated him. Blood and death. He wished he could watch this witch burn, but he dare not ask it. He drifted to sleep wondering whether the witch would be alive when they lit the fire. Animals were dead when they were spitted; would they poke a rod through her from mouth to arse? Or toss her screaming on to the bonfire, like a bundle of old rags?

22

Things, to Cnut's acute annoyance, had not gone to plan. London had been determined to hinder his ordered removal of such an auspicious man from their care and although they had lost the fight, protestors jostled and harangued those who dared move the holy remains. More than one stinking egg had met its target and plastered the monks who had come from Canterbury to exhume the bones, but with the King's troop of housecarls as escort, the belligerent crowd had done no more than jeer and throw what they could. London Bridge, however, had caused the greatest problem.

Turned out in their hundreds to watch the unique spectacle of a woman being burnt alive – it had been an interesting show, the woman cursing Cnut until the thick smoke had enveloped her and even then her shrieks had continued for some good while – the crowds had elected to remain and pay respect to the Archbishop's coffin as it passed by. Only, the solemn entourage found the bridge blocked by so many crowding the roadway, making headway impossible. Furious, unsure whether the ploy had been a deliberate ruse or mere coincidence, Cnut had commandeered a ship of his fleet, moored on the downriver side of the bridge, to sail the coffin across to the Southwark side, there to continue its holy progress, accompanied by prayer and song, to Rochester. On the evening of the tenth day of June Emma, with her children, joined her husband to be ready, on the morrow, to accompany the procession those few final miles to Canterbury.

'Are you asleep?'

Emma roused, relaxed, drowsing, her body glowing from the aftermath of pleasure. The King's quarters were cramped here at Rochester, but sufficient, particularly as far as his bed was concerned. 'Not quite,' Emma mumbled.

'I have chosen my new Earl and Archbishop.'

Half asleep: 'Oh? That's nice.'

'I thought you would like to know before I inform Council on the morrow. My choice in both will be loudly obstructed by Ælfgifu.'

Full awake. 'Oh?' Emma propped herself on her elbow, her loose hair tumbling across her shoulders and breasts. She scrutinised his face in the dim light that filtered through a few narrow chinks in the bed curtains.

'Christ Church is in full support of my decision,' he said into the semi-darkness, his fingers stroking the smooth roundness of her shoulder. 'But then,' he added with a shrug that Emma felt rather than saw, 'they are obliged to owe me a favour for my consenting to return their Archbishop's bones.'

A lopsided grin spread over Emma's lips. 'So Canterbury will not gainsay your choice for York?'

'No. Alfric Puttoc is sincerely approved.'

'Puttoc? Alfric the Hawk?' Emma spluttered, full awake now and sitting up. 'But he is a Bernician priest, a firm supporter of Uhtred. Was it not Puttoc who condemned Ælfgifu's father and approved Æthelred's blinding of his sons – despite him being a kinsman of the family?'

'Ja, it was Puttoc.'

Emma puffed her cheeks, ran her hand through her hair. Ælfgifu could very well do more than protest!

Cnut touched his lips lightly into the hollow of her neck. '*Elskede*, beloved, there is more.'

'More?' Emma said languidly, tipping her head, *mmm*, she wanted more.

'I am appointing Uhtred's son Ealdred as Earl. He has proved his worth serving as an under-earl of Bernicia beneath Erik. He has earned the whole glittering jewel for himself.'

She had been sinking into the delight of his caressing hand, sat bolt upright, pushing his hand away from where it had dropped to her breast. '*Guds skyld*, Cnut! He killed Thurbrand; you could be stirring that bitch to rebellion!'

Cnut chuckled and pulled her down beneath the furs, his hands straying over the curves of her body. 'That is my intention. I am doing what you have wanted me to do. Giving her the opportunity to speak out against me, or for ever remain silent.'

'And if she denounces you? Will you hang her?' Emma asked challengingly, again pushing his hands away. Remained unconvinced when, between kisses, Cnut nodded.

When not annoyed with him, she enjoyed the pleasure of his lovemaking, but at this moment her responses were slow, dullwitted, for her mind was many miles to the north. In Northampton. Oh, Emma was in no doubt that Cnut had told her of only half of his intentions, that this ecstasy he was inducing on her body was to distract her from discovering all he had not told.

Through her numerous kindred – there were so damned many of them – Ælfgifu had been steadily and, as she assumed, secretively cultivating a hold on northern power; a bribe here, a favour given or called in there. She thought herself secure, subtly manoeuvring herself into domination, forming friendships and alliances, binding those of influence to her side; ready, waiting, to make her move if – when – anything happened to Cnut. Emma almost laughed aloud, skilfully changed the sound to a pretended gasp of aroused delight. With these appointments the bitch would lose all that she had so carefully built, as if the whole of it had been made of sand, washed away with one sweep of an incoming tide. She would lose everything but her small domain of Northampton, and that Emma could easily ensnare if need be. Perhaps it would be wise to start laying the traps now? Reward Ealdred, grant him favour; be attentive to the new Archbishop, fund his charities, finance the building of a few churches. Offer them both the undivided attention of the Queen. What was stronger, more exhilarating? The climax Cnut brought her to or the delight of triumph over Ælfgifu?

23

'I want to ride with Papa,' Harthacnut demanded from where he sat, bounced uncomfortably by the open-sided wooden-wheeled wagon as it lumbered over sun-baked ruts, his body craning forward to see his father riding ahead.

'Well, you cannot,' Leofgifu retorted, hauling at his neckband to stop him falling over the side. 'You are to ride with me and your sister. We will soon be there,' added, under her breath, *I hope*, as she choked down the discomfort of vomit. She hated travelling in wagons or litters, the swaying made her feel so desperately sick.

Harthacnut folded his arms, his face turning puce. 'But Ragnhilda is with Papa! It's not fair!'

'Ragnhilda is eight years old. You are not yet four. She is also a good girl and deserves to ride up with her father. You are a naughty boy and do not.'

Slumping into a corner, mouth pouting, Harthacnut sulked and planned ways of getting even with his half-sister. Cnut doted on her, always sitting her on his knee, cuddling her, giving her chunks of sweet and sticky honeycomb, tweaking her braids, tickling her – aye, and Gunnhild also, she received his attention as much as Ragnhilda! But him? How often did Papa give him shoulder-high rides? Swing him in circles, play chase or rough and tumble on the floor? All right, Gunnhild he could accept, she was Mama's too, but Ragnhilda was not even English – what right had she to Papa's attention? He had tried spitting on Ragnhilda and had earned a whipped backside for it; he glowered at the slow-passing countryside, Papa was laughing at something Ragnhilda was pointing to. Harthacnut scowled deeper, he could see nothing worth looking at, not unless you actually liked cows and skipping calves. Girls' stuff! He was surprised at Papa for being so taken in.

More reason to hate her. She was not wanted, not by her half-brother anyway. Why could Mama and Papa not drown her and be rid of her, like those feral kittens the cook at Thorney had drowned in a bucket last week?

Pleased that his mother had been wearing a bright, full smile all morning, Harthacnut had hoped for good fortune this day, was rewarded by permission to walk with his parents into the Cathedral and sit beside them for the whole of the ceremony. On the understanding that he sat quiet and still. 'No fidgeting, no grizzling or getting bored!' Emma warned.

'No, Mama,' he emphatically assured. How could he grow bored when at any moment those bones might rise up out of their coffin and wail and protest, casting curses and doom over everyone present? That's what they had been saying would happen in London and Harthacnut could well believe them! Only, he sat and waited and it did not happen. Gunnhild had promptly curled herself on the floor and fallen asleep at Papa's feet the moment the service had started, and Ragnhilda sat alert and erect, listening intently to the entirety of it all. Harthacnut began to find the whole thing tedious after the first slow-passing five minutes.

Three times Emma muttered at him to stop wriggling. Four times Leofgifu prodded him. Once, Cnut himself hissed, 'Your sister is behaving. If you cannot sit as still as her, then you had better leave.'

Harthacnut slumped forward after that, his elbows on his knees, refusing to listen to another word, bending his thoughts, instead, on a myriad of horrid things that could befall Ragnhilda.

Then, delight! A chance revenge presented itself almost directly on their leaving the Cathedral. It had been raining, a steady drizzle from a pewter-grey sky that puddled and muddied the streets. Demurely Ragnhilda walked beside Papa, who also carried Gunnhild, Harthacnut's hand held tightly by Emma, as King, Queen and royal family made their way down the steps and progressed along the street towards the palace, the people lining their path cheering and shouting their pleasure. Petals were tossed, coins, bread, anything; hands came out to touch, to bless, to praise. Graciously, Cnut and Emma acknowledged the tumultuous adoration, urging their children to return the waves, the smiles, the good-natured laughter. And Harthacnut saw his chance. Papa had to skirt a large sprawl of mud, separating himself from Ragnhilda. Easy for Harthacnut to stick his foot out, trip her.

How he kept from laughing he did not know, she came up, pushing herself to her knees from where she had lain flat out, dripping, covered in dung-soiled mud, her hair oozing with it, cheeks spattered, gown ruined. Everyone crowded close, lifting her, dabbing at the mess, comforting her embarrassed tears, but for once, Harthacnut did not resent the attention. Worth it, to put the horrid runt in her place, put her where she belonged, among the sludge and debris of the sewage gutter.

24

When Cnut was busy, as more often than not he was, Emma passed the day in Gytha's company, for her own friendship and that of the children. They were the family that Emma had always wanted, the laughter, the enthusiasm, the love that she had been denied by the austerity of her rigid upbringing. Gytha was a natural mother, love pouring from her spirit as easily as milk came from her breast – she fed her own children, would have nothing of a wet-nurse. 'They are my childer, I bore them, I'll suckle them.' Swegn, in his third year, was weaned and a terror; Harold, two years the younger, still in demand for his mother's teat. Godwine humoured her, guessing that the inclination would wear thin once several more infants came along. He would jest proudly, 'She's happy with sleepless nights with only the two of them – you wait 'till we have our own home-bred army to feed! We'll be employing wet-nurses by the score then!'

'If you're thinking on producing that many children, husband,' Gytha would quip back at him, 'then you can go sire them on someone else to labour through birth! I'm not a brood mare!' And they would smile at each other secretly, knowing she wanted as many children as it took to fill the house-place to the rafters with laughter.

'Cnut works too hard,' Emma said, thinking aloud, as she held the naked babe, Harold, above the stream, bobbing his toes in and out of the sparkle of cold water, making him gurgle and chuckle with delight. She shrugged her shoulders at Gytha, sitting on the bank, keeping a watchful eye on the others, playing in one of the wider, shallower pools. 'He hates the thought of sitting still, always has to be occupied, doing something. He gives me a headache with all that fizzing energy of his.'

'I think men are only truly happy when either planning a battle or lying flaccid and spent in a woman's bed,' Gytha answered brightly.

Emma laughed and, holding Harold high, stepped out of the stream. 'One and the same thing to some men!' She passed the child to his mother and, releasing her gown from where she had hitched it through her girdle, sat on the spread blanket, began drying her wet feet with a corner of it.

'Harthacnut!' she called, looking towards the children, 'do not splash so. Swegn's smaller than you, he does not care for water in his eyes.' If her son heard her gentle admonishment he paid no heed.

Pulling her hose and boots on, Emma said, 'We have had word that Thorkell is willing to talk peace.'

'Word with truth behind it, or wild rumour?'

'I think the truth. Cnut is planning to sail for Denmark again come the autumn, to over-winter in Roskilde.'

Gytha settled Harold more comfortable in her arms. He was a good baby, easy to nurse, to amuse, quick to settle into sleep. Swegn, her firstborn, was an entirely different barrel of salted fish, what a lad for temper! Even his mother, who doted on him, admitted she would be wary of meeting him in the dark once he became a man grown.

'I will never understand Thorkell's thinking,' she said, rocking the baby in her arms. 'He had an exalted position, second in command to Cnut, had the world at his feet, yet he tossed it all into the midden – and for what? To come crawling on his belly, seeking forgiveness?'

There came a cry of rage from the stream, a sudden flurry of a squabble. Leofgifu thrust aside her spinning and hurried to her feet to separate the two furious boys, Harthacnut and Swegn, both of them haggling fiercely over the ownership of a toy boat. As fast as it had arisen the storm subsided, the two, at Leofgifu's insistence, sullenly agreeing to share. All the same, Harthacnut deliberately splashed Swegn again by bringing his palm down fast into the water. Swegn cried, Harthacnut laughed.

'I'm telling you, boy!' Emma threatened, 'stop splashing! If I need remind you once more you will be away inside until you can learn to behave yourself.' To Gytha, resuming their conversation, said, 'The doing was all Wulfhilde's, hers was the insistence behind the trying for more. Like her father, she always was a self-centred madam.'

'So her death at Easter past may explain Thorkell's change of heart?'

'I would assume so. If he has any sense he will lay the blame squarely at her feet and plead insanity through beguiled lust! Oh, for Heaven's sake, boy!' Emma scrambled up, strode to the stream and hauled Harthacnut, kicking and yelling, from the water. 'What did I say to you?' she scolded, slapping his leg, 'how dare you disobey me?'

'But he splashed me!' Harthacnut wailed, attempting to wriggle from her grasp. 'He splashed water right in my face!'

'Do not go tale-telling to me, lad, I plainly saw you! Now, get you inside and stay there until I think fit to release you!'

Screaming his protest, the sound squawking like a hen-house full of fox-chased chickens, Leofgifu bore Harthacnut away, mindful of his whirling arms and kicking feet.

'I reckon my lad and yours both need a switch around their backsides,' Gytha observed.

'Aye, but it is the fathers who let them get away with it,' Emma answered wryly. ' "They're just being lads," they say and give them no more than a frown and a pat on the head.'

Gytha nodded amused agreement. Unless the sin was truly serious it was not she who was the soft one in the household but Godwine. Comforting to know Emma considered the situation to be the selfsame in the royal Hall.

For two hours Harthacnut sat nursing his resentment, hunched in a corner watching the intricate efforts of a spider repair a torn web. Come the lowering of evening, they all trooped in from the stream, his mother, Aunt Gytha, his sisters, Swegn, all laughing. Laughing at him. He swept his hand down through the new-completed web, destroying the hours' work, stumped from the Hall and out into the evening air, not caring that his mother was sharply calling him back.

He headed straight for the stream, but it was deeper now, filling, like the entire inlet, with the flood tide. Men were down at the boats, making ready to sail, fishing boats, trader's craft – Bosham was a busy harbour, with or without the King in nearby residence. He wandered down to the shoreline, stooping halfway along to retrieve the toy wooden boat that the argument had been over. Trust Swegn to leave it behind, it would have been there all night, then forgotten and lost. Well, it was Harthacnut's now. Swegn could mither all he liked, but he would not get it back!

A wagon stood outside the open doors of the mill barn, half emptied of its load of grain. Much of the harvest of the King's and Godwine's land in these parts came straight to the mill for grinding, the flour stored in great barrels raised off the ground to keep them dry and vermin-free. To allow room for the cats and weasels to creep underneath hunting for rats.

The bread baked was coarse-ground stuff, flat and often burnt to one side, doughy to the other. Their bread within the household, was made from wheat flour, that gave the flat loaves more of a rise than the poor man's diet of rye or barley bread, although many a nobleman insisted barley was food fit only for horses or the fermenting of beer. The water-turned mills had been a rarity a few years past, but their value had spread as rapid as their building; every lord had ensured a mill was installed in at least one of the villages; the King had one near every residence. For the villagers, like the plough teams, the mills were a communal facility, jointly operated, their worth adding to the economy and an easier life.

The massive, water-driven oak-wood wheel with its elm gear-wheels, transmitted power through the solidity of a shaft, also of oak and banded with iron, and all of it turning with creaks and groans, the great, round, grinding slabs of the quern-stones. The mill-wheel turning slowly, with the force of several horses, better and more efficient than a single woman using her arm to grind the corn laboriously to flour.

The wheel was not turning, its huge brake rammed in place, for it operated one way only, on the ebb tide, a faster, more controllable push against the paddles. Wandering over for a closer look,

Harthacnut stood at the edge of the open culvert, a deep, narrow channel, especially dug with sluice gates to regulate the flow during high tides. The gates were open, the scummy water flooding in. He ought not to be here, the children were not allowed near the mill, but then, children made a habit of going where they were forbidden.

'Harthacnut? Harthacnut!' Ragnhilda's voice, floating on the lazy breeze. Damn her.

'Harthacnut? Where are you? Supper is served.'

Stubbornly, Harthacnut stayed where he was, allowing the darkening evening to enfold him like a shrouding cloak. The girl spotted him. She was a serious child, who accomplished her expected chores and duties in earnest and with a willing heart, doing anything to please her papa and the woman who was his wife. Ragnhilda was aware Emma was not her natural mother, but who else had she to love and cherish? Perhaps if Papa were not so often gone from home . . . ah well, as Leofgifu often said, if perhaps were a horse, then all would ride.

The sun had been hot today and she had enjoyed playing in the stream, but now she was hungry and tired, wanted only her supper and her bed. She had been irritated that Leofgifu had sent her to seek Harthacnut. Why should she? She was not a servant. But Leofgifu had asked her in a kindly way, saying please, indicating that she was busy with the babes; and Ragnhilda was a child eager to help those she loved. A pity it was Harthacnut she was sent to find; she did not much love him.

'Leofgifu says to come now. Everyone is soon to be seated at table, we are to have ours first in the kitchens.'

'Go away. I'll not eat in the kitchens. I'm not a servant like you.'

'Don't be silly. You know full well we always eat in the kitchens, Harthacnut.'

'I'm a prince. I should eat at table.'

'And I'm a princess, but you don't hear me complaining. Now come on!' Irritably Ragnhilda lunged forward, aiming to grab the child's arm. He swung away, her fingers missing, but knocking against the toy boat which flew from his grip and spiralled into the churning, bubbling water filling the mill channel. It sank, rose,

576

bobbed on the surface, twirling with the force of the eddying current.

'You stupid dolt!' Harthacnut shrieked, 'you sham-legged, poxed whore!' As with all his swearing, he was astute at picking up phrases that adults frequently used and were beyond his comprehension of meaning. Wildly he flung out his hand, clawing at her hair. 'You fetch it back!' he yelled, kicking and punching at her. 'You climb down there and fetch it back!'

'Let me go!' the girl shouted, furious, frightened. 'You let me go! Papa shall hear of this! Let me go!'

'Fetch it back! Fetch it I say!' and Harthacnut pushed, with all his weight, with all his strength he pushed, slamming into the girl, toppling her off balance. She fell, screaming, down into the green darkness of the water, and, like the boat, she went under but she was heavier than a wooden toy, she wore skirts and boots. Unlike the boat, she did not come up again.

Harthacnut stood, frozen, watching the tumble of water, the splash and churn as it flowed past the wheel. When they came to fetch him in, he pointed silently and said nothing.

They found her when the tide had ebbed out. The great wheel, for once, held still and silent by its brake, the men prodding with poles and sticks, dreading what they would find. The undercurrent had taken her up against the wheel itself and her hair had been caught between the worn cracks of a submerged paddle. They hoped that she had been dead before then, had drowned quickly as she first went under, not slowly, entangled and submerged, unable to escape.

With Cnut away, it was Godwine's duty to ask the boy what had happened; the Earl found him, sitting alone on the stone steps that led down from the wall surrounding the manor yard to the causeway which at high tide was covered to halfway up by sea water. Harthacnut was tossing pebbles at a post, attempting to hit it, missing every throw.

'Did she fall, boy?' Godwine asked gruffly.

'Of course she fell,' Harthacnut answered, his head lifting, mouth pouting, defiant. He was afraid of Godwine, for he was a large, gruff-voiced man who often bellowed and raged when things went wrong.

577

Several times he had seen Godwine whipping Swegn; once, only last week because he had caught the boy deliberately stamping on a nest of duck eggs. Cnut had never struck his son, he laughed and ruffled his hair when Emma sent him to his father for some misdemeanour or other, declaring boys were boys. Emma occasionally smacked him on the legs, which stung but was bearable. Once, she had paddled his backside with her house slipper and Harthacnut had cried for an entire two hours, before Leofgifu had come to cheer him with a beaker of milk and sticky honey spread on new-baked bread.

'What happened?' Godwine asked again, standing below the boy, his arms folded, expression stern.

Harthacnut shrugged his shoulders, lied. 'She slipped.'

'And you did not think to shout? To come and get anyone? Get help?'

'I thought she would get out.' That was truth, he was not aware of what drowning meant. He had been told of the danger of water, but he was a child, the adults' constant babble of warnings went over his head with no more notice than when the wild geese took wing.

Godwine stared suspiciously at the boy. There was something about Harthacnut that he did not like. No, it was not like or dislike, more something about him that he did not trust. Swegn, his own son, was wilful and naughty; Godwine was the first to admit he was going to be difficult to control in future years, but Swegn admitted his offences, was almost proud of them. Harthacnut lied too easily.

'God help you, boy, if you are not telling me the truth of this,' Godwine said. 'I have to tell your father when he returns from London that his daughter is dead. It is not a task I relish. He loved Ragnhilda, we all did.'

Harthacnut did not believe him. Why would father be sad? She was nothing but a useless girl and he had Gunnhild, another girl, anyway. He, Harthacnut, was the important one, was he not?

It came as a shock for the boy to discover that his father could weep. Troubled him when Cnut, on his return to Bosham, walked straight past him and went to stand, for hours, beside the millstream, his shoulders hunched and shaking, great sobs bursting from his mouth. More of a shock when, attempting to approach him, Cnut had snarled at Harthacnut to go away.

Emma was at a loss what to do. Her husband would allow no one near him. Harthacnut kicked and scratched at anyone who went within distance of his reach, and little Ragnhilda lay so alone and cold before the altar in the church. What could she do? What would any mother do at the sudden loss of a child? She left Godwine to persuade her husband out of the dark of the night and into the warmth of the Hall. For herself, Emma slipped quietly into the children's sleeping quarters and huddled with her daughter, Gunnhild, who sobbed herself to sleep, her mother's tears silent, but as many.

25

'They are saying', Godwine said, offering more chicken to his King, 'that you are a saint, the chosen of God.'

Cnut took the chicken breast, bit into the succulent white flesh. He preferred chicken to most other meat. Lamb he liked, although it occasionally tended to be fatty, and beef was enjoyable, provided it was not overcooked and dried, but the white meat of chicken never gave him wind or burnt around his heart.

'Then they are saying fool's talk,' he responded dourly. 'I am a mortal man, no more than are they, whoever "they" might be.'

'Oh, it is all of us, Sir!' Ulf piped from down the table. 'We think it nothing short of a miracle what you have achieved! To avert a war with words alone? That could not be a task completed by those as simple-minded as us.'

That Ulf, the proud coxcomb, should think of himself as simple-minded Cnut found hard to believe, but he held his silence.

'It seems, husband,' Emma said, curling her fingers into his and smiling at him with fond approval, 'that because you have conquered Thorkell into submission with only your voiced command the populace are overawed by your power.'

'Stuff and nonsense,' he countered, genuinely bemused. 'I have done nothing more than show him my strength and that I will not hesitate to use it. He has used his common sense and submitted to my superiority. Where is the miracle in that?'

'All the same,' Ulf added, 'that is what the people are saying.'

Cnut puffed derisory air through his pursed lips. Concentrated on his meal and sat, brooding a discontented mood for the rest of the evening.

'They are only meaning to compliment you,' Emma said that night as they lay together. 'They are pleased – relieved – that there will be no fighting, no death or bloodshed, and for that they praise you.'

'But it is not a compliment. Can they not see that? Who am I to compare myself with sainted men? With men who heal the sick of body and mind? With the saints who have been blessed by God's Grace? I have issued threats that I know I can follow through. Where is the saintliness in that?'

Emma sighed, snuggled closer to the delight of his naked body. 'The years of war and deprivation under Æthelred took their toll, Cnut. We, all of us who suffered through it, vividly remember his inability to defend and protect. Now, here you are, strong and powerful. You stand with your sword drawn and your shield raised, and you send our enemies from us with the ease of snapping your fingers into the wind. Is it any wonder the people think of you as almost a God?'

'Oh, enough!' he roared, hurling the bed furs from him and swinging his legs to the floor. He reached for a mantle. 'I have more than I can stomach of this from those fools out there,' he flicked a hand contemptuously in the general direction of the door, 'without hearing it from you also!'

'You do not hear it from me,' she rebuked softly. 'I am merely attempting to explain how others feel, that they delight in the ongoing peace that you have brought to us in England.' She shuffled forward, twined her arms around his neck, kissed his cheek, her fingers curling into his red-gold hair. Whispered seductively into his ear, her touch wandering lower down the fine hairs of his chest and into the bush above his manhood. 'I am not calling you a God. How can a man who loves the pleasures of his bed have the chastity of a saint?'

He laughed. Enjoyed proving her point.

'God's Grief!' Cnut groaned as he peered across the sea-flooded inlet early the next morning. 'What are all those people doing over there crowding the wharf at Bosham? Is something amiss, do you think?'

Emma came to stand beside him, shielding her eyes against the dazzle of the morning light. 'There are dozens of them! Are they waving – look, yes . . . and here comes Godwine. He seems in a hurry, what can have happened?' Her first thoughts, as with Cnut, being that Thorkell had changed his mind and that his ships had been sighted somewhere off the coast. Automatically, Emma turned her attention towards the sea, expecting to find the striped sails of a Viking fleet coming up the creek.

Godwine himself was rowing the small inshore craft, his lean, muscular arms pulling steadily on the oars as he negotiated the channels; they were deceptive in this inlet, what often appeared to be deep water lying no more than mere inches above treacherous mudbanks. All was safe, provided a man kept an eye on the pig's bladder marker buoys.

He hailed his King and Queen, who had moved down to the jetty, ready to catch the rope he threw. 'What is happening, Godwine?' Cnut called. 'What is amiss? Is it Thorkell?'

'Thorkell? No, my Lord, nothing is amiss,' the Earl panted, out of breath from his exertions. Gytha had remarked to Emma only yesterday that Godwine was beginning to wear the paunch of a padded belly.

'The folk from hereabout have come to beg favour of you, Sir, that is all.' Godwine spoke lightly, belying the fact that he was troubled and did not care for this unwanted mission or the intrusion of so many people clustered around his manor. 'I'm afraid this whole business has fermented out of the beer barrel and is bubbling over the brewery floor.' He accepted Cnut's proffered hand and jumped ashore. Scratched, embarrassed, at his moustache. 'They have come with their ills and sores, their maladies and disabilities. It seems you are equal to a saint who can cure all things sent by the Devil.'

Had he been in a better frame of mind, Cnut might have seen the jest of it, might have laughed, but his mind was muddled and bruised, and his soul was still mourning for the loss of an innocent child. He could find nothing to jest or laugh about. He rammed his hands against his head, groaned aloud, a heart-rending sound.

'Do they not think, were that true, that I would have revived my own daughter from drowning? That I would have raised her from the dead? That, instead, I am enduring this utter, complete agony of her loss?' He shouted the last, his arms flinging wide, tears pouring from his eyes and his grieving soul.

'I am no more a saint than you are, Godwine,' he pleaded, hands held low, open. 'With all my heart, for the sake of Ragnhilda, I wish I were, but I am not. I am not!'

Godwine, too, held his hands wide. 'I've told them that, my Lord. Since they started appearing at dawn I've been pleading, telling, shouting, but they'll not listen. We lived too long in fear of the Viking killers, you see, to believe that one man can so easily ensure that they do not come again.'

Cnut buried his head in his hands. 'What do I do?' he groaned. 'Tell me, what do I do?'

Emma linked her arm through his, turned him away from the jetty and the milling, expectant people on the far side of the creek. He looked tired and broken, grey was beginning to tarnish his hair and beard, the skin beneath his eyes to sag. He was seven and twenty years of age, looked seven and sixty.

'Come into the Hall,' she said. 'No one shall bother us here at Cnut Bourne, it is a private place.' *And thank God for it!* she thought.

The children were chasing the hens from the Hall, their laughter shrill as the creatures, with feathers puffed and comical, waddling gait, squawked and clucked their indignation. They were not supposed to annoy the fowl, but chickens were such tempting creatures to incorporate into a lively game and Leofgifu had said she wanted to sweep the old rushes away from the floor, lay new; all the trestles and benches had been removed, that left only the chickens to shoo out.

'Leave them alone, children!' Emma chided. 'Let your father have some peace.'

Gunnhild dropped the hen she had grabbed, allowing it to scuttle, complaining, away, Harthacnut stood, quiet, his thumb in his mouth, resentful at having the fun stopped, frightened of his father's presence.

Nothing had been the same since Ragnhilda had fallen in that water, and Harthacnut could not understand why. For two weeks after they had buried her near the chancel arch in the church at Bosham no one, aside from Mama, had seen Cnut. He had shut himself in his bedchamber, here at Cnut Bourne, refusing to come out, see anyone, do anything. Twice Harthacnut had stolen as far as the door, meaning to go in, needing to see his father to tell him that he was sorry, that it wasn't his fault that Ragnhilda had fallen, truly it wasn't. But the sound of his father sobbing had turned him away and no other opportunity had presented itself. It all seemed too late now, somehow.

He had tried to say, the day they had buried her, that he had not meant her to go under the water like that, that he had expected her to bob up again, as his boat had. No one had listened to him, though, they had all been so busy. He was worried, too, that Papa was going to die – he understood death now! Death was confusion and being ignored, and adults behaving strangely. Death was fear, a white face sliding silently under the water. It was screaming at night in your sleep and wet bedding come morning. Gytha and Leofgifu had absently answered his question about his father but had not satisfied him.

'Is Papa going to die?'

'Of course not. What gave you that idea?'

But then, why did Papa have a second grave dug next to Ragnhilda's? Leofgifu said it was because it was prudent to have your eternal bed made ready. But why bother if your were not intending to use it? He was too young to understand a father's grieving and a gesture of commitment, made on the spur of the moment.

Cnut sat in his chair on the dais. Emma brought him a tankard of the strong barley beer he occasionally liked to drink, one for Godwine too. Harthacnut walked across the expanse of floor between them, his boots sounding loud on the cleared and swept timbers. Slowly he mounted the three steps, went to stand before his father, pleading to be noticed, to be reassured that everything was all right again. Emma saw him first. 'Come along, son, get you out into the fresh air. Papa is not feeling well.'

'I only wanted to tell Papa . . .'

'Not now, Harthacnut. Later.'

'Yes but . . .'

'You heard what your mother said, boy,' Cnut shouted at him. 'Get you gone.'

Harthacnut stamped his foot. He was fed up with this. All he wanted to know was one thing. 'But I want . . .'

'Harthacnut! Go away!' Cnut's hand came out to slap his son's face.

Crying, startled, the boy ran, setting the group of hens, busy pecking through the pile of dust Leofgifu and the servants were sweeping, into fresh squawks as he scattered them. 'I hate you!' he shouted. 'And I hated her! I'm glad she drowned!' He ran on, out of the door, added to himself, 'I only wanted to know if they've found my boat in the mill-race yet!'

Leofgifu stood, her hands on her hips, shaking her head at the dust that would need resweeping. That boy was a mystery unto himself. Such a strange little man.

'Don't be too hard on him,' Emma said to Cnut with a sigh. 'He is a child who is bewildered by what is going on. We are, all of us, upset. How do you think he is feeling?'

'You see,' Cnut answered, setting his drained tankard down on to the table with a thud. 'I don't know how to handle my son – what sort of saint could rebuff a child because he is bewildered and frightened?'

Godwine was not so sure of that. Bewildered? Frightened? Not if he was any judge of children. He had seen the same look in Harthacnut's eyes that night as in his own son's face whenever Swegn was caught doing something wrong. That sullen, it's-not-fair, glowering look of unrepentence. It was there whenever Swegn was caught pulling the dogs' tails, or kicking over the fresh-drawn milk. Innocent things, aye, but naughtiness carried out with a determined streak of something that went beyond mischief. Malice, almost. And it had been there in Harthacnut's expression that night when Ragnhilda had drowned. She had fallen, Harthacnut had insisted, tripped and fallen over the edge, but no one had asked what they had been doing there beside the mill-race in the first

585

place. No one else had seen that damned toy boat bobbing about in the water. Through narrowed eyes, Godwine watched Harthacnut stump out of the door. He was not sure about his honesty. Was not sure at all.

'Right!' Cnut said suddenly, thrusting to his feet. 'Get my boat ready, I am going over there.'

'Cnut, why?' Emma said, trying to persuade him to sit down again. 'You are tired, you need to rest. Give them a few days and they will forget about this nonsense.'

'No, they will not. Like weeds the rumours will flourish and grow more rampant than ever if not hoed and thrown on the dung-heap.' He clicked his fingers for a servant, ordered his crown fetched, called to another, 'My chair here, take it across to Bosham.'

The servant frowned, uncomprehending. 'Now, man, before the tide turns. Put it in a boat and have it rowed across.'

'What are you planning, my friend?' Godwine asked curiously.

'When the tide turns back in, I shall hoe the weeds, to show the truth and stop the rumour. Go with my chair, Godwine, set it below your manor steps beside the sea-line. You, Emma, shall assist me to dress, I need my finest robes, the best of all I have. Today shall be an unexpected crown wearing.'

No one particularly minded the King's quirk of odd behaviour; in fact, it drew more crowds as men, women and children from all the outlying villages made their hasty way to Bosham to watch the tide come in. He sat on the causeway, a yard or so below the steps that led up through the back wall of Godwine's manor-house courtyard. Come high tide, the water would slap below the top steps, allowing for boats to moor there, for Godwine to board or disembark, whatever the height of the sea. Sat rigid in his chair, his mantle draped around his shoulders, his crown on his head, watching the tide creep slowly nearer, ignoring the whispers, the murmurings, the speculation. With polite gratitude he ate, drank, whatever Gytha brought him, but he refused to move from his chair.

'You think I am equal to God?' he exclaimed. 'Then let me prove, once and for all, that I have no more powers than any one of you.'.

586

And he sat, waiting patiently as the sea edged in higher. Clouds scudded over the sky, the wind turned. Gulls screeched and squabbled, waders, busy about their foraging, quartered the mudflats until the sea reclaimed the land; the moored boats, leaning drunkenly on their unsupported keels, waited forlorn, abandoned, with their sterns outward to where the sea had gone until gradually, trickling and gurgling, the water began to meander up along the channels, turning the reed-strewn mudbanks to whispering, rippling water, bringing the slumped ships awake.

'My Lord,' Godwine said, becoming anxious, 'Sir, it is not wise to sit here below these steps. It may seem that it creeps like a scared mouse, but in reality the tide can gallop in. Especially on a day as today, with the wind full behind it.'

'I know, Godwine, I know,' was all Cnut said as he sat there.

The excited, cheerful chatter of the swollen crowd, that had vied with the noise of the gulls, lessened to a baffled mumble. What was he doing? What was he intending to prove?

Again, as the tide lapped at the cobbled causeway, Godwine came to Cnut, worried. 'Sir? I beg you to move, it is unsafe here!'

Cnut had been dozing. He startled awake and for a moment Godwine closed his eyes in prayer. Thank God! The King had heard reason! But no, Cnut was having none of it. He half turned, stared long and steadily at the array of people, gathered now at a safer distance. They fell silent, all eyes watching him, awed by his presence, convinced that here was a man about to perform a miracle.

'You think I am God?' Cnut boomed. 'You think I dare to compare my humble self with the Lord Christ's Father in Heaven? For myself, I would not be so conceited as to agree with you, but you are, all of you, honest and brave people. Many among you read and write, are learned men and women – who am I to gainsay what you must know above me? I am one, you are many. You say I have the power of a saint, then let me see it for myself!' The water was lapping at his feet, swilling on to the folds of his cloak, seeping into its rich embroidered binding, the salt irreparably staining its plush, expensive wool.

He sat, his hands resting on the carved, gold-gilded arms of the chair, feeling the wet coldness of the tide seep into his boots. He raised a hand, glared at the running water, coming ever faster now, in full spate. 'I am a God, they tell me!' he boomed. 'As a God I make command of you, the sea! I tell you, you wicked, murderous tide, to go back! Get you gone! I command you, the waves, to cease, to stop your invasion of my land!' Nothing happened. A wave, higher, rolling with the eddying current splashed against the chair, sending spray into the air.

Solidly, Cnut sat there, unflinching, unmoving. The tide was to his knees, his lap. Again he boomed his command for the tide to recede, his voice running over the concerned murmuring. Beyond the roll of the tide relentlessly sweeping inwards nothing happened.

'My Lord, you must come!' Godwine, kneeling on the top steps, stretched out his hand imploring, Gytha at his side, weeping. Where was Emma? Oh, she ought be here, drum sense into the stupid man! 'Cnut, this is naught but folly! Come away! Now!'

'I command again!' Cnut bellowed to the swell of water. 'I demand you heed my word and retreat, that you cease from the flood and turn away. I order it!' The sea was to his chest, spluttering into his mouth, soaking his beard. All talk had ceased, was turning to cries of alarm and fear, a woman began to scream, another to cry. Many were on their knees, praying. Godwine himself was shaking, the housecarls, his own and the King's, arrayed behind him along the manor wall, alarmed, afraid, uncertain what to do. Cnut had bade them be still, to do nothing whatever might happen, but surely he had not meant for them to allow him to drown?

'Pull him out!' Godwine stuttered, unable to bear the tension any longer. 'Let us pull him out!'

'Leave him!' A voice called from the courtyard. Godwine swung round, saw Emma walking towards him. She had come at last, thank God! She would talk sense into her husband!

'My lady, he will drown!'

Emma climbed to the top step, stood, observing her husband sitting rigid, stubborn on his chair n the sea, the water almost up to his chin. 'Damn silly way to prove your meaning,' she muttered.

'My Lady . . .!' Godwine begged, falling to his knees as she stood there, immobile.

'Hush, man, have more faith in your Lord King!' Emma snapped.

She rarely wore her crown in public, only on feast and holy days, when it was essential to show the full regalia of queenship. Today she wore it with a pure white linen veil that fluttered to the shoulders of a gown that was a turquoise blue, the sleeves of the under-tunic a darker colour. At her throat, her wrists, gold jewellery, studded with rubies and gems as vivid as her dress. Standing on the top steps, she lifted her hands as a preacher would.

'My Lord God,' she cried, 'may you see this day that our King is a wise and humble man, that he shows to you that although he is anointed with the Chrism, that although he is touched by your hand and your blessing, he can but command the men and women and children of this land, not the wind or sea that is upon it. That he can command but mortal things, for he himself is but mortal!'

She stood down into the water, descending the first three steps, and reached out her hand to Cnut who rose from his chair, sodden and cold, took her fingers in his own as he waded through the swirl of the sea and climbed the steps.

'You see,' he roared, lifting his arms to the crowd, 'I am a King by the Grace of God, but I am not God himself!' With an extravagant gesture, he took his crown from his head and hurled it into the tide, let it drift there, significantly poignant.

He walked away, striding towards Godwine's manor-house, as dignified as he could, considering the weight of his heavy, sodden clothing.

'You had me scared my lord,' Godwine admitted as he personally stripped the clothes from his King in the privacy of his own chamber.

'I had to show them in a way they would understand, my good friend, and this was all I could think of.' With a half grin, through chattering teeth, he added, 'I knew full well what I was doing – though I had not bargained on the water being so bloody cold!'

Did not admit, even to Emma, later that night as he huddled into her warmth, that he had considered staying there, remaining seated, of going to join his drowned daughter, of trying once again, to see her sweet, smiling face. But sense had prevailed. He would see her again, one day, at a time of God's choosing, not his own.

26

The rain squalled in across the harbour, battering at the manor that sat on the rise of ground above the town, the ships bobbing in its wake as if they were impatient to be off and away, out into the open of the sea. A busy place, full of activity, as each ship was made ready to sail; fresh water put aboard in barrels, food, weapons, spare clothing wrapped tight in waterproof bundles of seal or otter skin. The shields were already out along the sides, some of the crews ready to run out the oars, hoist the sail. Always, that excitement when the fleet was making ready.

'And when', Emma said, her fists on her hips, face contorted in outrage, 'were you planning on telling me? Were you going to send a messenger, once you were clear of the harbour?'

'I only finally decided this morning, *elskede*. If I had made my mind earlier to take him I would have said,' Cnut lied.

Folding her arms, Emma stared confrontationally into her husband's exasperated face. He had difficulty meeting her eyes, sure sign of a guilt-ridden conscience. 'Yet Harthacnut seems to have all his belongings packed and made ready.'

'He has little to take, a few clothes, spare boots. Leofgifu knew what to sort for him.'

'Ah, so Leofgifu knew you intended to take my son from me, but not I. Am I the only one not to know?'

Running his hand through his wind-tousled hair, Cnut sighed, attempting to keep his ebbing patience. The tide would be on the turn soon; he must be making way. 'Look, Emma, I would have consulted you, but I knew you would be saying all these things. I wanted to save you hurt . . .'

Emma slapped his face. 'Don't patronise me. You are to take my son to Denmark, to offer him as a hostage to Thorkell, to bring peace between you. You are using *my* son – with the history of how you Danes treat hostage sons?'

Cnut spread his hands. What could he answer? 'That was me, Emma, I made the wrong decision to mutilate those boys, not Thorkell. I have paid the price for making that mistake ever since. Will carry it to my grave.'

'And what if Harthacnut, too, has to pay? What then?'

Cnut went to put his hands on her arms, but she brushed him angrily aside. 'He'll not be harmed, *elskede*, trust me. He will not.'

'Trust you? Trust you! I'd as soon trust a wild boar caught at bay to lie down and purr like a contented kitchen cat!'

Harthacnut ran up to them, his face glowing with excitement, one of Cnut's housecarls, assigned as the boy's bodyguard, close behind. 'Mama, I am to go on the *Sea Serpent* with Papa! I am to sail all the way to Denmark, is that not wonderful?' He ran off again, overflowing with happiness, to lean over the sea wall to watch another ship pull away from the harbour and join the flotilla waiting to make sail out in deeper water.

Cnut tried again, put his hands firmer on Emma's shoulders, gave her a light, loving shake. 'Trust me. I know what I am doing. The lad has to grow up some day, beloved, has to become a man soon. How is he to learn to become a king if he sits at home with the women all day?'

Emma attempted to bat his hand away. Shook her head, unable to reply.

'I intend to agree for Thorkell to rule Denmark as my Regent. I will need to show him that I am willing for such a treaty to work, for the sake of Denmark I must.'

'Then why not take one of *her* sons?' Emma said, her voice catching with tears. 'Why take mine? I loved Ragnhilda too, you know. I am sorrowing as much as you for her loss. And what of Gunnhild? How will she feel to be losing her brother so soon after her sister?'

More diplomacy. 'I am taking one of Ælfgifu's sons. I take my firstborn, Swegen, with me. He too needs to learn how to become a man.' He did not add that for Swegen there would be no remaining in Denmark, that he would be returning home with his father, that Harthacnut would not. That amount of courage the King did not possess.

'It will be all right, dear heart, please believe me.' How could he tell her his full plans? She would not repeat them, would not betray a confidence he shared with her, but Cnut could not, for what he intended to do must lie with his own conscience alone, for God would not be liking its doing.

Cnut kissed Emma's forehead, nodded for the boy to go aboard. 'Look how eager he is, Emma, how much he wants to stop being a little boy and start the path to becoming man grown.'

Emma did look, she looked until the tears blurred her sight and Cnut's ship was nothing more than a black speck on the distant horizon. Was this what it was to be a mother? To have to learn to let go, to bear the pain of losing a child that was no longer just a child? To have to accept that his face was full of laughter, that he was delighted to be going? That he had not even hugged or kissed her before he stepped aboard that ship? Did Harthacnut, then, love her, his mother, so little?

'He's a child,' Leofgifu said at her side, reading her thoughts, 'an excited boy who has no idea what it means to be leaving, to be going on an adventure with his father.'

Emma nodded. Leofgifu was right, of course she was right. But oh, it did so hurt!

How could she be knowing that Harthacnut was relieved to be leaving England? To be going away from the image of a girl's open-mouthed, silent, screaming face, sinking, slow, beneath the run of a mill-race? To be leaving behind the suspicious glare of Earl Godwine and his father's deep, unexplainable sadness? Perhaps, in Denmark, it would all be different and he could forget Ragnhilda. Live a new, better life. Harthacnut knew he would be happy, content in Denmark. That, if he had a choice, he would never return to England again.

Come the Nativity, Cnut sent word to his Queen of sad and grievous circumstances. Thorkell he explained in his self-written private letter, was dead. He died peaceful in his sleep come the rise of a Sunday, a Holy Day, morning. A good day to go to his Lord.

Emma closed her eyes as she read, thanked God, for fear had so filled her. Reading his letter, her hand shaking, her tears of relief streaming down her cheeks, Emma wondered at how she could have doubted Cnut's asking for her trust. Died peaceful in his sleep? Aye, with a death contrived and planned!

She set the letter aside, smiled, began to dress for the midwinter celebration of the longest night, a celebration of bright, blazing fires, spiced mead and gaiety. Harthacnut would be home soon, before Easter at least, Cnut had assured her. Whether he was wise to set his sister, Estrith, and her husband, Ulf, as joint regents in Thorkell's place was another matter, one she sincerely thought was a wrong choice. Estrith was more than capable, a woman Emma would trust her life to, but Ulf? Ulf was as trustworthy as a starving dog set to guard a haunch of roasted meat.

27

Standing, with her hands and weight supported on the table, Emma was stunned into silence, could not believe what she was hearing. 'You have the nerve,' she finally said, the suppressed anger quivering in her voice, 'to tell me that you have left my son in Denmark?'

Cnut stood to the other side of the trestle, his hair dishevelled by the gale wind blowing outside, his boots muddy, cloak, as ever, thrown askew across a wooden chest. 'I have this moment returned home, having battled with a bitch of a storm, have not yet been five minutes within your company and yet you already rail me?' he snapped in answer. 'What form of loving greeting is this?'

'It is no greeting if I am not also to greet my son!' Emma shouted back, her anger rising with his apparent indifference. 'You promised me that Harthacnut would not be taken from me for long, that our parting was a temporary arrangement only. Do you, then, break your promises as easily as did my first lying husband?'

'I made no promise to you about Harthacnut,' Cnut countered. 'I wanted him to be joint King of Denmark.' He swung away from the table and seated himself before the hearth fire which, because of the wind blustering through every possible crack and opening, was a sulky, smoking effort that offered no warmth and less cheer. 'I would have thought you to be pleased that your son is already a King, that he has the assured security of a crown before him.'

'I want my son as King of England, not Denmark!' Emma retorted, banging the flat of her palm on the table. 'What has Denmark to offer me?'

'So this is about you, not Harthacnut?'

Firmly, Emma set her hands on the table; felt the roughness of the wood beneath her skin, the solidity of the table itself. Very much did she want to grab hold of its edge and send it sprawling across the room. Very much did she want to scream and shout, and slap one of these hands against Cnut's face. 'No,' she said, drawing a slow breath, 'this is not about me, it is about England.'

'I am here in England, I require someone of my name in Denmark to ensure Ulf remembers his duty and his station. It will do Harthacnut no harm to begin the learning of his trade, that of kingship. As I so began at his age.'

'I am not disagreeing that he must learn the complexities of being a king, merely that he should do so here, in England, not Denmark.'

Cnut slammed to his feet, knocking the chair over. 'Enough! I am King, I have decided that my son is to remain in Denmark. You have no say in the matter!'

There was one thing that had served Emma well through all the years she had lived in England, one thing that she had cherished as a lifeline against insanity and the plunging depths of despair. Pride.

Tall, elegant, she faced her husband. With Æthelred she would have been hiding her fear, the dread of enticing into the open one of his furies. Cnut raged, for he had a temper that could bluster with all the pique of that gale mithering outside, but he was never cruel or spiteful, not towards Emma, anyway. For Cnut, there would have been no honour in beating a woman. Aside, as he had often jested, were he to strike Emma there was every possibility that she would strike him back with twice the ferocity.

'So,' she said with all the authority of her dignified self-esteem, 'you do not consider me worthy to have a say in my son's future? Because I once set aside two of my sons for your benefit, you think I am able to do so again without a thought or qualm? That because I must accept that my daughters be married to lords who live many miles distant, that I can readily accept the disappearance of my son? Well, think again, Cnut. I am Queen of England and I have an opinion as able as yours. Either you value me as your partner in marriage and rule, or you do not. You clearly do not, so get on with it, but do not come crawling to me when you need advice on how to circumvent some difficulty that you cannot fathom for yourself.' She walked across the room, lifted her cloak from its peg on the wall. 'If you so enjoy being King on your own, then I shall leave you to it. I go to Winchester, where I know I shall receive the respect that I am entitled to.' And she swept from the chamber, calling for Leofgifu and her maids to begin packing.

Cnut slapped his hands on to the chair arms, swore. How could he have told Emma the whole truth? It would have hurt her beyond healing. Ja, he had wanted Harthacnut to be crowned as a boy king for Denmark, for all the reasons he had said, but there had been no urgent need for him to remain there, not with Estrith as joint regent. But Harthacnut had refused to come home to England. He had screamed and shouted, had proclaimed he wanted to remain with his Aunt Estrith, that he did not want his mama because Mama insisted on treating him like a girl. He had not expressed himself well, for he was too young a child to have the vocabulary necessary, but Cnut had known what he meant, for he had come to the same conclusion. Emma overprotected the boy and coddled him.

And there was that other thing that Cnut had never confided in Emma, the matter of Ragnhilda's death. Godwine had been determined to keep his counsel, but Cnut had dragged it from him, that there was something odd over the manner of her death. As reluctant as Cnut was to accept Godwine's unspoken suspicion – he had not been able to force more exactness out of his Earl of Wessex – Cnut had his own scepticism that the girl had slipped or fallen. Cnut was well aware of his son's acts of spite and his jealousy towards the girl. The boy needed to be put firmly into a man's world, to be removed from the niceties of a woman's. In the real world there was no room for dwelling on what was, or was not, fair. Life was harsh and every moment of it had to be fought for. How to explain to Emma that the boy did no longer need his face and hands wiped of sticky honeycomb? That he could not be having the crooning and petting that was due to daughters? That if he were to become an effective king in adult life, he must begin the following of the road that led to maturity and manhood now?

Damn it, how could he have told Emma, without causing immense pain, that it was kinder for her to be separated from the boy now, before he grew too far away from her, taking with him all the memories of childhood that, this way, she could keep close and cherish?

He let her go to Winchester, let her grieve alone a while. He would go to her in a week or two. By then he might have thought of something sensible and comforting to say.

28

Gytha gave Godwine another son, Tostig, and Emma, two months later, miscarried of a five-month son for Cnut. At seven and thirty it was hardly surprising, for childbearing was a hazardous business for a woman. Age did not make the sadness of loss any the easier, however.

'I am only glad she is safe,' Cnut confided to Gytha as they sat, one each side of a brazier, sipping Godwine's best imported wine. Instead of August being its normal benign, hot month, the rain had fallen in sheets these last three days and the nights clung damp and chill. The sea had tossed, melancholy and aggressive, longing for the clearer, warmer days of summer, and Cnut's ship, coming up the creek, had been forced over towards Bosham, for the wind had been too recalcitrant to allow him to tie up over the way at Cnut Bourne.

It was late, gone ten at night, many of the servants settled abed, Gytha too had been preparing herself, her hair unbound, stripped to her under tunic, when the King had walked in as bold as a full-pronged stag, asking for shelter and something warming for an empty stomach.

'It has been a bastard of a sea voyage from London,' he apologised. 'My wife urged me to stay a while, but I have the law court at Winchester to attend. If this wind had not grown more tempestuous than I had reckoned, I would be safe there and not bothering you this night.'

What could she do? Turn him away? Deny his hospitality?

'My husband is not at home,' she stammered, covering her immodesty with a hastily grabbed mantle. 'He is at Southampton, supervising the fleet with my brother, Ulf. Alas, I have been left alone to find my own entertainment this last week around, although I had hoped him home this evening. No doubt he will be here early on the morrow.'

Cnut frowned. Ulf was proving to be not very useful; in God's name, he spent more weeks here in England than he did in Denmark! He claimed that it was because he felt honour bound to bring personal word of progress to Cnut and that Estrith was capable of seeing to government. All true and worthy, yet Cnut had the suspicion that Ulf used the voyages as an excuse to be gone from his wife, to be visiting other more enticing ladies, and to make money from illicit pirate trading. Ulf was always one for preferring adventure over staid duty.

Feeling awkward with Cnut's presence, Gytha reasoned sense: she was not alone, she insisted her women stay in the room, and this was the King, not some ruffian good-for-nothing outlaw. She was safe in his company. Surely? She served him wine, Godwine's best, and ordered food to be brought, guessing at the grumbling that would erupt from the kitchen at this late hour.

'Leofric of Mercia has had a second son delivered of his wife, did you know?' she asked, attempting to think of conversation. Why talk of Leofric? Godwine detested the man, nor was she impressed by him.

Cnut nodded, his eyes on Gytha. He was tired and this night, oddly, lonely. For one reason or another he had not been to Cnut Bourne or Bosham these last two years, not since that summer when they had laid Ragnhilda to rest and he had shown, by the only way he knew, that although he wore a crown, he was no more of a man than any of them. He ought not have come here, he realised that, but he would look the fool to leave now and Gytha was such an understanding woman.

'He has called the boy Hereward, I believe,' Gytha added, 'an old Mercian name.'

'A name belonging to the ancient kings of the Little Folk, so I hear tell,' Cnut growled. 'I trust Leofric is not lusting after more than he is entitled to?'

'Surely not!' Gytha answered quickly, wishing she had never started the topic. 'He and Godgiva are staunch followers of God, I would say it is His favour Leofric is intending to purchase, not yours.'

Cnut laughed. 'That I will agree with. If the man founds any more churches in the Mid Lands he will end up as poor as a pauper. Mind, he collects his taxes with a fervour that will easily balance the scales.'

Gytha motioned for a servant to top the brazier with charcoal. 'I will have my husband's bed made ready for you, my Lord King. I think you will find it comfortable.'

'Not without a woman to warm it for me, I won't.' The words slipped past his lips with the tiredness, the drowsing warmth and the strong drink. He shrugged, realising that he might have offended her, but suddenly not caring. God, he envied Godwine! He had healthy children, a charming wife, everything. Did they ever quarrel? Did they ever go for months barely speaking a civil word between them? Were there times when Gytha loathed Godwine?

'I have been advised that it would not be wise to lie with Emma for several months, that should she conceive again she will not survive the pregnancy. What is a man to do in such circumstances, eh, Gytha? Ignore a physician's orders or become a monk?'

What could she answer save the candid truth? 'It would harm no man to follow celibacy for a while. And if he cannot control his urges, then that, Sir, is what whores are for.'

Cnut saluted her with his empty goblet and a mocking grin. She was right, but how in God's name did he go to Northampton without his wife knowing of it? Ah, it was memories of this place that brought this unreasonable melancholia over him. The whispering of Ragnhilda's spirit drifting, lost and bereft, like a rudderless ship, in with the incoming tide.

'I may need to return to Denmark with your brother when he goes,' he said gloomily into the silence. 'For all it pains me to say this to you, Gytha, I do not think I can trust Ulf to keep faith with me.' He looked up sheepish, attempted a weak smile of contrition. 'I confess I did not wholly admit the truth to you, Lady. Had we tried harder, we could have moored across the way, but I found a

601

sudden need to hear answers to doubts that are clogging my mind.'

Gytha sat opposite him, straight-backed, proud. She was aware of her fortune in marrying Godwine, for he was a kind and generous man who doted on his wife and family. If he took whores to his bed, as all men did when away from the home for any length of time, he was discreet about it. Discretion being a thing her brother had no interest in. He might be the husband to a king's sister, but of what use would that connection be when the idiot man wasted his position on some foolish moon-seeking quest of his own? Which he would. Gytha knew him too well to believe he would stay sensible and grateful for what he had been given, not hanker for the more that he could, perhaps, obtain. Like Cnut, she was annoyed with his constant underhand forays away from Denmark; Ulf had never been one to take responsibility seriously. With a sigh she saved Cnut the embarrassment of asking his question, for she had already guessed it.

'You wish to ask me if Ulf can be trusted in continuing to rule Denmark in your name? I can answer you simply. No, he cannot. He lusts too much for the pleasures in life and grows too easily bored with the mundane issues of routine.' *Please*, she thought, her discomfort growing, *you have what you wanted from me, now go!*

Cnut was sitting leaning forward, his elbows on his knees, twirling his goblet in his hands. Looking at her with an intensity that was unnerving. 'And can I trust you to be loyal to me? Or are you like your brother also?'

'I am loyal to my husband,' she answered succinctly, 'and he is loyal to his King. I must therefore follow in his wake, for I am tethered to him by love and duty.'

Cnut waved her sensible answer aside. That was the sort of diplomatic thing Emma would have said, but he did not want quick wit and courteous, clever answers this night. He wanted warmth, comfort and the passion of a woman, the heat of sexual unity.

Shaking the drowsy muzziness from his head, he forced himself to concentrate. 'For my sister's sake I must allow Ulf to continue with this regency. If I do not, he may well declare war.' He laughed. 'For want of something exciting to do. By allowing him to do what he wants, and not make comment on his indiscretions and failings, war is narrowed to a possibility, not a certainty.'

Gytha did not agree, but held her council.

'You are a very beautiful woman, Gytha,' Cnut said, holding his goblet out towards her for more wine. As head woman, it was her duty to pour for him, but she indicated for a servant to do it.

'I thank you for the compliment,' she answered, 'but I beg that you will forgive my candour in answering that you do not see straight, for you are a little tired and a lot drunk.'

Cnut laughed, a slurred sound, rose unsteadily to his feet. 'I would forgive you anything for one kiss.' He patted the air in the direction of the servants. 'Send them away, I would talk to you in private.'

When she did not respond he ordered them out himself, but she countermanded quickly, her voice high, breathless. 'Remain. I do not wish you to leave and, Sir, I remind you this is my house. I give the orders to my servants.'

'And I remind you who gave you the house in the first place, and who could take it back as easy as this.' Cnut tried to snap his fingers, but his co-ordination was blurred. He laughed, took a step forward and collapsed in a crumpled heap to the floor, his arms going out to grab at something to steady the fall – Gytha. He clutched at her mantle and the under-tunic, which tore and pulled away from her shoulders, revealing her breasts beneath – and Gytha's brother, Ulf, walked in through the door.

They stood for a long moment, staring open-mouthed, at each other, Ulf recovering his surprise first.

'So this is how my sister entertains herself when her husband is gone from the manor?' He walked further into the room, sat, insolently hooking one leg over the curved arm of Godwine's favoured chair. 'Does your husband know of your liaison with our King?'

Composing herself, Gytha covered her breasts, ushered the servants from the room; this was how gossip spread and malicious rumour was tattled. 'Don't be a fool, Ulf, nothing has happened. The King has overdrunk of my husband's wine and stumbled, that is all.'

'Oh, I know what I see, sister.' Ulf leered at Cnut, sitting in a crumpled heap on the floor, attempting to extricate himself from a tangle of legs and arms. 'I wonder what Godwine will make of it when I tell him?'

Gytha's face, reddened from embarrassment, pinched white at the nostrils. 'You dare talk of this, Ulf, and I personally will geld you!'

Insolent, Ulf rose, strolled to Cnut and helped him to his feet, brushing floor rushes from his tunic. 'You are drunk, my Lord King, let me assist you to bed. I am sure my sister will ensure you are made comfortable, eh, Gytha?'

'Leave him, the servants or his housecarls shall see to him,' Gytha snapped.

Ulf deposited Cnut back on the floor and, bending, smiled into his blurred and vacant vision. 'Sleep well, my King, dream of what you can do to buy my silence about this unfortunate indiscretion.' He walked to the door, a smirk playing across his mouth. 'I'll seek my own bed for the night, shall I? Your husband will be here shortly, I rode on ahead to tell you that he is on his way. As well I did, eh?'

Come the morning, Cnut nursed a sore head and, apologising to a bemused Godwine for the inexcusable intrusion into the household, made arrangements to sail with Ulf to Denmark.

29

June 1026 – Rochester

'Do I cut here?' Gunnhild asked, indicating the curved line chalked on to the length of cloth spread out across a trestle table in the Hall. The double doors were thrown wide open to allow in the light, two chickens sitting inside the threshold, their wings and feathers fluffed, to make the most of basking in the sunshine.

Emma peered up from the seam she was pinning, nodded. 'Cut carefully, though, child; that is the shoulder end of the sleeve and if you cut it wrong you will find it difficult to sew it into the bodice.'

Careful, her tongue peeping through her lips in concentration, Gunnhild cut along the chalked line.

'You mind those shears, girl, they are sharp,' Leofgifu added, sternly watching her. 'Don't put your fingers so near the blade – aye, that's better, that's what handles are for, eh, lass?'

Gunnhild was a quiet, thoughtful child, a girl who, like her mother, enjoyed her books, but unlike Emma at that age, was enthralled by the mysteries of learning how to become a woman. At eight years old she was young enough for Emma to coddle, yet old enough to be a companion during the long months that Cnut was abroad, and he was so often abroad. There were nights when Emma lay awake, unable to find sleep, that she cursed Denmark to the fire pits of Hell. For taking her son and her husband, for being so much of a damned, bloody nuisance. On the spear side, Gytha had once said that she envied Emma the months of freedom from the confine of marriage, to do as she wished, without thought of a husband. It was a compensation, but not one, with Cnut, that Emma would have elected by choice. Had it been Æthelred, ah, then months apart would have been eagerly made welcome.

The gown they were making was for the midsummer festivities, the first time Gunnhild had been permitted to help with the completing of her own dress from the start of marking the cloth with the pattern, cutting it and sewing it. She had held pins before, threaded needles and made tiny garments for her wooden doll from scraps, but this was different, this was to be a gown to match her mother's and she was to help with it from start to finish – she had even woven some of it on the loom that stood in the corner of Mama's chamber. Although Leofgifu had only allowed her to do half a row, for she had dropped the shuttle and somehow two of the ring-weights at the end of the dangling warp threads had become tangled. Finished, Gunnhild handed the length of cut cloth to her mother, who inspected it, smiled approval.

'I will cut this last bit,' Emma said, 'then tomorrow we can begin sewing.'

Carefully, Gunnhild helped Leofgifu fold the pieces, and put the shears and pebble of marking chalk away in Emma's sewing box. Gunnhild loved looking in there, at the needles, the thimbles, the threads and wools for sewing seams and darning holes, the bundles of coloured silks that Mama used for her embroideries.

Suddenly, unexpectedly, the girl asked, 'Mama, is Papa dead?'

Emma was clearing the remnant scraps from the table, stopped, stood absolutely still, staring at the child. 'Of course he is not,' she said, astonished. 'Whatever made you think he was?'

Shutting the sewing-box lid, Gunnhild chewed her lip, slowly lifted her head, her face troubled, eyes wide, frightened. 'I heard Leofstan talking to some of the men. They said Papa had been defeated and that his ships had sunk.' She stared down at her boots, not seeing them through the mist that was gathering in her eyes. 'They said that man in Norway had sent a great flood of water over Papa. And water is dangerous isn't it? Papa never lets me go near the edge of a river, or allows me to paddle in the sea with it any deeper than my ankles. My sister drowned in water, didn't she? I don't remember it very well, but I remember Papa crying and then Harthacnut going away. I don't want Papa to have been drowned like Ragnhilda.'

Emma dropped the bundle of material and walked quickly to her daughter, knelt and enfolded the child into her arms. 'Papa is not dead, he has not drowned! The *Sea Serpent* is a beautiful ship, nothing, not even a whale leaping from the waves or a flood as deep as the one Noah faced, could sink her!'

'Then why has he not come home?'

Ah, why indeed!

Emma motioned with her hand for someone to bring her a stool. She took it to the doorway, shooshing the chickens out of the way with her foot, sat, much as they had, in the sun. Patted her lap for Gunnhild to climb there. 'Now, my lamb, let me tell you what happened from start to finish. Ulf, who is husband to your Aunt Estrith, did a very wicked thing. He decided that Olaf of Norway was a better man than Papa . . .'

'No one is better than Papa!' Gunnhild interjected hotly.

'Of course not, but Ulf, you see, was a very stupid man. Papa could not allow him to be so stupid, so he had to take the fleet and follow him. Only the man, Olaf, thought he was clever and that he would trick Papa by enticing him into a narrow part of the river by pretending to run away. He had ordered the river to be dammed and at the right moment, he released the held water and sent a flood whooshing downriver. Papa lost many men and ships, but the *Sea Serpent* is a fast, safe ship and he escaped. He is very, very cross, but he is not hurt.'

'So why hasn't he come home?'

'Because Ulf is now dead and Aunt Estrith is a widow. Papa has to see that she and your two cousins are safe and well.'

'Did the flood kill Ulf?'

'No, he died at another time, in another place.' In his bed, his throat cut; cut, so rumour said, by his enraged and humiliated wife.

'And Harthacnut?' Gunnhild asked. 'Aunt Estrith looks after Harthacnut with her two sons, doesn't she? Is he all right?'

'Yes, dear, Harthacnut is growing into a fine young king.'

Harthacnut? How would Emma be knowing anything of Harthacnut? He never came home to England, rarely wrote, what letters he did send were polite missives about what he had been learning from his tutors, or what the weather was doing in Denmark. Emma could not give a clipped coin for if it was raining or snowing! How was he? Was he growing? How tall was he, how strong? Was he handsome like his father, or had he the shape of Emma's nose? Her father's jutting chin? Emma sighed, no use thinking that way, she had to accept that Harthacnut would not be coming home to England, that he lived in Denmark. But at times such as this, when she thought of him, missed him, it was a hard acceptance to swallow.

'So will Papa be home soon?' Gunnhild asked, snuggling into her mother's warmth. 'I do so miss Papa.'

'I miss him too, sweetheart, and I miss Harthacnut.'

Gunnhild wrinkled her nose. She didn't! Harthacnut had been a bully, always pulling her hair or poking her with sticks or putting live mice down the back of her gown. That frog in her bed, she was certain Harthacnut had put it there, for he had done nothing but giggle all the next day. No, Gunnhild did not miss Harthacnut one bit!

Affectionately, Emma kissed the tip of her daughter's nose. 'Papa will be home as soon as he can.'

Gunnhild was pleased. As long as he did not bring Harthacnut back with him.

30

September 1026 – Thorney Island

'So, now that your brother has gone to God and Normandy left to his eldest son, I hear your nephews have fallen seriously foul of each other?' Cnut said, as he languished on the bed nibbling small, soft, sweet red apples piled in a dish that was propped on his belly. 'Who has opted to support the younger, Robert? Men of note, or worthless flotsam?'

Emma was attempting to do something different with her hair, twisting the braid and looping it round her head. 'He apparently has some eminent followers, the vicomte de Conteville; d'Arques; Avranchin and Blessin, le comte de la Mortain; Ivry and Eu. The family Montgomerie.'

Cnut raised his eyebrows. Montgomerie? He was impressed.

'Those who cannot stomach Robert and that slut of his are either with Richard or have cut their losses and sailed for the New Normandy in southern Italy.' Her brother would be turning in his grave if he knew the turmoil his sons were setting, between them, for Normandy. Ah, let him turn, it was no more than he deserved!

She tumbled her hair loose, began rebraiding to try a different style. 'Alfred says that given the chance, Edward would have sailed with them.'

Cnut said nothing, bit into his third apple.

'You'll give yourself bellyache,' Emma warned.

Cnut grinned, tossed the core at one of the dogs who ate it as if he were starving. 'Damn sure this hound thinks he's a horse.'

Coiling her hair at the nape of her neck, Emma laughed. 'He's certainly as big as one!'

'What if . . .' Cnut said slowly, pausing with the next half-chewed apple in the air. 'What if the sickly, always ill, Richard dies?'

Emma looked at him, blinking patiently. 'I assume the question is rhetorical?' she asked after a long pause.

Cnut waved the apple animatedly, 'You know what I mean; *when* Richard dies – it's a forgone conclusion, after all – what do we do about Robert?'

Putting her comb down, Emma sat with her hands folded in her lap. What do they do about Robert?

'I know very little of him,' she confessed. 'I knew virtually nothing of them until those few months of exile with Æthelred.' She smiled. 'I was thirteen when I married him, you know.'

'Word on the wind is that Robert is very much like his father in many ways, stubborn, self-opinionated. That he has a desire to be thought of as clever, to have men respect him.'

Emma snorted. 'Then perhaps he had better find himself a suitable wife and forget this tanner's daughter whore of his!'

Wiping juicy fingers on his tunic, Cnut set the fruit bowl aside, sat up. 'Exactly what I was thinking.' He stood, walked over to her. 'Estrith is in need of a husband.'

'Estrith', Emma answered indignantly, 'is in need of no such thing. She is only too pleased to be recently rid of the last one.'

Frowning, Cnut unpinned the hair that Emma had just so patiently set in place. 'Exactly. Oh, she has always denied it, but I am sure, down to the marrow in my bones, that it was Estrith herself who took that knife to Ulf's throat. She would never have tolerated the way he turned traitor against me.'

'So reward her with a life of her own choosing.' Emma took the pins from his hand, irritably began replacing them.

'The reward of being Normandy's next duchess is not to be sneered at.'

Emma laughed repugnantly. 'This is my cousin, Robert, we are talking of? If he is half as bad as my brother then that will be twice too much! My brother was a cynical, officious worm. Normandy is the better for him to be gone, and I suspect men will think the same of Richard and Robert in years to come. You cannot marry Estrith to Robert.'

'But think of the alliance, *elskede*, think of that.'

Emma slammed her hand against the table in front of her, making the array of jars and bottles leap and rattle. 'They said that same thing to me! I like Estrith, I will not permit you to inflict misery on her!'

Cnut shrugged, prepared to drop the subject for now. 'Well, the decision is with God. Mayhap Richard will rally from his sickbed, and Robert will come down with a dose of the pox and be the first to die, then all will be settled.' He kissed the crown of her head. 'When I travel to Rome next year,' the excitement at the prospect ticked in his voice, 'I may well decide to visit Normandy, see how the tide turns for myself.'

Emma made no answer. She was pleased for him that he had received this invitation to attend the coronation of Conrad as Holy Roman Emperor, second of that name. He would be guest of the Pope, meet with the senior dignitaries of all Europe – but oh, he was already so often gone and Rome was so far away. For his sake she had to match his enthusiasm, look to the event with eager delight. How good an actress she was becoming!

'I'm off to see about the breaking-in of that grey colt,' Cnut said, the cadence of his voice as jaunty as his step. At the door he turned. 'I prefer your hair as it usually is. A single braid hanging down your back.'

Emma loosened all the pins, dropped them into their box. Aye, she did too.

31

‘ "*My dearest wife,*

*How it is in my heart to have had you here with me in Rome!
Rome! I can scarce believe that I have been there, seen its glories,
touched its past and witnessed its holy present! How can I begin to
describe the beauty, the richness, the grandness of that place that I
have seen with my own eyes? Words scratched upon a parchment
cannot do justice, such a task is impossible!*"

'Needless to say,' Emma stated with a laugh, and looking up from
the multi-paged letter she was reading aloud to her daughter, and
the Earl Godwine, his wife and their children, 'he then goes on to
describe in great detail, and with poetic language, that very
impossibility.' She read on, describing her husband's ecstasy over
the ancient city that had once been the centre of the Roman world
and was now the centre of God's.

‘ "*The seven hills were lush and green, dotted profusely with olive trees
and vines; through it all the meander of the river – alas I cannot say it
sparkled blue, even in the dazzle of the sunshine, for the Tiber is more
of a murk and mud colour, much as our Thames where it passes
through and beyond London. They told me it is the colour of the sky
before it reaches the city, where there is no settlement, muck or
sewage, but I did not have opportunity to witness this for myself.
There was so much to do in Rome, so much to see, so many people to
talk with and discuss matters of personal interest and political import.
The river stinks, by the by, though this is only early in the year!*"

'As does the Thames,' Gytha remarked. 'I wonder if it is as bad or
worse come summer?'

'Oh, worse, I should think,' Godwine commented, 'the heat is more in Italy.'

'Go on, Mama,' Gunnhild urged. 'What does Papa recount next?' This though she had heard the letter on a dozen occasions already.

Emma scanned through a few paragraphs, selecting suitable reading material:

' "It was most odd to wander among the ruins that once served as functional buildings. Temples, houses, shops, marble-clad archways. The towering circle of the Colosseum, where so many Christians were martyred in blood. Rome is all glorious churches with ruined monuments scattered about. The Forum, where the Basilica and all the grand and important legal buildings stood, is nothing more than broken pillars of stone among the marsh meadow where cows now freely graze, It is called the Campo Vaccino, the Cow Field. It shows that no matter how imperial you may be, it is possible to end up covered in cow shit!" '

The children laughed, Godwine and Gytha smiled.

'It is true, that last,' Godwine admitted, 'it is very true.'

'Cnut goes on to talk of his audience with Pope John, nineteenth of that name, and all the people he met at Easter, on the six, and twentieth day of March at the coronation of Conrad the Second as Holy Roman Emperor. Alfric Puttoc was there, too, of course, having at last travelled to Rome to collect his pallium from the Pope. It was he, coming home ahead of my lord husband with greater speed and urgency, who brought these letters.'

Although he did not make mention of it, Cnut was especially proud that Pope John considered England to be important enough, now, to welcome in his holy presence not only the senior archbishop from Canterbury, but the representative of York as well.

'Is the King coming home soon?' Harold, Godwine's second son, asked, engrossed in brushing Cnut's favourite hound, Liim. The dog was on his back, eyes closed in bliss, his paws limp, tail occasionally thumping as the boy patiently searched for fleas, gleefully cracking each one that he found.

'He is on his journey home,' Emma answered, 'that is why he writes us, to tell us he will be with us soon.'

'Is he to stop in Normandy again?' Gunnhild questioned, skewing her neck round to squint up at her mother from where she sat, curled at Emma's feet. 'Will he meet with Goda, your other daughter?'

Emma smoothed her child's fair hair. She was nine now, a pretty lass, with wide blue eyes and dimpled cheeks. 'No, dear, Goda is not with Count Robert.'

'Read me what he says of the husband he has found for me, then, Mama.'

Emma obliged: '"*I have spoken at length with Conrad and have made the most wonderful arrangement for our beloved child, Gunnhild. I have achieved, my dear wife, an agreement of betrothal between her and Conrad's own son, Henri. Think, Emma! Our daughter, in maturity, will be the Holy Roman Empress!*"'

Gunnhild was not certain whether she would enjoy being a Holy Empress. Mama's chaplain often said she was not holy at all, especially when he caught her idling her thoughts when she ought to be reading her Bible, or when she sat daydreaming during worship. Henri sounded fun, though, and anyway, it was not to happen until they were both grown.

'I assume', Gytha wondered aloud, 'that the King does fully intend for this marriage between your nephew, Robert, and his sister Estrith to go ahead?' She sighed. Poor Estrith, when told of Cnut's agreement, she had apparently been horrified at the suggestion. To have escaped the nightmare of being wed to Ulf – and if anyone had the right to agree with Estrith on the vile nature of Ulf's character it was his own sister, Gytha – only to be wed to an equally pompous man such as Robert of Normandy . . . Gytha sighed. Such was the fate of royal widows.

'Estrith is to sail to Normandy and meet Cnut there,' Emma confirmed. 'How else can he neutralise any interest Robert may show in England? And Robert, despite his protesting that he has no wish to take a wife, must agree to the betrothal. His war with his elder brother is at stalemate; with patronage from England, Richard stands no chance of lingering.' She shook her head. Why were men so damned impatient? Richard always had been prone to illness and agues, since their father's death had barely been from his bed for more than a few days at once. He would no more survive for long as Duke of Normandy than would a handful of snow near a heated brazier. All Robert had to do was wait, but no, he wanted the power and the ducal coronet now. For that, he was willing to sacrifice his conscience, his whore and his indulgent lust for boys.

She made no mention of the reason why Cnut was so eager to back Robert's cause. Her sons by Æthelred were both of age and Robert, unlike his brother or father, was a man who wanted more in his mouth than he could easily chew. It would be so easy for him to decide to fight for the boys' right to the English crown. The only thing restraining him from such rashness was Normandy's overlord, the King of France, who was, as with Richard, an ailing man of poor health. If Robert could not have Normandy, however, he might decide to look elsewhere. Neither Cnut nor Emma could be having that. A tethering alliance through marriage was therefore inevitable, with poor Estrith the sacrificial goat.

Tactfully, Godwine returned to Emma's letter. This was her own personal version. Others had been sent to the Archbishop of Canterbury to be copied and sent throughout the entirety of England. 'It is interesting that the King has managed to procure more suitable arrangements for our pilgrims going to Rome. The tax levied against them at certain places on the journey was a scandal that ought to have been negotiated long ere this. Few except those of high means could contemplate going on pilgrimage, but now Cnut has opened the way, he is to be praised.'

'And to obtain a relaxation of the charges made to our archbishops when in Rome to collect their pallia; that, too, was an outrage, one that for all these months had denied Puttoc the honour,' Emma added, delighted at Cnut's triumphant political achievements.

She had resented his going when first Cnut had said of it, but the pride he had expressed in receiving the invitation to attend Conrad's coronation had made her hold her tongue. The first King of England to be welcomed in Rome, the honour he had obviously felt at the prospect of being received by the princes of all the peoples between Apulia and the North Sea – for everyone of importance was to be there and he was to be counted among them – how could she deny him that pleasure? Cnut, who had raided with his father as a barbarian, Cnut who had been charged with murder and bloodied deeds, now recognised as a sovereign king worthy of audience with his eminence the Pope. She could not have denied him all that, even if it meant his going away. Gods, she saw so little of him! What with him touring his kingdom for the making and passing of laws, the seeing to an outbreak of minor restlessness in the North, more unrest along the borders with Wales. The patrolling of the fleet, the consecration of churches that he had ordered built. Constantly busy, constantly on the move. The lack of a woman's passion was no bother to him, either – huh, he still had his Northampton whore! That he visited her was only to be expected, but Emma consoled herself with the thought that the bitch must be ageing now, was probably getting crow-foot wrinkles beside her eyes, sagging breasts and a broadening backside. And then he had taken himself off to Rome. At least *she* was deprived of him also!

Emma's delight at receiving his letter was evident to all who knew her. The sparkle returned to her eyes, a lightness to her step; once or twice servants had even heard her singing. The only part of it which troubled her was his brief outline of future plans. To go, more or less immediately, and make an end of the war with Olaf of Norway. She would not have been pleased, either, to have learnt that he had written separately, if not in as much detail, of his intention to Ælfgifu.

To Emma he had sent, '*And therefore I wish to make it known to you, my beloved wife, that I return by the same way that I went, through Normandy, to oversee the result of my negotiations with Robert, comte d'Hiémois. I then have intention of going straightway to Denmark to conclude, with the aid of all the Danes, a peaceful and final treaty with those nations and peoples who wished to deprive us both of the kingdom and of life.*'

He had been so angry when Ulf had betrayed him, and joined

616

with Olaf of Norway. Ulf was dead for it, Olaf was not, and Cnut now had the official blessing, and backing, of the Pope and Conrad III to do something about that. Let Olaf in his professed Christian grace go against him a second time!

He had signed his letter with such pride and determination. God was on his side and no one was going to stop his intended retribution against Norway.

'*May He in his loving kindness preserve us in our sovereignty and honour, and scatter, and bring to naught, the power and strength of all our enemies.*' And his signature for Emma, had been '*Cnut, your beloved and devoted husband*'. For his official letter to England, in case any were in doubt of the blessed authority he now possessed in the name of the Holy Roman Emperor and of God, through His representative on earth, the servant of the holiest of saints. To England, and to Ælfgifu, he had signed '*Cnut, dear to the Emperor. Close to Saint Peter*'.

Emma's grievance was that he had made no mention of Harthacnut. The boy was at Roskilde with Estrith. Was he to stay there when Estrith left? Would Cnut be bringing him home to England? She wanted to see her little boy, to examine with her own eyes that he was well.

Another resentment against that Northampton slut. She had her sons constantly with her.

32

The marriage of Count Robert de Hiémois to Estrith Sweinssdaughter was a matter of distaste for himself, his betrothed and her brother. Rarely were noble marriages expected to be of agreeable favour to the couple concerned; as rarely, were they as instantly hostile as this one.

'It was a moving ceremony,' Cnut observed untruthfully, as the celebration feasting entered its third hour of entertainment. For the prestige of his reputation there was nothing that Robert had left out. The food had been the most sumptuous ever prepared and served in Normandy; the jugglers and acrobats the best money could buy, the dancing bears expensive, the harpers unprecedented and the decoration of the Hall, a displayed mass of gold and silk, weaponry and jewels, breathtaking. A pity the sullen faces of bride and groom spoilt the proceedings.

Robert made no answer to Cnut's comment, but clicked his fingers for more wine to be served. If the day had to be endured, it could at least be helped along by the potent comfort of a good grape.

Cnut had swallowed the insult of being ignored for most of the day, longer than that, for the three days since his arrival here at Fécamp. Had it not been for the utter necessity of this alliance, he would have returned to his ship and left this Norman to his poxed fate. As it was, he swallowed his pride and attempted to be civil to his new brother-in-law.

'It will be good for our lands to be further united in property,' Cnut tried again, his eyes still roving the stone-built castle's Great Hall for sign of the two young men he sought. He was not surprised he could not find Emma's sons; Edward and Alfred would be prize fools to be here. He would dearly like to see the scrawny brats, to decide for himself whether they would ever be a match for his own sons, but given the open nature of his preference to see the both of them dead, it was no wonder they had declined any invitation to attend.

'For treaties to hold,' Robert said with narrowed, hostile eyes, 'the men who made them must be willing to uphold the agreements. To do that, the parties involved must have wanted the thing in the first place.'

'As we do,' Cnut answered, stubbornly positive, 'do we not?'

This arranged marriage was nothing more than one of political convenience, for unlike his brother, who would do the bidding without question of his overlord, the King of France, Robert was a wild, unbroken horse, who insisted on galloping his own trail. France, England, Rome could, collectively, go to Hell.

'I would remind you', Cnut said slowly and with barely disguised menace, 'that my sister is not a woman to be treated poorly. She will not allow dishonour or disrespect, neither will I.' How to convince this proud peacock that he would need to bend his knee to the command of his superiors if he wanted to successfully replace his brother as Duke?

Robert did not give two pickled eggs for what Estrith or Cnut wanted. All *he* wanted was the legal right to wear the ducal crown and for that, Richard had to be removed and himself set as Lord of Normandy. Above that wanting, he had a list as long as his arm for what he did not want. He did not want Estrith as wife; he did not want Cnut's patronage, nor the Pope, or the Holy Roman Emperor's interference. All he needed was for Richard to die, the rest would be simple, but damn the bastard, he refused to step into his grave and this despite spending months of his life abed with illness. Ah, that was the rub, when had Richard ever been truly ill? Always he had developed a stomach- or headache when something was required of him that he would rather not do. Robert had never known a man who could vomit to command with the absolute proficiency of his brother.

Robert was of the firm opinion that, given adequate arms and men, he could convince Richard that exile would be preferable to death, but to raise an army he required finance and that he did not have, for Richard, as crowned Duke, held the treasury.

Reading Robert's thoughts, Cnut spoke his own observations. 'I will undertake to back you in whatever the future may dictate for Normandy, whether that be at God's instigation or your own. In return, you will advance no military aid to the sons of Æthelred, should they seek it. We are brothers now, Robert, united through my sister. Consummate the marriage and treat her with respect, that is all you have to do. Beyond courtesy to her, I care not what you get up to, whether it is to make war on your brother or love to your whores, be they the tanner's daughter or beardless boys.'

Prudently, Robert made no comment and neither, sitting nursing her own thoughts on his left-hand side, did Estrith.

She was not a young woman, nor especially handsome or intriguing. Her quality was in her kindred to Cnut, and in her impeccable sense of loyalty and honour, the mainstay reason for her toleration of this sham. She had accepted her brother's wanting of this marriage because of his need of alliance. Estrith had adored her father, as she now adored her brother, for either of them she was willing to sacrifice her life and, as in the case of Ulf, her conscience.

In England, Gytha, her sister-in-law, had promised to take great care of her young son Beorn, sent to Bosham this past month. The eldest boy, Svein, was to remain in Denmark alongside Harthacnut. Beorn would be safe, well educated, and cared for by Gytha and Godwine. Strange that Gytha, unlike her brother, was such a reliable, trustworthy woman. But then Gytha, too, had detested Ulf, with his scheming and plotting and penchant for treachery. Under her guidance the boy would know of his birth, that he was Beorn Estrithsson, taking his name from his royal-born mother not a dishonoured father.

This marriage was not to Estrith's liking, but what woman was fortunate in having her wishes taken into consideration where a husband was concerned? She had dispatched one husband for his unacceptable behaviour, would have no qualms in doing so again, were it to prove necessary, as Robert would discover, should he attempt to humiliate her or Cnut. Whether she would count his dalliance with the whore Herleve she would yet have to decide. A man's past was his own and God's concern, of previous indiscretions Estrith would be tolerant and forgiving. The same applied to any future bedding for the practicality of need, as with any woman trapped in a loveless marriage that was not of her own choosing, better by far to have your husband occupied elsewhere in an insignificant whore's arms than suffer the risk of pregnancy and unwanted attention. A long-term mistress, however, was another matter entirely, particularly a woman who had already given the man children. Herleve's child had been a girl, no threat, no consequence, but the relationship must end and remain at what it had been, not what it could continue to be.

How was Estrith to know that Robert had no intention of setting Herleve aside? Or that at the time of his marriage a second child was already one month planted in her womb?

For Robert, the alliance with Cnut was essential for the single reason of funding, but God could be a cruel jester with an obtuse sense of humour. On the night of the fifth of August, scarcely two months after the marriage, Robert's brother was stricken with a seizured flux that emptied his stomach, his bowels and his body of life.

There were those who suspected poison at the hand of Robert, but equally, the fish at supper had tasted rancid, although none other had suffered symptoms akin to the Duke. But then, Richard had always been prone to eat more than was good for him.

33

A son. Herleve had given birth to a son. William, he was to be called. A lusty healthy boy. Estrith had learnt of his existence eighteen days after his birth, after her husband had returned from Falaise, and boasted of him to her and others of his Court. If he had assumed Estrith would not care, then he assumed wrong.

'You will not see that slut again,' Estrith said, standing in front of Robert, her arms folded, her back rigid, face set. 'I forbid it.'

Robert laughed. 'That slut, as you call her, is the mother of my children.'

'They are the bastards of a whore. This boy will never be anything more than the by-blow of a tanner's daughter. I am your wife, not her.'

'And I wish to God she was!' Robert roared back. 'She is good and kind, she gives me pleasure, gives me love. What do I get from you? *Dieu*, there's more warmth in a block of ice than there is in you.'

'Do not blame me for any failure in bed, Sir, the fault is yours. How you can believe that boy was sired by you is beyond comprehension. How did you manage it? That flaccid cock of yours has as much chance of siring children as a mule in a herd of mares! I've seen more life in a dead chicken than in your pizzle!'

That hurt, for it was true, all of it. Robert rarely visited Estrith's bed and when he did, usually when he was so besotted with drink he'd not know whose bed he was in, nothing happened. Yet he was never impotent with Herleve. Why was that he wondered? Because she was young and beautiful, and made no demands of him?

'Either you avow never to see her or the boy again, or I shall ensure the child never sees his first birthday.' Estrith was not bluffing.

'You'd not dare . . .'

'Would I not? I dared to cut my husband's throat for his humiliating me. I could as easily do so again with a child.'

'I'll have you locked up, have you flogged, starved, beaten . . . I'll . . .'

Estrith laughed. 'You can do nothing to me. If my brother should ever learn of any harm inflicted on me by you, then you will surely know the meaning of suffering. Not only this bastard son shall be killed, but his whore mother also. Her death shall be slow, after all of my brother's army have used her, after she is made to watch as this son of hers is ripped to pieces by dogs, or dropped alive into a vat of boiling oil. Lay one hand on me, Robert, and all that shall happen.'

Robert raised his hand, went to strike her.

There was no fear in her face, she did not flinch, did not blink. 'Do it,' she whispered, 'hit me, give me an excuse to prove what my brother is capable of.'

Angry, powerless, Robert ran, retching, from the room, did not stop running until he reached the upper walls of the castle. High above the town he leant his arms on the parapet wall, let the wind sting his eyes and bring the tears. No one would think he was weeping, not like this. How could he give Herleve up? But he would have to, he had known that; from the first when he had lain with her he had known he could not keep her. She was a tanner's daughter. How could he make her duchess? And he had no doubting that bitch who was the Duchess had meant every word. *Dieu*, if only he knew of a way to be rid of Cnut! Assemble an army, conquer England, take it by force, make it his. Huh! Hopeless dreams! Unless . . .

Robert's fingers gripped the stone, his nails digging in, bruising, painful, but he did not notice. Unless he could do it another way? What if he were to do as he had once, in half-jest, suggested? What if he were to put Edward back on the throne? He would need approval from his overlord, the French King, of course, but that should be easy enough done. He would need allies, too. How could he get them? How?

He relaxed, released the tight grip, rubbed his hands, thinking,

thinking . . . *Oui*, it might work. Had not that old lecher, Herluin, Vicomte de Conteville, always envied Robert his mistress? Herluin was wealthy, he wanted Herleve as wife, he said so often, had again and again offered Robert incentives to give her to him. What if the price was an army, and agreement that Robert could see his children and their mother whenever he wished? With Herleve legally married, what possible impropriety could occur?

Huh! Let Estrith parade her high-and-mighty indignation about that!

34

There is something about a great leader of men that makes him shine above all others, a different thing for different men. For Cnut, his talent was the aptitude to use his brain. If something went wrong he would analyse it, look at it from every angle, decide why it was a failure and what best to do about it. Never, during the entirety of his life, did he make the same mistake twice.

Olaf of Norway had got the better of him once, he would not be doing so again. The usurper had lured Ulf and other such scum into his employ and had won the day by trickery, a ploy that Cnut admitted had made him look an incompetent. On that occasion Olaf had used his brain; when he was ready, Cnut used his. Sailing from England in the late autumn of 1027, he took fifty ships to start the bringing of Norway under his control. He was not expecting too much of a fight, for there was more than one way to destroy a rat's nest. His ploy would take longer, all winter and spring, maybe, would be less exciting and more tedious, but it would be wholly effective.

From as far away as Rome Cnut had begun putting tactics into place: a subtle word here, a bribe there; sowing seeds, scattering whispers and grumblings into the wind. Olaf was not a great leader, nor was he especially liked. How simple for Cnut to build on the growing resentment against his austere rule, and his paranoia of rooting out all heathen and pagan practices. The people of Norway had nothing against the Christian God, many of them happy to embrace Him along with Thor and Odin, but they did not take kindly to being ordered when it came to the personal belief of worship. They preferred to make their own choices, their own decisions and, if necessary, their own mistakes. No lord, no matter how powerful or how devout, would sway the *i-víking* opinion by force. Olaf's mistake, Cnut's advantage.

So hated was Olaf that by early summer Cnut found he could sail along the entire coast of Norway and not meet a single ship in opposition. At each landing place he gathered more men and ships, until at the most northerly point, at Nidaros, all men of importance were willing to submit to Cnut as the undisputed King over all Norway, Sweden, Denmark and England. Recognising defeat when it leapt up and snapped at his backside, Olaf shrugged his shoulders and, with his family, fled temporarily into Russia, until fortune would swing again in his direction.

For Swegen, sailing with his father, the moment of triumph was exhilarating.

'My God, Father, is it so easy to achieve revenge? Why my mother goes on so much about it I cannot imagine.'

Raising an eyebrow, Cnut turned, with his arms casually folded, to observe the boy seated and stuffing his face with roasted meat to the far side of the cooking fire. Did he never stop eating? Either he was chewing, gnawing, running his fingers round the residue of a bowl, or searching for something to fill his already paunched belly. He was in his fourteenth year, yet had the girth of an old beer-barrelled man. Ælfgifu's son. Cnut's firstborn. A worthless hunk of whale blubber.

'So you think war is easy, then, do you, lad?'

Through a mouthful of wheat-bread: 'Ja. Look how easily you've made an empire for yourself.' Swegen chewed, swallowed. 'And a future kingdom for us, of course, for Harold and me.'

How odd that his three sons were all so different. Swegen here, lazy, greedy, expecting everything to be provided for him – so much like his mother, the very image of her, even down to the nasal whine when circumstances did not go his way. Harold. Harold was the fighter, the athlete, the wrestler, the one who always had to be better, braver, stronger than everyone else. They called him Harefoot, his friends, for his fleetness at running. Cnut did not deny him the praise he deserved for all those attributes, but where was the counterbalance? Where was the willingness to acknowledge others as good, the humility of losing? And Harthacnut. Still a child, not quite nine years, but with a streak of ruthlessness about him that would, when he became a man, bode ill for an enemy. He was the quiet one, the one who accepted that it was as important to read books as it was to learn how to use a shield and spear. That poetry and languages sat side alongside with the tactics of war. Swegen the acquisitor, Harold the warrior and Harthacnut? Harthacnut was the thinker. The one who, although the youngest, would, in Cnut's opinion, one day make the better king. Although Ælfgifu would never see it that way, but then, she was not a woman who could see anything except her own narrowed vision and her ceaseless lust for vengeance.

Cnut scratched at his beard and set his boot on the brick hearth ledge, leant forward, his arm resting on the raised thigh. 'I may decide that only one of my sons deserves to step into my boots when I kick them off. Then where will you be?'

Sullenly – there it was, that whine – Swegen complained, 'Mama says you want all this to come to us. Denmark and Norway for me, England for Harold. That is why you came to Northampton to fetch me and bring me here with you on this campaign. That is why you left Harold in England. You brought me with you because you wanted me at your side when you transferred the body of your father from York Minster into your new-founded church at Roskilde. To show your men that I am your eldest son and that I am the chosen ætheling.'

This time it was Cnut who laughed. 'You think all that, do you? Or rather, your mother does? Your walnut-sized brain has been busy! Her extent of imagination never ceases to amaze me.'

Swegen's scowl deepened. He disliked being laughed at.

'And what of Harthacnut?' Cnut asked. 'What is there in this grand scheme of yours for him? Do you conveniently forget that before we sailed here to Norway I had him standing on my other side when we laid your grandfather to rest in his beloved homeland?'

The boy said nothing.

'Let me enlighten you to another way of thinking!' Cnut snapped, the easy nature disappearing as he came to attention and stormed around the hearth to lock his hand into the boy's neckband. 'I brought you here because there is no point in a man having sons if those sons do nothing more than fill their bellies or brawl with others half their size. Nor am I interested in building an empire. As King of Denmark I control the narrow entrance from the Kattegat into the Baltic Sea. With Norway mine, I have command over the open waters that lead to that entrance. As King of England I rule the North Sea, which is a necessity for trade and fishing. I dominate the great trade routes which lead from the Bay of Biscay to the eastern Baltic. No one who wishes to trade in my waters can ignore me. *That* is why I am recognised as an equal in any European Court, *that* is why I am respected and listened to. And that is why neither you nor Harold will receive any of it solely for yourselves. If you think you can hold a kingdom then I suggest you get off your fat arse and start learning how to do it!' He shouted the last and, releasing his hold, cuffed Swegen's ear. The boy slumped on to his stool, miserable and resentful. His father would not have dared hit him had his mother been here. And as for Harthacnut, what, that twisted runt of a shrimp? Swegen could eat him for breakfast. Or at least Harold could.

'I'd do a better job than Harthacnut,' Swegen grumbled, scowling up at his father. 'He's nothing more than a milksop babe.'

'He will grow.'

'As will I!'

Cnut was impressed at that, the lad was more proficient at shouting back than he had realised.

35

Cnut poked his head round the storeroom door, his eyes adjusting from the bright sunlight into the dimness. 'They said I'd find you here,' he announced as, ducking, he walked through and down the three steps, reaching out to take one of the apples off the table.

Emma smacked his hand. 'If we ate them all there would be nothing to store!'

'One will not go amiss, surely?'

On every shelf, bench, ledge were rows of crocks and jars. On the floor, larger pots, their openings covered with greased parchment, the string ties sealed airtight with a mixture of clarified butter and oil. Barrels, wooden chests, small boxes, all of them, every one, crammed with the year's harvest. Boiled, honeyed or dried fruit; rose-hip preserve. From the roof beams hung bunches of drying herbs. Nuts, berries, root vegetables.

'Not that one,' Emma said sharply to one of the servants, pointing to the apple in the girl's hand, 'it is mouldy, put it with the others for the pigs.'

She turned back to Cnut. 'What is it you want? You can see I'm busy. With Gytha about her woman's work I have the two households to oversee, my own and hers.'

'Having had a daughter last time, Godwine is hoping for another boy,' Cnut offered as conversation.

'Godwine will get what the good Lord and Gytha together give him.' Again she attempted to shoo Cnut out; there were all these apples to store in the bran barrels, then the last of the plums to cover in honey and seal in jars. The fruit had ripened well this year, the crop offering a good yield. Everything that was not to be eaten immediately was to be stored in sealed containers, for rats and mice could make short work of a storeroom during a harsh winter, despite the employ of cats, ferrets and weasels.

'I need to talk,' Cnut admitted as he finished the apple.

'What, now?'

'It is a fine, clear day. Will you walk with me?'

'What is it you need to talk about?'

Cnut nearly answered with snapped impatience, *Just stop what you are doing and listen*, the words hastily bitten before they left his mouth. 'Anything and everything, Emma,' he said, 'but mostly my sons.'

Emma passed another handful of apples across to be packed in the bran. There was maybe a further half an hour's work to be done here, but these girls were sensible, they knew what to do and aside, this was only a favour she was offering Gytha. Once the babe was born and she was on her feet again . . . 'Finish here,' she ordered, 'and see you tidy everything away. I shall be checking.' She unfastened the sacking apron from her waist, presented herself to her husband. 'To where do we walk?'

Outside the storeroom he offered his arm, pointed to the meadows. 'I thought we could walk home by way of the fields. I have taken the liberty of saying our farewell to Godwine.'

'He knows to send if Gytha needs me?'

Cnut nodded. Emma threaded her arm through his.

'The swallows are gathering,' he said as he noticed the birds perched along the ridge of Godwine's manor house. 'They will soon be flying away. I wonder where they go and how they know to get there?'

'I expect it is like you when you sail your ship; they follow the wind, know the currents; watch the stars and the path of the sun.'

'I hate seeing them go,' Cnut confessed. 'The swallows fly away, the leaves turn gold, the cattle are readied for slaughter. Autumn can be a beautiful season, but I do so dread the onset of winter. It is so dark and cold for so long. When Yule approaches I wonder whether we shall ever see the sun again.'

Offering his hand, Cnut helped Emma climb over the stile, flicked his hand at several cows approaching too close and called the dogs to heel. His favourite, Liim, was getting old, slower with his running, his age showing in a pronounced limp and deafness to his ears. The pups leaving him far behind when they ran, all save for the smallest one of the latest litter, a white-pawed runt that clung adoringly to Cnut's side.

'You are to tell me that you cannot send for Harthacnut to come home,' Emma said after a long pause, during which they crossed half the meadow.

Cnut stopped, twined his fingers through hers, lifted his shoulders, let them fall, slowly, again. 'You do not like him being in Denmark, I know, but he is happy there. I have the right men looking after his and Denmark's needs. As King he must know the land, the people, how can I recall him to England and risk losing all I have?' He kissed her fingers, one by one, then leant forward to brush his lips against hers.

Easing her fingers from his grip, Emma continued walking. 'What you are trying to tell me is that not only can I not expect to see my son, but you, too, are to disappear again.'

'If I leave Norway open and vulnerable . . .'

Emma stopped abruptly, whirled to face him. 'Yet you leave England so! You leave me! How much have I seen of you these last years? A day here, a month there. Last year I even doubted whether I would recognise you were you to ride through the gateway!'

'*Elskede*, dear heart, I . . .'

'My son is gone, Cnut, and I see nothing of you . . . you say you dread the coming of winter. How do you think I feel when the nights grow longer than the days and I am alone? While you are off chasing rainbows, all I have is a hearth-fire and a gaggle of servants.'

'That is what it is to be a king, or queen. I am sorry.'

The tide was creeping in, half the creek flooded with water, the other half, the mudbanks, waiting to be covered. A small boat, her sail flapping, was out on the water, Godwine's eldest two sons, Swegn and Harold, their voices floating on the clear breeze.

Was this what she had wanted, those years ago, when she had decided on keeping a crown? She was the Queen, the most powerful woman in all England; she could do, have, whatever she commanded . . . except she could not have her son and her husband.

'I have, all these years, resented you taking Harthacnut to Denmark, making him a boy king of a foreign country. I want him here, as King of England, but equally, I am proud that he is becoming a good boy, that he is learning well and that he should follow in your steps and grow as bright as you.' She walked back to where Cnut had remained standing, set her palm flat on his chest. 'Go to Norway, as I know you will, but return as soon as you may. Do not leave me alone too long, not again. I have such fears for you, and for England, while you are not here.'

Cnut wrapped his arms around her, he was so fortunate to have this woman as his wife. She hated most of what he had to do, but accepted it. She missed Harthacnut, but realised that to be King he could not grow up under her skirts. How unlike Ælfgifu she was! Opposites, chalk to cheese, day to night, sour to sweet.

There was not a month went by that some messenger or letter arrived from Northampton demanding Cnut recognise his sons and offer them some position of worth to suit their rank. From that point, it had been a mistake to give Denmark's crown to Harthacnut, for Ælfgifu wanted the same for her own boys. Dare he do it? Dare he give Ælfgifu what she wanted and risk losing everything he had of Emma? Yet to crown Swegen and Harold now could be as useful as Harthacnut being joint King of Denmark; and were he to do it, then might there be a slender possibility that when he was gone there would be no fighting and brawling between the three for who was to have what?

'There is a log here, let us sit.' Gallantly, Cnut removed his cloak, spread it. 'There is no reason for me to sail for Norway until next spring. Olaf can scarce gather men together over the winter, but come spring it will be a different catch of fish. I will sail . . .' he pondered a moment, studying the sky, the run of the tide, as if the signs could tell him how the intervening winter would fare. 'Probably I will sail in April, after the Easter calling of Council.'

'You wish me to be your regent? Are you satisfied with how I have governed your kingdom in your past absences?'

Cnut laid his hand against her face. She was forty years old, a streak of silver was in her hair now, the lines at her eyes deeper, more marked, but her eyes were as bright, her figure as slim. Her wit as sharp. 'Do you need to ask? England is yours as much as mine, while I live.'

'England will be mine even after!' she shot back at him. 'Through Harthacnut I will remain Queen!'

'Yes, yes of course, I did not mean . . .'

'What did you mean, then?' Angry, Emma pulled away from him, stood, took two steps. 'Spit it out, Cnut, there is something you are finding difficult to say. You may be gone from me for seasons at a time, yet I know you all too well after these years together as husband and wife. What is it you are afraid to tell me?'

Must this wretched woman always be so astute?

'When I sail to Norway I am taking Ælfgifu and Swegen with me. She is to have Norway until he comes of age.' To Cnut's mind it seemed a suitable compromise. Ælfgifu got what she wanted, Norway was kept under Cnut's thumb and Emma, *ja*, well, he was not certain about Emma.

'And Harold? What of him?'

'I have not yet decided for him.'

'He will not have England, Cnut. By my life he will not!' Emma jerked her arms apart, palms outermost in a gesture of finality.

Cnut raised his eyes to the sky, confounded. 'Damn it, Emma, I thought you would be pleased. I am removing Ælfgifu and one of her sons from England. I am sending her away so that she can no longer annoy you!' That was the other advantage of the idea; as loath as Cnut was to admit it, even to himself, Ælfgifu and her demands were like mud cloying to his boots. By sending her to Norway he could be rid of her without raising a hurricane of temper.

'If you had set her aside, as our marriage negotiations had agreed, she would not annoy me anyway! If you had disinherited her brats, seen nothing of any of them, had her arrested for treason on the numerous occasions that she has stirred trouble against you, she would not annoy me. And despite all that you reward her with a kingdom and think I will not be angry? I suggest you think again, Cnut!'

633

'Oh, Emma, Emma! Please! Can I never satisfy you? I give Swegen and his mother Norway, that will content her and him both. She can do what she likes with it, provided she holds in my name keeps the waterways open and free for trade. Do you not think I have puzzled on this for months now? I have thought so hard it has felt as if my head would burst from the effort of it. Ælfgifu has only ever wanted a crown. Let me give her the next best thing and she will be content.'

'Content with a regency? Ælfgifu! I doubt it!' Emma turned on her heel, walked three steps, then swung round, her finger wagging as if she were admonishing a child. 'I warn you, Cnut, if either she or those sons try for more than this then they will regret the day they were born. My sons are the æthelings, Harthacnut is your heir, and after him come my other sons, Edward and Alfred. You, and she, may have forgotten their existence. I have not.'

36

Three years of peace and three years of Cnut, more or less, being as a husband should be, at home with his wife. That had its downside, of course, for Emma was not a person who minded the solitude of her own company and Cnut was not a man who pursued conversation for the sake of talk alone. On inclement days he had fussed and huffed his boredom, on hot days yearned for the freedom of the sea, but England enjoyed his presence and, on the whole, so did Emma. The few days that he was gone, for a kingdom needed to see its king, she did not mind, but admitted to missing him and his minor irritations.

Engrossed in sketching a new pattern for an embroidery, Emma did not hear Cnut come into the chamber, only a swirl of wind rustling through the rushes on the floor and a flutter of the wall hangings alerting her to someone entering. She assumed it was Leofgifu, who had gone to visit the privy.

'Did you fetch that drawing charcoal for me?' Emma asked without looking up. 'I need more if I am to design flowers for this corner.'

Cnut stood behind her, peering over her shoulder at the spread of low-quality parchment. 'It looks well enough to me, without an embellishment of flowers.'

Emma squealed, taken by surprise and spun around, her face lighting into a smile. 'You're back, oh, I am glad! I did not expect you until the morrow!' She was on her feet, charcoal, sketches and embroideries quite forgotten, her arms going about his neck, their lips meeting. 'Did it go well?' she asked, giving him another squeeze before releasing him, and sending her maids off to fetch refreshment and to heat water for a bath.

'You stink of travel grime and sweat.' She laughed, wrinkling disdain at his indelicate aroma.

'And it is cold out there, hot water would warm me. *Ja*, the law courts of the Dorset Hundreds went well, although I do not feel comfortable making judgements upon men and women.'

'If they have committed a crime they deserve punishment,' Emma observed, pushing him into a chair and bending to pull off his boots.

'But that is the problem, is it not? *If* they committed a crime.' He sighed, allowed her to rub warmth into his hands, the wind was bitter outside and this room, although heated with several braziers and hung with heavy furs and embroideries on the walls, was scurrying with malicious draughts. 'I wish there could be a way of discovering whether the truth was being told. To take one man's word against another is not always satisfactory.'

'Under oath a witness, or the accused, is compelled to answer the truth to King and God.'

Affectionately, Cnut kissed her. 'Ah, but not all of them fear their King or their God. Some prefer the prospect of greed. If I could find a way to ensure that my law courts were not corrupt and that there was proven evidence for murder or rape beyond one person's word against another, I would not feel this prick of conscience that I might have sent an innocent to hang, or allowed a wrongdoer to walk free.'

Emma smiled, hugged him. 'Someone I know once went to great depth to prove he was not God!' she said. 'All men face a final judgement. If innocent they shall find peace in Heaven, if guilty in the fires of Hell. You can but do your best as a mortal man and leave the rest to God.'

The maid returned with food and wine, others began preparing a wooden tub of hot water, the bustle and business of a lord returning home, even if this was only temporary accommodation here at Shaftesbury. The nunnery was a favourite place of both Cnut and Emma, the lodgings, despite the persistent draughts, were comfortable, the company pleasant, the table appetising. And Shaftesbury was so convenient for travel, being set, as it was, on the crossroads for London and Exeter, Bath and Bristol. Built on the rise of a seven-hundred-foot-high plateau, the abbey gave a breathtaking aspect across the Vale of Blackmoor. It was one of those places where, on a clear day, it seemed as if the whole of England could be viewed. Alfred, the Great King, had founded Shaftesbury for his daughter, Æthelfigu, and she, with those coming after her, had made a pleasing job of creating a place of peace and prosperity. More than three hundred and fifty people resided here, nuns, novices and lay servants; Cnut and Emma always being made welcome as resident guests, their patronage appreciated. Æthelred had had his own King's buildings further down the hill, but Cnut refused to use the ramshackle place. Too many of that king's manors and palaces were in need of repair, Thorney Island, for instance. One day Cnut intended to pull it down, rebuild palace and monastery alike.

Not until late evening did he find an opportunity to speak in private with his wife; supper had been served and the nuns, after Compline, had gone abed until their next requirement of calling to chapel, Matins at the second hour of the morning.

'I do not want you to gloat.'

Emma glanced up from concentrating on transferring her sketched outline on to a yard-long stretch of linen. She was not sure, yet, whether this embroidery would be used as a table cover or backed on to heavy sacking to become another wall hanging. It would depend, she supposed, on how satisfied she was with the finished article. The scene was of the Blackmoor Vale, the abbey itself to one side and the view, complete with meadows, woods and river, running across the spread of linen. She had decided against the flowers in the corner. 'I do not gloat. Gloating is for mean-minded people who want more than they can have.'

'No, well, I do not want you to be smug, then – and before you say it, you are perfectly capable of being smug.'

Leaning back to see if she had the proportion of abbey roof and outer wall correct, Emma did not contradict him. She did not consider herself smug; self-opinionated maybe, self-satisfied when she was proved right? She would agree to those. Smug? Was she?

'In only three years Ælfgifu is failing in Norway,' Cnut said with a bold tilt to his head, his arms folded, legs apart. Defensive. Expecting – challenging – her to make some disparaging remark.

Emma thought carefully, keeping the smile from twitching at her face. Perhaps gloat and smug were correct after all? She did not, however, trust herself to say anything, for the crow would be there, too easily heard in her voice.

Closely watching her expression, Cnut elaborated. 'When I established her as Regent of Norway the region of Trondheim welcomed her and Swegen with open arms. They had, after all, in my name defeated Olaf's attempt at reinstating himself by annihilating him and his army near Stiklestad.' What a triumph that had been! The shouts and cheers, the bellowing of their names, Cnut! Ælfgifu! Swegen! The very sky had rocked from the echo of it all. What was it that had brought such pride to Cnut? He was already a king, had won battles, had experienced the splendour of being praised and the elation of being the centre of adored attention. Had it, on this occasion, been the knowing that the people desperately wanted Cnut as their King, their choosing of him over Olaf? That they accepted, without question, his choice of regent? Or had it been the adoration, the sheer goodwill and love that had been generated, like heat blazing from a fire? Or the wonder on Ælfgifu's face? Her delight that Cnut had given her what she wanted, his trust? Emma had said that Ælfgifu would betray that trust and destroy the love that the people of Trondheim had been prepared to give. Had said that sour could not turn sweet, or the rotten taste good and palatable. He had not wanted to believe her because, for some perverse reason, he was fond of Ælfgifu, even if that fondness only went as far as pandering to his sexual need and the pride of knowing that he had sired sons. There again, she was rich and her wealth, tied to him as the mother of his sons, bound the north of England to his rule.

With a sigh he admitted the truth. 'Norway is regretting that welcome, regretting acceptance of her.'

'Why in particular?' Emma asked. 'Because she is a woman?' It seemed the most diplomatic answer to make. The others running through her mind she kept to herself, for none of them were complimentary, nor suitably fitting for a queen to orate.

'The people think her too harsh and autocratic. Worse than Olaf, apparently.'

638

With the final touches added, Emma began selecting embroidery silks, laying samples on the linen to decide which colours ought to go where. 'You knew she was like that before you sent her, Cnut, this can not come as a surprise.' The nearest she would come to saying I told you so.

'I had hoped that to give her what she craved would appease the lust, that for Swegen's sake she would temper her arrogance. I was wrong, you were right.' When had Ælfgifu ever shown sense or judgement or compassion, or had even listened to what people were saying, let alone take heed of advice? 'I have sent an emissary to tell her to be more diplomatic, although whether she will take notice . . .' He trailed off, wandered around the room, began drumming his fingers on the table, then against his cheeks, amusing himself with the hollow sound. He was bored. What he ought to do was summon out the fleet and go direct, himself, to Norway, but what signals would that send? That he had no faith in Ælfgifu? That he did not trust her? The answer that no, he did not, was not one to broadcast publicly. Nor would Emma receive the suggestion with favour and he did not want to push the wheel off the cart, as it had been running so smooth of late. Apart from the rumbling gossip that was draining, like stinking sewage, from Normandy.

He ambled across the room to regard her handiwork, changed a skein of dark-blue silk for a lighter shade. 'That looks better, do you not think? Are you going to add a few swallows in the sky? It would add movement?' He pointed to the top right-hand corner.

She had not thought of that, lied, 'Yes, I am, I forgot to add them.'

'There is gossip coming from Normandy, much of it, I believe, set deliberately astir by your nephew, Duke Robert. I admit to never liking that man.' Selecting a stick of the charcoal, Cnut sketched in three swallows. Emma did not want them there, but said nothing, she would change it later.

'Yet you were happy to ruin your sister's life by marrying her to him.' Her remark was scathing. Had she not, more than once, told him that she knew all about loveless, hopeless marriages?

'Estrith is content. She has her own palace, her own servants, can do more or less as she likes.'

'A man would say that,' Emma retorted with a snort of scorn. 'She is forced to say nothing about the open way her husband cavorts with his tanner's whore, is powerless to stop the snide and unjust things he says about her. Can do nothing against the way he flaunts his bastard son and daughter. He is my nephew, but he disgusts me.' And she had entrusted her sons into his care – had that been wise? Well, no, that was not accurate; they had been entrusted to her brother and they were grown men, now, Edward and Alfred, could take care of themselves. Were they, she wondered, behind this rising gossip against Cnut? If they were, why now, after all these years of silent inactivity?

'Ja, ja, I agree with you!' Cnut snapped testily, aware that against Emma's warning he had made another mistake in forcing Estrith to marry Robert. 'Do you want wine?'

Emma shook her head. Cnut poured for himself.

'There is unrest brewing in the South, here. It happens every year around this month, I know; those who were loyal to Edmund Ironside mark the anniversary of his death with respect and remembrance. I have no objection to that, he was a brave and honourable man.'

'But?' Emma prompted, realising there was more and that it was deeply troubling him.

'But,' Cnut said, puffing his cheeks, sitting, his fingers automatically going to fondle the nearest house dog, the one with the white paw, who, with groans of content, immediately lay at his feet, belly up, paws in the air. 'But the whispering is louder this year. Word is that I have no right to be wearing Edmund's crown, that his true heirs, his sons, reside in exile somewhere.' He paused.

'Were you serious', he asked, not daring to look across at her in case he read something he did not wish to see in her face, 'when you said that you would bring Edward and Alfred to England if Ælfgifu attempted to set either of her sons on the throne?'

The question threw Emma; she did not know how to answer.

640

That had been something that she had tossed at him in a moment of piqued temper, a threat aimed at Ælfgifu, not Cnut. Rarely did she think of the two boys in Normandy, occasionally she heard from Goda, a Countess with two sons of her own, but no letter ever came from Edward or Alfred. Emma chewed at a snagged fingernail, did it prick her conscience, that for the most past, she forgot their exile? They were well cared for, had their freedom, their life. Had she tried to keep for them the one thing they could not have – England – would they not have, instead, a cold and lonely grave? But as for Cnut's question, would she, if she ever needed to, suddenly remember them again?

Sometimes it was best to answer with the truth. 'If Harthacnut was dead, then yes, I would send for Æthelred's sons.'

'But you would give Harthacnut every chance to fight for his own kingdom first?'

She put her hands on her hips, head cocked, affronted. 'I would never place them above our son! Never!' But would she? If her back was against the wall, would she seek all the help she could get? She shrugged the thought aside, not wishing to think on it. 'What are you suggesting? I remind you, Cnut, that I did not want Æthelred as my husband, that I have not once grieved over his death and that I did not want to bear his children.'

'You do, however, want to keep your crown.'

She laughed, breaking the sudden rise of tension. 'I have never made any secret of that!'

A discreet knock on the door: Leofgifu.

'Lady, Sir.' Leofgifu bobbed a polite reverence to the King. 'There is a guest arrived, seeking the shelter of the nunnery. She wishes to speak with you, my Lord, urgently.'

Cnut puffed his lower lip as he tugged at his beard. It was late and he was not far from seeking his bed.'

'Who is she? Can it not wait?'

'No, Brother, it cannot!' A woman swept into the room, still wearing stained travel clothes, riding boots, thick mantle. She stripped off her gloves, handed them to Leofgifu and swept the King and Queen of England a dignified curtsy.

641

Emma sat motionless, her mouth open in shock, as if she had seen a spirit walking from the afterlife. 'Estrith!' she breathed.

'Estrith?' Cnut queried at the same moment. 'What are you doing here?' He peered over her shoulder. 'You have not brought Duke Robert with you, I hope? I am in no mood to entertain him this night!'

'And what would I be bringing him for?' Estrith tossed back, scathing, as she unfastened the brooches of her mantle and passed that also to Leofgifu. 'I have no wish to see the bastard ever again.'

One eyebrow raised, Emma exchanged a glance with Cnut, asked Leofgifu to find servants to bring food and replenish the wine. 'Is a room being made ready for you?' the Queen asked.

Waving her hand, Estrith nodded. '*Ja, ja*, that is not important. My situation is.'

'Come, Sister.' Cnut, kicking the excited dogs aside, brought a stool nearer the hearth-fire, patted its red cushion. 'Sit. Explain. You look pale. What is wrong?'

'Robert has gone too far. For your sake I put up with his adultery. For you, I bore the insults he hurled at me, but this, this I will not tolerate from him!'

Cnut hunkered to his heels in front of his sister, took her hand, rubbing it, much as Emma had done for him earlier. That Estrith was distressed was obvious, her face was grey, tears brimmed in her eyes, she was shaking.

'Has he hurt you? I will not permit him to lay hand on you.'

'Yet you permit him to ridicule me? To slander my reputation?'

To that Cnut could make no answer.

Estrith gathered her breath, gratefully accepted the wine Emma had poured, sipped. 'I tolerated him because I knew a treaty of peace between England and Normandy was important to you.' She looked at Cnut, her eyes imploring, one of the tears escaping. 'For you I would do anything, you know that, but I could not, cannot, remain as wife to a man who is planning to invade England!'

Cnut slammed to his feet. 'What?'

Swallowing her emotion, Estrith managed to stammer her

distress. 'He is preparing a fleet. He intends to support Edward, Æthelred's son, in a bid for retrieving his crown. The alliance is broken – he threw his marriage band at me when I challenged him on what he was doing, said the treaty was void anyway as he had never taken me as wife, that I was a shrivelled hag and a cold fish. That Herleve, even married to another, was the only woman he would ever bed and that if I did not like the war he was about to unleash on England then I could go to Hell – or to England, whichever I preferred!' She broke down, sobbing, her face in her hands, the humiliation too much to endure.

Emma was appalled. Was this why Cnut had been questioning her? Surely he did not think she was involved in this?

Pacing the room, Cnut thought rapidly, strategy, tactics, hurtling through his keen mind. England was not in imminent danger, not with the winds blowing as they were. A fleet would not risk sailing when such tempests were threatening.

'The rumours are true, then?' Emma said, forcing herself to remain calm. 'They have been deliberately sown to stir the blood of discontented Englishmen.'

Embarrassed at her lack of self-control, Estrith patted her face, wiped the tears. 'You have knowledge of Robert's plans, then? I was not aware you did. I came with all haste to warn you.' That was true, but the haste was also an excuse to abandon Normandy and a hopeless marriage. To leave before she was stopped, or before her courage had drained.

'I have heard only speculation, Sister, but someone has been stirring a pot of rancid stew. Talk of Edmund Ironside, of my usurpation of his crown and such. A bishop, while visiting Edmund's tomb at Glastonbury Abbey, has had a vision of God crowning the true ætheling, Edward Æthelredsson.'

Sucking in her cheeks, as Emma had a habit of doing when she was desperately thinking, she regarded Cnut. Did he imagine she was behind this plot to rebel against him? If he did, then she must nip out the lie as if it were a tainted bud on an orchard apple tree. 'Harthacnut is to be king after you. No one else,' she stated, reassuring him, paused, her eyes bright, connecting directly with

Cnut's. 'Would this bishop, by chance, be a man who was educated at Jumièges in Normandy?'

Cnut nodded.

'The Bishop of Ramsey?' Estrith enquired, knowing him well. 'He has been to Robert's Court and is a close friend to the Abbot of Jumièges, a man called Robert Champart, have you heard of him?'

Emma had, through her spies. 'Champart is a close friend to my Edward.' Added, with disgust, 'There has been speculation as to how close.'

Cnut added charcoal to the brazier. Could he trust Emma? Was she telling the truth? Ælfgifu's betrayal had shaken him, was Emma, too, to let him down? Ælfgifu had convinced him that she would make a good regent, that Norway would flourish and prosper beneath her rule, that he would be proud of her and his son. It had all been lies and illusion. Was Emma's complacence the same? Would she, if he were to die tomorrow, abandon Harthacnut and favour the sons of another man? All he had worked for, all he had achieved – all that he still had to do – all of it would come to naught, would come crashing down like a poorly built barn in a storm, to be left in a forgotten heap of rubble. He did not want that. He wanted to be remembered as a good and loving king, to have his son follow him and his son after that. To be the first of a long and illustrious dynasty. He had been so certain that Emma wanted that too. Was it reasonable to suppose that, just as he had three chances of fulfilling his dream, through Harthacnut, Swegen or Harold, Emma had the same choice? Harthacnut, Edward or Alfred? Damn it! She could have waited until he was dead!

Seeing the doubt, the flicker of suspicion in his dejected face, Emma stated, 'We have not heard of the building of any fleet. I have a network of men and women who are my eyes and ears. No word has come to me of such a plan.'

'Are you sure of this, Estrith?' Cnut asked, making an effort to shove aside these groundless suspicions.

Estrith was cold, tired, hungry. Mentally she had been abused, although not physically, Robert had never deigned to touch her in need, love or anger. 'He told me of it himself.' She rubbed her hands over her face, her eyes; unpinned her wimple and clutched it in her hands. 'He could have been lying. I suppose he could have been taunting me, to make me react as I did.' Another tear wavered down her cheek. 'I have fallen for his bluff, haven't I?' Utter despair overwhelmed her. Two marriages, two husbands, twice the years of misery.

Emma put her arm comfortingly around her sister-in-law's shoulders, knowing well her inner grief and pain. 'Let us get you fed and to bed. Once you have rested you will feel better.' She smiled at Estrith, at Cnut. 'Thank you for trying so hard to keep the treaty alive, but once something is dead it is best to bury it before the stench goes fully foul.'

Putting Estrith into the capable hands of Leofgifu, who was all too willing to use her talents of comfort and care to best advantage, Cnut sat silent, brooding. 'Is it bluff do you think?' he asked at length.

Emma had been considering the same question. 'If his fleet is assembling along the Breton coast, then we could well not have heard of it. He may also know of the trouble brewing in Norway and have hopes that you will be otherwise occupied.'

Cnut nodded. Exactly as he assumed. 'The question is, how do I outmanoeuvre Robert?' *And how do I know if I can trust you?* He might not have said the last but Emma read it in his eyes.

She crossed to him, knelt, took his hands in her own, kissed the fingers that were not as supple as they were when first she had known him. The joint ache was etching into the knuckles, particularly on the right hand, the sword hand. 'Edmund willed England into your capable hands, Cnut. You were ruling as King alongside him before he died. By right of strength, by right of law, you hold England. I would suggest', she added, putting her palm to his cheek, 'that you pour cold water on sparking embers. Soak the kindling and the blaze will not catch.'

He smiled, kissed her, light, on the cheek. 'I burnt a witch once, because I feared she had the power to turn the minds of men to her will. Ought I to burn you also?'

'No, dear heart, just Robert's scheming plans.'

'Edward's you mean!'

Feeling the sudden crisis begin to ebb away, Emma laughed, her head back. 'Edward could not organise a drunken spree in the brew house. If it were Alfred I would be more concerned. He at least knows which end of a spear to hold.'

'So what do I do? Ensure gossip of a counter kind is spread about?'

Emma returned to her chair, sat, crossed her wrists and ankles, Cnut marvelling, as he often did, at how elegant she always was.

'Make some grand, public show of your affection for Edmund,' Emma suggested after a moment of thought. 'You regarded him as your brother, you loved him and you mourn his death and his memory. We must remind the populace of that.'

'I was considering attending the service at Glastonbury to pray for his soul on his death-day. Would that be enough do you think?'

Emma nodded, perhaps it would, but it needed something more. 'You could take a suitable gift to place on the tomb. A sword perhaps?'

'No, not a sword . . .' Cnut, his spirits rising as he rubbed his beard, pinched his nose, thinking, thinking . . . 'I have it!' He hurried across the chamber, knelt at one of the great chests and, lifting the lid, began rummaging inside, pulling things from it – cloaks, tunics, a folded bolt of expensive silk. 'Where is it?' he mumbled, his head deep inside.

'What are you seeking?' Emma tutted, retrieving the strewn items, many of them elaborate, precious and irreplaceable.

'That cloak, that splendid embroidered cloak Conrad presented me with in Rome. Remember? The one with the peacocks?'

Her face glowing with pride and pleasure, Emma knelt beside him, helped him find it. It was there, at the very bottom, crushed, musty, but not damaged by moth or mice.

Cnut shook it out to reveal its detailed intricacy. In golds and blues and greens the bird, a peacock, its sweeping, bright-coloured, eyed tail resplendent, bragged of its glory. It was a cloak that could never be worn, for the decoration was too heavy, its opulence too great, but as a statement it was superb. The peacock, the symbol of the resurrection of the flesh. The transferring of sovereignty from a dead king to his chosen successor.

'I shall weep for Edmund, and mourn his passing and his greatness, then I shall place my crown on the crucifix of Glastonbury's altar and declare that who, aside from Edmund, was worthy to wear it?'

'And, of course,' Emma added with a wry smile, 'there shall be those among the pilgrims and congregation to declare immediately that they remember Edmund loving you as a brother, and that he entrusted his crown and his kingdom to you and only you.'

Cnut grinned sheepishly at her. How could he be so stupid as to doubt her? At every step she was there, beside him, supporting, encouraging and approving; giving herself and her love. Æthelred? What a fool that man had been!

'So,' Emma said, leaning forward to put her hands either side of his face, give it a gentle shake, 'you no longer doubt my loyalty, or my love?'

He kissed her, agreed, no, he did not. 'I still think you are inclined to be smug, though!' He laughed as he kissed her again. 'I shall send to Robert, protest at his insulting my sister and demand he repay her dowry.'

'That he will not do.'

'Then if I am so inclined, I have the excuse to go and get it.'

What a pity, Emma thought, *that the nuisance of Ælfgifu's sons could not be so easily dealt with.*

37

May 1033 – Avranches, Normandy

Henry of France, twenty-five years old and temporarily in exile after quarrelling bitterly with his mother, was fond of Robert, Duke of Normandy, a part cause for the disagreement with his mother. She did not approve of his friends, nor his determination to rule France without her interfering. Henry did not like his mother. Edward of England had every sympathy with him. Nor did the young French King appear as overenthusiastic as Duke Robert with this idea of invading England when Cnut sailed for Norway to prevent Olaf's son, Magnus, from establishing himself.

Alfred was in the mews, inspecting his birds; in particular a merlin that had damaged her flight feathers during yesterday's hunting.

'Ce n'est pas grave,' Alfred declared, setting the bird back on her perch. 'The feathers are not too badly torn, but she will not fly again until the next moult.'

Edward, seated on a pile of dried bracken, had his chin in his hands, looking glum.

Alfred laughed, feeling happier than he had for many months. 'Just think, Brother, when next I fly her we will be in England and you will be King!'

Edward was trying not to think of it. 'Alfred, without men to back us . . .'

'Oh, fah, the fyrdsmen will flock to our banners. We are English, they are full to here,' he indicated his eyebrows, 'with Danish foreigners.'

'In Denmark,' Edward offered, trying again, 'Cnut is known as Cnut the Great.'

'In Denmark, *oui*, but not in *L'Angleterre*. Robert says Cnut may think of himself as omnipotent, but he cannot defend two countries at once. Our ships are ready in the harbour, and as soon as this wind drops we cross the Channel Sea and hit hard and quick. You will have England by summer's end.'

'I doubt Mother will be too pleased.'

'Mama will be delighted!' Alfred stated, so sure of himself, so unwilling to consider the truth. One hundred French and Norman ships rested their keels on the mudflats of a low tide, that was all the truth Alfred needed. That and Duke Robert, finally, at last, honouring his promise to help his cousins return to England.

'You do not think that Robert is saying and doing all this merely to impress Henry, do you?' Edward suggested, half hopeful. Robert was ever the braggart.

'Why should he? What has he to prove to Henry?'

Edward did not answer. Perhaps Alfred was right, but what if he was wrong? Could the Duke's interest be to appear as a great hero in Henry's eyes? To show that he had the power to put exiles on to their rightful throne? Edward sat straighter, folded his arms. He would have his say in this, voice his thoughts.

'I think Robert has no intention of helping us. He might take us to England, but he will not land, and if he does not, then neither will his men. We will be alone and we will be roasting on a spit before we have walked from the landing beach. That is what I think.'

'Oh, nonsense, Edward. Robert knows what he is doing.'

'You all think because I am quiet and because I do not always have the courage to speak what is in my mind, that I am some sort of moon fool. What if Cnut does not go to Norway? And what of Mother? Will she welcome us with open arms or with a poison-tipped spear?'

'Mother will be . . .'

Edward lost his temper. He stormed to his feet and kicked over an opened sack of corn. 'Do not dare to say she will be pleased, Alfred! You know damn well she will not! Mother, if she knew we were coming, would order out the fyrd to arrest us and have us strung up by our privy parts!' He turned on his heel and stumped angrily away.

Alfred opened his mouth to protest, closed it. Loath as he was to admit it, Edward was right.

It all came to nothing. The wind changed, but brought in rain that poured down as if there was a hole in the bottom of a well. They did sail, eventually, but only the handful of miles along the coast to the bay of Mont Saint-Michel. Robert wanted to show Henry the monastery's building progress and after that, he lost interest in the expedition because Henry decided to go back to France. Magnanimously Robert said his cousin, Edward, could make use of the ships if he wanted them.

Edward did not.

As well he did not, for at the end of the month they heard that Cnut had decided to allow his Northampton whore to sort her own problems and had elected to stay in England.

38

Emma had been unwell for several days, nothing serious, a sore throat and a dry cough, treated with so many herbal concoctions that she professed she would sprout shoots and grow into a medicinal plant. Their fussing she did not care for, but the order to rest and be cosseted she accepted, for the weather outside was foul, and her depressed melancholia was suited to a warm bed and Leofgifu's motherly pampering.

Her daughter, Gunnhild, had gone to Henri, son of Conrad, Holy Emperor of Rome, soon after the Nativity festival, to meet her betrothed and become accustomed to the ways of his Court before the wedding, which would not be until the summer of next year. Emma envied her. If only she had been permitted to discover Æthelred before she had been forced into marriage. Ah, but would that have been worse? Knowing you were to marry a warted toad, with no way out of the agreement? At least, if what she had written in her lengthy letter was accurate, Gunnhild appeared to like her future husband. All the same, Emma missed her company. She would have liked to attend the wedding, or visit Harthacnut, had got as far, last autumn, as the quay at Thorney Island but no further. That step on to a bobbing ship had been too much. Instead, she had waved farewell to Estrith, who was now back at Harthacnut's Court in Denmark. Emma had a suspicion that Cnut intended to replace Ælfgifu and Swegen with his sister and her eldest son, Svein, but he was keeping his plans close concealed to his chest. Something would have to be done about the Northampton Bitch, for Norway was now all but lost. What a pig's ear the stupid woman had made of things! And she had wanted to be Cnut's Queen? Hah!

Grumpily, Emma punched at the goose-feather pillow behind her back, reached for the goblet of honey-sweetened watered wine, found it empty. The chamber was empty too, not a single servant; they must have left her to sleep in peace, kind of them, but where were they when she needed them? She tried to call out, but her voice came in a bleated croak. She lay for a while, watching the light fade from beyond the glass windows. The panes were small and distorted the view, but she had insisted on the best for her house in Winchester and was pleased about it now. The shutters would have to be closed soon, but it was comforting to lie quiet and watch as night settled outside. Noises from the street below had died away with the setting sun, it had been a market day and Winchester had been crowded, with people scurrying home as soon as the frail light began to fade. She had enjoyed listening to the busy, bustling sounds of life.

She called again, wanting a drink, feeling the hard swelling of her throat, the uncomfortable desire to cough. Pulling away the top fur, the yellowish white pelt of a polar bear, she swung herself from the bed, hitched its heaviness around her shoulders and went to the door. No one was beyond in the solar either. From below came a shout of laughter, raucous merriment. Someone celebrating something? Ah yes, Godwine had another son born and had treated most of Winchester to free ale. How many boys was that now? Swegn, Harold, Tostig, the daughter Edith, and this one – what had Godwine said they were to call him? Leofwine? That had made Emma laugh, this morning when he had told her of the news.

'Leofwine?' she had huskily whispered, 'but that is the name of Earl Leofric's father and you are a mortal enemy to Leofric!'

'I'd not say a mortal enemy, my Lady,' Godwine had chortled. 'I merely cannot abide the man.'

'You would not be saddened to hear he had befallen some fatal accident, though.'

'Well, no, I grant you that!'

Godwine would be over at the King's palace now, or at his own lodgings with his wife and newborn son. It was good to know that some marriages worked.

Crossing the bedchamber, and then the solar, was tiring. Emma was weaker than she had realised, her legs were shaking, the breath rasping in her chest, but even at the head of the stairs she could not attract attention. The guard stood at the bottom, laughing at the frivolity going on in the Hall. She did not begrudge them their pleasure, for the winter had been long and dreary, and it was not over yet. Godwine had said they were expecting more snow soon, had been pleased the child had come before bad weather closed in. Winter laughter was always welcome.

The bear fur was heavy and unwieldy, twice it slipped. She went down two stairs, holding tight to the rail, her body beginning to shiver, though sweat stood out on her forehead. She tried to call. The fur slid, caught between her legs and she was falling, tumbling down, somersaulting, unable to stop herself, unable to scream. Pain shot through her arm, a blast of red fire crashed through her head and she knew no more.

Cnut ran. He had not stopped to fling on a cloak or change soft indoor shoes for heavier outdoor boots. They had sent Leofstan to fetch him, knowing Emma's Captain of Housecarls would gain instant access, would be listened to immediately.

'The Queen has fallen down the stairs!' he had gasped, breathless, anxious, barely bothering to kneel, so great his distress. 'We fear her dead, Sir!'

Cnut, too, had been helping Godwine celebrate the birth of his son and was more than a little drunk, but Leofstan's white face, his spilled words, sobered him as surely as a thrown bucket of ice water. He was on his feet and out of the Hall, running up the street as if the Devil were after him. Head back, arms pumping.

The High Street was level at the palace end, but began to rise well before Emma's house, and the wind was blowing down from the hill, bitter and cold. Halfway up, Cnut felt his chest heaving, the breath coming in gasps, his head dizzy. The crowd of men with him had to slow, some overtaking him, Godwine was at his side, taking his arm, urging him to walk.

'Gain your breath, my Lord, we will get there as soon by walking quickly.'

Cnut waved him away, ran on, his face ashen, dread churning

with every step, every panted gulp of freezing air that burnt and seared at his lungs. In his mind he saw his father lying at the bottom of a flight of steps, his body twisted, blood trickling from his nose, mouth and ears, his eyes open, staring, blank, up at the sky. A sight that had never left him in all these years. He had thought he had shut the memory of that day away, but here it was resurrected, vivid, this cruel finality screaming at him as he pushed his labouring body to run, run!

Torches were blazing, the gates flung wide, people milling, voices muted, frightened, concerned. A few of the women crying, men murmuring. Cnut had been forced to slow to a walk as the hill rose steeper, but now he ran again, in through the gate, across the courtyard. He leapt the two steps up to the open-flung doorway, forced his protesting body to move, move across the Hall, through the parting, silent, grey-faced crowd.

She lay at the foot of the stairway. Someone had covered her with the white fleece of a polar bear that had spots of bright blood smeared on it. The physician was there, kneeling beside her, and Eadsige, Emma's chaplain. Leofgifu stood to one side, her face buried in her hands, shoulders shaking, soundless tears damping her fingers.

Cnut knelt slowly, feeling as if he were moving through a marsh bog, his feet leaden, body weighed as if with armour twice as heavy as expected. Knelt, lifted her cold, limp hand. The Hall, the men and women, all seemed far away, clouded in a shrouding mist.

'Emma?' he said, reaching forward to brush a strand of hair away from her face, 'Oh, God, Emma.'

He had to sit, there on the rushes of the floor, for his legs buckled, his body surrendering to the pains thrumming in a tightening band across his chest, and he let the tears fall as he held her hand, tight, so tight in his own. Tears of relief, for her eyes had flickered open and she smiled, weakly, apologetically, up at him.

'You scared me.'

'I'm sorry.'

'They said you were taken ill,' Emma admonished, her voice still hoarse, wincing as she carefully moved her bruised body.

Cnut made light of it. 'A combination of too much ale, the cold air and my fear for you.' He grinned sheepishly. 'I could not get my breath, that was all, I have been well since.' He had, in fact, collapsed in a heap, the world shrinking away from him as the blood had roared in his ears and pain had ripped from his chest and down his arm. They had made him sit, recover himself, had wafted a burnt feather beneath his nose until his senses had rallied. Rest? Sit quiet? He had lurched, angry, frightened, to his feet, pushing them aside, forcing them away, cursing their well-meaning good intentions, had demanded to see his wife. Godwine, sensible, practical Godwine, had calmed him, told him he must collect himself, she was in good hands, was being tended. Had it been anyone else but Godwine, Cnut might not have listened, or believed, but Godwine loved Emma almost as much as Cnut did. Godwine would not lie, not about Emma.

'You should take more care,' Emma advised, patting his hand, and Cnut, sitting on the bed beside her, laughed.

'You tell that to me? You, Madam, should take the care, particularly when negotiating stairs in an overlarge draped bear fur!' He fell serious, his hand clasping and enclosing her fingers. 'God's Eyes, Emma, they told me you were dead!'

'A sprained wrist, a few cracked ribs, and these.' Gingerly with her bandaged free hand, she touched the egg-sized lump on her head and the ugly swell of bruises on her face. 'Nothing more. Although my throat is as raw as it was and my side is now even more painful when I cough.'

She did not remember falling and getting out of bed seemed a distant memory, as if it had been a half-waking dream. The first she recalled was being carried up the stairs by, of all people, Cnut's newest-made earl, Siward of Deira, a great bear of man in build, temper and smell. She had been astonished to find herself in his arms, his concerned face peering into hers, the northern burr of his Viking accent reassuring her.

'Rest easy, lass, you have hurt yer'sel'.' Emma had thought she had gone to Valhalla and was being lifted by Thor himself, a thought she kept strictly to herself now she was full conscious in the real world. It would not do to have an English Christian Queen fancying herself taken off by a pagan warrior. Although she guessed that Siward, with his strong links to an ancient Danish ancestry, would have been pleased, would have taken it as a compliment.

She searched Cnut's eyes, looking for what he was not telling her. He was never ill, was always vigorous and strong. Solid. Dependable. Hers had been an accident that could have had serious consequences, but had, fortunately, resulted in nothing more than a few aches that would eventually pass. He was waving aside any concern for himself, but she was worried, for there was that one thing she remembered, in that confusion of the red mist that had sent her consciousness reeling between awake and asleep. She remembered someone saying, in a wild, panicked cry, 'It is a seizure of his heart!'

'You dreamt it,' Cnut insisted, and so did Godwine, Leofgifu and Siward when she asked them.

'You dreamt it, lass d'not fret yer'sel'.'

As the days rolled into weeks and the weeks to months, her bruises healed and the incident became forgotten, shut away, perhaps to be remembered and talked about on cold winter nights when memories swarmed behind closed shutters and demanded to be dusted off and discussed.

Do you remember when . . .? A good start to a good story, to while away a dark and tedious snow-bound evening.

Only occasionally did Emma frown and show concern, when after some particular exertion she heard Cnut panting for breath after he had been running, or ascending a stairway or steep slope, but he assured her it was caused by the extra girth that was starting to expand at his belly.

'My belly is beginning to paunch and I will soon lose sight of my manhood beyond it.' He would laugh, adding, 'I am not as young and fit as I once was. My bones are creaking and I have the joint ache in my fingers and knees, a sure sign of growing old. I will be getting grey hair, too, before long!'

And she would laugh with him and remind him that if he was old, then she must be in her dotage, for was she not several years his elder? Beyond their laughter the fears were set aside and forgotten, for there were other things to occupy busy days and loving nights. Who cared to dwell upon the stalking shadow of death while the sun shone?

39

July 1035 – Roskilde

The wind, blowing from the sea, caught Harthacnut's shoulder-length hair and added a few more tangles to its already wind-rumpled appearance. He scooped a lock out of his eyes and, using his hand, shaded his vision to look more carefully out to sea. She was definitely a Norwegian boat, but too far out, yet, to see her pennant or crew clearly. She was no trader's craft or merchant ship, but a war boat. Just one? A feeble attack, if that was what she had in mind.

Harthacnut shrugged, turned his attention to the repairing of the sea barrier, clutching at his cloak as the wind tried again to wrestle it away. 'That breach made last night will have to be mended before the next high tide,' he said to Scavi Redbeard, the man responsible for the upkeep and care of the barrier. 'If we leave it and this wind should pick up again, the whole lot could go.'

'*Ja*, Lord, we are doing all we can, but as you see, it is not easy with the sea as wild as it is.'

'Do your best, Scavi.' Again Harthacnut glowered out at the ship, battling her way through the temper of what remained of a two-day storm. He turned to the Captain of his Housecarls, Thorstein, pointing to the ship. 'Keep an eye on her, will you? I do not feel easy about the set of her sail.'

Thorstein, too, was watching the craft. There was nothing unusual about her: thirty-oared, a blue chequered sail, heavily reefed in the gale that was blowing out there. And yet . . .

'I shall be at the church, should I be required,' Harthacnut said, as Thorstein nodded acceptance and his other companion, Feader, fell into step beside him. The three of them were tall men, lithe of limb, strong of muscle – arms and shoulders that were used to taking a turn at the pulling of the oars developed a natural strength, and

Harthacnut had never shirked his fair share of crewing a ship. At nearing six and ten, he had turned into the image of his father, with perhaps his mother's nose and her ability to assess someone's worth within the first few minutes of meeting. His companions, Thorstein and Feader, were more than friends; men of ten years his senior they were, between them, guard, tutor, mentor and comrade. Harthacnut had known them for all the years he had been in Denmark. Their fathers had served Cnut, their fathers' fathers had served Grandpapa Swein. Under their eye the Danish boy King had learnt to use sword and axe, shield and spear. Had learnt to straddle a pony and not fall off too often; to handle the subtle moods of a boat and read the signs of sky, wind and sea. Thorstein and Feader had aided Harthacnut from innocent child to maturing adolescent. There was no one, outside of his own father, whom Harthacnut could trust more.

'You are thinking that ship could have something to do with Magnus Olafsson?' Feader asked as he strode with his King along the timber-boarded walkways of the narrow street. Timber houses and workshops stood to either side, the daily noise and movement of a busy wharfside town, with all the attached smells and sounds. Baking bread mingling with fresh dung, women talking, children laughing; the geese, dogs, the cries of the gulls wheeling in the sky as the fishing boats unloaded their catch. Over it all, the insistence of the wind as it scurried and squinnied, infiltrating into everything, permeating everywhere; rocking wattle fences and walls, lifting the edges of reed-thatched roofs and dislodging loose-set shingle tiles; flapping at doors, blustering inside to irritate hearth-fires and wall hangings, scuttling through the pots and pans, and sending the loom weights swinging and chattering.

Traders' stalls were set with silver and copper jewellery; Harthacnut stopped to examine an amber necklace. His aunt, Estrith, enjoyed wearing amber and this was exquisitely made. 'I'll take it,' he said, the craftsman beaming pleasure that the King himself had bought from his wares.

'Magnus Olafsson is squeezing Norway bit by bit, like a woman pressing fresh-made cheese through a sieve. Soon, as revenge for his father's death, he will have it all for himself and I am powerless to do anything to stop him. What worries me, my friend, is that once he has wrung Norway dry, will he turn his hook nose towards Denmark? I am not best pleased that I may be facing a war.'

They turned into another street, where the glassmakers tended their craft, then left again into a narrower way behind the rear of a row of houses that led to the Bishop's Gate and the Church of the Holy Trinity. Roskilde had been the first Danish town to have the proud boast of a stone-built church. Cnut had founded it, in his own and his son's name, and when finished had laid his father to rest before the altar. It had been Swein Forkbeard's desire, always, to return to Denmark; it had seemed fitting to bring his body from England and pray that his soul had followed. Harthacnut had not known his grandsire, but there were those in plenty in Denmark who had, and the nights were never lonely or boring when there were tales of the deeds of Swein Forkbeard to recount. The people of Roskilde, and of Denmark, were as proud of the grandson as they had been of the grandfather. Harthacnut, although young, had taken the position and responsibility thrust upon him with serious equanimity, particularly as he reached the verge of manhood and the full spate of his duties fell upon him. There had always been men to advise and guide him, good, loyal men, and his father too, of course, whenever he came to Denmark, but those trips had been shorter, less frequent as Harthacnut grew older, and he had found a firmer footing. Cnut was proud of him, Harthacnut would make a good king for Denmark.

Whenever he could, Harthacnut visited the Holy Trinity to pay respect to his grandfather's tomb. Often he could not come, for there was always some matter of Court that needed attention, and since he had reached the age of manhood they had grown more insistent and complicated. He realised now, how much of a burden his father's appointed advisers and clerics had taken on board on his behalf.

On his knees, he willed himself to relax, shoulders to sag, breathing to slow, to become calm. His mind to empty. It was no good talking to God if there was a background noise of jangled thoughts niggling and nudging for attention. The Bishop had taught him how to pray, and Harthacnut valued these few treasured moments of silence and solitude, when there was nothing and no one except him and Christ.

Boots scraping on the tiled floor. A discreet cough. Thorstein, Harthacnut would recognise the throaty growl anywhere. He finished the prayer, crossed himself, rose, 'Well? She is in harbour?'

Thorstein nodded, looked grim. '*Ja*, Lord, she is. In both senses. The Lady Ælfgifu and her son, Swegen, your half-brother, seek sanctuary at your Court.'

Ælfgifu stood rigid, as if her body had been turned to stone. She was cold, hungry, scared – the sea crossing had been as much a nightmare as the final desperate days in Norway. When Death stares you in the face, its hot breath sulphurous on the skin, few are brave enough to wave it aside without a qualm and Ælfgifu was no exception.

'They hounded me,' she complained, 'threw sticks and bones and dung; spat and called me vile names. Not one man, not one whore-poxed, bastard-born turd came to help me or my son. Not even the men supposed to act as my guard! Not one!'

Her attempts to govern had failed miserably, her rule already becoming synonymous as a period of oppression and wretchedness. The cause of her failure: her rigid determination to introduce a heavy burden of taxation and to demand excessively severe penalties for violence and committed crime. Her desire to dictate an imposed regime on the most fiercely independent people in the entirety of Europe was vehemently obstructed, as was her inclination to introduce customs and traditions based on the Danish way of life. Norway was not Denmark and the Norwegians, having had enough of her arrogance, solidly informed her of the fact. Olaf had been an autocrat, but never had he found the audacity to attempt to alter the fundamental relationship that united the role of king with his people. In comparison with Ælfgifu, Olaf attracted the memory of better times; he had been a bastard, but he had not been hated. He even had some qualities to be

661

admired, his obedience to the following of Christ as instance. Olaf, the people of Norway decided, had been wrongfully murdered. No matter, they would make him a saint, kick out the detested Ælfgifu and her rat of a son, and adopt Magnus, Olaf's son, as their king instead. What Cnut or Harthacnut thought of the decision they did not particularly care. And Ælfgifu, *ja* well, she had a choice. Leave Norway or hang.

'I demand a fleet and your best crews to take us back, to enforce my rule. Magnus must be defeated, the will of Cnut, your father, must be imposed.'

Harthacnut was staggered at her presumption. She had barely waited to be announced into his Hall, but had swept in through the doors like a blast of winter wind, Swegen, her miserable plump, rag of a son, scuttling at her heels. She had conceded a small inclination of her head, but given that Harthacnut was the legal crowned King, a full obedience would have been more proper. Nor had she waited for the politeness of formalities, but had launched immediately into a tirade of abuse and condemnation against the Norwegian people, followed by her demand for assistance.

For a full minute Harthacnut sat, staring in disbelief at her audacity, saying nothing.

'You have the effrontery, Madam, to burst uninvited into my Hall. To that you add demands of my crews and ships, without any suggestion of financing such a nonsensical expedition. Why should I bale you out of a sinking ship? What are you to me? What have you been to my mother, save a festering thorn that ought have been poulticed and plucked before I was born?'

'You dare talk to me so?' she snapped at him. 'I am your father's first-taken wife. This', and she shunted Swegen forward, the boy wiping at a dripping nose, 'is your father's firstborn son. Cnut set us to rule Norway. It is your duty to fulfil his wishes.'

'My duty is to Denmark. If Magnus Olafsson cares to bring a fight to me, then he shall feel the edge of my blade, but I am not in a position to take the sword to him. Not for myself, my father, nor, and most especially, for a whore and her bastard-born by-blow.'

Ælfgifu took one angry step forward. Just one, and found herself surrounded by the sudden standing to attention of Harthacnut's housecarls, all of whom cradled an axe or a spear. Had she made that two steps, the second would have been her last.

'Your father shall have something to say about this when he hears!' she hissed, fury oozing from every pore.

'Then I suggest, Madam,' Harthacnut answered laconically, 'that you reboard your ship and go personally to tell him.'

She was a proud woman, who had no idea how to admit defeat or to show humility. The years of bitter hatred had wormed into her, the cruelties she had witnessed seeping like black pus from her heart to contaminate her soul and every fibre of her body. Hate breeds hate that can never, once it has anchored, be sated.

'You shall suffer for denying me, Harthacnut, both you and that bitch you call mother shall feel the agony that I shall unleash upon you.'

'Get her from my sight,' Harthacnut ordered, 'come sundown, I do not wish to see her ship in my waters.'

Swegen sat hunched, miserable, in the stern of the ship, a walrus skin pulled close to his shoulders and head. It was supposedly waterproof, but how did he stop the slop of the waves from breaking over the side of this wallowing ship? The runnels of water gushing along the deck? He was wet, cold and uncomfortable, and he had not liked Norway, not the land, the mountains nor the people. He never wanted to eat another fish, smell the stench of another oily dead seal or whale ever again. Swegen loathed the sea and he had been useless at government – what little chance he had had at it. His mother had done most of it, making charters, judging law, dictating this and that. Swegen could barely read, although the tutors had attempted to beat into him the letters and sounds that scrawled across the pages. Harold was good at all that, but not Swegen. All he was good at doing, as she often told him, was annoying his mother. She blamed this present predicament on him too, of course.

She said that they were to return to England and demand that Cnut call out the scyp fyrd to redeem her honour. Swegen could not see Cnut doing it, but who was he to gainsay his mother when she was flying one of her rages?

He looked out at the heave of the sea, the white-topped waves that rose and fell as the ship lurched up and down from trough to trough, her keel rolling with the heavy swell. He felt sick. He did so hate the sea. And his mother. Scrabbling to his knees, he leaned over the side, his belly spewing bile. He knew the crew was laughing at him; Cnut's son, the useless dog who spilled his guts as soon as he set foot aboard a ship. Did not care. His only thoughts were of despair and discomfort, of the hopelessness of everything.

Whether the high, wind-driven wave that shook the boat and tossed her, as if she had been no more than a delicate child's toy, knocked him overboard, or whether he let himself fall, no one knew. One moment, as the ship rose, he was there, the next, he was gone.

Ælfgifu screamed that they were to put about, but the sea was rough and cold, and although they looked and called until nightfall, they could not find him.

Perhaps he had not wanted to be found.

40

The fear that Edward had felt when Duke Robert had threatened to invade England had been nothing to this. This was a gut-wrenching, cold, clammy terror, for the Duke, Robert, was dead and Edward did not know what to do. He had died at Nicea on the third day of July, returning from a pilgrimage to Jerusalem. Herleve, hysterical with weeping, declared over and over that she had begged him not to go. The child, William, had sat, withdrawn and silent in the same window seat for nigh on four and twenty hours now, and Edward? Edward was close to panic.

Already Normandy was crackling with the sparks that threatened to turn, in the next breath, into a burning blaze of war, for the men who had professed to love and respect Robert were greedy to sit in his empty chair. Whereas Edward and Alfred had always been welcomed at Court, suddenly they were being regarded with distrust and suspicion. Who could blame the noblemen of the Duchy? The only heir was an eight-year-old boy, born illegitimately of a tanner's daughter who now had a nobleman as husband; anyone who was able had the chance of claiming Normandy for his own. A count or viscount, or an exiled, English ætheling, son of the dead Duke's aunt?

Edward wanted a duchy as little as he wanted a kingdom, but to profess his lack of interest would be to open himself to ridicule. These harsh-minded, warmongering men of Normandy struck with an axe first and asked questions later, if it occurred to them to ask. They were not the sort of men who would believe a thirty-year-old exiled prince would not want to take power for himself if opportunity presented itself. Edward had tried convincing Robert of it, to no avail – even Alfred could scarce accept that his elder brother did not want a crown or coronet, only a monk's cowl.

'What do we do, Alfred? What do we do?' Rocking backwards and forwards hunched into a ball, his arms clamped tight about his knees, Edward's plea was pitiful. 'You can fight, you are skilled with sword and shield, but I am not. Could we go to Henry, do you think? Would France protect us?'

Alfred doubted it. 'Henry will have his hands full keeping this lot on a tight leash without the need to bother with us. We would do better to attach ourselves to the strongest lord and brazen it out. Offer our swords in service.'

That idea did not appeal to Edward at all. Tentatively he suggested, 'We could go to Jumièges? Robert Champart will take us in.'

Alfred threw his hands in the air in despair. 'A life of celibate boredom may suit you, Brother, but it has no appeal to me. I enjoy my women too much, even if you do not.' Edward said nothing. Women frightened him; he had, so far, had very little to do with them.

They were in the Great Hall of Falaise castle. Herleve, who had always regarded it as hers, had shut herself away in the solar, up at the top of the corner stairs, the servants going about their daily tasks as if nothing had happened. But then to them, Edward supposed, once the initial excitement had been exclaimed over there would be nothing different, a change of lord, that was all. Routine would be the same, the daily, weekly, monthly drudge. Get up, do your work, go to bed. The shakes began in his body again, trembling through his arms into his hands. 'We could always write to Mama?' he said, knowing it was a stupid thing to say as soon as the words left his mouth.

'Why not write, instead, to Cnut?' Alfred slammed back at him. 'Ask him what would be his preferred way for us to die? Shall we hang ourselves, or fall on a dagger? I am sure he could make a few useful suggestions.'

Edward hung his head, chewed his lip.

'It's the lad I feel sorry for,' Alfred remarked, nodding towards William. 'He is trying to be a man and keep the tears from falling; he worshipped his father, though he saw little of him. At least he should be safe. No one much bothers with a by-blow, least they will not, once a new duke is inaugurated and settled.'

Edward attempted a wan smile. 'Not unless he grows like you and hankers over what he could have had.'

Alfred, missing the sarcasm, shook his head, wrinkled his nose. '*Non*, the boy is too base-born to rise higher.'

Privately Edward disagreed, but held his tongue. William, apart from his elder sister, was Robert's only child, and there was no one else of the line who could boast a legitimate claim, outside of a disabled nephew and a distant cousin or two.

Noises filtered in from the courtyard, the sound of a retinue arriving, horses, voices, the chink of chain-mail armour. Someone else arrived to see for himself what was happening? To ensure that the husband of the Duke's whore did not pursue ideas above his status? Expecting a count, or an estate holder, Edward was surprised to see a man of far more importance stride through the door. Removing his cloak the man bellowed for the mistress of the house to attend him.

'Where is the woman Herleve?' He gestured to a maidservant. 'Fetch her, I would speak with her immediately.'

The maid bobbed a curtsy, scuttled off up the stairs.

This was a chance Alfred could not ignore. He grabbed Edward's arm and propelled him forward. 'We must speak to him and ask his protection. He'll give it I am sure.'

Edward was not as certain, but already dragged halfway across the Hall, he could not escape. Robert of Rouen might be the Holy Archbishop, but he was also styled *le comte d'Evreux* and had the reputation of being as formidable a warrior as any armour-clad cnight. On the obverse side of the coin he was their mother's second brother and therefore he had a duty to acknowledge his nephews.

'Sir?' Edward stammered, wary. 'I give you greeting. Until the Lady Herleve can prepare herself, may I offer you refreshment?'

'Ah, *oui*, the exiles,' Robert said, turning to look at them through slit eyes and the length of his long hook nose. He was a tall man, well padded with flesh around the stomach and cheeks. A man who did not experience first hand the leaner years of a poor harvest. 'You could be useful to my purpose, stay close. I shall wish to speak with you when I have finished with Duke Robert's woman.' Without barely a pause, his eyes flickering around the busy hall, added, 'Where is the boy? William?'

'Over there, Sir, in the window recess,' Edward said, obligingly pointing.

The Archbishop nodded his head once, curt, and strode across to the lad, booming that he was to stand up and cease snivelling.

Archbishop Robert terrified Edward more than a horde of besieging warriors, or a gaggle of sniggering women. He was ferocious and dogmatic. There was no way that Edward would volunteer to serve under him. This was it, then, his mind was made. 'I am going to Jumièges,' he declared to Alfred. 'I am going to seek sanctuary with Robert Champart.'

Alfred thought his brother a prime fool, but then he had known that ever since they were toddling children.

For most of the afternoon the Archbishop of Rouen was closeted with Herleve and her son within the privacy of the upstairs solar. As dusk began to fall the servants were summoned and a great activity began, the preparing and packing for a journey. Alfred heard of the reason and destination first and hunted for his brother, finally tracing him in the castle's kennels admiring the recent litter of one of the hunting dogs.

'She's a good bitch, this one,' Edward said, looking up as his brother, holding the lantern high, walked quietly in and shut the door behind him. He indicated the heap of straw he was sitting on, patted it, inviting Alfred to sit. Offered a wineskin and half his chunk of goat's cheese. Gladly, Alfred accepted the sharing of this sparse supper.

'That is the only thing with entering the abbey.' Edward sighed. 'I shall miss my hunting and hawking. I do so enjoy the chase.'

'Then do not commit yourself to anything permanent,' Alfred advised. 'Go to Jumièges by all means; in fact, I think the Archbishop would welcome your gesture, but go as a royal guest. That way you have the best of both lives.'

Edward frowned, suspicious. Alfred had never encouraged his desire before. 'You want me to go?' he queried. 'Why?'

'I agree, she is a marvellous bitch. If you were to ask Lady Herleve, I reckon she would give her to you as a gift. She's in the mood for giving anything asked of her at the moment.'

Edward leant forward, his arm on his thigh. 'I say again. Why?'

Drawing a long, slow breath through his nose, Alfred sat up straight, pulled his tunic more comfortable through his waistband. Stalling. 'Because I am to ride into France with the Archbishop and William, so that the boy may lay his claim and pay homage as vassal to Henry the King.'

'William?' Edward echoed, incredulous. 'William is to be Duke?'

'It seems his father arranged it so with both the Archbishop and King Henry before he left for Jerusalem. Henry owed him a favour, after all, for the months he spent in exile here with us. If it were not for Robert, he might never have climbed on to his throne. Robert, apparently, called in the debt.'

Suspicious again, Edward asked another question. 'Why are you to go with them?'

Alfred puffed his cheeks, embarrassed, rubbed his thighs. 'I have offered my sword, as I said I would, to the Archbishop – well, to him in his capacity as comte d'Evreux.' He cleared his throat, continued, 'The Archbishop is to inform our mother of her great-nephew's inheritance and is to ask her to ensure no foreign prince shall take a lustful eye to Normandy as an expansion to an already large empire while the Duke remains a child.'

Edward's eyebrows shot up. 'You mean he is warning Cnut off? That's taking a risk, is it not? Such a direct approach may be misconstrued as an insult and give cause for Cnut to act!'

Alfred shook his head. 'Archbishop Robert thinks not. Cnut will be busy with Norway – Magnus Olafsson has laid claim as heir to his father and is making overtures to annex Denmark as well.' He grinned. 'Our poor half-brother, Harthacnut, could soon find himself in serious trouble.' Added vehemently, 'My heart bleeds for him.'

Edward picked up one of the pups that had crawled over to

investigate the scent of his boots. At three weeks old, his eyes had opened and he was beginning to take an interest in the world beyond his mother's milk teat. A fine, sturdy dog, good legs, good head.

'You still have not explained why you will be going to France.'

'Have I not? If Cnut is to agree not to interfere with Normandy, King Henry and the Archbishop, acting together as guardians to the young Duke, will agree not to interfere in any way with England.'

'In particular with an inheritance issue?' Edward asked, his head lifting, eyes brightening with relieved delight. No more expectation to claim a kingdom? God be praised!

'*Oui.*' Alfred paused, added, 'I also get a captaincy in the Archbishop's army.' For Alfred, that was all he had ever wanted: recognition.

Edward set the pup down and ushered him towards his siblings. 'I may ask Herleve if I can have the pup. I like him.' Then said thoughtfully, 'Though William as Duke? He is but a boy of eight years. Will he survive do you think?'

Alfred stood, brushed the straw off his woollen tunic. 'How old was our father when he became King? Not much older. He managed it.'

41

Cnut's horse went lame a mile from Shaftesbury.

'A stone, I reckon,' he said, jumping from the saddle and lifting the offside foreleg to inspect beneath the hoof. With his dagger, he scraped at the dried mud accumulated between the shoe, prodded at the exposed sole. '*Ja.* Here, it is bruised.'

Godwine had dismounted and, passing his mount's reins to a servant, bent to look, agreed. 'Will you take my horse instead, Sir?' he offered.

Straightening, Cnut laughed. 'No, Godwine, it is but a short walk up the hill to the abbey.' He patted his belly. 'And to lose some of this will do me no harm!'

'My Gytha says it is my appetite for ale and honey cakes that has caused mine.' Godwine grinned as he ruefully examined his own extended paunch.

'Funny, that.' Cnut grinned back, clicking his tongue at his horse to walk on. 'Emma believes the same!'

Out of respect, Cnut's housecarls had dismounted, offered their horses as Godwine had done. Cnut dismissed them with the same reply.

'If we stay the night here with the good nuns, then proceed on our way at sunup, we shall reach Sherborne in good time,' Cnut declared, as he started up the hill. The nunnery was at the top of the plateau, the climb steep. At least the road was cobbled and dry underfoot; to slog up here in deep mud was never a welcome experience.

'I only hope the abbot at Sherborne does not intend to keep us too long. Sign these charters of covenant and be on our way home, I say. The skies are gathering too grey for my liking. It will rain by the morrow's dawn, you mark my words.' Godwine agreed with his

King, he sniffed at the air, swore he could smell the moisture.

'If I did not know you better, my friend,' Cnut chuckled through panting breath, 'I would say you are having second thoughts on granting land to the abbey.'

'What? No, no, Sherborne needs that manor more than I. It is the journey here that irritates, not the deed. I had hoped for the Abbot to come to me, not the other way around.'

'He has not been well, Godwine; we can hardly expect him to travel abroad with heavy rain expected!'

Godwine laughed at the jest – the Abbot of Sherborne was known for his reclusive ways – was grateful when Cnut halted halfway up the hill to catch breath. 'I could run up here when I was a lad, you know,' Godwine puffed. 'Can scarce walk it now!'

'Old and fat,' Cnut gasped, his hand on his chest, his heartbeat thundering in his ears, 'that is our trouble.'

Godwine chuckled. 'Or so our lady wives would have it! Muscle this is,' he said, patting his belly, 'muscle.'

'Flabby muscle? Be there such a thing?'

Cnut found he had to stop a second time before he reached the abbey gate, and was pleased to be made welcome with a comfortable chair and goblet of the Abbess's best imported wine. The nuns served good food, well cooked with a variety of menu, but he found he was light of appetite and, as evening fell, felt an extensive tiredness creeping over him.

'Are you not well, my Lord?' Godwine asked. 'You look pale.'

'Ready for my bed I think, Godwine, it has been a long day and I have an uncomfortable touch of indigestion. I will send for a herbal draught and get some sleep. Ensure I am woken an hour before dawn, for us to be on our way by sunrise.'

But Cnut, his heart failing while he slept, was never to see the morning sunlight flood over England again and Godwine, galloping his horse to return to the Queen at Winchester, did not see the dawn for the blur of tears that scalded his eyes.

PART FOUR

Emma

Anno Domini 1035–1041

And men advised that Emma, Harthacnut's mother,
stay in Winchester with the housecarls of the King, her
son, and hold all Wessex for his hands. And Earl
Godwine was her most faithful man.

Anglo-Saxon Chronicle

1

The Queen, Emma, knew from the grey pallor on Earl Godwine's face and by the way he stood, one step within the threshold, that something was wrong. Horribly wrong.

'My Lord, you are wet through?' she said, a question in her voice, although the statement was obvious. A second question, of why he had come to Winchester so unexpected in such torrential rain, hovered unspoken. Rising from her chair, set for comfort beside the fire, she indicated with her hand that he could enter into her private chamber, come closer, warm himself.

To her handmaid ordered, 'Fetch wine and food. Broth. My Lord Earl will require something hot.'

The girl bobbed a curtsy and, squeezing past the Earl, scuttled from the chamber, but Godwine remained at the door, his thumbs depressing the iron latch. How was he to tell her? How could he repeat news that would break this good lady's heart like shattered pieces of glass?

'My Lady Queen,' he finally stammered, 'I have ridden at the gallop since dawn.'

He shook his head slowly, held out both hands, palms uppermost, pleading for her to read what was in his mind to save the pain of having to say this thing aloud. How could she guess? No one in England could have foreseen this. No one. His arms fell to his side, a tear slithering down his cheek. His hair was rain-matted, his cloak and boots sodden. His chin beard-stubbled.

In despair, quick, with one breath, 'My Lady, your husband is dead. God took the King from us during the night.'

Emma stood perfectly still, barely breathing, her face draining of colour. She licked her lips, shook her head, denying what she had heard.

'No,' she said, backing away from Godwine and stumbling over a footstool, her voice rising to a scream. 'Oh, God! No!'

He hurried after her, took hold of her shoulders. 'We could not rouse him from sleep. His physician, who knows of these things, believes it to have been a seizure of the heart. I assure you he looked to be at peace, did not feel pain or discomfort.'

Emma, *Regina Anglorum*, Queen of England, remained silent for several long moments, her mind, eyes and heart blank. Empty. Numb. Then, with a steady calm returning, graciously thanked Earl Godwine for his trouble in riding to her on this cold, wet day. 'It was good of you to come to me personally, not send some mere messenger. You have always been loyal.' She spoke with a smile. 'I am grateful for that and for your friendship. Attributes that may, I fear, be sorely tried in the weeks that must now lie ahead of us.' She faltered, the control collapsing into the sham it was, her lip trembled, tears welled. Her breath catching, tight, in her throat.

Snatching up her cloak from where it lay across a chest, she muttered, 'Please, dry yourself before the fire. I would walk alone a while.' Pride had been her only comfort and salvation for too many years; she was not about to alter that schooled endurance now.

Before Godwine could remind her of the bad weather, she had disappeared from the chamber and was running down the wooden stairs, her gown lifted with one clutching hand. Ignoring the sudden hush of the crowded Hall below, she flung on the cloak and stepped out into the rain. She did not mind the rain; rain masked scalding tears and the pain of gut-wrenching, heartbroken grief.

Godwine made to follow her, reached as far as the Hall's outer doors, but here he halted, watched Emma walk across the mud-puddled courtyard towards the shelter of the stables. Retracing his steps into the Hall, he intercepted the handmaid, took the bowl and goblet to the nearest trestle. He had ridden straight to the Queen, had not waited to break his fast before leaving Shaftesbury, nor barely eased his stallion from the punishing gallop he had set. The horse was ruined, of course, his wind and legs beyond repair, but what mattered one horse when the King was dead? When so many more horses, and men, might soon be beyond saving? Earl Godwine ate, drank. Did not notice the taste of either broth or ale.

He would leave Emma a while to mourn alone, respect her need for privacy. Later would come the time for the murmuring of meaningless platitudes, the empty words that everyone muttered when the unwelcome shadow of death visited.

'He was a good man. A good King . . .'

'You have your memories . . .'

Memories? What good were memories when you so desperately wanted the solid feel of a man's arms around you or to hear the sound of his voice, see the quirk of his smile? The sparkle of laughter that shone from his eyes? Knowing, all the while, that you would never, never meet with him again.

Huh! Memories! Emma buried her tear-streaked face deep into her mare's bushy mane. She harboured enough memories to fill the Christian world twice over, but how did memories mend a torn heart? Ease the dread, dark chill of grief?

2

Emma heard a quiet footfall, a discreet cough. Godwine, come carefully to find her. She lifted her head from the mare's warm flank, brushed ineffectually at the tears. Godwine had faced the doing of some hard things during his lifetime of two-score years; having to tell his Queen that her husband, his King, was dead, he had found to be the hardest of all.

'I'm sorry,' she apologised with a false laugh. 'I am being childish and silly.'

'It is neither childish nor silly', Godwine answered, 'to weep for one who was loved and has gone.'

'I cannot believe what you are saying is true, it is as if this is some horrible nightmare and I shall awake from in a moment, see Cnut coming in through that door, cursing the rain and the leak in his boot. Or if not today, then he will return tomorrow or tomorrow, be gone some weeks, months, mayhap, but he will return. He has always come back to me. Always.'

Godwine was unable to find the words to respond – what did you say when someone was breaking apart? Instead, he spread his arms wide, half a gesture of helplessness, half an expression of support. Emma stepped forward then, uncertain, stood lost, unsure what to do, how to behave, how to react. Godwine had always been there, had always provided a rock of solid friendship, but they had never crossed the boundary into the close intimacy of touch. Suddenly, anger filled her, the overwhelming anger of misery.

'How dare he do this to me?' she gasped. 'How dare he hurt me so, let me down? He has always been so selfish, thinking of himself, his kingdom, what he wants, what he needs. How dare he! Oh, how bloody dare he?'

The tears freely falling, unchecked, unstopped, Emma went

into Godwine's arms, accepting the offer of his embrace for what it was, an unspoken mutual request for comfort. Her face ducked into his shoulder and the tears tore from her body as she wept great, gulping sobs of desperate sorrow, the pain so intense that it burnt. The unacceptable disbelief, incredible and all-consuming.

Kindly, gently, Godwine stroked her back, her hair, letting her cry, not caring to keep in his own tears. Two people, deep in the pit of grief, linked by their years of friendship and the gaping, aching chasm that had ripped open before them.

After a few moments – it was only a few moments of raw anguish – Emma pulled free, embarrassed. She went to turn away, but Godwine touched her shoulder, stopped her.

'It is all right to cry. Sometimes, it is best,' he advised compassionately.

'Yes,' she answered with a pale smile, 'but not always wise. I am the Queen, people expect me to be their strength. If the foundation should falter the building may fall.'

Godwine reached forward, very delicately put his finger to her cheek. 'I am not people, Emma. I am your friend.'

The initial shock receding, her smile strengthened and she took his hand, squeezed his fingers. 'That you are and I am so very grateful for it.' She took a deep breath, puffed the air from her lungs and, secreting away the grief, pretended a stoic public face as she smoothed the front of her gown for want of something to do with her hands. 'And I expect I shall be even more grateful during these next weeks to come. I will be in sore need of friends, for a variety of reasons.'

The stables were a refuge, they were also, apart from the horses with their steady, soporific sound of chewing the hay, deserted. There was no one to hear, no one to see.

'Tell me what happened, to the last detail; I wish to know, have to know. Is anything amiss suspected?'

Emphatically, Godwine shook his head. If she thought murder, then he could most certainly reassure her against that dark menace that so often stalked kings. 'No, Lady, he died in his sleep, at peace and knowing nothing of it.' He told her of yesterday – God, was it only yesterday – of the lame horse, the pleasant walk up the hill that in hindsight was shouting a warning. The breathlessness, the tiredness and chest pain of the evening.

'It was his heart, Lady, it stopped beating.'

Emma nodded, digesting the information. 'It is good to know he did not suffer, I would not have wished pain on him, he was too good and caring a man for that. He will be greeted well by God.' She was recovering, achieving the public face above the private grief. 'Has word been sent to my son? He must be informed as soon as possible.' Inside the outer calm was a great gash opened, numb as yet, but would be aching and throbbing for many a month to come.

Harthacnut, there, Godwine could be of service. 'I dispatched the Captain of my Housecarls, my most trusted man, he is to take my own ship and sail as close to the wind as he can to Denmark.' It did occur to Godwine, now that he had a chance to think on it, whether anyone would bother taking word to the other sons, Edward and Alfred in Normandy, but there were not many in England who retained a loyalty to the old King: a few monks, one or two abbots, no one of great importance. With the Duke of Normandy being a boy neck-deep in his own troubled pile of shit, it was unlikely there would be any Norman aid offered to two forgotten exiles. No, the difficulty would be coming, when it came, from Northampton. Godwine's mouth thinned; this was not the moment to be talking of it, but if Harthacnut did not come with all haste to England, his half-brother, Harold Ælfgifusson, would be making claim. England was open and vulnerable, a ship without a master, floating with a bewildered crew, eager to welcome aboard a leader who knew how to plot a course and read the wind. Harthacnut or Harold? Which one would outmanoeuvre the other?

Emma was a queen. She had been wed to three husbands, Æthelred, Cnut and England, and she was no fool. Her thoughts had leapt to where Godwine was only prodding. 'Then, while we await the new King we must ensure his succession. There are others who will be wanting a crown that is not theirs to take.'

Godwine half smiled, incredulous at this wonderful woman's resilience, at how the black-and-white necessities of life were taking over Emma's emotions. The practical and sensible things that needed attending. Arrangements, notifications.

'Word must be sent to all the lords, Godwine, reliable messengers selected. The Archbishops of Canterbury and York informed. As you know, my husband had a grave dug and made ready to receive his body at Bosham, beside his daughter, but he has become a great and beloved king since that early day of his reign. He must have something better for his place of rest, I would have him buried at Winchester, before the altar of the Old Minster, as is right for a king such as Cnut was. I would be buried there too,' she added, her eyes beseeching Godwine's as her steadiness faltered, wavered. 'When my end comes, I would be beside him.'

'That will not be for many years yet, my Lady, I assure you.'

Her voice cracked as she answered and she swallowed down fresh tears. 'Not too many years, Godwine. I pray God not to separate me from Cnut by the passing of too many years.'

With effort, she recovered her composure by taking gasps of air, as if she were drowning or asphyxiating, continued, after a moment, with the practicalities. Easier to think of those, to give orders, make decisions. To tread the familiar ground and pretend that the other – this new, unwelcome and unwanted thing – did not exist. 'You will please make arrangements for his body to be brought here and for all the nobles of the Witan to assemble as soon as may be? Harthacnut must be crowned King of England as soon as he makes landfall.' Angrily, she kicked at a stable door, causing the horse inside to snort and toss his head. 'I did not want Cnut to take Harthacnut abroad! For this very reason, I did not want it!'

Godwine did not agree, but said nothing. For his own judgement he did not like Harthacnut, had always found him a sullen, indolent boy who let lies fall too glibly from his mouth. But was he being ungenerous? Harthacnut had been a lad, then, when Godwine had known him. He was grown to a young man now. Perhaps he had learnt the subtle wisdoms of honesty and truth; could differentiate between a man of worth and one not worth knowing?

'Harthacnut', Emma said with finality, 'must come to England. He must be here for the calling of Council.'

Now with that Godwine did agree.

3

'You will find it difficult to take the Treasury from Emma, she will not be an easy obstacle to negotiate,' Earl Leofric said gravely, stroking his moustache and shaking his head. 'Assuming you get past her protector, Godwine, in the first instance.'

'The Queen is nothing!' Ælfgifu spat contemptuously. 'She has no more strength than I – and certainly not as much wealth to buy more, should it be needed.'

'It will be needed, Madam, I assure you it will.' Leofric of Mercia thought Ælfgifu's scheming for her son to be nothing short of madness. She had every right to put in a claim for the crown, Harold was, with all said and done, Cnut's firstborn son, but that small fact would hold little sway once Harthacnut landed in England. He was already crowned jointly with Cnut as King of Denmark; he had fought in battles, could adequately command a man and ship. The Witan would choose him without overmuch discussion. Harold, for all his mother's prolific adoration of him, was not the man Harthacnut was reputed to be. But then . . . but then, as Ælfgifu had so plainly stated, Harthacnut was not here in England, Harold was.

'What if Harthacnut should be delayed?' Ælfgifu said again. She had been saying so this last half-day, since Leofric's arrival in response to her urgent summons. 'What if the winds keep him in Denmark, so he does not hear for a while? She crossed her comfortably furnished solar to sit at Leofric's side, put her hand delicately on his arm. 'What if Harold does not wait for the Witan to choose? It is the one who wears the crown that carries the strength.'

That could be civil war, one faction against the other. England again trampled and bloody after all these years of peace. On the other side of the river, it could mean power and status, something

Earl Leofric, as much as his kinswoman Ælfgifu of Northampton, craved.

'There would be opposition,' he pointed out, laying his hand over hers. 'Deaths.'

'Theirs as much as ours.'

'It could ruin you. You could lose all you have, including Harold.'

'I could gain much, including a crown.'

Ah, Ælfgifu always had a persuasive answer.

'It is my son and you,' she said, her voice low, seductive, as if attempting to entice him into her bed, 'or her son and Godwine. Who would your rather have, Leofric? Who?' Her sweet breath fell like gossamer on his cheek and he was stirred. Not his manhood, not the wanting of sexual pleasure, but something stronger: the desire for the ultimate, for the highest of all powers. To be the man closest to the King.

'We will need to move fast,' he said, making his decision. 'Gather all we can to our side and descend on London. If we can get London with us we will find firm footing beneath our feet, for who controls London can control England.' He looked across the room at Harold, who sat, elbows on his thighs, his lips pressed into his clenched hands, his eyes watching, watching every move Leofric made.

Harold was one and twenty years, yet wore the look of an old man about his eyes, a narrowed, calculating vision that reminded the Earl of a snake's gaze. Harold's eyes, if ever you met them straight on, sent shivers tingling down the spine, as if an ice wind had blown in through an opened doorway. His mother wore the same eyes, the pair of them had the look of the Devil in their soul. All the more imperative, then, to go with them if the storm was going to gather. Better that than ride unprotected by shield or blade.

'Who will back us?' Leofric asked the question at Harold, although guessing his mother would answer. Harold had not spoken a word the entire afternoon, had just sat there, in the same position, brooding.

'Deira, Bernicia, the Seven Boroughs – all the Shires from the Great Wall down to the River Thames.' Alfgifu spoke with confidence, as well she might, for many of the thegns and lords were her kinsmen, either close related or, as with Leofric, distant cousins. However long or loose the tie, the blood of family could run thick when the possible reward was the greatest thing to be achieved, nothing came higher than a crown.

'Siward was Cnut's man,' Leofric countered, uncertain.

'Siward was content to serve Cnut, but not Godwine.'

Leofric was sceptical of Bernicia. 'Forgive my discourtesy, Madam, but I must say this bluntly. Uhtred's kin will never side with you, not after the shameless way in which he died.'

Ælfgifu had been expecting the comment, memories were long in the North. Memories, however, could be manipulated into being selective. Theatrically, she shook her head, sighed with exaggerated weariness. 'For how many years must I continue to plead my innocence regarding that dreadful day? I have been forced to remain silent of the truth for the sake of my sons. If I had dared speak within Cnut's hearing I would have risked my life and theirs. It has been hard to perpetrate a lie and bear the brunt of its carrying.' She stared levelly and confidently direct at Leofric. 'Cnut made use of the known enmity between my kindred and Uhtred's. The King was desperate to seek southern allegiance, but had first to be rid of Uhtred. How could he open his own hands and let England see the blood that was stained on them? So much easier to conceal the guilt and lay blame where it was conveniently diverted.'

She was clever, Ælfgifu, for she had lived through many years in which to practise the subtle art of illusion. She allowed a tear to trickle from the corner of her eye, her face to crumple into fragile sorrow. 'I carried a weighted burden for Cnut, bore vilification for the sake of my sons. But I cannot remain silent any longer, the truth must be told.' She patted the damp tears from her cheek. 'Cnut had Uhtred murdered, not I. I love the North, the strength we posses, the rights we ought to have and the independence we should be granted. Why would I attempt to destroy our unity? Cnut wanted to divide us, to set family against family, kin against kin, to create a blood-feud between us to ensure we would never unite against him.' She shook her head, seated herself on a chair. 'He succeeded only too well, for still the feud goes on, and in my name. Me, who had nothing to do with it.'

If he had no other regard for Ælfgifu, Leofric had to acknowledge that she was a believable liar.

'We must set aside our differences.' She sighed and her shoulders drooped, she dropped her hands into her lap, defeated. 'But it will never be. Our ancestors allowed the nobility of Wessex to walk all over us and we will never be rid of southern domination because we are too busy squabbling among ourselves, perpetuating old feuds that were deliberately calculated to tear our unity apart.' Carefully she did not raise her eyes, but kept her gaze downcast. Did she have him? Had she hooked him to her baited line?

She tried one last thrust. 'We have a chance of putting a northern king on the throne of England. If we do not act quickly, we may never see this chance again. England will always belong to Wessex, never, never to us.'

Uncertain, Leofric chewed his lips. Much of what she said was true, although as much of it stank more than fresh bullshit, but then, the North was used to the smell. He looked across at Harold, studied him. A lean-faced youth, so much like Cnut. A king had to shine, had to be more than ordinary. What was there about this boy that could inspire men to follow him into the Hell of death, if it had to be asked of them?

Harold gazed back, his stare rigid, unblinking. Unafraid.

'Why', Leofric asked, nonchalantly folding his arms, 'should I bother to put myself out and make you King, eh, boy?'

Ælfgifu held her breath, aware the answer Harold made would persuade the Earl's final decision that, once made, would not be about turned.

'Why', Leofric expanded his question, 'should I follow you as my lord and turn against Cnut's son? Harthacnut is already a crowned King and of more significance than you.' It was what they would all be asking. 'What is there about you, boy, to justify a war?'

Slowly, almost lazily, Harold unfolded himself from the hunched, morose figure he had depicted. He walked slowly towards Leofric, stood before him, confident and assured, his fists on his hips, legs spread. So much, so much like his father. 'There are things I could say that you already know. That I am the firstborn of my father; that my blood is Anglo-Danish, not tainted with Norman watering; that the crown is mine by right, but none of those would answer your question.'

Leofric shook his head. No, they would not.

'You will support me', Harold said, leaning forward, bringing his face close, so that Leofric could see for himself the conviction behind the words, 'because I intend to be King and I require the experience of a man I can trust to place as my second in command.'

The Earl was already convinced, he had been before he had arrived at Northampton. If he had harboured doubts about Harold he would not have ridden so fast from Coventry, but would have headed direct for the Queen in Winchester. All the same, he was not going to allow this scheming woman and her son to believe he was a man so easy led.

'And if the North were to declare you King, what would be the first thing you would do?' Another answer that was imperative to the unrolling of events.

For Harold it was an easy question. He knew exactly what he was going to do. 'I shall send an army to Winchester and demand the seizure of the Royal Treasury. And then, as you have endorsed, I shall secure London.'

A slow, calculating smile crept over Leofric's face. He stood, regarded Harold eye to eye, then knelt before him, bent his head in submission to his King.

4

Aghast, Emma glowered at Godwine. 'You are not seriously suggesting that I comply with this treasonous outrage?'

That was exactly what Godwine was suggesting.

'Your Earl of Wessex, my Lady, has the sense to realise that there is very little he can do to prevent me,' Leofric drawled, irritated that Emma had not given him permission to sit and that he had been standing during the entire hour of interview. He was no old man, but the ride had been long and hard, and his thighs and back ached. A seat would have been welcome, as would a bite to eat and a tankard of ale, but he supposed it reasonable for a queen to refuse a charitable welcome to the bringer of her imminent downfall.

'The Earl of Wessex', Godwine snapped back, 'is full aware that there is much I can do! I have a value for the lives of men who remain loyal to their King, that is all.'

Leofric shrugged. 'I am in agreement, why waste blood when there is an alternative? A pity your loyalty is misguided, Godwine. The King will be grieved to hear of it.'

'So he shall!' Emma hissed, furious with both of them, the one for his audacity, the other for his indiscretion. She would never have believed it of Godwine, that he could turn his back so quickly and easily on both her and his King. 'I assure you I shall repeat every word that you have vomited from your mouth to my son, Leofric.'

'I am pleased to hear it,' the Earl of Mercia answered as he swept her a low, mocking bow. 'When will he be in England to learn of it? Soon? Or does the rumour that Harthacnut may not answer your summons have any credence?'

The public Hall at Emma's Winchester house was crowded, mostly with Leofric's men, who had entered the city fully armed against no offered resistance. Again, Godwine's suggestion, another that had flown in the face of Emma's indignation.

'It is pointless to fight,' Godwine had said, as exasperated as his Queen and equally as determined to have his way. 'All it will achieve is the death of good men, and for what? A loss of public dignity? Without Harthacnut here in England we are like a holed ship. Provided we stay in shallow waters we will not sink, but once the tide floods, unless we can haul her higher up the shore she will be gone.'

Emma's own housecarls, and those of Cnut, had stood impotent, glowering, unarmed and helpless, as Leofric had, in effect, taken temporary command of Winchester. 'If the North unites,' Godwine had whispered into Emma's ear, 'then Wessex will burn as easily as a torch set to a summer-dried meadow. Without your son we can do nothing except appear to submit.'

That one word had alerted Emma to Godwine's intention. *Appear*. Sitting in what had been Cnut's throne – Harthacnut's now – Emma regarded Leofric with cool hatred. Godwine had never liked the man; she had been ambivalent towards him, for Cnut had thought of him as a reliable Earl who took the responsibility of Mercia as a personal and valued achievement. Under Cnut, however, Leofric's loyalty had never had to be tested.

'Harthacnut is the King of England,' she said. 'Not Harold. He has no say over the Treasury.'

'Once he is crowned he shall,' Leofric tossed back. 'And that, I assure you, shall happen within the week. With or without your co-operation. You either give what we want voluntarily, or Harold will come to Winchester and take it for himself. It is your choice, Madam. I doubt the people of Winchester will thank you for making the wrong one.'

And that was why, she realised now, Godwine had urged her to comply with this outrage. If they had been permitted an opportunity to discuss tactics and strategy, to plan and collude, she would have understood Godwine's thinking from the outset, but Leofric's arrival at Winchester's gate had come as a surprise, his demand unexpected. The Earl had caught them all with their guard down. What was it Godwine had said to her in those few moments of quick decision between barring the gates and allowing him entry? When caught in a trap, it was no use digging deeper, best to sit quiet and think of a sensible way to climb out.

What Emma wanted to do was take out Leofric's eyes, remove his tongue, his heart. Burn his entrails, hang him from the rafters of this very Hall, take an axe to his head – oh, she could think of a hundred unpleasant deaths. She did not want to capitulate to these humiliating demands, but then, neither did she want harm to come to Winchester.

'Very well,' she reluctantly agreed, 'you may have the revenue from the North, not all the annual tax has been gathered from Northumbria. If Bernicia will surrender it, you may keep it.' That in itself would busily employ these upstarts. The North was notorious for refusing to pay due taxation, it would be a small loss for Wessex to do without. 'For the rest, Harold may hold it until Harthacnut comes to reclaim it. But mark my word, Leofric, on your head rests the King's wrath.'

Leofric's smile was sardonic. This had been an easier task than he had expected. 'That fact I am already aware of. It just depends on which king we are referring to, does it not?'

Godwine felt a wave of relief wash through him. Thank God Emma had seen his ploy for what it was, a ruse to give them time. If war was to begin, and it would, sooner rather than later, he did not want it to break out here within the confines of Winchester. And not without Harthacnut to co-ordinate a retaliation and put this poxed bastard, Earl Leofric, in his place. Six foot deep in earth.

'You may encamp your pathetic army five miles from Winchester's walls,' Emma offered. 'Your usurper's share of the Treasury shall be delivered to you by tomorrow noon.'

'Dawn, Madam, would be the more practical,' Leofric countered. 'We can then break camp and be on the march towards London and King Harold by sunup.'

'Then break camp and be ready to move out,' Emma tossed back. 'The pack ponies, ready loaded, can fall into the column at sunrise.'

Leofric knew when to cease negotiation. 'Sunrise it is, then, and

689

you will be sure to include the crown and the royal sceptre in the load, of course? The King shall be requiring them for his coronation.'

Emma folded her hands, linking the fingers, her rings flashing in the reflection of the candle and rush light. 'If Harold wishes to use a crown, my Lord Earl, then he will have to find his own. He will not be using my husband's or my son's.' She smiled sweetly and flicked her right hand. 'As for the sceptre, it is in the safe keeping of my Lord Archbishop of Canterbury. Surely, Earl Leofric, you know that such a holy item is held within the sanctity of God, not among the chests of the Treasury?'

As bluff, it was a master stroke. Leofric was certain the Queen lied, but if what she said was true, how much of the fool would he be looking in the watching and assessing eyes of England?

'Sunrise,' he said with a curt bow as he turned to make his withdrawal. 'I expect delivery at sunrise.'

'Expect as much as you want,' Emma muttered through furious clenched teeth, 'but I'll not guarantee you will get it.'

'The sceptre is with Archbishop Athelnoth?' Godwine queried, one eyebrow raised, when the Hall had emptied of intruders. 'That is the first I have heard of it!'

Emma lightly shrugged one shoulder. 'Of course it is, Godwine, Cnut insisted upon sending it to Canterbury. I would not be surprised to discover that I am mistaken and find that his crown is with the Archbishop also. He is a such a good friend, he would never go against me, or Cnut's wishes.' Her smile was coquettish, some small triumph over Leofric and the wretched boy he represented. 'At least, if these things are not with the Archbishop at this precise moment, they soon shall be.'

She rose, walked unhurried to the stairs that led to her private upper chamber and the chests that stored the value of the Kingdom. 'You will help me decide what trinkets I can send this coxcomb and his bitch mother, Godwine,' she said, 'and you had best come up with an acceptable explanation for what almost bordered on treason.'

There was anger in Godwine's retort, had she not understood

after all? Was all that a mask to save face in an embarrassing situation? 'Do you not trust my judgement, then, Lady? If that is the case, what hope is there for Wessex and England? I can answer you immediate, without necessity to think of lame excuses. It is not treasonous to send an enemy away, having made him believe he has won a skirmish, leaving us opportunity to win the battle.'

She could see that, but it was the frustration of it all that angered Emma, the sheer inability to be able to do anything. Without Harthacnut here to lay his claim, her hands were tied and she felt as though she were shouting aimlessly into a storm wind.

'We need my son,' she said anxiously, by way of apology. 'We need Harthacnut.'

Godwine surrendered his anger. He was as humiliated as she. To bend to the demands of Leofric, of all people, God, how it stuck in his throat!

'So, until Harthacnut gets here,' he said, practical and with a hopeful smile, 'we must think of effective ways to scuttle the enemy's ships.'

'Oh, I have ideas, Godwine. Do not fear, I have already the ideas for that.'

5

25 November 1035 – Saint Paul's, London
Archbishop Athelnoth, called The Good for his devotion to Christ, was not best pleased to be summoned in all haste to London from Canterbury. Nor was he pleased to be ordered to perform a holy ceremony that went against the grain of legality in the eyes of the Kingdom and of God. To be consecrated as King was to be chosen by the Almighty, but first, when there was more than one contestant for the title, men had the deciding of the thing.

'I cannot crown a king without the express will of the Witan of all England,' the Archbishop said forcibly, standing proud and determinedly upright before the altar of the Cathedral of Saint Paul in London. It was a wooden building, humble in origin, large in status, built in the form of a square crucifix, with its high tower perched over the central transept, dominating Ludgate Hill and the sprawled city of London. For miles across the flat marsh lands of the Thames valley, Saint Paul's could be seen giving glory to God.

Ælfgifu, as a woman, found herself impotent to make redress to the Archbishop, her fury seething beneath the surface as she was forced to sit quiet and silent on a bench. She had never relied on others before, and found the experience both frustrating and humiliating. By God, even Cnut had listened to her! Now she had to sit, biting back the words that foamed in her mouth, while Earl Leofric and her son argued their case.

'Without a crowned king, England is open and vulnerable to attack. To riot and the wilful breaking of the law,' Harold stated passionately, convinced of his opinion.

'Without a crowned king the very sight of God is obliterated,' Earl Leofric added, not as hopefully as Harold, for he could recognise the stubbornness in this holy man's face, even if the boy could not.

Harold did not share the Earl's deference to God, Ælfgifu insisted that he was a man intent on buying his sway into Heaven with the building of churches and founding of monasteries. Give enough to God and you need not pay care to the consequences of sin.

'Leofric is the type of man who would sell his soul, were the reward sufficient,' Ælfgifu had often remarked, proved correct by his eagerness to assist Harold's claim. Done through the greed for power, not for love of his kindred.

God, thus far, had done little for Harold or his mother. Her father murdered, her brothers brutally blinded. Where had God been when his own brother had pitched over the side of a ship and disappeared into the sea? Where was God now?

'Despite Queen Emma's best efforts to stop me,' Harold said to the Archbishop. 'I will be King of England, as God is my witness I shall.'

'Very possibly,' Athelnoth responded graciously, 'but not until the Witan has been called together and the good noble men of this land have agreed it so.'

'You are refusing to crown me? I shall not judge that with favour in future months. Men either back me or go against me, Archbishop.'

The threat was subtle, but meant. Athelnoth did not miss its intensity. 'For the reasons I have stated, I refuse to crown anyone. The royal sceptre and crown are placed upon this sacred altar behind me and there, within the sight of God, they remain until judgement has been made.'

'Or trial by strength prevails.'

The Archbishop innocently spread his hands, 'Then that would be God's judgement, would it not?'

Athelnoth had no care for Harold, nor for his mother. In the sight of God her union with Cnut had been sinful, the children she had given birth to base-born. That one of them should have the effrontery to stand before this altar and lay claim to the rite of sacred consecration angered him to his very soul. And as for the woman, blood clung to her hands. She had made no attempt at penitence for the sin of murder. Had she shown remorse, been more charitable, as was Earl Leofric, or had the humility to take the veil, then the clergy might have looked more favourably on her son, but not a single chapel had benefited from her amassed wealth, not one nunnery or lepers' hospice had been grateful for her generosity. Generosity? Did the woman know the existence of the word? All she knew was hatred and cruelty, the route of evil.

'Then if there is no other way, we shall call together the Council,' Harold declared, exasperated. Leofric had said they would have to do so sooner rather than later, but his mother, stamping to her feet, unable to remain silent any longer, would hear none of it.

'We secure the crown, then go to Council,' she insisted, ignoring the Archbishop's severe frown of reprimand. A stubborn lady, who clung obstinately to her opinions and would not hear of alternatives. In his own mind Harold held the feeling that he would succeed quicker and fly higher were it not for his mother's interferences, but how to be rid of her?

'The Witan is already summoned,' Athelnoth declared, patient and politely hiding a triumphant smile. 'The Queen has sent word that Council is to meet at Oxford for the Nativity.' Gleefully added, 'Were you at home in your estates, my Lord Leofric you would have known of this, for the Queen's messenger went to your manor, I believe, and found you not there.'

Leofric made no comment. An earl could be stripped of title and lands and outlawed if he were not where he was expected to be, or if he ignored, without good reason, a royal command.

'Do not fret, Archbishop,' Harold leered, 'I will be there, with all who follow and support me. Be sure to bring my crown and sceptre to Oxford with you, old man, for we will be requiring them.'

While any suitable church would do for a king's crowning, London was the preferred place for coronation, for it pandered to London's pride and emphasised the importance of the capital city. The surest way of securing London for Harold. The gates had been opened to him without preamble, his fleet welcomed beneath the archways of London Bridge. Adequate payment, and the promised wavering of taxes, so often bought direct and desired results.

'As the Queen and Harthacnut shall also be there,' Athelnoth

694

countered, 'it is for the Witan to decide whether you be the stronger man than Cnut's legitimate son. It is not for your mother to be having that say.'

Ælfgifu rushed forward, her mouth twisting with aggression. 'I will see both that woman and you burn in Hell, old man, if you do not consecrate my son!'

The Archbishop smiled; he was not afraid of demons or their enslaved women. 'For that to be literally so, Madam, you will need be there with me.'

Ignoring the man's pedantic sarcasm, Ælfgifu turned on her heel and stalked from the Cathedral, announcing as she went, 'Crown my son, Archbishop, or face the consequences. I will not give way to that hag in Winchester, to you, or to God.'

'For the Queen and myself,' Athelnoth answered with equanimity, his stern voice ringing down the length of the nave, 'my answer remains the same: I shall bend only to the will of the Council. As for God, I do not fear Him. It is for you to challenge His will at *your* peril, not mine.'

6

The day started wrong and worsened into a progressive downward spiral through the morning and afternoon. First, Emma trod on a broken pot that had been overlooked from the evening before, when one of the maids had dropped a bowl of dried fruits. She had screamed on seeing a rat whisk across the corner of the chamber, let go of the bowl and it had shattered. Stepping from the bed, bleary-eyed and barefoot, the jagged shard had cut into the sole of Emma's foot, which bled profusely and was to prove tender and sore for several days to come.

At noon, her gown ripped on a nail protruding from the stairway. She had to return to her private rooms and change, which then made her late for an arranged meeting with the Bishop. Walking home from the Minster she had twisted her ankle on a loose cobble and now, early evening, she had discovered a ruby to be missing from a favourite ring that Cnut had given her during the first month of their marriage. She could have lost it anywhere and when. Today? Yesterday? Weeks ago? It was one of the rings she always wore on her right hand, with her marriage band and coronation ring on her left. It was only a small stone, set among a cluster of dark-green emeralds, would be of no difficulty to replace by a jewelsmith. All the same, Emma mourned its loss. Stupid to find herself crying over an inconsequential ruby; she had a casket full of rings, many of them given to her by Cnut, many more valuable, so why sit here crying over this one?

She remembered exactly where he had given it to her, the time and the place. The occasion. London, the seventh day of May in the year 1017. The sun had sparkled on the river as they had ridden across London Bridge, her mare close to Cnut's stallion, their hooves echoing on the wooden planking, but barely heard above the tumult of cheering. Surely every living soul in the city had turned out to greet their arrival that day? They had tossed blossom in their path, pink and white faerie flowers from the trees and hedgerows, so that the air was heavy with the intoxicating scent of hawthorn. The market stalls of London had been groaning under their weight of wares, pottery, tin and pewter pots and pans; leather goods, from bags to saddles to shoes; brocades, silks, linens and wools; furs, wooden furniture, tools and implements. Birds in cages, finches and magenpies, crowing cocks, cowering hares. Food of every sort, pies and pasties, haunches of beef, lamb and pork. Fish, barley cakes, sacks of grain. Jewellery of copper, silver, gold. Necklaces, armbands, bracelets, brooches. And rings.

Cnut had spotted the jewelsmith from the corner of his eye, a short, dark-skinned man with thinning grey hair, black eyes and nimble fingers. He was finishing a ring, setting the final central stone, a ruby, into a cluster of five emeralds. The sun flashed into the gem as the maker moved it in his fingers and Cnut stopped to admire the few items set to his table. Emma had said that she liked the colours of the ring, the red and the green, vibrant colours that shouted of the glories of life, and Cnut had purchased it for her there and then. The jewelsmith had wanted to give it as a present, but Cnut had insisted on payment, laughing that if every craftsman in his Kingdom were to give him gifts, he, the King, would be rich beyond measure and everyone else as poor as a church mouse. He had tossed a gold coin, and the ring, finished with a final polish, had been slipped on to Emma's finger, the crowd roaring approval, as if it had been the marriage band placed on her hand. Since then, she had never removed it.

Sadness aching, she worked the band from her finger, twisting it over the knuckle, wider and more swollen than it had been then, all those years ago. Stupid, stupid to cry like this! But suddenly she was weeping great sobs, her shoulders heaving, breath gasping in her throat as the tears fell. It was not the ring, not the stupid ring, but Cnut himself. The desolation of being without him, the lying there alone, night after night in their bed alone. Knowing never again would she feel his arms around her, the touch of his lips on hers. He had been her husband, but more, had been father, friend, brother. Lover. He had been everything, and now she had lost him, she had nothing.

Leofgifu, coming into the chamber and finding Emma crumpled to the floor, held her close and tight, as if she were a child, rocking her gently, saying nothing. Not needing words, for she understood. Leofgifu had lost her husband to the bitter loneliness of death, but she had known happiness throughout childhood, had not been forced to cherish only those few short years of marriage. Until Emma had been loved by Cnut, she had known nothing but emptiness.

'What am I to do, Leofgifu?' Emma said bleakly. 'How can I survive these days that echo as hollow as a dead oak tree? I want to see him walk in through that door and toss his cloak on a stool, for it to fall, as it always did, to the floor. To hear him grumble and complain about some nonsense thing as if it were a major catastrophe. To watch him tread mud into a new-swept floor and chastise him for it. God help me, he could tramp a whole pigsty of muck in here and I would not utter a word!'

'Aye, lass, I know.'

Her eyes watering with tears, her face pale, thin and drawn, Emma tipped her face up to Leofgifu, pleading, 'I cannot remember his voice. I try and try to hear it. I lie there at night, holding my breath, straining my ears, concentrating, thinking that if I can only be still and quiet I will hear it again, remember how it sounded, but I have lost it. Lost it for ever.'

Tenderly, Leofgifu stroked her hair, comforting in the only way she could, by being there.

'How am I to get through all this, Leofgifu? It has been but a month to the day since he died. How do I survive another month and another beyond that?'

Leofgifu shook her head. 'I do not know how, my dear. When we lose someone we love, carrying on is a thing we do, because we have to.' A pale answer, but it was the only one she had.

7

Opinion was equally divided. The North wanted Harold, the South Harthacnut. An impasse, where shouting, coercion, pleading and bargaining were not making any headway and civilised debate was on the edge of being abandoned.

The two women, Emma and Ælfgifu, were equally adamant to have their say and all niceties of femininity had long since been dispensed with.

'God give me a berserk warrior over a belligerent woman,' Leofric confided to the Earl of Deira, Siward, seated beside him on the eastern side of Oxford's Moot Hall. Siward nodded, amused at the exchange that was in full spate between the Queen and the whore. For all their outward respect of her, there was not a man present who did not think of Ælfgifu as anything less than that.

'Will it come to blows, do you think?' he asked, grinning, the spectacle of two women wrestling on the floor of this expensive, elite building stirring his male excitement. 'Those talons', he added, indicating Ælfgifu's manicured nails, 'look more lethal than a dagger blade.'

Exasperated that this Council meeting was rapidly turning into a fiasco, Leofric agreed. 'A blade can be less dangerous than their sharpened tongues, once a woman gets it wagging. God preserve us from ambitious mothers!'

'Or, at least, from mothers with sons,' Siward quipped with his Danish-bred humour. His own young wife had given him two sons, but they were babes in their cradles and, as yet, of no consequence.

Leofric did not echo his companion's amusement, nor, from Godwine's face, sitting opposite, was the Earl of Wessex enjoying himself. That was something, the day was going as bad for the opposition.

Godwine was tired, hungry, and his head thrubbed with the incessant talk that had, so far, got them nowhere. His comfort, Earl Leofric looked as worn and frayed as he did. There must, surely, Godwine thought to himself, be an easier way to crown a king than this fraught squabbling?

'My husband made no mention of a son to me,' Emma insisted, sitting rigid and proud in her place on the dais, although Ælfgifu had objected at the outset at the automatic assumption of seniority. Emma had scathingly set her straight: '*I am wearing the Queen's crown. My forehead bears the symbol of the crucifix traced there in holy Chrism. Unless there is another in this room who carries the same absolute blessing to call herself Queen, I shall remain where I am.*' An end to that particular argument.

'My son is the eldest surviving child of Cnut. As his mother I have the right of respect.'

'Then I suggest you act with respect and stop behaving like a harbour-side strumpet screaming aloud what she is trying to sell.'

Despite himself, even the weary Leofric smiled, hiding the reaction quickly behind a covering hand. Emma was no easy woman to argue with; nor, for that matter, was Ælfgifu, but the Queen was always composed. She delivered her pert answers without degenerating into obscenities.

'I take it you have proof that my husband was the father of your bastard son?' Emma said. She was dressed simply, in sedate clothing, her dark-green gown over an under-gown of dark-red, a white veil, minimal jewels, only her betrothal and consecrational rings to her fingers, and a brooch of emeralds and rubies to her shoulder. The only adornment her crown. By contrast Ælfgifu, bedecked in her finest, appeared gaudy and loud.

'I was wife to Cnut. A wife does not require proof,' Ælfgifu retaliated, irritated by the awareness that Emma was so easily getting the better of her.

'You were not wed in the sight of God. Your being bedded by him was as a consequence of transitory alliance arranged by his father. Cnut was not in England when you birthed the boy Harold, was very probably not in England when you conceived him.'

On the most part, Emma was conducting her prosecution with astute professionalism. As Regent in Cnut's place she had sat in judgement over many a law trial, listening to the impassioned pleas of men and women brought to stand trial by the majority verdict of a jury of twelve appointed 'doomsmen', thegns who were duty bound to present suspected evildoers to submit to the King's court of law. Trial by ordeal usually sealed the fate of those who could not be satisfactorily judged by other means. Good oration was an essential part of proving innocence or guilt.

'And how would you be knowing?' Ælfgifu thundered back, her strident voice triumphant, booming up into the rafters and dislodging trickles of years of accumulated dust. 'You had scuttled off to Normandy with your pathetic first husband. You had abandoned England for the sake of preserving your skin.'

'As Cnut abandoned you when Æthelred returned. Had you been an acceptable wife to him, would he not have taken you with him? Especially if he suspected you to be carrying his child?'

Ælfgifu turned her face to the northern lords, although few of them, now, were the same men as two and twenty years ago. 'Even I did not know I was with child when your predecessors went against the combined will of the fleet. Cnut, with his father, had released the North from the oppressive rule of Wessex, yet those men dismissed him in favour of Æthelred's return, to the consequential disaster of England. I faced the fear of death, for had Æthelred discovered that I carried Cnut's son, we would both have been murdered.'

There were difficulties in parrying some of the arguments, Emma found – how strange that after all these years of contentment, Æthelred's presence should once again be haunting her. She had to be careful in what she said, could not dwell on Æthelred, lest anyone remember that there were two other sons who could claim the title ætheling, although Ælfgifu, too, would not be wanting to mention that fact. Nor could she remind these men that Cnut had taken England by force, that he, technically, was a foreign usurper, although that too Ælfgifu would not be wanting to draw attention to. Harold, she could claim, had the more right of kingship through his northern English blood, a fact that her supporters already admired. Harthacnut did not bear a single drop of Englishness.

'Yet Cnut thought so much of you that he promptly took another woman, Ragnhild, as a lawful wife,' Emma said with scorn, directing attention back to Cnut abandoning Ælfgifu.

'How could he be knowing that he would return to England?' Ælfgifu snapped, disgruntled. That was the one thing that had annoyed her all these years. It was his leaving her behind in England to face the fear of Æthelred's retribution more than the taking of another woman as wife that made her so certain that he had never thought anything of her beyond her ability in bed.

'He had every intention of returning,' Emma countered, seizing her chance to amplify this other woman's ignorance. 'Strange how I realised that Cnut would not be leaving England to a sordid fate, but you did not?' She smiled, so irritatingly sweetly. 'He abandoned you dear, not England. The only way you could entice him back was to spread your legs for his occasional amusement and proclaim that the sons you whelped were his, even though it is well known your bed has always been as busy as a high street on market day.'

Many of the southern men laughed. A few of the northerners grinned.

Ælfgifu stamped to her feet, her temper rising. 'Cnut fathered both my sons. You only have to look at Harold's face to see Cnut there in him.'

Emma rose gracefully from her seat and walked with calm dignity to where Harold sat at the edge of the meeting hall. He was allowed to be present, but forbidden to speak unless specifically questioned.

'I find it difficult to believe he is your son, Ælfgifu,' Emma said with intentional amusement as she approached. 'Unlike you, he is able to sit still and quiet.'

More laughter.

Standing before him, Emma flicked her hand, asking Harold to rise, studied him, noting that he unflinchingly stared back at her.

'I am my father's son,' he said, his eyes boring into hers, daring her to contradict him.

She nodded and swept an arm towards the assembly. 'Yes, boy, but I see nothing beyond fair hair and blue eyes. Your father could be any one of the majority of men here.' It was not true; he was so much like Cnut, so very much. How Emma managed to choke down her tears she did not know.

Wessex and the South crowed laughter. The North scowled and argument broke out again, voices rising, the one side of the chamber squawking at the other. Lords, earls, thegns, bishops and respected merchantmen, each with an opinion determined to be heard. A few were on their feet, shaking fists, faces contorted, impassioned.

Emma quietly retraced her steps to her seat. She was shaking, her heart breaking all over again. It had been like looking again at Cnut himself.

The Archbishop of Canterbury, Athelnoth, stood, holding his hands high, patting the air, attempting to regain calm. 'This is doing nothing save giving us all blinding headaches. We have a situation where our decision is divided. Throwing meaningless accusations is getting us nowhere.'

Earl Leofric added his stout, strong voice, the bellow rising above the mêlée. 'As his son, Cnut took the elder boy, Swegen, to Norway . . .'

'And the boy's mother handed Norway to Magnus Olafsson on a trencher! I loved Cnut, but he was not above making wrong decisions.' That was a thegn from Sussex, a man loyal to Godwine and Emma both.

Leofric ignored the interruption. 'Why would Cnut accept the one son and not the other? Harold is Cnut's son. Did Cnut, while he was alive, ever deny that fact?'

Shouts of agreement, of jeering, the one faction against the other.

'Is it not plain', Leofric shouted, 'that Harthacnut has no interest in England? If he is so ardent to be our King, why is he not with us, here in Oxford?'

'Harthacnut is delayed by the weather, as you well know,' Godwine interceded, springing to his feet. 'Would you have him risk the uncertainty of winter storms and wager his life to suit your satisfaction? We are, most of us, seamen; we know the terror of the tides.'

'My son the King', Emma added forcefully, dipping her head in gratitude at Godwine's interruption, 'will be in England by Easter for his coronation. In the meanwhile, as God's anointed I am his representative.'

'And my son is here, now, and he can – will – command an army if any of you spineless lizards go against him!' Ælfgifu threatened.

Athelnoth tried his peace-making again. Found it difficult to be heard. 'Gentlemen, it is to us to decide. We must vote our preference.'

'With votes divided half for Harold, half for Harthacnut?' Ealdred of Bernicia chided in his strong northern dialect. His brother, Eadwulf, sitting beside him, declaring, 'The North will not stoop to electing a king who cannot bother to attend his Council.'

'And the South will not elect a king who is bastard-born, whether he be Cnut's son or no,' Godwine countered.

'Please, be at peace.' Athelnoth put his palms together as if in prayer. 'May I make a suggestion?' Reluctant, the agitated men settled, listened. 'To be true to our conscience, we must allow Harthacnut the chance to come to us in England. Earl Godwine of Wessex speaks correct, it may be that he cannot come. I propose we adjourn until Easter.'

Murmurs of agreement; for most of them sitting there, their backsides were becoming numb, their bellies rumbling for food, throats dry for ale or wine, but decision had to be concluded before Council could rise.

'By doing so we leave England open and vulnerable to attack. Someone must rule, must keep the law!' That was Ælfgifu, indignant.

'Attack from where?' a thegn asked, a northern lord. Scowling, Ælfgifu noted his face and his name, would deal with him later. 'There is no one to threaten us. Normandy is a boy, with his own troubles of staying alive; Henry of France is too lazy to leave his palace. Germany would never leave her land borders unprotected and Magnus Olafsson has Norway to secure.'

'Which leaves only Harthacnut in Denmark,' Emma chirruped, pleased that the thing had gone full circle. 'And I rule on his behalf as Regent. England is only vulnerable internally, from base-born usurpers. You must therefore elect Harthacnut as your King.'

'There is no must about it!' Ælfgifu shouted.

'Ladies, ladies!' Athelnoth boomed. 'I propose that the Queen, Emma, take care of the South until we meet again at Easter, and that Harold shall see to the safety of Mercia and northern England. To my mind it is a sensible compromise.'

To the minds of others also, for there was a sudden overwhelming and relieved shout of assent. The agreement carried, as swift and as quick as a hawk diving on her prey.

Emma was mistrustful of the idea, but on rapidly thinking it through, could see the sense. Once Harthacnut reached England, this shambles would be sorted and Easter was not too long to wait.

Rising from her chair, she inclined her head towards the Archbishop. 'It will be so,' she agreed and turned abruptly to leave, calling for horses to be saddled. She had no wish to remain in proximity to Ælfgifu a moment longer than necessary.

The men, pleased that a conclusion had been reached, broke into small groups, some discussing the issue and the outcome, others more eagerly anticipating the morrow's promise of good hunting.

Ælfgifu joined her son, her face triumphant, her fingers brushing at a lock of hair flopping over his forehead. Irritably he knocked her fussing aside. Did she still think of him as a small boy to be dressed and coddled in public? In Ælfgifu's mind, too, Easter was not long to wait. A lot could be proved and achieved in the interim.

At the door, Earl Leofric drew Godwine aside. 'I am surprised that you are so openly backing Harthacnut, in the light of what sort of man his father was.'

'And what do you mean by that, Sir?' Godwine could never remember liking Leofric, not even when he had been a child, brought to Court by his father. A boy who was always boasting of having the fastest pony, the most silver in his coin pouch and ensuring that others knew he had the better of them. A boy who took for granted that he would be Earl after his father had passed to God.

Leofric shrugged innocently, 'Only that I am amazed you remained friends with Cnut despite all. If that had been me, I would have danced on his grave.'

'I admired and respected Cnut, as I admire and respect his Queen.'

Leofric chuckled. 'Oh, we all know how you admire the Queen, Godwine. But is it only admiration, or are you hoping for more?'

Not liking the insinuations, Godwine's face began to blotch with red anger. 'I remind you I have a wife, I am wed.'

'I would not blame you for wanting to take Emma as wife instead. After all, you have just cause to set Gytha aside.'

Ignoring men pushing past to leave, Godwine curled his fingers into a balled fist. 'By which you mean?'

'That Cnut bedded your wife often enough for you to want to bed his.'

Godwine hit him, fast, straight, his knuckles direct into his face. Leofric falling, blood bursting from his nose.

Lifting one hand to stem the flow, and with his other waving concerned onlookers aside, Leofric scrambled upright, his blood-smeared face leering. 'Did you not know? What a jest, you did not!'

'I have no idea what you are talking about; if you are trying, in some warped way, to turn me from supporting Harthacnut, then you are miserably failing.'

'Your wife's younger brother told me. Eilaf. I saw much of him in Mercia before he died from that illness. He being a minor Earl with his estates bordering mine.'

'Told you what?'

'Told me what the elder brother had told him. Of how Ulf had caught Cnut romping with your bare-breasted wife.' Leofric took the hand away from his nose, inspected the amount of blood. 'You talk of Harold being bastard-born, Godwine? What of your sons? Are you so certain they are not all cuckoos in the nest?'

8

February 1036 – Bosham

Gytha knew there was something wrong, but had no knowing of what it was. She assumed her husband's moroseness to be the result of his ineffectuality at the Oxford Council, that the Queen was in some way displeased with him. They had argued again this morning, it was more of a surprise not to disagree these days. The slightest thing, the most innocuous remark, and Godwine would flare up like a torch set to marsh gas. All she had said was that the boys were going to be taking out the new boat they had made so much effort to build, and why did he not take advantage of a rare fine February day and go with them? Why he had so suddenly flared up and stormed from their bedchamber she had no idea.

'Mama, be this the right amount of flour?' the girl at her side asked. Edith, seven years old, a child who had a thirst for learning. Another few years and she would be sent to the nunnery at Wilton for a formal education. Gytha would miss her, but not as much as she would miss her boys once they found the impetus to fly the nest.

Peeping into the bowl – she was making bread with her daughter – Gytha nodded, smiling at the fact that more flour was on the bench than in the mixture. There had been tears from Edith, too, this morning, when Swegn had refused to take her out in the boat. She had as much a temper on her as any of the boys. It was only a small craft, two-oared, suitable for sailing the creek, not for going to sea, the boys had begun its building while Godwine had been at Oxford and Edith, helping with the tarring of its hull, had been most put out to not be allowed to sail in it this first launching.

'You are a girl, girls do not sail!' Swegn had jeered at her from his height as a six-and-ten-year-old boy who thought himself a man.

'I sailed as a girl on the fjords at home in Denmark,' Gytha stated, coming to her daughter's defence. 'I know how to reef and to row as

707

good as any of you three boys,' she had added, wagging her finger at Swegn and his two younger brothers, Harold, fourteen, and Tostig, eleven.

'Aye, but Mama,' Harold had impertinently retorted with a broad grin, 'that was when you were a young lass. You have too much girth around you now to row!'

Gytha had swiped his ear with her apron.

The dough mixed and patted into loaves, Gytha showed her daughter how to put them beside the warmth of the bread oven to prove. Then, wiping the girl's sticky hands, suggested they wrap themselves in warm mantles and walk down to the creek to see how the boys were getting on. Eager, Edith agreed.

The tide was full, the inlet at Bosham flooded, although even with the sea full in, care had to be taken, for some channels were shallower than others. Swegn, disagreeing with Harold, had insisted on tacking to the steerboard side. Smiling with a mother's fond indulgence, Gytha could hear her second-born berating his elder brother for his stupidity, his voice carrying clear over the water.

'I said not to, you dolt, there are reed banks here, you know that! Now look, we're stuck.'

'No problem,' Swegn tossed back, 'all we have to do is rock her free.' And he began jumping from side to side, pushing against the mast.

'You'll tip us over!' Tostig yelled.

'Don't be daft, she's too sturdy for that,' Swegn assured, leaping again. The boat dipped and he fell over the side, arms flailing, legs kicking.

Tostig screamed, Harold laughed.

On the bank, Gytha shook her head in exasperation. As well she had insisted they all learn to swim, full clothed, at an early age.

Crowing her mockery, Edith slipped her hand out of her mother's and ran towards her father, approaching from the church. 'Papa, Papa! Come see. Swegn was showing off and has fallen in.'

Dutifully Godwine answered her summons, gazed with a stern frown at the eldest attempting to sprawl, sodden, into the boat. Harold pushing him back into the water.

'Pull us off, while you're in there.'

'The water's cold, Harold, don't be such a shit!'

'You got us here; you get us off.'

'Are you not proud of your boys, Godwine?' Gytha laughed, turning to her husband, the smile faltering as he thrust an answer.

'My boys? Are they?' He stalked away, striding towards the stables.

Stunned, Gytha stood, hands on hips, confused. 'What do you mean by that?' Again, angry. Louder: 'I said what do you mean?'

Gytha set off after her husband, running to catch him up, ordering Edith to go to the house, fetch out dry clothing for Swegn. She caught Godwine as he was lifting a saddle to harness his stallion, lunged at his arm, made him face her.

She stamped her foot – rare for Gytha to let loose her temper. 'You have been as a hungry wolf prowling through dark woods these weeks, Godwine. What is it I am supposed to have done? Tell me!'

He shook her off, fetched a bridle. 'I go to Winchester,' he said abruptly. 'The Queen shall be wanting me.'

'You go nowhere until you explain your meaning.'

'Do I need to explain?' he scoffed. 'Is it not you who ought to be doing the explaining?'

Slamming the outer door shut, Gytha barred it with her body to stop him leaving. 'I do not know what all this nonsense is, but it stops here, now. You have been treating me and your sons as if we have the pox since you returned from Oxford. Tell me what is wrong.'

Godwine's jealousy had reared full to the surface, along with the anger and humiliation. He had loved Gytha all these years, rarely looking at another woman, save perhaps Emma herself, although he loved his Queen in quite a different way from how he worshipped his wife. To fear that perhaps she had not loved him in return, that she had lain with another twice his worth, with a king, was unbearable. Yet he did not have the courage to ask if it was true, for he might see the lie in her eyes when she denied it.

It had to come, though, he would have to know soon, because if those boys out there were not his sons, but the bastards born of a royal lover, then there was no way that he could be serving that other son, Harthacnut. Was that perhaps why Godwine had never cared for the child? Because he had, without realising it, recognised a likeness between Harthacnut and the boys he had thought to be of his own fathering.

'Tell me of Cnut,' he said suddenly, gripping her wrists in his clamped fingers. 'Tell me of the night your brother found you romping all but naked with the King!'

Gytha said nothing, stood, staring. What was he talking about? She shook her head, frowning, dismissive, then laughed, remembering the incident from so long ago. 'Who told you of that silly business? One of the northern men who had once been friends with Ulf?'

'Not Ulf, Leofric. Eilaf told Earl Leofric, who then told me, and I had no doubt he enjoyed waiting for the right moment to inform me. How he must have been laughing at my stupidity all these years!'

'Your stupidity? No, Godwine, his.' Carefully Gytha picked the tight fingers from bruising her skin any further. 'He told you false, husband. That you believed him makes you the fool, nothing more.'

'You deny you lay with Cnut? That he made love to you?' The hurt spilt from Godwine's mouth. How he wanted her to say yes, she denied it, and know she told him the truth!

Gytha put her hands each side of his enraged, suffused face and lovingly waggled Godwine's head from side to side, a calm and gentle shaking. 'Of course I deny it. It is not true. My brothers – both of them – always were able to see snow-capped mountains where there were only earthen molehills.' And she told him precisely what had happened those years ago, every detail, leaving nothing out. Of the King, drunk and lonely, of Ulf returning ahead of Godwine. Did he remember the night Cnut had slept, snoring fit to wake the entire Hall, in their bed?

Godwine furrowed his brow, thought back. Did he? No, he did not.

'Swear to me,' he said, taking hold of her hands, crushing her fingers with his urgency for knowing. 'Swear to me that my sons are mine.'

710

'Ask the servants about that night. Although they too, may have forgotten.'

Godwine's eyes desperately searched his wife's blue gaze for deceit, but he saw none, saw only her own hurt at being doubted.

'God's Teeth, that bloody bastard brother of mine made me swim to shore; would not let me in the boat!' The door slammed open, Swegn, dripping wet, shivering, burst in. 'Mother, Edith said you were in here. Where are my dry clothes? I need get out of these before my sodding balls freeze solid and snap off!' He stopped, realised his mother and father had been quarrelling, retreated, raising his hands in submission. 'I will find them, I'll manage.' Only Swegn, being Swegn, could not resist listening at the door. He was an avid collector of information, of things that were best stored away in the memory and saved there, until a time when, one day, they might be useful. He never said anything to anyone that his father suspected his mother of being unfaithful. Not until he was a man grown and, in a temper, dredged the long-forgotten overheard conversation into resurrection.

Gytha tentatively smiled. 'And you doubt that he is not your son? Even though he bears the image of your face and swears in the exact same manner? Still you doubt?'

Godwine slowly shook his head, slumped against the timber wall, attempted an apologetic grin.

'We are, all of us, using buckets full of mud to throw at our opponents. The Queen accuses Ælfgifu of lying over the parentage of Harold; Leofric accuses you of bedding with Cnut. As a goad to destroying loyalty, these tactics of deceit appear to work most well, do they not?'

9

Striding into his King's Hall, Harthacnut removed his cloak, and tossing it to a servant, walked towards his visitor with both arms outstretched in greeting. 'Godwine! I am so sorry to have kept you waiting! I have been inland. It is often a good time of year, as the ground is hard enough to ride on. Once it thaws we will be knee deep in mud.'

The two men embraced, hand clasped to arm.

'You were not waiting long I trust?' Harthacnut added, guiding his guest towards the hearth-fire and shouting for ale to be brought.

'I arrived yesterday, so no, not long.' Yesterday morning, a whole day, but no matter.

'And you are well? Aunt Gytha? Your sons? I suppose you know Aunt Estrith died last November?'

Godwine nodded. He did. 'Two days after your father, I believe?'

'Yes, strange that, was it not?'

Again Godwine nodded, yes, strange. Idle chat, surface gossip. Since setting out, Godwine wondered what he was doing coming to Denmark. He felt in his bones that this was going to be a fool's errand if ever there was one, but the Queen had pleaded with him to come, begged him to fetch Harthacnut home.

'I would ask a favour of you, Godwine.' Harthacnut was attempting to be jovial, the pleasant, welcoming host; yet the smile did not reach the eyes that did not meet with Godwine's. He held his body rigid and tense.

Making a jest of the undercurrents of discomfort, Godwine laughed. 'What? Favours already, and I have only just arrived!'

Harthacnut laughed, a chuckle more than a great belly-mirth. 'I would have you take Beorn Estrithsson with you when you return to England, for a season or two, if Aunt Gytha would not mind the having of him at Bosham? He is missing his mother and, being the same age as your Harold, it may be that the change of scene will cheer him.'

Godwine happily agreed. He had been going to suggest it himself, although not so soon upon arrival. To talk of when he returned within the same breath of giving welcome seemed to be a barrel-full of tactlessness.

'The eldest boy, his brother Svein, is taking the loss better?' Godwine asked.

'He has other things to occupy his mind. I have made him my heir, you know, should I not have children.' Harthacnut laughed, a mirthless, self-deprecating sound. 'Which, given that I never find the time to bed a woman, seems nigh on a certainty at the moment!'

Godwine wondered at that, but said nothing. Harthacnut was a good-looking young man. He had turned sixteen last birthing day, looked all of five or six years older. When he compared him with his own Swegn, God's Truth, how clumsy and immature his son appeared, although, as an opposite, having discovered the delights of women, Swegn could never find the time for anything else. On Harthacnut's part he was not going to be telling his personal secrets, that he had tried with women but found himself impotent. Who did you trust enough to speak of a matter like that? Certainly not a man who had sired a whole crew of sons.

There was no point in rummaging about the bush. Godwine decided he might as well come straight out with why he was here. Surely Harthacnut must have guessed, so why this pitter-pattering? Said outright, 'Your mother has sent me to fetch you.'

'More ale, Godwine? Your tankard is empty. Ah, good, they are bringing us food.'

Looking at him, Godwine realised that although he had an air of confidence, that he carried himself well, knew the right gestures, the rights words to say, Harthacnut was too young to show much of a beard or moustache. The skin around his nose and forehead was blemished with adolescent pimples. He was a boy, nothing more than a boy, doing a man's work.

'In public, your mother hides her grief, but she often has red-rimmed eyes of a morning and sits for hours gazing at nothing, her fingers fiddling with whatever she holds in her hand.'

Harthacnut chewed the meat pasty he had selected, wiped crumbs from his mouth with a linen cloth. Denmark was his home; to the green hills, the blue fjords, the freedom and exhilaration of the open sea. He knew so very little of England.

'My father brought me to Denmark when I was a child. From then, I saw him perhaps for a month once a year, occasionally longer. How can I miss a man I did not know?'

'It is not for your father that I am here, but your mother.'

'I am not a hound to be whistled to heel, Godwine.'

'We never thought you were, lad.'

Harthacnut's sudden-risen hackles settled. 'All I know of England is a manor house here, a town there. I remember nothing of it from childhood. I was not born until I came to Denmark.'

What he said was not quite true – there was much he remembered of England but all of that he had tried, very hard, to forget. He remembered Bosham, with its white church and tower, the way the sea crashed in across the causeway and rushed, booming, up the mill-race. Oh, he remembered the mill-race and a girl beneath the water. Her hair floating, her white face staring up, her mouth open in a silent scream. He remembered Godwine bending over him, his face very close, very angry.

'I thought you were going to hit me,' Harthacnut said suddenly, tucking his hands between his knees, his head bent down.

Godwine was confused. He had not raised his hand, made any movement, had he? 'When, lad? You've lost me.'

Harthacnut's face was full of pain as he glanced up. 'When Ragnhilda died.'

Shaking his head, Godwine's confusion deepened. 'That was a long while ago.'

'You were so angry with me.'

'Not angry, son, frightened. I did not know what the Hell I was going to tell your father. Have you not realised, now, as an adult, that the first thing we do when we are scared, or in the wrong, is to shout long and loud?'

714

Very quietly Harthacnut said, 'It was so hard, as a child, to accept that your father loved his daughter more than his son.'

'Nonsense. He loved you equally, boy, which is why we are in trouble in England now. Cnut could not willingly set aside any of his children. If he had, Ælfgifu would not be attempting to claim the throne for Harold.'

Godwine had never liked Harthacnut. He had been a sly, scheming boy, a whining child, throwing a temper when he did not get his way. He saw before him a thin young man with no colour to his face and no substance to his body. How could this boy outwit someone like Ælfgifu, or beat a warrior such as Harold in battle? Yet he had held Denmark all these years, although, for that, he had the good support of solid men behind him.

'You have no intention of coming to England, have you, boy?' Godwine said abruptly, realising the truth.

For answer, Harthacnut stood, beckoned Godwine to follow him outside. Beyond the door he pointed at the view. The tree-covered hills, the fjord, the ships in the harbour, the sprawl of the town. 'England is not my home, this is. My first loyalty is to Denmark and, if I can get it back from that thieving Magnus Olafsson's hands, Norway too. To the north there is Sweden, which I rule, and Finland looks to me for protection. I command the fjords and the seas. Every ship that enters these waters or wishes to sail north does so at my permission, or did until Olafsson poked his nose over the horizon. If I leave Denmark and sail for England, he will seize his chance and take all that is mine for himself. I cannot be risking that.'

'Nor can you risk losing England.'

Testily Harthacnut answered, 'England can wait. Mother can hold it for me.'

'No, Harthacnut, she cannot. Not for long. We can stall until the summer at the most. Come to England, secure your crown, then pay the English scyp fyrd to help you against Magnus Olafsson.'

'The English would not be doing that, Godwine, and you know it.' How could he admit the truth without this proud and capable man assuming him to be a weakling coward? How to say that he had

715

no interest in England, did not want it. 'I am King of Denmark, I have no ambition to be King of England also.'

Godwine felt as if the wind had been taken from his sails. He shook his head in disbelief. 'Are my ears hearing wrong? You are refusing to come?'

The sun was low, although it was not far past midday; in Denmark, in winter, the days were short, the nights long. Staring out into the fresh, brilliant sparkle of blueness, Harthacnut knew he could not leave, whatever Godwine said or thought.

'I had a letter from my sister,' Harthacnut said, hooking his thumbs through the broad, bronze-studded belt at his waist. 'From Gunnhild. She is settled and appears happy at the German Court. I wish her well in her marriage. In this letter she said that Mama was desperate for me to go to England. Why, Godwine? Answer me why Mother wants me there. For my sake or for hers?'

Godwine's answer was succinct. 'For England's sake, lad. This is for England.'

Harthacnut shook his head, returned inside to the warmth of the Hall. The day was bright, but the air cold. 'No, Godwine, I have seen precious little of her, but I know my mother well enough to understand that it is her crown she wants to preserve, not mine.' He pushed the heavy door shut, closing out the light and the chill. 'If Mama wants England, until I am certain that Denmark is secure she will have to do her own fighting.'

10

Emma stared uncomprehendingly at Godwine. 'What do you mean, he is not coming? He has to come, he has to be consecrated.'

'He cannot leave Denmark; Magnus Olafsson is too much of a threat.'

'Not as much a threat as Harold Ælfgifusson!' she barked.

Godwine could only keep his thoughts to himself and shrug. He agreed, but short of trussing Harthacnut up in rope and carrying him aboard a ship, what could he have done?

'Ælfgifu is working to deprive my son of his kingdom. Are you aware, Godwine, that she holds feasts and entertainments for anyone of influence from the North? Thegns, bishops and the earls, of course. She buys gifts and pretties herself to persuade them to swear loyalty to her and her bastard. Beds them, too, I do not doubt.'

The anger she felt was to hide the hurt. How to explain it? Cnut had been taken away from her without warning, leaving her to fight alone for survival. Now Harthacnut was refusing to accept the responsibility of duty to his kingdom and his mother. She slumped into a chair, rubbing her aching forehead with her hand. 'What am I to do, Godwine? What do I do? Cnut never foresaw this.'

Godwine was tired. The voyage from Denmark had not been easy, for the wind had been tempestuous and the waves strong. Nor had he relished this interview. He had taken the opportunity to bathe and change, to eat, but had not known how to prepare for telling Emma that her world was crumbling to dust. His world too? Ah, that was what made the difficulty. His life could, if he went the right way about it, continue much as it already was, whatever Hathacnut's ambiguities or Harold's ambitions. Provided he made his mind as to which path to follow.

'Your support consists of those beholden to you through your own held land. Their allegiance will transfer to Harthacnut through you. Archbishop Athelnoth is also loyal to you, although he must tread careful not to confirm that aloud. Despite this, my Lady, your position is becoming insecure.' He lifted his shoulders, wearily let them fall, the defeat plain. 'Without Harthacnut here to shout his cause,' he shook his head, 'there is nothing we can do to salvage the situation.'

In Harold's view he was the legitimate king; with his brother dead, he was the eldest of Cnut's sons, the most able and the most competent. Where was the controversy in this? Emma's opinion, by contrast, was that he was an illegitimate usurper; the force behind his claim his mother. That she herself was the same force behind her own son was immaterial, she was the Queen, Ælfgifu was not.

'I hear that Harold is willing to offer you the respect of a king's widow,' Godwine said carefully. He had heard this from Gytha not more than half an hour since. 'Is willing to leave you a portion of the Treasury and for your lifetime, your dower lands.' He rubbed at his moustache. 'If he has so offered, I would judge it to be without the knowledge of his mother. Ælfgifu would never consent to such generosity. Harold, in this, is showing considerable sense.'

This was a double blow, the knife stabbed in and twisted. Emma felt her stomach churn, her head reel. Her hands were shaking; she gripped her fingers into the chair arms so that Godwine would not notice. 'So,' she said with false civility, 'you also are to abandon me? You are contemplating turning to Harold?'

Godwine all but ran to her, took her hands. 'No! No, Lady, I did not say that! I convey only the facts. Will stay in this with you to the end, but without Harthacnut's commitment to England, what choices are left us?'

'Yet you judge Harold Harefoot to be honourable?' she rebuked. 'He will imprison me within my own house.' If she did not hide behind scorn and anger she would be sobbing; she could not, could not, allow defeat to consume her, for once she let go her hold on sanity, she would tumble into despair and never find the courage to climb out again. She had to stand firm, steel her resolve and fight.

'I do not judge him, not until, on your behalf, I find chance to talk further with him.' Godwine smiled jestingly. 'Perhaps we could ask for his mother as hostage?' he slumped, tired, into a chair.

Emma was not in the mood for frivolity. She waved him to silence. Her good friend's loyalty was faltering. Could she blame him? Without Harthacnut, as far as the men of England were concerned there would be nothing tangible to fight for.

'I will never accept any offer of Harold's over the rights of my son, Godwine. It is foolish of you to think I would.'

Aye, Godwine had known that.

They sat quiet a while, each nursing their own thoughts. Emma, annoyed with her son for being so selfish and stupid. Godwine wanting his bed and his wife.

'I have an alternative choice,' Emma said at last. 'I have two other sons who may, perhaps, have greater claim than even Cnut's whelps.'

Suddenly wide awake, Godwine looked up sharply from the doze he had been drifting into. 'Edward and Alfred? Lady, you cannot be serious? There is not a man in this land who would support the either of them!'

A man? Mayhap not. But the Queen would.

11

Edward was furious that his mother had written to him demanding help. 'How dare she send her "maternal greetings"? What is there maternal about her? I barely remember her as a mother!' Contemptuously, he skimmed the offending letter across the floor.

Alfred rescued it from a flutter of cackling chickens who thought anything thrown down had the possibility of being food. 'She sounds distraught,' he tried diplomatically.

'Distraught! Distraught? Did she care that we were distraught when Father died? When we were sent, running for our lives, from England? If she thinks I am going to risk my life to keep her head in high glory, then she can damned think again!'

'Mon *dieu*, she says nothing of risking our lives, Edward,' Alfred countered. 'She wishes to discuss the difficult situation in England, that is all.'

'Do not swear in God's name, we are within an abbey,' Edward admonished. 'Are you such a fool? I thought I was supposed to be the naive one! Tell him, Robert, explain what an imbecile he is.'

Alfred felt like retorting *bugger God, and bugger Abbot bloody Robert Champart!*

The Abbot of Jumièges, Robert Champart, rubbed at his clean-shaven chin. Edward had been a guest of his since Duke Robert's death, for the Court was unsafe, even for the present Duke. The boy, William, was not expected to remain as Duke for long, for already he had survived several attempts at assassination. If this young Duke William managed to reach maturity, it would be a miracle. Mind, if he did, men would alter opinion and be eager to follow him, for it would be obvious that God was protecting him as His chosen for a purpose yet to be disclosed.

Robert Champart was a man who had pledged his vows to God

and believed in His divine intervention, but did not think that William would see adulthood, not with so many experienced warmongering men so openly against him. Men who, if there aim was achieved, would not be tolerating those who had devoted their loyalty to the previous dukes. If – when – William was slaughtered, the likelihood would be that Robert Champart would be one of those in danger; he had no intention of remaining in Normandy when that happened. Nor did he want to throw away his carefully pursued position of prestige. This unexpected situation in England could be a gift sent from God, one Robert intended to exploit to the full for his own gain.

'Your brother speaks aright, *mon ami Edouard*,' Robert said, soft-spoken and with a small, sorry shake of his head. 'I believe your mother is thinking of England above the personal issues. But, if you are entitled to the crown and there is no one else fitting to wear it, then, alas, it is your duty to God to go to England.'

Edward mumbled a protest. That was not what he had meant on asking Robert to interfere. Why did this wretched issue of a crown insist on re-emerging every so often? How often did he have to state he was not interested in England? And to have this final insult of his mother, all of a sudden, apparently missing and wanting her sons beside her? Edward was, he admitted, gullible and soft-hearted, anyone could get anything out of him if they appealed to his easy emotion, but even he could see the ambiguity in this! Mama had been abandoned by her favourite, Harthacnut, and all she had left to cling to were the sons she had wantonly and callously abandoned to suit her own purpose years ago. To go running to her, open-armed and all-forgiving, was not an option. Not now. She had left it too many years too late.

'I do not want a throne,' Edward stated. 'Not for myself and most certainly not for the purpose of assuring her security. If Mama wants that, then I suggest she come to Normandy. There are some most suitable nunneries for widows.'

Impatiently Alfred sighed. What he would give for his brother to show an ounce of worldy sense! 'Our mama, Edward, is not the sort of woman to pass the rest of her days contemplating God in a nunnery.' Alfred did not see eye to eye with his brother over this zealous attitude towards prayer. In his view a monastery was a comfortable and safe place to live as a guest, but it was not an entire way of life.

Robert held out his hand for the letter, read it through after Alfred gave it to him. He rubbed again, thoughtfully, at his chin. He must tread carefully in this with Edward. There were two ways to catch a trout: hook him on the line and struggle to bring him, thrashing and squirming, ashore, and risk the line being broken, the fish lost for ever; or lie quiet on the grass on a hot, sunny day and feel, with gentle, stroking fingers beneath the rocks. Soothe the fish to sleep and catch him, quick, before he realises it.

Alfred was the bold one, who acted impulsively before thinking; Edward would need delicate cajoling and manoeuvring. He could ponder for ever, never committing himself. The one brother as opposite to the other as vinegar to honey.

'Your mother says that there are many who would support you over Harold Ælfgifusson. She urges you to hurry to England, for the usurper is buying his way to favour with gifts and great promises. Where he cannot purchase support, he issues black threats and warnings. It is your choice, of course, Edward, but unless you act now, England shall be lost to you for ever.'

'I do not want England,' Edward tried again, but Robert hushed him.

'It is not always for us to choose what we do or do not want, my son. That is for God to decide. You are the eldest-born of a king, the grandson of a duke. Why do you think God has so carefully attended your safety all these years?'

Edward hung his head, chewed his lower lip. 'I thought He wanted me to become a monk.'

Robert patted Edward's shoulder sympathetically, 'Yet I have never encouraged you in that. Ah, *mon brave*, you have another, greater, commitment to God. To serve Him as King of England, to hold the authority to restore His justice and will. To build churches in His name, to . . .'

Annoyed, Edward erupted to his feet. 'I am sorry, Abbot, but I have no intention of going to England. This summons', and he struck the parchment in Robert's hand with his knuckles, 'this outrage is a ploy of my mother's for her own benefit, not for ours. I will have nothing to do with it, or her. Neither shall Alfred.'

'I can speak for myself!' Alfred blurted out, suddenly as annoyed. 'All my life it has been Edward this, Edward that; always have I had it rammed down my throat that you are the eldest, that you are the one most likely to wear a crown. Never me, never Alfred, yet I am the more capable, I am the one who can fight; I am the one with sense and a brain. All you can do, Edward, is prance around with an angelic look of piety on your damned cherubic face!' The outburst swelled, let loose after so many years of being suppressed; a horse set free to kick his heels, a dog allowed to chase after hares without restraint – a younger brother always shouting for the value of his worth above an elder. 'You may not want England, Edward, but I do and I intend to have it!'

Ordinarily, Edward abhorred conflict and disagreement of any kind, but he was also a self-centred, vain man who could not abide being treated as second best. 'God gave me the right of the firstborn, Alfred. It is for me to be King, not you.'

'You would not last a single day without me!' Alfred exclaimed in retaliation at Edward's contrary petulance. It was near the truth. Edward, at thirty and one years old, possessed the emotional passion of a child. Insecure and uncertain, he relied on the familiarity of routine and the advice of others to make up his mind in almost everything, even to the wearing of his clothes. He had no dress sense, often matching colours that went sickly together, and although fashion was not a priority within the abbey at Jumièges, there had been occasions, at the Duke's Court, when Alfred had despaired of his brother's ability to cause embarrassment. Yet Edward was learned in his reading and writing, was compassionate and attentive to the detail of the written word and, a rare thing in a man, Edward was willing to sit and listen attentively to another's outpouring of problems without interruption or sanction. Nor would he make judgement without first hearing all sides of the argument. For a king, such skills were to be admired.

723

'If I decide to answer Mama and go to her,' Edward whined, his bottom lip pouting, 'I shall not be taking you, Alfred. It is me she is asking for. I was the one she sent the letter to.'

Robert rolled his eyes Heavenwards. Were these two men adults or children? Infants trapped within a man's grown body?

'She asks for the both of you,' he stated, pointing at the relevant section in the letter.

'I am perfectly able to attend my mother without a squirt of a younger brother trudging behind me!' Edward declared, his belligerence aroused beyond reason by Alfred's unexpected stance of defiance. Robert was carefully concealing a smile from touching his lips. Edward was so predicable!

'I have no intention of trailing in your wake!' Alfred hammered. 'I am able to think for myself and make my own plans!' Furious, he slammed from the room and, before he had stalked ten paces, regretted the outburst. As brothers, they had done everything together, laughed, cried, suffered, and yet, and yet . . . Alfred slumped against the cloister wall. Beyond the colonnades the sun was shining, the heat beating against the cobbled courtyard; while here, beneath the covered walkway, the air was chill. Somewhere beyond the outer wall a lark was singing, the song as high and sweet as Heaven itself. Alfred covered his face with his hands, felt the sweat trickle down the small of his back. He had never done anything without Edward. Was that why he felt this great heavy pit of empty space in his belly? Why he felt so worthless and useless? It had not mattered, as children, that they had been regarded as nothing more than items of furniture, a chest, a chair, to be carted from castle to castle with the rest of the Duke's accoutrements. He had not minded, then, the patronising smiles, the toleration of Emma's sons being there, unwanted, forever underfoot. Had not minded, even, the whispers of contempt, for most of the spite had been directed at Emma, not at her abandoned sons. But the whispers had become more frequent, the contempt more aroused as they had grown. Still Alfred had not minded, always thinking, always hoping, that perhaps tomorrow his mother would suddenly have need of him, would send for him, or come for him herself, come and explain that it had all been a mistake, that she had sent them both into Normandy to wait until it was safe to return, that she had done all that she had done for their benefit, out of love for them. Stupid, stupid to think that! Edward was right. Until this moment, when her future was in peril, their mother had forgotten their existence. Despite that knowing, Alfred wanted to go to England, wanted to show his mother what he had become and what he was capable of. Could Edward not see that? Did Edward not realise that if they hurried across the sea and saved Mama, she would be eternally grateful to them and would have reason to love them again?

12

'What', Emma asked her firstborn son with acerbic scorn, 'is the use of one, solitary ship? How in Heaven's name can we fight and win a war with one bloody ship?'

That was her greeting to her eldest son, having not seen him for twenty years. It was not what Edward had planned, but then, neither had Emma foreseen that the boy would mature into a man even more useless than his father had been.

'You asked for me to come to you to discuss your future,' Edward protested, finding a voice through his bitter disappointment. 'You said nothing of fighting and war.' He had imagined hugs and tears, and an outpouring of lost opportunities and regrets, a rainbow of emotion. Had not bargained for scornful disdain as the first words to leave his mother's lips. Like his father, he had no ability to see beyond his own feelings, had no sense of realising why others spoke and behaved as they did. Could not see that his mother was equally disappointed.

'I had no idea that I would be expected to spell it out for you. I advised you to come for your crown. How do you expect to do so without an army? Do you think Harold will take fright at sight of your face and meekly hand it over?'

They stood on Winchester's busy wharf beside the River Itchen, traders' and merchant craft moored alongside the modest ship that Edward had hired to bring him from Normandy; the smell of fresh-caught fish pervading the other dockside aromas of tar, sewage and unwashed men. Edward's annoyance had started to swell the moment the crew had tossed the mooring rope ashore, for the Harbour Reeve, hurrying from his house at the far end of the quay, had refused to allow them to disembark.

'I am the Queen's son!' Edward had proclaimed with indignation, aggrieved that he was not instantly recognised and welcomed.

The Reeve's answer was humiliating. 'That be Harthacnut. I knew him as a lad, afore 'e went to Denmark and you be not he. Nor be that his banner flying from your mast.'

'No, that is my father's banner, the white boar of Wessex. I am Edward, King Æthelred's son.'

'Harthacnut be our King. You canna' come ashore.'

'Send word to the Queen,' Edward demanded, controlling his inclination to stamp his foot. 'And do not come whining to me when she orders you flogged raw for this impertinence!'

Unimpressed by the threat, but mindful of his duty, the Reeve did so and Emma had come personally, sure that the message she had received was incorrect, that her son's *ship*, from Normandy, was in harbour, did she wish him arrested? Had she realised that it was, indeed, ship singular, not ships plural, perhaps she would have been tempted to stay within doors and agree, aye, lock him in a cellar somewhere until the next tide, then throw him back to the sea as if he were a worthless shrimp.

Edward objected to Emma's accusation. 'You did not ask for an army. You said I had plenty of support here in England.' Strange how he had thought that he had forgotten how this woman looked and sounded, worrying, through the voyage, that he might not recognise her, that she would be as a stranger. Unnecessary concern, for she had not changed. *Oui*, her hair, showing beneath the wimple, was paler, not the vibrant blonde he remembered, her skin was wrinkled at the corners of her eyes, the face fuller, particularly under the chin; a little plumper at the waistline? The same exasperation in her voice, the look of weary impatience in her eyes. Would he have recognised her instantly? *Oui*, he would.

A crowd had gathered, curious, as men and women were when there was gossip to be made from listening to family conflict. Someone pushed through, roughly shoving aside those more reluctant to move, a large man, broad of shoulder and girth, his temper as hard-edged as his elbow. Godwine.

'What in the name of God is this?' he bellowed, stamping to a halt before Emma and Edward. 'What the bugger is he doing here?'

There was no doubting who the boy was, for he was the image of Æthelred, save for the absence of a beard. 'Do not tell me you sent for him, Madam, please do not!'

Emma was about to lie, say no, she had not, when Edward, folding his arms and standing square in front of Godwine, countered, 'And why should she not?' He was not certain who this man was, Edward could barely remember anyone from his life in England beyond his family. That he was a man of importance was obvious by his tone and style of dress, although, even as an exile within a ducal Court, Edward had been used to more reverence than this bloated whale offered. Affronted, Edward added, 'I am the son of Æthelred, the second king of that name. I am ætheling. I have every right to be here.' Disdainfully wrinkling his nose, he looked Godwine up and down as if he were a begrimed beggar-boy 'And who, Sir, might you be?'

'I wanted my sons with me, is that not a reasonable thing for a mother to want?' Emma said quickly, belatedly aware of the storm rage that was glowing over Godwine's face and that she might have made an enormous mistake. 'Harthacnut has ignored my summons. You are deliberating the possibility of abandoning me.' She flicked her hand, desperate, uncertain. 'I thought it prudent to call my other son to me.' When Godwine made no answer, protested loudly, 'I cannot allow Harold to walk in through an open gate without pause, can I? I must try all I can before facing defeat. I am prepared to fight this thing through to the end, Godwine, even if you are not!'

Godwine stared at Edward, at the cut of his light-blue tunic and darker hued mantle. At the ermine trimmings, the curled, combed hair, the slender manicured fingers. If he had shown the curve of a bust and braided hair, Godwine would have sworn he was looking at a woman.

'To fight?' he echoed scornfully. 'What? With this delicate bluebell?'

'I have returned from exile into my kingdom,' Edward declared, annoyed, drawing himself straight and thrusting his face close to this man, Godwine, who he instantly disliked. 'It is obvious I have

728

been too long abroad, for Englishmen, even those of questionable nobility, appear to have forgotten their manners.'

Godwine stared at him, speechless.

'Let England rejoice at my homecoming!' Edward shouted to the crowd, raising his hands, the sun sparkling on his adornment of rings. 'Let the fyrd take up their arms and march with me!' He was enjoying being the centre of attention, although it would have been more encouraging if the cheers had not been so thinly scattered. How wonderful it would be when he had the chance to parade before all these onlookers with the crown on his head and the sceptre in his hand! He was quite looking forward to the pomp of all that. Was this another reason why he had never taken that final step into a monastery? Because he liked the thrill of pageantry and glory, abhorred the thought of always having to be humble and ingratiating towards others. Realised, suddenly, that he preferred the knee bent to him, not the other way round.

Blandly ignoring the imbecile, Godwine spoke direct to Emma. 'There is barely a man in Wessex who remembers Æthelred with anything more than contempt. No one will lift a spear to aid this peahen runt, except perhaps to quicken his going back to Normandy.'

'They will if I command it,' Emma snapped, knowing he was right. All these years she had shut the thought of Edward and Alfred away, not daring to let them out of the box she had buried them in, lest she betray the guilt she concealed. For the girls, her daughters, although she missed them she did not mind their going. Girls grew into women, women must wed. But boys, boys were supposed to grow into handsome, heroic men. Men who could sweep a woman off her feet, could ride into battle and kill ten enemies with their bare hands before dawn. They were not supposed to become effeminate dolts.

'If you command it, aye, the fyrd will answer you,' Godwine said, 'but their hearts will not be in it and you will bring down the full force of an armed North against you. Harold will see this for what it is, an outright threat, and he'll retaliate without pause to first ask question.'

Emma was close to tears. The frustration, the disenchantment, the sheer enormity of being alone to face all this. 'He would not dare bring an army into Wessex against Harthacnut's Queen!' she said, with more conviction than she felt.

Godwine was disappointed, too, in Emma, in England. In Harthacnut. Why did the damn boy not set sail? The anger bubbling over, making him forget all sense of position and diplomacy, Godwine shouted at his Queen, 'He will not be bringing an army against Harthacnut, it will be against a usurper, against Edward.' He pointed his hand at him. 'Do you seriously believe this lacklustre standing before you would last ten minutes against Harold? He may be the son of a woman you detest, but whether you accept it or no, he is also the son of Cnut. Harold's father ensured he was taught to read, write and fight. This lamb here may do well at prayer and dancing, but does he know how to use an axe or a sword?'

Edward did not care for being spoken about so rudely. He attempted a stammered protest that floundered into silence. He had never cared much for warfare, either. On balance, if it were a choice between the two, he would opt for this man's blustering. 'Alfred can fight,' he said suddenly, eager again. 'He always was better at it than me.'

Disdainfully Godwine turned round slowly, faced him, hands on hips. Said, with his back to Emma, 'I do so hope, Madam, that you have not issued a similar invitation to your other son? If Alfred comes to England, the hornets' nest will be well and truly kicked over.'

'Mama wrote only to me. Alfred was most put out about it. So cross, in fact, that we had the most dreadful argument.'

Emma closed her eyes, thankful that Edward was the simpleton he appeared to be. The letter had been intended for the both of them, had he not seen that? As well he had not!

Blithely unaware of possible implications and his mother's discomfort, Edward prattled on. 'Alfred raged about it for hours, saying he had as much right to come to England as me. He always did think he knew best above everyone else. In fact, he even threatened to go to Goda and her new husband for aid. You don't know *le comte de Boulogne* do you, Mama? Eustace is an ambitious sort and would welcome a chance to expand his authority, although he is far too brash and ambitious a man for my liking. Goda appears content with him as husband, though.' Realised, belatedly, that everyone had grown strangely silent and was staring at him with horrified eyes.

'Do you mean to tell me', Godwine growled, his breathing coming in quick, anxious rasps, 'that your brother may be bringing a Norman army into England?'

'That's what mother wanted me to do,' Edward exclaimed. 'She has this half-hour been scolding me as if I were a swaddled child for not doing so!'

'I hope to God, Madam,' Godwine said with vehement passion, his eyes staring into hers, 'that your second son is as pathetically foolish as this firstborn. I will not be held responsible or accountable for any of this. You did not seek my advice or opinion, you went behind my back, and that of every one of your advisers and supporters. What were you thinking, woman? If Alfred comes, then he is on his own. I will not offer my sword in support, nor shall anyone else.'

Emma's throat had drained dry. She tried to speak but no sound came. This was not what she had intended! Oh, damn it, what had she intended?

Annoyed, grieved that he had not been consulted, Godwine was turning away from her.

She caught his arm, pulled him to a halt. 'Godwine,' she said, pleading, 'I am so tired of trying to pretend that everything is all right, that I am managing.' She swallowed tears, her lip trembling. 'That I do not miss him.'

He turned back to her, touched his finger to her cheek. 'Ah, lass,' he said softly, 'we are all missing him.'

Emma shrugged, wiped a tear that had escaped. Took hold of his hand. 'I was afraid, God as my witness, I was afraid that I was to be left entirely alone with not a soul to help or aid me. Can you blame me for trying the one option I had left?'

Shaking his head, Godwine kissed her hand, then let it go. 'I cannot blame you for thinking of it, Lady, but I do blame you for doing it. You know nothing of war or fighting. Leave the tactics to those of us who know what we are doing.'

'And if you desert me? Who do I entrust with the tactics then, Godwine?' Emma hurled back, angry at his response. 'I know nothing of war? I witnessed it first hand when I watched Cnut besiege London. I felt it every day when my first husband abused and ill-treated me. I have done, and I will do, all in my power to preserve my crown and my son's kingdom.'

'Then I suggest you get Harthacnut over here. Now. There is no other way. I will not topple England on to her knees for any other. It is a sorry fact, but if Harthacnut will not come for his crown, then he is not the best man to wear it.'

Godwine bowed briefly, walked away. A light rain began to drizzle, Edward huddled his cloak about his ears; he had forgotten how oppressively damp England was.

Emma stood, oblivious of her surroundings, numbed. Unless Harthacnut came, Godwine would go over to Harold. With him would go the other nobles and thegns. She had thought loneliness to be unbearable when Cnut had been taken so cruelly from her. What was crueller? To live in perpetual misery and never know the pleasure of happiness, or to find it, only to have it taken away again? Who was there, now, to ride in on his stallion and carry her to paradise? If Cnut's death was hard to bear, this second loss was worse, for she had lost her friend, adviser, companion and crown all in the one blow. This was the knife being plunged into the stomach and slowly turned and twisted. This was the pain of despair. This is what it really was to be alone: the knowing that there was no further possibility of hope.

'Well,' Edward said, brushing imaginary dust from his sleeve. 'I can see that I am not wanted here, that you lied to me. Where are the armies you said would be here to greet me? Where the fluttering banners, the trumpets, the horns?'

'Go home, Edward,' Emma said wearily, indicating the ship. 'Go back to Normandy and tell your brother there is nothing for either of you here in England.'

13

July 1037 – Guildford

Emma's daughter, Goda, had been widowed along with the young Duke of Normandy's mother, Herleve, for Drogo, *comte de l'Amiens et le Vexin*, her husband, had accompanied Duke Robert to Jerusalem and had died with him of the same illness. Being the daughter of a past king and a reigning queen, Goda had no fear of a lengthy and lonely widowhood, and was soon snapped up by a young man who welcomed a boost up the ladder of power. Eustace, *comte de Boulogne*, achieved a double advantage: Goda was a handsome woman and she had proven her worth for breeding by producing two healthy sons for Drogo.

Eustace was ambitious. To have a royal-born as wife was useful for his purpose of bettering himself and the opportunity to become that rare commodity, a kingmaker, proved too tempting for him to ignore. When asked by his wife's brother for aid, he agreed with alacrity, seeing his own possible prestige as an end result. Always cautious, however, he invested only five ships and crew, but Alfred thought that enough; his mother had assured Edward that there was widespread support in England. All he had to do was land and send out word for the fyrds to rally to him. That they would not do so never occurred to him. If there was support for a timid mouse like Edward, there would be support two- or threefold for a more charismatic, and able, younger brother. Or so he thought.

To gain Eustace's help, there were one or two half-truths that Alfred had told. And a few outright lies. One of them, the most condemning, that he had made agreement for the entire venture with Edward and that they had arranged to meet in England, Edward marching to London from the south, Alfred from Sandwich. The Count also believed that Emma knew of, and approved, these plans, and that England was eager to be rid of

Harold Ælfgifusson as soon as might be possible. The choosing of either Edward or Alfred as king would be for the Witan, but Alfred was thoroughly confident that he would be the first choice. Eustace of Boulogne had his own agreement in that, for he had met Edward and had formed not a very flattering opinion of him.

Doubt nudged Alfred when the initial welcome in England was not as warm as he had expected, a caution he soon shrugged aside. Sandwich refused him permission to enter the harbour; no matter, he sailed instead direct to London, where he assumed Edward would now be with the royal housecarls from Winchester. Perhaps it would have been prudent to have contacted his elder brother before leaving Boulogne? To have informed him of his intent? But Alfred was sick and tired of dancing to another's tune, particularly the sanctimonious Edward's dictate. He wanted to do this on his own, to show his brother, show them all, what he could do if given opportunity. If he was to become king, he would require initiative and independence, and the pride generated for him in his ultimate success would be unmeasurable. He would gain the respect of the English fyrd, of his brother, brother-in-law and, highest of all, his mother. All could realise, in one easy blow, his worth and adept ability. Emma, in particular, would grieve for all that she had missed through these long years, would beg his forgiveness and rue the favouritism she had mistakenly shown to Harthacnut, who had shown himself to be as worthless as Edward as far as reliability went. Alfred would be magnanimous to his mother, would allow her to keep Winchester. Perhaps.

The blow came to his ambitious plans when London also refused him entry, the High Reeve shutting and barring the gate in his face, the suspicion that everything was going horribly wrong suddenly beginning to dawn. Where was Edward? Surely he would have planned to head direct for London? It was inconceivable to think of taking England without gaining London, but then, Alfred knew full well that Edward was no military strategist and their mother was a woman, what would she know of the imperatives of war?

Refusing to believe that he had misjudged the situation, Alfred left the ships at Greenwich and struck out across land heading south, assuming to meet with his brother somewhere along the way. He would not consider that Edward might not have left Winchester and that Emma had exaggerated the situation. Would not believe it because he could not, there was too much at stake, too much involved. Too much to lose in admitting he was making an almighty fool of himself. This was his one chance to free himself from the shackles of being an exiled nobody; he was here in England, he had armed men marching with him and he was going to succeed.

He got as far as five miles from Guildford in Surrey, where he was intercepted by a furious Earl Godwine.

'So, you came,' Godwine said, hitching his leg over his mount's withers and sliding to the ground. 'I thought your brother to be the fool; now I discover the both of you are alike. Mayhap you are even worse than he is.'

Seeing the troop of men appearing from the south, Alfred had assumed them to be Edward's men and had quickened pace, eager, his face alight with a broad smile of triumph. How astonished, and impressed, Edward would be to see him here with all these able men! How delighted their reunion, that stupid argument they had raged through entirely forgotten, how the people of London would grovel and beg forgiveness!

Pleasantly: 'You have the advantage over me, Sir. You are . . .?'

Abrupt: 'Earl Godwine of Wessex.'

Alfred's smile broadened. He thrust out his hand in greeting. 'My mother's man! This is well met, my Lord.' He peered round Godwine's shoulder at the mounted men, expecting to see Edward among them. 'Where is my brother? Is he not with you?'

'He is not,' Godwine answered curt, ignoring the outstretched hand.

Embarrassed, becoming aware that something was amiss, Alfred withdrew it, wiped his damp palm surreptitiously on the back of his thigh. 'As you see, I have come with men to aid my mother in answer to her summons.' Alfred swept that same hand towards the straggled group of his own weary, uninterested men taking opportunity to sit and rest, to swig at pigskins of ale, or gnaw at dried strips of beef or hard rye biscuits.

Critically Godwine eyed the ragtag crewmen, a moth-eaten bunch of retrogrades scraped from the bottom of barrels by the look of them. 'You intend to fight for a kingdom with this lot?' He snorted derision. 'Can any of them stand upright, let alone fight?'

'We have marched without rest from London,' Alfred defended hotly, refusing to give ground to this large and arrogant man. He would see to it that this Earl was replaced as soon as the crown was secure. *Oui*, he knew these men left much to be desired, but *le comte* had been as generous as he was able, given the limitations of finance. Aside, Alfred had expected better men to be available here in England. 'Is my brother to follow behind you soon, then?' he persisted.

Gruffly: 'Your brother has left Winchester . . .'

The delighted smile returned. 'Then he is on his way!'

'. . . And has returned to Normandy.'

The smile faded, enthusiasm seeping away like melting snow. 'But he was to lead an army?' The bewilderment turned to anger. 'Damn him,' Alfred roared, kicking at the hard ground. 'Damn him, the coward has done it to me again! He has shit himself at the thought of fighting and, rather than face a few ragged outlaws, has run for cover! He would never make a king and I will tell Mother so when I meet with her. I am the better man, she must see that now. Who needs Edward, anyway? I most certainly do not!' The anger came quick, to hide the disappointment of ruined expectation. Alfred had been so anticipating Edward's surprise at finding him here in full array for battle. Well, damn him, let him skulk and run, there would now be no necessity to convince the Witan of the preference for a younger brother!

Godwine laced his fingers through his baldric, slung aslant across his chest beneath his mantle. 'You think that, do you? You and who else?'

Alfred spread his arms wide, indicating the Guildford countryside. 'England, of course. You, Wessex, and all others who would join with me.'

'Let me make this plain. There are no others, nor will I join with you. The sons of Æthelred are not wanted or welcome here. I

736

suggest you march at double speed back to your ships, and return to where you came from.'

One of Godwine's lieutenants hailed him. 'Sir? Riders approaching.'

Godwine swore. Ten, twelve men, coming fast at a gallop. Swore again when he recognised the horse in front and therefore the rider: a spirited dapple grey with black mane and tail.

'I advise you, boy, to keep your mouth shut and say nothing,' Godwine said hurriedly as he faced the new arrivals, bowed to the man who leapt from the grey and swaggered over.

'I am not a boy to be ordered by a traitor like you,' Alfred grumbled.

'So you have intercepted him, my Earl of Wessex,' Harold Ælfgifusson said, nodding approval. 'What were you to advise? That he make all haste from England so that I need be none the wiser of this pathetic attempt at invasion? Or were you to escort him to Winchester to aid the traitor Queen?'

'My mother is no traitor! How dare you slander her!' Alfred shouted, ignoring Godwine's good advice. 'She is the crowned Queen, I am her son.'

'I know full well who you are,' Harold drawled. 'I am most pleased with London for informing me of your identity and whereabouts. London supports me, not the despised sons of that King Æthelred, who soiled himself as he ran from my father and grandfather.' With a hand gesture, Harold dismissed Alfred and confronted Godwine. 'And so, my Earl of Wessex, what say you? Would you prefer to keep your title, lands and life by serving me, or do you side with this absurd turnip? I remind you, before you answer, that you are not at this moment in Wessex. Surrey is mine and any man who brings an army into my territory must face the consequences of sedition.' He waved his hand at the Earl's men, Alfred's. Not many more than one hundred men, enough to constitute an army.

Godwine was trapped. This was the reason he was so annoyed with Emma, this was what he had feared, what he had not wanted to happen: a war to start, innocent men butchered. What could he answer? Defend Alfred, to whom he had no loyalty, and betray his own men? Men who had followed him all the years that he had been Earl, aye, and for some of them beyond that, for the two eldest had sailed with his father on that last outlawed voyage. But betraying Alfred would betray the Queen also.

Harold was awaiting an answer. Best, where possible, to cover a lie with the truth. 'I am on my way to my recent-built manor in Southwark,' Godwine answered boldly. 'I came across these men by mere chance. As you see, they face south, I head north.'

'So you have no objection to handing these dissidents into my care, then, Godwine?'

Both of them knew what he was asking. In Harold's keeping. Alfred would be facing certain death, but then, was that not the ultimate risk?

It was not an easy decision to desert Emma. Godwine had given her everything within his ability. He loved her, yet she had gone behind his back in this; an ill move to bring Edward and Alfred to England, poorly prepared and as badly done. England could not be held to ransom because one woman would not admit the finality of defeat. Without Harthacnut, England was lost, Emma was lost. It was selfish, and mercenary, to attempt to save himself, but neither was it rational or common sense to spread his hands in surrender and give up all he had for a cause that was already dead. Godwine made his decision, for Wessex and for England, the good of the majority had to take precedence above one woman and one foolish exile.

'I have your word of honour that Alfred shall be treated with the respect due to a king's son?' It was a futile request, but Godwine felt honour bound to ask it.

'He will face a trial for treason. I can give no more promise than that.'

Godwine was in an impossible situation, and so was Alfred, but the boy was too shocked to realise the full extent of it. He had stood open-mouthed, incredulous, not believing what he was witnessing. 'If you hand me over to this lout, you go against all that you have pledged to the Queen. You break your sworn oath.'

The contempt, the anger, had gone; all that was left for Godwine

738

was an immense sorrow. He found it difficult to speak for the tears were caught in his throat, not for Alfred, for a foolish young man he barely knew, but for a woman he greatly loved. 'I break nothing that has not already been broken,' he said, meaning the trust they ought to have held between them, the protection he must show to his men and his earldom, for they also deserved his honour. It was not oath-breaking to perjure oneself if the honour and lives of others were at risk, if by not breaking oath there would be death and slaughter. Honour was a peculiar thing. To be truly honourable, a man had to place the majority above the self or individual. By abandoning her, Godwine would be breaking Emma's heart, but that, too, was already broken by Cnut and shattered by his son, Harthacnut. It had not been Godwine's doing.

Harold beckoned his men forward, their swords drawn to arrest the exile and the men who dared follow him. Was becoming King of all England to be so simply achieved, after all?

14

Misery. Pain, worse, the humiliation and weariness of enduring, day after day, this living through a nightmare that would not cease, not even in sleep.

Alfred lay, curled on filthy straw in a dark and dank cellar that was home to some broken barrels and a family of rats that did not mind the putrid smell of abandoned decay. The monastery at Ely was nothing more than a shuffle of insipid buildings clustered on an isolated island set amid the wide space of the desolate Fenlands of East Anglia. There was nothing here except a wind that bragged in straight off the North Sea as sharp as an axe blade, and the incessant whispering of the rushes, sounds broken only by the ghostly boom of the bittern and the grunting and squealing, at dawn and dusk, of the rail.

The sky had been leaden grey, low and endless, pressing down over the glimmer of water that was the cold steel-grey of chain mail. It had been dusk as they had entered through the low archway of Ely, leaving behind the colourless spread of land, stretching from horizon to horizon. An eternity of a place. The last thing, aside from his prison and the faces of his torturers, that Alfred had seen.

Ælfgifu had sent him here; his solace, that it had been against Harold's wishes, but she had got her way in the end and he had been brought to this place where no one, not even God, remembered its existence. She had ridden with them, straight-backed, aloof, at the head of the small escort column. Gloating her sickening triumph.

How had it all gone wrong? What step along the way had he taken as a wrong turn? To think he was clever and have the arrogance to claim a kingdom for himself, by himself? To have the nerve to live, the audacity to be born?

And where was Edward? Had he, as Godwine had said, left

Winchester, returned to Normandy? Oh, God in His Heaven, God who had forsaken him, Alfred prayed that it was so, that Edward was safe, and in the next difficult breath prayed that he had gathered together an army and was at this moment about to besiege Ely and set him free.

Alfred cried out, the sound of a wild animal caught in a trap, its leg gnawed half through by its own teeth. A heart-wrenching, gut-twisting sound of immense grief and hurt. A prelude to death.

His men, those sent by his sister's husband, Eustace, were dead, all of them maimed then slaughtered. Murdered, with Ælfgifu looking on as each one was questioned, over and over through the agony of pain. Why were they here? Why had they come? To follow Alfred! To make Alfred King! Damned questions. Damned answers.

Why are you here? They had asked it of Alfred too. He had not answered, except to spit in their faces and denounce the usurper who called himself King. And then he had been the last left alive and they had brought him here, to the bleakness of the Fens and the empty edge of the world, where no one would notice his futile ending.

'Why are you here?' Ælfgifu had repeated as they had held him to the floor. 'If it is to be king, then your mother is to be disappointed. For falling into my hands you will pay the blood price for all that my brothers endured. You shall fulfil the promise I made when they were blinded, that Æthelred's sons would despair as my mother despaired.' And she watched, cold and detached, as her men burst out Alfred's eyes with white-heated pokers, willing the revenge to flow sweet and sated through her veins, but she felt nothing beyond the iron hardness that had turned her, during the passing of time, to unfeeling stone.

She laughed as they threw him to the rats, laughed as she rode away from Ely, and left him to take six days to die from the cruel way that they had blinded him.

The monks buried him in a grave in the south chapel at the west end of their tiny inconsequential church. In a grave that, it soon came to be said, echoed to the sound of a woman's insane laughter that never achieved the solace of vengeance. Laughter that, even as she watched her son being crowned King of all England, glutted from her mouth.

Vengeance was not as sweet as they said it should be. Not when it was tainted by the sickness of madness, cruelty and malicious spite.

15

Emma stood, resplendent in the full regalia of her royal finery, on the top step of Winchester Cathedral; stood alone, flanked by no one. Erect, proud, watching the man ride towards her on his prancing white horse, her expression an unreadable mask of stone, her mind as blank as her face. Harold, the crowned King, rode into Winchester with banners flying and crowds lining the streets, but the cheering was muted, only roused by the spear-points of his insistent housecarls.

He halted, dismounted, handing the reins to one of his companions. Godwine was there among them, and Leofric. All of them, every single, last, traitorous bastard.

Harold came up the steps, his crown catching the sunlight, his mail armour new, splendid. He stood in front of her a while and a while, then dipped his head, brought his right fist up to his left shoulder in salute.

'My Queen,' he said, the smile fixed on his face. He was not going to let this woman know that his knees were shaking, that he wanted to piss himself. Aye, all those men down there might be ranged on his side of the fence now, not hers, but how many of them carried a dagger concealed beneath their mantles? 'It is good of you to welcome me into Winchester.'

Emma stared at him. Saw Cnut's eyes staring back. Cnut's face, the slope of his jaw, jut of his chin.

Harold had offered her pax. She could live, retired, in her own home in Winchester, provided she never stepped outside the walls, and provided she handed him her crown when it came for him to take a wife.

'Tell him', she had said to the messenger, 'I will not let it go to the whore that is his mother.'

'Tell her', his reply had come, 'that neither will I. My wife, when I find one, shall wear it, and my son, Cnut's grandson, shall wear mine after me.'

A pity, Emma had thought, if things had been different, if it were not for Ælfgifu, perhaps she could have liked Harold. He had so much of his father in him.

'I do not welcome you, Sir. How can I welcome the man who had my son cruelly murdered?' Alfred, poor, stupid Alfred. She had indeed bred two fools for sons from Æthelred. Two simpletons. Edward, gone back to Normandy with all of the world calling him coward, and Alfred so brutally dead and already forgotten. For Edward Emma had given no second thought. He was his father's son, not hers. Looked like him, sounded like him, was as useless as him. Alfred? She had offered a prayer for Alfred, paid to have Mass said in his name and believed that God had taken him to Heaven, where all his pain and suffering was ended. She had not wept for him. How could you weep for a fool? 'I cannot welcome the man who is to take all I have.'

'Your son invaded my Kingdom. He knew the risk of war, the penalty of failure.' Harold's stomach was churning. How he wanted to say that Alfred's death had sickened him as much as her, that it was all his mother's doing? But how could a king begin his reign by falling to his knees and begging forgiveness? 'Nor am I taking everything from you. I have given you your house and, within Winchester, your freedom. I give you your life. There are not many queens who have been granted such honour. There are not many kings who would have been so generous.' Nor as many so stupid, his mother had said, but Harold would not, *would not* have any more blood shed at the start of his reign.

Nothing would induce her to set foot aboard a ship, Emma had said, so many, many times. Harold's offer of peace between them had come as a gift from God. Aye, she would be prisoner within her own town, but anything, anything was preferable to crossing that sea . . . except, except Harold did look so like his father. How could she, day after day whenever he was in Winchester, whenever she touched a coin that carried his likeness, how could she not see, instead, the beloved face of Cnut? Not touch it, caress it. Not remember it?

'I thank for your offer,' she said, 'it is generous of you, but I shall not be accepting it. England is my son's, Harthacnut's. It is not fitting for me to take bribery from the one who usurps his throne.'

Harold shrugged mildly. 'It is your choice, Madam.'

'I choose exile. It will be of but short duration.'

16

This was too much, one straw too heavy for an already overloaded wagon. Ælfgifu had interfered because of her petty squabbles and vengeances once too often. Harold had reached his fill of her. Her insistence on imposing her insane will on an independent and proud people had been the reason behind Norway's rebellion. Her second son was not prepared to lose England for similar reason. She had queried every move he had so far made, had belittled him in public, criticised him in front of his Council and disparaged him in the eyes of the Church. There was only so much a man could stand when it came to a woman undermining his authority and this latest, an incitement to murder, Harold would not tolerate.

'I remind you, Madam, that Thurbrand the Hold was your man, his feud with Bernicia was of your making. Blame for the murder of Ealdred sits square on your doorstep.'

'By appointing Ealdred's brother, Eadwulf, as Earl of Bernicia in his stead does nothing but perpetrate the feud. Thurbrand's son, Karl, is most aggrieved.'

Harold noticed that her protestations against his decision did not include mortification at being implicated in the outrage of murder. He did not give a damn for what Karl Thurbrandsson thought, Ealdred had been a good man and had kept a firm hand on the rippling unease of the borders with Scotland. He had also worked well alongside Siward of Deira, in itself no insignificant accomplishment, for the two areas of the North always had been antagonistic towards each other, except where Scotland was concerned. And Scotland, of course, always took advantage of any weak links. Cnut's authority had brought an uneasy settlement of peace; with his death all the old border raids were beginning again. It was a damned bloody nuisance to find Ealdred murdered through a nonsensical reason of revenge that had long been forgotten and supposedly forgiven. Harold had needed Ealdred to ensure the lasting protection of the Border Country; he did not need his mother continuously taking every opportunity to prod and poke life into dead embers.

'Ealdred was one of the few lords to speak against your crowning,' Ælfgifu retaliated. 'You ought to be pleased that he is gone, ought punish Eadwulf for his brother's disloyalty, not reward him.'

That course of action could well unite Bernicia with Scotland. It would not take much doing, for Cnut's adversary, Malcolm, was dead these past four years and his grandson, King Duncan, was touting for all the support he could get against the rising power of Moray and King Macbeth. Now that he had Gruoch as wife, Macbeth was daily growing stronger, for allied with the mac Alpin clan there would be nothing to stop him once he decided to make his move. Both Duncan and Macbeth were intent on playing out the game to its bitter end; if one side could manage to sway Bernicia, a distinct advantage could be created. For Scotland, not for England and the North.

While Scot bickered with Scot, England was safe, but steps needed to be lightly trod where the North was concerned, not committed to the heavy stamp of nailed boots. With his mother recklessly waving a lighted candle near the hay, the whole of the northern borders could erupt into flame.

'My father passed months of patience achieving peace between Ealdred and Karl Thurbrandsson. Putting an end to the bad feeling was one of his greatest accomplishments.'

'Ealdred had considered supporting Harthacnut. The bribes I paid him were tenfold to any other,' Ælfgifu intoned, as if that said it all.

'That was no reason to manipulate his murder! Godwine supported Harthacnut, too, as did virtually the whole of Wessex. Are you to manufacture several hundred deaths, then? Am I soon to be depleted of the entirety of my southern lords through a whim of yours?'

Ælfgifu resented being shouted at, it was a habit her son was growing into of late, she would need put a stop to it. The accusation of her being involved in this murder was exaggerated also, but there was no point in her denying it; when Harold was in one of these moods there was never any way to make him listen to reason. He had been the same as a child, to remedy it she had locked him in some dark, small place and kept him there until he apologised.

'You are being ridiculous,' she scoffed. 'I had nothing to do with Ealdred's death. As I understand it, the two men were heavy in their drink and the Earl made a careless remark against the memory of Karl's father, Thurbrand. Naturally, Karl took offence.'

Harold was not content to accept her censured version of events of a month past at Karl's steading of Rise Wood. 'God damn it, Mother, the pair of them were preparing to go on pilgrimage together!'

'As well they quarrelled here on English soil, then, not on the road to Rome.'

'They quarrelled because someone threw a flame into a pot of oil.'

'You have proof of that, do you?'

'I have proof that you have been promising Karl an earldom as soon as one becomes vacant!'

Ælfgifu made no answer, for she was not totally innocent and, wisely, she steered clear of saying more than was prudent by saying nothing at all. He could not have proof, this was bluff. She never set anything down in writing and her messengers were carefully chosen men who would not dare utter word against her. Not unless that fool, Karl, had said something. Had he? Had his fury at being overlooked in favour of Eadwulf addled his sense? If the man had sense in the first instance, which Ælfgifu doubted. The only mind that men possessed existed in their privy member, the capacity between the ears being nil compared with the life that manifested itself down below. Men were born fools, lived as fools, died as fools. Thurbrand's son had not done anything to convince Ælfgifu otherwise.

'Who the Hell is King here anyway?' Harold exploded. 'You or me, Mother? I distinctly remember the crown was placed on my head, not yours!'

748

'And who gave you life? Me! Who nurtured you through the uncertainty of childhood? Me! Who taught you everything you know? Me, me, me!' With each word, Ælfgifu prodded her own chest. 'I fed you at my breast, nursed your fevers, soothed your bruises and grazed knees. I endured the humiliation of your father abandoning me for that bitch Emma, suffering his patronising visits, pretending that I welcomed him, that I missed him when he was gone. For you, I surrendered to his pawing and poking, acting that I enjoyed his feeble lovemaking. For you, Harold, for you to become King, and what do I get as reward? As thank you? Accusations and ingratitude!'

'Oh, you make me weep! I was wet-nursed; I barely saw you from one week to another because you were always too busy about some plot or other with whoever happened to be your lapdog of the month. When you did deign to notice your sons it was always Swegen you preferred, never me.'

'As a child you were as pompous as a barnyard cock, always bragging your futile worth! You have not changed in manhood, I see. You would not be sitting there preening if it were not for me. My voice influenced the northern nobles to back you, my bribes, my cajoling. I could as easily break you, boy, as easily as I can snap a stick in two.'

How often had he heard this? Every time he made some law, some suggestion that went against his mother's grain. Would she never cease her interferences, her incessant comments and criticism? Do it this way, Harold, sign this, appoint him. On and on! God's Breath and she wondered why Cnut had so very rarely visited her? It was a wonder the man had come as often as he had!

'I know full well that it was you who planted the idea of becoming Earl of Bernicia in Karl's mind, Mother,' he countered acerbically, 'perhaps not personally, but you are adept at ensuring the right words are whispered in a chosen ear. You cannot bear to allow men to follow their own path, can you? Cannot tolerate peace and friendship. With you, everything has to be hate and spite and bloodshed. Even with us, your own sons, you could never encourage gentleness and caring, it was always killing. You made me watch as

749

kittens were drowned, made me stand at the slaughter pens at autumn. I was six years old when I first had to watch the cattle have their throats cut. I cannot smell or see blood without feeling sick. Did you know that?'

'You were always a weakling. I did it to toughen you. A king cannot afford to be squeamish.'

Quick, with loathing, Harold rounded on her, dribble spitting from his mouth in his sudden lurch of hatred for the hag who was his mother. 'Nor can a king afford to be as spiteful and vindictive as you are!'

Ælfgifu's eyes narrowed. 'You are a worthless wretch. You are nothing compared to your father, aye, nor your brother!'

'And you are nothing as a mother! I rule as king, and I will not allow more of your picking and prying at my judgements and decisions.' Harold marched to the door of this, his private chamber and, flinging it wide, bellowed for the captain of his housecarls to be summoned. The man came running, his mouth full of cheese, his fingers hastily lacing a half-undone tunic.

'I suggest, Madam,' Harold continued with iron coldness, 'that you get you gone from my Court and return to Northampton. You are no longer wanted here.'

Ælfgifu was aghast. 'But the Council . . .'

'. . . Can function full well without your presence. The only woman required to be at Council is the Queen. You are not she.'

Outrage was beginning to consume Ælfgifu. What did this boasting jay know of government? What did he know of law and politics? Aye, she had ensured that he had learnt reading and writing and numbers from the best tutors, that he knew his history and his geography, had learnt to navigate a ship and read the stars, to plan a battle, fight with sword, axe, fists and feet, but she had always been in command; hers had been the decision-making and the final word. It was a consuming lure, this necessity to be all powerful.

She sucked in her breath through clamped teeth. 'I am the King's Mother, until you take a wife and have her crowned as queen, I have the right.'

'That right exists only in your mind, Mother, and in my complacence in bending to your will. Both must stop.'

Drawing herself straight – puffing herself up like a pigeon, Harold thought – Ælfgifu answered with disdain, 'No one tells me what I must do, not since the day I saw my father carried in, covered in blood from where he had been butchered, not since I heard my brothers screaming for mercy when their eyes were blinded!'

The hunting party was returning. Harold could hear the noise and clatter filtering from the courtyard and so, too, could his dogs, disturbed from sleep, their tails wagging, growling and barking, milling at the closed door. 'Be quiet,' he yelled, at them. 'Go lie down, it is nothing to do with you!'

Most of the Witan members were already arrived here at Woodstock for the Easter calling of Council, but before business started in earnest, the King was obliged to entertain his guests. He had wanted to go hunting with them, but there had been important things to attend that could not wait: a letter to Henry of France, another to Baldwin, Count of Flanders. Neither would be answered, for both refused to acknowledge Harold as King. That was Emma's doing, her influence. The stretch of her authority and reach of her voice were staggering; she might be in exile, but her command was as much adhered to outside of England as ever it had been. Trade was suffering, for there was an effective blockade that stretched from Normandy to the Netherlands, export could not get out and import not come in. Unless he negotiated agreement soon, England would be facing financial deficit. There was only one way to outmanoeuvre Emma's meddlesome plotting and that was by forming his own alliance of convenience. Henry and Baldwin had daughters, young daughters not yet of marriageable age, but readiness for a marriage bed was no hindrance to a betrothal. Emma herself had proven that the offer of a crown was a magnetic lure for a pretentious count or king. A wife could relieve the trade embargo. She also had the advantage of ridding him of his mother. And as for Count Eustace, would it not be ironic if he were to negotiate a betrothal with his infant daughter? That would make Emma Harold's grandmother-in-law. He appreciated the jest.

'I politely suggest, Mama, that you get yourself gone from my Court and from my life.'

'You will not survive a season without my guidance.'

'I have other advisers. They are called earls and bishops.'

'Pah! Such men are duty bound to their own advancement; not one of them can be trusted to put your interest first and foremost.'

'Unlike you.' Harold busied himself with pouring a generous tankard of strong-brewed barley beer, something to do with his hands, something to break the tension that was as sharp as a whetted blade. His back to her, so that she might not see his face, nor he hers, said, 'I wish you to be gone, Mother, if not at your own initiative, then at mine. My Captain is waiting to escort you to your horse. It is saddled, your possessions are at this moment being packed.'

Ælfgifu looked from her son to the Housecarl. The ungrateful bastard had planned this! Had arranged it all! Dignity was the one thing that had allowed her to survive through the horrors and torments that had plagued her life. Dignity and a determination to ruin the lives of those who had ruined hers. She lifted her gown, stepped over the annoying array of dogs that her son insisted on keeping near him, great brutes of things that stank, particularly when their coats were wet. They would stretch out and sleep in the most inconvenient of places. Wisely, she refrained from kicking the biggest, a black-coated dog with razor-sharp teeth. She had tried it before, had been bitten for it. One day the cur would not be returning from a hunting trip; opportunity for the man assigned to the task had not yet arisen.

'I shall return to Northampton,' she said, 'but do not come whining to me for aid when something goes wrong and you are suddenly in desperate need for my wealth. You will find that my coffers are locked against you. As will be my door.'

'I'll not come whining, Mother.'

'You will,' Ælfgifu jeered as she swept from the room. 'You will.'

Alone, Harold drank the ale down in one gulp. Found his hands were shaking.

17

What had been worse? The panic in fleeing Winchester? The leaving of virtually all she possessed? Or the sea crossing? Her kinsman, Baldwin of Flanders, adored the sea, was always expounding the virtues of his prized warships, exclaiming the talent of his crewmen. Rivers and the sea might be a part of Baldwin's heritage and his future, too, for all Emma knew, but if he attempted to entice her aboard that cursed ship of his once more . . .!

Flanders had been the natural choice for exile. Normandy, with its boy Duke, was unstable and as Baldwin was the stepson of one of Emma's favourite nieces, he was kin and, more to the point, powerful. Baldwin, fifth of that name, ruled control of the Flanders sea lanes, held the key to the silver trade and was nigh on independent of any other country; and Bruges was a suitable base from which Emma intended to court allies to aid her return to England. France and Boulogne were worth cultivating, although she doubted Count Eustace would be willing to aid her, not after Alfred's bungling. King Henry of France Emma did not know personally, whereas Baldwin had been a guest of Cnut's Court on several occasions and had often professed to be fond of England's Queen. His Countess, Adela, was distant kin to the French King, Henry. The two had been married for eight years and had an expanding brood of children, the first two boys, the last a girl, Judith, and another one due any day.

Emma had no interest in the children, but Adela's condition did at least give her ideal opportunity to refuse Baldwin's insistence that she come sail with him.

'My Lord, I appreciate it is a rare fine day and the wind blows well from the direction you require, but how can I be so impolite as to leave your good wife's side when she is so near to birth? I would never forgive myself if her labours began the instant we were enjoying ourselves beyond the harbour.'

It worked. Graciously Baldwin submitted to her womanly sense. With a sigh of relief, Emma retraced the route up the incline to the Burgh, leaving the wind to billow the unfurling sail and abandon its persistence at tugging at her veil and cloak. She clicked her fingers to the dog, Cnut's hound, Whitepaw, who nudged her hand with his nose. He had not been an especial favourite of Cnut's – a pup of his best hunting dog, Liim, he was smaller than the others, less bold – but Whitepaw had been the dog to stay at Cnut's side, to lie at the foot of the bed; Whitepaw had always been there when the other dogs were more interested in chasing hares or scenting deer, squabbling for the heat of the fire or nosing after food. Whitepaw's first love had been Cnut and he had pined almost to death after he had gone. Stupid to have bothered with the animal; it would have been kinder to slit its throat, end its misery, but Emma, too, had been pining, she knew what it was to not want to eat, to want to curl into a corner and grieve. Knew what it was to want only the fond touch of his hand, hear the laugh in his voice. Through their mutual despair, and her persevering to make him eat, Emma and Whitepaw had become inseparable friends, down to both being dreadfully sick for the entire sea voyage here to Bruges.

Entering the doorway to the upper first-floor Hall of the stone keep, Emma almost collided with Adela. They apologised in the same breath, laughed.

'You had no hope of missing me, my dear.' Adela chuckled, resting her hand on the bulge of her belly. 'I am almost as wide as this entire Hall. The next time Baldwin comes near my bed, I swear I shall cut off his manhood. It is all right for the men, they do not have to wallow like an air-filled pig's bladder for nine months.' Adela threaded her arm through Emma's. 'I am about to walk along the river. I have a headache and I thought fresh, clean air might clear it; will you stroll with me?'

Emma agreed, for she found the confine of Baldwin's castle oppressive. Was it the castle or the overbearing good intention of its occupants? They made her so welcome, bade her treat the place as if it were her own home, but neither Baldwin nor Adela understood. She was safe, she was comfortable, was with friends, what was there for her to worry over? Nothing, save she wanted her crown and position. She could not make Baldwin realise that, here, she was his guest, obliged to the whim of others; in England she was the one to be deferred to.

'I hope the child is a boy,' Adela said. 'A boy shall mean so much more to Baldwin. Girls are for marrying, they grow and are gone. Sons bring their wives to Court, they do not leave.'

Saying nothing, Emma allowed Adela to walk ahead through the narrow gateway that led to the river path. She was not a woman to enjoy the feminine chatter of wives and mothers; children, as a conversation topic, had limited value to Emma. But what else was there to talk about in this dull place? The weather?

'Sons, too, have a habit of deserting you, I have discovered,' Emma said mournfully. She was feeling sallow this day, why was that? Her monthly courses had entirely ceased, although the symptoms of losing her womanhood irritatingly persisted, the hot flushes, the feeling of being as swollen as Adela, the so annoying loss of memory. She even found, occasionally, that she forgot what she was saying in mid sentence, and as for remembering where she had put anything – God's Grace, she was beginning to believe that were it not fixed to her neck she would one day soon, forget her head.

Fatigue caused it, Adela said, an opinion confirmed by the physicians. It could be that; Emma had barely slept these months, dozing, gaining two hours at the most, only to wake, fretful and soaked in sweat, longing for England and Cnut. For her own mind, Emma was convinced her memory and this baffled fug that clamped her brain into a stupor was the result of boredom. There was nothing to do here! Nothing to stimulate her, except those damn boats bobbing in the waterways, or the interminable walks alongside them. Adela was content with her domestic chores and her children. Emma, who had ruled a kingdom as Regent, never had been, never would be.

Relinking her arm, Adela gave Emma an affectionate squeeze. 'I am sorry, I forgot your Edward in exile in Normandy, and your poor, poor Alfred.' Overcome, Adela wiped at her eyes. 'How that lad suffered, how you too, must be suffering for his soul.'

Kindly meant, kindly taken. Emma said all the right things by way of reply while hiding scornful thoughts. Feel sorry for Alfred? The damn silly fool had brought it on himself. Come prepared direct to Winchester, Emma had said, so what do the pair of them do? Edward turns up with one ship and Alfred stumps off on his own course into the line of arrow flight. When stalking a deer you did not go downwind of it, nor did the marksman show himself during the drive. Bloody fools! And what had Edward to say? He had offered her the opportunity to be abbess of a nunnery near Jumièges so that she might pray for Alfred's memory and his peace. God in Heaven, the last place on this Earth that Emma wanted to be was near her incapable, idiotic, firstborn son!

'I thank you for your sentiment, my dear friend,' Emma said diplomatically, 'but I was thinking of Cnut's son, Harthacnut.'

Maternally, Adela patted her arm, although she was younger by fifteen years. 'So difficult to have control of more than the one kingdom. Baldwin does never find the hours to govern Flanders. How Cnut managed three is comparable to a miracle.' She said nothing direct of Harthacnut, Emma did not expect her to. The Count despised her son, for reasons of disagreement over trading and control of the sea routes, and what Baldwin thought, Adela unwaveringly echoed.

'Madam?' a voice called from behind. Adela and Emma turned round, the Countess assuming the hail to be for her, but it was Leofstan, Emma's dear, loyal, sensible Captain. He was running, waving a parchment. 'Lady, there is a communication for you!' he called, his voice caught and tossed by the wind.

Adela found a fallen tree as a seat, invited Emma to sit beside her while they awaited the man to catch up, but Emma shook her head, walked forward to meet him, patting her side for Whitepaw to follow. A letter? From Harthacnut? Please, Holy God and Mother Mary, let it be from Harthacnut! She ran a few steps, controlled the foolishness, forced herself to stop, stand, wait. Whitepaw whined, sat.

Leofstan, breathing hard, bowed, handed her the scroll. He was putting on weight, his hair starting to show the first frosting of grey. Emma smiled to herself. Gods! Had they, once, all been young?

Eagerly she took the thing, her hand almost grabbing it, her eyes going straight to the seal – her joy leaping. Harthacnut! Yes, it was from him! Her fingers fumbled at the seal, tore it open, her eyes scanning the words, looking for when he was coming, how many ships he would be bringing.

The anticipation dwindled, faded and a lonely tear trundled down her cheek. There was not much written there, a few lines of hastily scrawled script. Emma handed the parchment to Leofstan. 'It was kind of you to bring this to me. Please, read it.'

Frowning, puzzled, Leofstan did so, his face falling into concern as his eyes scanned the words. He did not finish reading it though, there was no need. 'Lady,' he said, tentatively reaching out to touch his Queen's arm, 'I am so sorry. So very sorry.'

Emma attempted a brave smile. 'Thank you, my friend,' then, 'I think I would be on my own. May I ask you to convey my apologies to the Countess? Offer to escort her either to the Burgh or on continuation of her walk. Explain to her?'

Leofstan nodded. 'You shall be all right, my Lady?'

She smiled, so sadly. 'I shall come to no harm. I have Whitepaw with me, he is all the company I require for a while.' She ran her hand across the smoothness of the dog's head, was rewarded by licked fingers. 'Inform the Countess that I shall retire direct to my chamber once I have walked and that I would be grateful for only a light supper to be brought to me.'

Again Leofstan nodded. He would do anything for his Queen, if only he could protect her from this new grief.

'There is bad news?' Adela enquired of him as he saluted.

'*Oui, Madam*,' Leofstan answered in French, the prime language of Baldwin's Court, 'the Lady Gunnhild, my mistress's daughter, has died of a pestilent fever.'

Adela shook her head, was there no end to Emma's grief and torment? She stood, wondering whether to walk further, decided against, asking Leofstan to see her home. Her back ached and her limbs felt heavy. If she was not mistaken the babe would soon be on its way.

Emma wept private tears for Cnut's daughter, for Gunnhild, called for that other woman from so long ago, Gunnhilda, wife to Pallig. Wept for the loss of a child, the loss of all that was dear. Wept for this new tearing of her heart. Whitepaw lay beside Emma on her bed, occasionally licking her face, his warmth and presence comforting, not minding if her arm was heavy, her hold too tight, or that her tears soaked his coat.

By next morning, from the floor above Adela's birthing screams filled the upper chambers of the castle. A short labour, three hours. She produced a girl, Mathilda, and asked Emma some days later to consent in being her Godmother. Emma agreed out of courtesy to her hostess; agreed, too, that although the babe was small – she looked more like a baby rabbit than a girl child in Emma's opinion – she would be destined for great things.

'Perhaps a king or a duke shall seek her hand in marriage!' Adela boasted, proud.

'*Oui, peut être,*' Emma replied, thinking the child was no more than a few days old and already her mother planned her marriage. That might be the sensible option, though, she reflected, when she was once again alone in her chamber, with only her dog and her despairing thoughts for company. Might it not be sensible to dispense with children the moment they were born? Aloud she said, 'That way, the hurt is over and done with the cutting of the cord.'

Whitepaw, with his liquid amber gaze, thumped his tail in uncomprehending agreement.

18

Godwine's hacking cough was painful to listen to; Gytha had tried, to no avail, infusions of coltsfoot, wild garlic and sage. His face remained grey, the cough barking and wheezing in his lungs, and still he had insisted on going out in today's downpour of rain. The meeting of Guildsmen at the Merchants' Hall might have been important, but so was his health.

'If you catch your death,' she had warned, 'do not expect me to be able to save you with my herbs and potions. I have nothing more to use.' Yet he had gone, and had come back wet through, shivering and burning a fever. Gytha had put him straight to bed and was steeping rose petals in hot water and honey, the smell from the simmering pot sweet and fragrant, when a visitor arrived at the Southwark manor. Tovi, who some called the Proud because of his supercilious nature and extravagant, colourful and highly expensive dress. He shook himself like a dog and crossed the Hall quickly, arms outstretched to greet Gytha warmly with a kiss to both cheeks.

'My dear Countess, I observed this afternoon that your husband is not well. I have brought you something to help,' and he ushered the servant accompanying him forward, to place a leather-wrapped package on the nearby trestle table. 'Spanish liquorice root,' he announced grandly, opening it to reveal the contents. 'The juice is guaranteed to cure the stubbornest of any bronchial cough.'

Gytha clapped her hands in delight. She had tried the ordinary liquorice root, but the Spanish variety was purported to be the better for medicinal value; she had intended to scour the London wharfside for it on the morrow.

There were many who scorned Tovi, for he was a wealthy man and his office to Cnut as Staller, a high-ranking Court Official, had been envied and, in some cases, condemned by those who claimed he had been given the position for his financial worth, not his ability. Among them, originally, Godwine himself, although that opinion had altered since Cnut's death, for Tovi had resigned his position and excused himself from serving Harold. In consequence, Godwine's path had crossed with Tovi's in a more social equitable manner, for the Staller had a lavish estate on the fringe of Lambeth, across the river from Thorney Island, and now that Godwine had his own manor built at Southwark, the opportunity to meet outside of tedious Court business had occasionally arisen. Godwine had discovered that, far from being an autocrat, Tovi was a man of convivial humour and unlimited generosity. Remove the necessity to keep your head above water, and the aggression, at Court, and a man became ordinary. Mocking himself, Godwine had observed to his wife that it was very possible that Tovi had previously held the exact same opinion against himself. 'We are, both of us, the better men for altering our biased opinion of each other,' he had confessed after a particularly enjoyable evening of laughter and entertainment at Tovi's manor.

Now this gift, personally brought in the discomfort of the rain. He could as easily have sent the liquorice with the servant, but no, how typical of Tovi to bring it himself. Was that not an indication of his charity and congenial nature?

Tovi sniffed at the infusion of rose petals, nodded approval. 'Use some of this, after it has cooled, to bathe his eyes, they looked most red and tired to me. It may help to cool his fever, too.' He smiled at Gytha, took her hand in his own. 'But then I am telling you of something you already know, and probably far better than I.'

'You are very kind and I thank you. I confess I am concerned for Godwine. He is unwell, and he will not listen to my pleading to stay within doors and coddle himself for a few days.' She shook her head, concealing the deeper thoughts, that Godwine was driving himself to a grave for the want of his conscience. Alfred's death weighed heavy in his heart – on many nights since that dreadful ordeal Gytha had awoken to find him out of bed, sitting alone in the dark, weeping.

Suddenly making up her mind, Gytha decided to unburden

760

herself. Who else could she talk to about this? Certainly no one of the King's Court, for everyone trod carefully in their expressed thoughts these days, not for fear of Harold, for he was doing his best, to be fair to him. No, the wariness was reserved for Ælfgifu, who took the smallest opinion to be the largest criticism.

'It is not this cough alone that bothers me, Sir.' She gestured for her guest to be seated, sank, herself, to a bench. 'But his state of mind. He frets and worries, cannot rest or sleep; always, always he thinks on the Queen or Alfred. He blames himself for both, you see.'

Tovi hauled a stool close, squatted on it, smoothing the lay of his moustache with his thumb and forefinger. He was not a young man, in his mid forties, with receding hair and a coarse-skinned face. He had vast wealth but had worked hard to obtain it, not expecting any man to take the responsibility of his merchant trading that ought fall to his own concern. That ruling, of assuming money could not be harvested from the ground but had to be gleaned from honest and steadfast toil, had set him well for the position of authority that Cnut had settled upon him and, it had to be admitted, consequently alienated him from many others. Not all men took responsibility with serious industry: why work yourself when God provided servants and slaves to do it for you?

'He was devoted to Queen Emma – begging your pardon for any misunderstanding in my saying that,' Tovi added with haste, 'as, similarly, I was devoted to Cnut.' He shook his head regretfully at the memory of what had once been. 'I understand that Harold is attempting to rule with the dignity and courage of a king, but until he gains the courage to bar his mother from his Court, I fear England will suffer the consequences. He expresses good ideas for the making of laws and legislations, but each and every one is shredded by his mother's superior authority. It is a king of substance we want, not a man too weak to demur to a dominating mother.' If it were not for Ælfgifu, Harold could have found that he had a chance, in time, to become as beloved as his father, but while he pushed her from Court with one hand then relented with the other and allowed her return, he would never be gaining men's respect.

Tovi patted Gytha's hand. 'We, all of us, Godwine included, privately bemoaned Cnut's faith in Emma when he appointed her Regent when he went abroad, but there are few among us, on this side of the hedge, who now doubt her ability. Aye, she could be caustic in her sarcasm and capable of whipping a man to his knees with her tongue, but she was fair-minded and just in her decisions. Until Harold learns that yea and nay are words to be uttered and vehemently adhered to, England shall continue to spiral into decay.'

Tovi sympathised with Godwine, for the decision to abandon Emma and serve Harold had been a hard one, one many shared in different degrees. Aye, Tovi was independent and concentrated on his merchant business – primarily the buying and selling of wool, a useful excuse for not being close concerned with King Harold – but for all that, Tovi had to tread carefully and bend his knee when it was required of him. Had he been a braver man, he could have stood by his conviction of support for Harthacnut and taken himself off in exile to his other estates in Flanders or Normandy, for Tovi had the wealth to have a finger poked into several pies, but he had elected to stay, another man among the many disappointed and dis-illusioned at Harthacnut's failure to claim his crown.

'If only Harthacnut would come to our aid . . .' Hasty, realising what she had said, Gytha covered her mouth. To speak thus was treason, if said before the wrong person would mean certain death by burning alive, a barbaric execution that Ælfgifu favoured. And what if Harthacnut did come? How would he value the men who had turned their backs on him in support of his rival?

Embarrassment was saved for Gytha by the noisy entrance of two young men, who burst into the Hall amid a cloud of sodden cloaks and barking, excited dogs. They were arguing, although the tone was amicable banter more than bad temper.

'And I say that the peregrine is the better bird than the gyrfalcon!'

'Nonsense! How can you compare any plumage with the gyrfalcon's royal ermine? I have seen the most beautiful birds, snow-white with flecks of black, reminding me of letters upon a bleached

762

parchment,' Swegn, older by two years, sparred with his younger brother, the two similar in appearance, already taller than their father, Godwine, Harold with hair a darker shade than the corn-gold of Swegn's

'Beautiful, I grant, but merely decorative against the speed and grace of the peregrine,' Harold persisted, noticed Tovi and immediately came over to him, his hand extended in welcome as he hailed a third opinion.

'Hie, brother, here is a man who shall surely settle our disagreement! What be the bird of your choice, Tovi? Peregrine or gyrfalcon?'

Tovi the Proud had not been in Cnut's employ without reason; his sense of diplomacy was unequalled. He threw his hands up and answered promptly, 'For my mind, my young adventurers, you cannot beat a plump roasted chicken basted with herbs and served with new-baked bread and thick, golden butter!' The jest went well, the laughter whirled to the rafters.

Leaving her sons to talk with their guest, Gytha gathered the liquorice root and asked a servant to begin their preparation, then went to tend her husband.

'We have visitors?' he said through a fit of coughing, 'anyone of import? Had I best come?'

'It is Tovi, brought us some Spanish liquorice; I am much obliged to him.'

Already Godwine was thrusting the furs from him, swinging his legs from the bed. 'Kind of him, I must thank him.'

'Where do you think you are going?' Gytha scolded, pushing him backwards and covering him again. 'If you think you are leaving this bed until I give you say so then you can have second thought!'

'But we have a guest . . .'

'Who saw you not two hours past at that damned meeting you attended and could not possibly have anything further to say to you, nor you to him. You are ill, you remain where you are!'

'Well spoken, my Lady Gytha. You listen to your wife, Godwine, or you shall answer to me in addition to her!'

Tovi ducked through the curtain into the chamber, assuring

Gytha that he had no intention of remaining long. 'I come to satisfy myself that Godwine is obeying his wife and doing all he can to get well as soon as he may.'

'Ach, I am not the invalid. I have been nursing a cold that has left me with this cough, nothing more serious than that.'

But Tovi could hear for himself the rasping wheeze in Godwine's laboured breath, sounding like a holed blacksmith's bellows. His face was grey, sweat standing out on his forehead, his hands trembling.

'You have had the physician bleed him?' Tovi asked Gytha, who nodded the affirmative. She had, although it appeared to have no effect beyond tiring Godwine even more.

Satisfied, Tovi bade his friend farewell and a full recovery. 'Take heed of my advice,' he said, his eyes twinkling, 'enjoy the undivided attention and pampering of your wife. Women forget the importance of their husbands once they have bairns hovering at their skirts; take advantage while you may, my friend, take advantage!'

Godwine attempted to laugh, dissolved instead into coughing.

Later, much later, he awoke from a fitful, sweating sleep, Gytha stemming the heat that was flowing from his body with cold water and linen flannels. The liquorice had helped, easing the cough, but the fever was growing worse. She was worried, but what more could she do?

Godwine caught her fingers, his thumb brushing the smooth skin across the back of her hand, his smile feeble but earnest. 'I need nothing more than a night of undisturbed sleep and God-granted peace from this turmoiled mind,' he said after another heavy fit of coughing and sipping at the soothing liquid Gytha offered him. 'Constantly, I see my Queen's face in my dreams and my sons agonising in torment, their eyes being blinded.' His breathing was harsh, difficult. 'What physics have you, my dear heart, against that?'

Gytha stroked his wet hair, admitted that she had none.

19

Tolerance between the Earls Leofric and Godwine had never been exceptional, their mutual wariness amounting to a polite curtness and nothing more. They met as little as possible, confining their crossed paths to the essentials of Council and the King's feasting, where they would contrive to be seated as far from each other as practical. Occasionally, avoidance was inescapable, especially when one man had a bone to pick over with the other.

'Godwine!' Leofric hailed his adversary as the noblemen were filing from the King's Council Hall, a stuffy, smoke-filled room to the west side of the Hall. The complex of royal buildings at Thorney had been lavishly extended by Cnut, although his attention had been attuned to the modest monastery and the private apartments which, even after rebuilding, remained susceptible to the slightest draught. The island was reclaimed from marsh and no amount of drainage could eliminate the damp, which permeated into the timber walls and up through the earthen floors, even those that were elaborately tiled.

Godwine hesitated, in half a mind to pretend not to have heard, but Leofric called again, hurrying towards him.

'My Earl of Wessex! I would speak with you!'

'Then you have my attention, although I would ask you to be brief. The King's decision-making was long and arduous; I have an inclination to visit the midden and then quench a raging thirst.' As ever, polite, but to the abrupt point.

'This will take but a moment. Good day to you, Lord Bishop,' the last to the Bishop of Durham, a slight man, totally deaf and incapable of staying awake during these lengthy meetings.

'The morrow we discuss an important issue, that of raising the tax levy,' Leofric said, sidestepping another group of men queuing to leave the Hall. He took Godwine's arm, guided him to a quieter corner. 'It will not go down well with the people.'

Earl Godwine shrugged, barely anything that the King's mother made demand on went well with common people or noblemen alike. Taxes never endeared any king – or king's mother – to anyone. Simply, Godwine said, 'Then we oppose the demand for their raising and refuse to comply. It has been done before now.' Not with much success, however, and usually as a prelude to civil war.

Leofric cleared his throat, that was not an option for him, as Godwine well knew. The King required financial funding, money could only be raised through taxes. Importation tax at wharf and dockside had increased by two pennies to the pound under Harold's rule. Trade, as consequence, was suffering, a trade that had already dwindled because of the sea blockade by Flanders organised by Emma.

'I cannot ask more from my tennants, Godwine,' Leofric confided with a defeated sigh. 'We are in danger of facing rebellion if we demand more than can be given.'

Godwine cocked his head to one side, was he hearing correct? Leofric making appeal to him for aid? No, there must be a sting in the tail somewhere.

'All we can do, Leofric,' Godwine answered neutrally, 'is vote down the King's proposals and take the hot breath of his mother's venom, or agree to it, collect in the revenue and face the wrath of the people.' He scowled ruefully. 'I think the expression is that we are caught between a rock and a hard place.'

Leofric himself suddenly very much also wanted a drink. He detested this man he was speaking to, thought of Godwine as a low-born pirate's son who grabbed handfuls of all he could to promote his own cause of importance. 'I cannot vote against the King, you know that full well.'

Godwine spread his hands, began to walk away. He did most desperately require that midden. 'Then why seek my counsel when you know already what I would say? I bid you good day.'

'No. Stay.' Leofric stood in Godwine's path, visibly deflated, his shoulders sagging, head drooping. 'Ælfgifu is not a lady to gainsay, not when she has her estate slap in the middle of your earldom.' He laid a hand on the Earl's arm. 'I would defy even you to deliberately antagonise her, where she to reside in Wessex.'

Despite the history of animosity, Godwine nodded; to that he would agree. 'As I see it,' he said, speaking honestly, 'we cannot continue much as we are. I have been bold enough to say it before and I say it again, here to you. Harold must rule as a king, not a puppet dancing on his mother's whim, or he must face the consequences.'

'I cannot back a rebellion, Godwine, I would forfeit everything if it were to fail.'

As would they all, but as things were, was there soon going to be much worth keeping?

Leofric folded his arms. Rebellion was not what he had intended to talk about. 'It is not easy to placate a woman, is it?' Before Godwine could answer, added, 'I recall it was Countess Gytha who insisted you remain abed for more than the month when you were ill? Or was rumour false and it was your decision, alone, to stay cosseted until mid July?'

Godwine cleared his throat, mumbled something about it being Gytha's order not his own preference. Not that he had put up protest. The cough had left his lungs severely weakened, even now he felt the breath wheezing heavy in his chest when the evening was damp or fog lay thick across the countryside.

'What is it you require of me, Leofric? If there is something specific, then spit out the gristle. I have urgent things to attend.'

Drawing in his breath, the Earl of Mercia unleashed his problem. 'I can do nothing to avert the King from his determination to increase these blasted tax levels, but I can attempt to placate my nagging wife.'

Godwine managed to hide the smirk behind his hand, pretending to scratch at his nose. He knew something of that already, Gytha had told him. 'As I understand it,' she had shared with him, last night in the privacy of their Southwark bedchamber, 'Godgiva is threatening to toss Leofric from the marriage bed if he dares raise the taxes again in Coventry.'

'Then if I were Leofric I would parade the woman naked through the streets and have her beg my forgiveness.'

'What?' Gytha had exclaimed. 'And risk her greater scorn? Godgiva is as much the harridan as Ælfgifu. Mind, the two share the same line of kindred, so is it any surprise?'

'I am afraid your wife is not my concern,' Godwine said to the Earl, 'Mayhap you ought curtail the expenditure of these churches she is prolifically building in your name. That would ease the financial burden somewhat, would it not?'

'Damn it, Godwine, I am attempting to be reasonable here! If you are going to resume your usual obnoxiousness I shall not bother with you!'

Once again Godwine turned away. 'Suit yourself. I am surprised you are bothering with me anyway. You usually find it easier to talk to the midden boy than to me.'

With great difficulty Leofric swallowed down his indignation. Against his better judgement his wife had insisted he have this talk with Godwine. On top of this taxation issue he dare not antagonise her further by setting the issue aside. In one of her rages, Godgiva terrified him more than any prospect of battle, torture and trial by ordeal put together. As compensation, he had suspicion Godwine shared a similar boat where Gytha was concerned.

What was it about this Wessex whoreson that annoyed him so? He was a dedicated earl, who never failed in his duties or service. He was just, generous, hard-working. But also, he was irritating, officious, opinionated and overbearing.

'I would chance to be able to set my wife's mind at rest over something this Nativity week,' Leofric stated. 'If I cannot offer her a truce on the matter of the King's taxes, then mayhap I can ease her mind on a more homely issue. She does, after all, think more of her sons than the business of government.'

Godwine raised his head, a suspicion of what was coming dawning on him. 'By which you mean?'

Aware that he had to be tactful, not offend, Leofric tried his best to put his request in reasonable terms. 'We bring our families with us to these meetings of the Witan, most especially to this, the

768

Christmas Gather. It is good for our wives to have the opportunity to exchange gossip; indeed, women appear to thrive on tongue-tattle. Good also, on occasion, for our sons to mingle, to hunt and wrestle and sport with each other.'

Godwine's turn to fold his arms, certain now of the direction of this interview, noting with suppressed glee that Leofric was becoming embarrassed.

'There is some sport, however, that is more suitable for the older lads. Not for youngsters,' Leofric said, the superciliousness rising.

Intentionally, Godwine decided to interrupt and be annoying. 'I would not say that. It depends on the nature of the lad, does it not? Some mature earlier than others. Now my Harold showed an inclination to want to fly his own hawks earlier than Tostig. Harold had his first merlin when he was, what, nine years old? Tostig is showing no sign of being interested in falconry even now he is three and ten. The same age as your Hereward, I believe?'

Bang. The nail hit on the head. Leofric scowled. 'Aye, the same age. Too young to be visiting a Lambeth brothel in the accompaniment of your eldest, Swegn!'

Swegn. How had Godwine known this was to be a complaint against Swegn? Feigning surprise, he lifted his hands and shoulders. 'Is it? I had my first whore when I was twelve.' When were the complaints not about Swegn? The surprise came when an entire day passed and only one grumble had reached Godwine's ears about the boy's outrageous exploits.

'But you are the son of an outlawed pirate. My son is blood kindred to the King!'

'By which you mean, Sir?'

At Godwine's rising anger, Leofric's horse also bolted. 'By which I mean, Sir, that I would have you restrain that damned eldest son of yours from influencing my lad with his bad habits and disgusting pastimes! Each night this week Hereward has come home drunk and stinking of a whore's cheap perfume. If he catches the pox, Godwine, I shall hold your Swegn responsible!'

Godwine laughed, intentionally misinterpreting Leofric's meaning. 'Have no fear of that, Swegn has too much liking for the ladies to be bedding boys. If that is your son's inclination, however, then I do not see how I can be held responsible.'

Trust Swegn to be shepherding the boy into ill repute. No doubt Hereward needed little leading, was wallowing in the freedom he would not be getting within the bounds of his mother's pious household in Coventry, but all the same, Swegn ought to know better. Ah, Swegn and common sense were as ill-matched as a thief in a mint.

'I demand that you send Swegn from Court, Godwine, else I shall be forced to make complaint to the King. Give him some task to do, make the boy face his responsibilities. I will have no hesitation in ensuring he is outlawed if not.'

Never one to rise to threats, Godwine stalked away, heading for the door and the last of the men to leave the Hall. 'My sons have natural high spirits. I doubt you will find the King willing to punish me, or them, for that. Mayhap it is your eldest son who is the poor influence? He is not spring-clean innocent. I have heard that where Swegn is, Alfgar often is also.' Annoyed as he was, Godwine was as angry with Swegn, for Leofric was right, he ought to be showing signs of responsible manhood. Send him from Court? How could he justifiably do that without belittling the boy or upsetting Gytha? On the other hand . . . An idea was forming in Godwine's mind. The morrow would unleash a high rage among the Witan, for Harold had no alternative but to press through his demand for more taxes and Leofric had been right in that also. Ask too much of England and the English could rebel. It was no easy thing to be rid of a king, not unless that king was there by default and another king was ready to supersede him. What if Harthacnut were to be told that Harold was failing? That, more than likely, England would, within the year, be ready to welcome a new king? The risk with raising rebellion was in being found out too soon. If word was to be sent to Harthacnut, then it must be with a voice that was wholly trusted. Aye, perhaps it was time Swegn was given his own ship and a decoy trading route. It was worth thinking on.

As final word on the subject Godwine said, 'I am unable to help you, Leofric. Absolve your conscience with your wife another way, not through the natural high spirits of young men. I would suggest, if you do not wish for a spirited colt to kick up his heels, do not allow him into the meadow, but keep him tethered in the stable.'

20

Leofgifu was dying. At three and sixty her passing was no unexpected surprise and indeed, the pain that was creeping through her emaciated body caused her to welcome death. It was Emma who could not let go. What would she do, how could she face life here, now, without her good friend to share it with? What would be left her? She rented her own house, a modest manor a mile distant from Bruges, had sufficient wealth to see her living comfortable for many years to come; loyal housecarls who refused to leave her, and the good will and opinion of Count Baldwin and his lady wife. What more could she want? Oh! Her friend and her crown!

Emma massaged the drain of tiredness from her aching eyes and face, the night had been long, with little sleep for either herself or Leofgifu, who had suffered much pain during these hours of darkness. At least she was sleeping now, the herbal draughts at last releasing her from consciousness. The priest had come at dusk, Leofgifu's last lucid moments, to hear her confession, had written down her will. To her nephew she had left land at Bramford in Suffolk, land that Emma had generously given her as reward for dear service. To Emma various sundries and the return of gifted land at Belchamp near Sudbury, also in Suffolk. She had nothing more to leave, no one else to leave it to.

'Shall I empty this night bowl, Madam?' the serving girl asked, indicating the piss pot. Emma nodded. Leofgifu's urine had been brown and bloodied, the flux emanating from her bowels more water than solid. 'Can I fetch you anything as I return, Ma'am? You have not eaten this past four and twenty hours.'

Emma smiled. The girl was young and immensely loyal. If she were ever to go back to England Emma would take her with her. 'No, child, I do not want for anything.'

'A bowl of chicken broth, perhaps? Or an egg custard? That will tempt you, surely?'

Relenting, Emma nodded. She really did not feel like eating, but the girl was trying her best to be of help. 'An egg custard, then, and some watered wine.'

Alone, Emma bathed Leofgifu's hot face. The skin clung to the bone, making her appear as if she wore a skeleton mask; the breath rasping in her throat. Emma did not wish her to suffer so and had, through much of the night, prayed for God to be generous in His compassion. Had He heard? Did He care? How often had Emma prayed these last years, begged and pleaded for His aid? Nothing had happened, no sign, no word. On empty and desolate dawns such as this, Emma found herself doubting that God paid heed to women.

She sank into her chair, a wicker, high-backed affair softened by feather-filled cushions; closed her eyes to ease the ache that throbbed behind them. There were those who said she was vain and contemptuous, perhaps she was in public, but those same people had never had opportunity to see her where she need not put on the show of pretence. People who would never believe that this same woman would sit through a night easing and comforting the last hours of a cherished friend, no matter the stink, the mess or the abhorrence of it all.

Emma exhaled with a weariness born of despair. Why chase a rainbow end when she knew it would always be moving those few yards ahead of her? To clutch at moonbeams, gather the stars? All of it was impossible, as impossible as regaining her crown. Huh, perhaps Edward had been right, perhaps she ought to consider the seclusion of the nunnery; if she took the Veil she would know what the morrow would bring, and the day after and the day after. Suddenly she was crying, her head bent into her hands, her shoulders shaking, the tears falling. All of it undone. Unravelled. Finished.

Leofgifu stirred, a gasped moan, and Emma was on her feet, hurrying to the bedside, her hand going to clutch, desperately, at the cold fingers of her friend. The breath was rattling from Leofgifu's throat, as if she could not take in air. Emma ran to the door, flinging it open, screaming for someone to come, someone to fetch the priest, fetch help. Please, please, God, do not take her! Emma was not ready for being alone and friendless. Do not take her, not yet. Not yet!

Leofstan Shortfist, Emma's Captain, burst into the room, followed by others of her guard, the maidservant and a stranger Emma did not recognise, although he appeared vaguely familiar. She pointed to the bed, to Leofgifu, her hand trembling, her fingers covering her mouth to keep in the second scream that wanted to be let out.

Quickly Leofstan realised the situation and sent the maid running for Emma's chaplain, and bending over the woman in the bed felt for the life-beat in her neck, found nothing, bent his head to her open mouth, felt no exhale of breath. He crossed himself and, shaking his head, said quietly to his Queen, 'I am sorry, Lady she has gone to God.'

The stranger found Emma in the church dedicated to Saint Saviour within a short walk of the manor. It was quiet within the solitude of the stone-built chapel, the heady perfume of incense and beeswax candles filling the still air, only the sound of birds twittering outside disturbing the silence and the murmuring of Emma's prayer. She knelt at the altar, aware that someone had entered but ignoring the intrusion. This was a holy and public place, any were welcome to speak to God within this sanctuary, but she wished they had chosen another time.

Finishing her amen, Emma rose, dipped God a reverence and walked, head bowed, down the nave.

A young man was sitting near the door on the end of a bench, not looking as if he had come to pray earnestly for the forgiveness of his sins. He too arose, swept Emma a low bow. 'My Lady Queen, it is not appropriate to address you at this moment of sorrow, I am well aware, yet I feel it may cheer you to hear the news my father sends.'

Emma regarded him sternly, the intention of sending him on his way with a sound thrashing hovering on her lips, yet that look about him was familiar. The set of his eyes, the jut of his chin, even the cadence of his voice.

'Godwine's son?' she whispered. 'You are Swegn Godwinesson. What be you doing here in Bruges? Are you exiled too?' She snorted laughter, a sound close to delirium. 'Your father always said you were a rogue who would be sent in shame from England one day. I never took him seriously, perhaps I ought to have done?'

Swegn grinned impishly at her, twiddled his seaman's cap in his hand. 'I am sorry to disappoint you, Madam, I am not here in disgrace.' He glanced aside, acknowledged the crucifix upon the altar, made a brief and hasty genuflection. 'Least, not wholly,' he admitted with a grin. 'I am merely at mid journey. My father, the Earl of Wessex, thought it appropriate that I rest the men here at Bruges for a while before continuing on up the coast; aside, the wind was blowing hard, we feared a storm, I had no choice but to put ashore.'

Emma detested ships and the sea, but knew enough of both to be able to read the weather with accuracy. The sea had been benign and calm this week around. Why did this boy have need to lie?

He glanced again around the chapel, not in reverence or apprehension, but to ensure they were alone.

'Only God and His saints can listen to us in here,' Emma said, noting the path of his eyes. 'We are quite alone.'

Swegn fiddled some more with his cap. He had been thrilled when his father asked him to do this thing, the adventure, the risk, the excitement – he had been willing to set off there and then, months ago now, but Godwine had held him back, sent him out with the ship to other places first: along the coast to Dover, then up to Ipswich and as far as York. Further, to France and Normandy, taking wine and horses, grain and hunting dogs. Yes, the trading routes were under blockade, but not to those who knew how to slip past the enemy ships, or had the gold to pay for closed eyes and ears. And now Godwine deemed Swegn ready, he had sown the false trails, had distracted the scent. Now, when Swegn took his father's ship out on a trade run, no one remarked upon it, no one noticed or cared, some, particularly fathers and husbands of pretty young maids, relieved that he would be gone a while from England. No one would notice, or realise, that his ship, this time, had gone north along the foreign coast, not south, had gone to harbour in Bruges.

'England, Madam,' Swegn said, eager at last to deliver the message of secrecy that he had been entrusted to impart to the Queen. 'England grows restless for a true and competent king. Rebellion buzzes in the air like hatching mayflies. If meaning were to be given to the English noblemen and the fyrds, then they would rise as one man. If there is a man who would be willing to replace him, then Harold could be toppled without undue argument or spilling of blood. All the South, and much of the North, is ready to rebel. I am on my way to Denmark, to give word to your son, our King, Harthacnut, that England is ripe for plucking.'

The tears seemed to fall easy this day; was it so simple to turn the depth of despair into an ember of hope?

'My father warns', Swegn added, forgetting that he was told to say this earlier, before raising false impression, 'that it may be some while yet, several months, mayhap a year or more, for the way has to be felt carefully, as if walking along a darkened passage without candle or lamp. When we rise, it must be as one, and Harthacnut must be in position with his ships and army. Arranging a war of conquest cannot be undertaken in the blink of an eye or drawing of a single breath.'

Emma took her hands away from her face, wiping at the tears that she did not care about being noticed. 'I have lost a dear friend this day, I will see about her burial and the saying of prayers for her journey to God, and meanwhile you shall go to my son in Denmark and tell him that his mother awaits him here at Bruges with the greater part of the English treasury at his disposal. That I look forward to greeting him and his fleet.'

Swegn bowed, accepting her order, but did not turn to leave. 'Lady, my father bids me tell you also that he begs your forgiveness for his weakness and his stupidity. That all the while he has not forgotten nor deserted you. That from Harold's Court he has been attempting to place the right man on England's throne. He says it has been slow and delicate work to chip away at the block of stone, but at last it is cracking and soon it shall splinter and break into pieces.'

Emma's chin tilted, her eyebrows dipped. Forgive Godwine? Could she ever do that after his betrayal, after his allowing Alfred to fall into the hands of that murdering bitch and her bastard-son? But if she did not have Godwine as friend, who was there to walk with into the uncertainty of the future?

'You may tell your father', she said succinctly, 'that only when I stand on English soil shall I consider his forgiveness. Not until then.'

She waited the year around, from March until March. Waited, often impatient, filling her time with plans for invasion and daily prayer, her heart high with hope. Waited for her son to leave Svein Estrithsson, the eldest son of Cnut's sister, in charge of Denmark, waited for Harthacnut to gather his fleet and sail to Bruges.

And then he came, in the month of March in the year 1040, sailing into Bruges as a cold wind blew a drizzling rain across the squall of the sea. He came, bringing ten ships into harbour, the rest, the other fifty and two, lying at anchor at safe distance in a sheltered inlet, lest the Count Baldwin misinterpret his intention. Emma greeted him with a smile that was as high as her pride and expectation. She was going home. Soon, very soon, she would be going home.

21

17 March 1040 – Thorney Island

Ælfgifu of Northampton was two months dead. She had died from a cause unknown within the limited medical knowledge of the physicians, although they were certain it had something to do with the lump that had been swelling on her breast for several months. Harold's emotions were mixed. He knew the men around him, his earls, thegns, housecarls, were not grieved at her passing, although they did not openly show it and had dutifully attended her funeral. Duty. Was he mourning her because of duty? Because it would not seem right not to do so? Who cared about rights and duties! Harold did not. So why this gut-wrenching mourning for a shrew and a harpy?

A roar of shouted laughter as the two wrestlers in the centre of the Hall fell heavily in a tangle of arms and legs, accompanied by several derogatory insults from the jeering crowd. At the side of the Hall a juggler was entertaining the ladies by keeping six eggs in the air at once, skilfully tossing them from one hand to the other; at the far end the lesser thegns concentrated on the beer. A normal Easter of feasting at the King's Court. Huh, what was normal about it? In appearance, aye, it was, but if the undercurrents could be seen, if the whispers could be heard, the quick, flashed looks interpreted? If all that could be done by some means of magic, then there would be nothing normal about this coming gathering of Council. Ælfgifu's death had changed everything, scurrying a charge of energy through everyone as if they had been struck by lightning. Because of his mother's death, something had altered within Harold's earls: they were less wary, talked louder and appeared more at ease in his presence, he knew not why it was, although he could guess at it. Rebellion, the wind said, as it slithered through the grass and rustled through the bare branches of the winter-clad trees.

Rebellion and conquest. The sea rippled and murmured its own warning, swishing on to the sand and rattling through the shingle. *Harthacnut is coming, Harthacnut.*

But the whispering had subtly altered since Ælfgifu had died. Were men not so sure, not so eager to overthrow him? Were they willing to give him a chance, try him as his own man, not as a moulting songbird, caged by his mother?

Her death could be his salvation, his survival; she had irritated and angered him beyond endurance, had mithered and moaned and demanded and ordered – so why in all the names of all the gods did he sit here this evening, outwardly enjoying himself and inwardly aching for his mother's attention? He was a grown man, damn it! He ought be thinking of finding a wife, siring children, ought to be thinking of running his country as he wanted it governed. So why was she haunting him like this?

It was not the first time she had abandoned him, had tossed him aside like a piece of old, stained rag. He remembered, as a child, running to her with some plucked flowers, pretty colours gathered from the hedges; remembered how she had wrinkled her nose and tossed them into the ditch declaring they were bedraggled weeds. How old had he been? Four? Five? Remembered how he had tried to please her with learning how to ride his first pony and she had retorted that he would not be a rider until he was old enough to sit a big horse; how he had tried to do things for her to please her, only to be told not to be a clumsy nuisance, to get from under her feet. Had she ever hugged him? Nursed him when he was ill? Praised him? Not that Harold could remember.

Swegen had been her favourite. Swegen had received all her attention and adoration, her interest only transferring after he had drowned at sea. Harold had always been jealous and envious of the love their mother had lavished on Swegen, not on him. No, that was not true. Ælfgifu had not known how to love, only to hate. Everything she touched had turned black and withered. Everything about her stank of evil and the consuming desire for revenge. Yet Harold mourned her, because she was all he had of his own. Even this Kingdom was not his, it belonged to his earls, his nobles, the

Council, the Church. To Harthacnut? If they decided to unite and rebel against him, there would be nothing he could do about it; not while Harthacnut lived and threatened his security. Not while Emma planned and plotted in her rented house in exile in Bruges.

'We are to have horse racing on the morrow, are we not?' Earl Siward, sitting on his right-hand side, asked him, breaking his gloom-bound thoughts. 'Across the flatness of the marshes? I have a fine grey. I'd suggest there will be few beasts able to outrun him at flat gallop.'

'Godwine has a grey, too,' Harold answered affably. 'I have seen him, a superb beast, dappled at hocks, knees and hindquarters. His stallion master has groomed him to perfection, his coat glistens as if it has the sun shining full upon it.'

Siward nodded approval. 'It is no easy thing to gain a shine on a grey's hide. I must have word with him, find his secret.'

Overhearing, Godwine, seated on the King's other hand, guffawed. 'It is no secret, Siward. It is nothing more than good feed and hard work with the grooming brush.'

'I'll gladly lay a wager with you for the morrow – my grey against your horseman?' Siward offered hopefully.

Godwine chuckled. 'That is a wager that would be painful to lose! Good horses can be bought anywhere, not so good horsemen. Let me think on it.'

Amused, Siward agreed.

'I would hazard,' Harold eased himself from his chair, patted Siward's shoulder, 'this will be a risk our friend, Godwine here, will not be fool enough to take!' The atmosphere was convivial with pleasant banter and good-natured jesting, giving Harold hope that the tide had turned, that his kingship was being accepted. Dare he hope for that? Was it yet too soon? It would take time to win them all to his side, but he was a man who held the firm opinion that if something was worth doing it was worth putting full effort behind it. He could gain their trust, now that he was a free man to do things as he wanted. To gain their friendship as well, though? Ah, that could be a harder task.

Leaving the Hall to visit the midden, Harold verbally batted aside the jibes at not being able to hold his bladder with the same quantity of ale as everyone else. Several of his earls watched him go, a moment of silence suspended in the air as each man nurtured his thoughts, wondering whether to speak, hoping it would be someone else to say the thoughts aloud. Godwine raised his goblet of wine, toasted the air and said quietly, 'So? Do we still send for Harthacnut?'

His mind concentrating on what he was doing, Siward cut a chunk of soft white mare's cheese, offered some to Eadwulf of Bernicia. What better place to discuss treason than at the King's own table with all England observing? To meet in secret where suspicion might be roused was foolhardy; best out in the open, where conversation would not be remarked upon.

'Now that the mother is gone, mayhap he will make a better job of things,' Eadwulf ventured with a quick look along the table to ensure Leofric was engaged in earnest conversation with the Archbishop.

'Or mayhap he will show the true extent of his incompetence. Had he the balls he would not have been all this while impotent against her,' Godwine countered.

'I vote we give it longer. Give him the year, let him prove his worth.' Eadwulf, who had no love for either Harold or Harthacnut, was happy to wait, to let Wyrd – fate – choose the path.

'Happen we ought to let Harthacnut decide?' Siward suggested, finishing the cheese and brushing the crumbs from his moustache. 'We have indicated that we might be interested in supporting him if he finally plucked the enthusiasm to do his duty and come to England. I am not intending to hold my breath in anticipation of it. He will receive nothing from me until he steps on to English soil.'

'You are backing out?' Godwine answered, mildly annoyed, his anger directed at Harthacnut as much as the man sitting beside him. If Harthacnut did not get off his backside and come soon . . . Harold was winning them over, now that that bloody woman, Ælfgifu, was dead. Huh! Her fault again! If it were not for her dying, none of this loss of impulsion would be happening. 'Harthacnut will not be

781

pleased to hear that Harold is gaining in popularity. He is in the process of assembling a fleet. I have good authority on that.'

'It takes more to conquer a kingdom than set a few ships bobbing in a harbour, Godwine,' Siward answered placidly.

Earl Godwine scowled, probed Eadwulf: 'You think along the same course as Siward? We abandon Harthacnut?'

The Earl of Bernicia shrugged. 'I had no love for Ælfgifu; she was a bitch and I trust she is burning in Hell. But I have no love for Harthacnut either. I would not grieve to learn his father is dancing to the same jig as Ælfgifu. I am for giving Harold a chance to prove himself, now that he is his own man.'

'Harold has been our king for four years and . . .' Godwine paused, worked out the exact date. He was quick with figures, as were most merchant-trained men. 'Four years and sixteen weeks. If he has not shown us his worth already, is he likely to show us now?'

To himself, Siward agreed, but he liked not the thought of opening raw wounds. England had been at peace, excepting the regular skirmishing across the borders from Scotland. 'I say we wait,' he said, nodding a warning towards the side door and Harold returning. 'We wait and see.'

Godwine was not pleased with the answer, nor would Harthacnut be, but his hands were tied; he had no knowledge of what the lad planned, if he planned anything. All he knew was that a fleet was assembling; what Harthacnut was intending to do with it was anyone's guess. All to the good for strategy, but it would have been useful to have some small knowledge of intention. Or did Harthacnut not trust any of them, not even Godwine? A reasonable assumption, given that Godwine, privately, was beginning to warm to Harold and inclined to agree with what appeared to be the consensus of opinion. Ah, but that was Harthacnut's fault and choice. Were he here, were he trying his Goddamned hardest to be here, he would not be losing those who ought to be firm ranked behind him. But as it was . . .

Swegn had said that Emma would consider his forgiveness when she stood on English soil, much the same as they were all saying for Harthacnut. England was the pivot of it all. Swegn had laughed,

782

made a jest of Emma's words, had not realised the anguish this was creating in his father. Nothing bothered Swegn save for where to lay his next whore or get his next drink. He was young, he would learn.

'By Christ, it is cold out there!' Harold declared as he sat, rubbing his hands. 'There is a sharp frost, the stars pock the skies like a thousand eyes watching us.' He clicked his fingers at a servant, signalling for the next course to be served.

'What? There is more?' Siward guffawed, rubbing his already bulging belly.

Always difficult to present a feast worth the eating during the lean days of Lent, but the royal cooks were expert at their job and, so far, no king had ever been let down, even with a menu that consisted almost entirely of fish.

'We have pike served in a wild garlic and butter sauce I believe,' Harold remarked, looking critically at the servants beginning to file in with silver serving platters held high. He was not much impressed by pike, but some men were fond of it and the cook had assured him the sauce would be the finest ever tasted. These last days before Easter had to go well in all areas, from discussion to dinner. This was all Harold's doing, none of it could be claimed by his mother. Nor blamed on her if things went awry.

Earl Leofric pricked the fish set before him with his eating knife. He, too, was not keen on pike. 'Pike gives my lady wife bellyache,' he observed.

'That's you poking at her that does that,' Harold mocked, his voice loud and carrying, more than a little drunk, drawing laughter from the rest of the table. Leofric scowled, he disapproved of lewdness. Disapproved, too, of disrespect, even if the remark did come from the lips of a king.

'How is your son now?' Godwine asked Leofric blithely. 'Your second-born, the lad Hereward? We have not seen him at Court much of late. Is he still alive? Or did the whore-pox kill him?'

Siward raised his eyebrows. What was this? Some ongoing dispute that he had not heard tell of? It sounded interesting.

Annoyed, Leofric frowned at Godwine. 'Hereward is at Ely,

studying with the monks. Studying the meaning of loyalty and trust, and duty to God and King. A pity other men's sons do not show the same sense.'

It was not what he said that roused Godwine's anger, but why he had said it. Ely. Why send Hereward to the Isle of Ely? Why talk of it so pointedly?

Leofric read the thoughts, suddenly realising the implication for Godwine, said snidely, 'Ely is on my wife's lands. It seemed the most fitting place to send our son. There, he is gone from the influence of your eldest, for Ely is the last place where any of your brood will dare tread.'

Siward locked his fingers round Godwine's wrist, gripping hard. For good measure kicked him under the table. 'Leave it!' he hissed. 'Leave it, I say!'

Ely. If ever there was a reminder guaranteed to rile Godwine's conscience and anger, then it was Ely, where Alfred had so cruelly died.

Another of those awkward pauses, when men had nothing that was not either belligerent or caustic to say.

Harold himself broke the silence. 'I have decided to search for a wife,' he declared as he cut the steamed fish open and began to separate the meat from the bone. 'A pity your daughter is not of age, Godwine.'

Godwine's head shot up, as did Leofric's and Siward's, all three for differing reasons.

'My daughter, Edith, is in her eleventh year, Sir,' Godwine answered, barely able to conceal his excitement. 'She is not long from marriageable age. At present she is receiving education at Wilton. The Abbess says she is an apt and careful student.'

'Ah, but is she pretty?' Harold asked through a mouthful of hot fish. 'I'll not take a hag to my bed, you know.' He picked a bone from his teeth, swallowed.

'If Godwine's daughter has anything like the ill-mannered temper of her eldest brother,' Leofric interceded, furious at the singling out of favour towards Earl Godwine, 'then her looks would not be of the slightest importance. Although I hear she is very plain.'

'And could there not be some objection on grounds of kindred?' Siward offered, as alarmed at the prospect of Godwine being so closely allied. Working alongside him as an equal was one thing, as father-in-law to the King not at all acceptable. 'Her mother is sister-in-law to Cnut's sister. Might not the Pope object?'

'Even if he does not, I most certainly shall!' Leofric railed, slapping the table with his palm.

'It will be nothing to do with your decision, but entirely the King's, will it not, my Lord?' But Godwine got no further, for Harold was rising from the table, tipping over his chair in his haste, his hand clutching at his throat. His breathing was gurgling, his face turning red as he signalled with his eyes, his fingers clawing at his neck, trying to cough, trying to spit out the fishbone caught there. Siward thumped his back, hard, between the shoulder blades. Someone suggested laying him down, another getting him to bend forward. All the while, Harold was gasping for breath that he could not suck in, the redness of his face turning blue. He fell to his knees, his right hand imploring someone to help; no one knew what to do, all they could do was stand, watching, suggesting futile ideas, helpless and hopeless. Someone – Harold, Godwine's second son – ran to find a physician, someone else to fetch the priest, but it was too late. Harold Ælfgifusson sprawled forward and lay dead, choked on a swallowed fishbone.

22

Emma fell to her knees, kissed the planks of the timber wharf, her heart thundering with happiness and relief. The happiness because she was home, in England, with her tall and handsome son Harthacnut; the relief because the ordeal of exile and a sea crossing were both ended. Those two, exile and sea voyage, Emma vowed, as she knelt, offering a thankful prayer to God, would never, *never* be repeated. She would rather open a vein than suffer the humility of either ever again.

Gallantly, Harthacnut offered his arm to help her rise. She flashed him a smile of gratitude, revelling in the marvel of how beautiful her son had become in manhood. He was, every inch of him, Cnut, save for being leaner, thinner. His hair perhaps a shade lighter? His voice a slight higher pitch? All else was the same. His eyes, his laugh, his strength. His smile. Cnut, Emma thought, would be so proud of him! If he were here, her husband's laughter would be echoing up to the very sky; he would be slapping everyone on the shoulder, asking after wives and children – calling for his best hounds to be brought forward, his favourite stallion, so that he might show them off. That was a difference. Harthacnut had no inclination to boast before others, to show what he could do and how clever he was at doing it. Perhaps because Harthacnut did not have the need to prove that he would be a great king? He already ruled Denmark with fair justice, discipline and authority. He was loved there for his strength and command. Cnut had never lost that inner unsettled need to prove himself to England. She put her hand down to Whitepaw who leant heavily, afraid, against her legs, the dog trembling at the noise, the new smells. Emma rubbed his ear, received nuzzled fingers in return.

The crowds pressed close, straining to hear the words of welcome offered by a succession of Church clerics, Bishop Lyfing of Worcester among them. His eloquent speech was intriguing, for he had opposed Harthacnut from the outset, championing Harold Harefoot and, as rumour wildly speculated after the event, had been party to the vicious blinding of Emma's son Alfred. Although it was false rumour, it was one that had the tenacity to cling as if it were spattered mud. The crowd was interested, also, to witness the reunion of the Queen and the Earl of Wessex. Not as interested, if only they knew, as the Earl himself.

Godwine had authorised the Bishop of London, Alfweard, to go immediately to Bruges on the first tide's sailing after Harold's death, before they had even buried his body in the grave near the chancel arch in the modest Thorney Island abbey. Before the body was cold, some said, though they did not say it loud for fear of being heard by the wrong ears. The Bishop had been as eager to go, for he had been a monk at Evesham, an abbey revered by Cnut, was himself a kinsman to that past king and had suffered personally from the vindictive nature of Ælfgifu of Northampton. He had been no friend to her or her by-blown sons, welcomed the chance to take word to Harthacnut that his kingdom was ripe for the plucking without murmur of bloodshed to the contrary.

Seven nights before midsummer – a significant celebration for the Danish, who associated the shortest night with rebirth and fertility, the ending of the old, the coming of the new – Harthacnut stepped on to English soil again. Godwine came forward at a slow walk, his head bowed, hands low and wide, his naked sword spread bared across them to show he made no threat, was suppliant to any wish or command, whatever it might be.

Godwine had never been frightened of anything, only that time when his father had faced trial by ordeal, but that was fear for another, not for himself. If you were to count that, there were all the births Gytha had laboured through, the childhood illnesses his boys had suffered; the death of men by drowning, the sinking and wrecking of ships . . . so many dangers that life and God, together, could throw at you. This fear was for himself. This could be the last day he felt the sun warm his face, heard the birds squawking and clamouring in the trees, taste the saltiness of sweat on his tongue and feel the dry rasp of a throat that would not swallow. Tomorrow he could be dead, hanged or worse. That was not what he feared, death was an inevitable thing; it might come sooner rather than later, could come quick and painless or in slow agony, but death was not eternal, only the afterlife was that. The process of death, whatever its manner of arrival, would eventually end. If the Lord Christ could bear its pain, then so could he. But could he survive Emma's scorn? Her ridicule? How could he endure it if she were to turn away from him, treat him as *nithing*?

He was before them, standing in front of the King. He sank to his knees, head bowed, spoke with the words choking in his mouth. His memories recalling this man before him as a boy, a boy who had gloated at cruelty, who had gloried in watching something that was alive suffer. Godwine had known exactly what the boy had been capable of then, and knew what he could do now, as a man, if he so wanted. Emma had never seen the streak of malice that had ran through Harthacnut as a child, neither had his father; at least, he had never made mention of it – or had he? Looking up into the young King's face, Godwine saw the features of the old. Cnut stared back at him through the same eyes. Had Cnut guessed? When Ragnhilda had drowned, Godwine had suspected that it had been no accident. The girl had been too sensible a child to wander near the edge of the mill-race, the boy too jealous of her. It occurred to Godwine, all these years later, why it was that Cnut had taken his son off to Denmark: to teach him respect and control, to fend for himself away from the niceties and fripperies of a Court that was spoiling the boy, as if he were meat left to rot. Had Cnut, too, suspected the truth behind Ragnhilda's death?

Had the plan worked? Had Harthacnut become man or monster now he was grown? 'My Lord King, I offer my sword and my loyalty, do swear my oath to you and beg your favour for my foolishness in doubting your coming to England to free us from the tyranny of a usurper king and the stupidity of our misguided error.' He offered the sword to Harthacnut, who took it, gave it to his housecarl, Feader, standing upright and straight at his side.

'Break this sword,' he commanded in stentorian voice, 'so that I may symbolise the ending of what has been.' He took a new sword given him by his other companion, Thorstein, held it towards Godwine. 'And take this in return as my gift to you, as your Lord and King, to signify the future peace and prosperity of my Kingdom, my rule and the well-being of my people.' He lifted it, kissed the round pommel and presented it to Godwine, who took it with a shaking hand.

Formal, Harthacnut set his hands to Godwine's arms, raised him, kissed him on both cheeks. The crowds cheered, petals were thrown, green-leafed branches, flowers. Joy, spreading like welcome sunshine emerging from behind black clouds.

Godwine turned, bowed again to Emma, the Queen, and again sank to his knees. Offered her the sword.

'My Lady, how can I beg your forgiveness for the part I played in the death of your son? I am a humble, worthless wretch, and I beg you to punish me now by ordering the striking off of my head with this, the sword presented me by my Lord, your eminent son, the King. I do not deserve to use it, only die by it.'

The cheers became louder, reached higher to the sapphire blue of the cloudless sky for Godwine, and his father before him, had always been popular here in the South. And crowds loved a brave hero.

Emma's stomach was still turning like a butter-churn, although this voyage had not been as bad as she had expected. Countess Adela had been responsible for that, with the potion of some steeped herbs that had tasted vile and bitter, but had settled the worst of the seasickness. For Emma, too, this was an anxious moment. With the whirl of excitement and activity that had been in progress these last four weeks, she had barely had opportunity to think of how she would react to Godwine. There had been the envoys to send to England, the promises that Harthacnut would be welcomed, that there was no threat of hostility; the hostages to be secured, for Harthacnut was not the fool to make harbour in Sandwich and come ashore with nothing to secure English assurance.

They were held aboard a ship, their hands bound, but otherwise treated with respect. At Harthacnut's signal, would be allowed ashore, to return to their families, but not until all was confirmed as secure and safe.

Harthacnut had made no protest at Alfred's slaying, beyond that of general disgust at the method of it. 'He is as much to blame for being captured as is Godwine,' Emma's son had said when first she had discussed it with him. 'As are you, Mother, for summoning him to England in the first place. You ought to have known Harold would think on it as an invasion, as attempted conquest, and treat it as treason, the penalty for which is death. Your son wagered on winning, he lost. That is the way of things.'

Emma's answer had been hot protest. 'I did not summon him! He was tricked into coming to England. Edward made mention of a letter that talked of them coming to me. I had no knowledge of any such communication. How could I? It was you I was fighting for, your name as King, not theirs.' It was not quite a lie; she had not summoned either of them, outright, to fight. The bending of the truth was permissible, for she had the well-being of her people at heart. Or so she told herself and would tell her final confessor, and God, when, inevitably, she met them.

But Godwine? What was she to do about Godwine? Harthacnut bore him no grudge, he had merely been doing his duty and her son was philosophical about accepting that. 'It was not Godwine's fault that I could not leave Denmark to defend herself from any threat by Magnus Olafsson. He acted in the best interest of Wessex. That is how he is supposed to act. Can I fault him for that?'

It was all well and good for Harthacnut to be so sublime; he had not been forced into exile, he had not suffered the humiliation, the degradation, and so Emma had told him, shrilly and soundly.

'But Mother, Harold had offered you peace. He would have allowed you to live quiet within your own manor at Winchester, yet you rejected his offer and refused to comply with his demands.'

'To give him the Treasury? To part with everything that was ours? I was not about to do that! To lose everything to that whore's bastard-born!'

'It would not have mattered.' Harthacnut had shrugged, that first day of his arrival at Bruges. 'I have got it all back again now, have I not?'

Gods! Why were men so absurdly infuriating?

They were waiting for her to say something to Godwine, to acknowledge his plea of forgiveness one way or another. Harthacnut was tapping his foot, impatient to be getting on and finished with these formalities.

'What do I do about Earl Godwine?' she had tremulously asked Harthacnut before they had boarded the ship that brought them home. 'When he asks my forgiveness, do I give it?'

'That is for you to decide,' Harthacnut had answered, not especially concerned. 'Alfred was your son, not mine.'

Her son. Æthelred's son. The three of them, the unholy trinity, Æthelred, Edward and Alfred. Incompetent, inept and ineffectual.

'Oh, get up, Godwine, for the sake of God, get up,' she said, impatient with herself as much as Godwine.

He eased himself from his knees, in four years he would be fifty, would have lived half of a century, no longer a young man with supple joints and lithe ability. His kneebone cracked as he stood, the pain of the joint ache swarming down his thigh from his hip. 'I know not what to say to you, Lady, or how to say it.'

'Then say nothing, but ensure that you serve me better in future.' She leant forward, touched her cheek to his.

The watching crowd went wild with delight, all but mobbing their new King and the Queen, his mother, as they walked the short distance to the royal house. Within, there were formalities to be completed, discussion to be decided, plans to be made. On the morrow Harthacnut would be riding to London and Saint Paul's to be crowned as King of all England, but that was for the morrow. As far as the people of Sandwich and the men of Harthacnut's fleet were concerned, this was today, and there was ale and wine to be drinking, women to be wooing.

Countess Gytha was delighted to greet her friend, Emma, but dismayed to find that the friendship had faded and that the trust and love for each other had been diluted. 'Will you be coming to

Bosham, do you think?' she asked of the Queen. 'It has been a duller place without your presence these years.'

Emma shook her head. She was tired, wanted to retire to her chamber and rest, the sea crossing had wearied her, the tension, the anticipation, all taking their toll. She was one and fifty, no longer a spring lamb. God's Mercy, they were all growing old! Soon she would be in her dotage, a toothless crone with nothing to look forward to except the next bowl of milk-sopped bread, days and nights confined to a bed and the indignity of incontinence. And people feared death? Emma most certainly did not, providing it came swift, unknowing and did not announce its presence. There would not be opportunity for her to rest, however, for there would be the ritual of spiritual cleansing for Harthacnut through the night in the sight of God in His house. The morrow, the journey to London and the crowning, then feasting and jollity. When would she meet sleep again?

'I have no care for Bosham or my old home now, Countess,' she said wearily. 'They are places where I shared happiness with my husband and some memories, once they have been tainted, are best left to lie quiet.'

Gytha said no more, realised that never again would there be that full and easy friendship between the Queen and her husband Godwine.

23

He had been the crowned King of England for the week and already he was missing Denmark.

Harthacnut stood at the edge of the River Thames, watching four ducklings paddling frantically after their mother to safer waters, his approach having disturbed their feeding among the reeds. Further along the bank, where the willow and ash trees formed a cool, green copse, the sedge warblers were creating, between them, a tapestry of sound, their musical notes integrating with harsh croaks that bore sampled snippets of impressions of other birds. Harthacnut laughed when he heard among the trilling the distinctive whistle that Thorstein made when he called up his pair of wolfhounds. Another bird mimicked the tinny peel of the abbey's three bells for the call to service. All this, the wide expanse of the somnolent river, the high blue sky, the whisper of the breeze ripping casually through the grass and rushes, was beautiful to gaze upon, yet he missed Denmark. In Denmark, this night, the longest of the year, they would have built the bonfires high, rolled out the barrels of ale and roasted a mountain of meat. This was Midsummer Eve when in Denmark the old year ended and the new began. When men laughed with their wives and bedded their whores. When, in nine months' time, at the start of spring, a fine new crop of midsummer-blessed children would be born. England did not share the same custom. There was so much that was so different about England.

The day was hot, the heat haze shimmering over the marshes and sparkling on the iridescent hues of a dragonfly's wings as it patrolled the river bank, turned a perfect right angle and darted low over the water. The midges, too, were out, but unlike the solitary larger insect, hunted in swarms the size of an army, biting at his bare arms, flirting around his head. He slapped a few with his hand, mostly ignored them. When you lived with lice and fleas and bugs, insects became irrelevant, a mild nuisance rather than a persistent irritant. He sighed, puffed his cheeks, squatted to his heels and, picking a grass stalk, sucked at its sweet sap. Home, Denmark, with crisp clean air which crackled with frost in winter and smelt of drying grass in summer. Where the Northern Lights flickered and danced their gorgeous mystical patterns above the night horizon. The lights danced in England, too, but fainter, not so vibrant and alive with the immense magic of the heavens. A small boat was coming downriver, the two men aboard watching the water as they trailed a light fishing net, peasants by the simpleness of their dress and the mean quality of the rowed craft, although Harthacnut could not see them clearly. Their features and the plain colouring of their clothing was blurred, as were the distant trees and landscape; only slightly, but enough to make the haze of the marsh seem deeper than it was.

Harthacnut pinched the bridge of his nose, the headaches he often nursed seemed to affect his eyes. Tiredness, he supposed, and he was often tired these days. He called out to the fishermen in English, 'Hie there, is it a good catch you are making?'

'Nay, my Lord, the fish are all either down deep or in the shallows, seeking the shade.' The speaker sounded cheerful, though, content despite the poor result.

'We will trawl downriver, then wait for dusk. That'll bring them to the surface for to catch the flies,' the second man added. If they could find pleasure and happiness then why could he not do so also? These were poor men, probably with families to feed, problems and worries that would be twofold to men without adequate means: the illness of a child, the failure of a harvest. Where the next meal might come from, how to keep warm. He had none of that, none of the struggle to survive from day to day, yet Harthacnut could not feel the satisfaction of inner peace. Why was that? He sighed. Why was that?

'Then I wish you good fishing,' the King offered, swiping at a horsefly that was suddenly interested in the alluring scent of human sweat. Harthacnut batted again, as the damned thing became insistent. Was it any wonder horses were driven mad by them? Swatting at it with both hands only made the creature more angry and determined, and Harthacnut found himself in the ridiculous situation of running along the bank, being chased by a crazed fly the size of a large, fat wasp. He ducked into a clump of reeds, found himself up to his waist in water, swore vehemently in Danish. At least the horsefly had gone.

He sat on the bank, pulled off his boots and drained them – the rest of him would dry easily in this heat – laughed when he saw one of the fishermen leaping about in the boat and waving frantically at the air with his hat. Persistent little buggers, horseflies.

'Harthacnut? Be that you?'

He groaned beneath his breath. Mother.

'*Ja, Mor, det er mig.* I am here.'

Emma dismounted her pony and, handing the reins to Leofstan, loosened her gown from where it had been hitched for riding. Bidding her escort to see to the horses, she joined her son at the river's edge and patted her leg for Whitepaw to come sit with her.

'I have been to the market in London,' she explained unnecessarily, for that was obvious by the bundles laden on to the two pack ponies. 'I have a new tapestry for the Council chamber wall; it depicts Christ in Majesty above a merchant ship, quite a fitting subject, I thought.'

'I trust it was not expensive? I do not have the finances to go spending on sundries. I have a fleet to pay off, do not forget. I'll not be able to do so from my enemies' plundered estates, so will have to find the coin from elsewhere.'

Emma was irritated. Everything she had done for Harthacnut this week had been rebuffed by his surly words and frowned grimaces. To look at him you would think that to be anointed and crowned as King was a punishment, not a singular honour. 'I paid from my own purse,' she retorted. 'I did not touch your treasury.'

A long silence, during which Emma stroked Whitepaw's silk-smooth ears and Harthacnut brooded on his thoughts.

'I will have to return to Denmark,' he said to the marsh, his eyes on the sun-sparkle ripple of the river. 'I cannot be away long.'

795

'You cannot leave England!' Emma answered, alarmed and more than a little afraid. 'Not until you have established your authority here. It will not be safe, nor sensible, for you to leave!' All this hard work, all the anxiety to get him here and already he was talking of leaving? Ah no, she was not tolerating that!

'And I thought you were more than capable of being my Regent,' Harthacnut answered with heavy sarcasm. 'How have I managed to think wrong?' All he had heard from Emma since leaving Bruges was how Cnut had governed, what he had done and how he had done it. How he had relied on Emma, how good a team they had been, working shoulder aside shoulder for the good of England. Harthacnut felt as if he knew every minute detail of his father's life, down to how often he pissed and passed wind. 'Have you not said, often,' he drawled, 'how well you governed England for Cnut when he was away? Surely you are not incapable of doing so again?'

'You are being churlish,' Emma protested. 'I am past my fiftieth year and as much as I would like to, I will not live for ever, nor will your Council tolerate a Queen ruling on her own.'

'Perhaps I can formally appoint Godwine, then?' Ah, he knew that would rile her. Publicly she had forgiven the Earl of Wessex, but not privately. She had not, to the best of Harthacnut's knowledge, spoken to him beyond the requisite of expected politeness.

She scrabbled to her feet and called Whitepaw, who had started nosing among the reeds, to her side. 'I'll not sit here with you if you are to behave like a spoilt child,' she declared. 'I have more important things to do.'

'Like passing an hour or two in private with your new chaplain?' Harthacnut queried accusingly. 'People are talking, Mother. Stigand was not the best of choice. He is not, from what I understand, well liked.'

'Should confession and spiritual comfort be conducted in public, then? I think not!' Emma responded angrily. How dare her son criticise her personal preferences for her appointed servants? 'Stigand has been a good friend to me through the years, to me and your father both. He served well as priest at Ashingdon. Was one of the few men who remained loyal to me, who regularly wrote to me while I suffered the embarrassment of exile.'

Oh, here we go agan, Harthacnut thought, rolling his eyes towards Heaven. *We are back to the hardship and degradation of exile.*

His mother caught the expression, rounded on him. 'Stigand showed faith in me and, more important, in you. I considered it my duty to promote him into the service of my chaplain. Eadsige was a fine and loved priest, but with him gone to God while serving me in Bruges, what was I to do? Abandon Christ and turn heathen?'

'Yes, yes, so you have said a dozen times over.' Harthacnut patted the air, as if Emma were a larger, more annoying, horsefly. 'I merely recount that there are many who do not approve of him, nor of your friendship with him. Many think the man is too ambitious for his own good and is using you as a stepping stone to power. He is a manipulative and over-influential wretch, who thinks of nothing but achieving a means to his own end.'

That was nonsense, but Emma was not prepared to argue the point. Yes, Stigand was ambitious; yes, he wanted more. What was wrong with that? His opponents were those who already possessed power and prestige, who felt threatened by him because of his lack of guile.

'Men dislike Stigand because he makes no secret of where he would like his path to lead. As long as he is capable of doing the job he is appointed to do, good fortune to him, I say. Is there anything wrong in wanting more than you have got, if it is there for the pursuing? Some people, Harthacnut, follow their dreams and ambition with alacrity. Others accept what they have already been given, and sit idle on their backsides, enjoying the benefit of men's labour, expecting everything in the field to grow green and lush without care of ever tending the weeds.'

'Are you insinuating that I am lazy?' Harthacnut snapped to his feet, arms flailing, instantly annoyed at what was undoubtedly criticism against himself. 'I faced down God alone knows how many threats from Magnus Olafsson. I have kept peace in Denmark, allowed her to prosper and thrive. Trade is higher, now, more than ever it was with Cnut as King. There are some nights I barely see my bed because government keeps me so occupied. How dare you suggest I am a shirker!'

Exasperated, Emma flung her own arms in the air. Harthacnut favoured his father in looks, but what son and mother lacked in similar appearance was made up for in temperament. Both as potentially volatile as a grumbling volcano or a gathering storm wind.

'I have said no such thing! Are you so stupid to think I would? Oh, for pity's sake, Harthacnut, I do not want to quarrel!' She stepped forward, set her hands each side of his face and, bending his head, kissed his brow. 'Dearest, I do not want to quarrel with you.' She smiled, smoothed back the flop of hair that insisted on tumbling over into his left eye, said again wearily, 'I do not want to quarrel.'

Harthacnut pushed her hand aside, but gently, not with irritation. 'Nor do I, Mother.' He shrugged a half-laugh. 'I shall be quarrelling in earnest with my Council 'ere too many weeks pass for I must raise payment for the Danish fleet I brought with me. I can only do so through raising taxes, which shall be an unpopular but necessary move.' His expression turned sheepish. 'I would have at least one friend beside me, even if she is a woman who knows her own mind too much for her own good!' He leant forward, offsetting the words that could be taken wrongly by placing a kiss on Emma's cheek. 'Forgive my impatience and my sullen mood; it has been with me since I rose from my bed, has left me with a storm of a headache.'

Emma cocked her head to one side, astute, as ever she had been. When Cnut had taken her son into Denmark and left him there as the joint crowned King, she had been, at first, grief-stricken, then furious. In part, the fury had never subsided. She had always been angry with Cnut for not confiding his intention to her. Would she have agreed to Harthacnut's crowning had he asked? Probably not, but at least she would have had the foreknowledge and known the reasoning behind the decision before having to accept an already completed policy. Odd that the anger had now shifted ground somewhat.

'I loved your father,' she confided, 'but he could, on occasion, make my blood boil like it were a bubbling cauldron of rage. He took you to Denmark on excuse that it would be for your own good and for the security of his throne there. I oft-times wondered then, more so now that he is gone, whether it was, in truth, to punish me.'

Harthacnut was shocked. Emma had walked a few paces from him as she had spoken, had turned slightly away. He whirled after her, swung her round. 'Why would he do that? It was me he thought to punish, not you!'

Maternally patting his shoulder, Emma shook her head. She had never spoken of this before – had never even allowed the thoughts to filter near the surface, especially while Cnut was alive, but so many hidden memories and troubles had surfaced since his death, and she had had so much opportunity to dwell on them while in Bruges, that it was becoming difficult not to share them.

'He blamed me for his daughter's death. For Ragnhilda's drowning,' she explained. 'He never spoke of it aloud, but I could read it in his eyes. He had expressive eyes, your father, as have you, eyes that could never hide the truth from those who knew how to read it. He thought I ought to have taken better care of her, not allowed her to go seeking you that night.' She sighed, suddenly tired of it all, tired of the longing for him, the anger she felt at his so suddenly going away; at not saying goodbye to him.

Harthacnut was appalled. Not at what she had said but at the consuming inclination that he suddenly wanted to laugh, to toss back his head and crow his mirth to the sky. All these years he had assumed that his father had deposited him in Denmark to remove him from his mother, from his home, friends and from the only life he had known as a punishment for Ragnhilda. Assumed Cnut had taken everything from his son because everything had been taken from himself with the death of his daughter. Assumed that Cnut had intuitively known that her drowning had been at Harthacnut's direct fault. A guilty child's way of thinking in an adult, grown-up world.

'I was angry too, Mama, when Papa said I was to stay in Denmark and learn how to be a king, if I could.' He looked out over the river, watched a heron taking off, its ungainly legs trailing behind, three crows rising to mob it as it flew over their nesting site in the trees along the far bank. 'He said that he wanted me to learn how to be a great and good king and that there was too much hatred in England for me ever to learn it. I thought he was ashamed of me, abandoning me in a place where my failures would not be noticed, that you were ashamed of me too, that neither of you wanted me near because I had been the last to see Ragnhilda alive. I believed it, you see, because you had already deserted your other two sons because they had disappointed you.'

Emma wanted to deny it, to enfold him in her arms, hold him tight, but if she did that she would be endorsing a lie and it was too late in life suddenly to develop demonstrative maternal feelings that had been too long suppressed. 'Who knows what his motives were?' she said with honesty. 'I was married to Cnut for eight and ten years. I worshipped him at first, for he was like a god to me, after suffering so as wife of Æthelred. But I soon learnt that gods can be fickle in their behaviour. Mayhap that is why we abandoned them all for the one true God and the Christ, for unlike mortal men, they tell naught but the truth and honour their vows.' She was talking of Ælfgifu, Harthacnut guessed, for the way that Cnut had refused to set her aside, had refused to shun her two sons. If he had done so, how much different would it all be now? He would have known his father and his mother; would, perhaps, have known what love was.

'When Papa sailed from Denmark and left me there I made a vow. It was a secret one, known to none but myself and God. He had left a regent to take care of the Country, housecarls and tutors to take care of me. For those years I wanted for nothing, save for my father to acknowledge that he loved me first, above all others. Do you know what he said to me, Mama, as his ship caught the tide and her sail billowed? He called out, "Take more care of Denmark than you did of my daughter, Harthacnut."' He dipped his head, his body sagging. 'I have been too scared of not doing so ever since. That was why I stayed, that is why I must return. I cannot allow my father, whether he be in this world or the next, to think wrong of me.' How could he add, admit, that it was the only way he knew of making atonement for the great wrong he had done? He had to do it, whether he wanted to or no, had to take better care of Denmark than he had of Ragnhilda.

This time Emma did set her arms around him. They stood, linked together, heads touching, not weeping openly but allowing the tears of shared regret to fall inside, where they could not show.

'He was a man who did what he had to do, even though the doing could be harsh or cruel. He did as many bad things as he did good, but he will be remembered as a loved and wise king, and God help me, Harthacnut,' Emma concluded with a shaken laugh, 'I shall never stop loving his memory, nor stop this wanting to have him with me.'

The both of them braved a smile. Harthacnut, linking her arm through his, began strolling back towards the royal palace. Not that it looked more than a hovel of clustered deteriorating timber and reed-thatched buildings from here.

'I hate this place,' he observed suddenly, with deep feeling. 'It is so sordid and melancholy!'

Emma laughed. 'That is what Æthelred repeatedly said – and Cnut.' Wondered, had Harold thought it too?

'One day I will rebuild. Raze the lot to the ground and replace it with buildings of stone. A palace and an abbey to be proud of. How think you of that proposal?'

'I think of it very well, only do not take over long in the doing of it. I have heard the selfsame avowal for nigh on seven and thirty years!'

They laughed, the animosity forgiven and forgotten.

As they walked beneath the wooden arch of the wide-flung entrance gate, Emma shivered at the sudden cold, for the watchtower and platform above threw the tunnel into dark and damp shadow; it was as if a ghost had walked across her future grave.

'Promise me', she said, earnestly, clutching at him, 'that you will never leave me alone to face the threat of exile again.'

Harthacnut smiled. Strange, he had been thinking earlier of something similar, that to be here in England was to be exiled from Denmark. England was the dragon's breath for him, not the fear of ships and the sea, as it was for his mother. He missed those, God in Heaven how he missed the rise of a ship beneath his feet and the crisp, saline tang of an autumn-frosted wind in his face! Exile was a damnable thing, in truth, a far worse punishment than ever death would be. You lived while in exile, founded a new life, new friends, new challenges and achievements, but you never, ever stopped hoping that one day, one not too distant day, it would end.

'I promise I will do my best for you,' he said. 'I can do no more than that, but in return you must do something for me.'

Emma lifted her face enquiringly. If he asked to be allowed to return to Denmark, the answer would be a firm no.

'I want to bring Edward back to England.'

Emma stared at him blankly. 'Edward?' she queried. 'My son, Edward?'

Harthacnut shrugged. 'Do I know of any other called Edward who is abroad at this moment?'

To his surprise, Emma laughed. Her arms outspread, head back, a long shriek of high-pitched, hysterical laughter.

24

Emma sent for Godwine. It had taken her the afternoon and most of the evening to pluck the courage from thin air to do it, but do it she must. Who else was there to confide in? To ask advice and opinion from? Who else had as much to lose as she, were Edward to come home? Only Godwine, Earl of Wessex. She sent her loyal Leofstan to bring him, for he was the one man who would never tattle of it, who would lay down his life rather than betray a confidence of the Queen. In that respect her son had been accurate about Stigand. Aye, he was a suited chaplain, would become, one day not too soon in the future, a superb bishop, mayhap even higher than that, but to reach those dizzy heights he would not be above using any step to climb there. Betrayal among them.

Leofstan conducted Godwine into the chamber, discreetly closed the door, stood guard himself on the far side to bar entrance from any possible intruder. The servants Emma had dismissed, even her beloved Leofgifu, had she been alive, would have been sent to her bed.

'Madam?' Godwine swept Emma a low, formal bow. 'You wished to speak with me?'

Emma had dressed carefully. She had laid aside her crown, queen's robes of fine linen and expensive silks, wore a simple, plain gown and a light mantle of soft wool. Had removed her wimple, had no jewels, or decoration. None were necessary.

'It is time I dismounted my high horse, Godwine,' she said. 'The view is fine from up here, but the air is cold and it is punishingly lonely.'

He did not answer straight away, but replied, on an exhaled breath, with, 'Aye, Madam, I would expect it is.'

'I was angry with you because you had let me down, had abandoned me in my desperate hour of need.'

Again, Godwine considered his answer. He had no wish to quarrel with Emma; indeed, wished for the opposite, to be the greatest of friends again, but a friendship broken was a friendship hard to mend. The pieces could be glued together, but the cracks would always show, the thing would be always fragile and in danger of falling apart, and Godwine was not convinced, not now, that he could ever again trust her. She probably thought the same of him. Nor was he prepared to take the blame, to fall to his knees and beg forgiveness for what had been a situation of her own making. He could not do that, for his own pride and for the honour he carried for the earldom he represented. But Emma was a woman, she was also a queen, a damned powerful one at that.

'I was angry with you, Lady, for the same reasons.'

Emma indicated the wine flagon on the table, suggested he pour for the both of them. She sat on her chair beside the hearth-fire that did little to dispel the evening chill. It may have been a hot day outside, but these quarters were situated to the northern end of the royal compound, where no sun penetrated. Even on the hottest days it was cold in this chamber.

'I made an almighty fool of myself, didn't I?' she said with a candid honesty that made Godwine raise his eyebrows.

He sat, tactfully raised his goblet in salute as answer. Better an action that can have alternative explanation rather than committing a spoken treason.

'I have no excuse, Godwine. I was distraught, despairing to the edge of panic. Why in all Hell I thought it a good idea to summon Æthelred's sons, only God knew. I certainly did not.'

'Had you talked with me first, I could have told you that it would not be a viable option.'

'Which is why I did not talk to you,' came the wry answer. 'I knew full well it was a stupid idea and that you would condemn it, but I wanted to be doing something, anything.' She offered a placating smile. 'Even if it was the wrong something.'

Godwine sipped the wine, French. He preferred a Saxon grape if the truth be told, or better still ale, beer or mead. She was a handsome woman, Emma, even now that she had seen her fiftieth year pass by. Her hair was more silver than gold, her skin not so pliant, but her eyes were as bright, her figure as trim, her mind as alert. Not for the first time in his life did Godwine regret that she was a queen and he only an earl. Cnut, he had believed for a while, had once attempted to seduce his wife. It would not take much for Godwine to take Emma, not now that she was widowed and he had no husband's wrath to fear, but then, he still had Gytha and she was a good woman. It did not stop a man's wanting, though.

'Is there', he asked outright, shuffling the sensuous thoughts aside, 'a reason behind this interview? Or am I here to decorate the room?'

Emma laughed, had read the signs in his eyes, that glow of arousal. 'You know', she said candidly, 'that while Harold was trying to secure the crown, and again while I was in exile, he and that bitch mother of his attempted to black my character and name by spreading rumours of adultery?'

Godwine nodded. He knew.

Emma laughed again, pretending she had not cared, although, in fact, she had, for their foul-mouthed gossip had tarnished the sacredness of her marriage to Cnut. 'They said I had slept with various men, from cowherds to priests and bishops.' She raised her eyebrows. 'Though none went as far as slurring the name of an earl.'

'I did never believe one word of their malicious tale-mongering, Madam.'

Did you not? Emma thought. *But I would wager you conjectured on the truth.* She switched subject abruptly. No use raking over dead ash. 'Harthacnut intends to invite Edward to England, to rule as King Regent. What think you of that?'

'It will create a difficult situation for you, Lady,' Godwine commented, added truthfully, 'More difficult for me, though, I suspect. Alfred was in my care when we came across Harold.'

Emma sat silent. She was prepared to forget Alfred. What sort of woman did that make her? What sort of mother? Cold, hard, uncaring? A woman without love? Yet she had loved Cnut to the depth of her soul, cared for Harthacnut. Cared for this man, Godwine, despite the hurt he had caused her.

Quietly she asked, 'What were you going to do with him, Godwine? With Alfred? He was just a child, a poor, misguided child. I have wanted to know these months, these years that have passed since then. Were you, all along, intending to hand him to Harold? To use him to save your own skin?'

Godwine was before her, kneeling, his hands taking hers, his face appalled. 'No, Lady! Believe me no, I was not! I was full intending to march him to the nearest river, secure a boat and send him direct home to Normandy on his brother's heels. Do you seriously think I considered harming the lad?' He drew away a little, rubbed his hand over his forehead. 'God, Emma, for how long have you thought that?' He gripped her hands again, his eyes on hers, pleading. How could she think him so cruel? He brought her hand to his lips, kissed the fingers, laid his cheek against it. Tears danced in his eyes.

Emma touched his face, her palm caressing, a light, tender touch. 'I did not believe it, my friend. I only wanted to know.' She paused, touched the tips of her fingers to his lips. 'In another life, perhaps you would have been more than friend.' She shrugged. 'But this is the one we have and this is the way it must be.'

She withdrew her hand. Paused, exhaled. 'Harthacnut does not fully know of the stupid letter Edward received from me, begging him to come to my aid,' she said, trying to remember what she had said to Godwine at the time, those years ago. The trouble with lies, it was so easy to forget them, to be caught out by telling a different story later in the day.

'Is Edward likely to make much of it? That is, assuming he will come. Would you blame him if he did not?'

No, Emma would not, but Edward would come, for the same reason that he had come before. Because Normandy was in turmoil and when the boy Duke was finally murdered in his bed or in some thick forest or secluded alley, the fighting that would erupt would be volatile and horrendous. The English-born son of a Norman-born duke's daughter would not be tolerated, since he, too, would have legitimate claim for the Duchy. Edward would come for that, and because Harthacnut intended to entice him with honeyed words and mellow promises.

'Then I would suggest, if Edward talks of a letter, we deny all knowledge of it.'

'And if he produces it?'

'Then we claim it is a forgery penned by Ælfgifu or Harold. The both of them are dead, they are not here to refute the blame.'

Emma nodded her head, thinking. Aye, she liked the idea and it could work well in her favour, be another nail hammered into Harold's coffin to repudiate the lies spread in his reign.

'Tell me,' Godwine asked, 'is Harthacnut aware that Edward may be as ineffectual as Æthelred was?'

Emma's smile was resigned. 'May be? You think he only *may* be as ineffectual? My friend, it is a certainty.' She lifted her arm, let it fall, heavy, to her side. 'Aye, Harthacnut knows. He does inform me that I will be all the more eager to welcome Edward to England, knowing I can continue to wield my authority without interruption.'

Godwine grinned. 'He has a valid point there, lass.'

Emma sighed aloud, she wanted to laugh, for she could see the humour in it, but it was not power or authority she craved, she did not want to lose status, naturally, but she wanted the chance to enjoy the freedom of doing what she pleased, when she pleased. A luxury so rarely allowed any woman. To walk, ride, hold feasts and entertainments; write an account of Cnut's glorious life. She wanted to enjoy her advancing age secure in the position of being Dowager Queen, to sit and watch while others ran around like headless chickens.

'I only hope, for England's sake, that Harthacnut finds himself a suitable wife and immediately sets about breeding a ship's crew of sons,' she said with a mild laugh.

Her thoughts were running slow, addled by tiredness and so many years of disappointments. She needed to ensure that Harthacnut was the undisputed King, that Edward would not suddenly be remembered as one born to an older, English, king. How to do it . . . to write an account of Cnut's life? Or her own? Yes, that could be it, a record for all to read, from England to Rome and beyond. The *Encomium Emmæ*, In Acclaim of Emma, an account of her years, her struggle and hardships. Her marriage to Cnut of Denmark, the birth of her sons, but not Æthelred, there would be nothing of him, let him moulder and be forgotten. He would have no mention in the books. Some of her life would be altered, or plain left out, of course, but that could be managed. '*And Harthacnut called his brother to come from across the sea to be Regent of England, now that all was made safe and well. And good triumphed over evil.*' She liked the sound of that, would ensure whoever she chose to write it used that phrase, and she would choose someone good, someone with a talent for writing history.

Excited, she explored the idea with Godwine, outlining the content, the reason behind it. 'With such a written account,' she explained eagerly, 'Edward would not be able to usurp Harthacnut's place of authority, nor that of his sons, once they are born.'

She did not know that, for some days, it was for the reason of future sons that Harthacnut had been thinking about Edward. No one knew, Harthacnut himself was not certain of all of it. What he did know was that he was impotent, whether he was also infertile he had no way of proving. He had lain with women, whores at the brothel, serving maids, farmers' daughters; with not one of them could he raise his manhood to perform its duty. He had even tried, to his shame, a boy once. What point was there in taking a wife? There would be no sons to follow after him.

To prove to his father that he was as capable a king as he had been, he had to ensure the continuity of peace for England. Denmark had Svein Estrithsson and, although Edward was not of Cnut's blood, he was at least of Emma's, and for the sake of his father's memory and his mother's respect he must ensure that Edward was there, one day when it was required of him, to see to England in his stead.

25

June 1040 – Jumièges

Justifiably, after the last unnerving debacle, Edward was concerned about opening another letter from England, even if this one did bear the seal of Harthacnut as King. He was not sure that he wanted anything more to do with that violent place of death and murder. Abbot Robert Champart opened it, in the end, after it had sat on a side table for more than two days; he read it aloud, his jaw dropping in amazement and eyes lighting with excitement.

'You have been invited to England!' Champart declared, rewarded by an immediate horror-stricken response from Edward, who clutched his arms about himself and shuddered.

'Oh, no! I am never going back there! I have no intention of having my eyes burnt out and my body thrown into a pit to rot and be eaten by rats!'

The Abbot declined to correct him on the minor infringement of accuracy. Alfred had been buried in a Christian grave by the monks; the fact that had it been up to Harold or his witch mother the body would have been left as Edward said, however, made the exaggeration significant.

'No, my Lord, this is direct from the new King, from your half-brother Harthacnut.' Strange how suddenly he dropped the informality of calling the man before him by his name and inserted a more deferential title instead. Edward, however, did not notice his sudden promotion in verbal rank. 'He begins with apologies for not contacting you 'ere now and in offering his condolences for the shameful manner of your brother's death.'

'Does he apologise for these years of exile? For his father booting me out of my home and denying me the right of succession? No? Well, there's a surprise!'

Edward was usually mild-tempered, but he did have a habit of running off at a tangent if something upset him, rather like a placid horse suddenly taking fright at something unusual and bolting off across the meadow, heels kicking, trumpeting neighs of indignation. And as hard to pull to a halt.

Retaining his patience, Robert continued, 'Your half-brother begs to inform that England misses your presence, that he very much wants you to join him there and for you to consider his proposal to make you King Regent.' Champart's eyes were glowing with the anticipation of possibilities for the future, his thoughts racing wildly. Thoughts for himself, not for Edward.

'And why would he want to do that?' Edward queried acrimoniously. 'For what purpose? To humiliate me publicly? To string me up by my nether regions in order to be certain that I could never act against him? To lock me away in a cell somewhere, never to see daylight again?'

'Sir, if he had design to be rid of you, it would be better to his purpose to leave you here, to remain forgotten at Jumièges. I would read this,' Champart waved the parchment, 'as an indication that he wishes to make lasting peace.' He smiled placatingly. Robert Champart knew well how to cajole Edward into doing what he did not want to do. It was as easy as enticing a child with a knob of sticky honeycomb. 'Harthacnut is also King of Denmark. Who can he leave behind to see to the government of England? There is no one – except you.'

Edward sat, pouted. 'There's Mother.'

Robert laid the letter aside. 'But, Sir, your mother is almost an old lady. She shall be sixty soon, think you she shall live 'till then? Do you know of anyone that old?' As it happened, Brother Albus had died two weeks previous, the oldest man in the monastery. He had been two and fifty.

'Do you not think', Robert continued, eager, putting emphasis into his words, encouraging excitement into his voice, 'that Harthacnut might want someone reliable to take care of England for him? A man of noble discretion, of wisdom and authority? A man who will maintain the justice and law of the land in his name?' Robert stared at Edward with a new measure of respect and admiration; with awe. 'Sir, this is a most wonderful opportunity!'

Any other man might well have cynically thought of asking for whom the opportunity was best offered, but Edward had not an ounce of deviousness or suspicion in his body. At five and thirty he was as naive and artless as he had been at five. He had no guile or instinct for subterfuge; he trusted everyone and believed everything. A devout man, Edward put his faith and personal protection in God; after all, it had served him well thus far in life. Never would it occur to him that Robert Champart, an ordained abbot, a holy man of God, would harbour secret ambition for himself and would be prepared to do anything to achieve it. Anything. Never would Edward have imagined, or believed, that Champart could be manipulative and malignant. Robert was his friend and Edward assumed that his friends were all as himself: mild-minded and trusting.

Edward loved Robert Champart, relied on him for advice, counselling, confession and companionship. He was grateful to him for always being there, for taking away the painful memories, for offering friendship and a secure home. Grateful for the returned love that Champart offered, which Edward thought of as genuine affection, not as a means to gain an end. Edward would have been appalled if he had realised that, additional to his ambition, Champart's affection ran a little too close to the wind for decency. He was an abbot, he presided over men who had taken vows of chastity and who had, for the most part, no intimate knowledge of women. That was not to say that some of them did not receive personal, and secret, relief from going with other men. Depraved thoughts and deeds were easy to keep sealed into privacy within the silent order of monks. With so many boys and innocents residing in close proximity, opportunity to enjoy sexual gratification was easy to come by. It would never occur to Edward that perhaps Champart had welcomed him as a friend because of his potential benefit for this purpose. The thought would have horrified him. It did not particularly bother Champart, who publicly condemned the homosexual act, but nevertheless occasionally enjoyed the personal fantasy of a vivid and exciting imagination.

Had Emma known that Edward was afraid of women, that he found their presence alarming and embarrassing, that he grew red-faced and tongue-tied if ever left alone with one, she might not have worried that he could be a threat to Harthacnut. Robert had never witnessed Edward alone with a woman, nor heard of his wish to be. There had been a girl, Alys, the daughter of a minor nobleman with whom Edward had shared a passing fondness once, but to the best of Robert's knowledge there had never been anything more than a shared interest in the psalms. Was certain that Edward was as innocently pure as on the day of his birth. In Edward's view, beyond religious fervour there was good reason for his wanting to become a monk. Taking vows satisfactorily omitted the proximity of women.

If he were to return to England as Regent, Edward would be obliged to take a wife. Champart shrugged the obnoxious thought aside. So what? Once the girl was breeding she could be sent off to a manor with the children, he could persuade Edward of the benefits of that. Remaining as an obscure abbot with no reward save that of a grave at the end of it all was not what Robert Champart craved. He wanted more, in this life not the next, and intended to have it. If he could organise it, he was going to the very top of the ladder and with Edward as King, who knew how high that ladder might reach? Certainly its stretch ran higher over there in England than it did here in Normandy.

'I'll not meet with my mother again,' Edward declared, his bottom lip protruding. He was clean-shaven, as most men were in Normandy, with his hair worn short, although not shaved at the back as soldiers preferred. He would have liked the monk's tonsure, but was not allowed it unless he had taken his vows and Robert had never permitted him to take those.

A slight suspicion crept into Edward's mind. He frowned, rumbled, 'You've not been stopping me from declaring myself to God for this reason, have you, Rob?'

Champart looked mortified. 'My Lord! How could I have known of it? This offer from Harthacnut is unprecedented!'

'This offer might be, but you might have harboured some hope that I would be going back to England in one guise or another.' Becoming more suspicious, Edward leant forward, his arms folded, brows a deep V of disapproval. 'You were most keen to send Alfred and me back.' He flung his arms wide. 'And look where that nearly landed me.' He stabbed a finger at Robert. 'Very nearly in my grave!'

Champart sank to his knees, palms open in supplication. 'Sir! I beseech thee! I did no such thing, shame on you for suggesting it!' His mouth dropped, a hurt, pained expression suffusing his face, a tremble to the lip. Oh, Robert Champart was good, was very good! 'I would never, never do anything to harm or hurt you, Edward. Have I not befriended you all this while? Taken you beneath my wing, offered you the sharing of all I have? How could you be so cruel as to believe some filthy lie of me?'

It worked well. Filled with remorse, Edward fell to his own knees, weeping his own tears, begged forgiveness. 'I cannot face England, Robert, I cannot,' he confessed. 'What should I do there? I have no idea of government, I have no knowledge of meting judgements!'

The Abbot shook his head in indulgent amusement; he was winning the argument, as he always did. 'Not know? Oh, my Lord, but you do! You possess a heart that would melt the deepest snowdrift, a generosity that would fund an entire lazar house; a kindness and humility of spirit to equal the Christ himself! You would make such a Regent that the world has never before seen, nor dreamt of.' Robert took Edward's hands in his own. 'You will become a Regent that the rest of the world will envy and admire. Oh, my Lord.' Robert bowed his head, held Edward's hands to his lips. 'How it shames me to know that I do not have it within me to emulate the extent of your noble and magnificent humility!'

Edward preened. There was nothing he liked more than unadulterated praise.

'And think on this,' Champart added as his final persuasion, 'as King Regent it will be your directive as to what is to be done with the man who was foully and brutally responsible for the murder of your brother.'

Pressing his lips together in the full flourish of sudden anger,

Edward hissed, 'With that bastard born of a whore, Harold, you mean? Aye, I would be told where they buried him, so that I may tip him out and leave him to rot as he would have left my dearest Alfred.'

Robert Champart had actually meant Earl Godwine, but no matter.

26

Godwine sent one of his own ships to collect Edward from Normandy. Not one of his shorter, stout merchant vessels, but a full dragon-length warship, complete with crew and fluttering banners. It was his gift to both the ætheling and the King, his contribution towards the royal fleet – and to ferry Edward home with eager welcome.

Edward had last seen London in the midwinter of 1016, a black, moonless night. Remembered, more than anything, the smells and the sounds. The crisp tread of boots on the frost as it had cracked in the freezing puddles; the steam of mens' breath, the stench of the decaying rubbish rotting in the river, as Earl Godwine had helped the two boys, himself and Alfred, aboard a craft that stank as pungently of sheep shit. Earl? No, Godwine had not been an earl then, that was an honour the usurper, Cnut, had bestowed upon him. Godwine had been his mother's friend then, nothing more than a wealthy merchant, a man Edward had barely known. How could she dare call him friend now, after knowing of his involvement with Alfred's death? It had been Godwine's ship, too, that night; Edward remembered complaining that it was not a dragon craft. Remembered also quarrelling with Alfred about becoming king.

He wiped at tears that welled suddenly in his eyes as the ship's crew back-swept the oars and hauled the craft in a neat and tidy angle towards the wharf. He missed Alfred, had not realised it until this moment. Alfred had cried on that cold, uncomfortable journey down the Thames, had hidden the fact by huddling into his blanket and shuffling as far away from Edward as possible. Alfred, braver than his elder brother, had disliked anyone knowing he was capable of shedding tears. Had he wept while they were torturing him and putting out his eyes? Had he begged and pleaded for mercy? Edward buried his face in his hands, his shoulders heaving with the sobbing tears. The crowd, gathered at the wharfside to welcome him, assumed the tears were for the overwhelming emotion of his home-coming. They cheered, loving him for that, waving their green-leafed branches, craning to see the better, pushing forward, hands reaching out to touch him, to toss flowers and petals, everyone wanting a part of the magic of the occasion.

Emma stood with Harthacnut, Godwine and the rest of England's southern earls – the North had not been able to come, for trouble was grumbling along the Scots border again, or so Eadwulf claimed. There, too, among the party of nobles, the two Archbishops of Canterbury and York, as formally robed as the King and his Lady Mother, the Queen. Emma looked magnificent, dripping with her jewels that sparked and winked in the sunshine, dressed in silks and brocades. Harthacnut, although it was August and a warm day, wore his favourite mantle of a cream polar bear fur. It had been a magnificent beast, its pelt more than fitting for a king to wear.

A hero receiving a hero's welcome, Emma thought with scorn. How fickle people were! Three years past, London had wanted nothing to do with her sons, had shut their gates to Alfred and shunned him. And Alfred would have made a better king than this feeble mouse. Even his hands, those long, slender fingers, looked too thin and fragile to be of value – if anyone grasped them too tight, would the bones not break?

Edward reached the King, his face, bemused at the unexpected euphoria of the reception, beginning to spread into a conceited grin as he realised the extent of the pleasure being shown for his return. Harthacnut was smiling. Edward hesitated. Was he doing the right thing? Was this a carefully planned, cruel trap? He glanced anxiously over his shoulder at Robert Champart, received an encouraging nod and a smile. Champart had come as his chaplain, a role the Abbot had humbly, but eagerly, accepted the instant Edward had, with a little guided prompting, offered it to him.

Seeing the wariness, Harthacnut strode forward, arms out-stretched to embrace Edward, two men, both the sons of one woman, who had never met.

'My brother!' Harthacnut beamed. 'It is so good to greet the man I always wanted as my friend and companion. Welcome to England, Sir, welcome!' And he kissed Edward on both cheeks, held him close in a bear's hug of delight and Edward shed a few more emotional tears.

'Come,' Harthacnut said, 'I must not have you all to myself. Mother, Edward has come to us. Is this not a glorious and happy day?'

The smile on her face appeared sincere; indeed, the upward-turned lips were genuine, but the delight did not come wholly from Emma's heart. Too much was uncertain, too many questions were rambling about, questions that did not yet have satisfactory answers. And too many sleeping memories joggled into lurching wakefulness. Edward was too much like his father, particularly now that he sported a new-grown moustache that drooped either side of his mouth. The face, if not the body, reflected too much of Æthelred.

'My son, you have been gone too long from England, it is with gladness in my heart that I see you come home again.' Emma presented her cheek for a kiss, the response from Edward dutiful but nothing more. He might tolerate this young man, Harthacnut, for he knew nothing of him, but his mother? Oh, he knew and remembered her well enough! Her austerity, her coldness. The disgust with which she had greeted him that last occasion at Winchester.

But no, Robert had schooled him not to think of that. To put it behind him. '*Look to the future with fresh eyes. Cast a new beginning,*' he had said.

'And you are, Sir?' she asked Champart.

He bowed low, submissive. 'Robert Champart, recent abbot of Jumièges. I accompany, at his explicit request, my Lord Edward.'

Champart. A parasite who clung to dead meat. Instantly, she detested him and recognised in his eyes that the feeling was mutual.

The parade through the London streets, once all the formality of greeting had been completed, was slow and seemed everlasting, for the crowds would not allow Edward through before they had been permitted full inspection of him and had offered their unequivocal allegiance. He soaked it up as if he were a cloth drawing in water. Waving and nodding his head, acknowledging their delight, he rode a pure white horse bedecked with fine harness and coloured ribbons, a horse with flowing mane and tail that pranced and sidestepped, and snorted dragon's breath at the flowers and green branches being strewn in Edward's path.

Riding behind, Harthacnut was grinning, pleased with the adulation. He had wondered whether this was to be one of his better or worse ideas. Thank the Lord it appeared to be the former, though why these Londoners should be so ecstatic over this frail-looking, thin and bemused man he could not comprehend. He was not a warrior type, one gust of wind and he would be blown over. As for wearing armour, would Edward be able to stand upright in a chain-mail hauberk? Lift a sword, wield an axe? Harthacnut had the clear impression that Edward had never handled such weapons. Quite possible, for the Norman dukes would not have been wanting to encourage a potential rival in the art of warfare. A poor idea, then? Would Edward be able, or willing, to defend England in time of crisis? His father certainly had not, but then it would not be Edward making any ultimate decision, and there were always men like Godwine, Leofric and Siward to guide him. And Mother, of course.

By the time they reached Thorney, dusk was closing in. Harthacnut had planned a huge welcoming feast, his King's Hall was strewn with splendour in honour of his brother; Edward was to be seated side alongside him at the centre of the high table. But first, Edward insisted on attending God.

'We have Mass to celebrate your coming at the Cathedral of Saint Paul, on the day following the morrow,' Harthacnut explained. 'Although, naturally, if you also wish to pray this evening . . .'

'I do, Sir, I insist upon it. Do you not attend Compline? Shame on you as a Christian king if you do not.'

Harthacnut did not, least, not always. Often there were already too many demands on his day without attending every service designated by the Church. 'I attend Mass before noon,' he explained, 'more, where and when I can. I need rely on my chaplain for all else of spiritual comfort.'

Edward was insistent and there was nothing else for it. Instead of heading direct for the awaiting feasting Hall, the party proceeded towards the abbey that spilt light from its numerous rush candles through the line of small, slit windows.

A small, humble place, built by Cnut, admittedly in stone, but nothing grand or imperious, wholly different from the churches Edward was familiar with in Normandy. Those were huge and magnificent buildings, cathedrals, soaring into the sky for the sole purpose of glorifying God. This, in comparison, was a peasant's bothy. Edward saw nothing, however, beyond the golden crucifix central to the altar, the serene faces of the twelve monks, the beauty of their soaring voices as they sang praise to God. Emma noticed that Champart was the one to pucker his mouth and flare his nostrils, disdainful and patronising.

Proceeding up the nave, Edward suddenly stopped, a shriek of rage issuing from his lips as he hurried forward the last few yards to the chancel steps. 'What be the meaning of this? What outrage is this? Get it gone! Get it removed!' Agitated, he waved his arms, stamped his feet.

Nervous whisperings from some, silence from others. The Archbishop of York, Alfric Puttoc, presiding this night in honour of his position as the officiating priest, hurried forward, enquiring, puzzled as to what was amiss.

'My Lord Edward, be there something that meets ill with your approval?'

'I say there is! How dare you insult me, how dare you!' and Edward rushed forward. Stamping and kicking at a stone slab on the floor, he fell to his knees, began clawing at the edges set into the tiles, tears falling freely from his eyes.

'Dig it up! Remove it! Get him out of here, how dare you bury my brother's murderer here within the sanctity of God's Grace!'

Harthacnut was appalled. He glanced at Godwine, at his other earls who stared back at him, blank-faced. It had never mattered to any of them that Harold had been buried here in ceremony by the monks less than four and twenty hours after his death, buried in the place usual for a king, before the chancel arch with his name, Harold, etched into the stones. No one had said not to, for by the morning after his death, most of his Court had scattered to the four winds, Godwine to send immediately for Harthacnut, others to their own estates.

Not one of them had given thought to how Edward would react, for the grave, in truth, and the man within it, had been almost entirely forgotten.

'Dig it up, I say!' Edward shrilled again, close to hysteria.

Alfric Puttoc whispered hastily to Harthacnut, 'I would do so, my Lord. It is, I grant, a most embarrassing situation and it would do you no harm to show England that you value the son of your mother over the bastard son of your father.' He added wryly, 'After all, Harold did not have right to this honour; he was illegitimate born.'

'He was also a consecrated king,' Harthacnut murmured, balking at the wilful desecration of a grave.

'Dig him up,' Emma declared, sweeping to his side. 'Edward speaks right. It is insulting that he should be buried here; he does not deserve a Christian grave.'

Tools were fetched, pickaxes, spades. The stone slab lifted easily, spewing dust and soil, there was no coffin, only a shrouded body that issued a foetid, choking smell of rotting decay. Thank God, Harthacnut thought; it would have been difficult to explain this despoiling to Harold's past supporters if the body had been discovered to be incorrupt.

'You,' Edward squeaked, his voice high and uncollected in his agitation. 'You, Godwine. You were responsible for my brother's death . . .'

'Sir, I beg you to not think so. May it please you, I had no choice I . . .'

'Do not interrupt me!' Edward bellowed, stamping his foot again in his rage. 'I know what happened. I was here!'

The church fell silent. Few had been aware of Edward's part in the suspected uprising against Harold, Harthacnut included. He glanced quizzically at his mother, who raised her eyebrows, shrugged innocently. There would be some explaining to do after this, but she suspected that she could manage it.

Godwine meekly bowed, surrendering to the inevitable. Edward, he judged, was not the sort of man who would forgive a digression. He was too much the child for that, too immature fully to let go of the interference of binding feelings. 'What is it you would have of me, Lord?' he asked, suppliant, resigned to fate.

Disdainfully Edward pointed to the body. 'You will remove that . . . that thing and appropriately dispose of it.'

Godwine spread his hands, at a loss, his eyes seeking command from Harthacnut. 'What do I do with it, Sir?'

An uneasy silence. Harthacnut had no idea, although he was vividly aware that to do the wrong thing could bring the wrath of England, particularly the Mid Lands of Northampton, down upon him.

The Archbishop, Alfric Puttoc, anticipated the dilemma by saying, hastily and with conviction, 'In our sight, Harold was a bastard usurper who committed treason against our true King. There was, or so I heard tell, concern that he was not the son of our great and mourned King Cnut, as we had been led to believe.' He shifted his gaze to Emma for confirmation and permission to continue. She nodded. 'I have heard', he continued, 'that it was very possible that the whore, his mother, did fake her pregnancy and birth, and did smuggle in the orphan brat of a peddler into her bed, in order to trick Cnut into believing that she had borne him a son.'

Gasps of incredulity and horror. Was this so? Was this true?

Earl Leofric, standing somewhat toward the back of the crowd, bowed his head, thanked God that his wife was not here to witness these shameful lies. But what could he do? Speak out? Shout that Harold was Cnut's true son? Lose his earldom for the trouble of it? He said nothing. Not a word.

Harthacnut had to act. 'Lift the traitor out!' he bellowed, his strong voice filling the stone church from floor to rafter, reverberating in the cluster of three bells swinging in the tower above the transept. 'Lift the traitor out and toss the remains into the marsh. Let the filth of the bog take their own!'

Godwine carried the burden in his arms, his nose wrinkled against the stench. Not normally a squeamish man, he resolved to strip to his skin as soon as this deed was completed, to bathe, scrub himself with goose fat and lanolin soap. Burn these clothes he wore, no matter that they were made new and had cost a fortune.

They walked a short way to where the Tyburn River edged the marshes, crossed the water by way of the bridge and, without ceremony, dropped the enshrouded body into the bog. It disappeared slowly, the bubbles rising, the gloop of sound indecent. Harold was gone. His reign finally ending in indignity. Edward's homecoming was complete, he was satisfied. Champart had been right, this had been his chance to reap vengeance for his brother's wicked slaying. So what more would there be for him to do here in England, now that he had accomplished what he had come to achieve within the first hour?

27

The Michaelmas calling of the Witan Council to the High King's Palace at Thorney Island was to be an acrimonious one. With the euphoria fading of Harthacnut becoming the crowned King and his half-brother, Edward, instated as the King Regent, the serious business of the day became of prime importance. The Witan was about to discover that Harthacnut might not be as docile a king as they had anticipated and that Edward was as ineffectual as his father had once been. Emma, sitting on her own Queen's throne, was not surprised by the second discovery, but was as alarmed by the first as her son's entire Council.

Argument had raged for most of the day.

'I brought the boy to your Court, Sir, with the intention of establishing a full army of support for his plight!' Siward growled his rage. For an hour, now, he had been pleading his case. For an entire hour, it seemed, his words had fallen on the King's selectively deaf ears. Edward appeared to be asleep.

On the fourteenth day of August Macbeth of the Isles had slain Duncan, King of Scotland, in battle and had taken upon himself the mantle of King of Scotia. Duncan's young son, Malcolm Canmore, had been hurriedly brought south to seek the aid of England and sanctuary with Earl Siward, his maternal uncle. Eadwulf of Bernicia had refused him hospitality on his flight south. Siward, seeing possible implications fortunate for England, had welcomed a kinsman, no matter that he was a child. To aid the boy in regaining his crown could place Scotland in England's debt. Eadwulf had not wanted to become involved and Harthacnut, to Siward's intense annoyance, agreed.

'I have not the funding to pay my own armies for my own protection!' Harthacnut roared in final protest, becoming bored with the selfsame argument Siward was presenting. 'How in all Hell do you expect me to finance a boy to fight for his throne?'

Realising the hopelessness of defeat, Siward spread his arms in surrender. 'May I at least be granted permission to keep the boy with me? Allow him the sanctuary he seeks within my household?'

'If you agree to fund his cost and keep, then *ja*, you may do as you wish.' At last, amicable agreement, although not one totally to Earl Siward's satisfaction. It would have to do, however.

'To other matters,' Harthacnut announced, by his tone matters that would not be favourably welcomed. 'I brought with me a Danish fleet of ships. Soon I must return with them to ensure the security of my Kingdom over the sea. I cannot expect those men, who have served me well and who expect reward for their service, to remain empty-handed much longer.'

Rumbles of muttered talk, earl exchanging thought with earl, thegn with thegn. Only the bishops and clergy sat quiet, nursing their own disapproving thoughts. As ever, no one liked discussing the collecting and payment of taxes.

'I came to England at your invitation. I came in haste and with all expectancy of meeting resistance.'

'My Lord, we welcomed you, there was no blood shed, no murmur against your arrival . . .'

'Thank you, Leofric, I am well aware of that. All the same, I could not take that for granted. Only a fool would.' Unconsciously he glanced at Edward, who had slid into a crumpled heap in his chair, his chin firm on his chest, mouth open, a light snore emanating from his nose. Only a fool would come into a kingdom seeking a crown with no army at his side. Twice Edward had tried it. Their mother had said he was a fool. Their mother was, as usual, right. Harthacnut turned back to his Council and his demand for tax.

'Had certain areas of England not turned traitor to me in the first instance,' he bellowed, his voice suddenly loud and penetrating, startling most of the assembly alert and waking Edward, who reddened and quietly asked the cleric at his side what he had missed, 'I would not have needed to come with an armed fleet.'

No one spoke outright in defence, although the chamber again rumbled with mutters and chagrined indignation. It was no easy thing to speak out against a crowned king; to disagree with what he said. Not if you valued your head and your life.

'I wish to pay off my fleet and make my displeasure known both at the same time. I therefore shall raise the money to pay them from the areas that did defy me.'

Gasps, shouts of no and shame – there were some things that did rile men into action, into strong denial, despite the danger.

'You mean to tax the North but not Wessex for this?' Leofric barked, stamping to his feet. 'Forgive me, Sir, but the proposal is outrageous. Godwine did defy you also!'

'No, he did not, Leofric! He supported me until, through my own inability to come to England, he could no longer remain in a tenable situation,' Harthacnut tossed back viciously. 'It was you who aided Ælfgifu to get her son crowned; you who incited rebellion against me.'

Leofric clenched his fists. He had been expecting this ever since Harthacnut landed at Sandwich, expecting punishment and retribution. Shameful of the man to leave his judgement so long, to play with his earls as if he were a cat stalking mice.

'With respect, you cannot lay blame entirely at my door!' Brave of Leofric to defend himself. 'If you are to do so, I request that you do it with honour and not impose suffering on the peoples of my Earldom who would fall foul of any increase in taxation. I must take the burden of punishment, if there is to be punishment, upon my own shoulders.'

Harthacnut sat easy in his chair; he was good at this, at government, had inherited the knack of it from both parents. 'Then you are willing to hang?'

Leofric blanched pale, managed to nod.

Harthacnut swiped the air, impatient, with his hand. 'I cannot afford to lose my earls,' he said. 'I began my reign without a drop of blood being spilt and I intend to continue it so. You will not be hanged or exiled for going against me, Leofric. As with Godwine, Siward and all others, I judge you to have acted in the best interest of England. Misguided interest, but come the end, you saw the error of your decision.' He motioned for his cleric to stand, to read the declaration of the additional tax to be raised, on top of the usual annual rate, during the October month.

'Tax is to be assessed at eight marks to the rowlock, eight marks to be awarded to each crew man,' the cleric said, amid the rising uproar.

'Sir! You brought two and sixty ships!'

'At sixty men to a ship, that is four hundred and eighty marks!'

'No, nigh on six hundred and forty – he brought the great dragon ships, do not forget!'

'Three hundred and twenty pounds of silver per ship – Christ God, my Lord King,' Leofric pleaded, appalled. 'You request nigh on nineteen thousand pounds of us!'

Harthacnut, familiar with the added sums, nodded agreement. 'I do. That is the cost of betrayal, Leofric. Be thankful that is all I demand.' He rose, a satisfied smile playing on his mouth. He had been used to getting his own way in Denmark since he came of age. Was not going to change the habit now. Everyone else had to come to their feet, no one sat while the King stood. Edward was the last to rise, having entangled his mantle somehow between his legs. Emma glared at him impatiently.

'I declare Council closed,' Harthacnut announced. 'Business is done.'

For the earls it most certainly was not, but the King had the last official word. Always did, always would. It did not stop the aftermath of mumbling, however.

'We could never raise the portion that would be required in Worcester,' Lyfing, the Bishop of Worcester, declared to Leofric. 'We cannot, nor will not.'

'Best thing for England,' Earl Eadwulf remarked, overhearing, 'when he be gone back to Denmark. God rid us of him, I say!'

Within the privacy of Harthacnut's chamber, Emma tore off her wimple, throwing the flame-coloured linen to the floor in her rage.

'How dare you decide such high rate without consulting me!' she shouted, thumping the table before her with her clenched fist.

826

Edward hastily caught a wine-filled goblet before it rocked and fell. 'This could raise rebellion against you; certainly it will cause unrest. And you are about to swan off to Denmark and leave me to gather up the shattered pieces? I had no idea you were such an idiot, boy!'

'Idiot, am I?' Harthacnut yelled back at her. He had received a bellyful of his mother's interferences these last weeks. Do this, do that, your father would have acted like so; well, he was not his father, nor was he some slumbering dormouse like Edward.

'What would you have me do?' he challenged. 'Let my men loose on the countryside? Allow them off the tight rein I have kept them on, let them choose for themselves what they would like to carry home with them? A few women, maybe, or the riches from churches? Where shall I suggest they raid, eh, Edward? What of Ely? They deserve retribution, do they not?'

Edward attempted to bluster a diplomatic answer, but never managed to finish his sentence.

'I said nothing against raising a tax,' Emma snapped back, 'but not at that levy. It is a ridiculous proposal!'

'So first I am the idiot, now I am ridiculous? And you so wanted me to be King of this sodding Country – have you so easily altered your mind?'

Emma gathered her breath to retaliate; the angry, churning words filled her mouth, but she swallowed them down, she exhaled, sat, ordered Edward to pour them wine.

'Whether I approve or not', she said more reasonably, 'is immaterial. What you have decreed must be obeyed. I suggest, however, that you grant longer than the one month for the gathering. Certain areas have been sore hit by the rains this harvest season. If next spring's sowing be as badly affected, we may face famine. The Shires of Worcester and Leicester have been most sorely pressed.'

She had done her best, but her son, she belatedly realised, was a man forged of unbendable iron and stone. He could be just and lenient, but like his father could be as stubbornly determined. And he carried a cruel streak of ruthlessness that, once his mind was made up to it, would not be assuaged. As had Cnut.

Harthacnut sailed for Denmark as September crept into the autumn-coloured month of October. He left behind the two men he most trusted, Thorstein and Feader, to collect this additional forfeiture of tax and to bring it, as soon as the winter storms abated, in his wake. If they did not come with the stipulated amount, he would return by Easter to take it by force. A threat that was not idle made.

28

October 1040 – St Mary's Church, Worcester

'And I say no! What do we do? Let our women and children starve? See their bellies swell and their tongues blacken for lack of food? What in God's name do we pay this foreign tyrant's taxes with? Our blood?'

The mood was ugly, the opinion united to a single voice. Worcester would not pay the King's demand. Under any circumstances, threat or punishment, it would not.

'Our bishop, Lyfing, for speaking on our behalf has been stripped of his authority and shamed before the entirety of London – are we not to condemn that?'

'If this King expects us meekly to accept his unjust decrees, he can think again, damn his eyes, I'll not be paying!'

The church of Saint Mary erupted into a crescendo of sound as man after man leapt to his feet and stated his piece. Tradesmen, craftsmen and merchants, innkeepers, farmers, bakers, butchers, potters and smiths. All had come, all to rage and protest. To say no to the King's demand.

Saint Mary's was the only place to meet, for Worcester had no Merchants' Guild Hall, and the church nave was the largest suitable indoor enclosure. The smith's forge had a large barn, but more often than not it was stacked with grain and liveried horses. Neither was Garth Handfast overly conscientious on how often he cleaned the muck out. Saint Mary's was clean, if not warm, was central for all to reach. They used the church often for meetings and gatherings, for legal judgements – and for the annual gathering of taxes.

Most of the menfolk of the town and the outlying farmsteads were here, only the old or infirm staying, reluctantly, away; even a few of those had hobbled and stumbled along, so afired was their indignation.

'So what do we do?'

The response was unanimous. 'Refuse!'

The talk had resounded and grumbled for most the evening, not until full dark did the church begin to empty, the stars shining bright and clear in a frosted sky, the moon rising lazily over the horizon. On the morrow the King's Housecarls would be here, their entourage with their wagons and oak chests and great books of names and detailed information of house, trade and livestock, passing the night not more than ten miles distant in a moderately comfortable roadside inn. On the morrow Worcester had planned a welcome that they would not be expecting.

'Set the tables here,' Thorstein directed officiously, the moment he stalked into the church. The benches had been cleared to the side, trestle tables left for use by the King's officials. 'That one over there; they can enter at the main door, make their mark here under Feader's administration, pay their due here at my table and leave through that side door.' As he spoke, Thorstein unpinned his cloak but left it hanging from his shoulders, it was cold in here.

'You!' He pointed to a man slyly disappearing through the door at the rear that appeared to lead into the tower. 'Fetch us braziers; we wish to be warm, not have our balls frozen off.'

The man bowed meekly, hiding his expression. Aye, he would see that they were warmed right enough!

'So much for all the empty air these peasants ranted on about.' Feader laughed as he perched his backside on the one erected trestle and watched the men begin to unload the reams and piles of official documents. 'They run like frightened hares!' He lifted one of the scrolls, the names of men who held freehold property in the Hundred of Worcester, glanced at it. Turbrand, coppersmith. Edmund, brother of Edwine, potter. Osbern Fairbrow, fuller. Bored, he tossed it aside. He so disliked tax gathering. There was always trouble of some sort.

'Might be an idea to send for a barrel of ale,' he suggested, 'a few pasties alongside it?'

'You filled your belly not more an hour since, man! You worm riddled or something?' Thorstein tossed at him with a laugh. The door to the tower flung open with a crash that resounded and echoed throughout the church, men were running out, their boots clattering on the tiled floor, their voices yelling.

'What the Raven . . .?' No chance for Thorstein to say more; he drew his sword, heard Feader yell a stout warning, turned to parry the thrust of a hunting spear as four solid-built farming men came at him. There were more behind him, to the side, ahead. The church filled with armed, angry men intent on spilling blood. Feader was bellowing his rage as he swung with his axe, the group of eight King's Men with him fighting as hard and desperate, their breathing sharp in their chests, hearts hammering, sweat wet on their palms, throats dry. Concentrating on staying alive. Blood ran, limbs bloody and mashed, scattered the floor. Men fell, screaming, whimpering, the nave of Saint Mary ran thick with the sticky ooze and the stink of death.

Feader went down, his arm severed, bright blood frothing from the artery. Then Thorstein, fighting to the end, though his stomach was pierced through. They struck his head off from behind. He never saw the blow and, even if he had, would not have been able to stop it.

The carnage was intense, quickly over, savagely done. The men of Worcester said they would not pay the King's damned taxes and they were men of their word.

What would happen next, no one knew, but they were prepared to wait and find out; prepared, too, to fight again if necessary. And again, and again.

29

Edward was playing at threading cat's cradles round his fingers with a knotted stocking lace, a game he had enjoyed since childhood. He hummed to himself a hymn, as he twisted his lean fingers in and out of the braid, pausing occasionally to suck his cheek in concentration.

Emma was busy reading the book presented to her as finished. Her *Encomium*, the justification of her life and that of her son, Harthacnut. She was impressed. It was a delicate balance of prose, intertwined with the right amount of fact and detail. He had been clever, her chosen author, the monk and scholar Bovo of Saint Bertin's in Flanders, for he had skilfully managed to gloss over the facts that she had not wanted included. Despite the mention of her two sons, their father, Æthelred, was not referred to once. Nor were Cnut's indiscretions against the English. He was made to appear the hero, the benign Christian conqueror who had saved England from the wrath of God; the admired politician rather than the feared warrior.

She particularly admired the desperate scene of Alfred's arrest and murder, the letter, the one she had sent to Edward summoning him to Winchester, was posed as a forgery, written in her name. There were none to contest the lie. More than ever, the account of Cnut's death was essential, for Harthacnut, far away in Denmark, was daily becoming more unpopular. Barely anyone had spoken out and condemned that bloody and wicked murder of the King's housecarls in Worcester; few blamed the murderers, many quietly admired them. What Harthacnut would say and do about it when he returned was anyone's guess. And return he would, for he was expected within the week, sooner if the winds were favourable.

The frontispiece for the *Encomium* was particularly charming: a drawing, skilfully penned, showing herself enthroned, with her two sons, Harthacnut and Edward, standing beside her and Bovo kneeling at her feet presenting her with his work. She intended to recommend Bovo to Saint Bertin's as an ideal candidate for their new abbot. He deserved her patronage.

'Bother!' Edward dropped the link and the criss-cross pattern twined through his fingers fell apart.

The book was a political work, inaugurated by a highly motivated political woman who was determined, at all cost, to retain her place at the centre of politics. Emma ensured that she and her sons were depicted as an emulation of the trinity, their rule as a united maternal and fraternal power, intent on bringing peace, loyalty and honour to England. A pity that, in reality, Edward behaved like an infant and Harthacnut had no interest in the English Kingdom.

Edward had read it, but had refused to comment. Secretly, he was thrilled at being one of the central characters, but he harboured a grudge against his mother for her continuation of friendship with Earl Godwine. Edward had wanted the man stripped of his title for his part in Alfred's death, Emma had refused to allow it. True, she had not absolved him of any crime, but nor had she condemned him, publicly, privately or in her damned book. If anything, the Earl appeared on the pages as much the victim as Alfred and knowing how many of the passages were blatant lies, how could Edward believe otherwise of that particular part? He thought his mother vain for wanting the thing written, although he did admit that it was better done than the work of her father's life written by Dudo of Saint Quentin's.

'Do you think I might have a book made about my life, Mama?' he asked, liking the idea as he said it.

Emma did not look up from her reading. 'I doubt it, dear,' she said. 'You have to be a noble and loved king for that.'

Edward pouted. Who said he might not be that one day? Also irritating, this annoying habit of calling him dear, as if she were indulging an infant. If he could find the courage, he would demand that she ceased doing it. Huh, what was that sentence near the end of this wretched book? Aloud, he quoted, '*Qui fratris iussioni obaudiens Anglicas partes aduehitur et mater amboque filii regni paratis commodid nulla lite intercedente utuntur.*' Edward recited it perfectly.

Raising her eyes from the book, Emma stared at him, surprised. 'You have read it thoroughly, then?' she remarked. 'Or did you only take heed of the parts about yourself?' Edward scowled, he had not intended for her to know that he had any interest in the thing.

Edith, Earl Godwine's twelve-year-old daughter, was sitting to the far side of the chamber, playing *tæfl* with her elder brother Harold. To his chagrin, she was winning again. She was returning to Wilton soon after Easter and Emma had taken it upon herself to welcome the girl into her household for these few interim weeks of the Holy Festival. Edward's objection to Godwine did not extend to the family. Harold he admired; Edith was amusing.

Making her next move, Edith translated Edward's quote into English. 'Obeying his brother's command, Edward was conveyed to England, and the mother and both sons, having no disagreement between them, enjoyed the ready amenities of the kingdom.' She placed her piece, won the game. Smiled brightly at Emma. 'I think it is a beautiful book, Madam, there are passages that made my heart beat with fear and others where I wept.'

Edward scowled. He made little effort to use English, preferring Norman French, a more civilised tongue, he claimed. How his mother had the gall to sanction that phrase, *no disagreement*. Not a day sailed by without harsh words and bickering passing between them, and the rows that had occurred between his mother and Harthacnut before he had departed for Denmark had been spectacular. Still, he did admit to enjoying the available amenities here in England. The hunting was superb.

Harold was studying the board. The first game he had been lenient, had let his sister win, but not this second or third. 'As God is my witness, Edith, how you did that I do not know.' He stretched and pushed away from the table, shaking his head emphatically when she urged another match. 'No way, Miss – and have it four in a row? Leave me some pride, eh?'

'Edward, will you play?' Edith asked, beckoning him towards the table.

'Tæfl? I am not so good at that, I but I will happily play chess with you.'

Edith frowned, she was not so adept at chess, it was too slow a game for her liking. Edward usually spent so long over deciding his moves that Edith grew bored with it, and the Queen hated the game. She said she would prefer chess more if the piece depicting her rank could have more moves and not be such a weakling. As guest in her house, Edith did not like to offend Emma; then she had a tactful idea, brightened. 'Bovo taught me a new game; we play it on a slate with chalk, wait . . .' She ran to a small wooden box placed on a side table, rummaged in it and brought out the items she required, questioning with her eyes if she had permission to use them. Emma nodded assent.

'I will be seeing to my stallion,' Harold said, taking leave. 'The mud and wet that we have endured this winter has severely irritated a hind leg, it is quite sore.'

'Best not pick the scabs off,' Edward advised, 'that could make it worse. Keep the infected area dry, though. Use plenty of goose grease.'

Harold nodded, that was precisely what he was already doing. He bowed to Emma, who nodded, returned to her reading.

'See, Edward,' Edith said as he joined her at the table. 'I mark a grid like this, horizontal lines, crossed by two parallel.' The tip of her tongue stuck out slightly from the corner of her mouth as she concentrated on drawing four perfectly straight lines on the slate. 'Then we each take turns at play. I mark a circle and you place a cross. The idea is to block your opponent from gaining three of each symbol in a row.'

'Oh, that sounds easy,' Edward said eagerly.

'You go first, Sir.'

Boldly, Edward marked his cross in the top left square and gave the slate and chalk to Edith, who marked her circle in the bottom left. The slate passed back and forth, Edward frowning in concentration; then, delight spreading across his face, he yelled. 'Three crosses in a row! I win!'

'How did you do that?' Edith queried. 'I did not see that space!'

Emma glanced up as Edward cavorted triumphantly, saw Edith's smug smile. She was a clever one, this daughter of Godwine, had a brain in her head and used it. Very sensible to let Edward win.

The door opened, Harold hurried in, breathless, rain spattered on his hair and shoulders. 'Lady?' He crossed to the Queen quickly as, frowning, she half rose. 'Your son has arrived back in England.'

A flush of a smile darted across Emma's face, hastily stifled as Harold plunged on. 'Word has come that the King sailed direct for London and marched west without pause.' His colour was as white as the block of chalk Edward and Edith were using for their game. 'Lady, he has taken an army to Worcester.'

30

Harthacnut marched direct to Worcester-Shire the day after he arrived in London; no pause, no rest, he would not indulge in either until his friends and comrades were avenged for their bloody death. Earl Leofric, at Coventry, received orders, sent ahead by swift messenger, to meet his King with a gathered army at the hill of Oswald's Low, a suitable place to encamp and wait. Leofric balked at complying as long as he could, but had no option to disobey, resented having to punish his own people for something that they had been provoked into doing. How many of the King's earls had expected that something like this would happen? Had advised against that damned insulting tax? He would have to explain why he had not acted thus far to bring reprimand for a savage murder that had happened within his earldom, but he had his excuse for that. Harder would be his reason for taking a mere fifty men with him. He intended to claim that was all he could rouse at short notice, which he knew Harthacnut would not believe.

Oswald's Low was an ancient burial mound, a local landmark, to the south-east of Droitwich, from where Leofric's main source of personal income was acquired, aye, and for many another lord. The natural brine that welled up from the underground springs there were one of England's richest areas for inland salt production. From the complex of salt pans and furnaces, the industry radiated outwards by means of well-travelled routes, the Saltways, tracks and roads that had been in use from a time and time before the Roman Red Crests had come; from when the British had worshipped the sun and built their great circles of stone.

Harthacnut travelled quickly from London, using the broad way of Sealtstræt that led from Oxford towards the Vale of Evesham. He marched quickly, covering more than forty miles in one day, for the weather was mild and the roads easily passable, although outriders, going ahead, had a thankless task of moving the slower traffic out the way; the strings of pack ponies, laden with salt, the ox-carts labouring under the weight of the wagons, peddlers, travellers, traders. The salt drew them all.

Away to the west, the horizon was dominated by the prominent ridge of hills that bordered the Hwicce, the Welsh Border Shires that had once been a noble and glorious Anglo-Saxon kingdom. Cnut, during his reign, had amalgamated the Hwicce lands within the one great Earldom of Mercia, giving its ultimate command first to Eadric Streona and eventually to Leofric. Riding at the head of the vanguard, Harthacnut wondered whether that giving had been one of his father's unrealised mistakes, but then, Leofric had been a loyal man to Cnut. Not so to his legitimate son, it seemed.

The ancient rocks of that distant ridge reared above the flat of the Worcester-Shire plain. Beckoning them westward, the hills grew steadily nearer, hills that still bore the British name that had been given them before the English grandfathers of grandfathers had come from their Saxon lands over the sea to settle and farm the land. Malferna, the 'f' pronounced as in the Welsh tongue, as 'v', the Malvern Hills. Away to the right of the road the high, whale-backed hump of Bredon Hill. Harthacnut drew rein, camped for the night, content to sleep with his men, rolled in a blanket, curled beside the fire. On their way again by sunrise, over the higher land of White Hill, to Pershore Abbey in the Evesham Vale, where Harthacnut agreed to pause a while and allow the ponies and men to rest. A short indulgence, but necessary, for he had covered the miles faster than he had anticipated and preferred to rest in comfort within an abbey rather than wait, kicking his heels, at Oswald's Low with nothing more than densely forested trees and a handful of shabby farmsteadings.

The Abbot served him well, but uneasily. There was no need to ask the purpose of the visit, not with an accompaniment of more than four hundred men, all of them the King's permanent army of housecarls, full armed and clad in chain-mail armour. He provided a sufficient table to his King, although it was Lent and limited to fish and plain fare.

'I notice more than several cattle and sheep lay dead in the meadows,' Harthacnut commented as he explored the contents of a pie, discovered the filling to be lamprey. 'Many others appear ill, with sores to their mouths and udders, lame too. Be there a problem?'

The Abbot shook his head sorrowfully. 'Alas, Sir, it is a plague that affects the cloven-hoofed creatures. Swine and deer, as well as sheep and cattle. It starts with blisters to the mouth, oft-times, within days the animal is dead. Carcasses that have been butchered show the blistering to have spread down the gullet and into the stomach.' He shook his head again; in whatever form, plagues were always a sorry thing. 'Like any pestilence that affects man, this one travels, spread on the spit of the Devil's own, who dance on the dead one night and tread with the healthy the next.'

'In my eye, then, it is foolish to leave the dead lying where they fall, Abbot. See to it that the wretched creatures are butchered more speedily.'

'But Sir, there are too many to deal with; they die quicker than they can be used – most the villages within a day's walking of here, those spread along the Saltways, have lost their entire herds of livestock. It is a calamity to equal any flood or tempest that destroys the harvest. The lambs being born in the fields are dead within the week. There will be no calves born later this year, no meat to eat, no milk to drink. No wool, no swine. All we will have is an excess of leather and render.'

Harthacnut frowned, concern beginning to register that this was no small and local problem. 'You have lost the abbey's stock? I noticed your fields are empty of grazers. I assumed the land was lying fallow.'

'We have one cow and five sheep left. Nothing more, all else is dead.' The Abbot rested his head in his hands, close to despair. 'What we are to do to survive the next winter I know not . . .' And he had to say it; for the sake of his soul and his conscience could not, any longer, hold the words back, for the death of farm stock was too awful a thing to choke back words that had to be released. 'Already the Shire is bereft, for it was hard to raise the tax you demanded. Forgive me for saying it, Sir, but there will be many a family unable to replace their beasts who will starve. We are left with nothing.'

Harthacnut grimaced displeasure. 'I hear your words, Abbot, but the Shire has a debt to pay.' Added grimly, 'And a plague among cattle shall not reprieve those who have murdered or who harbour murderers of that due debt.'

The Abbot lowered his head, picked at his food. Said no more.

At the Salt Brook, the Salter's Spring, they watered the ponies, then pressed on. Leofric, awaiting them, rode out to meet his King, the excuse he needed for having so few men ready on his lips.

'I have not the men I would wish for, Sir, for there is plague among the farm stock. I could not take men away from the disposal of so many carcasses.'

'This cattle plague affects you in Coventry, too, then?' Harthacnut asked, taken aback. 'Is it so widespread?'

Leofric nodded. 'Alas, aye, it is, my Lord King. The disease affects both foot and mouth of the creatures. All we can do is watch our animals die, or cut their throats to ease the suffering.'

'And there is nothing that can be done?' What was the use of being King if you could not find answers to problems? But then, as his father had once discovered, he was only a mortal man, some things were for the Heavenly King of all Kings alone.

The Earl mournfully shook his head. 'No, Sir, there is nothing we can do, although there are a few farmsteaders who are not allowing any man or beast to enter through their gate; but the Devil spreads his evil by wing and wind, roping gates closed is no answer. All we can do is pray for God's mercy and sprinkle Holy Water throughout our byres.'

If Leofric was hoping to soften his King's heart he failed. The death of his two most favoured and cherished housecarls, Thorstein and Feader, had angered and sickened him, and while a plague was to be feared, the healing of that was for the monks and priests to sort. He was here to deal with the breaking of the law, to show that bloody murder was not to be tolerated. Had someone done

840

something about it before now, his anger might have been assuaged somewhat, but as it was, no one cared, no one had bothered. The lack of justice seen to be done was as a sore that had not healed, a slight against the command of the King. He would have vengeance for his friends and obedience towards himself.

'Perhaps', Harthacnut remarked drily, as he prepared to give the order for the combined army to move out, 'this plague among the stock is sent by God as punishment? I doubt He is no more pleased than I over murder committed within the sanctity of His House.'

Leofric rode at his King's side, said nothing. That thought had occurred to him, too. He ought to have done something to reprimand the Shire of Worcester 'ere now but Edward, as Regent, had wiped his hands of any order for retribution, saying that the murdered were not his men but Harthacnut's. Aside, it would have been nigh on impossible to have discovered those who were guilty of the crime and to hang innocent men on top of the demand for excessive tax went against sense. Already the rumbling talk of rebellion was rearing its ugly head, spreading on the most part form the North, for Eadwulf was not a man who kept his grumblings to himself.

No, if Harthacnut wished to set the torch into the dried furze, that was for him to do; Leofric would not be holding the blame for igniting England into war.

There were few killed, a handful of dead only, for Worcester had been warned of the King's coming and the folk had fled to the island of Bevere in the River Severn, admirably able to defend themselves within their makeshift fortress. Harthacnut could not afford the time to lay siege and contented himself with bringing a more effective suffering. He burnt Worcester to the ground, firing all buildings, houses, shops, barns, all except God's churches were destroyed, the pall of smoke hanging like a cloud unwilling to move on. He then harried the Shire; for five days, the sky glowing orange at night. Without mercy, he ordered the killing of anything that lived, horses, dogs, fowl; sheep, cattle, goats and pigs, all that had escaped the blisters of the plague. By necessity he must be back at

841

Oxford for the Easter calling of Council, but he was satisfied that justice had been done.

He rode slower for the return journey, not so much need for haste, and the burst of blood rush that had accompanied the necessary punishment had tired him. He tired so easy these days, had noticed it shortly after Yule, assuming the fatigue and the thundering headaches were the result of excessive merrymaking and the wayward indulgence of feasting and drinking. But why so tired now? He would feel better once he reached Oxford and found opportunity to rest. The sword slash to his left thigh, a minor wound, nothing of importance, would heal faster there, too, once he was out of the saddle.

Although he could not know it, the order to slaughter all the livestock had halted the spread of the cattle plague from rampaging further south on into Wales, but for himself even in Oxford his wound proved damnably slow to mend, the pain and irritation niggling like an itch beyond reach of scratching.

31

Eadwulf, Earl of Bernicia, returned to his family home, the seaward fortress of Bamburgh, enraged and full of venom. All the journey north from Oxford he had cursed the name of the man he was forced to call King. King? Him? More a passed turd than a man! Eadwulf had hated that slut, Ælfgifu, loathed her by-blown son, but at least they had known how to try to win a man. Their praise might have been hollow, might have been padded with honeyed words and purses of gold, but at least there had been praise!

'He did rant on and on about Worcester,' he complained over again, to his long-suffering wife. 'It was all he was interested in and by God, if he had mentioned that slash to his leg the once more I would have drawn my sword and hacked the sodding thing off to put an end to his misery. Men carry the discomfort of their wounds in silence; least, a warrior does. Him? A warrior? By the Raven, my worst breeding sow could fight better than him!'

'The Council did not go well, then?' his wife ventured, instantly regretting the question.

'No, it did not! He was not interested in the North. I tried, *Guds skyld* how I tried, to inform him in detail of my plan to campaign in Scotland. Do you know what he said? He said he had not the finances to pay for needless skirmishes with Scotland! His exact words, needless skirmishes!'

Sigrida poured her husband strong ale, a special brew she made with malted barley; it put fire in his heart and often, thankfully, sent him to sleep.

'I have fought and beat the Scots, have sent them running with their backsides white to the sky, yet do I get praise? Do I get reward? Do I be damned!'

He drank the tankard down in one gulp, gestured for another. 'If he dares offer me some sop of an apology, once he realises Scotland must be kept under firm rein, I'll not be accepting it. I'll not play the fool for him. I had no liking for making him King and Siward agreed with me, the turn-face. The whole bloody lot of them make me sick. If he orders me to secure the Borders, I'll tell him where to stuff his security. To his face if need be, aye, to his very face!'

Harthacnut was having a similar conversation with his Earl of Deira. Siward, at Harthacnut's private request, had remained behind at Council, only discovering its reason after his rival. Eadwulf, had left for the North. And he was a rival. As kin to the man Uhtred and the great families of kings from the North, Eadwulf was having ideas above his place in the hierarchy of the King's nobles. Siward was the higher Earl, not Eadwulf, and he liked it not that the man was attempting to reverse the role.

'What do you think about the situation with Scotland?' Harthacnut asked him, inviting the Earl to sit, pour wine. They were alone in the King's chamber, not even servants in attendance.

'Scotland can be a volatile mix,' Siward said cautiously, aware that not many months before, Harthacnut had shown no interest in Scotland. 'At the moment it lies quiet, but who knows what storm may blow on the morrow? Macbeth is well entrenched, but he is not secure. It would only take someone with guts and determination to overthrow him. His wife is not liked.' Alluding to Ælfgifu, added, 'We ourselves, here in England, know what it is to have such a woman behind the throne.' He held his breath. Was Harthacnut to consider attacking Scotland, then? Damn him if he was, for it was too late to strike now; had he listened those months ago . . .

'It is not Scotland that concerns me,' Harthacnut said, pouring his own wine and sampling its taste. 'It is Eadwulf.'

Ah.

'You do not care for him?'

'No, my Lord, I do not. He is not the man Uhtred was. He was a man of honour and skill; Eadwulf is a braggart who thinks the world owes him a favour because his distant kindred once wore a crown.'

For a while Harthacnut turned the subject to other matters,

unimportant issues and conversation. Then said what he had been aiming for all along. 'I do not like my earls to disagree with me.' He held his hand to stem an answer. 'Do not get me wrong. I do not object to criticism and I am well aware that it is Council's duty to advise where need be, even if that advice runs against my opinion. It is sheer bloody-mindedness that I will not tolerate or allow.' Harthacnut leant forward, refilled Earl Siward's goblet, the red wine glugging from its jar. 'Deira is a comfortable earldom,' he said, looking at the wine as he poured, not at Siward. 'It is in my mind, however, that it was the better earldom when it was amalgamated with Bernicia. Northumbria as a whole, I think, would be a more efficient earldom to govern.'

Siward raised his goblet, saluted. Drank. Said not a word.

32

As the sun blazed high, Eadwulf, Earl of Bernicia, sailed into York. There was a brief flurry of courtesy at the wharfside, but Siward had sent only ten men as escort, as York, on its main market day, was a busy place without having to accommodate the arrival of a disliked lord. To further annoy him Eadwulf found that he had to walk from the river to Siward's manor. It was not a long nor difficult route, but he thought it beneath his dignity to be forced to go on foot.

'No guard of honour? No ponies? Do you not recognise me as a man of nobility then, Siward?' he grumbled before even the formalities had begun. 'I would have offered more respect to a Scotsman than you have to me.'

Siward ignored the contempt, held his guest by the shoulders, kissed both his cheeks. Steadfastly ignored the reference to the Scots, thankful that his nephew, Malcolm, was too young to understand the intended slur.

'I sent no guard, my friend, deliberately,' he countered jovially. 'What? And have you think I had reneged on my word of safe conduct?' Siward guided Eadwulf into his home, a large and extravagant complex of buildings gathered beside the Minster, that itself stood out, high and proud, like a dragon craft amid a flotilla of coracles. 'I gave my word, Eadwulf, that until the King comes himself, you will be secure here in York.'

Eadwulf growled beneath his breath, helped himself to a generous tankard of ale. 'And what of after? Eh? What of after the King has come? Shall I remain safe then?'

Siward laughed, gestured for the Earl to sit, commanded food be brought.

'That is for you and Harthacnut to decide, Eadwulf, not me. The King is to return to Denmark come the September month. I believe he wishes to leave England secure and prospering.' Siward glanced around, ensuring no one was listening, leant forward, whispered, 'I believe he has lost all faith in that turnip-head of a brother. Edward is useless for England, but the King is reluctant to allow too much power to fall into Godwine's hands.'

Eadwulf also leant forward. 'So he is looking to the North?'

Siward nodded once, briefly, imperceptibly.

Settling into his chair, Eadwulf was satisfied. About bloody time that someone recognised his ability and worth.

Annoyed to discover that his quarters were to the far side of the complex of buildings, not close to the main Hall, the churlish mood later returned. 'I am Earl of Bernicia,' he growled, 'I have a right to a main chamber.'

Earl Siward's steward had sufficient answer, however. 'The Earl thought it might be rowdy close to the centre. Unlike yourself, the men of York are not men of learning and tend to favour horseplay after supping and drinking. It is quieter in this corner, more private. My Lord has a chamber along here also, which he uses when he is not required to be closer to his Hall.'

Eadwulf nodded reluctant approval, ducked inside the room and met with ten men, Siward's men, who ensured that he would not be coming out again.

Harthacnut sailed direct to Denmark, had never intended to break his journey at York. There was no need; the North was safe in the hands of one man, the new Earl of Northumbria, who agreed with his King that it was worthless to deal with those who always saw the rain, never the rainbow. But then, neither of them, King nor Earl, thought to look beyond the rainbow at the clouds that swept, black and ominous, into a storm sky.

With Eadwulf's murder, the blood-feud that had raged between the families of the North was perpetrated and Harthacnut's reign was further tarnished by blood. Men of England, particularly those of the Church who wrote the *Chronicles* of these things, began to wonder whether he would ever do anything worthy of a king.

33

'You are not well. It would be foolish to attend this wedding feast as you are.'

'Oh, Mother,' Harthacnut complained, weary of the same argument. 'I am a man grown, I am perfectly able to take care of myself. I have a headache, that is all.'

'You are thin, your face is pale.' Emma walked close to her son and sniffed his breath. 'Your guts smell foul.'

'Why thank you, Mama, it is always splendid to hear such compliments tripping from your lips!'

Emma flounced away, irritated, began to rummage through her clothes chest with her handmaid, finding something suitable to wear for the afternoon of celebration.

'Well, if you must go to Tovi's wedding, then I shall not stop you, though Edward and I between us could easily represent you.'

'And have everyone wondering why I cannot be there? I think not, Mother!'

Emma dropped the austerity as she held a red gown to her for effect. No, too brash. The blue perhaps? 'It is only that I care for you, my dear, that I worry for your health.'

Harthacnut relented, *ja*, he knew that.

His relationship with his mother had improved through the last year, possibly because he had been in Denmark for most of it. A good way of doing things, spending the summers here in England, the winters in Denmark. It was colder there, admitted, darker during that part of the year, but England was so damp; he would rather have six months of snow than the incessant drizzle of rain. His mother ruled England well during those months of his departure, hindered more than aided by Edward, who regarded the hunting of deer, hawking and attending Mass as more important than making legal judgement, signing charters and all the myriad of necessary government duties that were tedious but essential.

He would make a hopeless king, yet who else was there to follow on?

Emma had returned to stand in front of her son, was straightening the crooked fold of his tunic. As if reading his thoughts – mayhap she had, he tended to frown whenever he thought of Edward – she said, 'Is it not time we sought out a wife for you? Tovi has made a good choice in Algytha, the third-born daughter of your fleet commander. Can we not find someone as pretty and equally intelligent?'

Harthacnut smiled at her, brushed her hands from fiddling with the appearance of his clothing 'One day, Mama. I will think on it.'

'What if we send an envoy to Kiev? An alliance with the Rus would be to our advantage. Or alternatively Spain or Italy? There are enough Northmen settled there to farm a whole host of wives. Alliance with any one of those great lords who have control over the eastern trade routes would have benefit to us. Think of the riches to be had in the trade of spices.'

'No, Mother, I am not ready for marriage.' Already, Harthacnut was beginning to regret this marriage of his friend and occasional mentor, Tovi, called the Proud. Always when someone they knew became wed, he went through this same routine with his mother.

Emma uncharacteristically stamped her foot. She more often displayed her temper by word of mouth, not action. 'This is not about whether you are ready or not, boy! This is about securing the succession! You need a son to follow you, several sons, and unless you start breeding soon you will be getting dangerously close to leaving a decision to God!'

'And is He not trustworthy in deciding, then?' Harthacnut quipped, knowing his flippancy would annoy her more, but might divert her to a different subject.

'No, He is not!' Emma declared, ignoring the sharp intake of breath from her handmaid at the blasphemy. 'Not where the matter of my crown is concerned. I trusted Him once before, and look where it got me!'

'Here in England, with the crown perched high on your head, Mother, and with two sons running to your every beck and call. Why not pester Edward to produce grandsons for you? He is, after all, not as busy as I am. I am sure, if he were to tear himself away from his hounds, he could find a spare moment to service a wife.'

'Don't be absurd,' Emma snapped back.

Harthacnut laughed. 'No, I suppose you are right, Edward would not know which part of a woman he was to serve. He thinks all women were born to be nuns and all men monks! A damn fine king he will make when I am gone!'

Emma drew in her breath in a sharp gasp of alarm. 'Do not say that!' She crossed herself; as an afterthought did it again and muttered a liturgy against the sin of her blasphemy. 'I meant, do not be absurd about Edward being King. He has no head for government. Unlike you, he has not been trained for it.'

Walking across the room to select a handful of early gathered wild strawberries from a dish, Harthacnut leant close to Emma, whispered, 'And whose fault was that? Not mine. It was not I who left him so long unattended in Normandy.'

Pouting, Emma whisked away to find a more suitable gown to wear for this wretched afternoon's event. She did not like weddings: all the false frivolity, the pretence of shared happiness, of wishing good fortune, with all the while, everyone drinking too much ale and wine, eating too much and envying either bride or groom, depending on who held the more wealth. The boasting father, the simpering mother. The reason for her cantankerous mood, of course, was that weddings brought to the surface her own memories. Her marriage in the Cathedral of Canterbury to a man she had instantly loathed on sight; then the second wedding, to Cnut, when he had summoned her from the nunnery in Winchester and led her to the steps of the Minster there, pledged his vows, his hand holding tight to hers, his blue eyes dancing with a happiness and pride that radiated from his very soul. She had loved Cnut. Loved him still, would never cease loving him.

'What if I cannot have children?' Harthacnut suddenly said,

looking up at her from across the table, his eyes so reminiscent of his father's.

'There you go being absurd again,' she huffed. 'Of course you will have sons, you are the King.'

'Yet I have had none yet.'

'You have not, yet, a wife.'

'The one, Mother, does not necessarily need the other.'

Emma chose to ignore his bland statement. 'If we are to go to this damnable festivity this afternoon, then get you gone from my chamber and dress yourself as befits a king. I do not know what you have done with that tunic, but it is as ragged as a bear-pit attendant's.'

Suddenly feeling a great sweep of affection for her, Harthacnut crossed the room and placed a kiss on her cheek. 'I know you have my well-being at heart, Mama, but there is nothing I can do to alter what God has decided for me.'

She smiled, laid her hand against his cheek. He was growing a beard, a fuzz of blond fluff sprouting from his chin. 'You can do whatever you want, Harthacnut; you are the King.'

He did not argue. What was the point? She would never listen to reasoned argument, not once her mind was set.

For her part Emma was genuinely worried for Harthacnut's health. He was thin, yet he ate well; tired easily, though he slept reasonable hours. She had noticed that he visited the privy more than other men, but mayhap that was because he often had a thirst – yet the days were hot, she herself had emptied the wine flagon of its watered grape once already this morning, of course he would chase a thirst.

'The mustard-yellow and the green, I think,' she said to her maid, 'the colours suits me. And I shall wear those new shoes. They are not yet comfortable, but must be broken in some time if ever I am to wear them at all.'

34

7 June 1042 – Lambeth, south of the River Thames
Was all of London invited? There were so many guests in Tovi's
Hall that Emma could not help thinking it was as well he was a man
of wealth – a smaller building and they would be packed like salted
herrings in a barrel. Thankfully, the day had cooled with the onset
of evening and if it were not for the irritation of the midges, she
might have preferred to be outside where most of the younger guests
were gathered. They were dancing on the grass that had, earlier,
been an immaculate part of Tovi's lovingly tended garden, the slope
down to the river not quite inconveniencing the more daring
couples as they whirled and leapt to the beat of the drummers and
the trill of flute and lute.

Harthacnut came in, his arm draped across the shoulders of the
bride's father, Osgod Clapa, a good man, though one who on
occasion spoke his mind a little too close to the wind. Harthacnut
trusted him implicitly, however, as had Cnut before him, but then
they had both been men of the sea and it took a sailor to recognise
a sailor. Edward, on the other hand, detested the man and secretly
Emma suspected it was because of a similar reason to her own
mistrust of him, for the opposite reason as Harthacnut's deep
friendship. A dislike of ships and the sea. Edward had never said as
much, but Emma had noticed he was always ready with an excuse if
stepping on board a boat was required.

Harthacnut was drunk, but then, who was not? He waved to her,
indicating that he had come in for another tankard of beer. Tovi's
best, brewed with hops and barley, potent stuff. A pile of men were
already slumped, snoring, against the far wall, their womenfolk
disdainfully ignoring them.

'I am proud of my son,' Emma said to Godwine, seated beside her.
He too had come within doors to escape the midges and to catch his

breath. Circling and stamping at a fast pace might suit the younger ones, but he had not the breath or stamina for it.

'Rightfully so, my lady,' Godwine answered, 'he has the making of a fine king, provided he remembers to listen and learn from those who know better.' He looked at her with a steady, solemn face, then suddenly winked and laughed. 'But then, how many sons care to listen to their mothers these days?'

Emma accepted the compliment by raising her goblet and saluting him. She would never wholly trust Godwine again, but had forgiven him. She needed friends and with the majority of those at Court wanting only to better themselves, whatever it took to do so, real friends, who did not take without giving, were a blessing. There were only a few she could count as such, could count them on the fingers of one hand, and all, save for Godwine, were dead. Pallig, his wife Gunnhilda, Leofgifu and Cnut, and now Leofstan, gone to God in his sleep two months past. Five beloved people whom she would cherish unto her grave. Did she cherish Godwine? No, but she was fond of him well enough for it not to matter.

Harthacnut yelled a bray of laughter, spluttering beer from his mouth at the lewdness of the jest Osgod had just recounted to those gathered around the beer barrels. Harthacnut had many friends. Emma supposed it was easier for men; they could form relationships without implication or innuendo.

He had made a shaky start, that business of raising the tax had been a sorry one and was best forgotten, aye, and Eadwulf's murder at Siward's hand, but had Cnut begun his reign any differently? Crews had to be paid, traitors and troublemakers had to be removed.

Another great shout of laughter. Emma glanced across at the rowdy group, saw that Harthacnut was dancing some odd jig of his own making, that his friends were standing about him, clapping, jeering at his foolery, laughing.

And then the laughing stopped. Harthacnut was sliding to the floor. A woman screamed. Was it Emma? After, she never could remember the series of events, who said and did what. She recalled running, dropping her goblet to the floor, hitching her gown high and tearing across the rush-strewn floor to her son, who lay at the centre of a circle of suddenly sober men, his limbs twitching and jerking, bloodied froth foaming from his mouth, urine and faeces seeping through his breeches.

Curiously, the dancing went on outside, the merrymaking, the celebration, for none out there knew what was happening in Tovi's great and grand Hall.

Edward had been dancing with them, the only time he did not mind the close proximity of women, for he loved the gaiety of holiday, the chance to prance and preen. His thirst, like so many others beforehand, drove him inside. He stepped into the Hall, stood a moment for his eyes to adjust. It was quiet inside, people spoke in whispers, were gathered at the far end. Some women were clinging to their husbands' arms; some, men and women, were kneeling in prayer.

A man rushed past: Godwine's son Harold, running, moving quickly, his face ash-pale. 'I must fetch a priest,' he cried to Edward, seizing his arm and giving him a shake, as if it were he who was frozen into stillness within the tableau. 'It is your brother, he has suffered a seizure. My God, Edward, your brother. I think he is dead!'

35

Emma stood alone beside the tomb within the Old Minster of Winchester where kings were buried, her veil pulled close around her face. Though there were none to see, she would not have anyone witness her weeping. She had seen three and fifty years of life and what had she to show for it? A heart heavy from misery, eyes red from tears and a stone tomb that contained all she had cared to live for.

Yesterday they had laid Harthacnut beside his father, and one day the tomb would be opened again for her to rest there also. If only she could, she would lift that slab and lie down with them now. What use was the rest of her life if lived alone, without them?

She brushed at a tear that was wandering down her cheek. What had it all been for? Of what use? To what purpose? All she had done and tried to do come so suddenly to nothing. What wasted effort.

Harthacnut had lived the day around after the convulsions had racked through him, but Emma's youngest son did not wake or speak again. They said his soul had already left his body, that it was only the shell draining of life that remained. He had already gone to God and his earthly father, who were waiting for him in Heaven. He had been King two years wanting ten days. So short a span of time in so short and unfulfilled a life.

England would march on, to a tune played on a different drum. One played by Edward. He could do that, play tunes, make songs, dance, but could he reign as king? She was not yet old or ailing, had the full use of her mind and her body, but could she rule as Queen and guide him? She would have to, there would be no hope for England if she did not. Edward had Godwine, it was true, and his sons. Harold, if not the eldest son Swegn, was sensible. They would make good earls, Godwine's sons.

Ah, she was so tired and she did so dislike Edward, for he conjured nothing that was good or loving from her past. She had her memories, they said, meaning to help her in their kindly way. Those you love may live and die, but they leave behind their shadows to walk, always, with you in the form of memories.

Decisively, Emma turned away from the tomb, walked through the empty hollow of the Minster, her boots tapping and echoing on the coloured tiles of the floor, the sunlight streaming through the windows, making the dust motes skitter and twirl as she passed by. No one had, yet, managed to take away her crown, nor would they, not until God called her to join the man, and the son, she had loved in life. But they, she, must wait for that meeting, for she must forget the past and see to the well-being of the future. While she lived it was her duty to do so, for she was Emma Ælfgifu, the anointed crowned Queen of Saxon England.

She paused, placed her hand on the supporting solidity of a pillar, closed her eyes, choked back tears. Memories. When you had nothing, no one to love, no one worth enduring for, what comfort was there in trundling out old memories? Memories that would be best shut away and forgotten. How did memories make an incompetent into a king? Help a tired, disappointed woman rekindle the strength that had sapped from her bones with the death of a beloved son? A son who had not seen many more than twenty, short, years of life.

She sighed, wiped at her wet cheeks, removing private sorrow from public view. Shut the memories away with the abandoned hopes and dreams. She would start afresh. She had done so before, could do so again. But with Edward? With that fool, Edward? Huh! Life turned full circle!

Drawing in her breath, she stepped through the door out into the sunlight. Memories? When you had nothing left, what good were damned, useless memories?

Author's Note

As with most kings or queens of Anglo-Saxon England, the documented life of Emma is sparse on detail, little more than a framework of basic fact – yet her CV is a rainbow of colour as intricate, and almost as controversial, as that of the later more famous (and more documented) Queen, Eleanor of Aquitaine.

Of Norman birth, Emma was a link between England and Normandy, a link which eventually led to the conquest of England in 1066 by her great-nephew, Duke William. She was wife, and queen, to both Æthelred II (the Unready) and the Dane, Cnut, and the mother of two more kings: Harthacnut and Edward (the Confessor). She was involved in political intrigue, fled into exile twice, was implicated in the murder of her son, Alfred, and was, later in her life, accused of treason by Edward who, soon after becoming King, confiscated her wealth and property. Conjecture and interpretation surrounds any analogy of Emma, but was her position in England that of a pawn, used as a bargaining power for the making of treaties and the gaining of crowns, or was she a queen in her own right, commanding the political power to rule as regent during Cnut's absences? We shall never know the truth of it, although I see her as something in between. Undoubtedly she wielded power during the short reign of her son Harthacnut, gaining her feel of managing a kingdom during the long periods when Cnut was abroad. There is some discrepancy as to where Emma was when Cnut summoned her to be his wife, in London or Normandy. Cnut would have sought Duke Richard II's permission to marry her, but beyond propriety there is very little evidence to show that she had fled, at that time, to Normandy. Indeed, it does not make logical sense that she had, for once out of England it would have been almost impossible for her to hang on to what she had got – England and her crown. The cross that Cnut and Emma presented to the Minster at Winchester is fact, but it was not necessarily given at their marriage.

Emma was the first English queen (to our knowledge) to have her biography written. She produced it as an act of political manipulation to accompany her son, Harthacnut, in his claim to the English throne – Early Medieval spindoctoring! The *Encomium Emmæ Reginæ* is a narrative that deals with her marriage to Cnut and the glory of his reign. She is obliged to mention her two sons, Edward and Alfred, but skilfully manages to conceal totally her fourteen-year marriage to their father, Æthelred, and the fact that Cnut was originally nothing more than a foreign invader.

Prior to marrying Emma, Æthelred had at least ten children by either one or two concubine wives. We know, in comparative detail, what happened to Athelstan, Edmund and four sisters, but others are mere shadows in history. Because there are so many characters involved in *A Hollow Crown*, by necessity I have had to abandon those who would, at best, have enjoyed only a brief walk-on part. All we know of one son, Edgar, for instance, is that he was at Ely and exiled or killed by Cnut. He has had, therefore, to remain in obscurity as far as my novel is concerned.

It is certain that Athelstan quarrelled with his father, for we have him seeking Æthelred's forgiveness in his will. Edmund 'Ironside' also quarrelled with Æthelred, for after the murder of Sigeferth and Morcar, he did indeed rescue Sigeferth's wife from the nunnery and marry her, thus gaining her dead husband's estate and the loyalty of the North, but I met with a puzzle when it came to her. Ealdgyth is recorded by the *Anglo-Saxon Chronicle* as Morcar's wife, yet Edmund married *Sigeferth's* widow – so why was she not the one to be named? Was there an error? Were they both called Ealdgyth, perhaps? On matters such as this, imagination and interpretation win the day. I therefore used the name for Sigeferth's wife.

Personal names have proven to be a difficulty for there seems to have been a limited cache of ideas for parents of Anglo-Saxon children to choose from. Technically, Emma was known as Ælfgifu, a more English name than the Norman Imma or Emma, but she appears to have referred to herself privately as Emma, and as there are other characters in this story named Ælfgifu I have kept to 'Emma' throughout. As for all the variations of Swein . . .!

England was a wealthy and well-organised kingdom, particularly where the collection of taxes was concerned. Despite the almost annual increase in the Viking demand of the payment of heregeld (only called Danegeld *after* 1066) the money was always quickly and efficiently raised. One way of getting the cash, as duly recorded in an Anglo-Saxon charter, was through the selling of land to any interested party of whatever nationality. Æthelred's failure as a king was through widespread corruption and his inability to lead with deliberation. Misdemeanours were punished by the forfeiture of land, and it was all too easy for Æthelred and his appointed officials to fabricate or exaggerate crimes, seize land and sell it on for a fat profit.

A contemporary source complains that the organisation of the fyrd (the army) was abysmal. The English were never in the same place, at the same time, as the Danish. Edmund was to prove that, with skill and determination, it *was* possible to be an effective leader and to drive the invaders back, that the Vikings were not invincible. Had Eadric Streona not turned tail and run, and had Edmund not been mortally wounded at Ashingdon, he might well have succeeded in defeating Cnut. Another of those snatches of history when everything of the future could have changed. The location of that battle is not certain, there are other contenders, but I have chosen the site on the River Crouch in Essex, purely for the reason that it is the nearest to where I live.

Most of my characters existed, although beyond the simple recording as a written name on various charters, wills and documents, we know only bare facts about them. Pallig was real, and has been recorded as a traitor who went over to the Vikings and was possibly the husband of Swein Forkbeard's sister. I needed a dashing, heroic type to be a friend and guide for Emma, and Pallig fitted nicely, so truth regarding him and Gunnhilda in the real structure of things may not be accurate, but after all, this *is* a novel! Hugh was the name of Emma's Exeter reeve, although I have invented de Varaville; Leofstan was recorded as Emma's man in her will, as was a nephew of the woman Leofgifu, who had served for many years. Eadric Streona was the scapegoat for Æthelred's ineptitude. He may not have been as bad as the *Chronicles* painted him, but every novel must have its villain, so Eadric remains typecast. Surnames in Anglo-Saxon England did not exist. Second names were descriptive terms as in Thorkell *Havi*, the Tall, or as 'son of' – Godwine *Wulfnothsson*. 'Streona' means acquisitor and may not have been used until after Eadric's death, as also is the case of Æthelred 'the Unready', *Unraed* is a play on his name, meaning 'ill-counselled', and he was not necessarily called this during his lifetime, but it was certainly used very soon after. Leofric's wife, Godgiva, later became acclaimed in legend as Lady Godiva; however, there is no authenticity to her riding naked through the streets of Coventry in protest at high taxes, although the high taxes themselves certainly were an issue. Godwine's remark is the nearest I will come to that particular tale.

The dates I have used have sometimes been arbitrary as the *Chronicles* so often record different versions and dates for the same episode, and confuse ranks, titles and names as well as time and place. For instance, in one version Ulfkell is referred to as ealdorman, in another document he is not. Where I have used exact dates, e.g. 7 June 1042, these were as they were recorded, but for various deaths when only the date and place are known, I have made up the reason or the doing. We know that Cnut passed away while at Shaftesbury, that Harold Harefoot died suddenly and that Harthacnut fell to the floor in a fit after imbibing too much ale at a Lambeth wedding, and died on the 8 June 1042. For Harthacnut, my use of the symptoms of diabetes seemed a logical assumption for a cause.

For a few minor things of interest: siege warfare at this time was not very sophisticated; later sagas depict Swein Forkbeard as using mangonels, but these were written in the twelfth century and cannot be regarded as authentic. The blood-feud between Uhtred and Thurband is well documented; it continued into William's time and was an important element in northern politics. Unfortunately there was not the space to use this tragic and complex side of human nature in more depth here.

There is no surviving record for the year 989 and so there is no mention in any English chronicle of the appearance of Halley's Comet; however, it was well recorded in France and across Europe; unless England had three entire months of bad weather (not impossible!) it would have been seen. The Comet next appeared in 1066 as a portent of doom. One comment forwarded to me from a reader of my previous books was that I mention the weather quite often. A very British trait, I'm afraid, possibly because our climate is so changeable. Weather was very relevant to the early years of the first millennium, when several instances of famine and flood were recorded. I have included the desperate plague that affected the beasts and, having recently witnessed the awful devastation of foot and mouth disease, I have used this as the cause of one of them.

Edward presented the birthing girdle used by Emma, said to have belonged to the Virgin Mary, to Westminster Abbey. Supposedly, it was subsequently used by other royal English mothers.

The dictate of a nationwide religious Mass lasting several days is authentic, even down to slaves being given time off to participate. It is interesting that human nature does not change; the first millennium brought fear of the wrath of God, the second the wrath of the computer. Whether the people of the Lake District actually gathered at Grasmere to climb Helm Crag is conjecture. The story of King Dunmail is local legend and, while climbing the Crag during a downpour, I saw those three astonishingly beautiful rainbows arcing across the Raise below Helvellyn. No bore tide rides up the Thames now, but it did in Anglo-Saxon times. I have borrowed the details from other similar tides.

I must add a note on a few of the Anglo-Saxon terms: *ealdorman* was a Saxon title, which became *jarl*, corrupted into the English equivalent of *earl*, under Cnut. *Housecarl*, or personal bodyguard, is also a Danish term. Trade reeves – what we would now call customs and excise men – were technically known as *port reeves* in early Saxon, 'port' meaning trading place, which was not necessarily a sea harbour, hence my use of trade reeve to avoid modern confusion.

Æthelred was, on the whole, responsible for the shiring of England, it is from *Shire Reeve*, the man appointed to keep order in the Shire, that we get the later Norman title of *sheriff*. Much of Æthelred's law-making still survives as a basis of modern law, as does Cnut's. Both men implemented practical means through which the legal order of the realm could be secured. Æthelred's agreement to be a better king when he returned from exile in Normandy was the first recorded pact between a government and a king. The very early beginnings of democracy.

Emma is the only woman to have been an anointed, crowned and reigning queen to two different kings, yet she is barely known in history. I find it very frustrating that the rich, varied and wonderful culture of England pre 1066 has so casually been swept aside by those who wrote of and recorded the post-1066 kings. Particularly during the Victorian era, so much of our history was twisted to suit their ideas of romantic fantasy. It is the Victorians who altered Cnut's name to Canute, to make it sound more English, although the irony is that in his determination to prove his worth and value Cnut had, by the time of his death, become more English than the English. It may have been the Victorians who distorted the famous 'King Canute and the Waves' story. As I have included here, Cnut's intention was to convince his people that he was only human and did not have the power of God to turn the tide. Whether this scene was indeed at Bosham (pronounced Bozzum) is unrecorded, but Bosham itself lays claim to the honour and the tide does come in most superbly there – as anyone who has been unfortunate enough to leave their car parked on the seafront has discovered!

A mention here on the word *Viking*, probably another Victorian distortion. Viking, literally, means to go raiding – *í-víking*. The Danes would never have referred to themselves as Vikings, although for ease of use I have commandeered both terms. Another Victorian invention – they did not wear horned helmets!

Cnut very conveniently, for latter-day historians and novelists, wrote several letters to England. One was to explain his expedition to Denmark in order to keep England safe from his elder brother

Harald. Whether he did murder him is conjecture, but is highly probable, for he was never heard of again and there is no other explanation of death. Cnut was the first King of England to be formally invited to Rome, quite a coup for a man who had invaded and conquered with not an entirely clear conscience.

The cliffs at Robin Hood's Bay (*Green Man Bay*, as I call it) are high and formidable. Emma's climbing of them is my invention, but not the incident. My grandmother, also an Emma, was cut off by the tide and climbed to safety carrying her baby in her teeth. This was done in Edwardian dress, probably complete with stays. The baby was my father, Frederick Turner M.M. The fact that I am here to write this story proves her courage. Sadly, she died many years ago and as a teenager I never had the patience to talk in depth to a very deaf old lady. What a waste of a chance to get to know a most remarkable woman.

There is a grave at Bosham that contains a young girl and strong tradition assumed her to be Cnut's daughter, who drowned in the mill-race. Her resting place denotes her as being of royal or important birth. I have invented her name, her mother, the manner of her birth and the details of how she died. There are other suggestions. Recent discoveries have located another grave close to hers which is very possibly the final resting place of King Harold II, butchered by Duke William's men at the Battle of Hastings. It was common for men and women of importance to plan ahead for their death by constructing a burial chamber during their lifetime, and it is the suggestion of John Pollock, local historian of Bosham, that Cnut, in the early years of his reign, may well have had his grave dug at the same time as that of his daughter's burial. As it happened, Cnut became a much-loved and respected king, deserving a grander burial place within Winchester Cathedral and so his grave at Bosham was not needed – until 1066 when Harold's mother, Countess Gytha, was desperate for a private and secret resting place for her son. She would have known of this place prepared for a previous King. Emma, Cnut and Harthacnut remain in Winchester Cathedral, but they, and all other important Anglo-Saxon burials, are now nothing more than a jumbled collection of bones kept in chests that sit above the screens near the medieval altar. I wonder if her bones are mixed in with Cnut's? I do hope so.

What happened to Edmund Ironside's wife, Ealdgyth, the sons she smuggled from York, Edward's long reign, Earl Godwine and his sons and the end of Emma's fascinating life, is told in the novel I wrote before this one, *Harold the King*. I have discovered that it is extremely difficult writing a prequel to a story already told, as new ideas do not always fit into what has previously been imagined and written. I apologise for any errors of continuity.

Helen Hollick, 2004

If you enjoyed A Hollow Crown *why not try further titles by Helen Hollick . . .*

Harold the King

England 1044. As dawn breaks over a summer's landscape, Harold Godwinesson is riding east. One of seven sons of the noble Godwine family, he is newly created Earl of East Anglia. But marrying for love sets him against his family and his king.

In France, William, the bastard son of a duke, is hungry for power. A charismatic leader, he cares nothing for the hypocrisy of court, only his next victory. Matched by his determined wife Mathilda, he casts his eyes towards England.

King Edward is alternately influenced and angered by his powerful mother, the Dowager Queen Emma. Manipulated into a marriage of convenience with Harold's sister, he is at the mercy of his nobles – and he lacks an heir . . .

arrow books

The Kingmaking

The year is 450AD, and there is only one who can lead Britain from the chaos of darkness into a new age of glory. Protected since birth by a false identity, he is revealed as the new Pendragon – Arthur. A young boy, powerless and lacking an army, he must serve a hard apprenticeship under his enemy if he is to succeed . . .

Pendragon's Banner

Arthur is king of Britain. At just twenty-three years old, he rules the kingdom he has dreamed of and fought for with Gwenhwyfar at his side. But retaining the royal torque is far from easy and will test his strength to the utmost . . .

Shadow of the King

Arthur Pendragon is dead! Or so the cry goes up from the battlefields of France. His widow, Gwenhwyfar, left at Caer Cadan with their small daughter, faces overthrow by the powerful council headed by Arthur's uncle. But, unknown to her, Arthur has survived and is nursed back to health in France. And events abroad mean a far mightier battle for the Pendragon throne – and the very future of Britain itself – lies ahead . . .

arrow books